MISSED

APPROACH

❖❖❖❖❖❖❖❖❖❖❖❖❖❖❖❖❖❖❖❖❖❖❖❖

MACK ADAMS

To
Rio Adams
Our beloved rescue canine companion.
We loved her dearly...and forever will.
(March 17, 1996—September 9, 2013)

MISSED

APPROACH

ONE

RioAero, SA

FRIDAY, FEBRUARY 20, 1981

"Flight operations...we have a problem." Captain Franco Rameros' voice came through loud and clear on the secure RioAero factory communications frequency.

While the incident was occurring only seconds before, little action could be taken from the cockpit. The event was over virtually within a blink of an eye. Now at ten thousand feet, a frustrated Captain Rameros had everything under control. But an enigma still remained as the WindStar lumbered back to the airport, laboring from the confounding incident.

As chief test pilot for RioAero, SA, Rameros was a highly qualified aviator. His career as a pilot spanned over twenty years: beginning with the Brazilian Air Force for eight years, then with RioAero. During that career, he had encountered almost every imaginable problem an aircraft could have. He had seen total power-plant failures, cabin/cockpit fires, fuel tank explosions, jammed flight controls, structural failures, a variety of landing gear malfunctions, and two crashes. Today, his in-flight situation was different than anything he had ever experienced. What had just happened simply could not have happened, but indeed it had.

The turbo-prop aircraft he was flight-testing was neither a prototype nor an experimental aircraft. There was no reason for anything unexpected to occur. During the previous three years, RioAero had painstakingly designed and manufactured a new generation of aircraft—like no other available. The WindStar-100 had been rigorously tested and recently certified. Over twenty aircraft were already in military and commercial service. Rameros was now merely performing a routine pre-delivery flight check of a WindStar destined to join others already in the Brazilian Air Force fleet. He was verifying that every system was operating in accordance with standard specifications. One system certainly had not.

"Advise on your problem," a voice came back over the company frequency. It was the dispatcher at Flight OPS responding to Rameros' radio transmission.

Franco Rameros, a wiry man in his early forties, was perhaps the best known pilot in all of Brazil; that is, next to the late Alberto Santos-Dumont, the country's famed patriarch of aviation. Rameros was a perfectionist with a can-do attitude. Unfortunately, he was also rather arrogant and abrupt. His ego was as legendary as was his reputation as a skilled pilot. His spiritedness tended to overpower his occasional charm. He was direct—too direct—about matters involving RioAero and its aircraft programs. He had no qualms about making statements critical of others. He had no tolerance for lines of authority—he did not care who you happened to be. He was, however, invariably and gallingly correct on any position he took. Few would guess that underneath the tough crust, a loyal and staunch heart dwelled.

Tall and lean, Rameros was once a handsome man; that was ten years ago, before the fiery accident. A sudden hydraulic failure in the prototype aircraft he was taxiing produced an immediate total loss of both braking and nose wheel steering. As a result, the aircraft collided with a parked fuel truck filled with avgas. The ensuing explosion and fire caused second and third degree burns to seventy percent of his body. Nine months of skin grafts and rehabilitation at the Burn Unit of Rio de Janeiro's Saint Christopher Hospital allowed Rameros to be functional again; however, the deep scarring of his body—and especially the permanent disfigurement of the left side of his face— also annealed his personality. He emerged from his ordeal even bolder and brasher; more relentlessly aggressive. He chose to have few close friends. He was more irascible than ever before.

But lately, Franco Rameros irritated even himself. He began finding most of his test flights tedious and monotonous. Unchallenging. BORING. Today, however, his flight was far from commonplace. His problem was real—very real.

"It is an engine problem," Rameros matter-of-factly advised OPS. "Well, it is really the prop. We will be cutting this test flight short and coming back for landing with only one engine operating. The right power plant was developing zero thrust. We had to shut it down."

"So, the prop went into feather and everything is under control?" the dispatcher queried, knowing the WindStar had excellent single-engine performance capabilities. Under most circumstances, the aircraft could fly for hours on only one engine. When feathered, the propeller of the failed engine automatically angled its blades directly into the airflow like a knife and ceased to rotate. Very little drag was created.

"Roger, everything is under control, but we will have to install a new prop after we get back to the hangar. The one that stopped working is now a piece of junk." Rameros paused, still leaving his microphone open, effectively controlling the dialogue he was having with Flight OPS. "And by the way, I better not see any emergency equipment or curious bystanders out on the tarmac when we land. We have a very delicate situation here. No publicity."

"Understand your request," the dispatcher responded.

Rameros' face reddened. "It is not a goddamn request," he shot back. "Make sure it does NOT happen!"

There was no response from Flight Operations. None was necessary. Rameros had made his position perfectly clear.

Of all days, today Franco Rameros happened to have a special guest on board who was being allowed to serve as first officer. On test flights, the company's policy typically permitted only pilots type-rated in the WindStar to be first officers. Major Osvaldo Paulo was an exception. He was the newly appointed director of procurement for the Brazilian Air Force. The major was an experienced pilot (transport category jets), but now spent most of his time flying a desk. He knew very little about the WindStar, except that the Air Force had already integrated ten WindStar aircraft into its operations and was expected to take a dozen more soon. The aircraft in which he was flying today was due to be one of the additional WindStars for the Air Force fleet.

Major Paulo was being afforded the VIP treatment. Earlier that morning, he had been given a red carpet tour of RioAero's impressive facility. Following coffee in the executive dining room, Salo Montero, RioAero's Chairman and CEO, had suggested that Paulo join Franco Rameros on the test flight of the eleventh WindStar that the Air Force would be accepting delivery of on Monday. Of course, the major eagerly accepted the invitation.

The factory's VIP approach to the major's visit was more of a courtesy than a necessity. In actuality, the major's role in procuring aircraft for the Air Force was simply to follow through on decisions already made by military top brass. Even the Air Force itself had little choice when it came to selecting an aircraft. The government's mandate was that if any aircraft manufactured by RioAero came even close to meeting the needs of the Air Force, an acquisition would be made. The same dictate applied equally to every other Brazilian agency or commercial enterprise that used airplanes in any way. The military controlled the country. The military owned RioAero. It also owned many of the country's other major industrial enterprises.

"Do you have any idea why it happened?" Paulo asked.

Franco shrugged. "It could be a manufacturing defect. It could be faulty installation. It could be damage in shipment. It could be lots of things. It is really too early to tell."

The major craned his neck to look out the side cockpit window and then back to the wing where the engine was mounted. This he had done over a half a dozen times since the incident occurred. The slick, black deicing boots glistened, contrasting against the mirror-like, white Alumigrip paint of the wing and engine nacelle. Everything seemed perfectly normal; that is, everything except for one very important item.

The major was confounded about what he saw—actually, about what he did not see. There was no propeller attached to the engine. The entire eight-foot diameter, four-bladed prop assembly had separated from the shaft that attached it to the engine gearbox. Nearly five hundred pounds and over a hundred thousand dollars worth of propeller components had mysteriously plunged to the ground. Amazingly, there was no damage to any part of the aircraft. Now to the eye, it appeared as if someone had simply forgotten to install the prop assembly onto the right engine.

TWO

St. Croix, U.S.V.I.

B y nine o'clock that Friday morning, Rick Harris had already checked out of the Hotel Caravelle in Christiansted on St. Croix, the largest of the U.S. Virgin Islands. He was now on his way to the airport in a rusted-out Volkswagen taxi that rattled along the city's still sleepy streets. He gazed aimlessly at the harbor's old buildings. Then, a sudden overwhelming feeling of anxiety engulfed him for no obvious reason. His face felt flush. His mind shouted out: *What the hell have you gotten yourself into, Mr. Harris?*

No calming voice answered.

Harris abruptly shook his head much like a dog stung on the ear by a bee. He inhaled deeply, and then groaned a slow exhale. Had he made the right decision? He hoped so, but knew he could not be sure. Not yet.

Rick glanced at the laminated business card ID tag attached to the handle of his leather travel bag. It read: *Richard A. Harris, Director of Aircraft Sales, Empresa Rio de Aeroespaço, NA*, a.k.a. RioAero, NA. He smiled for a fleeting moment, allowing the reality of it all to sink into his mind. He was keenly aware that his recent decision to join a young Brazilian aircraft manufacturer heading up North American sales for its new and as yet unproven airframe would certainly provide for more than enough challenges. Though Harris had always thrived on challenges—on pressure—this time an unsettling feeling was nagging at him. It was a feeling he had never experienced before. He was beginning to sense his upcoming task would be more formidable than he had initially thought. Still, he hoped his tingling sensations were wrong.

R ick Harris had always been involved with aircraft. As a native Texan and son of an Air Force lieutenant colonel, Rick grew up in Seguin, a small town near Randolph Air Force Base just northeast of San Antonio. During his formative years, he received the type of discipline and direction that would serve him well throughout his entire life. By the age of seventeen, while still a senior in high school, he had earned his private pilot license. Later, he attended Texas A&M for a degree in engineering, had a four year stint as a pilot with the Texas Air National Guard, and as the final part of his formal education he received an MBA from SMU in Dallas. While in graduate school, he worked part-time at the local airport and became a flight instructor. That quickly led to his involvement in selling small single-engine planes, then larger piston twins, then even larger turbine-powered aircraft. He had worked for such companies as Cessna, Piper, and Fairchild.

It had been just four months earlier, during a breakfast meeting at the Commuter Airline Association of America (CAAA) convention in Chicago, that Rick first met RioAero's Chairman and CEO, Salo Montero. Salo was so impressed with Rick that by the end of the convention Harris had an offer from Montero that Harris simply could not refuse. So now, Rick Harris had advanced to a high visibility position with the Brazilian airframe manufacturer's newly established North American subsidiary.

Rick and Salo had overlapping backgrounds. Montero, a former colonel and pilot in the Brazilian Air Force, had been sent to the United States by his government to study aeronautical engineering at Texas A&M during the early '60s. But Salo's trajectory was much different than Rick's.

Salo Montero was highly-placed in the Brazilian military establishment. He knew everyone who was important. He was held in high regard. The Brazilian military was a club of sorts—a very exclusive and powerful one indeed. In Brazil, unlike the United States, the military controlled or influenced everything—government and industry. So when Brazil decided to expand its industrial base by designing and manufacturing aircraft, Salo was well-positioned and was quickly tapped to head up the venture.

Salo Montero was innovative and hard working. The small aircraft company he had formed in 1968 flourished. While much credit for RioAero's accomplishments had to go to Salo, the Brazilian government basically guaranteed the success of the company. The government supported RioAero by placing onerous restrictions on all compeititive aircraft imported into Brazil. Essentially, RioAero was a favorite son: if RioAero did not have some part to play in manufacturing an aircraft, that aircraft was unlikely to be sold to fly in Brazil.

In its early days, RioAero just manufactured a variety of light single-engine and twin-engine aircraft under license agreements with foreign corporations that wanted to sell aircraft in Brazil. During the process of manufacturing those aircraft and interfacing with major aerospace firms around the world, RioAero was able to advance its own aircraft design and engineering capability, as well as implement cutting-edge production technology.

Now with thirteen years of experience under its belt, RioAero was rapidly becoming a mainstream aerospace corporation. Major airframe component contracts with Lockheed and Boeing promoted tremendous expansion. The company's facilities had grown to over forty-five acres, and included research and development, engineering, marketing, as well as production. RioAero even had South America's only Level IIIC wind tunnel to test aerodynamic designs. Nearly seven thousand people were employed at RioAero's sprawling facility near the outskirts of Nova Iguaçu, a city of almost a million people just northwest of Rio de Janeiro in the Sarapuí River valley.

Boldly, three years previous to his meeting with Rick, Salo had made a calculated gamble. He believed that the deregulation of the airline industry in the United States would create a need for a reliable and truly efficient nineteen-seat commuter airliner. Because the U.S. Airline Deregulation Act of 1978 would slash enormous federal subsidies and allow major air carriers to pull out of unprofitable markets, Salo envisioned an influx of fledgling airlines rushing to fill in the gaps. He was adamant that a new generation of commuter and regional airlines would need hundreds of smaller, new technology aircraft. So, and of course with the Brazilian government's backing, Salo bet his reputation and his company on his vision—a vision that would evolve into the WindStar-100.

It took over $500 million to design, engineer, certify, and tool-up for production of the WindStar. That was more than the company had earned during its entire thirteen-year history. Beyond the startup expense, a completely new facility had to be built to manufacture the aircraft. And now, even though it had been only four months since the WindStar had received certificates of airworthiness from both the *Centro Técnico Aeroespacial* (CTA) in Brazil and the Federal Aviation Administration (FAA) in the United States, the factory was turning out an astounding number of aircraft—nine each month. These aircraft had to be sold—sold in large numbers and sold quickly.

Unfortunately, sales had been slower than anticipated. Initially, the Brazilian government could only absorb a couple dozen of the new aircraft in its military operations. The North American market seemed averse to jumping on the bandwagon for a brand-new aircraft from a relatively new company. RioAero had yet to complete setting up a fully stocked and staffed support operation in the United States. The result was that for each of the nine aircraft manufactured every month, five remained unsold. At well over a million dollars per aircraft, that type of sales lassitude could not continue.

Twenty "white tails"—unsold aircraft, many painted base-white—lined the factory's ramp area. Some aircraft had avionics and interiors installed; others were unpainted, unfinished or "green." Major vendors to RioAero were beginning to slow delivery of critical parts needed to produce the aircraft. Many vendors had not been paid for over six months. Both Salo and government officials were becoming unnerved.

This was where Rick Harris entered the picture. He had been hired to do a thing he did best—sell aircraft. Rick knew exactly what the company's situation was. The task was enormous, but by no means impossible. Rick and Salo respected and trusted each other's skill and judgment. Still, the challenge at hand would test both to their limits.

R ick repositioned his body, attempting to stretch out his legs within the confines of the VW's tiny back seat area. He tried not to think about the four additional hours of flying it would take to reach Fort Lauderdale. This would be the last segment of the almost twenty total flight hours required to get home. Indeed Southern Brazil was a long, long way from South Florida. He wearily closed his eyes. Then before he realized it, he was at the airport.

"Uhh," Harris said stirring himself from his reverie as he began to instruct the cab driver, "just drive on the ramp past that big gray hangar."

Security was rather lax at most smaller airports outside the continental United States, especially in areas designated for general aviation operations. St. Croix was no exception. There were no guards to confront and no locked gates to contend with. Access to the general aviation area was easy and direct.

The cab slowed as it neared the weathered-gray hangar. The driver's eyes focused on an aircraft that stood out from all the rest. "Haven't seen one of those before," the driver remarked. "Ya know what kind of plane it is?"

"Sure do." The suddenly invigorated Harris beamed to the driver. "It's a factory-fresh, brand-new 1981 WindStar. She does three hundred knots and can carry nineteen passengers. She's a state-of-the-art air taxi. You, sir, are now one lucky man. Not many people have seen a WindStar. This one's number thirty-four off our production line at RioAero in Brazil."

The cab driver grinned. "Air taxi, huh," he said, mulling over a phrase well known to him.

"Yup," Rick acknowledged, keying into the driver's apparent interest. "While the WindStar is an air taxi when it's used for on-demand flight, others label it a commuter or regional airliner when it's operated on a regular flight schedule. But no matter the nametag, the WindStar is a symbol of air travel freedom…a versatile alternative to…" He paused, hearing the aircraft sales pitch rolling off his tongue, no prospective client here, but he finished with flourish anyway. "…a versatile alternative to large airliners."

Rick handed the driver his fare as the cab stopped near the nose of the WindStar. He unfolded himself out of the taxicab's uncomfortable back seat, exited the cab, and then reached back inside to pull out his well-worn leather travel bag. As he purposefully pushed his double-gradient Ray-Bans up the bridge of his nose, he zeroed in on a flight line crew that had just completed fueling the WindStar's tanks.

Rick smiled. "All topped off?" he asked, making his way toward the line chief.

"Roger that," came the reply. "By the way, nice plane." The line chief nodded three times in genuine admiration. "Would you mind if we took a look inside?"

"Not at all," Rick said radiating pride as they walked toward the aircraft. He loved everything about the WindStar. It was a pilot's dream. It was a passenger's delight.

The plane's snow-white Alumigrip paint glistened in the morning sun. A band of five cobalt-blue stripes ran the entire length of the fuselage. The crisp lines streamlined the aircraft. Initially tapering at the nose cone, the striping flowed backward along the fuselage, first gradually broadening, then dramatically expanding in a rapid upward sweep at the tail before bluntly ending at the rudder. On the tail, in twelve inch-high black lettering just above the striping appeared the FAA registration: N100WS. The aircraft's overall appearance gave it character; its registration provided unique identity.

The airstair door leading to the cabin was a fully integrated part of the WindStar's fuselage. It was a three-by-five-foot plug located just forward of the left engine's propeller; its lower fuselage attach point was about shoulder height. Rick reached up and rotated a handle connected to the latching mechanism; five bayonet-like rods that extended into the fuselage structure immediately retracted back into the door. With a slight pull on the handle, the door's counter-balance and gas-spring actuating system allowed it to slowly open from the top by pivoting on its lower mounted hinge.

The line crew eagerly followed Rick up the entry door stairs. Their appreciative glances quickly took in the spacious stand-up cabin and the three abreast leather-covered seats configured for nineteen passengers. The new aircraft smell was intoxicating.

Rick flipped on the master power switch in the cockpit—the aircraft came alive. The slight clicking that occurs as the fluorescent cove lighting first illuminates the cabin was barely noticeable. He switched on the cockpit cassette tape player typically used for giving prerecorded announcements to passengers. But instead, he inserted a special tape for his visitors. Rhythms of Sergio Mendes were broadcast over the cabin sound system.

"Very impressive," complimented the line chief. And he really meant it.

Pleased, and taking the praise as much for the aircraft as for his own performance, Rick nodded. "Thanks, that's always nice to hear." He followed his visitors out of the aircraft.

As the line crew drove away in their fuel truck, Rick began a perfunctory preflight inspection of the WindStar. He was looking for any leaks of oil, fuel, or hydraulic fluid; any damage that might have occurred to the aircraft during the night. Everything seemed fine during the cursory check. It did not need to be exhaustive. Rick knew finding a flight-grounding item on an aircraft with less than twenty-five hours entered into its log would be very rare. Besides, if he found any significant problems with the aircraft, he knew he would be stranded in St. Croix for at least two more days until parts arrived from Brazil. That was not going to happen. No problems. Not here. Not today.

THREE

RioAero, SA

"This type of incident could be a real disaster for the company," Paulo said to Rameros. The major grimaced; he knew that RioAero's future weighed heavily upon the success of the WindStar. A lone prop incident might not seriously affect sales in Brazil, but then again, the country could only absorb so many WindStars. By far, the largest and yet untapped market for the WindStar was the recently deregulated airline industry in the United States. And, the audience grew even larger since the entire worldwide aviation community was closely monitoring how the new WindStar was performing.

"*Disaster* for the company?" Rameros sarcastically parroted the major. "It is going to be more like a friggin' catastrophe." He clenched his jaw, shaking his head slowly, first up and down, then from side to side. "Yes, this one is going to be hard to keep quiet…from the press, I mean." Rameros paused, unnecessarily fiddling with the rudder trim that he had set and reset three times before. The more he thought about the incident, the more noticeably disturbed he became. He knew once word was out that a new WindStar had had a propeller simply fall off during a routine flight, the press and RioAero's competitors would have a field day. Questions would be asked. Airline operators would be skeptical about ordering the WindStar. Passengers would be apprehensive about flying in WindStars already in service. But WindStars had to be sold. The company's very existence depended upon it.

"Hopefully," the major continued, "Engineering and QA will quickly be able to determine the cause."

Rameros remained silent. He knew there could be a lot of buck-passing and finger-pointing. RioAero might blame Dayton-Standard, the propeller vendor, for design flaws or manufacturing defects. Dayton-Standard might blame RioAero for improper installation or faulty rigging. And, of course, if the FAA or Brazil's CTA thought that the aircraft might now be unsafe for any reason, the entire fleet of WindStars could be grounded—or worse, the airworthiness certificate for the WindStar could be revoked. Even false rumors of problems concerning an aircraft type could spell disaster for an airframe manufacturer.

"I wish I could agree with you, major," Rameros finally said with a sigh, "but I know how the system works. Weeks could easily pass before anyone knows why what happened, happened. I truly hope I am wrong and the cause of the problem becomes obvious. But first, we need to get this bird on the ground and take a good look at the engine gearbox." Rameros paused, then switched from the secure company communications channel to the Tower frequency. "Good afternoon, Tower, WindStar Papa-Tango-Sierra-Bravo-Whiskey is fifteen miles southwest for landing."

Although the aircraft's speed was now only slightly more than half the three hundred knots of which it had been capable, it was still operating very well on only one engine. Rameros saw no reason to tell the Tower that the right engine's propeller had fallen off and into the Sarapuí River some thirty miles southwest of the airport. He knew that if he announced his current "single-prop" situation to the Tower, he would likely be able to watch his landing later today on the evening news. The press always had the Tower radio frequency programmed into their scanners. A reporter would be on the scene in a matter of minutes with videotape rolling.

The Tower acknowledged the aircraft's registration, position, and request for landing. It also advised of a wide band of thunderstorms fifteen miles north of the airport that was rapidly moving to the south. This, of course, Rameros had been monitoring with his in-flight weather radar. The controller concluded his transmission by saying, "Report passing the Outer Marker for a straight-in approach to Runway Three."

"Thank you, Tower," Rameros responded. Then reflecting upon the propeller incident, he said to Paulo, "You know, major, we should be thankful it was not the left propeller assembly that failed. The left prop would have caused a much more serious problem for us."

"How so?" From Paulo's perspective, a propeller separation was a propeller separation. What did it matter if it was on the right engine or the left engine?

"Think about it." Rameros smiled, breaking his own tension by toying with the major. "Oh, sorry, I forgot that you are used to those heavy transport category jets—the ones without propellers."

"Still," the major said, dismissing Rameros' snide remark, "it should not make any difference which propeller it was. Should it?"

"Why yes, it really does." Rameros presented the major with some basic information about turbo-prop propulsion. He explained that most aircraft engines were mounted with propellers facing forward which turned in a clockwise direction. He noted that during rotation, the descending blades created most of the thrust. "So you see, major, if a right propeller assembly separates from the engine gearbox of an aircraft in flight, it would tend to move down and away from the fuselage. But on the—"

"Okay, now I understand. That explains why there was no damage to the aircraft after the right prop broke away from the engine." The major, glad for the intellectual diversion, eagerly grasped his new found knowledge. However by not taking it a step further, he was still truly unaware of the gravity of the situation that would be posed by a left propeller separation.

"But on the other hand," Rameros continued, somewhat irritated with the major's lack of intuitiveness, "if the left propeller assembly were to have separated, it is very likely that the blades of the detached rotating disc would also have moved away from the engine and to the right. That means the blades would probably have slashed somewhere into the left fuselage before the whole assembly—hopefully—completed its fall to the ground."

"Or..." the thought finally dawning on the major, "the blades could have remained embedded in the fuselage?"

"Exactly."

"So now, Captain Rameros, what is the probability of having the left propeller assembly separate and rip into the fuselage?"

"That could happen any second now," Rameros said deadpanning.

The major's eyes widened.

"Nah..." Rameros said with a grin. "Two propeller assemblies on the same day, on the same flight? Not to worry, major," he chortled, "it will never happen. We have a better chance of anything else happening: fuel flow blockage, hydraulic failure, even a heart attack of the pilot-in-command."

Franco Rameros knew that the WindStar propeller assembly was manufactured by one of the most reputable companies in the United States—Dayton-Standard. Like most parts incorporated into the WindStar, propeller components were manufactured to exacting tolerances. The testing and inspection was in accordance with rigorous procedures approved by the FAA and CTA. Entire propellers simply just did not fall off an aircraft in flight. However, Franco Rameros knew that if one propeller assembly had improbably and mysteriously broken away from an engine gearbox, a second propeller failure could also occur. The odds certainly weighed astronomically against having a second failure on this flight, but the odds had also been heavily against the first failure.

"Are you sure the left prop will stay attached to the engine long enough to get us back to the airport?" Major Paulo asked with new concern.

"Absolutely, positively!" There was no reason for gloom and doom. Frankly, there was nothing that could now be done about it anyway. Franco Rameros casually reported passing the outer marker to the Tower.

FOUR

St. Croix, U.S.V.I.

T he same Volkswagen taxi that had ferried Rick to the airport almost an hour earlier slowed as it once again approached the WindStar. The cab stopped just twenty feet from the left wing tip. As the passenger door opened, a lithe brunette in her early twenties emerged.

"Good morning, Rick."

"Good morning, Vicky."

Victoria Montero was the daughter and only child of Salo Montero. Rick had met Victoria just the week before his scheduled departure to the States. He was in Salo's office discussing his North American sales program when Victoria interrupted by abruptly walking in and announcing that she had just crashed the new WindStar simulator—twice! Rick had jokingly replied, "As long as you don't break the contraption, crash it as many times as you like." Everyone laughed.

Despite Victoria's family aviation history, her true love was medicine. She was enrolled at the University of Miami, and had accepted her father's offer to hitch a ride with Rick in the new WindStar Rick would be ferrying up to the United States for customer demonstrations. Salo had convinced her that by joining a highly qualified and experienced pilot like Rick, she could both get back to her course work in Miami and learn more about aviation along the way. The dutiful daughter also knew garnering more familiarity with the WindStar during the flight would very much please her father.

The night before the departure, Salo invited Rick to join him and Victoria for dinner at his hilltop compound overlooking the city. They talked for hours about aviation: everything from J-3 Cubs to swing-wing Tomcats; and indeed, at great length, about Rick's many anticipated future sales to airlines. The convivial evening and shared dreams led Salo and Rick to joke that someday, somewhere, there would be a regional airline with an expansive fleet of RioAero aircraft called "WindStar Airlines." Laughter filled the air as lofty dreams were toasted with cups of espresso capped with lemon twists.

At the end of the evening, Rick took the opportunity to brief Victoria about the upcoming three-day flight. It would involve a lot of flying: up the Brazilian coast to showcase the new Windstar at Salvador, Recife, Fortaleza, and Belém; then, onto Port-of-Spain in

Trinidad, and Christiansted in St. Croix; and finally, ending in Fort Lauderdale. It would be, he remarked, a long, long flight.

Now, no one watching Rick and Victoria stroll toward the WindStar could have guessed they were not friends of long acquaintance. It was obvious that what was normally expected to be a tedious and boring trip had become enjoyable with time passing quickly. Throughout the trip, common interests had spurred many lively conversations. The trip had jump-started and cemented a friendship. But the realization had suddenly set in. This was the last flight segment; soon their journey would be over. The end would be both welcome and regrettable.

After re-entering the aircraft and securely closing the cabin door behind himself, Rick followed Victoria to the flight deck. There, each settled into one of the cockpit's two imposing and remarkably comfortable sheepskin covered seats. The metal tongues of seatbelts and shoulder harnesses clicked into the respective buckles. Rick attached the airport taxiway chart to the clip on his control yoke. Entries were made in the aircraft's log. He handed Victoria the day's flight plan and two low altitude charts for enroute navigation.

"Let's get down to business," Rick said.

Victoria nodded in agreement while pantomiming fanning her face. The mid-morning sun was beginning to heat up the cockpit like a greenhouse. Once the engines were started, bleed air taken from the compressor sections would allow the air cycle machine to cool the aircraft's interior.

The master power switch once again energized the aircraft. Noise from dozens of peripheral system switches, buttons, knobs, and levers, each with a unique hallmark sound, flooded the cockpit as Rick's deft hands seemed to float through the air, checking, setting, and rechecking positions and functions. The whirling sound of gyros feeding critical information to key flight instruments increased in pitch during spool-up. The multitude of annunciator lights on the master caution panel, just below the center window glare shield, illuminated in hues of red or yellow—some flashing, some not—as the press-to-test switch was activated. Rick double-checked the fuel gauges and made sure the fuel-used indicator was set to zero. This was a long flight; his fuel reserve would be little more than the required extra forty-five minute amount.

Harris continued on with the engine start checklist. The WindStar was designed to be a simple and straightforward aircraft. The two full weeks of day and night training he had received from factory test pilots made him comfortable and capable—but not cocky—with the aircraft and its systems. His years of experience made him confident.

Rick had accumulated over six thousand hours in airplanes, and half of that time was in turbine-powered equipment like the WindStar.

On the overhead panel, Rick moved the right-engine-start switch upward. A low-pitched humming sound increased in frequency as the starter began to rotate the engine's compressor section. Focusing on the instrumentation cluster located just above the engine control pedestal, he murmured: "Oil pressure, check; speed stable, twelve percent." He advanced the fuel condition lever forward. Igniter plugs of the automatic ignition unit emitted a rapid clicking noise as high voltage current arced across contacts. Then like a blowtorch, the kerosene fuel being sprayed into the engine's combustion chamber lit off. Digital numbers on the ITT (Internal Turbine Temperature) gauge flashed by, rapidly rising, peaking at 750°C, gradually backing off to 550°C. The Dayton-Standard propellers slowly came out of feather and then droned at 1,100 rpm. Everything was normal. The second engine's start only slightly increased the noise level in the cockpit. TurboAirTech had designed a remarkable new technology engine. It was as extremely reliable as it was relatively quiet.

The avionics master switch was flipped on. Both Rick and Victoria donned their headsets. Rick punched in the "Hot Mic" button on the avionics select panel. He and Victoria could now leisurely converse through the cockpit intercom without having to compete with the low, but still present, engine noise.

"Anything we forgot?" he quipped over the intercom, glancing at Victoria.

"Does *we* mean *me*? As in, did I remember to bring coffee from the hotel?" She knew Rick really liked his coffee. "Well, the answer is negatory on the 'forgot.'"

"Thanks." He smiled. "I'm really glad you decided to come along on this flight, and I don't mean just as the major coffee procurer." Pressing the small round button on the top left side of the control yoke, he said, "Ground Control, November-One-Double-Oh-Whiskey-Sugar is ready to taxi VFR (Visual Flight Rules), Fox-Lima-Lima (FLL)."

"Roger, Whiskey-Sugar, taxi to Runway Two-Seven; wind, three-one-zero at one-two; altimeter, twenty-nine-ninety-nine. Say aircraft type."

"WindStar One Hundred."

"Nice!"

The line chief gave Rick a thumbs-up as the WindStar taxied past the fixed-base operations hangar. By now, half a dozen mechanics had walked out onto the tarmac to see it taxi by for takeoff. The mid-point of Runway 27 was a mere three hundred feet from where the on-lookers stood.

As Rick slowly taxied east to the beginning of the runway, he made a thorough pre-takeoff check of the aircraft, its systems, and its flight instruments. With typical Caribbean weather, there was no need to file an IFR (Instrument Flight Rules) flight plan. Going VFR with occasional radio contact with San Juan Center would make this last long flight segment less tedious and more enjoyable despite strong forecasted headwinds. When he was two hours out of Fort Lauderdale, he planned on checking in with Miami Flight Service to see if the weather was improving as forecast. Then, he would work his way into the air traffic control system with Miami Center.

"Good morning, Tower, Whiskey Sugar is ready to roll, Runway Two-Seven," Rick casually announced.

"Roger, November-One-Hundred-Whiskey-Sugar; wind, two-eight-zero at one-zero. Cleared for takeoff."

Rick taxied out to the departure end of the runway and lined-up with the centerline. He knew that the line chief and the group of mechanics assembled in front of the hangar would be watching.

It's showtime, Rick thought to himself. Then over the cockpit intercom, he briefed Victoria. "This takeoff will be max performance. I want the folks here in St. Croix to remember and then talk about the WindStar for months to come. There will be some abrupt maneuvering and a bit more noise than normal. So be prepared. Don't worry, though, it's perfectly safe."

"Are you sure?"

Rick shrugged. He had absolutely no reason—at least at this point—to believe it would be otherwise.

"Fine," she acknowledged. This should be exciting. She was eager to see what a maximum performance takeoff would be like in the WindStar.

With brakes firmly held, Rick smoothly advanced the power levers until the engine torque read seventy percent. The aircraft vibrated under the strain; the prop wash striking the tail buffeted its structure. The cockpit noise level increased significantly.

"Here we go," he said over the intercom.

As the brakes were released, the aircraft surged forward, pressing Rick and Victoria back into their seats. He further increased the power to bring the torque to one hundred percent with propellers rotating at 2,000 rpm. Now, each engine was developing its full thirteen hundred shaft horsepower.

Thirty knots...

The wheels thumped over expansion joints in the concrete runway.

Sixty knots...

Acceleration dramatically increased.

Eighty knots...

Though poised to leap into the air, Rick held the WindStar on the runway a split second longer.

Rotate.

The WindStar pitched up at just over ninety knots. While the gear slowly retracted, Rick allowed the aircraft to quickly accelerate to its best twin-engine angle of climb speed before rocketing skyward. All assembled eyes focused on the aircraft as it climbed out at nearly a thirty-degree angle from the runway. It had the performance of a lightly loaded Learjet.

"Say altitude," the Tower queried.

"Passing through three thousand."

"Extraordinary," was the comment from the controller. "You are clear of our airspace; frequency change approved at pilot's discretion."

Rick grinned. *Great aircraft!*

FIVE

Destination: Fort Lauderdale

S even minutes after takeoff from St. Croix, Rick Harris leveled off at 16,500 feet. He watched the aircraft's true airspeed rise to three hundred knots, then he reduced the engine power to long range cruise and adjusted the props to 1,500 rpm. The cockpit noise level markedly quieted. Navigation instruments were double-checked. The autopilot was engaged.

Flight conditions were perfect. The cloudless pale-blue sky blended into the distant horizon, converging with the ocean below. Although the aircraft was moving along at a rapid pace, it seemed motionless—fixed in space and time. There was no meaningful outside reference to indicate its speed. Even clusters of islands dotting the azure waters below gave no clue as to the rate of the aircraft's true forward movement.

Slightly behind the left wing tip, the landmass of Puerto Rico could easily be identified seeming to lazily float upon the water. The Dominican Republic appeared as a mere shadow in the distance much farther to the west. Rick entered a frequency into the aircraft's navigation system to receive signals from the VOR (VHF Omnidirectional Range) transmitter located ahead on the tiny, yet still invisible island of Grand Turk. Quite remarkably, given that the plane was still nearly three hundred miles away, the aircraft's receiver locked onto the signal. He turned the WindStar seven degrees to the left, settled back into his seat, and began tracking direct to Grand Turk.

R ick yawned, then glanced toward Victoria who had just returned to the cockpit from the cabin's small galley area. She had poured two more cups of coffee from the thermal jug the hotel had filled earlier that morning. She handed him a cup.

"Still that Brazilian java?" he quipped.

"Why, of course!" She scowled, her nationalistic Brazilian pride momentarily affronted. "You know, we grow over half the beans that you folks use." Then, adding with a tsk, less seriously, "Do not believe what that Juan Valdez guy and his Colombian friends may say."

"Oh, that's just advertising," Rick said. He took a sip. "Mmmm…most of us who drink coffee in the States really have no idea where it comes from. It just tastes either good or bad." He grinned, then admitted, "You know, mostly we have little appreciation of how good or bad it does taste. We drink it anyway." He paused. "Someday North Americans will become connoisseurs of really good coffee as people are in Europe and South America. But in the meantime—"

"You are really glad I came along or you would just drink whatever you were served!" Victoria knew Americans' habits.

He shrugged, then keyed his mic. "Miami Radio, November-One-Hundred-Whiskey-Sugar is on one-twenty-three-thirty-five." He had just passed Grand Turk and was looking for a weather update from Miami Flight Service.

"Go ahead, aircraft calling Miami Radio."

"Miami, WindStar One-Hundred-Whiskey-Sugar is requesting the current terminal weather and forecast for Fox-Lima-Lima."

"Stand-by one." The flight service station operator gathered the latest data and relayed it to Rick. Although FLL was now in the clear, a frontal system that had essentially shut down its air carrier operations for most of the morning had only moved twenty miles to the southeast—directly into Rick's flight path. There was no way around it, especially considering the strong headwinds and limited fuel reserves on board.

"Thanks for the info." Rick paused, mentally reviewing the mechanics of the IFR flight plan data he was about to give Miami. He keyed his mic again. "Miami, we'd appreciate your re-filing us for IFR to cruise at Flight Level one-eight-zero, RNAV direct Fox-Lima-Lima."

"Roger, Whiskey-Sugar, we will amend your VFR flight plan as requested and put the information into the system for Miami Center. So long."

"Well now," he said to Victoria, "looks like we're in for some actual."

"Actual? Actual what?" a perplexed Victoria asked.

Pilots are known to communicate about flight activity rather cryptically; some say in the interest of reducing radio frequency congestion when talking with air traffic control. Although pilots and controllers fully understand what is being said, those not intimate with aviation talk typically find many of the truncated words and phrases confusing.

"Oh, sorry," Rick said, instantly realizing that she had no idea what he was talking about. "The weather in Fort Lauderdale is beautiful," he began explaining. "It's sunny and unseasonably cool. But a frontal system that had the airport socked-in earlier this morning has moved directly into our flight path. We'll have to penetrate the front. That will mean a bumpy ride and some *actual* instrument flying."

The previous flight time in the WindStar on the trip up from Brazil had all been under excellent weather conditions. Now, Rick thought, the last hour of the flight would be more challenging—at least for him. He also knew flying IFR would give Victoria a better perspective of what being a pilot was all about.

Rick disengaged the autopilot and slightly re-trimmed the WindStar for straight and level flight. "Okay, Vicky, how about some real practice?"

"Sure!" Victoria was excited, but apprehensive. She had "flown" the simulator at the factory, and some of those sessions had not ended so successfully. However, her confidence had largely been restored when she had flown the WindStar at various times during earlier segments of this trip. But during the past two days, there had been no significant weather with which to contend. "Now remember, I am only a private pilot. Don't let me scare myself."

"*No problema,*" Rick said. "I won't let that happen." The way he had learned how to really fly was by being a flight instructor. If he had been given to paranoia, he would have concluded that his students were always trying to kill him by attempting to crash whichever aircraft was being used for instruction. Nowadays, he felt habitually prepared for anything.

SIX

RioAero, SA

F ranco Rameros surveyed his approach. From four miles out, the airport was in plain view. The two hundred foot wide, nine thousand foot long runway was ahead and slightly to the left. RioAero's massive facility was located just to the north side of the runway. A dozen buildings and nine large hangars were edged by expanses of tarmac ramp areas and concrete taxiways. A huge inventory of WindStars, positioned wingtip-to-wingtip, sat temporarily stored along the side of Hangar Seven (Final Assembly) and Hangar Eight (Interior Finishing). All the aircraft had bright yellow wooden chocks bracketing their nose wheels and heavy-duty nylon ropes looped through mid-wing tie-down rings to secure them in place. This inventory of unsold aircraft was an embarrassing testimonial to the dismal sales record of the aircraft since its certification. Airframe manufacturers always strive to have strong order books with many dozens, if not hundreds, of sold aircraft backlogged but yet to be manufactured. However, RioAero's aggressive manufacturing schedule, anemically supported by an inept sales program, now resulted in the very opposite situation.

Although production of the WindStar was still going strong, logic would soon have to rule. Unless a major order came in for the aircraft within the next few weeks, the WindStar production line would likely be severely cut back or, even worse, shut down. For now, though, RioAero's facilities were still operating at high capacity.

"Roger, Sierra-Bravo-Whiskey, not in sight," the Tower responded. "Wind is three-one-zero at one-eight with gusts to two-niner, altimeter three-zero-one-one. There is no traffic. You are cleared to land."

"Thank you, Tower," Rameros came back.

The airstrip at Nova Iguaçu generally had little flight activity. During weekdays, most of the traffic was generated by factory pilots testing recently manufactured aircraft or prototypes still under development. There were also a variety of military aircraft operations from the Air Force base located on the south side of the field. Commercial traffic was almost nonexistent, since those flights typically used Rio de Janeiro International or Santos Dumont Airport, both a short distance away.

Rameros completed his pre-landing checklist, reserving both flap and gear extension for when the aircraft would be on a short final to the runway. Naturally, even in perfect weather, single-engine approaches always required more caution than did normal twin-engine approaches. In the event a go-around was required prior to landing, a "clean" aircraft could more quickly respond to the limited power available from just one engine. But today's gusty conditions created a formidable task even for experienced pilots who were operating aircraft with two functioning engines.

Major Paulo was very much aware of the challenges that the weather presented to Franco Rameros. He watched Franco further position the nose of the aircraft to a generous twenty-five degree "crab" angle into the strong winds that were now blowing almost directly across the runway. Still, the WindStar was slowly drifting to the right. Experience told the major that as the aircraft descended, the effects of the wind on the aircraft would be magnified.

Rameros knew that in order to safely land, he would have to muscle the WindStar onto the runway, all the time being sure that proper airspeed, directional control, and descent rates were maintained. Although the current wind conditions had been tested to be within the WindStar's twin-engine operating limitations, the crosswind component now exceeded the aircraft's demonstrated single-engine landing criteria. A further problem was that the factory's huge hangars bordering the northern side of the runway's touchdown zone were known to create unpredictable wind shear conditions.

Within one mile from the runway, Rameros set in fifteen degrees of flaps. Then he moved the gear handle down and continued to rest his right hand on the switch as he briefly waited for three green lights to appear on the lower instrument subpanel, indicating that the gear was down and locked. He throttled back slightly to allow the airspeed to bleed off to one hundred thirty knots and set the rudder trim to neutral.

"Well, major," he said unflinchingly, "looks like we have a tiger by the tail."

Major Paulo tried to respond, but words failed him.

As was anticipated, the wind was now having a greater effect on the aircraft's controllability during the descent to the runway. Vertical and horizontal components of the gusty conditions were seemingly at odds with the aircraft's intent to land. The major silently watched Rameros make constant and sometimes aggressive changes to the flight controls in order to cope with the aircraft's ever-changing pitch, roll, and yaw. Just as the WindStar would stabilize in its three-dimensional approach to the runway, a burst of wind would throw it off course. Within seconds, the same scenario would play out again.

Indeed, Franco Rameros was no longer a bored pilot. The WindStar was bobbing and weaving, fighting its way down to the runway. Layers of wind tore through space, surging, whirling, and hissing, almost as if mocking the WindStar's resolve to land. There were jolting air pockets with powerful bursts of energy. The effects were very visible, very real.

"Wind check, two-seven-zero at two-five, peak gusts three-five," the Tower controller broadcasted an update. The wind had intensified.

The major's eyes widened. The words "peak gusts three-five" seared into his mind.

Rameros added further power to the left engine. It was critical for him to maintain a specific margin above the aircraft's normal airspeed. He felt the relentless wind and its unpredictable gusts continue to menace the WindStar's approach. Now, the aircraft had to be firmly flown down and onto the runway, relying upon techniques like those used by Navy pilots during aircraft carrier landings.

Just after crossing the runway threshold and descending through two hundred feet, Rameros initiated his final maneuver to position the WindStar for landing. The aircraft's angled crabbing into the wind transitioned to a forward slip. The left wing was lowered into the wind to prevent the aircraft from drifting across the runway; the nose was aligned with the runway centerline using slightly less left rudder pressure than had been required before. Now positioned for landing and effectively compensating for wind drift, the aircraft was banked to the left, but flying longitudinally straight. It was awkward looking. It was awkward feeling.

The WindStar descended to within one hundred feet of the runway.

Fifty feet...

The aircraft veered to the right. Corrections were made, bringing it back on runway centerline.

Thirty feet...

SEVEN

Destination: Fort Lauderdale

Victoria adjusted her seat to be more comfortable at the controls. "Maintain heading and altitude?" she asked.

"Yup," Rick acknowledged, then reconfirmed, "three-five-zero and sixteen thousand five hundred."

Harris powered up the aircraft's weather radar. It was the latest digital system from Bendix—an RDR-1400. Bendix Avionics Division had consigned the system to RioAero for use in this new demonstration aircraft. The RDR-1400 was so advanced that helicopter operators in Texas and Louisiana used it under instrument flight conditions to make approaches to oil rigs in the Gulf. Definitely a great toy to have in the demonstration WindStar, but the radar's features and functions were overkill for most small airline operators.

He glanced toward Victoria. "You're doing just great, Vicky." It was true; still, reinforcement was always good to hear.

"Thanks."

"Remember," he continued in instructor mode, "try to relax and let the airplane fly itself. When it strays, just use light pressure on the controls to help it get back to where you want it to be." Rick knew that low flight-time pilots invariably became stressed when at the controls and facing unfamiliar situations. There was a tendency to unnecessarily muscle the aircraft to force reaction, rather than just coaxing with a gentle nudge now and then. "Think of it this way," he went on, "if these contraptions were too hard to fly, no one would buy them. Remember, pilots aren't brain surgeons or rocket scientists."

"I hear you, but it is not as easy as you make it out to be." Victoria was being modest about her capabilities. Her heading rarely varied by more than ten degrees, and she was almost always within one hundred feet of the prescribed altitude.

Rick studied the aircraft's weather radar display. It showed exactly what was ahead. The microwaves being pulsated from the radar transmitter penetrated the forward airspace. Each sweep of the parabolic antenna, located in the aircraft's nose cone, captured those waves that hit and then bounced back to the aircraft from pockets of moisture being developed by the frontal system. Shades of green, yellow, and red illuminated the CRT mapping out the weather.

Rick switched to COM-2. It was time to contact enroute air traffic control. "Miami Center, WindStar One-Hundred-Whiskey-Sugar is with you over Manta Intersection at sixteen point five; like to pick up an IFR to Fox-Lima-Lima."

Center promptly responded. "Roger, One-Hundred-Whiskey-Sugar, radar contact; cleared as filed, climb to and maintain Flight Level one-eight-zero."

"As filed, up to one-eight-oh." Rick motioned for Victoria to pitch up the aircraft.

The controller asked, "Whiskey Sugar, are you radar equipped?"

"That's affirm, we're painting the front some fifty miles down the road."

"If you need to deviate let us know."

"Wilco, Whiskey Sugar."

In a little more than ten minutes, Rick knew it would be a bouncy ride picking their way through the front. Several small isolated patches of heavy precipitation flashed in red on the radar screen. Narrow batches of yellow, indicating moderate precipitation and moderate turbulence, clustered near the flashing red targets. The entire picture was raggedly framed by a wide area of lighter precipitation depicted in dark green. Every two to three seconds, the sweeping radar antenna captured a new weather image as the aircraft advanced on the front.

"Better be sure your seatbelt is snug," he cautioned Victoria over the cockpit intercom. "We're gonna get jolted around. And, it'll be rather noisy when the precip hits the plane."

Her eyes repeatedly glanced at the ominous weather ahead and then refocused on the flight instruments in the cockpit. "I think you might want to take over at the controls," she said with a slightly nervous tinge.

"Nah, it'll be good practice," Rick said confidently. "Remember, Salo wanted this trip to be a learning experience for you. Indeed, it will be."

Rick twisted a knob on the radar indicator to adjust its range and paint what was just twenty miles ahead. Suddenly, the entire CRT lit up like a Christmas tree. "Hmmm…" he moaned, "looks like we've got another minute or so before entering the leading edge of the front." He paused, reducing the power somewhat. "Don't worry, though, you'll do fine. Just concentrate on the aircraft's attitude indicator with an occasional check on the altimeter and HSI (Horizontal Situation Indicator)."

The midday sun disappeared as the aircraft penetrated the weather. The bright whiteness of the clouds turned to turbid gray. Rick switched on the panel lights to better illuminate cockpit instrumentation. He flipped off the wing-tip strobes to suppress the annoying sequenced flashes.

"Miami Center, One-Hundred-Whiskey-Sugar would like to pick our way through this weather."

"Roger, Whiskey-Sugar, thirty-degree deviations from course approved at pilot's discretion. Descend to one-four thousand, expect one-zero thousand in two-five miles."

"Whiskey-Sugar is out of one-eight for one-four." Rick paused. Victoria had heard the controller and was already beginning the descent. "Vicky, turn left to three-three-zero so we can miss that weather cell up ahead." Moderate to heavy precipitation and its associated turbulence were flashing on the radar screen.

Just as the aircraft leveled on the new heading, it began to shake like a car on a washboard road. Then, it seemed as if it was hitting a series of gigantic potholes. Powerful updrafts and waves of turbulence began slamming and pounding the WindStar. Suddenly, three hundred mile per hour rain pelted the windshield and fuselage; sounding like birdshot, it peppered the aircraft's skin. The tumultuous precipitation intensified. Now, torrential streams of water separated from the air, blanketing the aircraft as the WindStar fought its way forward. The sounds were almost deafening. The aircraft felt as if it would be torn from the sky. But it was not. Victoria was doing a remarkable job at the controls.

Rick raised his brow in absolute surprise. "How'd you get so good, Vicky?"

"You know, Rick, that new full-motion WindStar simulator that FSI (Flight Safety International) installed at the factory—the one you used for part of your training..." She hesitated as she pitched the aircraft up slightly. She was getting close to her desired altitude. "Anyway, after I crashed it twice, I went back for more..." She hesitated again. "Sorry, but I don't think I can chitchat with you while I am doing this."

Now he understood why Victoria was doing so well at the controls. She had spent much more time in the simulator than he had previously thought. And, he knew that a flight simulator was always much more difficult to fly than was the real aircraft.

Rick eyed the radar screen. "Okay, only ten miles to go and we'll be through this weather. Take a heading of three-six-zero."

Just as Rick gave her the new heading, he knit his brow in puzzlement. His nostrils flared. There was a strange smell in the cockpit. It was pungent and distressingly identifiable. It was the hallmark odor of scorched wire insulation.

An instant later, he heard the distinct sound of a circuit breaker pop. It came from the primary electrical bus. The panel was located on the cockpit sidewall below his left elbow.

Suddenly, the radar display disappeared. The entire cockpit darkened. The constant chatter that filtered through Rick's headset as other aircraft communicated with Miami Center went silent.

His eyes shifted down and to his left, focusing upon the circuit breaker panel. He immediately realized there had been a catastrophic failure of the PSU (Power Supply Unit). The PSU was the heart of the aircraft's electrical system.

Instantly, everything electronic became inoperative. Red flags appeared on the attitude indicator and the HSI. There was no flight control guidance. No navigation. No communication. The cockpit intercom that fed through the master avionics panel no longer functioned.

"Damn," Rick exhaled as his eyes once again focused upon the circuit breaker panel.

But he had no time to concentrate, things began happening quickly—very quickly.

The aircraft rapidly accelerated. Descending in a tight spiral to the left, the WindStar plummeted into the turbulent sea of air and driving rain. The rushing sound of speed increased in amplitude and became earsplitting.

Engine propellers surged.

The IVSI (Instantaneous Vertical Speed Indicator) read six thousand foot per minute.

Airspeed was approaching redline.

THE AIRCRAFT WAS OUT OF CONTROL.

EIGHT

RioAero, SA

Major Paulo cracked a nervous smile in relief as the WindStar continued its single-engine descent through fifteen feet. Everything was looking good. The aircraft seemed ready for touch down.

But at that moment, just as everything seemed to be under control, everything changed. A violent gust of wind wreaked havoc on Rameros' intended landing. The aircraft instantly leapt twenty feet above the runway. Its left wing angled upwards nearly thirty degrees. The WindStar began pivoting to the right as its airspeed dropped to eighty knots. The ominous, heart throbbing, stall warning horn loudly echoed throughout the cockpit. The aircraft struggled to stay in flight—its airfoils buffeting; its control yoke shuddering.

Rameros reacted immediately by shoving the left power lever full forward, slamming it into the throttle quadrant stops. There was a slight delay in response. Then the lone operating engine roared as its turbo machinery transferred thirteen hundred shaft horsepower to the forward gearbox. Propeller blades bit angrily into the air. The WindStar yawed further to the right, perilously drifting to the side of the runway. Rameros kicked full left rudder.

But nothing happened.

Catastrophe seemed imminent.

The major had been transfixed by the ongoing events. He had not spoken since the flaps and gear had been extended earlier during the approach. But now the fingers of both of his hands had a death grip on the armrests of his seat. His widened eyes glazed. His body froze. Profound terror.

Rameros had to act quickly. His reactions sprang from pure instinct. There was no time for thought; no margin for error. Adrenaline surged. Pupils dilated. Even though he still held full left rudder, the WindStar had yet to respond. There was no turn back to the left. The aircraft was still drifting with the aggressive wind.

Ahead and to the side of the runway, the ILS (Instrument Landing System) glide slope antenna loomed large as an obstruction. A fully extended windsock beckoned like a Greek Siren. Five tons of aluminum, composites, hydraulics, and electronics were failing to answer control inputs.

Rameros ripped the power lever of the left engine to its aft flight-idle stop, all the time holding full left rudder. He simultaneously nosed the aircraft down toward the runway to gain airspeed and sharply banked to the left. Momentarily, the aircraft seemed to hang as if suspended. Then, abruptly responding, the WindStar pivoted violently to the left. The indicated airspeed fell to sixty knots—well below flying speed—as the pitot tubes were briefly blanketed from detecting forward air pressure by the rapid maneuver. With a sudden jerk back on the yoke, Rameros neutralized the descent and immediately added aileron to level the wings.

Amazingly, the WindStar had not yet crashed. It was now hazardously positioned just two feet off the ground over the grass apron that bordered the right side of the runway. Still flying, nearly colliding with a taxiway marker and runway edge light, the aircraft was heading directly into the wind. As the wing tips crossed the runway's edge, Rameros abruptly planted the landing gear down onto the runway's concrete surface. It was an unconventional landing— across the *width* of the runway. The airspeed indicator read eighty knots; however, ground speed was a mere forty-five knots due to the powerful head wind.

As ground contact further slowed the WindStar, Rameros angled toward a taxiway just ahead and slightly to the right. He locked into the sensations coming through the controls to him. Focusing on safely clearing the runway, his mind raced ahead. He was oblivious to the superfluous and, at the moment, incoherent mutterings from the major who was slowly emerging from his stark terror.

Immediately after clearing the runway, the WindStar began to shudder. Rameros could feel the sickening newly familiar oscillations reverberate through frames of the superstructure that held the sidewalls and floorboards in place. The entire aircraft now shook violently, uncontrollably. The vibration was so extreme that the instrument panel almost became a blur. A master caution warning on the instrument panel flashed, indicating a prop over-speed condition detected from the left engine gearbox. The sensations were *déjà vu* to those experienced only thirty minutes earlier with the right engine's failure. And it was all happening again within a split second.

Before a word could be said or an action taken, an explosive penetration of the left fuselage occurred with the heart-stopping intensity of a mortar shell. Then, eerie silence. The last thing that Rameros thought could happen, actually had happened. The propeller from the left engine had separated from its gearbox, striking the side of the fuselage and becoming embedded in it.

"Mary, Mother of God," the major shouted in Portuguese. "That, that…" he stammered, "that could have happened earlier. That could have—"

"Jesus Christ, major. *Silêncio!*" Rameros had had enough stress for the day. He had little tolerance for an Air Force major—and a pilot, as well—who was about to get hysterical about what was now history.

"Interesting landing," the controller commented over the Tower frequency. "Wish I could have videotaped it."

Keeping a level head, Rameros knew that the controller's reference was an empty remark about the WindStar's unorthodox approach to landing across the runway. The Tower cab, located on the far eastern side of the field, was well out of range for videotaping any aircraft after its touchdown on Runway 3. Apparently, the wild gyrations had transfixed the controller enough to overlook the missing propeller on the right engine, and it was physically impossible for him to have witnessed the after-landing failure of the left prop.

"Thanks, I guess," Rameros coolly retorted. "I assume we are cleared for taxi to operations."

"Roger that."

The WindStar, now without any engine power, yet still in motion by virtue of its previous momentum, coasted along the taxiway that led between Hangars Seven and Eight, slowing though as its inertia dissipated. Switching to the secure company frequency, Rameros radioed, "Flight OPS, Sierra-Bravo-Whiskey needs a tug." Pause. "We are on the taxiway just south of Seven and Eight." Pause. "And, by the way, you had better call Biega in Engineering and Martinez in QA. Have them come down to Hangar One right away."

"Wilco, Sierra-Bravo-Whiskey."

NINE

Destination: Fort Lauderdale

"**I** got the aircraft," Rick shouted out. "I'VE GOT IT!"

Victoria abruptly released her white-knuckled grip. Her fingers flew off the control yoke and locked onto the armrests of her seat, all the while her eyes remaining riveted to the meaningless outside view.

Rick ripped the power levers back to their flight idle stops. The engine noise faded. The propellers acted as massive speed brakes. A high-pitched buzz was emitted as the propellers reacted to the excessive airspeed. With both hands on the control yoke, Rick muscled a turn to the right. The wings leveled. A split second later, he eased the WindStar out of its dive by slowly increasing its pitch. He was relying on the aircraft's pitot-static vacuum system which powered his four primary flight instruments: airspeed, vertical speed, altimeter, and turn-and-bank.

The airspeed reversed direction. The noise level inside the aircraft markedly quieted. Then the engine noise increased as the power levers were advanced to climb settings.

By now, the number one NAV/COM radio was operational and the left instrument panel gyro horizon and HSI had fully spooled up. These, and a few other critical flight instruments and devices, were connected to the emergency electrical bus which was fed by a 24 volt nickel-cadmium battery. Emergency power would last for approximately forty-five minutes.

Voices crackled once again through the earpieces of his headset. "One-Hundred-Whiskey Sugar, this is Miami Center, radar contact lost." There was a pause. "One-Hundred-Whiskey-Sugar, do you read Miami Center?"

Rick hoped that this was Miami Center's first call. He really did not want to comment about his in-flight problem. Questions would be asked. He would have to file a report with the FAA. Skepticism could be cast upon the WindStar.

"Roger, Miami, Whiskey-Sugar is level at one-four thousand." He lied. The aircraft had lost over three thousand feet during the incident and was just now climbing past twelve thousand. Rick knew, with radar contact lost and an inoperative transponder, there was no way air traffic control could know his real altitude.

"Whiskey-Sugar, descend to six thousand, contact Miami Approach on one-twenty-eight point six. You should be in the clear shortly." Center's hand-off to Approach Control at this point was a standard operating procedure.

Rick Harris took in a deep breath. "Out of one-four for six, so long."

With his right hand, Rick twisted the Miami Approach frequency into COM-1. Almost like magic, the cockpit brightened. There was clear blue sky for as far as their eyes could see. Home was now so close that any thought of further problems was vanquished from his mind. He smiled and glanced over toward Victoria who was visibly shaken by all that had transpired.

"What happened, Rick?" she spoke more loudly than before, partly from fear and partly knowing that the cockpit intercom was inoperative.

"Well, we had an electrical failure." Rick responded casually, as if what had just happened was a normal occurrence, a mere slight inconvenience. Of course, it was not.

But while the electrical failure was obvious, it was not the whole explanation for how the aircraft got into such a perilous situation. In just the few seconds it took Rick to look down at the circuit breaker panel of the primary electrical bus, Victoria had let the aircraft get away from her. When the instruments she was accustomed to using had failed, she diverted her attention to the weather outside the cockpit. Then, she lost all perception of what was up, down, left, right—where the aircraft might be.

Victoria had allowed the WindStar to go into a graveyard spiral. But she had done it so smoothly that it was virtually unnoticeable until it was almost too late.

"So, an electrical failure makes an aircraft go out of control like that?"

"Well, yes and no." Rick was trying to be diplomatic. As pilot-in-command, he realized he was ultimately responsible for the aircraft's diving spiral. He should have been more diligent with Victoria at the controls, especially after the electrical failure in the storm. "Let me put it this way," Rick continued, "without the electrical failure, the aircraft would not have done what it did."

Victoria was very bright and perceptive. She knew Rick was side-stepping the gist of her question. "Remember, it was your job not to let me scare myself."

Rick forced a laugh and went back to his original treatise. "Unfortunately, sometimes systems problems like the one we encountered do happen. New aircraft have what we call teething problems. Those take time to sort out. But the real problem is…" he lingered for effect. "The real problem is, how are we going to get those darn coffee stains off the new cockpit carpet?"

"You are a crazy man," she said as she playfully punched him in the arm. Rick's inane comment about spilled coffee had served its purpose, both diverting her attention from the system's malfunction and reducing her anxieties.

He smiled, then put his forefinger to his lips. The universal sign silenced their conversation before his next radio contact. "Miami Approach, One Hundred Whiskey-Sugar is level at six thousand with the airport in sight."

"Roger, Whiskey-Sugar," came the response from Approach Control, "cruise three thousand, contact the Tower on one-nineteen point three."

The approach to Fort Lauderdale was always a pleasant sight for Rick, and today even more so. He first glimpsed the huge, red and white smoke stacks of Florida Power and Light towering just to the west of Port Everglades. Then, two massive cruise ships at the docks came into vision. Next, he sighted Pier Sixty-Six on the other side of the Seventeenth Street Causeway. After that, he briefly focused upon white roofs of houses clustered along the meandering Intracoastal inlets.

He checked in with the Tower, "WindStar One Hundred Whiskey-Sugar is with you on a three mile left base for Two-Seven Left."

"Roger, Whiskey-Sugar, follow the Aero Commander on a two mile final, cleared to land Two-Seven Left."

No more surprises, Rick thought to himself. But the day was still young.

Rick kept the Commander in sight while slowing the WindStar to its normal one hundred twenty knot approach speed. He selected fifteen degrees of flaps. The aircraft pitched up slightly as the flap extension modified the wing camber. Then, he eased a small handle shaped like a miniature wheel out of its locking detent and moved it downward to actuate the hydraulic system and extend the landing gear. Two red lights from within the translucent handle flashed as three elongated, two-piece doors opened up bays on the underside of the aircraft, allowing the landing gear to extend. The flashing red lights extinguished just after three sequential thumps were felt through the aircraft's floorboards. The anticipated three small green lights illuminated near the gear handle. The landing gear was down and locked into position.

The WindStar turned onto a short final. Full flaps were selected. The airspeed slowed. The power levers were advanced to a target engine torque required to maintain the aircraft's ninety knot over-the-fence speed. The pre-landing check was complete.

Crossing the runway threshold, Rick transitioned the aircraft to a slight nose-up landing attitude and began reducing the engine power.

A faint double chirp sounded as the previously stationary main gear tires contacted the runway and started to roll along the grooved concrete surface. The aircraft slowed to fifty-five knots. The nose wheel contacted the runway with a dull thud. Rick eased the power levers up and back past the flight idle stops and into the beta range. The propellers first buzzed, then deeply resonated with the reverse in pitch as the engines spooled up to further slow the aircraft.

"WindStar Whiskey-Sugar, contact Ground Control on point seven as you clear."

Rick smiled. Almost home, he thought. He twisted in 121.7 on COM-1, and was cleared to taxi to RioAero on the south ramp. "I'll bet you've never seen our North American base of operations," he commented. The facility had just been completed three months earlier.

"You are right, I never have." She was almost relaxed now. Her composure belied that just thirty minutes ago she had been sure they were falling from the sky.

TEN

RioAero, SA

T he clang of the metal tow bar hitting the concrete floor echoed throughout the factory's nearly empty Hangar One. The tug's transmission whined over its muffled engine noise as it slowly backed away from the hapless WindStar and then departed from the hangar. Two pairs of forty-foot tall electrically powered steel doors slowly converged from each side of the hangar's entrance. The doors rumbled along over tracks embedded in the hangar floor, occasionally creaking and squealing, until reaching their forward travel-stops with a thunderous bang. Now, the almost ghostly stillness that fell within the hangar was only penetrated by disembodied bits of monotone conversation droning from nearby the WindStar. Dozens of fans suspended from high atop the hangar's massive girders wobbled while silently circulating the searing summer's air.

Hangar One was the heart of RioAero. Every new aircraft designed by the company was painstakingly developed and perfected by engineers working in various sections of the hangar. Each aircraft evolved through a series of developmental stages. Initially, detailed engineering blueprints were converted into full-scale wooden mockups for a proposed aircraft. The wooden mockups were used to layout, test, and fine-tune each aircraft zone and system—cockpit, avionics, flight controls, landing gear, etc. Later, as many as three prototypes were custom-produced by Manufacturing for flight testing, structural analysis, and the all important certification process required by airworthiness authorities.

Six months ago, when both FAA and CTA approval of the WindStar's Certificate of Airworthiness appeared imminent, the factory began spooling up for full production of the genuine aircraft. However, concurrent with the optimistic decision to manufacture the aircraft at an aggressive rate, any new engineering programs had to be placed on hold. The extensive cash outlays that had been required to successfully complete the WindStar program and enter the aircraft into production had severely drained the company's financial reserves. So, belts had to be tightened.

Still, a few programs involving the WindStar had been kept ongoing. Serial Number 003 was undergoing fatigue testing in a separate area of the hangar—a required program for any newly certified aircraft; it would last several more years. Serial Number 001 was being modified for military special mission operations—a twelve foot radar antenna pod was being affixed to the fuselage belly; two seventy gallon extended range fuel tanks were being fitted to hard points beneath each wing. Serial Number 009, a full production aircraft previously delivered to the Brazilian Air Force, was being retrofitted for armament—short-range, air-to-ground missiles. Despite these aircraft modification programs, nearly two-thirds of the immense Hangar One remained empty. And now on Friday afternoon, when even the small crews needed for these projects had wound up their day and left, the entire hangar seemed deserted.

A small entrance door at the rear of the hangar slammed. The metal-to-metal impact resonated throughout the structure. Distant fast-paced footfalls slapped against the glistening gray concrete floor. Faster. Closer. Louder. The buzz of conversation from around the WindStar ceased. The footsteps slowed, and then silenced. A hulk of a man now stood just forward of the aircraft's left wingtip.

"Hello, Lou," Gabe Batista almost whispered as he quickly glanced up at Biega. Batista, the long-time propulsion engineering department manager, fully understood the ramifications of the problem at hand.

"I just got here a few minutes earlier myself," Jeffe Martinez declared defensively, knowing full well that his quality assurance department had ultimate responsibility for detecting any production line defects.

Lou Biega was almost larger than life. His imposing six-foot four-inch height was accentuated by a massive frame that supported nearly three hundred pounds of engineering savvy and personal obstinateness. Big Lou, as he was known, was as much of a physical and emotional individual as he was an aloof aerospace intellectual. Biega had joined Salo Montero as a senior engineer when RioAero was formed in 1968. Two years later, Biega headed up Propulsion, then Structural Design, and finally, in 1973, Big Lou was promoted to run all of Engineering. Next to Salo, Lou Biega was the most powerful man at RioAero.

"It looks like a structural failure," Batista flatly stated.

"Probably a defect in milling the prop shaft," Martinez interjected.

Biega's face remained expressionless. He pushed back his long, wind-tattered, pitch-black wavy hair with one hand and with the other hand removed an unlit, half-smoked panatela from his moist lips. He slowly walked up to the left engine nacelle and gazed at the gearbox—the sheared shaft, ragged. He cocked his head to the right, studying the propeller assembly that was still embedded in the fuselage.

"What do you think, Lou?" Martinez asked.

"What do I think? What do I think?" Biega slowly muttered in a disgusted voice. His body tensed. "I will tell you what I think," he roared. "I think some friggin' sonovabitch screwed up my goddamn airplane. Nobody does this to one of my birds. NOBODY. I am going to get to the bottom of this. When it is all said and done, the bastard responsible for this is going to pay. I will have his friggin' ass. You got me, Martinez? Dead meat!"

Martinez, visibly shaken, stepped backwards. He was new to RioAero, joining the company a little over a year ago after serving as assistant director of QA for a European airframer.

Biega's oral tirade boiled over into pure physical anger. His face reddened. His eyes narrowed. Uncontrollably, with the instep of his right foot, Big Lou kicked the lower blade of the propeller assembly that hung only inches above the hangar floor. He kicked it again, and again. The embedded assembly silently withstood the savage onslaught unmoved.

"Lou, Lou, wait!" Batista shouted, rushing toward Biega. "We need to carefully analyze every aspect of the damage. We need to preserve all the evidence. We need to learn what actually happened. We need to know why."

"Yeah, yeah," Biega grumbled. He knew Batista was right. Big Lou abruptly backed away from the fuselage, his arms windmilling to maintain his balance. "You know, this kind of shit just does not happen by itself. Somebody caused it to happen. Gabe, I want you to call Dayton-Standard and have them get their asses down here tomorrow. Tell them what happened. Tell them this is not some kind of joke. Have them bring whatever equipment they need to get the answers."

"But, I am not sure they can get here by then," Batista advised. "I think—"

"Call Willie Roth." Big Lou fumed, throwing his cigar to the ground and savagely grinding it into the concrete floor with his heel. "He is their goddamn president. He can make it rain. Tell him I want him and his best engineers down here no later than Sunday. Or tell him, if he prefers, I will personally fly up to Dayton and shove one of these goddamn prop blades up his friggin' ass."

"Okay, Lou, I will take care of it." A flustered Batista turned and hurried away toward an office near the front of the hangar.

"So, Mister Quality Assurance," Biega said searingly, turning to Martinez, "what the hell is going on? You guys in QA are supposed to make sure this kind of shit does not happen." He paused, glaring at Martinez. "Spending too much time in Rio with the samba girls?"

"No, no," Martinez stammered, "I cannot understand it. We have detailed inspections. We perform numerous tests. Each aircraft is signed off by over a dozen inspectors before being released to Flight OPS. It is not a quality assurance problem. I can tell you that."

"Yeah, right." Biega knew human nature. He found that engineers, like most other people, had a difficult time in accepting responsibility for problems that arose on their watch. "Tell me, Martinez," Biega continued, "who was the pilot of this plane when everything went to hell?"

A still uneasy Martinez grinned to himself.

ELEVEN

RioAero, NA

RioAero's new facility in Fort Lauderdale consisted of two identical, fifteen thousand square foot, two-story buildings connected by a glass enclosed walkway. One building housed administration and sales, the other customer service and product support. The complex's beige stucco exterior was accented by a broad band of cobalt blue—RioAero's trademark color—that visually divided the two floors of the two rectangular buildings. The barrel tile roof, also cobalt blue, was an uncommon sight for the topping of on-airport facilities that were instead usually quickly fabricated from inexpensive corrugated steel. The Brazilians had insisted on quality construction for their new presence in a new market. The choice of location in Fort Lauderdale for RioAero's North American operations was more for personal than business reasons—South Florida had a heavy Latin influence.

The company's nearby massive thirty-five thousand square foot hangar had been just a skeleton of steel I-beams when Rick had last seen it prior to his departure to Brazil. Now, it was a fully enclosed structure of bright-white corrugated steel topped with a sky-blue translucent fiberglass roof. The general contractor was presently installing six huge electrically actuated doors that opened horizontally, riding upon railroad-like tracks imbedded in the floor's concrete foundation. When closed, Rick noticed the doors transformed into a blue lettered billboard that read: ***Welcome to RioAero***. The company's trademarked comet logo underscored the lettering.

Rick taxied the WindStar around and then behind the hangar to a parking area near the administration and product support complex that had been specifically designed to showcase the company's aircraft. He set the parking brake and placed the engine condition levers in the fuel cutoff position. The engines spooled down. The propellers went into feather, slowly windmilling until their rotation stopped.

By now, employees were filtering out of the two buildings to get a closer look at the aircraft. Many of them had only seen pictures of the WindStar—never the actual aircraft.

Before Rick and Victoria even had their seatbelts unfastened, the cabin door opened. "*Tudo bom?*" greeted a voice using the Brazilian phrase "everything good."

Rick twisted his body to the right, peered down the aisle into the cabin, and spotted Joey Delgada, director of product support, entering the aircraft.

Though Delgada was Brazilian, he was very much like many of his country's professionals having been educated in the United States—MIT, in fact. Joey knew more about how to keep a fleet of aircraft flying than anyone Rick had ever met. He had the pragmatism of an airframe and power-plant mechanic, yet the intellect of an aerospace engineer. Joey was a short, stocky, boy-like man in his mid-forties. He wore light brown cowboy boots that clashed with the rest of his ensemble of navy blue slacks and burgundy oxford shirt. His thick, dark brown hair was wild and windswept.

"*Tudo bem!*" Rick responded. "I'd like you to meet Victoria. She's a private pilot and the daughter of someone at the factory." Rick chose not to divulge the fact that Victoria was actually the daughter of Salo Montero. He felt there was no need to do so. "Anyway, Vicky made sure I didn't get lost during the trip. Having her along was also very helpful in communicating with flight line personnel during our refueling stops in Brazil."

Joey and Victoria briefly conversed in Portuguese. Rick could pick up a few words here and there. He was fluent in Spanish, but, to him, Portuguese seemed to be a jumbled amalgamation of Spanish and Italian that largely proved unintelligible. However, Rick could tell that more than mere pleasantries were exchanged when Joey's eyes widened, his mouth fell open, and he turned to Rick with an incredulous stare.

Victoria excused herself as she exited the cockpit so that Rick and Joey could discuss the in-flight incident. She retrieved her bag from the forward stowage compartment and departed the aircraft.

Joey slid into the copilot's seat. "So, I understand you had some kind of an electrical problem."

"Yes, I was about to get to that," Rick said. "It was a complete electrical failure that occurred while we were pushing through that weather just half an hour before landing."

"Damn," Joey groaned, "bad timing for an electrical failure. You probably had your hands full for awhile." He hesitated while considering a playful jibe, but realized an attempt at levity would be inappropriate. "Hmmm...I hope it was not, but let me take a stab at it. Was it the PSU?"

"Yup."

"Hell, that unit performed so well for us during certification. I cannot understand it." Joey closed his eyes tightly, grimaced, and then shook his head. "Lucas is a good vendor. Their PSU has had an excellent MTBF (Mean Time Between Failures). I just cannot understand it." He paused again, trying to come up with a rational explanation for the failure. "I just do not know…cannot say. Hopefully, it was a bad connector. Maybe moisture got into the unit. We can find that out pretty fast. But on the other hand, if we are just learning that there may be a design problem with the unit, well, that is another story. Design problems take a lot of time to fix. You know, Rick, the WindStar program is small potatoes to Lucas."

Aircraft like the WindStar had dozens of vendors from all over the world supplying parts, equipment, and accessories that were incorporated into the finished product. Many of these vendor items were unique and designed to RioAero's specifications. Unlike Boeing and McDonnell Douglas, who turn out more than fifty aircraft each month, or Cessna with its hundreds of monthly aircraft shipments, RioAero manufactured a mere nine WindStars per month. With minor customers, vendors were typically slow to respond when problems developed in such limited production runs. Indeed, very little funding could be justified for product support. In first response, these vendors typically blamed the airframe manufacturer for exceeding an item's initial design capabilities, or the airline for improper maintenance or operational abuse. Unfortunately, despite the poor stepchild treatment, small airframe manufacturers had to accept what they could get. There were only a few vendors from among which an airframer could select a required item. It was a real catch-22 situation.

"You got a spare in inventory, Joey?"

"Not here, but you should have one somewhere in the cargo loaded on board before you left the factory. I will have the failed unit pulled while the cargo is being off-loaded, and then install the spare. We will bench check the failed unit; we will have the aircraft's entire electrical system checked out. We certainly do not want to have this kind of stuff happen when you have a hot customer on board."

"Thanks, Joey." Rick knew Joey and his tech support team would thoroughly inspect the entire aircraft over the weekend—nose to tail. "By the way, Joey, I brought back four cases of Brahma Chopp. Two cases are for you and your guys." Real beer from Brazil was always a treat. While the name was the same, many people privately thought that the beer imported for distribution in the States had little resemblance to the Brahma Chopp they drank in Brazil.

"*Obrigado*." Joey thanked Rick for his thoughtfulness. "I will have the other two cases put in storage so they do not sprout legs and walk off." He laughed. "You can pick them up whenever you like."

By now, half a dozen employees were on board the aircraft, combing through the cabin. On the tarmac, a much larger group was admiring the aircraft's exterior. Excited voices in both Portuguese and English were extolling the plane's virtues. Everyone was smiling. Rick acknowledged the crowd's presence by commenting in his limited Portuguese about what a joy it was to fly the WindStar. Grinning, he grabbed his travel bag from the forward stowage area. But as he approached the cabin door and was about to exit the aircraft, his face paled, his body froze. "What the hell is *he* doing here?" he snarled to himself, clenching his jaw.

TWELVE

RioAero, SA

"The pilot's name is "Franco Rameros," Jeffe Martinez confidently said to Biega in Hanger One.

"Figures," Big Lou said, still glaring at Martinez. "That hotdog was probably doing some kind of aerobatics that overstressed the aircraft. Have him get his ass down here. I want a few words with him."

"Will not have to." Martinez nervously half-smiled in relief, feeling about to be spared from Biega's wrath—at least for the moment. "You could not have noticed, but Rameros slipped into the hangar while you were, uh, examining the propeller assembly that is embedded in the fuselage. In fact, he is over on the other side of the aircraft by the right engine."

"Oh really! This is going to be great." Biega laughed acerbically to himself, relishing the opportunity to harangue Rameros over what hopefully would prove to be pilot error.

Most engineers and pilots seemed to clash. Cats and dogs. Some would say different cultures. Others would arrogantly and erroneously attribute it to different genetics. Seldom would either faction speak highly of the other. But Lou Biega was a rare engineer who had developed a liking for a pilot, and oddly enough to many outside observers, that pilot was the equally haughty Franco Rameros.

Over the years, Biega and Rameros had worked together on a variety of aircraft programs. During that time, both headstrong individuals had come to reassess biased perceptions about each other that had initially caused personal conflict. They now held begrudging respect for each other. However, their gigantic egos always seemed to quash any true close relationship that could have developed.

Big Lou turned away from Martinez and quickly moved around the front of the WindStar. Just as Martinez had said, there was Franco Rameros, standing on a small platform inspecting the upper forward section of the engine gearbox. Holding a magnifying glass in one hand and balancing a Styrofoam cup of Jack Daniels on ice in the other, Rameros was quietly grunting and clucking to himself as he twisted his body to clinically inspect the sheared-off propeller shaft.

"So, you are the sonovabitch who broke my plane," Biega suddenly bellowed, hoping to catch Rameros off-guard.

"Yeah, yeah," Rameros echoed back with barely a flinch and without repositioning his body. "Nothing personal, Big Lou," he continued, straightening his slightly hunched-over back, still focusing his attention on the propeller shaft, "but if you were not such a goddamn pathetic engineer, maybe there would not have been a problem in the first place."

Biega quickly retorted, "And, if you were not such a shit-ass pilot, I would still have a WindStar with two fans on its wings." Big Lou marched up to the platform where Rameros was standing. He paused for nearly five seconds, staring at Rameros' back, and then he said with sincerity, "How was it out there, my friend?"

"Honestly," Rameros smiled as he turned to Biega, "I have had better days. It was a little tense for awhile." He paused, slowly shaking his head from side to side. "You know, on top of it all, Osvaldo Paulo was flying right seat when everything happened."

"The major?"

"Unfortunately, yes." Rameros took a sip from the Styrofoam cup. "When things started falling apart, the goddamn major acted like a teenager at a whorehouse." Rameros snickered. "All excited, but too overwhelmed to know what to say or do. He just froze." Rameros swirled the ice in his cup. "At least he kept out of my way."

Big Lou's eyes narrowed. "And this is the very aircraft scheduled to join the Air Force fleet of WindStars?"

"Why, yes," Rameros said, nodding in agreement, "but that is probably not going to happen for awhile. Not until we replace the props, the prop shafts, do some metal work, and, of course, assure the major that what happened will never happen again."

"Where is the major now?" Biega inquired.

Rameros laughed. "He went home. Too stressed, I guess. He even passed up on some Jack Daniels just to get the hell out of here." Rameros raised his Styrofoam cup and smiled as he looked Biega in the eye. "Worry not, Lou, the major agreed to keep everything confidential. I told him we would talk on Monday."

"Good," Biega said, switching gears from earlier pure anger to an inquisitive mode. Shock and disappointment at the sight of the crippled aircraft was waning. His analytical mind was kicking in, and now curiosity was overtaking him. "Franco, tell me about the flight. See if we can put some pieces of this puzzle together."

Rameros stepped down from the platform upon which he was standing and began to detail each stage of his test flight in the WindStar, from takeoff to the event filled landing and subsequent second propeller incident. Actually, from his perspective in the cockpit, there was little information that could be used to pinpoint the cause of the propeller failure. Yes, the propeller assemblies did separate from their fractured gearbox shafts. Yes, cockpit instrumentation did alert Rameros to a propulsion problem. But the only warnings he received had occurred within split-seconds of each incident.

"Hmmm…" Biega exhaled, gloomily. "Looks like you had your hands full in safely getting this aircraft back on the ground."

Rameros shrugged. "I guess it comes with the territory. I have been through worse." Indeed, Franco Rameros certainly had. "By the way," Rameros said, lowering his voice as he came closer to Biega, "did Batista or Martinez notice anything peculiar about the sheared prop shafts?"

Big Lou frowned, pursing his lips. "Those guys had nothing meaningful to contribute. Just the typical speculation about structural failure and manufacturing defects."

"How closely did they examine the shafts?" Rameros squatted to glance under the WindStar's fuselage before receiving his answer or going on. No one was on the other side of the aircraft.

"Not sure."

"Here," Rameros said handing Biega his 10X magnifying glass. "Take a look. Tell me what you see."

Big Lou stepped up onto the platform, and then spent over a minute examining what remained of the cannular propeller shaft. "What are you getting at, Franco? What am I looking for?"

"You are the engineer, Big Lou. I am just a damn pilot." Rameros sighed and then stepped up onto the platform with Biega. "Now I suppose you want me to do your job too."

"Hey, Franco, I will get to the bottom of this sooner or later," Biega said, newly irritated with Rameros.

"Okay Lou, you win." Rameros saw no need to further agitate Biega. What Franco had noticed during his examination might not be worth even noting; but, then again, it could be a clue. "Look just inside the shaft at about the ten o'clock position…at the fractured edge."

"Uh-huh," Biega said, repositioning his body.

Rameros extended his hand. "Take this flashlight. It will help."

Full-feathering propeller systems, like those installed on the WindStar, are connected to the aircraft via a flanged, nickel-based alloy shaft. The rear or engine-side flange is attached to a gearbox that reduces the twenty thousand revolutions per minute generated by the power section of the turbine engine into a more usable propeller operating range of between 700-2,000 rpm. At the forward flange, the shank of each propeller blade is secured to a hub. Here, a system of levers, counterweights and springs allow the blades to change pitch and efficiently use engine torque to produce optimal thrust during various flight regimes. The shaft itself is solid except for its thin tube-like center. The narrow diameter of the center tube allows high-pressure oil from the engine to flow through the shaft to a piston located just forward of the propeller hub. A governor, mounted on the gearbox, adjusts the oil pressure that moves the piston forward and aft. Movements of the piston generate a force to a pair of levers that are attached to each of the four propeller blades. This, then, twists the blades to a specified angle or pitch. The propeller shaft is not a preflight checklist item. It is rarely inspected, except by mechanics, and then usually only once every year.

"Ah-hah," Biega said with surprise. "Yes, yes…I think I see what you mean. It is barely visible."

What Rameros had seen, and now led Biega to discover for himself, was a series of tiny discolored spots, smaller than the tip of a needle. Even with a magnifying glass, it was virtually impossible to determine anything about the spots except for their existence. But their presence was certainly a suspicious anomaly.

"Well, Lou?" Rameros queried. "What do you think?"

"Interesting…" Biega mused. "I have never seen anything like this before on a propeller shaft. But, then again, I have never had an aircraft lose one propeller, let alone two, due to a fractured shaft."

"Exactly," Rameros agreed. "And, if we take a close look at the shaft on the left engine, my bet is that we will find something similar, if not identical."

As Lou and Franco rolled the small platform to the left side of the aircraft, they saw Batista and Martinez approaching from the front of the hangar.

"So, when are those boneheads from Dayton arriving?" Biega scowled.

"Their tech support guy is trying to locate Mr. Roth," Gabe Batista said, apologetically.

Jeffe Martinez chimed in, "He is supposed to be coming back from some meeting in Detroit."

"Really," Biega said, sarcastically. "Okay, you two can do part of Willie Roth's work for him. Remove the prop shaft from the right gearbox and air express it to Dayton-Standard, ATTENTION: WILLIE ROTH. Got it?"

"Yes, sir," both Batista and Martinez said, almost in unison. They immediately departed for the right side of the aircraft.

"Now, my dear Franco," Biega continued, his eyes narrowing with anticipation, "I think it is time for us to take a look at the left prop shaft."

Big Lou slid the platform up to the left engine and took a step up. He turned to Rameros who handed him the magnifying glass and flashlight. A short ten seconds later, Biega exclaimed: "DITTO!"

A smile spread across Rameros' face. His hunch was correct. They had discovered a clue that hopefully could be linked to the cause of the propeller separation.

"Good work, Lou," Rameros said, cuttingly. "You engineers always seem to know what to look for."

"Yeah, sometimes we have a good bird dog and get lucky." Biega stepped down from the platform and slapped Rameros on the back. He knew that without Franco's help there was little chance he would have come across the evidence he had just seen, especially this early in the investigation. "You are a pretty perceptive goddamn pilot." He paused, pulling a new panatela from his shirt pocket and fumbling with its wrapper before continuing. "An ion microscope or mass spectrometry should provide us with the type of metallurgical analysis necessary to identify the why of what happened. Dayton has that capability."

"How long will it take to get the report?"

"We will know by Monday. I am sure Willie Roth will make it his top priority," Biega said, now glancing at his watch. "Tell you what, Franco, how about walking back with me to my office. There are a few phone calls that have to be made. I would like you to be there. Besides, I think you probably need a refill. I know I have your brand."

Rameros rattled the ice cubes in his otherwise empty cup and said, "I thought you would never ask."

THIRTEEN

RioAero, NA

R ick had glimpsed Dan Cole on the ramp below. Dan was standing with Roberto Menendez, the company's CFO.

"Get on down here, Harris, and say hello," Cole bellowed with a deep southern accent.

Rick disliked everything about Dan Cole. He found just the sight of him revolting. A short, heavy-set man in his late fifties, Cole looked like a paunchy aging bulldog that sported thick horn-rimmed glasses and a crew-cut hairstyle. Today he was wearing a gaudy tangerine guayabera shirt over gray, polyester Sansabelt slacks.

Dan Cole had been in aviation all of his life. He seemed to have worked for or been associated with almost every airframe manufacturer in the world. And, he thought he knew more about the aviation industry than anyone, anywhere—a supposed expertise he would never let a person forget.

At airline convention hospitality suites, Cole was a rude and obnoxious drunk. He bad-mouthed his competitors. He chastised airlines that spurned whichever aircraft he was promoting at the moment. As a businessman, he was frequently illogical and vindictive. There was not an ethical bone in Cole's body. Rick knew some aircraft sales executives who had worked for Cole. They all despised the man. Most industry professionals tried to avoid him. Those who did associate with him usually later regretted it.

Most recently, Rick had heard that Cole was heading up the North American operation of ComJet, a Spanish aircraft leasing company that now had an operation in Boca Raton. What Cole was doing here at RioAero would be something beyond Rick's wildest imagination.

"Hey there, my boy, I'm darn glad to see you," was the greeting with which Rick was assaulted as he exited the aircraft and put down his travel bag. Cole snatched Rick's right hand and began pumping it as if trying to get water from a well. "I was just telling Bob here," he continued, referring to Roberto Menendez who hated the nickname Bob, "what a fine boy you are, and that every now and then you get lucky and sell an airplane." Cole snorted, then gut laughed for what seemed to be forever. "Ain't that so, Bobby?" Menendez just rolled his eyes at Rick in silent shared pain. "Anyway, let's do dinner tonight. I'll catch you up on what's going on."

"Actually," Rick said, doing all he could to maintain a reserved countenance, "I've been out of the country for three weeks and promised my wife—"

"Yeah, yeah…I know, I know. Hey, we'll just get together at the office on Monday morning and go at it from there."

"Sure, fine, great seeing you," Rick said smiling with as much sincerity as he could muster. "Monday it is." Then he thought to himself: What the hell is going on? Did RioAero hire Cole as some kind of consultant? To do what? Rick picked up his travel bag and started to look for Victoria.

"She is upstairs with Silvia," Menendez said, guessing as to Rick's questioning glances around the assembled people. Roberto's secretary had taken Victoria to Rick's office.

"Thanks, Roberto…walk with me, please." When they were out of Cole's earshot, Rick said, "Roberto, I very much respect you and the company we both work for, but Dan Cole is another story. Would you be perfectly honest and tell me what is going on?"

"You mean you don't know?"

"Know what?"

"Salo didn't tell you?"

"Tell me what?" Rick was getting agitated.

"Well, I can tell you are not going to like—"

"*Roberto*, get to the point."

"Okay…" Menendez took a deep breath and stopped walking. "Dan Cole is the newly appointed managing director of RioAero, NA—he is our boss."

Rick dropped his travel bag onto the tarmac. There was silence.

The inside of the Administration Building was virtually empty of people. Indeed, half of both levels remained sparsely furnished. Only a small group—mostly Brazilians—had been initially hired to staff the new operation.

Rick left his travel bag in the lobby and trotted up the stairs to his office. As he walked down the corridor, he could not help but notice the name on the door of the large office just down the hallway from his own. It read: DAN COLE—MANAGING DIRECTOR. Brazilian companies often used European terminology for executive level positions. Rick knew that managing director meant the same thing as president. He gritted his teeth.

Rick entered his office. Victoria was at his desk just finishing up a telephone conversation. He walked past her to the bank of windows that framed the back of his office and gazed out at the WindStar below. There, near the aft cargo door, stood the man in the tangerine guayabera shirt. Dan Cole was pointing to the vertical tail of the aircraft. Two of the company's department managers flanked him. "What a shame, what a damn shame," Rick muttered softly to himself.

"Okay," Victoria said as she hung up the phone. "Everything is set. I am having a classmate from Hollywood pick me up." She noticed that Rick's attention was fixated on the WindStar below. He had not heard a word she said. "Are you okay?"

"Oh…sure, sure." Rick turned away from the windows, thoughts spinning in his mind, still not making eye contact with Victoria. "Will you be giving Salo a call?"

"Probably later this evening. I am sure he has left the factory by now and is on his way to the lake house. That is where he usually tries to spend his weekends during the summer. February is summertime in Brazil, you know."

"Well, when you do get hold of him, please have him give me a call at my home. He has my number, but let me give it to you anyway." Rick wrote the number down on the back of a business card he picked up from his desk. He handed the card to Victoria. "It's just business," Rick continued, "but it's very important that I speak with him as soon as possible."

"I will be sure to let him know." Then changing the subject, she continued, "I want to thank you for the lift to the States. It was educational, and then some." She paused, adding politely, "Let's keep in touch."

"Okay, sure," Rick replied, his mind still preoccupied with Cole. Victoria gave him a quick hug and left the office.

Rick glanced at his overflowing in-basket and the stack of pink message sheets near his phone. A twelve-foot long blackboard on the wall to the left of his desk detailed an extensive listing of airline prospects he would be contacting during the following week. He was hardly in the mood to do any business. Yet it was just past four o'clock in the afternoon, and there was lots of work to be done. But not today.

With a sweeping motion, Rick pulled some paperwork together and stuffed it into the leather briefcase he snatched from under his desk. "I'm outa here," he said aloud to himself.

Rick marched defiantly out of the office.

FOURTEEN

RioAero, SA

The side exit door to Hangar One was pressured shut. Blustery northwest winds assaulted the hangar—penetrating between the door and its metal jamb. The winds hissed as if seemingly eager to again create turmoil for the crippled WindStar. Big Lou twisted the handle and pushed against the door. It opened slightly, then slammed shut as a strong gust rattled the entire side of the hangar's corrugated steel siding. He frowned in disbelief. Then putting his shoulder to the door, he overcame the wind's force. But before he could steady the door in his grasp, it flew wide open, flailing against the hangar's siding, banging again and again. "You were actually flying in this shit?" he shouted to Rameros who had followed him out of the hangar. Lou muscled the door closed.

Rameros' retort was unintelligible, squelched by the howling wind.

They walked determinedly, occasionally teetering against swirling gusts, to the Engineering Building that was a short distance from Hangar One. The piedmont area to the north was darkening with an unsettled summer atmosphere loaded with moisture. The air rose, then cooled, then rose once again, working its way up thousands and thousands of feet into a boiling sky. Ascending water droplets became ice crystals, forming anvil heads of cumulonimbus clouds that pointed in the direction of their travel—directly toward the airport. Lightning arced, dancing from cloud to cloud. Distant thunder roared. Pellets of hail began to descend, bouncing off the ramp areas and walkways. Without a word between them, Lou and Franco sprinted the last few yards to the building's side entrance door.

"Summertime in Brazil," Biega said, invigorated from the short walk and mad dash to the door.

"Good timing," Rameros commented, as they both entered the building. A bright flash and near immediate clap of thunder punctuated his remark.

Three flights of steel-lipped gray-tiled stairs angled up to a brightly lit corridor that led to Biega's corner office at the other end of the building. Along both sides of the hallway were clustered mazes of modular cubicles broken apart by several large open areas where scores of engineers seemed frozen over massive drafting boards cluttered with blueprints. An occasional rustle of paper and sporadic words in Portuguese, frequently intermixed with English, broke the stillness in which the engineers worked.

The top floor of the building housed the GEA—*Grupo de Engenharia Avançado*. The advanced engineering group was a "Skunk Works" of sorts. All new aeronautical projects were born here. Any major problems arising from a product that RioAero manufactured, whether aircraft or subcontracted component, were analyzed and solved here. Indeed if Dayton-Standard could not determine the cause of the propeller shaft failures, GEA would. The some fifty engineers who worked at GEA had been handpicked by Biega. Their engineering skills were without peer. Their loyalty to Big Lou and RioAero was resolute. Biega affectionately called GEA his "Think Tank."

Projects under GEA development were always highly confidential. Competition among aerospace manufacturers was keen. All Think Tank engineers had top security clearances. They were a highly cohesive team of professionals who had the ability, creativity, and vision to produce cutting-edge aerospace programs. Their projects included both commercial as well as military applications. The W350X project was an advanced WindStar, stretched to accommodate thirty-five passengers. The WJ500X used a slightly modified WindStar fuselage, incorporated a newly designed high-speed wing, and had aft fuselage-mounted fan-jet engines. It resembled the Gulfstream II business jet, but was somewhat larger and had a proposed four thousand mile range. The JMX, a joint project with Pugliese Aerospace of Italy, was envisioned as the next generation of low-level military attack jets. Additionally, a special section within GEA was quietly working on laser and satellite technology applications.

Biega and Rameros silently walked down the corridor. Big Lou nodded occasionally, acknowledging a few of the engineers who caught his eye. With a quick point of his finger and sweeping motion of his left arm, he beckoned one engineer to join him in his corner office. "Everything seems to be humming along," he noted with satisfaction to Rameros. "I live to see my guys create new stuff." The pride was evident in his voice.

"Hello, Lou," said Gloria Soto, Biega's always busy secretary as she glanced up from the paperwork spread across her desk. "No new messages."

"Good," Biega responded with a smile. "Please get Willie Roth on the phone. Try his private office number. Then, see if you can reach Salo at his lake house. He should just be arriving there by now."

He walked through the doorway into his office. Rameros followed.

Biega's office was huge—nearly fifteen hundred square feet. It was larger than any other office at RioAero; it was larger than most houses in Brazil. When Big Lou took over Engineering nearly eight years ago, he consolidated all departmental functions under one roof. It made sense. A centralized engineering group could work more efficiently. It would assist Biega in fulfilling the mission he had been assigned by Salo Montero—to establish RioAero as a world-class aerospace company. And, it was happening. The company's technical expertise accelerated. The company was doubling in size every few years. Indeed, an expansive opulent office for the director of engineering in a newly constructed building was a small price for the company to pay.

Biega seated himself behind his immense reddish-brown mahogany desk in preparation for the telephone conversations he was about to have. Rameros remained standing, his eyes searching the room for that bottle of sour mash Big Lou had mentioned he had.

The back and left sides of the long, rectangular office were formed by sixteen-foot wide sections of double-pane tinted glass that stretched from the ceiling to a wide sill three feet above the short-napped blue-gray carpeted floor. The eight-foot tall, charcoal gray vertical blinds that hung from motorized ceiling tracks were slightly open. The walls were "Biega Beige," a creamy, softly textured hue reminiscent of *café au lait*. Clusters of tastefully positioned aircraft pictures and esoteric Brazilian art effectively belied the walls' expansiveness.

To the far right was the conference area. The satin smooth mid-tan hardwood table dominating the area could easily accommodate the twenty-five engineers and department heads that Biega met with on a weekly basis. To the far left was an oversized drafting table that he used less frequently now than he once had in the past. Discretely tucked into the recesses of his office were a small kitchen and a private bathroom with shower.

From the office doorway came a soft but raspy voice, "You wanted to see me?" It was Ronnie Trilliano, a short, frail-looking middle aged man. From his shoulder length hair, to his wire-framed glasses, to his rumpled ill-fitting clothes, Trilliano could easily have been mistaken for an indigent. He was not. He was Biega's right-hand man. Whenever a project bogged down or a critical problem needed to be solved, Trilliano was always involved. He got results. Quickly, almost like magic.

"Thanks for coming, Ronnie," Biega said, politely. Big Lou's disposition was mercurial. It was greatly influenced by his respect for the people with whom he interfaced. His Think Tank family was special. He related to them with the thoughtfulness and diplomacy of a statesman. "Ronnie," Biega continued, "we have a problem with S/N-35. The aircraft is in Hangar One right now. Apparently a metallurgic problem caused both prop shafts to shear a few millimeters from their gearbox flanges. The right propeller is somewhere in the Sarapuí

River; the left one is embedded in the fuselage. I am having Batista and Martinez send what remains of the right shaft to Dayton-Standard. I would like you to take a look at the left one."

Trilliano's eyes opened wide behind his thick-lensed glasses. "Yes, yes of course, I will certainly examine the aircraft," he said very quickly. Then, slowing his tempo, he squinted his eyes and continued, "Very strange…this is all very strange. I have never heard of a shaft fracture like this. Now you tell me we had both shafts fracture, and the incidents occurred during the same flight. This is very strange indeed."

"My thoughts exactly," Biega agreed.

"What else can you tell me about the failures?" Trilliano pressed. "Any information, however minor, would be helpful."

"There is not really much," Biega said, glancing for input from Rameros, who just shrugged. "Franco had little warning prior to the incidents. In all other respects, the flight was very normal." Biega paused. "But later in Hangar One, Franco and I took a close look at the fractures. What we were surprised to find was a series of tiny discolored spots at the fracture site on the inside of both shafts."

"Hmmm…" Trilliano intoned. He wandered toward the bank of windows that spanned the southern side of Biega's office as he contemplated what he had heard. It was just past five o'clock. The weather was improving, yet steady rain and heavy winds prevailed. Through the angled blinds, he could see production workers scurrying to the parking lot from Hangar Two (Wing Fabrication) and Hangar Five (Subassembly). He just stood there, gazing out the window. Frozen in thought. Minutes passed.

Biega clicked open his silver Zippo lighter and fired up the unlit panatela he had unwrapped earlier in Hangar One. The long slender cigar was dwarfed by his massive hands. "About that drink," he said to Rameros, motioning toward the small kitchen area. "Second cabinet to the left. Make one for me. Just ice will be fine."

Slightly over a minute later, Rameros returned from the kitchen with two coffee mugs half filled with Jack Daniels over ice just as Trilliano finally turned away from the windows. Rameros handed one mug to Lou.

"So, Ronnie, what do you think?" Biega asked.

Trilliano had had an epiphany. He was smiling, but grimly so. Watching scores of production workers hustle themselves from Fabrication and Subassembly had given him a thought. It was an ominous one. "Okay," Trilliano began explaining, "if we discount such obvious factors as defects in manufacturing the shaft or faulty installation…" He briefly hesitated and shot a glance toward Rameros before continuing. "And, if we eliminate the possibility of excessive in-flight maneuvers that could have caused stress, a possible explanation could be…" Trilliano's words stopped. "No, forget it," he shook his head and continued, changing gears. "I have seen propeller assemblies throw blades. I have seen improperly rigged props twist engines from their mounts…nearly tearing the entire assembly from the frame. I have seen lots of things. But I have never seen a catastrophic shaft fracture on an aircraft, let alone a new aircraft…and two on the same flight?"

"Well," Biega said, "well, it happened. Now, what was it that you were about to say before you said 'forget it?'"

Trilliano, however, forged on without addressing Big Lou's question. "Dayton-Standard is a fine company. Their manufacturing processes and quality control are second to none. Their product support is excellent. They have been in the propeller business for more than fifty years. They—"

"Get to the point, Ronnie," Biega almost growled, his tolerance and diplomacy wearing thin.

"Lou…" Trilliano hesitated. "I am not sure. I could be dead wrong."

"Ronnie…" Big Lou was persistent. "I need ideas. I need input. I need them now."

"Okay, okay…" Trilliano acquiesced. "But let us keep this among ourselves until I have done some research. I do not want to start an unfounded rumor that could later embarrass you or GEA."

"Consider it done," Biega said, leaning back in his chair. "Whatever you say stays between us until we have evidence to verify it."

Trilliano walked over to Lou's desk, picked up a blank memo pad and scribbled one word onto it with his felt-tipped pen. He handed it to Biega who glanced at what Trilliano had written and then eyed him skeptically.

"You think so?" Biega asked, soliciting affirmation.

Trilliano nodded. "It is quite possible."

Biega dropped his head as he re-read the single word Trilliano had written. He looked up at Rameros, and with a hushed tone carefully pronounced the word: "SA-BO-TAGE."

The room remained silent. Eyes repeatedly making and breaking contact as minds struggled to accept the concept. Not a breath taken.

Rameros' vague prior suspicions were strengthened. His words were first to puncture the silence: "What? No! Why?"

Trilliano shrugged. "There could be a lot of reasons," he answered. "Of course, it is still just a theory. That is why I did not want to mention it until I had taken a good look at the aircraft. But, when I saw the workers dashing from the hangars to the parking lot, something clicked. I remembered three years ago. That was before the former President of Brazil, General Geisel, allowed unions to strike."

Ronnie Trilliano removed his glasses and distractedly went through the motions of trying to clean them using the front of his baggy shirt. His small pale blue eyes reddened. It was unpleasant for him to recall a tragedy of the past. "I can still see in my mind's eye a large group of workers running away from the small assembly hangar that used to be where Hangar Two now is. Then, there was an explosion. The hangar was destroyed. The factory was shut down for over a week. The military locked everyone out. It is a different time now, but in many ways it is not. The military still runs the country. They still own RioAero. So based on what little information you gave me, there is a possibility that someone within the factory, or with access to the aircraft's components, could—I say *could*—have caused a weakening of the shafts. That may have led to premature fatigue—the fracture."

"Still, Ronnie..." Biega said, frowning, "WHY?"

"Again," Trilliano shrugged, "there are a lot of possibilities. You know the company's current situation. And, you know the Brazilian economy. RioAero has had a dismal sales record during the past few years. The company is in a tenuous financial position—little cash. Inflation has been running wild—triple digits, the worst ever."

"Yes," Rameros agreed, "but production workers' compensation is adjusted for inflation each and every month."

"Of course," Trilliano said, raising his eyebrows, "we all know that. But the adjustments have not kept pace with the current rate of inflation, and there is always a lag in paying the workers. Some workers are pissed. I have heard rumors. The Democratic Movement Party is well represented at the factory. Many workers feel it is time for a return to a civilian government. Sometimes there is little logic to the actions of a few of the more outspoken. Remember, all it takes is the right person at the right place with the right tools." He paused, looking into Rameros' eyes, and added ominously, "You know, Franco, the WindStar you were flying in was meant to crash. You had luck on your side...this time."

Gloria Soto appeared by the door. "Lou, I have Mr. Roth on Line Two."

"Thanks, Gloria, I will be right with him." Then to Trilliano, Biega said, "Take a good look at the left side of S/N-35 and get back to me as soon as you can."

Ronnie Trilliano nodded and left the room.

"Damn," Big Lou said in a disgusted voice, "that would be all we need, especially now...some dipshit assembly guys biting the hand that feeds them." Composing himself, he picked up the phone. "Willie, *tudo bom*?"

"Hello Lou," the distant voice crackled over the telephone line, "we're all doing just fine up here in Dayton. We have more orders than we've got inventory to fill. But you're not calling me to chit-chat. My people tell me that you had some kind of propeller problem."

"Unfortunately, that is true. Let me put you on the box. I have Franco Rameros here with me in the office." Biega pressed the button on the phone to the speaker and hung up his handset. Both Lou and Franco detailed events leading to the propeller incidents as they had done with Trilliano and would do with Salo.

"Sounds pretty bad," Roth said. "I'd rather not speculate at this point, but I assure you I'll do everything I can. Send up one of the prop shafts and we'll do a complete analysis. You'll have our report by Monday afternoon at the latest."

"Thanks, Willie, I knew I could count on you." Biega was relieved even though he had every expectation Roth would fully cooperate. He conceded to himself there was really no need for Roth or any of his engineers to fly down to the factory over the weekend. "The shaft is being disassembled as we speak. It will be air express shipped to you tonight. Talk with you on Monday, if not before."

"Have a great weekend, if you can," Roth said. The poor telephone connection was fading in and out.

"You bet," Biega called out. "At least we will try." He punched the button on his phone to disconnect the line. "That was easy," he said to Rameros, "but Salo is going to be a different story. He will be outraged when I tell him what has happened." Biega puffed on his panatela twice, and then took a sip from his mug.

"Think Trilliano is right?" Rameros quizzed Biega.

"He is right most of the time." Big Lou got up from behind his desk and moved to the windows overlooking the hangars. He glanced toward Hangar Two, below and to his left. The stream of workers hurrying to the parking lot was thinning out. Biega did not like the idea of sabotage at all. "Hell," he said turning to Rameros, "if Ronnie is right, we have big problems. We can never be sure what will happen next. It could be the landing gear, the engines, the electronics. We will have to reinspect every damn aircraft coming off of the production line and every white-tail parked on the ramp." Biega abruptly stopped talking. He saw Gloria standing by the door again. "I bet you have Salo on the phone," he said, not relishing his imminent conversation with RioAero's Chairman and CEO.

"That is correct," Gloria confirmed, noting the tension in the room. "He is on Line One."

"Great, like I really want to do this," Biega muttered almost inaudibly. Telling Salo Montero that both propellers of a new WindStar had separated from their shafts during a pre-delivery test flight for the Air Force would be a delicate matter. Hinting that his company could be falling apart due to disgruntled production workers would be worse. Salo loved the company he had founded and nurtured along for the military establishment. His involvement had been intense with the WindStar program from its inception. He had a personal attachment, if only psychologically, to everyone on the payroll. That today's in-flight incidents could imply the WindStar might have airworthiness problems would be disconcerting. But the possibility of internal sabotage would be devastating to him.

Biega pressed the button on his speakerphone. "Hello, Salo."

"*O que se passa, Lou?*" Montero's voice was slightly gruff, yet apprehensive. He had left the factory shortly after lunch only three hours earlier. A phone call placed by Gloria for Lou meant business, not pleasure. It implied a problem.

Biega immediately got to the point. "Salo, I am in my office with Franco Rameros and have you on speaker. We have a potentially serious problem involving the WindStar." He briefly paused for the impact of his words to sink in.

Montero remained silent.

Lou continued, "I will cut to the chase. Remember that ride you asked Franco to take Major Paulo on earlier today…well, things did not go as planned. For reasons yet to be determined, the aircraft had propeller problems. First, the right propeller sheared off from its shaft during a normal climbout some thirty miles from the airport."

"First? It gets worse?" Montero quickly questioned in disbelief.

"Unfortunately, yes." Biega proceeded. "Shortly after landing, the second propeller sheared from its shaft, embedding itself in the left side of the aircraft's fuselage. Needless to say, the major was a basket case."

There was a long silence on the line. "Diagnosis?" Montero finally queried, his tone amazingly stoic.

"None yet." Biega felt awkward. "It only happened a little while ago. We are analyzing everything. I have Ronnie Trilliano on the case. The prop shaft is being sent to Dayton-Standard. Except for speculation, we have nothing to report yet."

"What speculation?"

Biega was afraid Montero would ask. He decided to down-play his own mounting suspicion that the answer could be sabotage. "The usual—manufacturing defects, installation, damage during shipment..." Biega kept it brief.

"And, the press?"

"Rameros did a superb job of keeping the incident quiet. The Tower does not even know about it. We should be safe from the onslaught of reporters, at least for now."

"Good work, Franco," Montero said. "Let me know, Lou, as soon as you learn anything. Thanks for the call."

Biega pushed the speakerphone button to off.

"He took the bad news remarkably well," Rameros said to Biega.

"I suppose there was not much else he could do. But I will guarantee you one thing," Biega said, snuffing out his cigar in an ashtray, "come Monday morning, he is going to want to know why the WindStar had a problem. He will want all the details...details we must have."

Rameros nodded.

FIFTEEN

Pasador Ranch

The winter sun was slowly sinking in the clear blue South Florida sky. Distant rays swept the landscape, imparting a rich golden hue. Radiant beams filtered through massive banyan trees and towering royal palms. Shadows lengthened, spreading over the dormant, yet still green turfgrass.

In the pasture, a gray gelding snorted and then uttered a high-pitched squeal. He kicked up his hind legs, twisted his body, and momentarily left the ground altogether. The gelding enthusiastically embarked upon a self-appointed task. First galloping, then settling into a smooth largo gait, he drove the group of mares forward. They crowded together, then surged ahead.

Rick Harris slowed his silver BMW as the first section of black pipe fencing came into view. He rolled down the car's left tinted window and focused on the gelding herding the other horses. "*Qué brio*," he said aloud, admiring the gelding's spirited style. Rick continued to watch the Paso Fino horses thunder through the pasture with extended high-held tails on a curved path of their own design. They moved so effortlessly, so carefree, so naturally. Yes, Harris thought, it felt good to be home.

He drove ahead, turned left at the end of the road, and stopped at the beige stucco archway entrance. With the push of a button on his remote control, electric motors of the gate opener lazily droned and the two sides of the wrought-iron gate pivoted away from each other and opened. After Harris drove forward, the gate automatically closed behind him. He grinned broadly at the sight of the large house only a hundred yards more down the concrete driveway.

As he parked and stepped out of the BMW, two black and tan dogs suddenly came charging toward him. The rottweilers' massive frames and powerful movements would be heart-stoppingly intimidating for anyone. However, Rick Harris was calm, simply dropping to a squat in response to the charge. The dogs closed rapidly, now twenty feet away. Rick responded by clapping his hands. The dogs kept on coming; their mouths open, lolling tongues flopping with each downward thrust of their paws.

"Bruce…Jessica…" Rick called out. "Good dogs!"

Narrowly averting a collision, the dogs ran just past him before skidding to a halt. Then as deftly as they could, the dogs whirled and hurled their ninety-five pound bodies back toward him. Their uncommon, undocked tails wagged madly. Their bodies quivered. Snorting and whining sounds filled the air with a mix of excitement and greeting. The dogs were ecstatic to find their best friend home once again.

But as quickly as the dogs had come, the pair turned away and raced down a pathway that led to the stable. Rick followed, knowing that the greeting committee would soon be announcing his return to others.

The house and stable had been built slightly less than five years ago on a thirty-five acre site in Davie, just outside Fort Lauderdale. It was then about as far west as you could go without disappearing into the muck and sawgrass of the Everglades. The property originally boasted only a small grassy landing strip once used by drug traffickers who flew marijuana up from Jamaica in light single-engine aircraft. When U.S. Customs eventually seized the property and later put it up for auction in 1975, Rick and his wife, Gail Richmond, were the only bidders. Real estate developers were yet to be interested in land that far west. At $7,000 per acre, the property was an unbelievable bargain.

Although the three thousand foot landing strip still existed, it was barely identifiable as such and remained unused except for grazing by horses. Rick and Gail had built a Mediterranean-style house with an orange barrel-tiled roof near the roadside entrance to the property. Further improvements, located behind the house, included a fifteen stall stable, training ring, hay barn, equipment shed, and a duplex structure consisting of office space on one side, and living quarters on the other side for Domingo Sanchez, the ranch manager. The entire property was now enclosed by five-rung black pipe fencing specially designed to contain horses. All in all, today's Pasador Ranch was a far cry from the drug trafficker's original drop-off point.

Harris was halfway to the stable when he heard the staccato beat of a Paso Fino's hooves rhythmically hitting the sixty-four foot stretch of sounding boards located in the center of the sandy training ring. Similar to the fast moving feet of a flamenco dancer, the rapid clippity-clop of the Paso's four-beat gait was music to his ears. No other breed of horse was quite like a Paso Fino—so hot-blooded, so spirited, so muscular, yet so compact in size and so smooth to ride.

While highly popular in Colombia, Puerto Rico, and the Dominican Republic, Paso Finos remained rather rare in the United States. The breed, generally averaging a mere fourteen hands high, was a genetic mix of the Barb, Spanish Jennett, and Andalusian. Forebearers of the breed were brought to the New World by Columbus and subsequent voyagers and became one of the first equine species to once again live in the Americas after all horses had mysteriously become extinct over ten thousand years ago.

Gail Richmond had admired Paso Finos ever since she had learned about the breed in grade school. Later, through her practice as an equine veterinarian, she became increasingly familiar with the breed. She loved everything about them. Now, she and Rick owned ten Paso Finos, including three mares in foal.

As Rick arrived at the training ring, he observed his wife astride *Vuelo del Halcón*, a dark bay colt that had been foaled on the ranch just four years earlier. Gail saw Rick immediately. She waved an excited acknowledgement to him and then prepared for another pass on the sounding boards.

The young colt stammer-stepped to the side. Gail increased leg pressure to collect him. He bucked mildly, protesting her control. She commanded a slight turn to the right to reaffirm her authority, straightened him to his task again, and urged him ahead toward the sounding boards. With the clucking sound almost universal among riders, she prodded the colt forward into a classic fino-fino gait. The percussion of a rapid unbroken rhythm of hooves, each independently striking the narrow strip of wooden boards, dramatically punctuated the horse's natural movement. With the piston-like motion of his hooves pounding almost in place at two beats per second, the colt inched its way forward. His upper body was tense and virtually motionless. His neck sharply arched, ears pricked forward. The colt was fully focused. The exhibition was art in motion and in sound.

The cadence muffled to silence when the colt's hooves sank into the sandy soil at the end of the sounding boards.

"Well, stranger, what do you think?" Gail Richmond beamed, projecting her voice ahead to Rick as she settled the fired-up colt down and soothed the horse into a slow walk in Rick's direction.

His face glowed with pride. "Aside from being glad to be home, I'd say you've done a remarkable job with *Vuelo*, and bareback at that!" The two rottweilers were at his side, keenly interested in sampling every foreign scent Rick's clothing contained. "Have these canines been taking good care of you?" he asked, scratching one of the dogs behind the ear.

"Absolutely!" Gail crossed her right leg over the colt's withers and slid off the side of its sweating back. She detached the curb chain from the bit, unbuckled the throatlatch of the headstall, removed the bridle, and lightly slapped the colt on its shoulder. The horse sprinted away to freedom on the far side of the ring.

"So, Sky King," Gail said mockingly as she walked toward Rick, "these three weeks have been a long time." She hung the bridle on her shoulder and climbed over the fence. "You've got a lot of catch up work to do here at home this weekend. I hope you're not too travel-weary."

They embraced passionately. Even after ten years of marriage, the excitement in their relationship was very much the same as it had been when they first met.

"It felt more like three months to me," Rick bemoaned. Then, continuing apologetically and looking deeply into her eyes, he spoke: "I'll make sure it doesn't happen again."

"Thank you, Mr. Harris, I'll count on that," she said, hanging the bridle on top of the fence.

They walked, hand-in-hand, back to the house. The dogs followed.

SIXTEEN

Pasador Ranch

Rick was in the bedroom, beginning to unpack from his trip. Gail was showering. The phone rang. Rick was about to let the answering machine screen the call, but then he remembered that Joey Delgada or Salo Montero could be calling.

"Rick Harris," he answered in a business-like tone. Joey Delgada was on the line.

"We found the problem with the PSU," the voice said, getting right to the point. "The connectors were not locked in place."

"Uh-huh." Harris listened.

"Those connectors have a locking mechanism that prevents them from vibrating loose. And, as a further precaution, they are always safety-wired." Joey paused. Rick was silent. "Neither the input nor the output connectors to the PSU were locked or wired. Very strange." Joey paused again.

Rick waited, remaining silent.

"Well, what happened was when the input connector loosened, it created an electrical arcing at the plug receptacle. You probably smelled burnt insulation in the cockpit, right?

"Yes."

"And then, the circuit breaker blew."

Harris silently agreed. That was exactly what had happened.

"You know, Rick, it was just a matter of time before that aircraft had an electrical failure. It could have happened earlier during your trip from Brazil. Then again, it might not have happened until weeks from now."

"But why wasn't the connector locked and wired?" Rick probed.

"May be somebody at the factory doesn't like you."

"Huh? What do you mean?" Rick quickly asked, not sure what Joey was implying.

"You were the only one who was going to fly the plane away from the factory. And aside from the factory's test flight pilots, you are the only one qualified and authorized to fly that aircraft for sales demonstrations here in the States. So, if someone—"

"You can't be serious," he retorted, cutting Joey off. "I'm new with the company. Hardly anyone knows me yet. I certainly couldn't have pissed off anyone enough to sabotage the aircraft on my account."

Rick's shocked consternation had been Joey's playful intention. Goal achieved, Joey bit his lip, trying to hold back hysterical laughter. "I know, I know," Joey said. But now the ruse was up and he cackled. "Hey, Rick, try not to take me so seriously all the time. Sometimes you pilots need to lighten up." Then, more solemn, Delgada continued, "My bet is that some production worker was simply not paying attention and skipped a step in the install procedure."

"But how about QA?" Rick inquired. "Shouldn't they have caught it?"

"Yes, they are supposed to. QA inspectors are supposed to make sure Manufacturing turns out each aircraft in accordance with approved build specs." Joey was reciting what Rick already knew. "Sometimes they screw up, too. Do you like the sabotage explanation better?" Joey laughed, firmly believing that an oversight at the factory was the only explanation for the PSU problem. Sabotage, just a lame joke.

"No, no," Rick swiftly came back, but taking Joey's comment to heart. The last thing any pilot wants to carry in the back of his mind is the possibility of sabotage on an aircraft he is flying. "You'll let the factory know about the problem?"

"I have already sent a fax to Martinez in QA. He will handle it from there. And worry not, Rick, we will be doing a complete inspection of the aircraft over the weekend. I know you have big plans for the WindStar during the next few weeks."

"Thanks, Joey, I appreciate your help."

Rick hung up the phone just as Gail walked out of the bathroom and into the bedroom. His glance at her became a rapt stare. Gail's short damp auburn hair seemed sculpted to her head. Her firm, deeply tanned body was accentuated by a pink cotton demi bra and string bikini panties. Her freshly glossed lips glistened radiantly. She moved with the grace of a dancer. One excellent looking woman, Rick thought.

"Who was on the phone?" she casually asked, fluffing her moist hair, and further interrupting his thinking.

"Oh, uhh…it was just Joey Delgada at the airport," Rick stammered, closing his suitcase and removing it from the bed. His breathing rate had increased. His voice had a slight, but noticeable quiver.

"Problems?" Gail asked, perplexed by Rick's sudden change in behavior.

"Yes…NO…uhh, not sure." Rick seemed confused, but he really was not. He stretched his body out on the bed, propping his head on one of the pillows. A silly boy-like smile crept across his face. "If you come a little closer," he stage whispered to Gail, "I'll tell you about one problem I really do have…one that I think, with your help, could be solved."

Now, it made sense to her. Rick was making a clumsy attempt at being amorous. *Men,* she thought, sensitive and insecure creatures, all of them. "Well, Mr. Harris," she said with a bewitching smile, "let's just s-e-e what kind of problem you have." She moved slowly toward the bed, her hips swaying, her breasts rounded beneath the pink demi bra. Rick's eyes absorbed every enticing movement of her body.

"You know," she continued, now crawling onto the bed and straddling his lower body, "I'm a licensed doctor of veterinary medicine and you look like a poor animal that could use my help."

She unbuckled his belt. Her eyes sparkled. A seductive smile crept across her face.

Rick inhaled deeply and was about to speak when Gail put a finger to her lips indicating silence.

"I'm not really used to my patients talking. In fact, I've learned to read body language very well. So, just try to relax." She slowly pulled the belt out through the loops of his pants with her left hand and pressed her right hand against his groin. "My, my…you feel awfully tense." She gently bit down on her lower lip. "I can tell that extended trip to Brazil has really had an effect on you," she said in a resonating purr.

Rick could no longer bear it. His body felt like a steam boiler ready to explode. He had to react. With both hands, he reached up toward her, but before he could touch her body, Gail grabbed his wrists and pinned him back against the bed. She pressed her lower body against his, arched her back, and watched Rick's eyes capture the shape of her breasts. He moaned, "I want you so much."

Gail smoothly released his wrists.

They fell together.

SEVENTEEN

Pasador Ranch

In the kitchen, Gail was preparing dinner for the dogs. A lamb and rice dry dog food mixed with warm water made a succulent meal for the rottweilers. Rick was concentrating on making a mango punch in the blender—fresh mango slices from the groves in Homestead, Absolut vodka, Bacardi 151, grenadine, and lots of crushed ice. The fruity smell perfumed the kitchen air when he lifted the lid to add more ice to the whirring mixture.

"So, tell me about your South American expedition," Gail said to Rick as he turned off the blender and poured the golden pink slurry into two tall glasses. A couple of weekly phone conversations from Brazil had not been nearly enough to share all his thoughts.

Rick poked two straws into each glass of the punch and then handed a drink to Gail. "Brazil's an interesting country," he said, taking a sip from the glass and rolling the slurry on his tongue before swallowing. "Mmmm…pretty good." Fresh mango punch was one of Rick's all-time favorites. "You know, Brazil has more tropical fruit juices than you could ever imagine. Everybody in Brazil drinks fruit juices. Compared to what we serve here in the States, the juices there are sweeter and thicker. I've got to dilute those drinks with ice." He took another sip of his punch. "Anyhow," Rick continued, delving into his newly learned history of an area he had found fascinating to visit, "Brazil is a big country. It ranks fifth in both area and population among all other countries in the world. In fact, Brazil is bigger than the entire area of our lower forty-eight. And, like the States, Brazil has tremendous natural resources, so it has great potential. On the negative side of the equation, the country has serious internal problems. Drug use and trafficking is widespread—tentacles of Colombian drug lords are everywhere. The government is corrupt as hell—it's been a dictatorship run by the military since the coup in 1964. A third of the urban population lives in slums; only about seventy-five percent of the people can read and write; and, the economy is a disaster with triple-digit inflation. Black market moneychangers pay heavy premiums over normal bank rates for American dollars. Everybody knows the dollar is strong, and everybody knows Brazilian currency loses value with each passing day."

Gail intently listened to Rick's every word. "So compared to Brazil, even the high inflation and twenty percent interest rates we are now seeing here in the States are relatively benign," she opined. But she was finding herself puzzled by how and why a poor third world country like Brazil could afford to get into the highly technical and highly competitive aviation business. "With a third of the country's people living in slums and perhaps all but a small minority just getting by on a day-to-day basis, where did the billions of dollars come from to create RioAero?"

"Aah, that's an interesting question," Rick observed. He walked over to the kitchen table, placed his glass down onto it, and slowly settled back into one of the chrome-framed swivel chairs adjacent to the glass-topped table. Then, happily rubbing his open hands together, he began one of his typical animated dissertations. "Remember the 'Butter and Guns' analogy from Macroeconomics 101?" Rick paused.

Gail shrugged, rolled her eyes, and shook her head no. She was a veterinarian; he had the MBA in applied economics.

"Well, anyway," he went on, dismissing her nonverbal response, "the government of Brazil—the military in this case—decides how public monies should be spent. Of course," he raised both hands, almost knocking his drink off the table, "with a military dictatorship, there's no real voting—no say by the people. The military establishment has its own agenda—it does whatever it wants. In Brazil, the military is sort of a 'good old boy's club' with rights of ascension. You see, every four years or so, some club member—a general, of course—gets appointed as president. Most are hard-liners—Army guys who want to keep the dictatorship in place and the rest of the population as far away as possible from positions of political power. So to maintain their holds, the president and each branch of the military have their own cloak-and-dagger intelligence organization to repress any opposition. Hell, a differing philosophy is enough for someone to be vaporized, and certainly, perceived threats become extinct. But every once in a while, absolute power does not corrupt, and a levelheaded military leader gets a shot at the helm. Some of these guys even have good ideas now and then. Back in 1968, some mucky-muck general who became president had a brainstorm. That's the background, now get ready for the economics."

Gail groaned. "I was afraid you were going to get to that."

Rick feigned a wounded face and continued, "Anyway, this general essentially said, to hell with focusing upon quality of life for the people, which was pretty bad in the first place. In economic parlance, he said, forget about churning butter; let's make guns—super highways, hydroelectric plants, or airplanes in this instance. For the military, there was prestige and glamour in manufacturing airplanes. No glamour with butter, or, for that matter, with coffee or with orange juice. So, *voila*...almost overnight, an aircraft factory appeared just down the road from Rio de Janeiro."

Rick stood up, grabbed his near-empty glass from the table, and sauntered over to the blender on the kitchen countertop. "Short-term it made no sense at all—crime, poverty, and economic chaos were rampant in Brazil. Long-term—HA—the decision was brilliant. Brazil is a vast geographic territory. Air transportation truly is a critical factor to its future development. Why should the country continue to rely upon imported aircraft if instead aircraft could be manufactured in a Brazilian factory? It sure makes more sense for a country the size of Brazil to make aircraft than, for example, a country the size of Sweden."

Gail furrowed her brow. "I sort of remember you mentioning that Fairchild and Saab were talking about making a new regional airliner a year or two ago, with the Swedes taking the lead. But, why would Sweden be making airplanes?"

"Good question," Rick responded. "Perhaps for some of the reasons the Brazilians decided to get into the aircraft business— prestige and glamour. Nonetheless, the Swedes have typically made airplanes for military purposes with a very limited number for the commercial market. Then again, unlike Brazil, the Swedes have the alternative of joining NATO if they so choose. Even more unlike Brazil, Sweden is a small country with a stagnant population growth rate, high labor costs, and limited resources. Really, there's no true economic reason for Sweden to manufacture aircraft. The Swedes could easily do what most other countries do—buy aircraft from the French, the Brits, or the Americans. In the long run, the country would save a ton of money.

"Whether sensible or not, the Saab partnership with Fairchild Industries involving a thirty-seat commercial aircraft is in its early stages and appears to be on-track. Hardly revolutionary, that aircraft is essentially a slightly stretched and updated G-I Gulfstream from the late 1950s with new General Electric helicopter engines that have yet to be proven on a fixed-wing aircraft. Saab and Fairchild say they will capture twenty-five percent of the world market with this new aircraft within the next ten years or so—fifteen hundred aircraft. I seriously doubt that production will be more than 500 before manufacturing is shut down."

Rick poured the remaining contents of the blender into his glass and strolled back to the kitchen table. The Bacardi 151 was helping to enliven his presentation. "On the other hand, Brazil is prime. The country has a large domestic market and a government with the willingness to spend whatever it takes. Couple that with a recently acquired technical expertise and dirt-cheap labor costs, and RioAero becomes a company well positioned for the long haul. Its competitors are already nervous about the impact the WindStar will have in the market…how RioAero will adversely affect the competition's sales."

Rick was getting carried away. He knew it. Fortunately Gail was very much interested in the aviation industry and Rick's business activities. She always enjoyed his often emotional and animated discussions.

Gail spoke up, "So, everything's going well for RioAero and the WindStar program?"

"Yes and no," Rick responded. "The WindStar is a fantastic machine—technically advanced, highly efficient. The company has their engineering and manufacturing act together, but their sales and marketing expertise are virtually non-existent. For the past year, a worthless aircraft broker over in Dania has been retained to market the WindStar in North America. He's done virtually nothing. The only six WindStars contracted for and soon to be delivered to a U.S. airline were actually a direct result of the efforts made by the company's Chairman and CEO, Salo Montero, shortly before the aircraft was certified by the FAA."

Gail said, "Heck, that sad song is history now, what with RioAero's new facility here in Fort Lauderdale and you in charge of North American sales."

"Well, yes, but the factory has some two-dozen new WindStars built and stored as inventory. And, get this, aircraft are still being turned out at a rate of nine per month."

"What?" Gail started in amazement. "Are they crazy?"

"It's pure business insanity. They feel they have a great product, which they do; and, they feel it should sell, which it has not." Rick was shaking his head in disbelief. "They just keep making aircraft and continue tying aircraft down on the tarmac."

"Wow!" Gail said, astonished. "How long can that go on?"

"If things turn out as I've planned, within three months that inventory will be sold, the company will have a twelve month backlog, and may even have to up the production rate."

"Yeah, right," she said with an incredulous smile. "And just how do you intend to do that?"

"Ah-haa, that's the magical question," Rick said. "I have a plan."

Gail smiled and replied, "So, you think you're RioAero's White Knight."

The ring of the telephone broke in on their conversation. Rick was pumped up, on a roll, and tried to ignore the sound. However, Gail knew Rick was expecting a call from Salo Montero in Brazil. If this were that call, it was important for Rick to take. She pointed toward the telephone, gave him a thumbs-up, and left the room. The dogs followed her.

He picked up the cordless telephone and said, *"Boa noite,* Rick Harris."

"Speaking Portuguese, are you, Mr. Harris?" the voice on the other end of the phone quipped. It was Salo Montero. "I just had a brief conversation with Victoria. She said you asked for me to give you a call. She thought it was important."

"That's right, Salo." Rick was apprehensive about telling Montero what was on his mind, but felt he had to. It had been bothering him ever since he had arrived in Fort Lauderdale that afternoon. "Sir, may I speak freely?" he continued, reflexively relying upon his former military training and phrasing his words as he would when addressing a ranking officer.

"Why, of course, Rick." Cautiously feeling Harris out, Salo continued by saying, "You know you are the key to our success in the North American market...selling the WindStar...keeping the production line operating." Salo's words were flattering but also honest. He was banking on it being true. "So, tell me what is on your mind?"

After a brief hesitation, Rick spoke up. "I need to discuss a critical matter. Something I have great difficulty understanding, let alone dealing with."

"And, yes," Salo said, "what is it?"

"Two words," Rick said in response, trying to hold back both the frustration and anger that was developing at just the thought. "DAN COLE," he blurted out.

There was silence on the other end of the phone. Rick listened, but there was no response from Montero.

"Salo..." Rick continued on, warming with ire. "What the hell is going on?"

"Rick, this is difficult for me to explain." Salo's tone was regretful. "I wanted to brief you about it before you left the factory, but the timing was not quite right. Too many things were happening that day. Too many people were around. It just was not—"

"Goddamn it, Salo," Rick blurted out, almost shouting into the phone. Rick was now pacing the floor, his eyes darting from side to side as his mind kept flashing upon the image of the man in the tangerine guayabera shirt—the image of Dan Cole, managing director, RioAero, NA. "What the hell, Salo..." Rick's emotional state, mixed with Bacardi 151, was getting the best of him. His feelings of betrayal by Montero were raw. "So, you let me leave the factory only to come home and discover for myself that some scumbag blowhard is now managing director of the North American operation."

"Now, Rick—" Salo tried to interject.

"No, Mr. Montero, it's not 'Now, Rick.'" Harris was fuming. "I thought we had a deal. I thought you approved my program plans. I thought selling the WindStar in North America was my bag. Today, I find out that some damn ass has been appointed as managing director. An insufferable jerk who will screw things up." Rick's boiling anger erupted into physical action as he threw the now empty drinking glass from his hand into a trash container located on the floor near the end of the kitchen countertop. The glass shattered on impact. The sudden noise and angry voice caused the dogs to rush into the kitchen, barking, hackles up. Rick ignored the dogs. "Salo," Harris continued, "I have a great deal of difficulty in respecting this kind of decision-making. I thought more of you. I thought more of RioAero. Maybe I was wrong."

There was dead silence.

"Rick," Salo's calm, collected voice began, "I want you to listen very carefully. This is as difficult of a situation for me as it is for you."

Harris was clenching his jaw, grinding his teeth, trying to rein in his blazing anger. He had stopped pacing the floor and was now seated on one of the kitchen chairs. With elbows anchored to the table, he rested his forehead on one hand, and held the telephone tightly against his ear with the other hand. He was steeled to listen to Montero's explanation.

Salo continued, "Rick, sometimes things happen over which we have no control. Cole was not my decision. I felt the North American operation was just fine the way it was…without a managing director…without Cole. With Menendez managing finance and administration, Delgada in product support, and you handling sales, I was pleased with the company's initial structure."

Harris was slowly calming down from his earlier tirade. He was now ready to weigh Salo's information and judge what kind of decision-making could justify hiring Cole. "I'm listening," he said to Salo.

"Thanks, Rick," Salo replied and then went on. "The decision was not mine; it was made by General Carlo Cardella. You probably are unaware of it, but Cardella is a very powerful man here in Brazil. He heads up the Army's intelligence network. Although he works in the background, he has a great deal of influence over many of the ministers who report directly to the president himself." He briefly paused. "Frankly, I really do not understand why the general got involved in something as mundane as RioAero in Fort Lauderdale. Unfortunately, the reasons are known only to him. Nobody ever questions Cardella. It is just not done."

By now, Rick had composed himself. He spoke in a normal business voice. "But, why Cole? He's a charlatan."

"Like I said," Salo responded, "I do not know. I cannot say what Cardella's relationship is with Cole." He hesitated for a second. "The only thing I am aware of is that Cardella has been doing a lot of international travel. That is somewhat unusual for a man in his position. During the past few months, he has spent a great deal of time in Europe. My understanding is that France and Spain were his primary destinations. Maybe he is working on some military deal. Maybe it involves RioAero. Nobody knows."

Interesting, Rick thought. France was a major aerospace power. The country had advanced technical expertise. Located there were Dassault, Aerospatiale, and Snecma, among others, and the newly formed Airbus Industrie. In Spain, there was really only Barcelona Aeronáuticas, SA (BASA), established nearly fifty years ago as an airframe manufacturer. For the past ten years, BASA had manufactured the Avio-23, a smallish twin-engine, high-wing utility transport that had both military and commercial applications. BASA had responded to airline deregulation in the U.S. by updating the Avio-23's interior and offering it in both nineteen seat and twenty-three seat configurations. While the aircraft was still otherwise low technology and slow flying, BASA's aggressive and sometimes-questionable sales tactics had resulted in significant orders.

"But, Salo, what am I to do?" Rick, switching thoughts, quickly continued, "This Cole guy makes my skin crawl. I know his background. I'm going to have a hard time working with him. There's no way in hell I can work for him."

Montero fully understood Harris' point of view. He empathized with Rick. "Here is what we do," Montero said in a confiding tone. "My priority is to keep the production line running as it now is and to unload the inventory of aircraft that has been building up over the past several months. To do that, I need you to execute significant sales contracts for the WindStar with some major commuter and regional airlines. And, it needs to be done as soon as possible. We are running out of time."

Rick was fully aware of the precarious situation of RioAero and its mounting inventory of WindStars. He was confident his efforts to sell the aircraft would be successful. But Salo was sidestepping the Cole issue. "And, Cole?" Rick again roughly interjected.

"Unfortunately, for now, Cole is there." Montero's tone was melancholic. "You will have to work with him, or work around him. Dan Cole's responsibilities are basically administrative. His presence is more of an encroachment upon the activities of Mendendez and Delgada. You, as director of sales, report directly to me. General Cardella is fully aware of that aspect of the organizational structure.

We are in the middle of a critical push to sell the WindStar in the States. That mission will not be compromised."

Rick knew corporate politics. He had seen many aviation sales executives come and go due to changes in top management. One day they could be selling Fairchild Metros, the next day it might be BAe Jetstreams or 748s, and another day they could be hawking de Havillands. That was part of what industry insiders called the "Sporty Game"—the manipulation of people and money in the high-stakes arena of multi-million dollar aircraft sales. Sometimes these sales execs left on their own accord; other times they were forced out by a new president or managing director. In almost all cases, conflicts in personality or in philosophy were the ticket out the door. Both issues already existed for Harris with regards to Cole.

Rick took a deep breath. He did not like his situation one bit. It could easily undermine his sales efforts. He did, however, believe in RioAero and the WindStar. He knew he could be successful in selling the aircraft. He had to be successful—he was truly the WindStar's and RioAero's last chance. He felt his resolve steel. He was not going to let some Brazilian general wreak havoc upon RioAero by having Cole's presence interfere with a crucial sales program.

"Okay," Rick resignedly said, "I'll do what I've got to do. But, you'll have to help me."

"How?"

Rick had a simple idea for a short-term solution that would ease his frustration. "If you could get Cole down to the factory for a week's orientation, that would make my day. That would get him out of my face and off of my mind." Harris briefly paused. A tempting thought crossed his mind and a hard smile crept across his face. "And maybe, while he's down there, you might be able to have him sort of permanently disappear into the hustle and bustle of Rio or São Paulo. It happens, right?"

Montero chuckled. "Yes, people have been known to simply disappear in Rio or São Paulo, but you know it is not my style to have him disappear, at least not right now. However, it is agreed, I will make the arrangements to temporarily get him out of your way. Cole does need to pay us a visit here at the factory. You know, I have never met the man."

"It'll be a treat," Harris acidly said, "I guarantee it. And, by the way, make sure he flies coach. You wouldn't want to have him rubbing elbows with any of Varig's first class passengers." Harris sourly laughed. While not thrilling, Salo's words reaffirming Rick's standing in the corporate structure had brought a measure of relief.

"Now," Montero said, his voice taking on a grave tone, "I have some bad news. It is potentially damning."

"Worse than Cole?"

"I am afraid it very well might be."

Shit, Harris thought. This just is not my day. It was difficult enough to endure that total in-flight electrical failure, and then find Dan Cole as part of the welcome home committee. Now, there's more to come?

"Rick, you need to know this." Salo briefly hesitated. "Earlier this afternoon, I had a telephone conversation with Lou Biega and Franco Rameros." Salo paused taking a deep audible breath. "On a routine pre-delivery test flight of a WindStar scheduled to be handed over to the Air Force on Monday, we experienced a prop failure. Both—I repeat—both propeller assemblies separated from their shafts just forward of the gearbox flange. The aircraft was S/N-35. Fortunately, it made it home okay and is now in Hanger One."

"Damn," Rick gasped. He leaned back in his chair and stared at the ceiling. This was worse than he ever could have dreamed. He knew that such an incident could prove devastating. It could scuttle the WindStar program. All the creativity and innovation he had incorporated into his newly developed sales approach might be for naught. He listened as Salo explained further details of the incident and the measures that were being undertaken to determine its cause. When Salo finished talking, Rick asked, "Has anyone met with the company's folks in PR to discuss our corporate communications strategy on the incident?"

"Not sure," Montero said. "The incident is under wraps and remains highly confidential. Only a select few know anything about it."

"Trust me, Salo," Rick interjected, "there's really no such thing as confidential in this industry when it comes to in-flight incidents. It'll be just a matter of time before you read about it in the local newspaper and then later in the aviation tabloids with worldwide circulation. You need to be sure that Biega briefs PR on this. The company has to have a response, an explanation for the incident. We need to be proactive."

"I will be sure Biega gets your input."

Rick was about ready to end the telephone conversation when he realized that no reference had been made to the electrical problem he and Victoria had experienced in the WindStar just prior to landing at Fort Lauderdale. Perhaps Victoria had chosen not to mention it to her father. Perhaps Salo had decided not to revisit the incident with Rick. But the more Harris thought about it, the more a troubling connection formed between the two incidents. Maybe Delgada was right. Maybe someone was implementing a campaign of sabotage, but not against Rick Harris as Joey had joked, against the WindStar program itself.

"So, what did Victoria say about her flight?" Rick asked, probing for any reaction from Salo.

"Not much, except for the fact that it was long and that she enjoyed your flight instruction," Salo said, remembering his very brief telephone conversation with Victoria just a half hour earlier.

"Is that so?" Rick murmured, adding incredulously, "No mention of any electrical problems?"

"Huh?"

"A PSU failure while IFR."

"WHAT?" Salo was caught off-guard. Victoria had been on that flight only because he had prodded her to do so. If the aircraft had crashed, Salo never would have forgiven himself. He mumbled something in Portuguese, and then in English ordered Rick: "Tell me what happened."

Without replaying the entire event, Harris gave Montero a synopsis of the incident, including Joey Delgada's post-flight findings. "I've got a suspicion there's more going on here than we now realize," Rick said. "The WindStar I was flying was S/N-34. Two dissimilar, inexplicable incidents involving aircraft with consecutive serial numbers seems more than a coincidence."

"I hope you are wrong, Rick," Montero said, his tone indicating frustration and dejection. "I will run this past Big Lou." He paused noticeably disturbed. "Nothing else, I hope?"

"I think we've covered everything."

"Okay, Rick, hang in there. I will call you Monday afternoon, but let me give you my number here at the lake house in case anything comes up before then."

Rick scrambled for pen and paper and wrote down the number Salo provided.

As the conversation ended, Gail walked into the kitchen. The dogs followed at her heels, silently padding across the gray terrazzo floor. "Is everything okay now?" she questioned, observing Rick had calmed down from his earlier tirade.

Rick got up out of his chair and walked toward Gail. "Sorry," he said apologizing for his prior behavior. "Sometimes I get carried away." He paused. "It's been a rough day."

"I understand, but going ballistic as you did earlier on the phone serves no useful purpose. You—"

"Okay," Rick said, giving his wife a timeout signal with his hands, "I understand." Quickly changing the subject, he pressed on. "How about if we drive over to Pier Sixty-Six and have some drinks, fresh grouper, key lime pie, and even take in some dancing?"

Gail's eyes lit up with anticipation. Dinner and then dancing, she loved the idea. It had been three long weeks since they had been out on the town. "Great," she said. Just as she was about to leave the kitchen to change into something more appropriate than the tee-shirt and faded jeans she was wearing, she flashed a wink to Rick and said, "Hey, and along the way, what say we stop by the airport. You can give me a quick five-minute tour of the WindStar. Then, I'm sure I'll better appreciate why you're so enthused about this Brazilian flying machine."

"It's a deal." Rick was pleased she had shown an interest in the project with which he was so deeply involved. Gail had always been supportive of everything he had undertaken. Fortunately, the WindStar was no exception.

EIGHTEEN

RioAero, NA

Within ten minutes, Rick and Gail were driving east along SR-84, heading away from the serenity of the ranch and toward the bustling activity near the beach. The clear, star shimmering heavens above gradually transitioned to an amber hue. Brightly painted by city lights, a reflective sky pulsated with energy.

Rick pushed a button on the console of his BMW. The moonroof retracted. Nature's fragrances intermixing with cool fresh air gently swirled into the car. "Aah," he said, giving Gail a quick glance, "the night in South Florida is always a delight."

She smiled, then leaned her head onto his shoulder. The quiet hum of the BMW's engine and soft whoosh of the air rushing overhead were soothing sounds indeed.

Soon, the roadways they were traveling on became more congested with traffic. Street lights, traffic signals, and sprawling strip centers reached from each side to anchor the thoroughfare in place. Overhead, the passing roar of jet engines intensified as Rick and Gail neared the airport. Tonight, approaches for landing at FLL were being vectored in from out over the Everglades to the west. Air traffic controllers were sequencing arrivals and departures at a rate of one nearly every sixty seconds. Snowbirds by the thousands were passing through the Terminal Building each day. Tourist season was in full swing on the Gold Coast.

Rick turned onto Griffin Road and drove under Interstate 95 at the airport's southwestern boundary. He continued on toward RioAero's facility just off the south side of Runway 9-R, the non-precision runway primarily used by general aviation aircraft. Turning left into the company's nearly vacant parking lot, he drove past the Administration Building and headed toward the gated entrance of the secured Aircraft Operations Area.

Just beyond the eight-foot tall chain link fence, the WindStar stood alone, basking in the white-orange light of high-pressure sodium lamps that were affixed to eaves of the Administration Building. Rick stopped the BMW and lowered his window. He reached out, punched his four-digit password into the gate access keypad, and then watched the fifteen-foot wide gate jerk to the left and slowly move along its track paralleling the fence.

"Well, what do you think, Gail?" Rick asked as he drove through the open entranceway.

An old Learjet-23 had just lifted off Runway 9-R. The noise from its antiquated turbojet engines was almost deafening. By the time Gail could reply, Rick had driven to within twenty feet of the WindStar's left wingtip, stopped the car, and shut off its engine. He looked at her expectantly.

"My honest opinion?" Gail, being coy, slowly responded. She was deliberately letting Rick's intrigue build before giving her critique of the aircraft.

"Why, of course," Rick eagerly remarked.

The floodlights showcasing the WindStar momentarily flickered, then went dark. The only illumination now consisted of a pair of pole-mounted mercury vapor lights located over a hundred feet away. The WindStar took on a greenish-blue hue. Its silhouette still glistened, although detail and color were obscured by low light and shadows.

Gail said, "New aircraft always look superb, even under low light conditions." She paused and shrugged. "Older aircraft with a new paint job have appeal, too." She paused again.

Rick frowned, biting the inside of his lower lip, still unsure of Gail's perception of the WindStar.

"But *this* aircraft looks…" she dropped the act and was now smiling, "fantastic…fast…and sexy in an unabashed way. I know you were hoping I'd like its looks, and I honestly do."

"Excellent!" Rick said with relief. "You had me worried for a moment."

They got out of the car and hand-in-hand walked three steps toward the aircraft. Rick stopped and cocked his head. Muffled conversation seemed to be coming from the far side of the aircraft. He dropped to a squat and looked under the belly of the WindStar. Two men were standing near the right engine nacelle. Strange, he thought, who would be here at this hour? By six o'clock on a Friday evening, everyone who worked at RioAero would have left to go home or be out celebrating yet another seasonally pleasant winter weekend in Fort Lauderdale. It was now 7:30 p.m.

Rick motioned for Gail to stay where she was. The discussion he had had with Salo just an hour earlier was fresh in his mind. Was he about to witness another sabotage attempt? He could not be sure, but he needed to find out what someone was doing near *his* aircraft.

He cautiously walked toward the tail of the WindStar, occasionally stooping to assess the movements of the men near the right engine nacelle. A loud metallic clang rang out. Something heavy hit the ground. He froze in his tracks, briefly holding his breath, carefully listening. There was laughter, and then more unintelligible conversation. His pulse raced.

He hunched down below the dorsal fin that extended from the tail cone, and duck-walked toward the front of the aircraft, staying in the shadow that the fuselage cast below. He wanted to ensure his approach would be less conspicuous than the simple confrontation afforded by walking around the right wingtip. The conversation grew louder. A repetitive sound of metal-to-metal contact rang out.

When Rick neared the fillet at the wing's leading edge, he immediately knew the intentions of the shadowy men and what to do. The element of surprise was in his favor. The men had their backs positioned toward him. He smiled to himself and murmured, "This is going to be great."

Rick carefully inched his way from underneath the fuselage and stood erect. Then, in a deep theatrical voice he said, "Good evening, Mr. Delgada."

Startled, both figures flinched hard. The pair sheepishly turned toward him.

"You scared the bejesus out of us, Rick," Joey Delgada exclaimed. "Where did you come from? What are you doing here? What—"

"Relax," Rick soothed. "I've had a very strange and tiring day. At first, I wasn't quite sure who you guys were or what you were doing. Anyway, when I finally recognized you, I just had to be polite and say good evening." He chuckled. "Caught you off-guard, did I?"

Joey grunted something in Portuguese. The technician with Joey laughed; the pair of metal wheel chocks dangling from a rope in his hand clanged together again.

Rick continued, "So, what are you two up to?"

"We just came back from dinner at Dirty Ernie's on Federal Highway. Mario and I were about to move the aircraft into the new hangar. We are going do a complete inspection of the WindStar over the weekend."

Rick nodded. He recalled Joey's statement earlier that afternoon and the planned inspection of the WindStar. "Do you mind if I give my wife a quick look at the aircraft's interior before you taxi it away?"

"Go ahead, be our guest."

The three walked together around the nose of the aircraft and back to the closed airstair door on the left side of the fuselage. Joey and Rick continued on toward the BMW and Gail, who tensely awaited the outcome of her husband's gumshoe tactics. Meanwhile, Mario unlatched and opened the door, and then flipped a switch located on the lower doorjamb to illuminate the stairs and cabin entryway. As Mario continued to prepare the aircraft for boarding, Rick introduced Joey to Gail.

"Joey," Rick said, "I'd like you to meet my wife, Doctor Gail Richmond. She's smarter and lovelier than anyone I've ever known."

His words instantly relaxed Gail and she went into smiling executive wife mode. Salutations were exchanged. Gail accompanied them back to the WindStar and up the stairs into the cabin.

Joey turned to Mario and sent him out to be sure the engine intakes were clear and the other wheel chocks were removed. "Rick, go show your wife the fine interior of this aircraft, the kind that only Brazilian craftsmen can create. I will go up in the cockpit and switch on the power so you will have light in the cabin."

"Thanks, Joey." Rick and Gail stepped into the aisle of the darkened WindStar.

"Mmmm…new aircraft smell," Gail commented to Rick. "Nice to be able to walk upright. Other small commuter airplanes pretty much make you crawl to your seat."

In the cockpit, Joey settled into the left seat. On the overhead panel, his right hand intuitively found the master power switch. He flipped that switch on and quickly toggled two additional switches to illuminate the cabin. He noted the familiar clicking and humming sounds of various electrical devices activated by the master power switch.

But another faint sound—an unusual sound—was coming from the aircraft. A groaning, grinding sound. A sound that Joey had never heard associated with putting electrical power to the aircraft.

The sound became louder.

The entire fuselage began to vibrate, then shudder.

Joey immediately reacted by quickly reaching up and flipping the master power switch off.

The aircraft turned dark.

All normal electrical sounds ceased.

But it was too late.

"JOEY!" Harris shouted out from mid-cabin. Rick realized what was happening. He could feel the telltale signs through the cabin floor.

During the few short seconds while Delgada had the master power switch turned on, the aircraft's hydraulic system had somehow been activated. Hydraulic pressure stored in emergency accumulators had been redirected through the system's high-pressure lines. A battle was now taking place as the landing gear retraction pistons attempted to overcome down-lock mechanisms on the gear struts, forcing the gear up despite the aircraft's enormous weight. The WindStar was moving—not horizontally, but vertically.

The landing gear was RETRACTING.

Briefly, wheels of the main landing gear rolled forward on the tarmac before being pressured upwards into respective wheel wells located beneath each engine nacelle. Simultaneously, the nose gear snapped up into its bay just forward of the cockpit firewall.

Suddenly unsupported, the WindStar collapsed, helplessly falling five feet down onto the tarmac below with a sorrowful, metal-bending thud.

"What in God's name happened?" Gail called out. She had fallen to the floor between two rows of seats on the right side of the cabin. Now getting to her feet, she dodged dangling drop-down oxygen masks that had fallen from overhead compartments during the crashing impact.

"You alright?" Rick yelled from where he had been thrown flat in the aisle. He pushed aside a long section of ceiling panel that had separated and fallen from its upper fuselage attach points to make his way to Gail.

"I'm...I think I'm okay." Her forehead throbbed. The aircraft's free-fall had caused her to slam into the cabin's oval sidewall. She felt the contusion on her head. It was painful, but would not need medical attention.

Rick grabbed her by the hand. "Let's get the hell out of here." He was not sure whether anything else could happen, but he was not going to take the risk. Rick helped her climb out through the main cabin exit. The airstair door was now more horizontal than vertical. "I'll be right behind you, but first I've got to check on Joey."

In the cockpit, Joey Delgada sat motionless. His eyes blankly staring. Rick called Joey's name twice. Delgada blinked his eyes and shook his head, dazed. "What happened, Rick? What caused the gear to retract?"

"Don't worry, Joey," he said, "we'll find out. But first—"

From outside, they heard Gail shout: "Rick! Rick! I need your help!"

Harris and Delgada scrambled out of the aircraft and rushed toward Gail. She was kneeling over Mario who lay sprawled out on the tarmac just a few feet forward of the WindStar's nose. Mario's head was back, his mouth open, with his neck stabilized on Gail's rolled-up white sweater to maintain an open airway and to immobilize the neck.

His body was motionless. Lifeless.

"Rick, get the medical kit from your car," Gail commanded. She insisted that the trunk of Rick's car always contain a large yellow fishing tackle box containing an assortment of emergency medical supplies. "Joey," she pointed to the WindStar, "get some blankets from the aircraft."

The two men dashed to their respective tasks.

Mario coughed, then groaned. "What...What...?" His voice was weak and hoarse.

"Don't talk," Gail said firmly but comfortingly. "I'm a doctor; you're going to be okay. Just lie still until I can be sure that nothing is broken."

She had already checked his rate of breathing, his pulse, and for signs of hemorrhage. Her fingers rapidly palpated his body. There were no obvious signs of physical damage. She pinched the skin on his ankles, then his wrists. He reacted normally to the stimuli. She asked him to turn his chin toward his left shoulder; then, toward his right shoulder.

"Any pain?" she queried.

"Nuh, no," Mario answered.

Joey had returned from the aircraft's cabin with two blankets. He covered Mario with them.

Rick rushed back from the car carrying the makeshift medical kit. He opened it and placed it near his wife.

Gail reached into the open yellow tackle box and fumbled around with her fingers until finding a penlight. She clicked it on and studied how Mario's pupils reacted to the bright light. Putting the penlight between her teeth, she used both hands to carefully examine his head.

"Neurological signs good," she murmured. "No indication of severe concussion. Color good." She fished the stethoscope from the bottom of the tackle box and listened to his lungs. Breathing was shallow, but normal. No evidence of pulmonary wheezes, gurgles, or dullness.

Gail removed the stethoscope from her ears and said, "Okay..." She began nodding. "You probably feel like you've been hit by a Mack truck." She raised her brow and smiled warmly. "Somehow you were thrown away from the WindStar—most likely by the nose gear when it kicked forward before it retracted. If you had not been thrown away, you probably would have been crushed when the aircraft fell to the ground. You're a very lucky young man."

Mario smiled, relieved to hear that there were no obvious serious injuries.

Gail continued, "I'm afraid you'll be plenty sore for the next few days. However, I don't see anything that time itself shouldn't cure." She paused. "Nonetheless, you really should contact a physician to check you out further. I'm a doctor, but I don't treat people. I'm a veterinarian."

Rick and Joey helped a shaken Mario to his feet. "I'm alright," he said, slowly twisting his already aching body to verify that everything was indeed working properly. "Thanks, Doc, I appreciate your help." Then focusing on the WindStar, Mario said, "My God, there is going to be a lot of work to get that bird back in the air."

"Nah," Joey interjected, "there is really less damage than you think. In a week or so, this WindStar will be like new. There should be no structural damage. I'll have a team of technicians fly up from the factory. That will accelerate the repair process."

The arc tubes of the high-pressure sodium floodlights glowed, then brightly lit up the ramp area once again. Rick shook his head at the timing, not relishing the WindStar being showcased like a beached whale rather than the high performance aircraft that it was. "I'm going inside to shut off those floodlights." He thought for a second, and then said to Joey, "We should probably find a couple of tarps to throw over the aircraft until it can be moved into the hangar for repairs. We would not want any roving photographers capitalizing upon our ill-fortune."

Joey agreed and added that he would handle all the details concerning the WindStar and its relocation to the hangar for repairs. But first, he would be taking Mario to be checked out.

Rick turned to Gail. "Before I go shut off those floodlights, I want to take a quick look inside the aircraft. It will only take a few minutes." He was reluctant to ask her to join him in surveying the condition of the flight deck. A fall to the ground while in the WindStar would have a chilling effect upon anyone. Instead, he silently arched questioning eyebrows to her.

She matter-of-factly brushed away Rick's uncertainty. "Don't worry, that five-foot crash didn't bother me a bit. What does bother me, though, is not knowing why it happened. We need to figure that out." They both walked back to the WindStar. "This machine isn't going to explode is it?" Gail asked, mainly to lighten the mood, but also half-seriously.

Rick laughed. "Don't worry. There are no fuel leaks. This isn't Hollywood. Nobody's making a movie. Besides, I'm no Evil Knievel looking to be the hero of a fiery stunt."

They stepped onto the now near-horizontal airstair door and climbed into the WindStar. Gail followed Rick's lead into the cockpit. He settled into the right seat, she into the left seat.

Shining through the aircraft's front windshield, bright floodlights from the Administration Building provided marginal but sufficient visibility within the cockpit. Rick surveyed the right cockpit area. He nodded. Everything appeared intact and normal despite the tumble to the ground the aircraft had taken. There was no damage to the cockpit. He checked the right circuit breaker panel—normal. He moved to the center of the cockpit, leaned in front of Gail, and ran his hand across the left circuit breaker panel—all breakers were set. "Hmmm…" he mused, sinking back into his seat.

But why did the WindStar fall? Why did the landing gear collapse? How could it have happened? He continued to think. His eyes shifted to the center pedestal, and then to the left of it. Suddenly it became obvious. "Ah-haa…" Rick exclaimed. What he saw was very strange and highly abnormal. The collapse of the aircraft was beginning to make sense.

Rick caught Gail's puzzled glance. He pointed to the landing gear handle. "That switch with a wheel-like handle controls the position of the landing gear."

Gail immediately noted its setting. "Why is it in the UP position?" she asked.

"Exactly my question," Rick returned, and then went on. "No one in their right mind would ever put the gear handle in the up position when an aircraft is on the ground. When in the up position," he explained, "the gear handle electronically actuates circuitry for the hydraulic system to raise the gear."

"Then that's the cause. Why, of course, that accounts for the gear retraction," Gail said, thinking she had found the answer.

"Well, yes and no." Rick tilted down the dark green translucent sun visors located above the front windshield to reduce glare from the bright floodlights. "Just about all aircraft have safeguards against accidental gear retraction. Still, on a few older types of aircraft, it might be possible for someone who's getting in or out of the left seat to accidentally bump against and inadvertently push the gear handle to the up position. The WindStar is different." He placed the handle into the down position and asked Gail to push it upwards.

She tried to push and then force the handle into the up position. "It doesn't move."

Rick nodded and then demonstrated how to move the switch into the up position. "You see," he said, "you have to physically pull the handle out like this, and then bring it up. On the WindStar, moving the gear selection handle is definitely a conscious action. It can't happen by accident."

"I see what you mean," Gail said, mimicking his movements to successfully change the position of the gear selection handle herself.

Still, Rick thought, this accident was not just absent-minded stupidity. It should not have made any difference where the gear switch handle was—up or down. He went on to explain a further safeguard against inadvertent landing gear retraction featured in virtually all aircraft with retractable gear. "When the landing gear is down and locked and the weight of the aircraft is on its wheels, the gear struts are depressed. That causes small electronic displacement sensors, commonly called squat switches, to be depressed as well. And, when the squat switches are activated due to a depression of the struts, the GEAR UP command to the hydraulic system is overridden.

All commercial aircraft now manufactured with retractable gear are designed this way."

"So," Gail responded, "you're telling me what just actually happened, couldn't have happened."

"Well..." Rick was momentarily caught off-guard. "Yeah, but it did happen, and we need to find out why."

On the overhead panel, he flipped on the master power switch just as Joey had upon entering the cockpit. Then, he turned on the cockpit lights.

Almost instantly, a small red switch guard that was positioned low and to the left side of the landing gear handle caught Gail's attention. She pointed to it. "What's this doohickey?"

"This what?"

"This small red thing over here, near the landing gear handle."

"There shouldn't be anything there." The center pedestal had obstructed Rick's view.

"But there is." She leaned forward. "There's lettering that says: DOWNLOCK OVERRD."

"Damn." Rick groaned. He knew exactly what Gail was referring to and what the switch cover concealed. He knew it could be the cause of the WindStar's free fall to the ground. "Let me take a closer look."

They exchanged seats.

"Yes," he continued, "aah, yes, I'd almost forgotten about that little bugger." He hunched forward in his seat to more closely examine Gail's discovery.

Flipping the red switch guard cover up provided access to the knurled knob that lay beneath. Normally, the guard is safety-wired with a low tensile metal to make accidental access to the switch difficult. But Rick noticed that the guard on this aircraft was not safety-wired. He looked at Gail, then back at the red cover. He had a sinking feeling about what he would find when he lifted up the switch guard.

Rick held his breath as he lifted the switch guard. He saw exactly what he did not want to see. He sharply exhaled, then pounded his fist down onto the center pedestal. "Damn," he blurted out.

"What is it?" a startled Gail asked.

Rick abjectedly collapsed back into his seat. "Things like this make me wonder," he said, slowly shaking his head. "When I tell you, you are not going to believe it."

Gail was about to say how nothing else could further surprise her this night, but she waited.

Rick went on. "It's the downlock override switch, and it's positioned to the 'ARM' mode." He ran the fingers of both hands back through his hair and interlaced his fingers behind his head. He leaned back, briefly closed his eyes, and continued speaking, "I remember it from my flight training sessions in Brazil." He placed both hands on the armrests of the seat, readjusting his posture. Turning to Gail, he said, "The downlock override mechanism is a technical requirement mandated by the Brazilian Air Force. The Air Force operates out of some short unimproved strips that have no takeoff or landing overruns. Over the years, the Air Force has lost more planes than it would care to admit by using up too much runway during landing. The planes crashed into water at the end of the runway or simply went over a cliff. To solve that problem, the Air Force had a bright idea: incorporate a mechanism into the gear system that overrides the downlock squat switches and allows for gear retraction even when weight is on the wheels. Activating or arming that small switch would allow the pilot or copilot to retract the landing gear when the aircraft is on the ground and weight is on the wheels. So, then..." Rick paused to ruefully laugh. "Then, the aircraft could be bellied in for a quick stop."

Gail questioned, "Aren't pilots supposed to know how much runway is required to takeoff or land?"

"Under normal circumstances, yes; but in emergencies during military operations, there are no rules. You just do whatever it takes—whatever you're told. Even commonsense may not be part of the equation."

"Okay," Gail said, her analytic mind working, "so military operations may require this capability, but airline operations certainly don't, right?"

"That's for sure."

"Why was this switch installed in an aircraft intended for civilian use?"

"Good point." Rick remembered asking Lou Biega that very question. "Engineering's response was that it's easier and more cost effective to turn out identical aircraft from the production line than to custom build them. With very few customers to boast about, the company has no idea where each aircraft coming off the production line will end up. Many do go to the military. So, if the Air Force needs another WindStar in a hurry, the factory just taxis one from inventory over to the finishing hangar and slaps in one of three different types of military interiors."

Gail was now shaking her head in disbelief. "What kind of mess did you get yourself into, Rick? The company doesn't quite seem to have its act together. What you're telling me sounds quite bizarre."

"Granted, Gail, but this is the only crazy thing about the WindStar I can recall." Rick understood her line of thinking. "And, the gear override switch is supposed to be deactivated on all aircraft except those going to the military. On this aircraft, the switch was not supposed to work."

"But, it did."

"Yes, it did."

"Why?"

Rick raised his voice in frustration. "Damn it, Gail, how the hell am I supposed to know?" Rick was unnerved by Gail's probing questions. He did not have the answers. He could only speculate. "Maybe someone in production didn't disarm it. Maybe someone in QA didn't check it. But then again, maybe both production and QA did their jobs properly. Maybe someone reactivated the mechanism. Think about that!"

Gail apologized. Indeed, her intent was to help Rick, not to annoy him.

"No," Rick acquiesced, "I'm sorry for blowing up." He flipped off the master power switch. The aircraft interior darkened only somewhat. Bright floodlights still shined through the front windshield. The couple silently exited the WindStar.

"Now, what?" Gail asked as she retrieved her white sweater that was still lying on the tarmac. Rick closed, latched, and picked up the yellow tackle box. They walked to the BMW and stowed both items into the trunk.

"I'm going into the building and shut those spotlights off. Want to join me?"

"Sure."

NINETEEN

RioAero, NA

Rick swiped his cardkey through the electronic reader at the rear entranceway to the Administration Building. A small green light illuminated. He entered his four-digit code into the keypad. With a sharp click, a solenoid unlocked the metal-framed glass door. He pulled the door open and led Gail into the dimly lit building.

The sound of their footsteps echoed off the walls of the small, tile-paved foyer that quickly branched into a carpeted corridor. Rick turned left, passed the darkened employee lounge, and continued to the next door down the hallway. It was marked "UTILITY." Rick opened the door. The windowless room illuminated automatically. High intensity incandescent lights recessed into the ceiling provided the type of candlepower that would satisfy even the most demanding electrician. Inside the room, a maze of cables, wires, conduits, and pipes of various sizes and materials were arranged in an orderly fashion—all painstakingly identified. Clearly labeled on the left wall was a row of switches identified as EXTERIOR LIGHTING. Rick easily located three switches marked NORTH, and flipped all to the off position.

During the short time it took Rick to locate and switch off the north ramp floodlights, Gail had been intensely studying the layout of the room's equipment and wiring. "I've never seen such an assemblage," she said. "The building has a fairly complex communications system and even a high-tech security system." She moved closer to a tier of equipment stacked on metal shelving that was anchored against the right wall. "Rick, did you realize that there are four independent videotape machines that record feed from surveillance cameras?"

Rick had known surveillance cameras were installed on the building, but that fact had not entered his mind this evening until Gail reintroduced it.

"In fact," Gail continued, "one machine is labeled NORTH VIEW."

They turned toward each other. Rick and Gail had the same thoughts. Nothing needed to be said. The entire gear-up incident would have been caught on tape. In fact, Rick's arrival in the WindStar earlier that afternoon would also be on the tape. The possibility even existed that the tape might contain a clue as to why the WindStar had fallen to the ground.

"Check the cabinet under the shelving," Rick said. "Maybe there's a blank tape in it."

Gail dropped to her knees and opened the metal cabinet. "There's a whole box of blank tapes."

"Great, hand me one." Rick grabbed the new tape, tore off its cellophane wrapper, and slid the cassette out of its box.

"What kind of tape machines are these?" Gail asked.

"They're specially designed, variable speed VCRs that can provide anything from real-time video like we use at home to record and watch movies, to less animated, time-lapse recording used in surveillance that essentially captures a single frame every few seconds or so." Rick paused, taking a closer look at the machine and its settings. "Let's see...this machine looks like it's set to fully record an XL-10 tape in twenty-five days. That's pushing the limit of today's technology."

Rick hit the eject button. The recording sequence stopped. The program display flashed and the machine motorized the cassette out of a center slot. Rick removed the cassette, inserted the new one he had just unwrapped, and pressed the record button.

"How do you know so much about surveillance and videotape?" she asked.

Rick smiled sheepishly. "One day before I went to Brazil," he admitted, "I was going down the hallway to get some coffee. And just as I passed the door to this room, I noticed that a contractor was installing the system." He laughed. "You know how curious I am—that I used to be into this electronics thing as a radio amateur—so I hung out with the guy for a half hour. It's really interesting stuff."

Gail broke into a wide grin. "Yes, that sounds just like you, Rick."

He looked at his watch. It was just past 8:30. "Remember what I promised you?"

Gail eyed him quizzically.

"Drinks, dinner, and some dancing," Rick reminded her. "That is, if you're up to it."

Gail's head still throbbed from the hit to it she had taken when the WindStar's gear collapsed. "Drinks and dinner for sure, dancing...maybe a rain check."

"Consider it done," Rick said with a nod.

She grasped his hand as they left the utility room and strolled down the hallway. "Glad you're home," Gail said.

"I'm really glad to be here with you," Rick responded.

They exited the building.

TWENTY

RioAero, NA

A Lincoln Town Car was parked just behind Rick's silver BMW. The first letter on its rear license plate was "Z," the State of Florida's DMV designation for rental cars and motor vehicles for hire. The car was black, inside and out, but did not have the deeply tinted windows typically found on most South Florida cars.

Rick was puzzled by the car's presence on the ramp. He knew that FAA inspectors simply did not lease Town Cars. He knew of no one at RioAero who would rent a black Town Car. During intense South Florida summers, entering any black-on-black automobile would initially feel like an oven on wheels. Even during the winter, a black car could be too warm for comfort.

As he and Gail approached the WindStar it became clear that whoever had arrived in the Town Car was now inside the aircraft. He heard loud voices, then boisterous laughter. Rick cautiously approached the aircraft's damaged half-open door that rested on the tarmac. There was more laughter. Rick recognized the sound coming from one man. It was unsettlingly familiar: a bellowing gut-laugh, periodically broken by bursts of pig-like snorting.

Rick looked over his shoulder to Gail, and then walked two steps back toward her. He handed her the videotape and said, "I want you to keep this. Give it to no one."

Her face clouded with puzzlement, surprise, and apprehension. "What do you mean? What's going on?" she questioned.

Rick spoke softly, "I think I know who is inside the WindStar." He glanced toward the aircraft door and then back to Gail. "It's the new executive-type guy that RioAero just hired. His name is Dan Cole. It's a long story. I'll tell you more about him later. But for now, I need to find out what he's up to."

Rick left Gail standing near the left engine's propeller blades, two of which had been severely damaged during the accident. He moved to and quietly stood near the aircraft's main entranceway and tried to carefully listen to the conversation coming from the cockpit. The words were frequently slurred. It was difficult for Rick to grasp the gist of what was being said. But he was able to confirm that indeed it was Cole, and one other person who was being referred to as Felipe.

He heard movement from within the flight deck. There was some profanity and then more laughter. From the sounds of their actions, the men seemed ready to leave the cockpit. They would likely soon disembark from the aircraft.

Rick backed away from the entranceway and quickly moved to Gail's position by the left engine. He dropped to a squat as if examining the damaged propeller blade. Rick looked up to Gail and quietly said, "They're coming out of the aircraft. They sound pretty drunk." He paused still looking up at her. "Try not to hurt them unless they get really weird."

She nodded.

Rick knew that Gail had a short fuse when it came to drunk and belligerent men. He had seen how she had reacted to groping, foul-mouthed drunks in the past. She thought nothing of treating an out-of-line human as she would an ill-mannered, overly aggressive colt— grabbing an ear or lip and twitching it to the ground. To her, the outcome of a confrontation with a disrespectful two hundred pound *Homo sapien* was a foregone conclusion.

Dan Cole emerged from the cabin entryway almost falling as he tried to maneuver his portly torso and stubby legs along the damaged airstair door. He wavered, regained his balance, and clumsily stepped off of the door. Only then did he notice Rick near the left engine.

"Who's there? Is that you, Harris?" he questioned, not totally being sure in the low light and shadows.

Rick stood up and turned to face Cole. "Good evening, Mr. Cole," he brusquely replied. Cole was still wearing that gaudy tangerine guayabera shirt over his gray polyester, Sansabelt slacks. "Had a good happy hour or two, have you, Mr. Cole?"

"Absolutely, have we…we have," Cole stammered. "Fort Lauderdale has absolutely the best socializing establishments in the world. This place on Federal called Solid Gold, or Solid Platinum, or Solid something is a very friendly place." Cole was referring to an upscale strip joint a few miles north of the airport on Federal Highway. "On Friday evenings they have this fantastic all you can eat buffet, and they have some pretty fine meat on the hoof, too." Cole snorted a quick gut laugh. "Do you know Felipe Retegi?"

Rick was only half-listening to the tawdry account of Cole's foray earlier that evening. He was focused upon the tall, thin, slightly dark-skinned man in his mid-thirties who stood just behind and to the left of Dan Cole. Retegi had been openly leering at Gail ever since he had disembarked the WindStar. Rick's protective hackles were up. The introduction offered by Cole gave Rick an opportunity to confront Retegi.

Rick moved toward Retegi and said, "Rick Harris, I don't believe we've ever met."

Retegi extended his hand. Rick grasped it firmly and pulled Retegi uncomfortably close in a patently unfriendly handshake. Retegi stumbled forward, his eyes widened. There could be little doubt of Rick's irritation and the preemptive assertion of dominance over Cole's companion.

Retegi responded, "It's, it's my pleasure, Mr. Harris." He stammered nervously and with a noticeable Spanish accent.

Harris returned in Spanish, asking Retegi of his relationship with Cole and involvement in the aviation industry. Retegi replied that he was an engineer and leasing executive at ComJet, the organization that had employed Cole prior to his move to RioAero.

Cole, never having bothered to learn Spanish, initially just nodded. Then Cole interrupted the exchange, gesturing broadly at the WindStar. "So, what the hell happened here?"

Harris released Retegi's hand, stepped back, and eyed the WindStar. "Looks like we have a real problem, wouldn't you say?"

Cole was too drunk to want to spar with Rick. "Do you know what happened?"

"Aah...." Rick said, smiling contemptuously, "I know exactly what happened."

"You do?" Cole was caught flat-footed by the blunt statement. "Tell me about it."

"The gear retracted," Rick said flippantly. "I was in the cabin of the aircraft when it fell to the ground. Joey Delgada was in the cockpit."

Cole continued his probing, "Why did the gear retract?"

"It's rather complicated," Rick went on. "The cause lies within the electro-hydraulics."

"And...?"

"Well, I really can't tell you right now." Rick was enjoying toying with Cole. "There's evidence that has to be analyzed before I can give you the details."

"Evidence?" Cole seemed surprised. "What evidence?"

"Oh, you know..." Rick continued to improvise as he went along. Cole's intense interest and questioning provided more than enough motivation for Rick to be imaginatively creative in his response. "The usual, you know, factory build standard, QA documents, inspections, personnel, videotape—"

"Videotape?" Cole's eyes widened.

"Yeah, videotape." Rick casually shrugged, fishing to see if the videotape comment would tweak Cole's interest.

"What kind of videotape?" Cole persisted, now roused from his intoxicated state.

"Well," Rick came back, coolly continuing his ploy, "I really can't say right now, that would be premature. But I am certain it will unravel the cause of the entire incident." Rick lied. He had no idea what was on the videotape that Gail was now holding in both hands. Indeed, it could pinpoint the cause of the incident. Yet, then again, the tape might not have captured anything incriminating. In the back of his mind he had a notion that Cole was somehow involved, but he could not be sure. Maybe his animosity toward Cole simply raised suspicions about the man. Maybe Rick was just hoping for a convenient way to implicate Cole.

Cole's eyes drifted toward Gail and locked onto the videotape she had gripped in her hands. He clumsily took three steps toward her while saying, "I think I should have that."

Out of the corner of his eye, Rick saw Gail's protective reaction to Cole's approach. But before Rick could move, headlights flashed onto the WindStar as the white company van passed through the gateway onto the ramp and parked alongside the Town Car.

"Who the hell's driving in here at this hour?" an angered Cole growled the words, his attempt to obtain the videotape thwarted.

"It's Joey Delgada," Rick responded. "He's going to coordinate getting the aircraft back on its feet." Rick paused, watching Joey exit the van and open its sliding side door. "I'm sure Delgada will review his version of the accident with you if you ask. Right now," he said motioning to Gail, "I'm late for a dinner engagement."

Stepping away from Cole and Retegi, Harris and Gail joined Delgada at the van. Joey was connecting a light and battery pack to a video camera. He would be documenting both the exterior and interior condition of the aircraft prior to its move into the hangar. Engineers at the factory would be keenly interested in reviewing every aspect of how the WindStar had withstood its gear-up fall to the ground.

"The show is all yours," he said to Joey. "And, I've arranged to have a couple of assistants here to help you. They were in the aircraft when Gail and I returned from the Administration Building after turning off the flood lights."

"Who is the guy with Cole?"

"He's a Basque engineering-type who Cole worked with at ComJet."

"Thanks, Rick," Joey groaned, "like I really need those guys hanging around and grilling me about this mishap." Joey was still unsettled about the WindStar and its unfortunate fate. "By the way," Joey noted, "I phoned AeroMech at Opa Locka. I expect them to be here around midnight with jacks and inflatables. We should have the WindStar back on its gear and into the hangar before the sun rises."

"Excellent, Joey," Rick said. "Now, I'm off to my dinner, finally!"

TWENTY-ONE

Pier Sixty-Six

A s the time neared nine o'clock, Rick wheeled his BMW off Federal Highway and onto Seventeenth Street. The always heavily traveled six-lane boulevard was congested with activity. It was obvious that tourist season was in full swing on the Gold Coast. Rental car and out-of-state license plates branded almost half the drivers on the road as not being locals. Unsynchronized traffic lights slowed cars to a snail's pace. Restaurant parking lots overflowed. Young deeply tanned valets dashed along pathways to satellite lots. Groups of tourists leisurely strolled along sidewalks. Bicyclists whizzed by at a hair's breadth from the curbside.

Ahead, and just before the Intracoastal, the broad roadway narrowed to funnel onto A1A, an alternate route that for hundreds of miles snaked up along the beaches to the north. Tonight, all traffic seemed pressing for the northern beach route. In the opposite direction the boulevard was uncannily empty of traffic.

"There must be a problem up ahead," Gail commented. "I don't remember traffic being this bad when we lived near the beach."

Rick nodded in agreement. In the distance, he heard the long staccato ring of a bell. "Our timing isn't quite right tonight," he moaned to Gail. "You know, most Intracoastal drawbridges are allowed to open on demand after eight o'clock on weekends. All it takes is one big sportfisherman and a captain who's too lazy to take down his antennas or outriggers. He just blows his horn and the bridgemaster has to stop traffic, open the bridge, and allow him up the waterway."

"We may be stuck here for awhile," Gail said, now remembering the causeway bridge.

A stream of headlights began to appear in the distance ahead.

"Nah, not tonight," Rick smiled. "Looks like we'll be moving soon."

A few minutes later, Rick accelerated the BMW to merge with the traffic. His tires buzzed an echoing hum as the roadway changed from pavement to steel-grated drawspan and rose over the Intracoastal Waterway. At the crest of the drawspan, Rick saw his destination. To the left sprawled Pier Sixty-Six: first the marina; then, the resort complex; finally, towering into the starlit sky, the hotel and its revolving rooftop lounge. The facility was a Fort Lauderdale landmark—and a hallmark of Phillips Sixty-Six, the petroleum company.

Rick motored onto the facility's private driveway and up an incline to the hotel's porticoed entrance. Young valets, nattily outfitted all in white, sprang into action. Car doors snapped open. Rick and Gail were ready to enjoy their evening.

The hotel lobby was a beehive of activity. Boisterous conversations resonated throughout its elegant, expansive public areas. Arriving and departing guests and visitors mingled to relive their day's activities and begin planning their next move for a lively Friday night. Rick and Gail wove through the milling crowd and around the coveys of people, politely nodding and smiling while making their way through the high-spirited atmosphere. Midway through the lobby, Rick abruptly stopped in his tracks. He had heard his name being barked above the din.

"Harris…"

He turned toward the sound of the voice, eyes searching through the crowd.

The foghorn of a voice came again: "HAA-RISS."

It was closer, but the source was still unidentifiable.

Now, Gail also heard his name being called. "Meeting anyone here?" she asked.

Rick shrugged. "Hadn't planned on it."

"Yo, Harris," a second voice echoed. "Wait up."

Rick and Gail came to a standstill. They both surveyed the mosaic of faces around them.

Striding from the front desk area in the lobby, three large men were making their way directly toward Rick Harris. They wore black baseball hats, unmarked except for scrambled eggs on the bills. The men began to stand out from the crowd as they loomed closer. Gail was first to notice the men; she watched their advance warily. To her, they looked like professional wrestlers—massive shoulders, long hair, and a certain ruggedness. She had the uneasy sensation that these men were serious about their intentions. Although not calling out the name Harris again, the men intently eyed Rick as they rapidly closed in. They were the ones who had called Rick by name. She knew it.

Keeping her eyes locked on the three men, Gail alerted Rick. "Do you know three really big guys who like to wear black baseball hats?"

He followed her stare. He saw the men. "I'm afraid not, but I've got a feeling that we're about to meet them real soon."

The men pressed forward. They were strangers to Gail. Rick could not identify them.

"Harris, you sonovagun," said the first man to reach them. "Have you been trying to avoid us?"

The second man stepped up and said, "Where the hell have you been hiding?"

The third man clasped the fist of his left hand with his opened right hand. Knuckles cracked. A white toothy grin spread across his face.

Gail's mind leapt to defense mode, swiftly calculating the odds against them. Rick smiled and placed a restraining, reassuring hand on her shoulder. "If you three guys ever got serious about buying airplanes instead of just sucking my expense account dry, I would have come up to visit you more frequently." He laughed. They laughed.

Gail forced an uneasy smile, trying to regain her composure. Her heart was still pounding from the unexpected encounter. Not goons, friends instead; she took a deep breath and slowly exhaled.

The low-pulled baseball hats and rough clothing had initially prevented Rick from recognizing the three. He was used to seeing them in business suits, and without baseball hats. They were airline people: Kelly Long, President of Long Airways, Atlanta; Sammy Santelli, President and Chairman of InterState Airlines, Cincinnati; and John Andreas, President of Express Airlines, Boston. Rick had visited with each of them, played golf with all of them, and made an occasional aircraft presentation to all in hopes of cultivating a sale. During the past two years each had been indecisive about adding new equipment, despite Rick's prodding.

But with airline deregulation well underway and opportunities for growth seemingly everywhere, the thought occurred to Rick that perhaps his friends might now be receptive to what he—and RioAero—had to offer. Effortlessly switching to salesman mode, Rick quickly spoke out, "So, what are all you guys doing down here?" He smiled, relaxed now and delighted with the unexpected opportunity to see old acquaintances.

"First," Sammy Santelli said, avoiding Rick's question, "how come you haven't paid me a visit this year? You might not know it, but I'm finally ready for some new equipment."

"Fantastic," Rick came back, "and I totally agree it's about time you moved up from those old Beech 99s." Then, after quickly glancing at Kelly Long and John Andreas to be sure that they too were included in the conversation, he continued, "The reason I haven't visited with any of you guys is that I changed jobs early this year. I'm no longer with Fairchild. I now head up sales for RioAero."

"Good move," Kelly Long opined. "That means you're pushing the WindStar now, right?"

Rick nodded.

"I like the airplane," John Andreas added. "From what little I've heard about it, the WindStar seems to be a solidly built, screaming machine. It certainly has to be better than those Fairchild Metroliners you were trying to sell me for the past few years."

"You know," Santelli swiftly interjected, "airlines that operate Metros call them 'turbo tamales'—guaranteed to give you heartburn." He laughed. "But being the only pressurized nineteen-seat turboprop on the market, there was no choice."

Rick slowly nodded, sadly agreeing with Santelli.

Sammy continued, "Word has it that the cabin door never closes quite right, the engines are always in the shop for repairs, the wing fuel tanks leak like sieves, and that's only part of the story."

"Yeah," Kelly Long chimed in. "I've flown in them as a passenger while on the West Coast. The shape of the cabin was like flying inside a sewer pipe. If that wasn't bad enough, you literally had to crawl down the aisle and then wedge yourself into a tiny thing Fairchild called a seat. And, it was so damn noisy to ride in you could go deaf."

"I know, I know," Rick spoke up, raising both palms into the air hoping to stop the friendly and yet somewhat exaggerated verbal barrage. "But until now, guys, there wasn't a better mousetrap. I never said it was a perfect plane. To enjoy you fellas' company and keep grain in my horses' buckets, I had to walk the line to as fairly as possible present the Fairchild Metroliner for the factory, yet not misrepresent it to the customer. So when people like you asked about the aircraft's strengths and weaknesses, I did my due diligence by providing a complete list of operators—public information—and suggested contacting their mid-level operations people for feedback."

"And they spoke freely, very freely," John Andreas noted. "You're a straight-up guy, Harris. You never bad-mouthed the competition and you never lied about the Metro's faults. You just told us where to get the facts, for better or worse."

Prior to joining RioAero, Rick had spent two years with San Antonio based Fairchild Aircraft as the company's Eastern Region sales director. When Rick signed on with Fairchild, he cut a deal with their management that allowed him to remain domiciled in Fort Lauderdale. From the company's perspective, it really did not make any difference where their sales executives resided so long as aircraft were sold. However four months ago, a new management team at Fairchild began pressing Rick to move to the San Antonio area. Rick and Gail seriously considered relocating. Weighing in on the decision, though, was Salo Montero and opportunities at RioAero. The WindStar was far superior to the Metroliner. Rick did not regret his decision to join RioAero, not even after today's cavalcade of WindStar disasters.

"Oh, I am forgetting myself," Rick said apologetically. "Let me introduce you to my wife, Gail Richmond. She's heard a lot about and of you guys." Rick winked.

Sammy looked over to Gail, who was by now comfortably smiling along with the group. "Hope everything you heard was all good, and Rick did not belabor the truth too much, right, Rick?" He paused briefly as Rick sheepishly grinned. "Now, how about if you two join us for a couple drinks upstairs in the lounge so we can give Gail the rest of the story?"

Rick glanced toward Gail for approval, but before she could respond Kelly Long asserted, "We're not going to take no for an answer."

"But Gail and I haven't had dinner yet, and—"

"Neither have we," Kelly said, cutting Rick's comment short. "Don't worry, though, we'll scare up some food."

"Hell," said Sammy, "this is a damn hotel. If the lounge doesn't have a kitchen, we'll call room service."

"Okay, it's a done deal," concluded Kelly.

Together, they walked to a bank of elevators at the left of the lobby area. Rick pressed the call button for the express elevator, and stepped back from the elevator's highly polished gilded doors. With a smirk, he whispered to Gail, "You're in for a very interesting evening."

She whispered back, "It's been more than interesting already."

When the elevator arrived, the group entered and fell silent as the doors closed behind them. Then, like a slow-motion missile exiting its silo, the aerial tramway's glass capsule rose skyward departing the secure substructure of the hotel. Silently gliding upwards along the building's exterior, the ground seemed to sink deeply below with its landscaping swallowed by the darkness. As the capsule's elevation increased, a panorama unfolded. Glistening city lights were everywhere—various hues and intensities traced or framed surface features, gradually fading to black on the distant horizon.

Slowing as it approached the circular rooftop lounge, the elevator came to a stop with a slight jerk and shudder. Simultaneous with a muted flat-sounding ding, the doors retracted, sliding to the side. The group exited to enter an environment much different than the lobby they had departed exactly sixty-six seconds before. Here, the pace was much more subdued with a genteel atmosphere of hushed conversations and occasional laughter.

Sammy Santelli's eyes took in his surroundings. Except for the elevator entrance area, the sides of the lounge's geodesic structure were framed with massive glass panels. In the center, a huge pillar supported the umbrella-like roof. Within the dark paneled ceiling, the sparkle of hundreds of tiny high intensity lights illuminated the surroundings below. Several rings of plush seating arrangements were positioned on a slightly elevated platform that slowly orbited around the central bar. The rotation provided a phenomenal view of the entire cityscape, once every sixty-six minutes.

Santelli strode forward to the hostess' podium, hat in hand, and greeted the young lady who casually leaned forward. With a broad smile beaming through the stubble of an unshaven face, he commandingly proclaimed, "The name is Santelli. My friends and I are tired thirsty sailors who have a Hatteras tied up at your marina. Would you be so kind as to find us a place to unwind?"

The hostess contemptuously eyed Santelli who was dressed much differently than the other patrons already sipping cocktails in the lounge. Even though the light of day had faded to black nearly three hours earlier, tortoise shell Wayfarer sunglasses still hung on the gold-tone chain around his neck. From his wind-tattered hair, to his soiled bright pink polo shirt and lived-in khaki pants, Santelli truly appeared as the sport fisherman he professed to be. She gave the lounge a cursory glance, and then referred to her seating diagram on the dimly-lit lectern. "Hmmm..." the hostess murmured. She squinted. Then came the pre-programmed brush-off response: "You have reservations?"

"Why, of course," Sammy lied.

The hostess raised an eyebrow.

Santelli reached into the side pocket of his pants, all the time maintaining eye contact with the hostess. He glanced down momentarily, and then placed a crumpled twenty-dollar bill into her hand.

The hostess grimaced, almost physically recoiling from the grungy bill. She shot a glance toward the others who stood behind Santelli. Her eyes spotted Rick, who was conversing with Andreas. "Is Mr. Harris with your party?"

"You know him?" Santelli asked, suddenly awkward at her chilly reception to his bribe.

She smiled, catching Rick's eye, nodding to him. Harris was more than an occasional visitor to the lounge. Over the years he credited Pier Sixty-Six with assisting him in closing several aircraft deals.

"Mr. Harris is a gentleman," the hostess said, handing Santelli back his twenty dollars. "Please be kind enough to follow me to your table."

Dumbstruck, Sammy stuffed the bill back into his pocket.

TWENTY-TWO

Pier Sixty-Six Lounge

The drinks flowed as freely as did the group's conversation which was now livelier than that of the other patrons. Sammy Santelli regained his swagger when his food order was brought up from the hotel below. The light dinner of romaine with endive salad blanketed by layers of blackened grouper, clumps of stone crab, and slivers of mango and papaya was a welcome delight.

In most cases, airline executives and aircraft salesmen got along remarkably well. It was politically expedient. Both groups had an insatiable hunger for industry information that was not yet public. Each thrived on rumors, true or false. Innocent passing remarks could translate into important knowledge and a competitive advantage could be obtained. Indeed, an airline's new program plans, rarely announced to the media until the timing was just right, or internal problems, only made public when required for damage control, often slipped out in conversations over a round of golf or other social event. The give-and-take shook out similar information about airframe manufacturers.

Rick knew what a gold mine informal conversations were among people in aviation. Over the years he had become highly successful in his profession. He had placed over a hundred multi-million dollar aircraft with corporate customers and regional airlines. And, his success was not by accident. Rick was masterful in guiding a conversation. An astute listener with the capacity for remembering even the most casual details, he was attentive whether airline executives talked about their business or personal lives. His questions were never the uncomfortable, prying type that make people clam up. His audiences never failed to be impressed when he inquired about their wives, their children, or their pets by name, and were astounded when he made reference to seemingly impossible to recall birthdays, anniversaries, and graduations. Rick Harris' interest in his customers was genuine. He developed solid relationships and garnered a reputation for being more of a friend and confidant than simply a salesman.

Rick's business acquaintances trusted his judgment. Whether the decision being mulled was either to buy or sell an aircraft, Rick was sought out with the confidence a fair transaction would evolve. All the socializing Rick did in bars and in restaurants, or on boats and on golf courses, was an integral part of his business—developing and maintaining relationships. He had spent more than his share of time doing just that. Sometimes his workdays were nearly eighteen hours long. Today would be one of those days.

After the light dinner and yet another round of drinks, the conversation at the table became somewhat fragmented. Andreas and Long were filling Gail in on their backgrounds in aviation. Mutual interests had brought the three airline executives together. It had also solidified their friendship over the years. All of them had been athletically inclined in college. All of them had been aviators in Viet Nam. And, it just so happened, all three men shared an entrepreneurial spirit. Each had formed a small independent airline of his own. Common ground, common interests; the evening was turning out to be as interesting as Rick had earlier promised. Gail was truly enjoying herself.

Rick and Sammy, however, strayed into serious business discussions. The subject matter was the post-deregulation airline industry, and how airframe manufacturers were positioning to capture market share with larger, more efficient aircraft.

Now ten minutes into the conversation, Rick could sense that Sammy was in the initial planning stages of taking his airline to the next level. He felt confident that Sammy would soon be capitalizing upon new deregulation opportunities to expand route structure. Rick listened carefully. He noted Santelli continually made reference to city pairs that currently did not exist within the InterState Airlines route structure. The names of cities such as Chattanooga, Charlotte, Pittsburgh, Toronto, and Washington did not jibe with Santelli's current airline operation. The stage lengths from Cincinnati were essentially beyond the capability of Santelli's current aircraft fleet. The airline's eight Beech 99s and seven Navajo Chieftains would be ill-suited to the implied expansion. Speed, pressurization, and passenger appeal would be critical elements for Santelli's future success.

Rick smiled to himself. He knew that the WindStar had everything Santelli needed. Although an order for two or three WindStars from InterState Airlines would hardly be the large fleet order he needed to substantially reduce the factory's growing inventory, it certainly was a starting point.

But sometimes conversations are like icebergs. All the facts are not revealed. The consummate conversation miner, Rick was so focused on pitching the WindStar that he had not yet considered why his three airline friends had converged on Fort Lauderdale this weekend. It did not involve just fun in the sun. It actually involved serious airline business. During the past six months, Santelli, Andreas, and Long had ardently, but covertly, been discussing combining their companies to form one large regional airline that would blanket the

East Coast. This weekend the three had come together with the intent of finalizing the terms and conditions of a definitive merger agreement. It was highly confidential.

Sammy sat back in his chair and lit up his third cigarette of the evening. Even though knowing smoking was quickly going out of vogue, he found the habit he had acquired when in Nam difficult to kick.

"So, my good friend, Rick," Sammy said, blowing his smoke to the side, "everything you say about the WindStar sounds impressive." He took a swallow of his Scotch, and exhaled. "Now, when can I have a flight demonstration?" He looked Rick squarely in the eye.

Rick responded quickly, "Sammy, you know you've got a demo anytime you want one." He paused for a second, gathering his thoughts, and then went further. "I'd be delighted to bring the aircraft up to Cincinnati in a week or so. We could fly it on some of your routes, and have your OPS people crawl all over it. I'll bring some of my tech support guys."

In preparation to tout the aircraft, Rick had already told Santelli of the trip to the factory in Brazil and of bringing a new WindStar back to the States to use as a demonstrator for customers. Of course, Rick had carefully edited out any of the problems occurring to the aircraft earlier that day. Certainly the damaged WindStar, soon to be undergoing repairs, would not be airworthy for at least another seven to ten days.

"Now, now, Mr. Harris," Santelli said lightheartedly, crushing his cigarette out in a nearby ashtray, "I wouldn't want to put you to all that trouble. Cincinnati would be nearly a three-hour flight for you. This weekend, we're only a stone's throw from your operation at the airport. How about if we just take a look at the WindStar here in Fort Lauderdale?"

Rick forced a smile, remaining silent. Still emblazoned in his mind was the image of a hapless WindStar resting—gear up—on its belly on the tarmac at RioAero.

"Remember, Rick," Santelli continued, "I said *I'm* in the market for new equipment." He realized Rick knew most airlines made acquisition decisions through committees that spent months if not years analyzing every aspect of every aircraft that could possibly fulfill their mission requirements. Multiple flight demonstrations, detailed economic analyses, and protracted contract negotiations were *de rigueur*. Sammy Santelli was different.

"Rick," Santelli went on, "you know that whatever new aircraft flies in the InterState livery is the one I select. My OPS people—God bless them—make whatever equipment I buy work for the airline. It has always been that way, and it will always be that way." Sammy paused for a moment, raised his brow, and waved his right hand at Andreas and Long to gain their attention.

"What's up?" Kelly Long asked.

John Andreas smiled, then laughed. "Has Rick sold you a new fleet of aircraft already?"

"No, no," Santelli quickly scoffed at Andreas, "at least not yet, but he does have my interest."

Andreas laughed again. They all laughed.

"Rick Harris is an astute salesman. In fact..." Santelli paused for effect. "In fact, he's one of my favorite aircraft salesmen."

"And so?" Andreas queried.

"Well, he's made me an offer I can't refuse. It's that simple."

Rick rolled his eyes, not sure where Sammy was going with this conversation.

"Now," Santelli continued, "my question to you guys is this: Do you want a piece of the action?"

There was silence among the group. Sammy's intent was unclear.

Santelli went on, "You see, Mr. Harris has offered to take us on a flight demonstration in the WindStar." He extended his hand to Rick in an appreciative gesture. "And, I and my friends accept that offer." Andreas and Long responded with enthusiastic nods as Santelli knew they would.

"Great," Rick said, shaking hands with Sammy. "I'm sure you will be very impressed with what you'll see." He was well aware that getting the customer up in the air was a major step toward selling any aircraft. He was confident he could negotiate a deal with Santelli and possibly pave the way for future sales to the other two airline executives.

"Okay, then, how about early Sunday morning?" Santelli said rubbing both hands together in anticipation. "I get to fly up front and do at least one takeoff and landing, right?"

For an instant, Harris felt faint. His mind raced, attempting to ferret out a workable solution. How could he fly an aircraft that would be in the hangar propped up by a set of jacks and undergoing repairs?

Kelly Long broke in. "Let's make it midday, I'd like to make another run at some billfish a few miles offshore that morning."

Rick still remained silent.

"Then, it's a done deal," Santelli confirmed. "Right, Rick?"

"Absolutely," Rick spoke up. What else could he say? The solution would just have to be worked out later. "Gentlemen, you have got yourselves a WindStar flight demonstration." He raised his glass to Sammy in a toast.

"Here, here," Santelli said, lifting his glass. It was his sixth Johnny Walker of the night. Although Sammy's speech occasionally was somewhat slurred, his body seemed to have a high tolerance for alcohol. "Now, my good friend, I want to tell ya...yeah," he nodded, agreeing with himself while continuing, "how fortunate I consider myself...what by running into you and your wife downstairs. Ya know, if it were not for that, well I wouldn't be getting a ride so soon in the WindStar, would I?" Then, more earnestly, Santelli made an admission, "I must tell you, Rick...in all honesty...two other airframe manufacturers have almost been camping out at my office the past week or two." He laughed aloud. "Yeah, those 'turbo tamale' people from San Antonio are keen on doing a deal...keen, keen, very keen. And, those matadors from BASA...well, they gave me a highly attractive proposal for the purchase of five Avio-23 aircraft with options for an additional five."

"Really?" Rick said with frank surprise. Earlier, Santelli, Andreas, and Long had disparaged the Fairchild Metroliner. And the Avio-23 was slow, unpressurized, and low technology. Certainly Santelli could not be serious about either aircraft. However the real eye-popper, a potential order for now what appeared to be up to ten aircraft, was nothing to sneeze at. That is, if what Sammy had said was actually true.

John Andreas chimed into the conversation, "Rick, you need to know that those Spaniard peddlers make their aircraft tough to turn down. They're an aggressive bunch. They actually give you a chunk of cash if you sign up for one of their long-term leases." Then, Andreas laughed. "They call it 'integration funds'—cash to help you integrate their aircraft into your operating system. But with no accounting for the funds after the fact, they don't really care what you do with the money."

"Still, we're not stupid," Kelly Long spoke up. "It doesn't take a rocket scientist to figure out that anything an airframer 'gives' you with an aircraft is packed into the price or lease structure. Besides, the Avio-23 is—"

"Okay, guys," Sammy said, narrowing his eyes and shaking his head, "I'm sure Rick knows all about the sporty game that's played in selling aircraft. We need not bore him with details of discussions individual operators like us have been having with his competitors."

Rick flashed a big smile. He laughed. "Don't worry, you're not betraying secrets. I pretty much have a handle on the competition." Though truthfully said, he knew there was not such a thing as too much information about the competition. In a more serious vein, he continued. Rick had made a decision about the demo dilemma. "Gentlemen, I have a confession to make. It's not something any salesman likes to tell a prospective customer. But you need to know.

And," he grimaced, "I'd like you to keep it confidential, at least for the time being."

Quiet temporarily blanketed the table.

"Okay, confidential it is," Santelli acknowledged. "Right, guys?"

Andreas and Long nodded.

Rick leaned forward. With elbows firmly planted on the table and hands tightly clasped, he forced himself to talk about a subject he really wanted to forget, but could not. He knew it would be better if the group got the facts from him rather than from Fairchild, BASA, or the media. Rick spoke up. "Earlier this evening a mishap occurred to a WindStar...the one I brought up from Brazil." Rick's eyes focused on Gail. His pained expression revealed the turmoil he now felt about discussing the incident. A hint of a smile from her bolstered him onward. He looked over to Andreas and Long, and then back to Sammy. "We were preparing to tow the aircraft into the hangar for an inspection when something happened. We don't know exactly why, but for some reason the gear retracted. An investigation is underway."

"Ouch!" Kelly Long exclaimed. He shook his head. "Not good."

"Yeah," Santelli nodded, stunned upon hearing the news. "Aww, know how you must feel. I'm sure you'll figure out the cause."

"I think I may already have." Rick glanced back toward Gail. "But I don't have all the facts yet. One thing I can assure you of, Sammy, is that this problem will not affect any aircraft we may deliver to you. Guaranteed."

"And the demo?" John Andreas queried.

"Don't worry about the demo," Rick said with confidence. "I'm arranging to have another WindStar flown up from the factory over the weekend. As long as we can slide the demo by a day, everything could be set for Monday afternoon." Rick was being wildly optimistic. As of yet he had not even contacted anyone at the factory concerning the WindStar's latest damaging incident. Regardless, he knew another aircraft would be needed in the States to support his time-critical sales program. There were plenty of WindStars tied down on the factory's ramp. He felt confident that one would be provided—it had to be provided. But, by Monday afternoon?

"Now Rick," Santelli said somewhat skeptically, "if you can get it together, then fine. But if you can't, we'll all understand. I'll pencil the demo in for Monday afternoon." Sammy borrowed a pen from Rick and began scribbling on one of the cocktail napkins that cluttered the tabletop. "Here's the phone number on the *LOAD FACTOR*." He smiled, vainly. "Great name for a boat, huh? Anyway, just give me a call later to firm up a time for Monday."

Rick glanced at the number, and then stuffed the napkin into his shirt pocket. He was relieved. True to form, he had to be forthright about the WindStar and its problem. "Thanks for understanding. It's important to me that you all know what happened."

Sammy looked at his wristwatch. It was nearly midnight.

Gail hid a yawn behind her hand.

Hours of drinking had taken its toll on the group. Rick's bulletin on the WindStar now had a sobering effect.

Kelly Long keyed in on the lull in the conversation. "Let's pack it in for the night," he said. "We've got another big day ahead of us tomorrow."

"Good idea," Rick concurred.

"I'll get the check," John Andreas piped in.

"It's already been taken care of," Rick announced. "When you come to my town, the drinks are on me."

They thanked Rick for his hospitality; then, the group rose and departed the lounge for the hotel lobby below.

TWENTY-THREE

Destination: Pasador Ranch

D espite the late hour, the hotel lobby was far from deserted. The pace, if anything, was even more hectic than when Rick and Gail had arrived nearly three hours earlier. Weekend nights in Fort Lauderdale seldom quieted down until sometime after two o'clock in the morning.

Santelli, Andreas, and Long strolled to a bank of elevators that led up to their rooms in the hotel's tower section. Having been previous visitors, they knew that getting a good night's sleep on their boat at the marina was nearly impossible. Weekend party revelers were seemingly everywhere. Cigarettes and Scarabs continually trolled the Intracoastal. The deep resonating thumping rumble from the powerful twin-engine boats at idle was often overridden by the trumpeting roar of wide-open throttles. The merriment and noise would continue on for several more hours.

Rick and Gail wound their way through the lobby and out the front entrance to the parking valet. Luckily, the wait to have their car retrieved was only minutes. In her sweetest you-can't-say-no tone, Gail offered to drive. She had had much less to drink than he. Having accompanied Rick before while he was entertaining customers, Gail knew how to smoothly switch from date to executive wife mode. When donning that mantle, she usually prudently selected to drink Campari on the rocks with a big splash of soda. Its low alcohol content and bitter tree-bark taste made Campari her drink of choice whenever she wanted to maintain a clear mind throughout the evening. To her, Campari was a quaintly entertaining experience. She enjoyed leisurely stirring the drink, watching the melting ice slowly lighten the dark reddish color. Later, when the cocktail became diluted enough for her to actually drink, she would finish about half of it and then order another. The entire process usually took about thirty minutes.

As Gail drove the silver BMW away from the hotel, she could not help but think about various parts of the evening's conversation. Was Santelli actually ready to acquire new equipment? Or, was he just leading Rick on? How many aircraft might he order? Was the WindStar a prime contender? What part did Andreas and Long play in his acquisition program?

Rick reclined his seat and closed his eyes as the car's tires buzzed across the metal grates of the causeway. "So, what do you think?" he asked Gail.

"I was about to pose that very same question." She adjusted the rearview mirror from Rick's previously set position. The reflected glare of a pair of high intensity headlights from what appeared to be an off-road pickup truck had become irritating. "Are your friends for real, or are they just acting out their parts as airline honchos?"

Rick laughed twice, then opened his eyes and began to explain. "That is one of the things that is really hard to tell about most people. Is it all hot air? Or, is there substance to what they're saying? In some cases, there's no telling. But to answer your question, these guys are for real. Sammy is gearing up for a major expansion. I'm sure of it. Everything he said tonight points to it. And if Fairchild and BASA are putting a full court press on him, they can sense it too. For now, we just have to hope that the WindStar can hold itself together. We can't afford to have any more bizarre problems like we had today. Airlines tend to be a conservative bunch. The last thing they want to be near is an aircraft that seemingly has been cursed by some voodoo priest."

Gail ignored his comment about voodoo priest curses, not realizing that various forms of voodoo were actually practiced in Brazil. She continued to focus on Santelli and friends. "You sound rather sure about Santelli."

"I am." Rick quickly responded. "I've known Sammy for a good number of years."

"But if you had not run into him tonight, he might not have even considered the WindStar."

"Not the case. He knows far more about the aircraft than you would suspect. Sammy is one smart guy. But he hasn't been quite ready to make his move. He's still putting together his program plan. And in the process, he's exercising the competition. That's part of the game. He wants to find out how far Fairchild and BASA will go to get his business. Then, he'll give me a call. He'll ask for my bottom line. I'll give it to him. He'll know he's got a fair deal. Everybody will be happy. It will happen that fast. I know Sammy even better than Sammy thinks I do."

"Don't get cocky, Rick."

"I'm not." Rick understood how Gail could have gotten that impression. She was a brilliant veterinarian. She could read most animals by just glancing at them. "Look at it this way, Gail. You know horses. You can tell what a horse is going to do before it does something just by studying how it acts. When it swishes its tail and there are no flies around, a horse is most likely irritated. Then when it pins its ears back, you know it's really irritated. And, when its ears are flat and its muzzle is wrinkled, watch out…you're likely to get bitten. Am I right?"

"Well yes, but—"

"People are no different. When you hang around them and analyze them as I have over the years, you learn to read them—their body language; the types of words they use; their intonation. They give you all sorts of signals as to what they might be thinking, what they might do next. Of course, some people are more difficult to read than others. Some of them are pretty good actors who can camouflage their true intent. But even with them, once they're relaxed and feel secure in the scene they're playing, they often let down their guard, if only for a moment. Then, they're just as easy to read as a horse."

"You may be right, Rick."

"You know I'm right!"

"Now don't get arrogant on me."

"Sorry if I was, I didn't mean to be. I am very confident about Santelli. He's going to order some WindStars. The real question is how many? Unfortunately, I don't have that answer. Fortunately, he has the wherewithal to do whatever he wants. He and his family have deep pockets. They are well connected. That is also true for Andreas and Long, but not to the same degree. Sammy's family owns one helluva big trucking company in Ohio."

"Santelli Brothers?" Gail guessed. She had seen their ever-present big rigs on the Interstate. Their orange with black parallelogram logo was hard not to remember.

"That's right. And, you probably didn't know that John Andreas' family owns a string of breweries...some located in the US...some overseas. Then, there's Kelly Long. His family owns one of the biggest construction companies in Atlanta. These guys ain't flakes."

Gail had just driven by the north side of the airport and was now passing under I-95 on SR-84. The skies seemed even closer and more radiant than earlier that evening. Tranquility now filled the air. There was no rumbling thunder from approaching aircraft. Few scheduled flights operated much past midnight at FLL.

As they traveled farther west, road traffic quickly thinned out. Extraneous exterior sounds muted within the BMW. Radial tires lazily hummed, singing to the pavement below. Rick took a deep breath, slowly exhaled, and began to doze off. Gail knew he had to be exhausted. It had been a long, event-filled day. She was glad to see him relax. In another five miles they would be home.

Abruptly, Gail downshifted into third gear, rapidly accelerating the car to well above its previous forty-five mile per hour pace. The jolt from her shifting brought Rick awake with a start.

"What's going on?" he asked, repositioning himself in the passenger seat.

"I'm not sure," Gail responded. She was heavily concentrating. Her eyes rapidly shifted from the road ahead to the image in the rearview mirror as she analyzed what she had noticed. It was odd indeed, she thought. But she could not muster a logical explanation.

"Not sure?" Rick was confused. "Not sure about what?"

"When we left Pier Sixty-Six," she answered, "I readjusted the rearview mirror from where you had it set. Headlights from a pickup truck behind us were reflecting into my eyes. The lights were higher up and brighter than those of most other vehicles, and the lights had a bluish tint."

"Geez," Rick groaned. He anticipated Gail's next statement. "And that same truck is behind us now?"

"I am afraid so," Gail said the words slowly, distinctively pronouncing each syllable.

"And, it accelerated when you did?"

"O-o-oh, yeah!" She glanced at her side view mirror. "Now it's picking up more speed. Looks like it's going to pass us in the second lane."

"Damn..." Rick groaned. This evening's WindStar accident further heightened his concern. He did not like the possibility of what he felt could happen. Maybe too much TV and too many action movies influenced his thought pattern. He reacted instantly. "Turn here, onto Flamingo!" He pointed ahead and to the right.

Gail braked hard and jerked the steering wheel to the right. The BMW shrugged off speed, skidding, drifting left toward the far shoulder of Flamingo Road before gaining traction once again. Out of the corner of her eye, she glimpsed the black pickup truck zoom by, its brake lights almost immediately illuminating.

She swiftly slammed the transmission into second gear and punched the car forward. Its engine came alive, snarling, peaking at redline. The rear tires spun, screeching and shuddering as contact was repeatedly made and then lost with the road. Plumes of blue-white smoke and the acrid smell of blistering rubber spewed out from the car's wheel wells before full-power traction was regained. Tires tenaciously gripped the pavement like claws of a cat scampering up a tree, accelerating the BMW down the road and away from the ominous pickup truck. With its intended, now unstoppable forward drive, the car screamed down the smaller two-lane road that headed due north, burning past an old slow-moving van.

Rick's mind raced ahead. He knew that the BMW 633CSI was a remarkably fast and well-engineered high-performance car. But the black pickup truck was jacked-up, tricked-out, and highly modified. Soon it would be barreling down the road after them. Everything happening foreshadowed a dangerous scenario. He needed a plan of action. He needed it now.

Just then the answer came into view, Rick recognized it. He remembered driving past it on periodic trips up to Palm Beach County. Immediately ahead, and to the right, was an old cement factory, one of many that supplied the life-blood material to contractors busy in rapidly developing South Florida. Tonight the facility should be deserted. A good place for temporary cover. Hopefully the pickup driver would continue north, duped into believing that the van, which Gail had just passed, was the target.

"Slow down and pull off into this factory," Rick shouted to Gail as he braced himself against the front dashboard. Heavy braking caused the tires to sadly wail, tearing at the roadway's surface, trying to dissipate the BMW's forward momentum. He looked back down the darkened road as Gail followed his instructions. The van was still several hundred yards away from the factory's entrance. Farther back in the distance, a set of headlights was barely identifiable as an obscure, bluish-tinted single beam. It must be the pickup truck, he thought.

"Now, what?" Gail asked as she killed the headlights. Her adrenalin was flowing. Being pursued by an unknown threat was a real-life nightmare. But, why? Why was it happening? Not having an answer was most troubling.

The car rumbled onto a graveled expanse that abutted the paved entrance driveway. Rick strained his eyes to quickly scope out the facility which was lit by moonlight and random mercury vapor lamps. There were a multitude of places a car could park and be out of sight. But which place should it be? He had to make an immediate decision. And, it had to be the right one. Instinctively, he chose an inconspicuous area near the roadside. It was one that would allow for a quick exit if necessary. It was also one that he felt a pursuer would easily speed past without first investigating.

"Pull around to the side of that small equipment shed to the left," Rick commanded. "It's isolated from the other larger buildings and is close enough to the road for an escape if the pickup decides to pull into the factory." His head was throbbing. Too little sleep and too much Scotch were taking a toll on him. He hoped his decision on this location was the right one.

Gail responded, doing as she was told. She positioned the BMW, engine running, first gear engaged, foot poised on the accelerator.

"My bet is that the driver of the pickup will initially think that the van is us and pursue it. Then, when it's found out that the van is not us, the truck will hopefully go up the road a bit farther with the intention of overtaking us." He paused with a groan. "Or, less good...the driver could immediately double back to find out where we may have pulled off." Rick rubbed his eyes, and shook off an intruding yawn. "If I'm wrong, and the truck pulls in here first—"

"I'll be sure to put the pedal to the metal," Gail spoke out in uncharacteristic CB radio lingo. "By the way, how am I doing so far?" She grinned, trying to be calm and clear-headed, though her heart was still pounding.

"Damn good, so far." He tightened his seatbelt, and checked hers. "I'm sure glad I gave you that high performance driving course for your birthday a few years back."

"A few years?" Gail mocked him. "That was nearly seven years ago."

"You're welcome." Rick broke a smile. "You retain knowledge well."

"Thanks."

Seconds after the van passed the cement factory, the black pickup truck thundered by at what could have easily been a hundred miles an hour.

Rick slowly counted to five as he watched the truck's taillights swerve around the van and keep going. Then he said, "Okay, let's get the hell out of here. Keep your lights off and don't touch the brakes. With a little more luck, we'll be free of whoever is chasing us."

Gail pulled the BMW out onto the road, headed in the opposite direction from the truck's rapidly shrinking taillights, and smoothly sprinted her machine past seventy miles per hour. "Thank God for a bright South Florida night," she softly said almost to herself. A quick glance into her rearview mirror revealed no sign of the pickup truck.

"Anything behind us?" Rick asked.

"Nothing yet."

"Good." Rick continued on, "Okay, now here's what we do. When you get to SR-84 take a left and go east toward civilization. No one would expect us to go back from where we came. And even if someone did, there would less likely be a chance of danger there than there would be out here in the boonies."

Gail nodded, slowing, but not stopping, as Flamingo intersected with SR-84. She headed east, once again accelerating the BMW past seventy miles per hour. Things were looking up, Gail thought. In five minutes, they would safely be back to urban surroundings and much more secure than on a desolate highway where anything could happen.

Then, ill-fortune: something they had not expected; something that never entered their minds; but, something cooler minds might have anticipated.

Rick noticed it a split second before Gail.

"Shit!" he said, gloomily. "Bad timing."

"Oh, well," Gail added, "we were running only on luck. The odds were beginning to stack up against us."

"Yeah," Rick despondently agreed.

Alternating blue and red strobes filled their side view mirrors. A spotlight briefly stabbed through the BMW's deeply tinted back window. An abrupt whir of a siren underlined the need for an immediate response. The white with green, Broward County Sheriff's Department car seemed almost glued to their bumper.

Resignedly, Gail eased off the accelerator. "I suppose a few points on my license and a fine of a hundred dollars or so is easier to swallow than getting your BMW wrecked by some maniac in a pickup truck," she said, justifying the situation to Rick. Still, she did not like the idea of being busted by a Deputy Sheriff when she felt breaking the law was, in this instance, well justified.

"At least we're safe now," Rick offered.

"I suppose," Gail said bemoaning with a shrug. Then she smiled, more fully understanding Rick's consoling remark.

Ahead and to the right was a RoadWay Express service station that had just closed for the night. The station operator was pulling out of the parking area as the BMW, with police car in tow, approached. Gail dutifully put on her directional signal and coasted into the service station, stopping just before the filling pumps. The police car angled behind her with strobes still pulsating.

Gail had already exited and walked behind the BMW to stand waiting patiently in the headlights of the Deputy's cruiser even before the officer opened his door.

Finally, the Deputy, a tall, husky man in his mid-thirties who seemed to be poured into a tailored shirt that was three sizes too small, cautiously approached Gail. His right hand rested on the grip of his holstered gun. He knew full well that he never could be quite sure what kind of situation might lay in wait for him. A silver BMW with heavily tinted windows, driving recklessly at nearly one o'clock in the morning, indicated the possibility of serious trouble. South Florida was a key port of entry and a distribution hub for the country's rapidly escalating drug trade. The actions the Deputy had observed from Gail's driving fit the profile of both dealers and users of drugs, especially those attracted to cocaine.

But before the Deputy could speak, Gail said, "Boy, am I glad to see you," and beamed a smile.

The Deputy did a double take. "You're glad to see *me*?"

"Yes, yes, Officer Callahan," Gail said animatedly as she read his name from the silver nametag that was pinned just above his right breast pocket. "You see," she dove into her explanation, "we were being chased by some hooligan in a big pickup truck." She paused breathlessly. "I have no idea why."

"Hmmm..." The Deputy's eyes narrowed. In his years on the force, he had heard almost every conceivable excuse that could be told for violations of the law, but being chased by hooligans in pickup trucks was certainly inventive.

"I know I was speeding...I know my lights were off...I was trying to escape."

"Sure, little lady," the Deputy responded, still highly skeptical of her story, "trying to escape, huh?"

"Uh-huh..." Gail stammered, not knowing initially how to respond to his clear disbelief. Suddenly, the means to substantiate her story came to her. "Let me tell you exactly what happened. Then, go to the car and ask my husband what happened to us tonight. He will corroborate everything I say." She paused, scanning the Deputy's face to see if he would consider her proposal.

The Deputy briefly closed his eyes and began shaking his head from side to side. "Look, ma'am, I don't really have time for—"

"There...THERE!" Gail shouted out, pointing to the pickup truck as it thundered by.

The Deputy snapped his head around and zeroed in on the truck. "Okay, okay...go ahead, let's start with your story, then I'll hear what your husband has to say." A chink had been created in his doubt.

After all the story telling was over, the Deputy shrugged, raising his hands palms up into the air. "Amazing," he said, now smiling. "Your stories jibe." He closed his eyes and shook his head in disbelief. "I don't think you both could have made up such a bizarre tale." He paused, shrugged again, then went on, "My guess is that the pursuit was a case of mistaken identity. BMWs like yours are very popular among some of our less than upstanding citizens." The Deputy reached inside his cruiser and shut off the strobe lights. "Although there is seldom an excuse for breaking the law," he continued, "the reasons for your actions are, at least to me, plausible. So, I'm not going to cite you this time." While still somewhat unsure their tale was totally believable, the Deputy did offer an escort home in the interest of maintaining public safety.

Both Rick and Gail thanked the Deputy and slid back into the BMW's leather seats to await the escort. In the back of their minds, the mistaken identity theory offered by the Deputy just did not ring true. The unsettling thought they shared without voicing it was that the eerie chase had something to do with RioAero and the WindStar. What made them so sure, they just could not say. So many strange events happening during the same day made coincidence seem too far-fetched.

TWENTY-FOUR

Pasador Ranch

SATURDAY, FEBRUARY 21, 1981

The pastures at Pasador Ranch glistened as if with the sparkle of a million diamonds as the sun's first rays kissed droplets of dew clinging to the blades of Coastal and Bermuda grasses. A group of Paso Finos stood motionless, dozing and basking in the uplifting warmth of the early morning. The horses' elegant shadows silhouetted onto the weathered-gray boards of a tin-roofed run-in shed. Against an endless, bright-blue winter sky, three Snowy Egrets glided in from the neighboring Everglades, wings transitioning to a graceful flare allowing a two-step touchdown. Nature's art was silently captured.

Near the stable, an old Massey-Ferguson began rumbling along as it towed the loaded New Holland manure spreader to an isolated section of pasture that lay fallow. Domingo Sanchez stood proudly upright, his feet anchored to the floorboards of the tractor. His arms were comfortably folded across his chest, his thighs pressed slightly forward against the steering wheel. Cool air ruffled his long, thinning gray hair. He smiled, deepening the creases in his tanned, leathery face. The tension maintained by his legs on the steering wheel allowed the tractor to seemingly guide itself along the fence-line path. His world was complete and at his command. Domingo was a happy man.

Rick and Gail had first met Sanchez four years earlier. It was on their second trip to Medellín, Colombia, during their search for a young stallion. There, on one of the many horse farms, they noticed a middle-aged man working an obstinate colt in the round pen. The colt raced uncontrollably around the small ring, abruptly and repeatedly reversing direction, occasionally stopping long enough to emit an echoing snort of frustration. All the while, Sanchez remained calm, watching and allowing the colt to expend pent up energy. He knew horses well—far better than most people might even think they knew their fellow man.

Finally, Sanchez slowly approached the colt. While doing so, he began to almost sing a repetitive string of words in Spanish. With each tone variation in Sanchez's voice, the colt became more focused upon him. Masterfully, Sanchez slowly extended a hand and gently stroked the underside of the young horse's neck. The singsong words were now a mere whisper. The colt's breathing slowed, its body relaxed. Then, Domingo Sanchez casually strolled away from the horse, and, as if invisibly attached, the colt followed him. Together, the two calmly made a circuit around the training ring.

For nearly forty years, Domingo's life had revolved around horses—Paso Finos. To him, the Paso was the only horse worthy of his time and effort. His love for the breed and his skill as a trainer were evident. Gail and Rick were so impressed with the colt and Sanchez, that Rick and Gail exported both to Fort Lauderdale. It proved a winning combination. Sanchez was now the trainer and operations manager at Pasador Ranch. To him, South Florida was home. To Rick and Gail, he was an important member of the family. And the colt, now an impressive stallion, was the pride of the ranch.

The manure spreader's cam mechanism continued to click and clack with every turn of its slow moving wheels. Domingo glanced backward to reassure himself that the trusty old spreader was still in proper tow. Farther behind, he could see the gleam from the bright orange barrel-tile roof of the main residence. The predawn dew was slowly vaporizing. A thin cloud of mist rose above the house.

Within the residence, sunlight aggressively sliced through thin gaps between tall vertical blinds that masked the master bedroom from the center courtyard of the U-shaped structure. Facets on angled specks of crushed stone in the polished blue-gray terrazzo floor subtly expanded and energized each ray's spectrum of light. The room was beginning to come alive.

Gail leaned over Rick. She gently shook his motionless body which sprawled diagonally across the king-size bed. She nudged him again and again.

He finally moaned, clutched a pillow, and instinctively rolled away from her repetitive prodding.

She pursed her lips, then broke into a thin smile. Too much Sammy Santelli, she thought.

"Rick," she said in a business-like tone, "someone from the factory is on the phone."

He remained silent. There was no movement from his body.

"*Momentito, Señor*," Gail spoke her limited Spanish into the mouthpiece of the phone.

"*Bueno*, Doctor Richmond," came the voice from the other end of the line, "but I speak English very well."

"Oh, sorry—"

"Do not be, you had no way of knowing," the voice responded. "Did my good friend Rick drink too much Jack Daniels last night?"

"No, no," she chuckled, now recognizing that the caller was likely more than a casual acquaintance. "It was a combination of mango punch and Scotch, but the real factor is that he's only had a few hours of sleep. It's just past seven in the morning here."

"Oops," came the voice, "my sincerest apologies, I never can remember that our time is slightly ahead of yours."

"No matter," Gail continued talking into the phone, "I imagine that it's important for you to speak with him."

"Why, yes," the voice reassured, "yes it is."

"Whom shall I say is calling?"

"Franco...Franco Rameros."

"Franco, he'll be right with you." Gail moved closer to Rick, who seemed oblivious to her presence. She took hold of the end of the pillow, paused for a two beat count, and then quickly snatched it from Rick's loose grip. His head fell three inches, thumping against the firm mattress below.

"Aarrgghh," Rick gasped. "What's going on?" he mumbled, grumpily. Initially, he was somewhat confused. Then, he noticed Gail holding the telephone.

"It's Franco Rameros at the factory," she said. "Don't worry, I have the mute button pressed."

Rick tried to flash an appreciative smile, but could only manage a squinting grin as his eyes adjusted to the daggers of morning light that raked through the room. He knew he probably looked as bad as he felt. It was nothing new. He had been there before. A hot shower and a tall glass of cold milk were always an effective remedy. Rick shook off a yawn and rubbed both of his eyes, hard.

"Thanks," he said to Gail as she handed him the phone. He moved the pillow to the headboard of the bed and propped himself up against it. He pressed the mute button to off. "Franco," he said loudly into the phone, trying to be as upbeat as possible, "you're interrupting my beauty sleep."

"HA!" came Rameros' typically sarcastic response. "You would have to sleep for a couple of years to make any improvement."

They both chuckled.

"Listen, my gringo friend..." Franco's tone mellowed for a moment. "How would you like it if I paid you a visit?"

"Huh?"

"Well," Rameros continued, "it has been some time since I have been to Fort Lauderdale. Besides, I just learned that you and Joey Delgado broke one of our WindStars last night. Big Lou called me about it. In fact, it was at three o'clock in the morning, my time."

"Oh...oh, yeah..." Rick was now back to the reality of the situation. "It was a gear system problem."

"You know," began Rameros with another jab, "you should really keep your hands off that gear switch when the aircraft is on the ground." Franco paused, then, in absence of any rejoinder from Rick, pressed on. "Anyway, Big Lou's A-Team has been crawling all over a

WindStar that just came out of the Finishing Center on Thursday. They have checked and double-checked everything. He wants me to get the aircraft up to you ASAP."

"Excellent!" Rick was pleasantly surprised at how quickly the factory had mobilized, anticipating the need for another aircraft to be in place and on the ramp at FLL. "You guys are really on the ball!"

"Hell," Rameros interjected, "Big Lou can make it rain if he wants to. By the way, have you talked with Delgada since they moved the aircraft into the hangar?"

"Uh, no…"

"Well, according to Lou, that aircraft apparently has a bigger problem than just collapsed gear."

"What do you mean?" Rick immediately questioned.

"I do not know the total extent of the damage, but those folks from Opa Locka that Joey called to get the aircraft back on its feet…well, they accidentally put a screw jack through the left inboard fuel tank."

"Damn," Rick said, trying to restrain his ire. He knew that that kind of damage involved more than skin work and paint. There could possibly be structural damage. Now, it might take perhaps a month to get the WindStar back into the air.

"Sometimes shit happens," Rameros said, heedlessly.

"Yes," Rick regretfully acknowledged, "but I think you would agree that it's been happening a bit too frequently to the WindStar." Redirecting his interest back to Rameros' travel plans, he asked, "Tell me, Franco, what's your ETA for—?"

"Whenever we get there, my friend," Rameros scoffed. "A complete inspection of the aircraft is being finished. The tanks will be topped off shortly. I have repair equipment and parts in the cargo hold. Three engineers will be joining me to help revitalize that aircraft of yours that took a tumble onto the tarmac. I should be blasting out of here within the hour."

"So, you'll be here Monday night or Tuesday morning?" Rick speculated.

"No, no, my friend, we are not taking the scenic coastal route as you did," Rameros emphasized. "And, we are not holing up every night in some fancy hotel on the beach. We are flying through the interior and only stopping when the engines scream for more kerosene."

Rameros paused.

Rick remained silent.

"I will be there by Sunday morning. Is that good enough for you, Mr. Harris?"

Rick rolled his eyes in disbelief. It would truly be almost non-stop flying. "Sunday morning would be perfect."

TWENTY-FIVE

Pasador Ranch

T his aircraft sales business never has a dull moment, Rick thought to himself as he shuffled toward the bathroom. After a quick shower and light breakfast, he would be ready to begin organizing his activities for the next few days.

"Never a dull moment...never a dull moment," he continued to mumble to himself. Hot water rained down upon his body. Soothing. Invigorating. Even the seemingly banal act of shampooing his hair quickened his revitalization. After a long four minutes of grunting and groaning, Rick emerged a new man.

"Feel better now?" Gail handed him a towel.

"It's amazing how much self-inflicted abuse the body can take and spring back as though nothing had ever happened to it," Rick philosophized.

"Don't push it too far, though," Gail cautioned. "As remarkable as the body is, too much is always too much."

"Aye, aye, madam doctor," Rick quipped. He knew exactly what Gail was saying.

Rick quickly dressed: faded jeans; khaki shirt; well-worn, dark brown roper boots. In the kitchen, he gulped down a pint-sized glass of cold milk mixed with Ovaltine.

Gail had already walked down and back up the driveway with the dogs to retrieve the morning paper. She was now sitting at the kitchen table just finishing thumbing through the Front Section. She took a sip from her mug of coffee, then she glanced at the first page of the Metro Section. The image there hit her like a sledgehammer being dropped on her foot. First the shocking numbness, then the conscious pain.

Rick was oblivious to the almost immediate change in her demeanor. The two rottweilers, however, sensed her distress. Briefly, the dogs quietly whined.

"What's up, guys?" Rick soothingly asked noticing the dogs' anxious behavior.

Gail looked down at the dogs, then back up toward Rick. "Sit down, Mr. Harris. Please."

"Sure," he said, quizzically raising his brow.

"Remember last night when the WindStar collapsed to the ground?"

"It would be pretty hard to forget that experience," Rick lamented.

"Well, it looks like the *Sun-Sentinel* wants all of South Florida to know about it." She handed him the Metro Section.

He quietly stared at the black and white photo. The headline read: NEW AIRCRAFT COLLAPSES. A brief six paragraph story made mention of Brazil, the WindStar, and RioAero. Although it noted that the cause of the incident was under investigation, it rambled on about airline deregulation. The story suggested that foreign manufacturers might not be taking appropriate measures to safeguard America's flying public as the race to design and produce aircraft for an expanding North American market accelerated.

"Damn..." Rick exhaled the word. "We really don't need this kind of publicity." He pushed the paper away and gazed blankly at the ceiling. He sensed this would only be the first story mentioning the WindStar. Reporters would be asking questions, interpreting the answers in whichever way they and their editors saw fit. He was now thoroughly thankful that he had mentioned the incident to Santelli and the others the night before. It gave him credibility—both professionally and personally.

Gail was puzzled. "How could the press have gotten on to the story so quickly?" she asked Rick. "It only happened slightly after eight o'clock last night. No one knew about the incident except us, Dan Cole and his friend, and Joey and Mario. The contractor from Opa Locka couldn't have arrived on the scene until close to midnight. It certainly seems strange that the press would have a photo and some basic background information before their deadline. And, that couldn't have been more than a few hours after the incident itself."

"Very strange indeed." Rick stood up from the table. "I don't know what's going on here, but..." He shook his head, abruptly ending his thought. After standing frozen in silence, he began to speak again, "I'm really getting concerned; too many ill-fated coincidences in such a short period of time. I can't believe these misfortunes are coincidences at all. The odds are against that. It seems like a conspiracy. And, it seems to be accelerating. But, why? And, who's behind it? We've got to figure it out before it's too late, before the entire WindStar program falls apart."

"Where do we start?" Gail asked.

"Not sure," Rick cocked his head to the side and then slowly began to nod as if he had had an idea, which he did not. "Gonna take a walk, do some thinking. Don't worry, we'll sort this thing out."

Gail nervously smiled. She realized the gravity of the situation.

Rick placed a reassuring hand on her shoulder. He leaned over and kissed her on the forehead. "I'll be back in a half hour. Don't worry."

R ick grabbed a light jacket that hung behind the kitchen entrance
door and left the house. Walking toward the stable, his mind
shifted gears and began replaying events of the past twenty-four hours.
The crisp morning air and bright sunlight fueled his thought process.
There was the fresh smell of manure and the acrid scent of horse urine
as he entered the stable area. He heard the occasional snort of a stabled
Paso Fino clearing its nasal passages. Rick Harris walked on, deep in
thought.

"*Señor Rick*," came the voice from within one of the stalls,
"*buenos días*." It was Domingo Sanchez.

"*¡Hola!*" Rick acknowledged. "*¿Cómo estás, Mingo?*"

"*Muy bien, Señor Rick*," Sanchez said, exiting the stall, closing
and latching the lower half of the Dutch door behind him. "A beautiful
day, no?"

Rick smiled, placing his hand on Domingo's shoulder. "Mingo,
remember this," he said from his heart, "every day is a beautiful day."

Sanchez nodded. "I know what you mean. There is reason for
every day, even when the sun it does not shine."

Rick thought about what Sanchez had just said. "Mingo, you're a
perceptive man." Indeed the sun was shining, but a looming storm was
preoccupying Rick's mind. The dark clouds had gathered for some
reason. Now, he would have to figure out that reason, and soon.

Together the two men walked on, passing three empty stalls.
Domingo stopped at the end stall where a bay filly, marked with a star,
a snip, and two rear white socks, was leisurely nibbling on a flake of
hay. Rick peered into the stall, his face brightening with delight. She is
beautiful, he thought.

Sanchez saw the enchantment in Rick's eyes. "She moves with the
grace of her mother, the spirit of her father. She trains very well."

The filly looked up, recognized Rick, and nickered. She turned,
took a few steps, and extended her head over the closed lower half of
the door. Rick vigorously scratched the base of her forelock. The filly
drooped her head. Her eyes closed for the moment, for the pleasure.

Canción de Sacina was born on the ranch almost three years ago
to the day at five o'clock in the morning. Since it was known that her
birth was imminent, regular checks were being made on her pregnant
mother. Even so, Rick and Gail missed her birth. They arrived two
hours later only to find *Canción* already up on her stilt-like legs and
trying to figure out just how those long appendages were supposed to
work. Early imprinting and progressive training made the filly highly
receptive to people. In fact, she was more dog-like than horse-like in
personality.

"Take her out in the pasture, *Señor Rick*," Sanchez urged. "You
both will enjoy the diversion."

Rick agreed.

Within minutes, Domingo had the filly tacked up with a McClellan saddle, a halter, and reins.

"Thanks, Mingo," Rick said as he mounted. A slight amount of thigh pressure and a single cluck were all the filly needed to move out in the direction Rick desired. He passed the equipment shed and the massive near-empty hay barn with huge hangar-like doors. Then, he entered the narrow half-mile long pasture that bordered the Everglades to the west. The turf was firm and freshly mown.

Rick once again applied thigh pressure to urge the filly on. The three-year-old immediately launched into the expected largo gait, swiftly accelerating to nearly twenty miles per hour. Still, her rider remained virtually motionless in the saddle. The joy of a Paso Fino, Rick thought. Power and speed, but without the discomfort that accompanies non-gaited horses.

At the far end of the pasture, Rick dismounted. He appreciatively scratched the filly's throatlatch. She flexed, bending her neck sharply to the left, a sign of deference to Rick.

From above, he heard the faint roar of a distant airliner spooling up its engines for a power-on approach to FLL. Its highly polished aluminum skin was as brilliant as a star in the morning sky. The brief distraction redirected his attention to the problem at hand. What to do about the WindStar?

"You're insulated from it all," he said to the filly, now grazing on the pasture's grasses. "But I've got a puzzle to solve, and some of the pieces are finally coming together."

Rick remounted and headed back to the stable. First at a largo, then accelerating to a flat-out run. He broke into a wide grin as raw power from the filly's hindquarters propelled them both across the pasture. The balls of his feet pressed down on the stirrups as he leaned forward, clutching the reins and horse's mane. Thundering hooves pounded the compact turf. The rush of wind made his eyes water. A thin stream of tears began to flow backwards along his cheeks. All too soon the end arrived as the horse and rider exited the pasture and headed the last few hundred feet to the stable.

Rick collected the filly into a walk. She was still breathing heavily, her nostrils flaring, her eyes wide open. With adrenalin continuing to flow, she initially challenged his control by prancing to the side. Her thin delicate legs rapidly hammered the ground below, though only momentarily until she finally settled down.

Rick dismounted, still smiling. The ride was as much of an exhilarating rush for him as it was for his girl, *Canción*.

"You ride like a *caballero*, *Señor Rick*," Sanchez remarked.

"No, no, Mingo," Rick laughingly responded, "I ride more like a greenhorn…not being sure what's going to happen next."

Sanchez smiled, knowing full well what Rick had meant. "You need to ride more, then you will be as comfortable on a Paso as you are in an airplane."

"Yes indeed, but there are not enough hours in the day."

"*Comprendo, Señor Rick.*"

The two spoke for a few brief minutes. Rick outlined some tasks he wanted Domingo to complete by Sunday morning. Then eyeing the faded-red twenty-year-old pickup truck that was parked at the end of the stable barn, he asked, "How's the Chevy running these days?"

"Never better, but I drive it very little," Domingo replied. "Like the filly, it could always use some exercise."

"Good," Rick said. "I have a few errands to run. Do you still keep the keys to it in the ashtray?"

Domingo nodded.

"Then, *hasta la vista*," Rick said as he proceeded to the truck.

With a few pumps of the accelerator pedal and a twist of the ignition key, the engine fired up. The deep-throated resonance was the sound that only a big block V-8 could make. Rick shifted the transmission into drive. The pickup slowly rumbled away from the stable and along a gravel portion of the driveway that led back to the main residence. He stopped near the side entrance to the house.

Rick set the parking brake, leaving the engine running, left the truck, and trotted to the house. Rushing through the kitchen, he smiled at Gail who was sitting cross-legged on the floor intently brushing the teeth of one of the rottweilers. The dog's eyes followed as Rick passed through the room.

A brief moment later, Rick reappeared. In his left hand were three dark blue denim baseball caps embroidered with the lettering WINDSTAR and the company's trademark comet. His right hand held a well-traveled leather briefcase that contained, among other things, two videotape cassettes.

"Ready to save the world, Captain America?"

"Maybe not the world, good doctor," Rick responded. "Right now my focus is on trying to keep a portion of Brazil out of harm's way."

"So, you've got a plan?"

"Sorta." Rick shrugged. "Things are coming together, though slowly. First, I need to find out what, if anything, is on that videotape we stumbled across last night."

"How so?"

"Remember Tommy Maxwell?"

"You mean that quirky high-tech guy that used to work with some governmental agency up north as a spook?"

"Shhh…" Rick smiled with a quiet laugh as he slowly shook his head. "Tommy maintains that he was a cartographer, but we both know better. Even though he's really a different kind of guy, he is a master of the things he does. He's well positioned to find out just about anything I need to know. For the past couple of years he's worked out of a little shop on Las Olas, and although he may still do some government work, he does regular PI stuff mostly for the fun of it. I'm sure he'll be able to help me with some of the pieces of my puzzle."

Gail grinned.

Rick went on, "Then, I'm going to slide by Pier Sixty-Six to see Santelli and crew so we can firm up a time for that flight demonstration. Besides, I've got a new videotape from the factory that showcases the WindStar." He paused for a second. "Oh, yeah, and I will dress up their day and get rid of those morose black baseball caps in favor of the latest WindStar fashion from Brazil."

She glanced at the blue caps Rick was holding in his left hand. "Very chic!"

"Why thank you, fashion maven," Rick said with a wink to Gail. "Anyway, I should be back by mid-afternoon."

"…a quiet evening at home?"

"Absolutely!" He gave his wife a casual salute, turned and exited from the house.

Rick steered the old pickup down the driveway. Passing the entrance gate, he turned right heading east toward the beaches. The Chevy ambled down the roadway with a few shakes and rattles that age had bestowed upon it. Certainly not a BMW, Rick thought, but a refreshing change.

He pushed the accelerator down to the floorboard. There was a momentary lag, then a rushing sound from the Holley carburetor as air and fuel intermixed, aggressively vaporizing into the intake manifold. The mature V-8 engine sprang to life. The automatic transmission downshifted. The rear tires emitted a brief chirp just loud enough to be heard above the bellowing resonance from the dual exhaust. The truck seemed to flash a smile of youth as it sprinted down the road.

TWENTY-SIX

RioAero, SA

Heat generated from the mid-morning summer sun had pushed the temperature past ninety degrees. The thick, moisture-saturated air was a harbinger of what would be yet another afternoon of unsettled atmospheric conditions in southern Brazil.

On the ramp just outside the factory's delivery center hangar stood PT-SBY—WindStar S/N-36. Nearly a dozen technicians silently hustled about the new aircraft much like worker ants scurrying around the carcass of a grasshopper. The entire aircraft structure and its components were probed, assessed, and carefully scrutinized.

Even though these skilled professionals had now been at the task for almost five hours, their pace had not slowed as they attended to every detail. The nose to tail examination of this particular aircraft was ordered by Lou Biega. The director of engineering wanted to be absolutely certain that the plane would not be plagued with any—ANY—in-flight problems.

Now with the evaluation almost complete, exterior inspection plates were finally being refastened to the aircraft's glistening white skin. The nacelles were carefully refitted to frames surrounding the engines. The prop spinners were reattached to hub mounts.

Near the hangar door, a watchful eye intently focused on the activity. Jeffe Martinez had been standing there for most of the morning. He flicked the butt of yet another cigarette down onto the tarmac, compulsively crushing it out with the sole of his shoe as he had likewise done some ten times before.

Martinez was certainly under the gun, and he knew it. From all appearances, his QA department had been caught sleeping on the job. During the past few days, system failures had occurred to the WindStar at an alarming rate. So now, Big Lou's handpicked team of engineers and technicians were reassuring the integrity of S/N-36. And beginning Monday, that same team would begin to verify the reliability of all inspection reports issued by Martinez and his department. Indeed, Martinez was not a happy camper.

"*Tudo bom, Jeffe,*" came the booming voice of a man who seemingly appeared from out of nowhere.

Martinez was startled. He quickly turned in the direction of the voice.

The man who had spoken beamed from behind the obscurity of a pair of mirror-finished double-gradient Ray-Bans. His face was further masked by the short, dark brown bill of the khaki military-styled hat he was wearing canted well forward on his head.

"So, Martinez," the man spoke again still within the shadows of the hangar, pausing to slowly remove his sunglasses, "what do you have to say for yourself?" He cocked his head to the right. His scarred face was now recognizable.

"Well, uh...for a moment, uh, I did not know it was you," Martinez stammered, now fully aware to whom he was speaking. "You look, well, different. It is the uniform, I think."

"Aah, yesss..." the man spoke softly, though with a disdainful tone.

The two men now stood face to face. The the new arrival's eyes penetrated through the director of quality assurance like a laser. While only a few seconds had passed, Jeffe felt suspended in time. His face frozen, his eyes wide.

"Aah, yesss," the man repeated himself, and went on, "it provides an element of swagger, would you not say?"

Martinez responded with a slight nod and a nervous forced smile.

Franco Rameros carefully reseated the Ray-Bans on the bridge of his nose. Indeed, he did look quite different. His routine dark blue flight-line jumpsuit had been exchanged for what very closely resembled a military uniform. Khaki trousers, tight at the thighs, flared below the knee, fell in sharp creases over the top of a pair of highly polished, dark brown Wellington boots. The tailored, safari styled jacket was adorned with only a gold pilot's emblem over the left breast pocket and epaulettes embroidered with four gold pentastars which sat upon his shoulders. Franco Rameros' presence bespoke both confidence and uncommon authority.

"Later," Rameros grunted brushing passed Martinez and making his way to the WindStar. He was bristling with suspicion that in some way Martinez played a part in the double propeller failure S/N-35 had experienced less than twenty-four hours earlier.

As Rameros approached the freshly inspected aircraft's entrance doorway, he acknowledged a group of the technicians briefly with some words in Portuguese. Their team effort would assure a safe uneventful flight, at least from a mechanical point of view. He searched among the men who were now packing up equipment and toting away toolboxes. Not seeing the person he sought, he asked the lead technician for the whereabouts of Bjorn Svensson, a young Swedish engineer who was scheduled to accompany him on his trip north. Svensson also held a commercial pilot's license and would be serving as copilot while Rameros caught the shut-eye that would certainly be needed during various segments of the almost non-stop itinerary.

The lead technician pointed to the cockpit of the WindStar indicating that Svensson was already on board.

Franco Rameros strode to the entrance door, up the extended airstairs and into the aircraft. He turned left and went forward to the cockpit.

"*God morgon*," Franco spoke the few words of Swedish that he knew to the young man in the right seat.

"And, good morning to you, Captain Rameros," the young lanky engineer said in perfect English, lilting with a heavy singsong accent. "Although some weather is developing over the mountains just west of our course, we should have an uneventful flight to Brasilia this morning. By late afternoon, it will be a different story. But that is nothing new for this time of year." He paused for a few seconds. An arriving fuel truck had caught his eye. "Oh yes," he began speaking again, "I have filed us for direct at two-two-zero. It should take about an hour and a half enroute...make that one plus thirty-seven to be precise."

"Very good, BJ." Franco knew that Svensson preferred to be called by just the first two letters of his first name. The pronunciation of "Bjorn" was invariably perplexing and sometimes comical coming from non-Scandinavians, especially Brazilians.

Rameros left the cockpit and exited the WindStar to monitor the fueling operation as well as to perform a cursory preflight check of the aircraft. Even though he knew his walk-around inspection was truly unnecessary, since a crack team of professionals had just completed a thorough examination of the WindStar, experience had taught him that sometimes even the most obvious could be overlooked. He would never forget the time he attempted a taxi-for-takeoff in a high-performance twin-engine aircraft with pitot tube covers still in place. Fortunately, a fellow pilot noticed the zero-airspeed takeoff situation and quickly alerted him to the folly.

The lineman had just completed topping off both tanks of the WindStar and was reeling the long, flesh-colored hose back into its stowage compartment in the fuel tender. Franco double-checked the security of the over-the-wing fuel caps. He was very much aware that when in flight, a loose cap would allow fuel to be siphoned out of the tanks as low pressure was generated atop the wing. Again, chalk it up to personal experience. Little things were important. If overlooked, the little things could be both embarrassing as well as potentially catastrophic.

After signing off on the refueling order, Rameros re-entered the aircraft. He peered back into the WindStar's cabin, noting that the two other engineers scheduled to be on board were already buckled into the rear-most seats of the aircraft. That was the most comfortable place in the cabin—and where the noise levels were lowest. Franco grasped the handrail cable of the airstair door and, with one fluid motion of his body, pulled the door upward and inward until it made firm contact with the seals of its sill. A quick clockwise rotation of the latching handle thrust the bayonet-like retaining rods into frames, securing the closure.

Within two minutes, the WindStar was taxiing out for a departure on Runway 3.

"Enjoy yourself, BJ," Rameros said over the cockpit intercom after receiving takeoff clearance from the Tower. "I'll take care of the throttles, props, and gear; you get us out of here."

Svensson grinned at having the opportunity to do the takeoff. As a low time pilot, his only twin-engine experience had been in a Navajo Chieftain that the company regularly used as an avionics test bed. Even though he knew everything about the WindStar on paper, today was his first chance to fly the actual aircraft.

"Okay, here we go," Rameros said after aligning the aircraft with the runway centerline. He smoothly advanced the power levers to a target takeoff torque.

The aircraft rapidly accelerated, wobbling down the runway, weaving slightly to the left and then to the right, as Svensson overcorrected one way and then the other with rudder pedal pressure. Rameros did not initially comment, knowing that over-controlling was a common problem experienced by low-time pilots intimidated by larger unfamiliar equipment. He was allowing Svensson to learn by experience, only casually remarking over the intercom that smaller rudder movements would reduce the aircraft's yawing oscillations.

After the takeoff and upon reaching Flight Level 220, Svensson had no trouble engaging the autopilot and coupling it up to navigation waypoints that plotted their course to Brasilia. He settled back in his seat, now more relaxed. But the young copilot had one question that continued to puzzle him. He had started to pose it to Rameros several times before. Now, curiosity had gotten the best of him.

"Captain Rameros," Svensson said through the cockpit intercom, "I have an inquiry."

Franco looked up from the high altitude enroute chart he was perusing. With a raised eyebrow, he rephrased his copilot's request for information. "A question?"

"Well, yes," the young Swede hesitantly acknowledged.

"Go ahead, BJ."

"Your outfit...your clothing..."

"Yes?" Rameros replied.

"I have never seen you dressed this way before," Svensson blurted out. "It is some kind of uniform, but...its significance?"

TWENTY-SEVEN

RioAero, SA

Within the quiet of Hangar One, a somber eeriness prevailed. Rays of mid-morning light fought to penetrate through the large, translucent, corrugated skylight panels that had become crazed by both time and the elements.

On the gray hangar floor stood the propless WindStar. Its normally glistening white skin dulled by the hangar's near-opaque structure and the absence of illumination from artificial lighting.

Ronnie Trilliano liked to work in subdued light. It had a calming effect on him. He felt he could think better. And, why light up the entire hangar when he could see just fine for what he needed to do? He repositioned his small-framed body in a large, rickety wooden chair situated between two huge tables requisitioned from the company cafeteria. The makeshift office he had cobbled together just off the left front side of the WindStar was a war room of sorts. From this command center, he intended to get to the bottom of the problem— why both propellers separated from the aircraft.

Scattered across the two tables were a variety of computer printouts and blueprints, each customized for S/N-35. Trilliano swiveled his chair to the right and castered it along the floor to the end of one of the tables. Now facing four stacks of heavy-duty cardboard boxes piled three high on the hangar floor, he groaned to himself. Each box was carefully labeled: OPS/TRAINING MANUALS; MAINTENANCE I; MAINTENANCE II; MAINTENANCE III; SYSTEMS—HYDR; SYSTEMS—FLT CTR; SYSTEMS— ELECT… He slowly eased himself to his feet and began to more closely peruse the labels. The one he sought was on the very top of the third stack: POWERPLANT—INSTALL (PROP). He groaned once again, then wrestled the box away from the others, and lowered it down onto the hangar floor.

Trilliano unwound the string from plastic grommets that secured the top of the box and opened its flaps. He began rummaging through its contents, first slowly and methodically, then more quickly with almost random abandon. A flutter sound from above froze Trilliano's fingers in midair.

He angled his head upwards toward the hangar's tall ceiling.

There was nothing unusual.

Above and to the left, almost directly over the WindStar hung an ominous looking three-foot sphere similar to the ones which could be found in almost every hangar at RioAero. Workers called these globes *olho da morte*—eye of death. The sinister colors of dark reddish-yellow and deep purple against an ashen gray background mimicked the shape of a gigantic eyeball. The sphere swung slowly as high-mounted fans circulated the hangar air.

Trilliano had certainly seen these portentous globes before. He knew what they were all about. But an inadvertent chill still slid over his body. The silence was strange, different than before.

Then, he heard more fluttering.

He glanced toward the ceiling again. Still nothing caught his eye.

Suddenly a burst of wild fluttering. And again, silence.

Seconds later he heard a muffled thud.

A black, starling-sized bird had glanced off the radome of the WindStar disquietingly hitting the ground near Trilliano's table.

Ronnie Trilliano grimaced and closed his eyes tightly. His mind temporarily drifted from his task at hand until he was started back to reality by a voice coming from the side of the hangar. The words were undecipherable. But as the engineer squinted behind the thick lenses of his wire-framed glasses, he identified the man who was approaching. Ronnie firmly pressed his lips together with contempt.

The man was Jeffe Martinez—a man disliked even more by most people at the factory now than ever before. Indeed QA people, even when only quietly pursuing their function of verifying the integrity of each aircraft coming off the assembly line, were never really appreciated by Production or Engineering. QA people were viewed as nit-picking trolls, hiding in wait to criticize anything and everything produced by the factory. Their existence, however, was a mandate from airworthiness authorities. When QA inspectors worked as a cohesive team with Production and Engineering, aircraft were manufactured in seamless harmony. When out of sync, anxieties ran high.

Presently, QA was a pariah at RioAero. Not only did it seem QA had compromised the integrity of the WindStar through inadequate inspections, QA had assumed the protective position of absolving itself from post-production aircraft problems therefore creating further internal conflict. Martinez maintained problems recently experienced by the WindStar were due to engineering, either the vendor's or RioAero's own.

Martinez spoke up as he approached Trilliano and the WindStar. "Looks like the EYE has taken its toll on another bird."

Trilliano tried to ignore him.

"You know, Ronnie, those spheres really do not kill birds." Martinez laughed. "What does is a covert activity most people do not even know about."

"Avicide," Trilliano remarked, disdainfully. He knew full well to what Martinez was referring.

RioAero, like most airframe manufacturers, could not tolerate flocks of birds nesting upon hangar rafters. Production processes would be contaminated and compromised by corrosive bird droppings. Even post-production, a freshly painted aircraft spattered with bird droppings was something every airframer sought to avoid. So quietly, highly toxic poison was secretly and strategically positioned high atop a hangar's superstructure. The globes were mostly for show, a diversison for environmentalists and humanitarians who would likely go ballistic at learning the widespread extent to which avicides were being utilized.

So furtively were the poisons placed that almost every factory worker and visitor truly believed that the evil Eye actually scared birds away. In reality, most birds that ingested the poison conveniently died away from the hangars. Occasionally, as in today, a bird would plummet to the hangar floor. Of course, it was always thought to be a result of the Eye. No one—even those in the know—would offer to dispute that.

Jeffe Martinez turned away from Trilliano and took five paces toward the WindStar. He snorted. "That is a big one," he said, looking at the dead bird as it lay on the gray hangar floor. He rolled the bird over with the toe of his shoe.

Trilliano watched from a distance. He wished the bird would spring to life and attack Martinez. But he knew better. The bird was dead—very dead—just like the WindStar program would be unless he could come up with an explanation as to why both prop shafts had failed on S/N-35.

Finally, in rancor and in order to rid himself of Martinez who continued to hang about and who had begun to shuffle through papers laying atop the tables of the makeshift office, the normally reserved Trilliano blurted out: "I have no time for you today." He eyed Martinez and jabbed, "You see, I am just beginning to uncover information about why we had two propeller separations on the same aircraft. Soon I hope to understand why you QA people did not catch it and why QA seems unconcerned with the follies befalling the WindStars coming off the production line."

"You sonovabitch!" Martinez exploded like a bully as he verbally slashed at the frail engineer, something he would never have imagined attempting with Franco Rameros. "You goddamn pathetic sonovabitch. You will never find out why those shafts failed. You—" He abruptly stopped speaking realizing he may have said more than he wanted to in his angry outburst.

Trilliano smiled. "I will, you know I will."

"Hell," Jeffe continued, "those shafts were under specified. They are at the edge of their performance capability. They were never designed to handle all the power those TurboAirTech engines develop. It will be just a matter of time before each and every one of them falls off the wing. You damn engineers have your heads up your asses. You just do not get it. You will never figure it out."

Martinez stormed away, continuing with a loud slur of profanity in Spanish. Trilliano watched him exit the hangar. The side door slammed with a resounding bang.

Now in the silence of a near empty hangar, Ronnie Trilliano continued on with his work. While he felt fairly confident that QA truly would have been unable to have identified any irregularities with the failed shafts during the installation process, he could not explain the rash, if not defensive, behavior Martinez had exhibited. The words "covert activity" surfaced in his mind. The comment that he would "never find out" why the shafts had failed dredged up previous thoughts of sabotage. Trilliano feared that more problems could be hidden among other aircraft—perhaps in S/N-36, the one Rameros was flying to FLL. But could Martinez be involved in the wave of operational problems the WindStar had experienced? Maybe yes; maybe no. It was still too early to tell.

Throughout the afternoon Trilliano planned to review the propeller type spec and the results of Dayton-Standard's fatigue testing program. It was just a precaution to be sure that what Martinez was saying was wrong. All aircraft and QA documents would be reviewed. The complete history of these two prop shafts, and all of the others that were shipped to RioAero by Dayton-Standard during the past six months, would be examined.

Trilliano needed some clues. Any indication of irregularities would be helpful. Perhaps by Sunday, Monday at the latest, Dayton-Standard would have completed their metallurgical analysis of the sheared shaft. There had to be an explanation as to why it failed. Other WindStars currently flying could be affected by the anomaly that had taken its toll on S/N-35. Yesterday Rameros was lucky, today could be different. A propeller separation under the wrong circumstances would be catastrophic. The Amazon region of Brazil was an unforgiving environment.

Trilliano glanced at the propless WindStar once again and then upwards toward the hangar's rafters. Ceiling fans wobbled as their blades cut through the warm humid air. The evil Eye seemed to mock him as it slowly swayed from side to side. Ronnie Trilliano smirked wryly at the Eye, then nodded. Indeed, he thought, the obvious can easily obscure reality.

TWENTY-EIGHT

Las Olas Boulevard

T he Las Olas neighborhood was just awakening as Rick steered the old Chevy off of Federal Highway and headed east onto the tree-lined boulevard. To the west, new high rise offices and a government complex rose into the sky. East Las Olas Boulevard, however, held the charm born from a city that had been cut out of the mangroves some seventy years ago, subsequently was rebuilt after devastating tropical storms, and then finally began to flourish during the 1950s.

Anchoring the picturesque roadway were The French Quarter, The Reserve, Paesano, and several other *haute cuisine* establishments that Rick occasionally frequented with prospective customers. By midday, the area would be bustling with activity. Indeed, if the relatively new City of Fort Lauderdale had what could be called an old town section, it would be the neighborhood located along this thoroughfare bordering the New River.

As he drove farther along East Las Olas toward the beaches, the charming cityscape transformed. The quaint and the swank were replaced with an array of lackluster bars, hamburger joints, tourist traps, and small businesses occupying nondescript cinder block structures. The charming boulevard became a mundane four-lane roadway.

Up ahead on the right side of the road would be Tommy Maxwell's place. Rick remembered the rundown office building from the time he had initially met Maxwell. That meeting had occurred shortly after Maxwell established himself as a private investigator. Rick had needed Tommy's help for locating a customer who not only welshed out on a contract to buy a used Beech Queen Air, but whose bounced $30,000 deposit check then added insult to injury. Tommy came through for Rick a day later. Unfortunately, though, Tommy located the shady customer in the Dade County Morgue—an apparent drug-related homicide.

Rick slowed the Chevy as he spotted the building. It was much different than he remembered. The building had been totally renovated. Now, it sported a spotless light gray stucco exterior and new landscaping. He noticed that the sign affixed to the front of the structure said nothing about private investigations as it once had. The new sign read: MacroScientific, Ltd.

Damn, Rick thought to himself, Tommy is either out of business or has moved elsewhere. Nonetheless, Rick pulled over to the side of the near empty street and parked at the curb. "Let's see if I can find out where this Maxwell guy has gone," he grumbled, snatching the briefcase from the passenger seat and exiting the pickup.

He swung open the deeply tinted, metal-framed glass entry door to the building and was greeted by an ultra-modern reception area. The deep reddish-yellow Spanish-tiled floor flowed forward to surround a soft-gray modular reception station, and then met a charcoal carpeted corridor to the left. The off-white walls were decorated with framed art deco prints and two particularly eye-catching high-resolution transparencies of offshore racing boats that were backlit to an almost 3-D effect. Ceiling speakers filtered in up-tempo disco music from a local FM radio station, imparting the office building with a sense of vibrant energy.

Rick's eyes locked onto the black-outlined red lettering of the company's name that filled the wall directly behind the receptionist's work station. He thought: What the hell is MacroScientific, Ltd?

Abruptly his attention was diverted. From the corridor to his left, he caught a blur of movement. Rick's eyes followed an attractive, deeply tanned young woman as she glided to her station in the reception area. "This is a very beautiful building," he said to the woman.

She smiled acknowledgingly while seating herself.

"I know I'm at the wrong location," he continued, "but might you know the whereabouts of Tommy Maxwell?"

She smiled again, then politely asked, "And who would be interested in the whereabouts of Tommy Maxwell?"

"Oh," Rick said with a slight hesitation, "fair question. The name is Harris, Rick Harris. Tommy helped me out with a case a little over a year ago. I'm trying to locate him. I need his help once again."

She furrowed her brow slightly, remaining silent.

Rick had a sinking feeling in the pit of his stomach, still he pressed on. "Have you ever heard of Tommy Maxwell?"

The young woman shrugged.

TWENTY-NINE

Destination: Brasilia

Bjorn Svensson pressed the pitch-sync button on his control yoke. He eased the WindStar's nose below the midday outside horizon. Then referencing the cockpit ADI (Attitude Director Indicator), he positioned the yellow command bars of the flight director to minus seven degrees and released the button. The autopilot locked onto the command, further guiding the aircraft, now smoothly stabilizing its enroute descent rate at fifteen hundred feet per minute. Power levers were reduced from cruise setting to maintain the descent profile. The DME readout flashed a four hundred seventy-five knot ground speed and ninety-five mile range. Directly ahead, Brasilia was just becoming visible to the trained eye. ETA: less than fifteen minutes.

In the left seat, Franco Rameros smiled to himself. Svensson was doing a fine job of piloting during this, his first, flight in a WindStar. Rameros was pleased to be accompanied by a bright, yet open-minded, factory engineer who was also a commercial pilot.

"Ever been to Brasilia, BJ?" he asked his young copilot.

"Negative." Svensson shook his head.

"Well, I'm going to do you a big favor," Rameros sarcastically said. "You are really not going there today, just to the airport, about ten klicks outside the city. Even so, we are only going to be on the ground for about fifteen or twenty minutes to top off the tanks and re-file for our next stop at Georgetown."

Franco Rameros gazed over the nose of the WindStar and was just able to glimpse Brasilia International (BSB). "You probably cannot locate BSB quite yet," he said, "but it is just south of Lake Paranoá. See the lake?"

"Roger." Svensson nodded, but he was not quite sure. From the air, distant landmarks were always rather difficult to identify, even for experienced pilots, unless the route is regularly flown.

"You know," Rameros bitterly declared, "Brasilia is a damn white albatross!"

Svensson remained silent, unsure how to react to Rameros' unexpected acrimony.

The decision to move Brazil's Capitol from Rio de Janeiro to an inland location had not been a hasty one. Various regimes had weighed the idea for over a century to gain the benefits of staving off the possibility of a foreign invasion of the existing coastal capital as well as to provide an impetus for the development of the country's heartland. But the generations clicked by without a move being made until, in 1955, a burst of newly invigorated nationalism cast the die.

The country's new capital city was to be a city like no other in Brazil—totally planned, ultra modernistic. The design intent was for an ideal city to sparkle as the crown jewel for an ideal society—a showpiece of the country's technologic advancement, a proper entry card for Brazil among the powerful nations of the world. But in reality, Brasilia initially was an architectural folly—a fantasy city. While the city was beautiful on paper, no one in power cared about the needs of the people who might be living there. And this embarrassing lack of foresight was something Franco Rameros could never forget. What he saw in Brasilia was an impractical, unlivable city—a complete failure as a human habitat.

Nonetheless, construction was fast and furious. And in 1960, Brasilia was inaugurated amidst much fanfare as politicians touted the country's entry into a new era. However, four short years later, the ongoing momentum of building the city ground to a halt when a military coup brought construction to a standstill. There was even pressure to transfer the Capitol back to Rio. Franco Rameros, like many of his countrymen, strongly believed that the building of Brasilia had significantly accelerated the hyperinflation that was beginning to ravage the country. So thus, Brasilia became hyperbole for grandiose failure and for the excesses that were piled upon the backs of the common man. The original grand scheme turned into a nightmare; the new city battered the country's economy and saddled it with monumental debt—debt that was almost exclusively supported by loans from international banks. In short order, loan payments were made by simply printing more money. The economy was headed for virtual collapse.

Now, during the early months of 1981, construction surged again as the current government attempted to breathe life into a tattered dream. Nonetheless, it was common knowledge that the new Federal District became a veritable ghost town from Friday afternoon through Monday morning as the wealthy and most of the highly paid government personnel escaped to the more traditional social cities like Rio and São Paulo for extended weekends.

Looking at Brasilia, Franco Rameros only saw reminders of the toll the new city had taken on the nation, the sorrows endured by its people. Each time he flew to Brasilia, he choked with scorn and lamented its very existence. From the air, the city was designed to resemble a giant bird with outstretched wings. Rameros saw a millstone, an albatross. Over the cockpit intercom, he grumbled his thoughts again and again: *"albatroz bronco...albatroz bronco...uma cidade sem vida."* Indeed, Brasilia was a city without a palpable pulse—a city without life.

The controller broke Rameros' bitter contemplations with clearance to land. Approach flaps were extended. The aircraft was turned onto a short final to Runway 29. Franco Rameros extended the gear and then full flaps. He fine-tuned the power settings and began coaching Svensson on what to expect next, what to do next. Nonetheless, Franco still made sure that the WindStar was well-stabilized and almost flying itself down to the runway. Weather was not a factor. The wind was light and variable.

At fifty feet above the runway numbers, Rameros began assisting Svensson's first landing maneuver of the WindStar by slowly easing the power levers back to just forward of flight idle. The aircraft's descent increased. Svensson, taking the landing procedures back into his own hands, saw the long runway loom nearer...too fast, too close, he thought. Not wanting the aircraft to fly into the ground, he applied excessive back pressure on the control yoke. The WindStar quickly ballooned to ten feet above the runway. Then, twenty feet. The airspeed, now below targeted landing speed, continued to bleed off. A red light flashed on the instrument panel. Simultaneously, a disquieting chirping drone from the stall warning horn filled the cockpit. The airframe started to shudder in prelude to an incipient stall. BJ froze at the controls. With the WindStar on the verge of falling from the sky, Franco Rameros swiftly took over the controls, quickly advancing and then slowly retarding the power levers. The descent, cushioned by the burst of engine power, turned a free-fall into a decisively firm landing. The main gear solidly made contact with the runway's grooved surface with an aircraft-carrier-landing jolt and thud.

"That was a perfect full stall landing, BJ," a calm Franco facetiously said.

Svensson's widened eyes were still riveted to the runway ahead. Beads of perspiration slowly rolled from the sides of his forehead. "I am not sure that I actually knew what I was doing," he admitted, uneasily. "I thought I did, but..." He paused as Rameros guided the aircraft off the runway via a high-speed taxiway to the left, then Svensson continued, "This aircraft seems awfully large and pretty fast, at least to me."

"Not to worry," Rameros reassuringly responded. "Everyone needs time to become accustomed to a new environment. The more time you spend in the WindStar, the more comfortable you will be. Right now, though, you have a slight perceptual problem being reinforced with a little apprehension. Remember, airplanes are airplanes, just like women are women. All the same, but also all very different. You just have to develop a familiarity for the make and model you are involved with." Rameros grinned, proud of his analogy and hoping that BJ could correlate the intent.

The customary rapid-fire words were exchanged with Ground Control. The WindStar was cleared to the general aviation ramp.

After the parking brake was set and the engines spooled down, Rameros directed Svensson to monitor the refueling operation while he went inside the general aviation terminal to recheck the enroute weather and file a flight plan to Georgetown, Guyana. His two engineer-passengers from the factory followed him to the terminal. With a little luck, the ground time would be minimal.

But luck was not on their side today.

The fuel tender that arrived was an avgas truck. Svensson identified the error and stopped the line crew just before fuel nozzles began pumping the wrong fuel into the WindStar's tanks. He thought it was indeed strange that a line operation would mistake the WindStar for anything other than the turbine-powered aircraft that it was. Placards located on the two over-the-wing refueling points clearly indicated that Jet-A fuel was required. He distinctly remembered Franco's radio communication with the FBO just prior to their descent for landing. It requested a quick turnaround with Jet-A.

He sent the truck away and waited for the proper fuel to arrive.

Ten minutes passed, then fifteen minutes. There was still no sign of a Jet-A fuel tender. And, Franco Rameros had not yet returned.

Svensson considered leaving the aircraft and walking the short distance to the line operations office in the terminal. But he chose not to do so and leave the aircraft unattended, especially in light of the near error in fuel type. He wanted to be sure that there would no chance for further servicing errors to the aircraft. He knew that the next leg of the flight was a long one, and one that would require transiting the extensive and rather inhospitable steamy jungles of the Amazon. So, he sat on the lower step of the opened airstair door and waited.

The ramp area was quiet and seemingly deserted. A Learjet, a Westwind, and two King Airs were the only other transient occupants. There was no activity from equipment or personnel.

Svensson waited.

THIRTY

MacroScientific, Ltd.

T he young woman's smile quickly returned and broadened as she nodded to Rick Harris. She shrugged again and laughed quietly before responding. "Why, of course...of course I've heard of Tommy Maxwell."

"You know where he's gone?" Rick pressed.

She looked perplexed. "Gone?" she repeated.

"Why yes, I really need his help."

"I'm not sure what you're talking about." She furrowed her brow again.

"Hmmm..." Rick was puzzled by her apparent confusion. Momentarily unsure as to what to say, he studied his surroundings and was drawn toward one of the three-by-four-foot high-resolution transparencies of the offshore racing boats. He absently walked closer to the backlit transparency, trying to gather his thoughts, considering what his next line of questioning might be. His eyes widened, and he turned back toward the receptionist.

"That's him," Rick said, barely restraining his enthusiasm as he pointed to one of the men in the boat.

"Yes, yes it is," she said with a slight giggle.

"So," he grinned, "this is still Tommy's place, isn't it?"

"Yes," she declared, now warming to Rick. "I just couldn't understand where you were going with the conversation. Tommy's here. He's never left."

"Is he here, now?"

"Why yes," she said, picking up the phone and punching in three numbers. "You know Tommy, he never stops working."

"Yes, I know...he's one of a kind."

She paused for a short two seconds and then spoke into the telephone, "Mr. Maxwell, there is a Mr. Harris here to see you." She listened for a moment then placed the receiver back into its cradle. "He'll be right out."

"Great," Rick said with an appreciative nod, and with relief he began to slowly pace the lobby area in anticipation.

A minute later, Thomas Jefferson Maxwell appeared from the corridor and strode up to Rick. "Well, well, well..." came his smooth mid-baritone voice.

Maxwell was a tall, graceful, well-built, dark-skinned man in his early forties whose refined Caucasian features contradicted his

African-American heritage. Short-cropped hair, chiseled facial features, and an always-present sparkling white smile framed by thin lips gave him a dashing appearance. He had the presence of an accomplished politician and the tenacity of a Jack Russell Terrier. His can-do attitude allowed him to be successful at whatever he chose despite any barriers that crossed his path.

The two men shook hands.

Tommy spoke up, "Now tell me, Rick, how long has it been?"

"A year, maybe a little more…"

"Hell, it must be closer to two years," Maxwell said, shaking his head in disbelief. "But, no matter, it's still good to see you. Anyway, what brings you here?"

"I'm in a jam. I need your expertise."

"Airplane stuff, again?"

"Yes, but this time it's more complex."

"Hmmm…" Tommy pursed his lips. "I've got a few minutes." He cocked his head to the left. "Let's go back to my office and hear what's troubling you this time."

Tommy led the way down the corridor to the rear-most office in the building. He motioned for Rick to sit in one of two swivel chairs that were pulled up to a small circular rattan and glass table near the left side of the room. "Coffee?"

"Thanks, black would be great," Rick said.

Tommy poured two cups, placed one in front of Rick, and then settled himself into the other chair. "Okay, Rick, give me a thumbnail sketch of what's going on…what brought you here."

Rick took a long five minutes to highlight events involving the WindStar while Maxwell listened attentively without interrupting.

"That's it in a nutshell, Tommy," Rick said, ending his narrative.

"I see." Maxwell bit down on his lower lip, and then began to nod. "Yes, I believe you do have a problem." He put his right hand to his mouth and closed his eyes momentarily. "Rick," he looked across the table and began to speak again, "I'm sorry to say that I don't really do PI stuff anymore." He grimaced, head cocked to the side. "While there were times when it was a fun thing to do, there wasn't any money in it. It just didn't make any sense to continue that gumshoe fantasy."

Rick took a deep breath and then exhaled in soft frustration. "No exceptions?" he asked, hopefully.

"Well," Maxwell began, "let me tell you what I'm doing now." He swiveled the chair to the left and crossed his legs. "When I was with the Company up north, I was a cartographer of sorts, and a damn good one at that." He laughed twice. "At least I think I was. Anyway, I had access to all the high tech tools—the computers, the software, you know—but I was bored. The work was tedious. I got no recognition. I could see myself doing that same thing, with that same organization, for the next ten years. So, I quit and came south to become what you would probably call a Magnum PI of sorts."

Maxwell shook his head and then shrugged. "Unfortunately, my life wasn't a television program. I had no benefactor. And frankly, being a PI ain't even close to what is shown on TV. Besides, most of my casework turned out to be even more boring than the job I had up north. So, I stowed my PI tools and started hawking my skills in cartography. Actually, I specialize in marine cartography—acoustic tomography, complex subsurface sonar, that sort of thing. I got myself a couple of those new Apple Computers—a far cry from the mainframes we had at the Company—and hired a bright gal just out of the University of Miami to bounce a few ideas off and do some of the grunt work. Then as luck would have it, within a month I fell into a small consulting job with PetroMar, a fairly large player in the Colombian oil business." Tommy paused. "Let me know if I'm boring you to death."

"No, no…go on, I'm very much interested."

"Well, that small consulting job led to a major contract." He raised both hands into the air and gestured to their surroundings. "You can see what a difference positive cash flow makes."

Rick nodded.

"Along the way, I've met some high rollers in South Florida. I guess word gets out." Tommy grinned, unabashedly. "In fact, I'm just beginning to apply cartographic technology to locating sunken treasure, thanks to this guy I met down in the Keys named Mel Fisher. Ever heard of him?"

"Yes indeed, I remember reading a story the *Miami Herald* did on Fisher's operation in Key West."

"Well, what he's doing is exciting—truly exciting. Maybe I can be part of it. With a little luck he'll score the mother lode. I'm sure of it. But don't get me wrong, Rick, there were times when being a PI was exciting as well. I especially liked the high tech aspect of it."

Rick quickly spoke up, "That's exactly what I need, high tech PI stuff."

Maxwell grinned. "Okay, now exactly what do you propose that I would do for you? That is, if I were still in the PI business."

Rick pulled out the videotape cassette from his briefcase and placed it on the table. "For starters, I need this analyzed. Somewhere between 4:00 p.m. and 8:30 p.m. on Friday some important evidence was recorded. At least I hope so."

"Like what?"

"I'm hoping what is on this tape will show why a brand-new aircraft that was parked on a ramp at FLL had its gear mysteriously retract, causing it to crash onto the tarmac five feet below. And then, how the *Sun-Sentinel* was able to print the story—with photo—just hours after the incident."

Tommy glanced across the table at the cassette. "An XL-10, huh?"

Rick nodded. He sensed that Tommy was beginning to have an interest in his project. "Let me help to better pinpoint the times."

Tommy opened a spiral notebook that was lying on the table and plucked a mechanical pencil from his breast pocket.

Rick went on, "Sometime between 4:00 p.m. and 5:30 p.m. on Friday, I suspect that you may see a short stocky man with a tangerine colored shirt enter the aircraft. He should go into the cockpit and sit in the left seat. He'll be there for only about a minute or so, then he'll leave the aircraft." Rick thought for a second. "Oh yes, his mannerisms might look like someone preparing to rob a bank— cautious, concerned, wanting to be sure that no one is watching him."

Tommy grunted an acknowledgement as he took some notes.

Rick continued, "Later, slightly before 8:30 p.m., this same guy pulls up in a black Lincoln. This time he'll have an associate. My guess is the video will show that they took a photo of the aircraft. Somehow that photo got to the newspaper before its deadline."

Tommy briefly looked up from his notebook.

Rick pressed on, "The guy's name is Dan Cole. My gut feeling is that he's involved in a conspiracy against the WindStar. I really don't know why—maybe just money—but it's my bet he's part of a fairly large scheme against the aircraft."

"Okay, Rick, tell me," Tommy posed the question, "why are you taking the lead on this? Isn't this the factory's problem? Brazil's problem? Why not get them involved?"

Rick quickly responded, "For all I know, someone at the factory or within the Brazilian military establishment might be behind everything. Dan Cole is probably just a puppet. He's not smart enough to mastermind anything, especially considering the types of things that have been happening within the past twenty-four hours." Rick shook his head in frustration. "Over half a billion dollars has been spent to design, certify, and then ramp up full production for a truly remarkable aircraft. The recent happenings will likely scuttle the WindStar. Along the way, a fine company could go out of business and thousands of Brazilian workers could be thrown out into the streets at a time when the country is on the edge of economic chaos. No, this is my problem. It's my job. I believe in this aircraft. And, these incidents have gotten personal."

"That bad?" Maxwell bit down on the eraser of his pencil.

Rick slowly nodded. "I'm afraid so."

Maxwell's eyes flashed down to his notebook and then back toward Rick. "What would you do if I said I couldn't help you?"

Rick hesitated with his answer. From Tommy's behavior, Rick knew he had piqued the former gumshoe's interest. But was it enough? It was hard to be certain. Still, he had a feeling that Maxwell would help, somehow. He could see it in Tommy's face. Each time Rick laid out another layer of the intrigue, Tommy's eyes darted from side to side. Tommy's pupils dilated. Rick recognized that type of behavioral pattern as an unconscious, but heightened state of awareness that usually, but not always, indicated keen interest in the situation at hand.

Rick steeled himself and hoped for the best as he answered the question Tommy had posed. "Actually, if you can't help me, I'm not sure what my next step would be. But there is something I am very sure about, things are beginning to happen fast—really fast. I have barely begun to work on the problem and I'm already running out of time." He stopped and looked Maxwell straight in the eye. "Tommy, I honestly need your help. Give me just a day or two of your time. By the end of this weekend, we will solve the case or it'll blow up in my face. What do you say? Can I count on you?"

In silence, Tommy Maxwell rose from his chair, turned away from Rick, and walked to his desk at the opposite side of the room. Rick's eyes followed Tommy's every movement, trying to discern what the decision might be. Maxwell seated himself in front of a computer monitor positioned to the side of his desk and hammered some commands into the keyboard.

Tommy shook his head.

Not good, Rick thought.

"Please excuse me for a moment," Tommy said, and left the room.

Five minutes, then ten minutes passed.

Rick's mind raced ahead. Now that it seemed Maxwell was going to turn aside his plea, he tried to come up with an alternative plan of action for his problem. Maybe Maxwell would aid him to the extent of at least locating another investigator who could work on the case. He hoped so. Anything would help.

Just as Rick had given up on getting assistance of any kind from Tommy, the man re-entered the room.

Maxwell reseated himself at the table and, with an expressionless face, he abruptly slid the spiral notebook across the table to Rick.

"Here's what I want you to do," Tommy said. "Take this pencil and write down every person and every organization you think might be involved in this conspiracy; detail the events you spoke of earlier, identify anything—ANYTHING—that might be helpful, however minor. I am going to help you help yourself. You need to organize all your facts, identify all your suspects, set forth possible motives."

Rick did not like the path the meeting was taking. He was a pilot and an aircraft salesman, not a private investigator. Yet he complied with Tommy's directive and began to write. There seemed little choice.

Tommy left the room again.

In the notebook, Rick carefully wrote his thoughts:

SUSPECTS

- *Dan Cole/ComJet*
- *Competitors: BASA, Fairchild, etc.*
- *Factory Workers and/or Union*
- *Colombian Drug Lords*
- *The Brazilian Military Establishment*
...any combination of above.

INCIDENTS

- *Double prop separation (impossible)*
- *Total electrical failure (improbable)*
- *Gear collapse (definite sabotage)*
- *Screw jack damage (deliberate?)*
- *Newspaper photo and story (too convenient)*
...more to come???

THIRTY-ONE

Brasilia

In the distance, Bjorn Svensson's eyes locked onto and followed the movement of a short thin man who was dressed in an open-collared, white short-sleeved shirt and black trousers. The man had come from the vicinity of the Control Tower, which was several hundred yards to the left of the general aviation terminal. When the individual reached the door Franco Rameros had used to enter the terminal, he stopped and gazed toward the WindStar. Then, instead of going into the terminal, he continued on walking to the aircraft.

As the man neared, Svensson rose to his feet.

"*Você fala o Português?*" the man asked.

"*Não senhor, somente Inglês, Espanhol ou Svenska.*"

"Okay, English it will be...the international language of aviation," the man said confidently with a heavy Brazilian accent. His eyes turned away from Svensson and followed the lines of the fuselage from nose to tail. "A very nice aircraft you have. Brand-new?"

"Yes, brand-new, straight from the factory."

"And, where do you fly to?"

"Georgetown, with a final destination in the United States."

"Are you pilot-in-command?"

"No, no, I am copilot."

"And, where is the pilot-in-command?"

Svensson motioned to the general aviation terminal. "Filing a flight plan, checking the weather."

"I see," the man said, briefly turning toward the building. "I was in the Control Tower when you landed." He pointed to the ID badge that was clipped to his left breast pocket. The badge's design incorporated broad diagonal slashes of green and yellow, identical to the national colors appearing on a Brazilian pilot's license.

Svensson focused on the badge, immediately noticing the bold black lettering abbreviation—CTA—representing *Centro Técnico Aeroespacial*. He was very much familiar with the vast powers of the CTA. At the factory, RioAero had varying degrees of influence over the CTA. In the field, however, it was a different story. A CTA inspector could ground an aircraft or suspend a pilot at will.

"So, how may I help you?" a very polite Svensson asked.

"I must ramp-check this aircraft," the inspector curtly responded.

Out of the corner of his eye, Svensson glimpsed Franco Rameros leaving the terminal and striding toward the WindStar. Svensson nodded toward the terminal. "The pilot-in-command will be arriving shortly."

"Very well," the inspector responded as he carefully regarded Rameros' approach. He noticed the military-like uniform, the assertive carriage, and finally, as Rameros neared, the inspector's eyes locked onto the epaulettes with four gold stars.

Rameros was noticeably irritated because of the time he had had to expend to file a flight plan and be updated on the weather. The deeply furrowed brow spoke volumes. He dismissively glanced at the inspector and forced a thin smile at Svensson. "I assume we are ready to go, BJ."

"Uh, not quite yet. They sent an avgas truck. I am still waiting on Jet-A."

Rameros displeasured attention focused on the man standing next to Svensson. "Are you involved with this?" He scowled at the man.

"No, no," came a quick response, "I am Inspector Fernandes from the CTA."

"Good for you," Rameros shot back. "I suppose you have never seen a WindStar and want the grand tour."

Svensson quickly shook his head from left to right several times, trying to divert Rameros' attention. He was hoping to forestall any problems Rameros' blunt speech could provoke.

The inspector, intimidated, briefly stuttered, "Nuh-no...I, I have a job to do, Mr.–"

"It is GENERAL, Inspector Fernandes...General Franco da Silva Rameros. I am in command of all aircraft operations at RioAero. We design and manufacture this aircraft and many others at our factory near Nova Iguaçu. Now, what is it that you want?" Of course Rameros was not a military general, that was bluster; but Rameros was very much in charge of aircraft operations at RioAero, and that was absolute.

"I have orders to ramp-check your aircraft."

"Bullshit, Mr. Inspector." Franco Rameros snapped back at the man as few others would have done. He was well aware that a CTA ramp-check could involve anything and everything associated with the operation of an aircraft. Today, his agenda did not include spending an entire afternoon humoring a CTA inspector. "I am on a tight schedule and have no time for you today. Why not inspect that Learjet over there, or maybe one of those King Airs?"

"You seem not to understand, General Rameros. I have my orders."

Rameros glared at the inspector. He read his name from the ID badge: "Inspector Alonso Fernandes, is it?"

"Yes, sir."

"I do not give a damn who you are," he said, sharply turning away from the inspector and placing one foot on the bottom step of the airstair door. But rather than ascending the stairs, he stopped and turned back toward the inspector. "And, under whose authority were your orders issued?"

"Under the authority of the CTA."

Rameros marched back to the inspector. He looked down on the small man, who seemed still adamant about fulfilling the ramp-check mission. "No, no, Mister Fernandes, you are not listening," he said, slowly articulating his words. "I am not in a mood to play your goddamn bureaucratic games. Tell me exactly who at the CTA authorized this?

"That is only released on a need to know basis."

Rameros clenched his teeth and folded his arms across his chest, tightly. "And, just why would you want to bother ramp-checking a brand-new aircraft that was released from the factory only a few hours ago?"

"I have my orders."

"Let me put it another way..." There was a long pause from Rameros who slowly lifted his face and stared into the sky. Redirecting his attention back to the inspector, he sternly questioned: "What are you looking for? What do you hope to find?"

The inspector stammered. "We, uh...I received information indicating that this aircraft—PT-SBY—has errors."

"Errors?? HA!" Rameros glowered. "This aircraft has just been completely inspected by no less than a dozen factory engineers and technicians."

The inspector persisted, "It is not airworthy."

"What do you mean?"

The inspector continued, "I have a telex listing this aircraft as an unregistered aircraft. The CTA has not executed an airworthiness certificate for this WindStar."

"Of course not!" Rameros barked. He was very familiar with the documentation process for all aircraft manufactured by RioAero. "The factory has the authority to issue all paperwork for new aircraft coming off of its production line. That authority was granted by the CTA under our type certification approval. Your offices may currently be unaware of paperwork for recently released aircraft."

There was a blank stare from the inspector.

Rameros went on to explain. "Our chief inspector is authorized by the CTA to issue a temporary certificate, which is superseded by a permanent certificate that is issued within thirty days. It is the *permanent certificate* that is issued by the CTA." Rameros turned back

to Svensson. "Did you check the aircraft's paperwork before we left
the factory?"

"Yes."

"The logbooks?"

"Yes, all endorsements are proper."

"And those, are they on board?"

"Yes."

"And, did you check for the temporary registration and
airworthiness certificate?"

"Yes."

"And, they are on board, right?"

"Yes."

"Please bring them to me."

Svensson scrambled up the steps of the airstair door and
disappeared into the aircraft.

"So, my dear inspector," Rameros said with confidence, "I will
soon show you that we have all the paperwork that will allow us to fly
wherever we like, whenever we like."

A minute later, Svensson trotted down the airstairs. In his hand
were two half sheets of paper—one white, one pink.

Rameros took the papers and spent a brief twenty seconds in
careful review. Even though being very familiar with each document,
he wanted to be sure there were no errors. "Just as I thought," he
quietly said. A wide grin spread across his face. "BJ, go to the line
operations office and tell them to get some Jet-A out here,
rapidamente."

Svensson was about to depart, but stopped at the sight of a Jet-A
fuel tender slowly approaching the WindStar.

"BJ, make sure there is no screw-up with the refueling," Rameros
cautioned. Then returning to the conversation with the inspector, he
said, "Now, Mister Fernandes, I do not know what kind of telex you
have or who issued it. Frankly, I do not care. All of our paperwork is
in order. Take a look for yourself." He handed the documents to the
inspector. "This aircraft is totally airworthy and fully registered. We
can fly out of here anytime we want. And, this we will do."

"I must verify this information." The inspector was dragging his
heels. "There have been reports of many irregularities with aircraft
documents, especially for new aircraft leaving the country."

"Do whatever turns you on Mister Inspector, but once this aircraft
is refueled, we are out of here."

"General Rameros," the inspector said firmly, but respectfully, "it
seems you may have forgotten that this airport is controlled by the
CTA. You need clearance to taxi. You need clearance to takeoff. I can
make sure that does or does not happen. My orders are to hold your

aircraft until all documentation is verified. I must now report my findings. It seems that we may have been in error. The documents you have just shown me appear to indicate this." He handed the papers back to Rameros.

"Good, then we are cleared to go after we get refueled?" Rameros pressed the issue.

The inspector repeated himself, "You will be cleared to go when I receive the verification I need."

"When will that be?"

The inspector hesitated before responding. "Well, soon."

"Is this like a telephone call, a telex, or what?"

The inspector shrugged without answering.

Rameros wondered what kind of verification was required. Today was Saturday, and for all practical purposes the factory was closed. There could be no verification of the documents from anyone at RioAero. Rameros was also positive that the CTA would have no record of the documents now under scrutiny.

"We need to be in the U.S. by tomorrow morning," Rameros emphasized.

"This is not my problem." The inspector held his ground. "Still, you must wait until I have verification to release you."

"Let me ask you a question, Alonso." Franco Rameros was growing more and more irritated by the second. "How would you like to head up the CTA office in Boa Vista?" Boa Vista was a city flanked by Venezuela and Guyana in the northern most pocket of Brazil. Despite its name, the small city was a hellhole of a domicile for anyone associated with aviation.

The inspector frowned. "There is no CTA office in Boa Vista."

"I know," Rameros said with a smirk. "But I have friends in high places that can make it happen. And mark my words, they goddamn will make it happen unless you release us for departure within the next ten minutes."

There was silence.

Rameros continued by repeating himself. "Once this aircraft is refueled, we are out of here. So, my good friend, you better get that verification you need swiftly. And, there better not be any further delays. Be sure you understand what I am saying. Think about it very carefully. A rash decision could haunt you for the rest of your life."

Without a word, the inspector turned and retreated to the Tower.

Ten minutes later, fueling was complete. The two engineer-passengers, oblivious to what had transpired, had just returned from the terminal building and took their now customary places in the

152

rear of the aircraft. In the cockpit, Rameros ran through the checklist with Svensson and started the WindStar's engines. He contacted Ground Control, received his IFR clearance to Georgetown, and was cleared to taxi to Runway 29.

Everything was progressing smoothly. Even though what had been expected to be a brief fifteen to twenty minute quick turnaround at BSB had been drawn out to well over an hour, the WindStar would soon once again be on its way.

"Good afternoon Tower," Rameros said in English for the benefit of Svensson, "WindStar Sierra-Bravo-Yankee is ready for takeoff, Runway Two-Niner."

No response from the Tower.

The radio frequency was rechecked. There was no error. The transmission was repeated.

Then came the Tower's response. "Papa-Tango-Sierra-Bravo-Yankee, standby."

"Damn," Rameros said aloud over the cockpit intercom. "There is something strange going on here."

Svensson nodded.

Rameros groaned. "A near screw-up on refueling, then some worthless CTA bureaucrat delays us even more over nothing at all. Now, we are on a standby from the Tower." He groaned again. "The big question is: Who wants us delayed and why?" He shook his head, totally perplexed. "It is all very suspicious."

"WindStar Bravo-Yankee, Tower."

"Go ahead Tower," Rameros responded.

"WindStar Bravo-Yankee, expect an indefinite hold for takeoff."

Rameros, now enraged, slammed his armrests with the palms of both hands. He then looked over to the right seat at Svensson, who meekly shrugged.

Minutes passed. There was no communication within the cockpit. Rameros heatedly stared at the avionics stack above the center pedestal. He drummed his fingers on the control yoke. The Dayton-Standard propellers droned in the background. Rameros had a decision to make. If the hold were extensive, he would have to taxi back for more fuel. The flight segment to Georgetown was pushing the WindStar's range envelope, even with forecast tailwinds of one hundred knots.

Rameros finally spoke up to Svensson. "Here goes nothing." He keyed his mic on the Tower frequency. "*Olá*, Mister Fer-nan-des, I hope you enjoy your new assignment in Boa Vista."

There was no response.

Rameros pursed his lips and dug his fingers into the padded armrests.

Finally, a transmission came from the Tower, "Papa-Tango-Sierra-Bravo-Yankee is cleared for takeoff."

That was all Rameros needed to hear. "Buckle up tight, *meus amigos*" he said over the PA system to the two engineers in the cabin. Without any verbal acknowledgement to the Tower, he briskly advanced the power levers. The WindStar surged ahead, entering the runway. Using left rudder, he steered the aircraft onto the centerline. The power levers were further advanced until the engine torque read one hundred percent. The Dayton-Standard propellers aggressively sliced through the air, rocketing the aircraft forward. He keyed his mic, casually transmitting to the Tower: "Bravo-Yankee requests an immediate left turnout after liftoff."

"Approved," came the Tower's response.

Rameros beamed. *What fools they are*, he thought. A slight turn to the right—not to the left—would have put the WindStar directly on a course to Georgetown. Over the cockpit intercom he cautioned Svensson, "Do not ever do what I am about to do."

His copilot remained silent, not knowing what to expect.

At one hundred knots, Rameros rotated the aircraft, quickly retracted the gear, but now held the WindStar in ground effect—a phenomenon found close to the runway surface where air compressed by the wing creates greater lift, reduced drag, and more rapid acceleration. The aircraft's speed quickly increased to one hundred fifty knots…one hundred eighty knots…

Midway down the runway, and almost abeam with the Tower, Franco Rameros aggressively pitched up the WindStar and then snapped its ailerons for a seventy-degree banked turn to the left. The aircraft responded immediately, turning to the southwest.

The Tower's cab loomed above and directly ahead. The WindStar raced straight toward it, now at nearly two hundred knots. Despite the speed, everything seemed in slow motion to Rameros. He detected the silhouettes of three people in the cab. He clearly identified two antenna masts extending above the Tower. He noticed the silhouettes suddenly disappear as the people instinctively dove for cover below the waist-high control consoles that rimmed the interior of the cab. He saw a fleeting reflection of the WindStar's fuselage in the Tower's huge panes of glass. Svensson steeled himself for the unavoidable collision. And then…and then…just blue sky ahead.

Rameros laughed aloud. "Those CTA sonovabitches…" He laughed again. "Hell, they asked for it in more ways than one."

The WindStar continued its climbing turn to the north.

THIRTY-TWO

MacroScientific, Ltd.

Rick was still organizing his thoughts when Tommy Maxwell re-entered the room. This time Tommy was carrying a large cardboard box that was taped closed and marked FRAGILE in bold red letters. After carefully setting the box down onto the floor near the table, he glanced at the notebook into which Rick had been writing.

"Beginning to make more sense, isn't it, Rick? It always does when it's on paper. It helps you visualize it, add to it, change it, really work with it."

Rick looked up, half smiled, but said nothing. Orderliness was helpful, but he needed more than an exercise in organizing his thoughts.

"You know," Maxwell said, glancing toward the half page Rick had written, "any PI worth his salt outlines every case he works on. There's always a better chance of solving any problem when all the facts are in front of you rather than just floating around inside your head. Let's see what you've got."

Tommy picked up the notebook and settled down into his chair at the table. "Hmmm…" he said, "this Cole guy, I know nothing about him, but from what you said earlier, you seem fairly confident that he's a player. But, what is ComJet?"

"The company Cole was most recently associated with prior to joining RioAero here in Fort Lauderdale."

"I see." Maxwell paused, referring to the notebook. "Next, you feel that your competitors could be involved." He looked up toward Rick who remained expressionless. "Now that's difficult for me to imagine, hard to understand. Let me put that group of suspects to the side for the moment." Tommy's eyes glanced down to Rick's notes. "Factory workers. Yes, this item might be a real possibility. I could see some crazed individual, perhaps a handful of discontented workers— maybe even their union—being involved in sabotage. Workers and their unions have been known to initiate similar, bizarre actions against their employers. But from what you tell me, there appears to be a well-organized effort against your aircraft with some incidents not necessarily factory related. This might rule them out." He paused again, though only briefly. "And so far as the drug lords—the cartel or actually the cartels, I suppose you mean—yeah, these days there's always a possibility that they could be involved in anything. They're certainly a cold-blooded lot. But, why them? How do they figure in on what's been happening so far? What would be their motive?" Then, Tommy laughed in surprise as he zeroed in on the final suspect Rick had penciled in. "The military? Really? That doesn't make any sense. Doesn't the military actually run the country? Don't they pretty much own or control most of Brazil's industry? If they wanted to kill the WindStar program, couldn't they just cut funding? Couldn't they have had their airworthiness agency simply withhold certification of the aircraft or later revoke it?"

Tommy finally paused just long enough for Rick to interject. "You see, it's a pretty complex case. Everyone I listed could be a suspect, but it's the motives that are elusive."

"Exactly," came Maxwell's emphatic response. "Now I'm not saying that any of those you listed should not be suspect, I'm just questioning everything. We can't go off on the wrong track and pursue a wild goose. We don't have that luxury. As you said, we're working with a short fuse. The whole thing could blow up while we are chasing a bad lead."

Rick nodded. He liked the way Tommy had incorporated the word "we" into the commentary.

"Okay, let's go back to your competitors." Maxwell narrowed his eyes. "Is your business so ruthless that other airframe manufacturers would resort to such a high level of sabotage just to gain a competitive edge?" He shook his head in skepticism. "These manufacturers are big public companies, aren't they?"

"That's true."

"Damn, I just can't see big public companies behind the sort of thing you just described." Maxwell shrugged. "Yeah, I'm sure every player in your industry uses subtle tricks of the trade to make a sale at the expense of the competition. Hell, they might slander you, your company or your product, but they wouldn't be involved with the types of incidents that have occurred to the WindStar, would they? It could easily backfire on them. If someone, somehow uncovered the fact that a competitor was involved in a complex plot against RioAero, it would be devastating to that competitor. They might never be able to recover from the adverse publicity that would result or the possible legal actions that would likely be taken against them."

Rick disagreed. "No, Tommy, that probably would not be the case. The competitor would survive, perhaps without even skipping a beat. Sure, the press would have a field day. Sure, those people involved with covert initiatives against the WindStar would be canned. But the company would just maintain that there were a few bad apples in the basket. They'd say, steps would be taken to assure nothing like that could ever happen again. Then, the competitor would assemble a new management team. It would initiate a damage control PR blitz. Everything would blow over quickly. Business would soon be back to normal. But there would be one major difference—there would be no WindStar to compete against. And probably, RioAero wouldn't exist, at least not as we know it today."

Tommy snorted in frustration, not being able to argue with the possible scenario Rick had just set forth. "Goddamn, this is a tough nut."

"Absolutely," Rick agreed.

"And, you really want me to take on this case?"

"Positively."

"You're sure?"

Rick responded with a slow confident nod.

"Hell," Tommy said with almost the growl of a bear as he gnashed his teeth, "I think I must be crazy to even consider getting involved in this case. But I'll tell you what…you're on! We're gonna kick some butt. This is gonna be fun!"

Rick was relieved. A heavy burden had just flown off his shoulders. "Thanks, Tommy, I owe you."

Maxwell laughed, heartily. "You will owe me big time." His voice boomed, "Bigger if we're able to sort out this damn mess." He walked over to his desk, and still standing, picked up the telephone and punched in three numbers. "Monica," he said, "come on back here, it's showtime." He hung up the phone, grabbed a pair of scissors from atop his desk, and sauntered back to Rick.

Monica appeared in response to Tommy's call.

Tommy seated himself at the table and began to speak while using an opened blade of the scissors to slash through the tape that secured the cardboard box he had placed on the floor. Without looking up, he said, "I know you two have already sorta met. But let's do it proper. Monica Rice is my right-hand man—err woman—she's almost as smart as I am. He glanced up and smiled. "And, as you can see, she's a lot prettier than me." He nodded twice. "Monica, Rick Harris is an airplane marketeer who somehow always manages to have trouble find him." He winked at Rick. "Well, maybe not always. At any rate, Monica, we're going to help him save the day. And, he promised to reward us handsomely if we succeed. Right, Rick?"

"Indeed, very handsomely."

"Good." Tommy was now unpacking the box. He took the bubble wrap off of an array of what looked like some miniature electronic components and carefully placed each on the table. "Monica, I need you to do some fast but thorough research. Get everything you can on a guy named Dan Cole and ComJet, his former employer. Cole is Rick's villain, at least for now. Then, check out two airframe manufacturers—BASA and Fairchild. Financials, sales, top management, that sort of thing. Rick thinks there is a possibility that one of his competitors may be plotting to figuratively blow up RioAero, the Brazilian airplane company that he works for. And yes, find out who the hell AeroMech is. They're some kind of aviation services company at Opa Locka. They screwed up one of Rick's airplanes." Tommy stopped speaking.

"That's it?" Monica queried.

"Do you want more?"

"No, no."

Rick spoke up, "Monica, see if you can find out anything about a Basque guy named Felipe Retegi. He's an aviation engineering type with ComJet who is somehow associated with Cole. I think he may have a minor supporting role in this sabotage conspiracy we're trying to unravel."

"Fine," she said.

"Great," Tommy interjected. "And by the way, Monica," he continued on with a grin, "I'll need as much as you can get by 9:00 o'clock tonight."

She shrugged. It was never unusual for Tommy to ask for the impossible. "I'll do what I can." Monica quietly left the room.

"Okay, Rick," Tommy said, his arms crossed, head slightly cocked back, "I'll be reviewing this video tape and checking out a couple of other angles we haven't discussed. In the meantime, I need you to go to the airport and visit that office complex of yours. I have a task for you. Okay?"

"Sure, but what task?"

"See these gizmos." Tommy spread his hands apart, palms up, directing Rick's attention to the electronic paraphernalia he had arrayed on the tabletop.

"Tools of the trade?" Had to be, Rick thought.

"Exactly." Tommy looked at the electronic devices and smiled almost endearingly. "One of the most difficult things I had to do when I quit working as a PI was to mothball these buggers." He picked up the smallest of the black modules. "It's amazing what technology can do. This one can encroach upon anyone's conversation. It can be hidden almost anywhere."

"Do most private eyes use this kind of equipment?" Rick asked.

"No, no, not at all, what the run-of-the-mill PI might have would be much more primitive," Tommy was quick to respond. "Most private investigators don't even know these advanced types of things exist. And, even those who do know find this type of equipment very difficult as well as outrageously expensive to obtain." He grinned, only slightly self-aggrandizing. "For now, only a few of us James

Bond-types have access to this level of performance and miniaturization."

Rick thought about what Maxwell had just said. For some reason, he had always felt that Tommy was still involved in some kind of government spook stuff. Maxwell's earlier foray into the PI business and his current MacroScientific activities could easily just be a front for something much more complex. But there was no reason to pry. Tommy's business was Tommy's business. Rick was thrilled to have Maxwell's help.

Tommy handed Rick two of the smallest devices on the table. Each was about the size of a bottle cap. "I've just checked these out," Tommy said, "and they are ready to serve as our ears to that nefarious world of your dear Mr. Dan Cole. I need you to place one under his desk somewhere near his telephone, and the other one near any other telephone or meeting area he may have in his office. Just remove the backing from the tape and the device will stick underneath wherever you place it. Of course, be discreet. If the plot against your airplane is moving forward as quickly as you say, Cole will undoubtedly be in and out of his office throughout this weekend. When there, he'll likely be meeting with his cronies or making/taking phone calls. With an ear there, we'll be able to find out what kind of stew he's cooking up."

Rick nodded as he examined one of the bugs.

Next, Tommy handed Rick a device the size of a pack of cigarettes. "This is a UHF repeater. It will receive and then re-transmit anything the bugs detect. You see, the bugs themselves are the latest in ultra-low power, short range, sound-activated, intermittent transmitters. So, we couple them with a higher powered more complex transmitter that operates on a band of continually changing frequencies. This allows us to receive the signals at our base station. The whole process also does a good job of making gibberish out of the signals. All of that, my friend, makes detection tough even with today's state-of-the-art frequency scanners." Tommy broke into a theatrical grin. "I love this stuff."

"Where should I put the repeater?"

"I'll leave that to your imagination. Just make sure it's within three hundred feet of the bugs, but somewhere no one would likely scan for it."

"Fine."

"Now for one final item." Tommy pointed to three of the largest devices on the table. "We need to be in touch for a truly coordinated and effective effort against your bad guys. These devices are sort of clunky but work very well. Basically, they're just dual-band, handheld, ham radio transceivers. Operation is on both VHF and UHF bands. The two-meter, VHF band is pretty close to the frequencies that aircraft use; the UHF band is higher at seventy centimeters." Tommy took the newest looking transceiver and pushed the other two across the table to Rick. "We'll use one-forty-six-seventy-five on the two meter band to communicate with each other. The transmission is at about five watts—that's a lot less power than hardwired aircraft radios—and it's line of sight. Around here, that's good for maybe fifty miles. The NiCad batteries in the ones I'm giving you are about three years old, so use the second transceiver as a spare."

Rick nodded. "Anything else?" he asked, still not being totally sure what Tommy might have up his sleeve.

"Oh, yes..." Maxwell quickly responded. He leaned forward, halfway across the table. His facial expression, quite serious. "If you lose or break my toys, it will be really expensive."

"I understand," Rick said, carefully placing the electronic devices into his briefcase.

"Okay, that's it." Maxwell clapped his hands together once, swiveled his chair to the side and rose. "You do your part, I'll do mine. Let's get together tonight. I'll have some stuff to brief you on by then. How's ten o'clock sound?"

"Not a problem."

"Great, let's connect at one of my favorite hangouts. You know September's on Federal Highway, just south of Commercial?"

Rick nodded.

"Then, I'll see you at the restaurant there. Now get out of here, plant those bugs, and sell a few aircraft. I need to get to work on your case. The weekend is only so long, you know."

THIRTY-THREE

Destination: Georgetown

Twenty minutes after its delayed departure from Brasilia, WindStar PT-SBY had climbed to Flight Level 260 and was tracking outbound on the 343° radial of the BSB VOR. Power setting: intermediate cruise. True airspeed: 300 knots. DME readout: 125 nautical miles; 400-knot ground speed. Weather: CAVU—ceiling and visibility unlimited.

"Pretty amazing," Svensson remarked, pointing to the DME in the center avionics stack. "That is one excellent tailwind."

Franco Rameros cocked his head to the right, glancing at the digital readout. "Roger that, BJ, certainly not the norm. Still, I am not one to argue with Mother Nature. Her kindness should cut down our enroute time by about an hour."

Svensson retrieved a clipboard he had temporarily stowed on the glare shield above his flight instruments. "Let's see..." he said, his engineering sensibility prompting him to review the flight log that was attached to the clipboard. "The winds aloft are forecast to diminish somewhat as we travel farther north. So, taking that into consideration, I am estimating this segment should be just under four hours, three plus forty-one to be exact." He double-checked his numbers. "And yes, we will save about an hour of flight time."

"Unless," Rameros interjected, "that thunderstorm activity forecasted near Boa Vista costs us. Circumnavigating the build-ups may tack on another ten or fifteen minutes."

Svensson cringed at the implication that his painstaking calculations did not include skirting enroute thunderstorms. Disconcerting thoughts about uncontrollable variables entered his analytical mind. "Umm, how about if we use my general estimate of just under four hours?"

"That will be fine, BJ." Svensson's attempt to apply engineering precision to real flight prompted a smile from Rameros. "You know flying airplanes is not an exact science even though some folks may lead you to believe it is. Indeed, on a long flight like the one we are on today, anything can happen. Despite our most exacting estimates, the bottom line is always the same: We will get there, when we get there."

"Huh, interesting way of putting it." Ego still smarting, Svensson placed the clipboard back on the glare shield, and then briefly stared out the front windshield before changing the subject. "So, Captain Rameros, what is your take on the delay we took at BSB?"

"I was just wondering if you were as curious about that as I am." Rameros dropped his right hand down between his legs, disengaged the seat latching mechanism, and slid his seat back ten inches until making contact with the cockpit bulkhead. "I have been rehashing that whole rigmarole in my mind. It is a hard one to figure. But first, give me your impression," he said, throwing the question back to Svensson.

"Well," Svensson said, recalling the cascade of events, "it was almost as if everything was orchestrated to trip us up: the wrong fuel; the ramp-check; the so-called paperwork verification; the delay from the Tower. But, why? It just does not add up."

Rameros covered a yawn with his left hand. He had had only a few hours sleep the previous night. The jangling phone and Big Lou's firm insistence that Franco personally launch a second WindStar to FLL had totally destroyed his slumber. "Maybe my mind is not as sharp as it could be today, but I agree, it is all very puzzling. Line operations would never pump avgas into an aircraft the size of the WindStar. Just glancing at the engine nacelles tells the aircraft had to be turbine powered. While the WindStar's engines do prefer Jet-A fuel, turbine engines can pretty much burn almost anything including Bacardi 151. Still, that avgas incident was not an accident. And, that ramp-check stuff was a crock of shit. Every CTA inspector knows how airworthiness certificates and aircraft registrations are issued. That Fernandes guy was not new to the job. He himself did not take the initiative to ramp-check us. Someone above him at the CTA had orders to stop or delay our flight. Still, the question is why."

"Maybe it is you, maybe you were specifically targeted to have a bad day."

"Huh?"

"Well, you do have a reputation for being...uh, uh...less than tactful on occasion."

Rameros clenched his jaw. He knew Svensson was right. He did have a knack of irritating a lot of people, especially those at the factory. Perhaps it was payback time. "I guess that is always a possibility," he reluctantly admitted. But his intuition was stirring, and it said that that was not the full explanation. Any introspection on his own shortcomings was brief. In a switch of gears, Rameros shot a rapid unexpected burst of questions at his young copilot. "You were with the aircraft all the time we were on the ground, right? You watched like a hawk during refueling, right? You sampled the fuel after the tanks were topped off, right? You saw no one tamper with the aircraft, right? So, mechanically, we are a-okay?"

"Yes...yes...yes...yes...yes," Svensson very quickly responded, though somewhat confused. "Everything is fine, Franco. I never left the WindStar."

"Good, because I would hate to put down in the Amazon due to fuel contamination or anything else. The place is full of snakes, you know. And, snakes just give me the creeps." He feigned a shudder. "Anyway, the bottom line is the CTA did not stop our flight, just delayed it. Hmmm…I wonder if delay was the real goal. I will have to give that some more thought."

"But it was hardly much of a delay. We could have been stalled much longer."

"Aah, yes, certainly could have been. We might have been there all afternoon." Not lingering on his point, Rameros lowered his chin, his eyes twinkling over the upper frames of his Ray-Bans as he looked to Svensson. "Was mine a consummate performance as a bad-ass general?"

"Very much so."

"Now you are beginning to learn why I dressed like a starship commander."

The tension broken, they both laughed.

"You see," Rameros continued, for the first time delving into the reason for the unconventional uniform he was wearing, "rank—any rank—has its privileges. That is especially true when traveling through airports in South America. When dressing with authority, one usually gets respect. Even if deference is not shown, generally whoever is attempting to harass you is intimidated; that is, unless that someone is armed and has a machine gun pointed at you."

"Machine gun?"

"You never know. Our route includes some small countries that are politically unstable. Anything might happen."

"At Georgetown?"

"Nah, no worry. Georgetown was no problem last time I checked. We should be in and out of there in a blink of an eye." Rameros yawned again. "It looks like you have everything under control, so I will settle back and catch some shuteye. Remember, in another hundred or so miles we will be out of radar contact. You will need to fly the old fashioned way…position reports, estimates, et cetera, et cetera."

"Not a problem," Svensson reassured. "Just relax and recharge your batteries. If I need your help I will certainly let you know."

Franco Rameros reseated his sunglasses and slumped down into his seat. The low drone of the props, the soothing, almost imperceptible vibration within the airframe, the slight hiss of the wind past the pressurized door seals, the familiar sensations all eased

Rameros' state of mind. Within minutes, his neck drooped. He dozed off.

Svensson continued to monitor the WindStar's progress as the aircraft screamed across the central highlands toward the Amazon region. He repeatedly checked his position against the sparsely scattered ground-based navigation aids and diligently verified his estimates for crossing enroute intersections.

He keyed his mic on the Brasilia Center frequency: "Center, WindStar Papa-Tango-Sierra-Bravo-Yankee, Flight Level two-six-zero, over Tucano at zero-seven, estimating Bandeirante at fifty-five, Xingu next."

Center acknowledged Svensson's position report and advised him to contact Brasilia Center on a subsequent frequency when over Bandeirante.

The DME readout indicated 390 knots. Each minute, the WindStar covered nearly seven more miles. Svensson scanned the instrument panel and used the aircraft's low frequency ADF (Automatic Direction Finder) receiver to crosscheck the primary course VHF navigation system. He was now reminded how boring long cross-country flights could be. Still, the repeated checking and crosschecking of all instrumentation made time pass by more quickly.

Cumulous clouds were beginning to form below.

Radar showed no significant weather ahead for the next 100 miles.

Svensson made two more position reports, and once again changed the communication frequency as he entered yet another air traffic control sector of Brasilia Center.

The miles continued to click by.

The clouds thickened, becoming scattered to broken and covering fifty percent of the sky below. Sixty miles to the left of his course, tall cumulonimbus clouds provided a sign of what could be looming ahead.

His navigation system indicated the WindStar should be directly over the Amazon. He looked down, hoping for a glimpse of the world's second largest river, but all he could see were puffy white clouds with occasional patches of emerald green terrain. He reached toward the center of the instrument panel and increased the radar's range to paint 150 miles ahead. Ragged dark green with splashes of yellow appeared on the CRT. The colors marched closer with each sweep of the radar antenna. The aircraft experienced a slight jolt from the rising unsettled air surrounding it. Then a sharp but brief downdraft caught the WindStar, momentarily pressing Svensson up against his seatbelt.

Franco Rameros awakened. He groaned with a prolonged yawn. Temporarily removing his sunglasses, he rubbed his eyes twice. "Aah, how long was my catnap, BJ?"

"Almost two hours."

"Wow." Rameros was amazed how quickly time had passed. "Anyway, I am back. How is our progress?"

"We just passed the big river thirty miles back. Our ground speed is reduced only slightly. Our progress is excellent. Another five-fifty miles to go."

"Very good." Rameros moved his seat forward, and, out of habit, snugged up his loosened seatbelt.

"We are painting some weather up ahead. It is still too soon to tell how bad it might be. The clouds have been building along our route for the last couple hundred miles. The WindStar flies like a dream, too bad takeoffs and landings are still a nightmare for me," Svensson informed with a little self-goading.

"Ehh, worry not, you will be okay," Rameros reassured. After a brief pause, he added, "You know, I still cannot get Brasilia out of my mind. I went to sleep thinking about that Fernandes guy and our delay. The little weasel really pissed me off. For the life of me, I still cannot figure out why the CTA used that lame paperwork excuse to keep us on the ground. Maybe the delay was to ensure we would have a rough ride in the late afternoon weather." He laughed. "Awww, what the hell, at least we are making good progress thanks to those strong tail winds."

Svensson nodded in agreement.

Just as Rameros leaned forward to reset his altimeter to the standard setting of 29.92 used above 18,000 feet, he glimpsed a blur of movement out of his forward left windshield panel. The object rapidly increased in size. Within seconds the image filled the entire windshield.

THIRTY-FOUR

Pier Sixty-Six Marina

Sammy Santelli proudly sat in the massive fighting chair at the stern of his pristine Hatteras 53 Convertible. He swiveled the chair ninety degrees to the starboard and gazed out at the still quiet Intracoastal. Tilting his head up, he glanced toward the tuna tower that extended above the boat's bridge. The tower's highly polished anodized aluminum finish reflected the underlying energy of a grand-scale sportfisherman. Fluttering in the light breeze atop the tower was an orange with black parallelogram pennant, the symbol of the Santelli family trucking business and Sammy's pride. Well below the tower, the flawless white gelcoat finish glistened. He smiled to himself as he enjoyed the warming midday sun.

"Nice, very nice," Sammy softly said self-satisfied, "perhaps a little large, but still very nice."

A few steps up from the low-freeboard fishing cockpit where Sammy sat was the spacious custom main cabin. The salon was fashionably designed and comfortably appointed with a high gloss cherry verneer interior and a variety of furnishings including an L-shaped settee, several heavily bolstered swivel chairs surrounding a dining table, and an advanced audio/video entertainment system. A full galley boasted the ultimate in equipment and accessories necessary to satisfy the most demanding culinary devotee. The boat's sixteen-foot beam accommodated three spacious staterooms below.

The two-year-old Hatteras had been acquired during the previous summer from Oscar Renauld, the famed Miami restaurateur. Sammy's last boat, an aged Bertram 31, had been a delight over the years, but he had been ready to move up to twin diesel power and all the added creature comforts of which he had always dreamed.

Santelli came to own this yacht by virtue of being at the right place at the right time. A yacht broker at Pier Sixty-Six heard rumors that Mr. Renauld had been quietly unloading assets prior to an anticipated contentious divorce. The broker verified Renauld's pre-divorce selling spree and approached Sammy. The Hatteras was available, the price was right, and the deal was quickly done.

John Andreas stepped aboard from the marina's C-Dock. "Good morning Captain Santelli. Kelly Long is ten minutes behind me. He had to make a second run on Big Daddy's…forgot the Bacardi 151." John lowered two cardboard boxes that he had carried from the parking lot down onto the deck. Fishing into one of the boxes, he snatched out two cold beers. "It's never too early for an Amstel Light, is it?" He popped the caps off of both bottles and handed one to Sammy.

"Thanks, John," Sammy said with genuine feeling, "good business partners like you and Kelly are hard to come by."

"Yes indeed, that's because good friends make good partners." He raised his beer. Their bottles clinked together.

Santelli took a long swallow from his bottle and said, "Undoubtedly the best light beer ever made. It's a shame Busch and Miller have not come up with something that tastes this good."

John began to nod in agreement, but quickly caught himself and said, "Damn, I could have brought down a case of that Amherst Lager we just started making in our brewery in Norwood. Although it's not a light beer, you would like it even better than an Amstel. Unfortunately, we are not yet distributing in Florida."

"That's a shame." Sammy knew that small breweries like those owned by the Andreas family were basically regional. Unique local brands with distinctive flavor typically had narrow geographic distribution. Switching gears, Sammy mused, "So, I guess one of the only items left to decide upon is a name for our merged airlines."

"I thought that was already decided," John quickly returned. "Kelly and I think Express Airlines says it all. That's essentially what regional airlines provide…express transportation."

"Hell," Sammy shot back, "last night Kelly said that InterState Airlines was the moniker of choice. Besides, Express Airlines sounds like a lousy parcel company. My family would ridicule me if we selected a name like that for our new passenger airline."

John smiled, knowing full well no decision had been made, and matter-of-factly added, "Kelly is just miffed because he knows his choice was out of the running even before the selection process began. We both know Long Airways only makes sense if your name is Kelly Long."

"You're absolutely right." Sammy flipped open his Zippo and lit up a cigarette. "But there is an even bigger issue that needs to be resolved: What aircraft to select. We need standardization. We need a solid airframe. We need something that can grow with us into the future without being an economic burden to us now."

John Andreas nodded in agreement and focused on the matter of aircraft selection. "There is no perfect aircraft for our combined operations. Anything available is a compromise. The Shorts 330 is too slow, too big, and damn, it is one hell of an ugly airplane—a flying box with stuck on wings. Our Canadian friends at de Havilland pretty much make just STOL (Short Take-Off and Landing) aircraft with either eighteen or fifty seats. Beech still offers only an unpressurized fifteen-seater that really has no future for us. Cessna and Piper are peddling general aviation airframes into which they try to pack eight or nine passenger seats and call it an airliner. Then, there's Fairchild. They have a screaming nineteen-seater, but the fuel tanks always seem to leak and the engines aren't on the wings for more than a few months before needing costly repairs. Despite drawbacks, there are some aspects about the Fairchild product I like, but its cabin has zero passenger appeal."

Sammy nodded, fully in accord with the predicament.

"So," John pressed on, "aside from the British Aerospace Jetstream, which is still a work in progress and essentially will have the same damn engines as the Fairchild Metro, the other choice we're left with is the BASA Avio-23. But that aircraft barely does one-sixty knots, is unpressurized, and is basically an old technology military aircraft repurposed for the commercial aviation market. Even though BASA is as aggressive as hell in putting a deal together, their product doesn't seem like a long-term play for us. Besides, I really don't feel comfortable with the company or its people. There's just something unsettling about BASA I can't explain."

There was a moment of silence.

"So, your conclusion, Mr. Andreas?"

"Well, Sammy, my conclusion is that I don't have a conclusion, at least not yet. I am leaning toward one aircraft, though—the WindStar. All the research we've already done on the WindStar leads me to believe that it could be a winner for us." He reflected for a moment. "Maybe it was sheer destiny that brought us together with Rick Harris last night."

"Happy coincidence, but don't worry," Sammy commented, "although I was unaware that Rick was heading up sales for the WindStar, RioAero was on my contact list for this coming week. Our fortuitous meeting just accelerated things a bit. And from what I gathered during our discussions last night, his company has aircraft ready to deliver...bet they're hungry to do a deal." Sammy chuckled. "Rick Harris will probably crap in his pants when I tell him that we want his best and final offer for a transaction involving twenty firm with options for forty."

They both laughed, knowing full well that capturing an order of that magnitude would be a dream come true for any airframer in the business.

Santelli continued, "By the way, have you seen the morning paper?"

"No, not yet," Andreas said matter-of-factly. "Anything interesting?"

Sammy contorted his face. "Here, have a look for yourself."

John took the part of the paper Sammy handed to him. It was the Metro Section. "Hmmm…" John groaned upon seeing the headline and photo of the WindStar, although not with surprise. "It's just as Rick said last night. One of his planes lost its footing and crinkled some aluminum."

"Yeah, but shit like that shouldn't happen."

"I know. Still, I'm sure Rick will have an explanation; if not today, then by—"

"Speak of the devil," Santelli abruptly cut off John, "here comes crazy Kelly, and look who's with him."

John followed Sammy's eyes down C-Dock and spotted Kelly Long walking toward them. He was carrying a box of more provisions for the boat. Alongside Kelly was none other than Rick Harris.

"Now that's timing if I've ever seen it," John remarked. "Looks like we'll soon find out what kind of appetite his Brazilian company has for cutting an aircraft deal."

Kelly stepped off of the dock and onto the boat. Rick paused, temporarily placing his briefcase and the baseball hats down on the dock. He leaned against one of the massive pylons that supported the marina's superstructure and he slipped off his old roper boots and socks.

Santelli grinned and called out, "Not everybody knows proper boat etiquette."

"Well," Rick said in response as he boarded the Hatteras, "when you live in Fort Lauderdale, I guess it comes natural. Anything but boat shoes or bare feet can really mess up a nice deck." He paused, gazing at his surroundings. "Indeed, this is one hell of a fishing machine, Mr. Santelli. Congratulations." Sammy shook Rick's extended hand.

"Thanks," Sammy said, "she's the love of my life, at least until I can find the right woman."

Rick smiled, noticing the sparkle in Sammy's eyes. "Oh, you will, and she'll be a gem just like this Hatteras." Changing the subject, Rick continued on, "Since I was in the area, I thought I'd take a chance and see if you'd be on the boat. Here's some of the latest *haute couture* from Rio." He passed out the WindStar baseball caps. Next, he dug into the top of his open briefcase and pulled out the black VHS cassette. "Hot off the presses, the latest WindStar videotape. I think you'll enjoy watching it." He grinned. "I did the intro myself when I was in Brazil."

Santelli threw out a jab, "Hollywood Harris, huh?"

Rick shrugged.

John Andreas interjected an observation, "Almost seems like you think you might sell us some of those flying coffee makers from way down south."

"I'm always ready, John, it's my job," Rick responded. "But I won't hound you to death. I'm not one of those always-in-your-face aircraft sales types. I won't pressure you, as do most other manufacturers' reps. I will, however, represent my product as fairly and honestly as possible. I'll work with you in any way I can to fully answer your questions, to dispel any initial reservations. In the end, if my aircraft is right for your business plan, you'll buy it because you will have sold yourself on it. I'm just a catalyst. I try to help make your decision process both straightforward and accurate. I don't want you to select the wrong aircraft. That would be a big mistake for both of us."

"Wow!" John said, "They teach you that at Harvard?"

"Actually no, I got my MBA from SMU in Dallas, but that kind of stuff is not taught there either. Business philosophy is something one has to come up with by oneself…figure out what suits one's ethics. I sell airplanes only one way—the right way. You know, my approach is not standard practice within the industry. I guess I'm sort of a maverick. Still, my results please both my company and my customers. I know airlines have figuratively and literally crashed and burned by selecting the wrong aircraft type. I'm sure you know what I'm talking about." He paused with a nod. "Anyway, my intention is to not let that happen to you guys, not if you give me a chance to help you. I want your decision—whatever it may be—to be something that you'll be comfortable with in the long run."

"Atta boy, Rick," Sammy said, "you're talking my kind of language. Now, if you'd care to join us in the parlor," he motioned toward the main cabin, "we'd like to get down to some serious business."

"By all means," Rick agreed.

Destination: Georgetown

"**G**ODDAMN!**"** Rameros shouted, instinctively punching off the autopilot and reflexively positioning to shove the aircraft's nose down. But before he could put the WindStar into a dive, the object screamed past just above, leaving behind a deafening blast of noise.

Almost instantaneously, the WindStar began to pitch, roll, and yaw uncontrollably. The aircraft thrashed about wildly—violently—caught in a sea of turbulence five miles above the ground. Rameros could do little to stop it. But from what he had seen, he knew exactly what was happening and why. The two aircraft had been as close as possible in the airspace without having a fatal mid-air collision. The odds against such an incident occurring at high altitude over the Amazon were more than one in a million. The odds were impossible, yet it had just happened.

Rameros' skill and experience won out as he regained control and eased the WindStar up out of the wake turbulence.

"What was that?" a stunned Svensson blurted out in confusion, shaken by what had just happened.

"Close call," Rameros tersely replied. "A midsize jet—Gulfstream G-II, I think—with a camouflage paint scheme just overflew us by inches."

"Military?"

"Had to be."

"So, some Brazilian Air Force pilot was not looking where he was going?"

"True and false." Concern was written all over Franco Rameros' face. "Many pilots flying at high altitude seldom look outside the cockpit, because frankly, at Flight Level two-six-zero over the Amazon, it would be rare to see another aircraft. They just read a newspaper or magazine, chat among themselves, or play around with their avionics." He shook his head in disdain. "Some pilots are real asses. And, military pilots are the worst. I ought to know, I was once one of them. But based on that jet's course, it should have been flying at an odd numbered altitude, not twenty-six thousand feet. Those are the rules of the road. That would have provided adequate vertical separation, even if the pilot was snoozing on autopilot."

"Okay, so what is the 'false?'" Svensson furrowed his brow in puzzlement.

Rameros matter-of-factly added, "The Brazilian Air Force simply does not fly Gulfstream jets in camouflage colors. I am positive about that."

"Hmmm…" Svensson grunted, not yet realizing what the highly experienced, ex-military pilot was implying.

Rameros remained silent. He looked back into the aircraft's cabin to check on his passengers. The two engineers, somewhat shaken, waved their hands in an expression of being okay. He keyed his mic on the PA system and asked how they were doing. Each signaled a two thumbs-up. He commented about the rough ride and reminded his passengers about having seatbelts securely fastened.

Rameros then redirected his attention outside of the aircraft. He methodically scanned the horizon. His mind mulling over the Gulfstream jet: Where had it come from; why was it flying at an incorrect altitude. He tried to convince himself that the incident was probably nothing; perhaps, just a foreign dignitary flying in from Central America for a weekend of fun in Rio. He took a deep breath and slowly exhaled. After all, there now was little to see outside the cockpit except developing weather—lots of it—normal for the time of year.

Sixty miles to the west, an unsettled atmosphere continued to spawn cumulonimbus clouds, some now towering above forty-five thousand feet. The clouds' anvil heads indicated movement to the north-northeast. He pointed to the radar indicator which was painting dark green with numerous swatches of yellow and commented to Svensson, "Looks like we are in for a bumpy ride as we approach the mountains and cross into Guyana."

Svensson shrugged. "Nothing we have the right to complain about. It was all in the forecast."

Rameros nodded in agreement.

The weather was not enough to distract Svensson from the troubling near mid-air incident. "Any idea why we almost had a head-on with that jet?"

Rameros was about to say that he had absolutely no idea, when a low rumbling sound within the WindStar interrupted him. His eyes were automatically drawn to the master caution panel just below the center window glare shield. The panel was black; no annunciator lights were flashing any warning. He scanned the engine instrument cluster. There were no abnormalities. He reduced and then reset the prop rpm to be sure that the propellers were synchrophased. But the dull muffled noise continued.

Rameros considered that perhaps, in some way, the WindStar had been damaged when the military jet over flew by inches. An avionics antenna might have snapped loose from its upper fuselage mounting. It could be vibrating in the airflow, creating the peculiar sound within the cabin. However, the unexplained rumbling sound had begun only within the past ten seconds. It seemed to him that any sound resulting from fly-over damage should have occurred immediately following the incident.

Svensson honed in on the sound too. To him, it seemed to be emanating from the aft section of the aircraft. He leaned left and looked quizzically back into the cabin. The two engineer passengers were transfixed and staring at the upper aft section of the fuselage. The sound grew louder. Deeper. The entire airframe resonated, uncharacteristically. The control yoke began to vibrate, then shake. The rumble further deepened, intensifying. Suddenly, there was a thundering roar. The mysterious G-II ominously slid into view from above, once again filling their windshield.

The much faster, more powerful aircraft had circled behind the WindStar and was now descending in front of it. Then not totally unexpectedly, the jet developed maximum thrust and began accelerating in a delayed climbing right turn to the south.

The sound was deafening.

"DAMN!" Rameros shouted, fighting the controls as the WindStar went through a second series of wake turbulence gyrations. This time, though, the G-II stayed in sight long enough for Rameros to get a better glimpse of its fuselage. The full drab camouflage paint scheme without any registration numbers or other identifying markings was ominous. But another feature of the aircraft gave Franco Rameros even further cause for pause. It was disturbingly unusual—highly unsettling.

Svensson had noticed the feature as well. "What are those?"

"You really do not want to know," Rameros responded with genuine trepidation.

This Gulfstream was like no other production G-II. More than the aircraft's paint scheme, what unnerved both Rameros and Svensson were the jet's highly specialized after-market modifications. Two non-factory specified hard-points had been incorporated into the outboard structure under each wing. Mounted on each hard-point was a short-range air-to-air missile.

"What are those?" Svensson repeated, more urgently.

"Sidewinders," Rameros grimly replied.

The AIM-9 Sidewinder was the most widely manufactured and significant heat-seeking missile ever made. In service since the 1950s, the missile was now readily available on black markets around the world. The communists shamelessly reverse-engineered the American design and called it the K-13, code named the AA-2 Atoll by NATO. The awesome missile had a nearly sixty-second rocket motor burn and supersonic speed. The Sidewinder operated through a system of nose-mounted cassegrainian mirrors and moving reticles to actively seek out heat rays generated by the intended target. To avoid deflection to other heat sources, integral optical filters allowed only specifically desired infrared wavelengths to be processed. The missile could lock onto and track a targeted aircraft's hot exhaust from a distance of three to four miles. Once launched, it literally flew up the target's tailpipe. Warhead detonation followed with the deployment of rod fragments that ripped through the skin and structure of its victim like hordes of knife-wielding assassins.

"Bad news?" Svensson queried, but he really knew better than to ask.

"Very bad news," was Rameros' short response.

Over the Brasilia Center frequency they both heard a voice say, "WindStar...*va a la frecuencia uno dos dos punto nueve.*" It was a request in Spanish for the WindStar to come up on Multicom, the air-to-air communication frequency.

Svensson set the frequency into COM-2.

At first the only sound was the static noise of an open mic, then once again came the voice of the Gulfstream pilot, "*Buenas tardes,* WindStar. We come many miles to visit with you."

At that instant, everything started to click for Rameros. He recognized the dialect, and was now certain that the Gulfstream had to be Colombian. But it was not from the Colombian Air Force; they would never recklessly fly into the heartland of Brazil. Most likely, the aircraft belonged to a private military agency (PMA), one that was undoubtedly financed and controlled by the most influential of all organizations in Colombia—a drug cartel. The cartels maintained an extensive fleet of various aircraft types to protect cocaine production and distribution centers from attacks by anti-drug forces.

Pieces of the puzzle were coming together. Today's vexing aggravations were more close to aligning for Rameros. And, it was not a pleasant picture that he was constructing in his mind.

RioAero was South America's only major airframe manufacturer. Their aggressive, can-do engineering department was well underway with two classified aircraft modification programs involving the WindStar. Serial Number 001 was being modified for special mission operations—a twelve foot side-looking radar antenna was being affixed to the fuselage belly; two, seventy gallon extended range fuel tanks were being fitted to hard points beneath each wing. Serial Number 009, a full production aircraft previously delivered to the Brazilian Air Force, was back being retrofitted for armament—short-range air-to-ground missiles. These programs had been given the go ahead eight months ago by President Figueiredo, despite significant resistance from key members of his staff.

Rameros knew that these special mission aircraft would soon be certified and then marketed around the world. It was not a stretch to believe the aircraft would be used against members of the Colombian drug cartels. That was easy enough for anyone to assume. But Rameros did not like the tack his thoughts were taking. He was very much aware that cartels had no compunction about acting aggressively and violently against any perceived threat to their empire. The missile equipped Gulfstream was certainly not on a sightseeing flight over the Amazon. Its mission was to destroy the WindStar. Rameros was sure of it.

"We are a sitting duck!" Panic was written all over Svensson's face as the young copilot nervously scanned airspace to the east from his side window. "What can we do? There must be something!"

Rameros remained silent. He had no more of an answer to Svensson's question than he had a response to the Gulfstream pilot's transmission. He began to speculate why the Gulfstream was playing cat and mouse with the WindStar rather than simply splashing it. Pilot ego, perhaps. His mind continued to swiftly sort through what was happening and why.

The reason for the delay at Brasilia was now crystal clear to him. Someone at the CTA was ordered to make up an excuse—any excuse—to delay the WindStar's departure. Complicity was not at all unusual. Every governmental agency in Brazil was corrupt. The CTA was no exception. If RioAero and the WindStar were on a cartel's hit list, as Rameros now suspected, a few telephone calls would have been all that were needed to coordinate the launch of a missile-equipped aircraft to intercept the WindStar on its route over the Amazon. The CTA knew the exact route Rameros would be taking; to estimate where Rameros would be and when would have been easy. Even though air traffic control radar was unavailable over the Amazon region, the Gulfstream pilot needed only to monitor the Brasilia Center frequency and obtain the position reports faithfully radioed in by Svensson. Rameros figured that the jet had simply flown near one of Svensson's enroute fixes, entered into a high altitude holding pattern, and waited for the WindStar's arrival.

Rameros finally replied to Svensson. "What you said is true, we are indeed a sitting duck." In segue, he switched to the cabin PA system to dryly advise his engineer passengers of the situation at hand: "Gentlemen, please stow your tray tables, place your seatbacks in the upright and locked position, and be sure your seatbelts are fastened...tight. Within the next few minutes, some Colombian bastard is going to attempt—I say, ATTEMPT—to fire a couple of missiles up our engine exhaust stacks. This is not a joke."

"What can we do?" Svensson demanded.

Rameros lit up a Churchill-sized Monty. "Showtime!" he growled through clenched teeth, then took two puffs from his fat cigar. The cockpit quickly filled with the cigar's rank grayish smoke, much to Svensson's repulsed amazement. "I feel lucky today," Rameros continued. "Too bad no one is here to capture this on film. It is going to be interesting…interesting, to say the least."

"You are crazy."

"Looking death in the face makes me seem that way, does it not?"

"Yes, but…"

Rameros took a few more puffs on the cigar. "How much do we have stowed in the aft cargo compartment?

"We are light, just under seven hundred pounds."

"All securely tied down with 9-G netting?"

"Yes."

"Real secure?"

"Absolutely, I checked it myself."

"Good, I would not want that stuff to go flying through the ceiling if I have to pull some negative Gs." He grinned, clutching the cigar between his teeth. "Now, BJ, if you are a religious man, this might be a good time to say a few prayers. It could not hurt. It would be nice to have the Big Guy on our side for the next few minutes."

Once again a transmission came over the Multicom frequency. The background noise was distinct. It was the Gulfstream pilot. "*Buenas tardes, amigo*. Are you listening?" The mic stayed keyed for five seconds and then clicked off.

"*Buenas* afternoon to you, *compadrito*," Rameros came back in typically sarcastic form. He carefully adjusted the earpieces of his headset and turned up the volume to maximum. He wanted to hear every sound within the Gulfstream cockpit each time the pilot keyed his mic.

"You know, *amigo*," came the ever so smugly confident voice of the Colombian captain, "the WindStar aircraft causes my friends many problems."

The background noise from the Gulfstream cockpit provided no insight for Rameros. He wanted to run, but he knew that the jet had almost a two hundred knot speed advantage over the WindStar. He hesitated for a split second before making a critical decision that would seal his fate. Not really that he had a choice. All he could do was hope for the best.

Decisively, he retarded the power levers to flight idle. The huge propellers became massive speed brakes, buzzing in the air, quickly decelerating the WindStar from its three hundred knot airspeed, pressing its occupants forward against their seatbelts. At the aircraft's one hundred eighty-five knot maneuvering speed—the design limited speed at which full control deflection should not result in a structural failure—Rameros promptly placed the aircraft in an emergency descent attitude.

Background static from the Gulfstream was heard again over Multicom. "Ha-haaa…" the pilot laughed with arrogant self-assurance. There was more background static from the open mic, then a further verbal transmission, "*Amigo*, you can run, but you cannot hide. You will never reach the cloud bank below before I have my way with you." The transmission ended after a long pause.

The WindStar, now pitched down at nearly a forty-five degree attitude, had its IVSI (Instantaneous Vertical Speed Indicator) pegged at six thousand feet per minute. The relative wind surged past the propellers, which acted as giant near-static discs fighting against the uncontainable sea of fast-moving air. Rameros beamed, nodded once, and then abruptly jerked both condition levers back to their aft fuel-cutoff detents. Engine torque: zero. Internal turbine temperature (ITT): dropping, rapidly cooling. The power turbines spooling down. Both propellers would soon feather.

"What are you doing?" Svensson screamed out, fingers clawing into the armrests of his seat. "You just shut down both engines!"

Rameros' teeth clamped down onto his cigar. "Saving fuel," he smirked. "Sit back and relax, if you can." He was relying on his past aviation training and experience: fighter jet training with the Brazilian Air Force; US Naval Test Pilot School at Patuxent River NAS. He knew that his fate and that of the WindStar were totally in his own hands. Only seconds remained before the jet would trigger its missiles.

The Gulfstream pilot keyed his mic. The hallmark background noise transmitted from within the jet filled the cockpit headsets of the WindStar. The captain's voice came booming through to Rameros. This time there were only two words and a long pause: "*Adiós amigo…*"

Over the Multicom frequency, Rameros heard two metallic clicks among the background static. Next, a slight hissing surge as each missile was launched. Then, laughter. Then, the frequency went silent.

If indeed the missiles were Sidewinders, as Rameros had assumed, the launch would have most likely been at a range of two and a half to three miles from his aircraft. There was not much time remaining until impact—until the obliteration of the WindStar.

Franco Rameros glanced at the ITT gauges. The reading was now below two hundred degrees and falling. Little exhaust heat was being generated by the engines; hopefully, not enough to whet a

Sidewinder's appetite. But he could not be sure. He slowly counted to himself: one-thousand-one...

Rameros abruptly and resolutely hauled back on the control yoke. The weight of his body increased—two, three, four times—forcing him down, pressing him deeply into the cushion of his seat. His Ray-Bans immediately slid down the length of his nose before dislodging and tumbling to the floorboards. The airframe strained under the accelerated 4-G maneuver.

But the WindStar accepted the challenge, responding immediately, pivoting along its lateral axis, angling vertically, almost standing on its tail. The initial climb was rapid due to inertia and feathered propellers, yet as speed bled off, ascent markedly slowed until the aircraft was virtually motionless—seemingly suspended in space. Now an eerie silence permeated the cockpit.

Svensson heard a double whoosh sound. He glanced downward out of his side window. Two thin parallel ribbons of grayish-white smoke floated less than a hundred feet below. "The missiles...they missed!" he shouted out in a sudden burst of excitement and complete disbelief.

Rameros had no time to gloat. The WindStar was not an aerobatic aircraft. It was designed for utility—carriage of passengers and cargo for hire. The maneuver that he had performed was totally foreign and unapproved for the WindStar.

The aircraft was literally suspended as it hung vertically in the air. Rameros' timing had to be right. "Now," he quietly said as he jerked his head forward and kicked full left rudder. There was no response from the WindStar. Limited relative wind rendered the controls almost totally ineffective.

"Goddamn..." Franco groaned. A tailslide followed by an inverted spin was something he desperately wanted to avoid. Flight-testing had shown the aircraft was unable to recover when placed in such a flight regime. He groaned again, silently willing and desperately using body language to coax the WindStar into completing the hammerhead maneuver.

Still...no response from the aircraft.

And, Rameros could do nothing more... nothing at all.

The WindStar had to respond.

The WindStar needed to respond.

But, could the WindStar respond?

A split-second later, the comatose aircraft slowly came back to life, lazily rotating about its vertical axis, left wingtip knifing backward/downward, nose following in slow motion, now initiating the requested one hundred eighty degree change in direction.

As the nose passed down through the horizon, the airspeed indicator came alive. Forty knots…eighty knots… one-twenty knots… continuing to build. The sound of rushing wind was music to his ears. At one hundred-eighty knots, Rameros eased the aircraft out of its steep dive but continued the descent, angling for the clouds below and to the left.

As airspeed hit two hundred knots, Rameros proceeded to restart the engines. He quickly glanced at the right engine gauges on the engine instrument cluster. "Compressor speed…check." He set ignition to automatic and advanced the right condition lever forward. There was a momentary delay. Then the pulsating igniter plugs lit off the fuel being sprayed into the right engine's combustion chamber. Digital numbers on the ITT gauge raced upwards. The WindStar yawed to the left as engine torque was transferred to the right prop. Rameros went on to quickly start the left engine as he continued his sprint for cover in the clouds.

The foiled G-II pilot furiously keyed his mic, this time saying only one word: "*BAS-TAR-DO!*"

Rameros smiled broadly, stealing a second to savor the moment, then answered back, "*Y ustedes, también.*" He winked at Svensson, whose face was as ashen white as any Swede could get.

Within twenty seconds, the WindStar was securely cloaked in a bright-white bank of clouds. Almost heaven, Rameros thought to himself, or at least as close as he wanted to get to heaven right now. He adjusted the power levers for intermediate cruise, punched on the autopilot, set the heading bug to 350° and selected altitude hold.

Svensson finally found his voice. "That was really too close for comfort."

"*Ya-haw*," Rameros responded with a mock Swedish inflection, "very, very close, but that is all history now, BJ. How about you take over in the cockpit, monitor the autopilot, and be sure we stay in the clouds for awhile. That Gulfstream will no longer be a problem for us." He slid back his seat and unbuckled his safety belts. "I am going aft to relax for a bit, finish my cigar, and chat with our two friends in the cabin who probably think they have been to hell and back."

THIRTY-SIX

Pier Sixty-Six Marina

Inside the plush main cabin of the Hatteras, Sammy and Rick settled into swivel chairs to the right of the table; Kelly and John took positions in chairs on the left side.

"A beer?" Kelly asked Rick, whose eyes were taking in the impressive layout of the cabin.

"Uh, no thanks. After last night, I think it would be best to wait a tad longer before I have one."

"Okay, first things first," Sammy abruptly began the discussion in a serious business-like tone, looking Rick straight in the eye. "Much of what we're going to disclose to you is privileged information. Likewise, I'm sure that some of the things you have to say should be viewed as privileged as well. So, we all agree that what is said stays among us and remains confidential regardless of whether or not any transaction evolves. Agreed?"

It was unanimous.

John Andreas opened a stowage compartment and began placing several thick three-ring binders onto the table. Rick quietly watched. The binders were prominently identified: BA-23; SA-227; RA-100. All had the same descriptive element in common: the letters POH written across the covers in large bold type. Rick immediately knew that these were the Pilot Operating Handbooks of the three aircraft types that were seriously being considered: the BASA Avio-23; the Fairchild-Swearingen Aviation Metroliner; the RioAero WindStar.

"I'm impressed," Rick said. "It looks like you've been doing your homework." He knew that it was difficult—virtually impossible—to obtain a complete and current edition of a Pilot Operating Handbook for aircraft of this type and size. Airframe manufacturers simply did not pass these out. And, one could not be ordered unless you actually operated that aircraft itself.

"I suppose you're wondering how we happened to come by these manuals," John said to Rick.

Rick shrugged. "I imagine you do have your sources." He thumbed through the WindStar manual, noticing that various sections were highlighted in yellow. The serial number of the aircraft to which it belonged was redacted. "Yes, this is pretty much the current edition. There's only one minor revision that hasn't been incorporated into it."

"Damn," Kelly Long said with a snicker, "we'll have to get a partial refund for that."

"Still," Sammy interjected with a raised eyebrow, "our comparative analysis shouldn't be compromised, right?"

Rick nodded in agreement. "It should not."

"Okay, Mr. Harris…" Sammy took back the lead in the discussion. "Our conclusion is that any of these three aircraft can give us what we need. They all have strengths and weaknesses. All of them, except for the brand-new WindStar, have track records that detail their economics. All of them, except for the WindStar, have comprehensive support programs in place. All of them, except for the WindStar, have highly attractive acquisition programs. All of them—"

"Sammy," Rick broke in, "this is our first real sit-down on the WindStar. I know what Fairchild can offer. I know their aircraft inside and out. Remember, I used to work for Fairchild. I sold the Metro to operators up and down the east coast. The Metro is a fine aircraft, but it's no WindStar." Rick paused.

The group remained silent, awaiting his further comments.

"As for the Avio-23," Rick continued, "BASA makes a rugged aircraft. They've been in the airframe business for half a century. But BASA is not in the same class as RioAero. BASA is a company mired in stagnation. The Avio-23 is basically a low-tech commercial variant of a highly successful military aircraft. Neither Fairchild nor BASA are best suited for your combined operation." Rick smiled confidently at Sammy.

There was dead silence within the cabin of the Hatteras.

"What combined operation?" John Andreas asked.

Rick smiled again. "The one that you three are putting together."

"That's news to us," Kelly Long chimed in.

Sammy Santelli's face remained expressionless.

"Look," Rick said, individually making eye contact with each of the three, "I've known you gentlemen for a good number of years. So, when I see you all sit down together with an aircraft salesman to discuss what he has to offer…well, something's up. You don't have to be a Rhodes Scholar to figure that out. Remember, we agreed that everything discussed today is held in the strictest confidence."

"Okay, okay," Sammy finally said, shaking his head, "you're a perceptive man, Mr. Harris. What you've surmised is very true. We're combining forces. We made it official—handshakes and all—last night shortly after our dinner with you and Gail. We would have broken the news to you within the next ten minutes, but you've already figured it out and beat us to the punch."

"Sorry," Rick said, shrugging apologetically, "I had no intention to upstage your announcement. My apologies."

"Accepted without prejudice," Sammy granted.

"So now," Rick said, trying to suppress a wide grin, "how many aircraft do you gentlemen need and how soon?"

Sammy looked over to John and Kelly. They both nodded in agreement to forge ahead. "I'm glad you're sitting down. This could knock you off your feet." Sammy paused for effect. "How about twenty firm at a rate of two a month. And, of course, we'll need options—two groups of twenty. Our program plans call for those additional forty aircraft to be phased in during years two and three. Beyond that, it's a crapshoot...too hard to pin down an accurate number. And just for your information, we all feel fairly confident that the first option will be exercised some six months after we combine our operations."

Rick was caught totally off-guard by the magnitude of the transaction. He had hoped for ten firm, with ten options. A sixty aircraft deal was beyond his wildest imagination. He sat in stunned silence.

Sammy and the others waited for his reaction.

"Pretty damn aggressive," Rick finally said.

"Yes it is," Sammy acknowledged, "but it's also very realistic. Our three airlines currently operate over thirty aircraft. All of them are programmed for replacement under our business plan. As we expand, additional equipment will be needed."

Rick grimaced.

Sammy noticed and anticipated the concern. "Don't worry," he said, "we're not asking you to take in our old equipment. We feel we can do a better job ourselves in unloading our current fleet. We know how much airframe manufacturers hate to take on the responsibility of remarketing trade-ins. Undervaluation is rampant. We'd be shortchanged."

"Good," Rick said in relief. What Sammy had said was very true. Changing the subject, he asked, "By the way, have you divulged all of this to BASA and Fairchild?"

"No, no, we have not met with the other manufacturers as a group, only individually. Even then, my interest was only for five with options for five. Kelly and John never mentioned any numbers...just were chumming the waters to see what the sales guys would offer."

"I see." Rick was pleased knowing he had an edge on the competition, at least for now. "So, my good friends, since we're all dealing the cards face up, let me tell you what I can do. I'm going straight to the bottom line. I don't expect to have a second chance. I know how far I can go without getting canned or queering the deal. I'm willing to go that far. I need to sell airplanes as badly as you need to acquire them. And from what I gather so far, you've decided that the WindStar will perform well on your proposed route system.

Indeed, with the POH that you have, I'm sure your analysis is accurate. What you don't know about, however, are the economic enhancements I can offer—how I can make the WindStar even more attractive than it already is. Let me explain."

Rick was prepared to take as long as was needed to detail his aircraft acquisition program, a program he had spent nearly four weeks developing, nurturing along, and revising. The program he was authorized to set forth for a major fleet order involved elements never before offered by any manufacturer of this airframe class. Rick had made it aggressive. He knew he needed to be able to beat the competition on every avenue. He also knew it had to be realistic from RioAero's perspective. His company could not survive by giving aircraft away to flakes, only to later see defaults on lease or loan payments. He needed solid customers with sound business plans. He personally knew that Sammy, Kelly, and John were the type of operators he sought. Their merger plan made sense. He was sure that the business plan they would soon share with him would be sound. Rick Harris had to make the sale. He was confident he would.

He reached into his briefcase and pulled out a file folder. It was unmarked. From within the folder he distributed three copies of a four-page proposal to those he believed would be his next customers. The document was simply labeled "Model Airline Fleet Purchase." There was no mention of RioAero or the WindStar, only key elements of the deal. Rick wanted it that way. He always guarded against the possibility of a document like this falling into the wrong hands—the competition. This way, only those to whom he made his presentation would actually know what it was all about. Copies that might find their way to Fairchild or BASA would be meaningless—generic and could have been written by anyone.

As his audience studied the document, Rick made some brief comments. "Our financing is through a subsidized Brazilian export program called FINEX and is administered by *Banco do Brasil*. It is tied to LIBOR, the London InterBank Offered Rate, and not the U.S. prime rate. Currently, on a debt-financed program over seven years, you're looking at 8.75 percent. And, that's without any personal guarantees on your part. If you want a longer term, several financial institutions are willing to take our program and repackage it with one of their own and go ten or twelve years."

"Most other financing programs are at rates fifty percent higher than yours," Kelly Long commented.

"Even higher than that," Santelli corrected Long.

"I know," Rick responded, "and the competition is teed off at us for what they can't offer. They wish RioAero didn't exist. But we're here, and we're here to stay. So, they better sharpen their pencils and get used to some healthy competition."

"And, the down payments?" John Andreas asked.

"Under the program I just detailed, it's fifteen percent. Add a full percentage point to the interest rate, and only five percent down is required.

"WOW!" Andreas was taken back.

"But, that's only part of our package," Rick continued. "We've taken a few lessons from the big boys who sell heavy iron to the major airlines. We're offering cost guarantees that the competition won't even discuss."

Kelly asked: "You mean ASM guarantees?"

"In a way, yes," Rick went on, "but we instead use aircraft flight hour costs, which from a manufacturer's perspective, more accurately reflect the cost of aircraft operations. You can easily derive an Available Seat Mile (ASM) cost from our flight hour scenario. Of course, we're only talking about direct costs involving airframe operation, not pilots, administration, insurance, or the like. Also, fuel costs are not guaranteed, only fuel burn per flight hour, since oil prices could skyrocket tomorrow."

"Very fair, very attractive," Kelly admitted. "But how long is the guarantee period?"

"So long as the aircraft is operated under our FAA approved inspection program by the original airline…seven years."

"And, what if the guaranteed costs are exceeded?"

"We pay you."

"In cash?"

"Sort of…" Rick began to explain. "You keep an accurate monthly record of all expenses for each aircraft and submit it to us on at least a quarterly basis. If our guarantee is exceeded, we will credit your account with us toward the purchase of spare parts you obtain from us."

"No cash?"

"No cash." Rick was adamant. "We want to be sure that our aircraft are properly maintained in the event that payments in excess of the guarantee are required. Spare parts credits help do that. Cash has a way of being redirected away from aircraft operations. You know: setting up new stations; advertising; administration; indirect this and that."

"Understandable," Kelly confessed. "Cash does have a way of mysteriously disappearing."

"That's right, Kelly." Rick was pleased with the way the discussion was going. He smiled to himself as he prepared to further drive his point home on how an airline should select its equipment. He knew this would further bolster his case for the WindStar. "Most airlines acquire equipment—ground equipment as well as flight equipment—without truly considering the overall impact on the operation. When it's necessary to procure this or that, there are presentations from vendors, time necessary to play with the numbers, moaning and groaning for some deal concessions, and finally, after perhaps months and months of negotiations, a new fuel tender, a tug, an airplane, or whatever is bought. Despite the lengthy process, a flaw in the decision-making will usually come to light.

"Sure, when it comes to aircraft, what has been selected typically is able to do the job. But simply doing the job of carrying passengers on a route system is not enough. Aircraft are like busses with wings. Or, like conveyor belts that carry buckets filled with sand—but instead of sand, hopefully the seats are filled with passengers. An airline can be compared to a factory—a factory in the sky. However, unlike factories that contain costs to the penny, small commuter and regional airlines have not pressed their vendors for comprehensive financing programs and cost assurances. RioAero took that proactive initiative. We analyzed every component on the WindStar. We pressed our vendors for MTBF (Mean Time Between Failures) guarantees and imposed financial penalties for under-performing. If anyone knows what an aircraft can do from both performance and cost perspectives, it's the manufacturer. My company doesn't just sell or lease you an aircraft, we provide you with the capacity and capability you need, and at a known cost of operation."

"You'll undoubtedly be starting a trend, Mr. Harris," John Andreas noted.

"Yes indeed," Rick responded, "and that's exactly how aircraft should be sold in the future. Airline deregulation is new. Regional airlines are young. But as regional airlines become more sophisticated, they'll be in a much better position to make demands from their vendors for the types of things that are currently unobtainable. Regionals will be able to get the same types of things the majors can get from Boeing or McDonnell Douglas."

Rick spent the next forty-five minutes addressing a variety of items about which Kelly and John continued to quiz and probe him: training; route proving; maintenance; tech reps; spares inventory; consignments. Then noticing that the other man present had remained silent for longer than usual, Rick directed his attention to Sammy Santelli, who had just finished his third beer and fifth cigarette. Sammy was now once again carefully reviewing the document Rick had passed out during the beginning of the discussion.

"What do you think, Sammy?" Rick asked.

"Sounds good, so far. But I can only come closer to a decision after I've had that flight demonstration you promised me."

"Why certainly," Rick said, "that goes without saying." He paused, weighing John and Kelly's enthusiasm and animation during the discussion with Santelli's silence. Something was wrong— something was troubling Sammy. Or maybe his behavior was a negotiating ploy. "So, Sammy, what else would you like to know about the WindStar or RioAero?"

"Oh, I'm sure there are a thousand things that we could talk about," Sammy said off-handedly. "Your program has merit, it seems rather attractive. I can guarantee you that its consideration is a top agenda item for us."

It was not Santelli's words that unsettled Rick, it was more how the words were spoken. Maybe it was nothing, but Rick could not take the chance of missing a critical clue to landing the deal. An unspoken objection or an erroneous perception from a customer was something vital to know. And, Rick did not have the time to nuance an understanding.

"Okay, Sammy," Rick said, probing for an explanation of what he had read between Santelli's spoken words, "I know there are a thousand things that need to be addressed. This will be done. There's plenty of time for that. Aircraft deals are much more complex than what can be put on a few sheets of paper. But for now, I want you to be perfectly honest with me. I sense there's something important that we need to discuss today, rather than tomorrow or next week. What might that be?"

Sammy got to his feet, turned away from the group, and walked a few steps to the galley. He opened the refrigerator door, pulled out two beers, and slipped each one snugly into a slim leather cozy with a Hatteras emblem on it. After removing the tops, he returned, reseated himself, and handed one of the bottles to Rick. "I think it's time for a drink, my friend."

Obligingly, Harris took a small quick swallow from the mouth of the thin-walled amber bottle.

"Yes," Santelli finally admitted to Rick's question, "I do have a few problems. And like you, I'm going to lay the cards face up."

"Good." Rick Harris sat back into his chair. Though he hoped he could adequately address whatever was troubling Sammy, he could not be sure.

"To be honest, Rick, my main problem deals with betting our brand-new airline on a brand-new aircraft manufactured by a relatively young company like RioAero. What compounds the problem is that that company is located in a third world country which is currently having some serious economic difficulties."

Rick knew exactly what Sammy was saying. Brazil's hyperinflation and corrupt military government were no secret. The country's stability could certainly be questioned.

"Now don't get me wrong," Santelli continued, "from the research that we've already done on your aircraft and from what we have heard from you today, it looks like you have a winner with the WindStar. But I feel ill-at-ease putting so many of our eggs into one basket. With Boeing, it might be okay; with RioAero, it's a different story."

Sammy lit up yet another cigarette. Rick and the others silently let Sammy carry on.

Santelli nodded twice. "Maybe I'm just over-reacting, maybe not, but that gear-up incident disturbs me. And somehow, I have a feeling it's not the only inexplicable incident that the WindStar could endure." He took a shallow drag from his cigarette and quickly exhaled. "I don't know, Rick...I just don't feel I can jump on your bandwagon quite yet."

This was exactly what Rick Harris had feared most. Skepticism. Lack of confidence. And worse, the inability to adequately address Santelli's concerns. His mind shifted into high gear trying to find placating words. His mental focus was rapt on searching for anything to keep Sammy and the others in his camp. He found only a void. Helpless. No resolution; no ready response to be offered. His pulse pounded.

Kelly Long echoed Sammy's concerns, "Have you been able to determine the cause of yesterday's gear up incident?"

Rick clutched the beer bottle in his right hand and took a long swallow from it as he tried to time his response. Unfortunately, before he could respond, John Andreas chimed in with what seemed to be an innocuous follow-up. To Rick, however, the question was as devastating as an atomic bomb.

John asked: "Have there been any other inexplicable incidents with the WindStar since its certification?"

It was almost as if Rick had had a virtual rug pulled out from under his feet. He saw the very deal he was trying to weave—the one that could save his company—begin to unravel before his very eyes. It seemed now as though he had never had a chance, even from the beginning. His earlier confidence now seemed as ethereal as a shimmering mirage, ever so promising, ever so elusive, then totally vanishing...never to reappear.

A weighty silence fell over the group. Rick could hear the pounding of his own heart...lub-dub, Lub-Dub, LUB-DUB. Barely breathing, he consciously began trying to control his rate of breath. Slowly. Deeply. His bare feet suddenly chilled and clammy. His racing mind flashed back to earlier that morning and his horseback ride in the pasture. He remembered the sound of the faint roar from a distant airliner spooling up its engines for a power-on approach to FLL. He recalled the glint of its highly polished aluminum skin being as brilliant as a star in the morning sky. Suddenly narrowed, his field of vision darkened at the edges. His body unconsciously tensed—muscles contracting. His right arm dramatically, involuntarily, abruptly extended. He felt pain shoot through his right hand as his wrist glanced off the edge of the table. There was an accompanying sharp splintering sound as if his life's work was audibly exploding before the assembled group.

The beer bottle had shattered.

"GODDAMN," Santelli shouted. "You okay?"

Kelly used a towel from the galley to mop up the flow of beer. John grabbed a second towel from a stowage compartment. Startled back to reality, Rick looked at his hand. There was no blood. There were no cuts. The leather cozy Sammy had provided to insulate the bottle had contained the sharp glass fragments.

"Sorry," Rick said, now totally back in the moment, keenly embarrassed about what had just happened.

"Was it something we said?" Kelly asked, angling for some levity.

Rick slowly shook his head from side to side. Then with a frustrated laugh and after a deep inhalation, he said, "Nobody ever said selling airplanes was an easy job."

Sammy reassuringly slapped Rick on the back. "Okay, my friend, tell me what's going on...what's the deal?"

Rick quickly returned, "Sammy, the deal is a pretty damn big deal. Every hour it seems to be getting bigger."

Confusion silenced the group.

"We've got some cards on the table, but let me spread out the entire deck of cards, face up." Rick paused, briefly rubbing his sore, but uninjured right hand. The last thing in the world he wanted to do was reveal the problems that the WindStar had experienced over the past twenty-four hours; but now, he felt there was no alternative. "What I am about to disclose to you is extremely confidential. Some of it, though, is only still speculation. Please bear with me and hear me out. I think you need to know what's going on. I owe it to you."

Rick reprised the scenario he had presented to Tommy Maxwell just a few hours earlier. His three friends listened intently. When he had finished, there were silent nods. Everyone realized the gravity of the situation into which Rick, and now they, had been thrust.

"So, what are you asking us to do?" Sammy supportively asked.

"Just keep an open mind," Rick responded. "But please know that the WindStar is a sound and uncompromised aircraft. Someone or some group yet to be identified—people, organizations, working together or independently, I don't know which—are attempting to covertly sabotage my aircraft and my company. I have instigated initiatives to uncover the perpetrator. The problem will be resolved shortly. Perhaps by the end of this weekend. At least, that's what I'm shooting for."

"Fine," Sammy said, "we'll see you through on this."

"Good." Rick was relieved. "Now, about the demo. A second aircraft is flying up from Brazil as we speak. It's scheduled to arrive sometime late Sunday morning. I have some things to attend to prior to that, but would like you all to join me at my ranch for lunch. After that, we can head out for that demo flight. I'll have Gail, my wife, pick you up at the marina. How does 11:15 sound?"

The staggered response of agreement followed only a slight pause.

Sammy Santelli escorted Rick to the stern of the boat and then up onto the dock. While Harris pulled on his socks and slipped into his boots, Sammy again sincerely thanked him for the candor during the discussions.

As Rick Harris walked alone down the pier toward the marina's parking lot, doubts preyed upon his mind. He knew major obstacles had to be overcome before he could finalize the most important aircraft deal of his life. He had successfully dealt with customer skepticism before. But this time, he was doubting himself. Was he trying to move too quickly? Could he be risking his life, and the lives of others, with an aircraft that was compromised? He tried unsuccessfully to shake off these troubling thoughts. Was Rick Harris only fooling himself because he had bet his career on a company that was in the throes of economic disaster and an aircraft that seemed programmed for failure?

He walked on.

THIRTY-SEVEN

Destination: Georgetown

T he WindStar forged ahead surrounded by the security of clouds. There were no complaints about the choppy ride created by intermittent jolts of turbulence.

Svensson verified the aircraft's position and again recomputed his previous estimates for crossing enroute fixes. He monitored the weather radar, making occasional deviations from course to avoid moderate precipitation. His routine actions belied the fact that this was one flight he would never in his life forget. Never.

Just before the WindStar crossed the Acarai Mountains and entered Guyana airspace, Svensson contacted Georgetown Approach Control—standard procedure for a routine descent into Georgetown. It was over, he kept reassuring himself in relief, yet he still could not shake the terror out of his mind. He kept thinking about the missile attack. He was unable to stop himself from wondering if any other plots against the WindStar could be lurking ahead in Georgetown.

Franco Rameros finally re-entered the cockpit. "Our passengers are obviously a bit shaken up, but otherwise doing just fine." He reseated himself behind the controls.

"Do you think we really should continue on to Georgetown?" Svensson inquired.

"Good point, BJ. The bad guys may have devised a backup plan just in case the missile attack failed. Cartels are pretty smart these days. Gone are the times when their ranks were comprised of only lowbrow thugs. Indeed, a surprise very well may be planned for us when we land at Georgetown."

"That is exactly what I was thinking."

Rameros reflected for a moment and then continued, "But if they are that smart, they also might figure that we could divert to neighboring Suriname. So, heading there might be a catch-22 situation."

Svensson was at a loss for a response.

Rameros entered 123.0 into COM-2.

"Good idea," Svensson remarked, noting the use of the air-to-ground frequency typically tuned in for aircraft service communication at Tower controlled airports.

"Georgetown Unicom," Rameros began, "this is Learjet November-Triple-Two-Charlie." The misidentification an intentional subterfuge to avoid identifying himself as piloting a WindStar.

"Learjet calling Georgetown, go ahead."

"Triple-Two-Charlie is estimating Georgetown at zero-five, requesting a quick turnaround with Jet-A, over."

"Roger, Learjet Triple-Two-Charlie, we cannot—repeat, CANNOT—accommodate your request. Our Jet-A and avgas fuel tenders became inoperative earlier this afternoon. We apologize for not being able to service your aircraft."

Rameros laughed aloud. "Sonovabitch, those Colombian bastards are pretty thorough!"

Svensson nodded.

Rameros keyed his mic, saying, "Thanks for the info, Georgetown, Triple-Two-Charlie, out." He turned to Svensson. "Glad we checked in with Georgetown. Landing there would have cost us at least the night. Certainly, without taking on fuel, we could not have departed for anywhere." He paused, briefly. "And, there also could have been some additional surprises that I do not even want to ponder."

"So now, on to Suriname?" Svensson inquired.

"I am afraid so." Rameros bit his lip in concentration. He glanced at the enroute chart. "Cayenne..." he hesitated, glancing at the fuel gauges and digital fuel-used indicator. "No, French Guiana will be pressing our range."

"Any problem with Suriname?"

"Yes, our timing is not quite right to pay a visit there." He pursed his lips in frustration. "Anyway, there is no other choice."

Suriname, formerly Dutch Guiana, had only been five years independent when, in early 1980, the country's elected government was overthrown by a group of sixteen noncommissioned officers. The usurpers quickly seized control of the government, suspended the constitution, and abolished the legislature. The new regime now ruled by decree. Although a civilian filled the post of president, a military man named Desi Bouterse actually ruled the country.

"What do you mean?" Svensson asked. "Bad timing?"

"Remember my earlier comment about some small politically unstable countries in South America?"

"Yes."

"Well, Suriname is one of those countries. In fact, Suriname takes the cake. Do not be surprised if you see a bunch of kids with machine guns crawling all over the airport." Rameros momentarily paused. "Not sure which is worse, a Gulfstream with missiles or a bunch of kids with itchy trigger fingers."

"Any alternatives?"

"Afraid not, we are pretty much committed to landing in Suriname. Our refueling stop there should be very interesting to say the least."

THIRTY-EIGHT

RioAero, NA

Rick Harris weaved the old Chevy through the RioAero parking lot's maze of lush landscaped medians. He stopped at the access gate to the restricted Aircraft Operations Area, punched his password into the keypad, and watched the fifteen-foot wide gate jerk open to the left. As he drove through the open gateway toward the new hangar, he gritted his teeth. Regardless of how he tried, he simply could not shake the memory of his consternation at the meeting earlier that afternoon on Sammy Santelli's sportfisherman. It kept replaying over and over in his mind.

"Damn," he blurted out, sharply striking the steering wheel with the palm of his left hand. "I will not lose this sale...not to Fairchild...not to BASA...not to anyone." He took a deep breath attempting to regain his composure.

Although Rick had identified other prospects for the WindStar, those deals would take time to bring to fruition. Unfortunately, Rick Harris did not have time on his side. Santelli's decision regarding the WindStar needed to occur within days, rather than weeks or months. That determination would either place the WindStar on firm-footing within the airline industry or result in strengthening a competitor to a position untouchable by RioAero. Rick knew that penetrating the North American market was crucial. The long-term success of his aircraft and his company depended on it. He also knew he had a long, long way to go in convincing Sammy Santelli to bet an airline on a new aircraft from a young company in a country that was on the verge of economic disaster.

Still, for Rick's sales efforts to be relevant at all, his first critical mission was to resolve the issue of inexplicable incidents befalling the WindStar. He somehow had to unravel what he was sure was a coordinated web of sabotage that imminently threatened not only the WindStar, but the very existence of RioAero itself. And, that had to be done quickly—very quickly.

Rick pulled the Chevy into the open hangar and out of the mid-afternoon sun. Shutting off the engine, he left the truck and strode toward the hapless WindStar. Even though its gear had now been extended, three huge screw jacks were needed to support the aircraft above the hangar floor. The damage was frightfully obvious. Lower tips of both four-bladed propellers were badly bent. The lower fuselage antennas had been crushed. Gear doors were mangled. The airstair door was nearly twisted off its hinged attached point. Altogether, a sad sight.

The sound of a Delta L-1011 just lifting off from Runway 9-L slowed Harris' pace and turned him back toward the hangar entrance. The thundering sound of its three powerful engines sent him into a brief reverie. He thought how much easier his life would have been had he chosen to fly for the major airlines rather than sell aircraft. Airline captains received extremely generous compensation without facing the day-to-day realities of Rick's life: no tension; no stress; no possibility of failed deals; and, plenty of time off to pursue other interests. He brusquely shook off the thought and turned again toward the WindStar. Deep in his heart he knew that spending a good part of his life as a left-seat robot in a heavy jet would never have been the fulfilling profession, at least not for him.

"*Hola*, Rick." It was Joey Delgada rounding from the back of the WindStar.

Rick grinned as Joey approached. They shook hands. "How goes it, my friend?"

"Actually fairly well, now that the dust has settled." Joey smiled. "The damage is not all that bad, even with a screw jack penetrating a fuel tank."

"That's certainly good to hear." Rick's eyes scanned the WindStar, then he glanced back toward Joey. "How did Big Lou take the news?"

"Well," Delgada groaned, "as you can imagine, he was not pleased. I spoke with him just after we got the WindStar into the hangar. I really hated the idea of calling him, especially so early in the morning, but it had to be done."

"I'm glad you did," Rick said gratefully. "Most likely because of your call, Big Lou launched Franco Rameros in another WindStar almost immediately. He should be arriving here sometime early Sunday."

"Wow, that is fast."

"Indeed it is, and so fortunate for me. I have a flight demonstration scheduled at high noon on Sunday."

Joey smiled. "Anything serious?"

"Very much so." Rick's response was immediate. "I've got some prospects that are both serious and qualified. But keep it under your hat. The fewer people who know what I'm doing, the better I'll feel. Above all, I certainly don't want Dan Cole meddling around my customers."

"I know what you mean," Joey candidly said. "There is something about that guy. He just appears from out of nowhere to become managing director of this division. Nobody really understands why he is here." Joey slowly shook his head. "Rick, I just do not trust that man. Anyway, did you say something? Hell, I have already forgotten what you just said." He flashed a quick wink at Rick.

"Good." Rick smiled. "Oh, by the way, Rameros is bringing up some spare parts and a couple of engineers to help you get this bird back in the air."

"Great, I will accept all the help I can get."

"Okay, now here's the question of the hour," Rick said, changing the subject. He really wanted to hear Joey's analysis of the gear up occurrence. "Have you been able to determine the cause of last night's incident?"

Joey shook his head in dejection. "No, and that troubles me. Everything seems normal. At this point, I have no clue as to why the gear collapsed."

"Hmmm...." Rick was surprised. Joey should have immediately identified the anomalies in the cockpit that both Rick and Gail had seen just after the incident. "Tell me," Harris probed, "did you observe anything strange in the cockpit?"

"Strange?" Joey furrowed his brow.

"Yes, different...unusual...abnormal."

"No." Joey seemed perplexed.

"Nothing?"

"Like I said, Rick, everything was normal. Why? What are you getting at?"

"Let's take another look inside the cockpit." Rick motioned toward the aircraft. "Is it safe to climb aboard?"

"Sure, just standby for a second."

Joey was eager for any leads Rick might provide to solve the riddle of what had caused the incident. Delgada walked over to the moveable metal stairway that a mechanic had earlier used to inspect the propeller hub assembly. He rolled the steel-grated structure over to the main entrance door and locked its wheels in place. The two men climbed aboard the aircraft and seated themselves in the cockpit—Joey in the right seat, Rick in the left seat.

Rick glanced at the gear handle. Unlike the last time that he and Gail were in the aircraft, it was now in the down position. Understandable, he thought. It had to be placed in that position for the gear to be currently extended. Then, he focused upon the small red cover that guarded the gear downlock override switch. He could not believe what his eyes saw. His face was immediately cast into surprise and concern.

Joey noticed. "What is it?"

Rick shook his head. "Did your guys just put new safety wire on the gear override switch guard?"

"Huh?"

Rick repeated himself.

"Hell no, why would we bother to do that?" Joey was somewhat annoyed by Rick's cross-examination. The question did not make any sense.

"Please bear with me," Rick said, brushing aside Joey's irritation. "Last night, just after the incident, when you left with the injured technician, Gail and I went back into the aircraft to try and figure out why things went wrong. While sitting in the cockpit, we noticed that the gear handle was in the up position." Rick paused, glancing at a totally shocked, but silent Joey Delgada. "But what's worse," Rick continued, "we—actually Gail—noticed the override switch. Its guard wasn't safety-wired, and when we looked closer, we found that the switch was positioned to the ARM mode."

"That cannot be so." Joey paled. "Before the AeroMech people arrived and before we moved the aircraft into the hangar, I personally checked the cockpit. I am positive the gear selector was in the down position at that time. And, I distinctly remember checking the override switch guard. It was wired."

"I'm not saying that's not what you found," Rick went on, "but if the override switch was in the ARM position and if the gear selector was in the up position, wouldn't that have caused a gear retraction if someone flipped on the master power switch?"

"Absolutely. With residual pressure contained in the accumulators of the hydraulic system, the gear would retract and the aircraft would crash to the ground."

"I'm afraid that's exactly what happened last night."

"Are you serious?" Joey was incredulous.

"Dead serious," Rick sadly confirmed. "After we entered the aircraft last night to give Gail the cook's tour, you went up into the cockpit, flipped on the master power switch and turned on the cabin lights for us. Almost immediately, I heard a groaning grinding sound that was the gear beginning to retract. You, like me, didn't connect what was happening until it was too late."

Joey looked long and hard at Rick's facial expressions. "Okay, Rick, say I believe you, but who put the gear selector in the up position, removed the safety wire from the override switch guard, and then armed it to override the squat switches? Who would have made the WindStar an accident waiting to happen? Why? And then, how did the switches get back to the normal positions?"

"Fair, those are the tough questions I'm wrestling with, Joey. And while I do have a very strong suspicion about the 'who' is behind all of this, I can't answer the question 'why,' not just yet. When all the pieces of the puzzle come together, I guarantee that you'll be among the first to know. In the meantime, be careful. Strange and inexplicable things have already happened to the WindStar, more could be on the way." Rick paused. "By the way, did Big Lou mention the double prop separation incident that Rameros experienced?"

Joey painfully nodded.

"Add to that the suspicious electrical problem I had just before landing here yesterday afternoon."

Joey shook his head in frustration. Unfortunately, he could think of only one possible explanation for the chain of apparently unrelated events. "You are thinking sabotage," he flatly stated.

"That's my best guess for now." Rick crossed his arms and slowly swiveled his head first to the left, then to the right, trying to ascertain if their conversation was truly private. "Don't mention a word of this to anyone." He paused briefly and lowered his voice. "I just retained the services of a high-tech PI. We have a plan to get to the bottom of everything. In the meantime, there could be more sabotage efforts. Keep a sharp lookout for any unfamiliar people in and around the hangar."

Joey nodded again.

"I know I don't really have to say it, but before you release this aircraft back into service—"

"Worry not, Mr. Harris, I will be sure to disable the override switch."

Rick flashed Joey an approving smile. "Okay, then, I'm off to tidy up my desk a bit and try to sell some airplanes."

THIRTY-NINE

Destination: Suriname

N ow two hundred-twenty nautical miles southwest of the capital city of Paramaribo, home to over half of the Suriname's entire population, the WindStar was soon to make its initial contact with Zanderij Approach Control.

"Well, well, well," the upbeat Franco Rameros said over the cockpit intercom to his copilot, "Zanderij, here we come."

Svensson, still not fully recovered from the near-deadly experience over the Amazon region with the missile equipped Gulfstream jet, forced a weak smile in response.

It was not so much that Franco Rameros looked forward to landing in Suriname, for indeed he did not. Rameros was very much ill-at-ease with the recent military *coup d'etat* and the resultant uncertainties the event had created within the country. He did, however, look forward to exiting the aircraft and stretching his legs. Four hours were long enough for him to be wrapped in an aluminum tube with wings.

Over the cockpit intercom, he said to Svensson, "Before we say hello to Approach Control, we should check in with Zanderij Unicom and relay our refueling request. Why not give the call, BJ?" Rameros wanted to refocus his young copilot's attention from past events to the present.

Svensson twisted 123.0 into COM-2 and made a transmission.

There was no response.

A second transmission was made.

Still, there was no response from Zanderij on the Unicom frequency.

Puzzled, Svensson shook his head, shrugged, and turned to Rameros for advice.

"Eh," Rameros nonchalantly grunted in reply, "an FBO does not always monitor the Unicom frequency, especially if airport activity is really slow." He glanced at his watch. "Besides, it is dinnertime down there. The line chief is probably holed up somewhere chowing down."

"Maybe Zanderij will be like Georgetown." The apprehensive copilot rolled his eyes. "Maybe there is no Jet-A available there either."

"Try to be positive, BJ," Rameros cautioned.

"I know I should," Svensson sadly agreed after a deep inhale, "but I guess I am still wired about nearly being blown out of the sky over the Amazon."

"Understandable, that was a close one. But remember, BJ, when you are with the general—General Franco da Silva Rameros—everything will turn out just fine. Guaranteed!" Rameros gave a confident laugh. "Not to worry, there will be fuel at Zanderij. There is power in positive thinking."

A sheepish grin slowly crept across Svensson's face. "You are probably right, Franco. And, after what we have been through, refueling should be a non-event. If we can elude two Sidewinder missiles, fueling in Suriname should definitely be a cakewalk."

Positive thinking aside, Rameros knew there was not enough fuel in the tanks to take the WindStar anywhere else. They were committed to landing at Zanderij International Airport, like it or not. He paused long enough to attach an approach chart to the clip on his control yoke, then further remarked to Svensson, "Okay, even though nobody seems to be at home on the Unicom frequency, I am sure we can scare someone up at Approach Control." He switched to COM-1 and keyed his mic. "Zanderij Approach," he spoke slowly and distinctly, very much aware that English could be a distant second language to the controller, "WindStar Papa-Tango-Sierra-Bravo-Yankee, one-niner-zero miles southwest, Flight Level two-three-zero, landing Zanderij."

"Good evening, WindStar Bravo-Yankee," the controller came back immediately and very clearly with a smooth British East Indian accent, "cruise seven thousand, altimeter three-zero-zero-five, wind calm, expect a visual to Runway One-One." The controller paused with an open mic. "Why do you come to Zanderij?"

Very interesting, Rameros thought. An articulate British-educated controller was rather uncommon for a lower-echelon third world country like Suriname. But what he found even more curious was the controller's query: *Why do you come to Zanderij?* It was highly unusual. Indeed, controllers never—NEVER—asked pilots the "why" about an intended destination.

"They damn well better have fuel," Rameros muttered to no one in particular. Keying the mic, he responded to the controller, "Roger, Zanderij, we are out of two-three-zero for seven." He paused with his mic still open. "Our landing is for refueling only."

"Very well, Sierra-Bravo-Yankee," the controller came back, "have you checked in with Unicom?"

"We tried, but were unable to raise them on the frequency."

"I will see what I can do. Please guard the Unicom frequency. Report the airport in sight to the Tower."

"Roger."

As Rameros released his mic button, a clearly relieved Svensson extolled, "He seems like a very helpful controller. Maybe Suriname is not quite as bad as you have made it out to be."

Rameros did not want Svensson to be apprehensive. "Perhaps I was wrong in painting such a glum picture." But the landing in Suriname was a concern. Ramereos had read PIREPS (Pilot Reports) detailing difficulties aircraft crews had had when transiting Suriname. He felt there was a fairly high probability that something could happen at Zanderij. Still, there was no reason to ramp up Svensson's stress level.

As the WindStar began its gradual descent and further penetrated Suriname airspace, the weather markedly improved. Cloud cover rapidly dissipated creating a much more stable atmosphere. The sun slowly began to sink in the western sky. Rays of light diffused. Soon, late afternoon would transition to twilight.

On the overhead panel, Svensson switched on the aircraft position lights and wingtip strobes. He turned on and adjusted the cockpit panel lighting.

Rameros punched off the autopilot. "Go ahead and hand-fly this machine, BJ. You are going to do the entire landing this time. I will advise you as necessary."

"Fine," Svensson happily acknowledged, adjusting the elevator trim for a thousand foot per minute descent.

"Comfortable with night landings?" Rameros asked.

"Absolutely." The chance to focus on the purely mechanical allowed Svensson's can-do attitude to override his earlier apprehension. "I have done a lot of night flying in the factory Navajo."

"Good." Rameros glanced at the approach plate on his yoke. "The runway is fairly long and has an ILS associated with it. You could probably land twice, if you wanted to."

"Once will be fine for me."

The WindStar sliced through a thin cloudbank below as the altimeter momentarily indicated ten thousand feet. The outside light was now reduced by half. The ground and sky were seemingly airbrushed together in shades of gray. Clustered twinkling lights defined the city of Paramaribo in the distance. Thirty miles south of the city, the international airport's rotating beacon lazily projected alternating beams of green and white.

Rameros gave Svensson a thumbs-up and flipped the Tower frequency into COM-1. "WindStar Bravo-Yankee is established on the localizer for Runway One-One at thirty-five DME with the airport in sight."

"Hello again, WindStar Bravo-Yankee," came the same British accented voice. "There is no reported traffic. You are cleared to land Runway One-One...altimeter three-zero-zero-three, wind calm."

"Cleared to land. Thank you, Tower."

The WindStar continued its descent through seven thousand as Svensson eased back the power levers and began slowing the aircraft from its two hundred fifty knot indicated airspeed.

"Okay, BJ, let's see what we are going to do here." Rameros reviewed the approach plate clipped to the control yoke, and then commenced to brief Svensson: "Descend to and maintain four thousand while continuing in on the localizer. Then, extend approach flaps and slow to one-twenty knots. About forty percent torque should be all the power you will need. When the glide slope comes alive, dump the gear. That will help stabilize the aircraft and give you the additional drag you need to follow the glide slope down to the runway with only minor power adjustments."

"That is it?"

"Simple, huh?"

"Sounds simple," Svensson replied, a touch of incredulous in his tone.

"Yes, BJ, the WindStar is a dream to fly. Nonetheless, it is certainly a complex high-performance aircraft, and it does take some training and experience to properly fly. Still, having said that, we designed the aircraft to be as simple and as forgiving as possible. Did not want those low-time regional airline pilots to embarrass themselves too much." Rameros gave a hearty laugh and paused briefly gazing over the nose of the aircraft. "Even though we can clearly see the airport out there, about twenty miles ahead, using a precision instrument approach makes flying to the runway as easy as descending down an imaginary sliding board." He switched on the recessed landing lights located just outside the engine nacelles on the leading edge of each wing. Two shafts of bright white knifed through the dark gray sky that was quickly fading to black.

Svensson leveled the WindStar at the four thousand foot minimum safe sector altitude, added approach flaps and slowed to one hundred twenty knots while continuing inbound on the localizer. The combination of reduced power and decreased airspeed created a relaxing hush within the cockpit. The surrounding air, virtually as smooth as glass, added to the tranquility. It was a moment of calm detachment from the reality of it all—the reality of what could confront them in Zanderij.

When the glide slope indicator came alive, slowly drifting downward toward the mid-point of the HSI, Svensson extended the landing gear. A slight but noticeable bump was felt as powerful hydraulic actuators forced each gear strut to the down and locked position. Closed micro-switches sent electronic signals to the indicator near the gear handle—three small green lights illuminated. Immediately, airflow turbulence created by the drag of the struts and gear doors broke the cockpit's calming silence, though only slightly. The WindStar automatically pitched down in the sea of air, resolutely following the descent path specified by the glide slope.

"Like magic, huh?" Rameros beamed. "Now, all you have to do is go down that imaginary sliding board and the WindStar will pretty much land itself on Runway One-One." He laughed. "Naturally, you will have to make some minor adjustments here and there to keep the aircraft from wandering off course. And, do not forget to cut the power just before the wheels hit the runway. That is it!"

Over the final approach fix, the blue light on the marker beacon receiver began flashing on the instrument panel—first dimly, then more brightly, until fading to dark again. Simultaneous with the flashing light, the sound of the marker beacon's Morse code audio identifier briefly filled the cockpit: *Dah-dah-dah-dah-dah-dah...*

Five miles ahead in the darkness below, the Approach Lighting System (ALS) beckoned the WindStar forward. This Christmas tree-like array of signal lights was rooted at the landing threshold and extended some twenty-five hundred feet into the approach area. Multiple light bars, affixed to metal structures just a few feet off the ground, provided guidance to assist pilots in transitioning from their landing approach to the runway environment. Runway Alignment Indicator Lights (RAILs) sequenced a series of high intensity flashes that created the visual of a high speed ball of light traveling toward the centerline of the runway—twice every second. Runway End Identifier Lights (REILs), located laterally on each side of the runway threshold, repeatedly energized bright white strobes in unison. The runway itself was flanked on both sides with High Intensity Runway Lights (HIRLs), first in white, which changed to yellow in the caution zone at the last two thousand feet, then ending in a glowing bar of red.

"Tower, black the strobes and step two on the lights, please." Rameros requested the lighting intensity be reduced. To Svensson, he added, "That Christmas tree array with the rabbit relentlessly dashing toward the runway is just too annoying, at least for me."

Seconds later, the RAILs and REILs were shut down and the HIRLs were dimmed.

"Thank you," Rameros acknowledged on the Tower frequency.

Slightly over two minutes after passing the final approach fix, the amber light on the marker beacon receiver began flashing on the instrument panel. Its audio identifier fleetingly broadcasted within the cockpit: *Dit-dah, dit-dah, dit-dah, dit-dah...*

"Okay, looking good," Rameros reassuringly said as the WindStar passed the middle marker that was located slightly less than half a mile from the runway threshold. "Now, ease the power back some, and give me a target airspeed of ninety knots."

The WindStar gracefully descended down to the runway touchdown zone with its wingtip strobes pulsating in the early evening's darkness. The aircraft slowed to one hundred knots, gently floating just two feet above the runway. Powerful landing lights cast beams forward, illuminating the marginally maintained asphalt surface.

"Power back and just hold the aircraft off the ground until it settles," Rameros instructed.

Svensson eased the power levers to flight idle and smoothly applied a slight amount of back pressure to the control yoke. But the WindStar continued to float down the runway. He winced, flush with sudden anxiety. The white runway marker lights sped by, soon transitioning to a pale yellow. The distant bar of red lights loomed nearer.

"Power back," Rameros repeated in a more insistent tone of voice.

Tension pressed on Svensson. The power was back, but the aircraft continued to float ahead in ground-effect, unwilling to settle onto the runway. Frustrated, Svensson aggressively pulled back on the power levers once again. Unknowingly, he forced the levers behind the flight idle detent. The engines seemed to momentarily pause, but then groaned with a resonating guttural snarl.

"Goddamn," Rameros moaned, knowing exactly what had happened.

The once idling engines sprang to life. The propellers tore into the air. Yet, the WindStar seemed to have hit a brick wall.

Rameros' right hand swiftly accessed the throttle quadrant. He snapped the power levers forward and out of BJ's white-knuckled grip, advancing the levers from the aft position to just ahead of the flight idle detent. With his left hand, he commandeered the control yoke.

But it was too late.

The aircraft pivoted slightly to the right and descended to the runway like a rock. The nose gear contacted the tarmac first, then the right gear, with left gear following a split second later.

Svensson's pulse pounded. He knew that the aircraft had performed strangely, but he did not know why. From less than two feet above the runway, he had once again setup a firm, aircraft carrier-type landing—solid contact, unnervingly so.

"What ha-happened?" he demanded to know.

Relieved that the aircraft was safely onto the runway, Franco Rameros relaxed his grip on the control yoke and continued to guide the WindStar with the rudder pedals. He let his pent-up breath exhale. "Young man, you are going to make my hair turn white before its time!"

Svensson, confused, remained silent.

"I know you have no idea as to the 'why' of what just happened…" Rameros gathered himself. "Thank God we were just skimming the runway and ready to land anyway." He slowly shook his head. "Let me show you what you just did. Watch my right hand."

The WindStar was now slowed to twenty knots and heading for a taxiway exit. Rameros grasped the power levers and, with one fluid motion, lifted the levers upward and behind the flight idle detent. The engines spit out the same roaring growl as had been heard during Svensson's attempted landing. The propellers clawed the surrounding air. And, the aircraft came to an almost immediate stop without any application of brakes.

"What you did just before touchdown, BJ, was to put the propellers into reverse. Definitely not an approved in-flight procedure."

Svensson cowered.

"An honest mistake due to inexperience," Rameros allowed, "with an outcome of nothing more than a solid landing." He paused, cocking his head to the right, briefly eyeing his young copilot. "At ten or twenty feet above the runway, the result would have been, well, very much different."

Svensson now totally understood what he himself had done and the possible ramifications of his mistake. He bit down on his lower lip, still remaining silent.

"You cannot reverse the props of a Navajo Chieftain," Rameros lectured, "but on turbo-props you can. You just have to remember not to do it in flight. Never lift up on the power levers until the wheels are firmly planted on the ground. That is why there is a detent or stop on the throttle quadrant. It is supposed to prevent an unintentional reversing of the propellers. But, I guess, it is not absolutely failsafe. Worry not, though, had you gone through the factory's two week training program you would have learned all about that."

Svensson grimly nodded an acknowledgement. "But what made the aircraft continue to float down the runway?"

"Aah…." Franco Rameros suddenly realized the "why" of Svensson's actions during the imperfect landing. The crash course Rameros had been giving Svensson in the WindStar had almost become a crash, in fact. "We used only fifteen degrees of flaps, not full flaps as we did in Brasilia. That, combined with a slightly higher airspeed when the WindStar was in ground-effect, made the aircraft feel like it never wanted to land. Now I know why you wrenched back on the power levers as you did."

"Exactly." Svensson said decisively, relieved Rameros did not consider him to be just a fool.

The controller's voice greeted their arrival. "Welcome to Suriname. You are cleared to the ramp, park anywhere you desire."

Rameros acknowledged the clearance and then asked, "Any response on our refueling request?"

"Unable to make contact with line operations," came an immediate reply from the Tower.

Annoyed, Rameros responded with a double-click of his mic button. Indeed, it was not a good sign that even the Tower was unable to reach the FBO.

"Okay, BJ, you have the controls," Rameros said unbuckling his seatbelt and removing his headset. "Just taxi us over to the main ramp and shut us down about fifty feet from the terminal entrance."

Svensson nodded.

The ramp near the terminal was deserted—totally empty. Not an aircraft in sight, no movement of any type. Only a few scattered lights on metal poles illuminated the area.

Rameros left the cockpit, switched on the cabin lighting, and made his way toward the back of the aircraft for a visit with his two engineer passengers. During the hopefully brief time on the ground, he wanted the engineers to perform a detailed walk-around inspection of the WindStar. The unusual flight attitudes over the Amazon might have caused a shift in the cargo or perhaps even overstressed the airframe. The engineers would be able to quickly determine whether or not there was any obvious damage or irregularity.

As Rameros seated himself in the aft section of the cabin and began his conversation in Portuguese, Svensson brought the WindStar to a stop. With condition levers placed into the fuel cut-off position, both engines spooled down and the propellers windmilled. The parking brake was set. After taking a minute to make a few entries in his flight log, Svensson casually exited the cockpit, opened the forward entrance door, and descended down onto the ramp.

In the distance Svensson heard the poorly muffled engine sound of a rapidly approaching vehicle. The sound grew louder, closer. Tires squealed on the pavement. With the screech of well-worn brakes, the vehicle slowed. Suddenly a bright spotlight illuminated, shining directly into his eyes.

Svensson's body froze in the beam.

FORTY

RioAero, NA

"I don't give a rat's ass what the hell he says," Dan Cole shouted into the telephone in his office located the second floor of the Administration Building. "If that sonovabitch doesn't keep his nose out of the project he hired me to ramrod, we're all gonna be in deep shit. Too many things are happening all at once. That's not the way it was planned. We can't afford mistakes. All the money we've been promised won't amount to a damn dime if word gets out and our benefactor is shot dead in the streets of Rio. Have him chill out or we'll all be in big-time trouble." He slammed the phone down into its cradle and glared as his eyes cast up only to see Rick Harris standing in the open doorway. Cole's face reddened. How much of the conversation had Harris overheard?

"Problems, Mister Cole?" Rick slowly sang out as he took two steps into the office and waited for a response.

"What the hell are you doing here?" Cole gruffly bellowed. "Lurking around outside my office, were you?"

"Take it easy, DAN. Remember, I work here too. My office is just down the hallway from yours." Rick smugly strolled over to the two chairs arrayed in front of Cole's desk. "We all know that aircraft sales is a high stress, extremely competitive business. Everybody wants to make the big sale, but everyone won't. Still, Dan, we all have to take things in stride or we'll run out of gas and never hear from the fat lady."

Rick's blithe comments only stoked the simmering rage. Cole snapped back in his typical aggressive style. "What the hell do you know about selling aircraft? I've sold thousands of aircraft in my life. The process has never changed. It's all blood and guts. Nice guys never win a sales campaign. This is war, my boy. And, you're too much of a wuss to know how the real sporty game is played."

In response, Rick calmly selected and settled himself into a chair and crossed his legs. He serenely smiled, mildly amused by Cole's hollow arrogance and futile attempt at baiting.

While Dan Cole was deeply entrenched in the industry, Dan's techniques were from the old school of sales. In many respects, he was the epitome of a used car salesman transplanted into the airframe arena—from the gaudy attire, to the perennial gut-laugh, to the incessant glad-handing. His philosophy was simple: Get in the customer's face and stay there. The more face time you had with a customer, the more likely you would wear them down and close a sale. He told his prospects whatever they wanted to hear. He always presented his aircraft as superior to all the rest, despite any design deficiencies or performance shortcomings. Misrepresentations and outright lies were his stock-in-trade. One time he sold a customer a used Lockheed Electra, and then, in a highly unorthodox move, added outrageous charges for the engines, props, interior and avionics. Amazingly, despite these unsavory tactics, Dan Cole managed to continue to sell airplanes even to customers he had repeatedly duped and abused. The sole reason he was not drummed out of the business was simply because many other aircraft salesmen were just the same. Rick Harris was not.

"A very, very nice office you have, Mister Cole," Rick said toying, feigning being impressed with the surroundings. Harris knew both Cole and his reputation. He had frequently heard stories about the man from other aircraft salesmen as well as airline executives. He had encountered Cole from time to time at industry conventions. Now being eye-to-eye across the desk, Rick felt his garnered knowledge of Cole was far better than Cole would have wanted. Rick's perception of Cole's chameleon personality—how it dramatically morphed according to his audience—was unknown to Cole. When Cole dealt with those viewed as subordinates, Cole was as unabashedly pretentious and disdainful as he was cloying and ingratiating with those he viewed to be above him. In all, Cole was wholly unprincipled, defiantly greedy, and sometimes a dangerous man.

"So, what the hell are you doing here today?" Cole scowled. "I thought you'd still be sleeping off the effects of the partying you did last night at Pier Sixty-Six."

"Pier Sixty-Six, huh?" Rick knew he had mentioned to no one where he and his wife were going to dinner the night before. He was positive about that. "How'd you know I was at Pier Sixty-Six?"

The dilation of Cole's pupils and the momentary shift of his eyes away from Rick spoke volumes. There was an awkward moment of silence in the room. "Well, well you're the one who mentioned it just before you left the airport last night," he blurted out, trying to invent an answer.

"Is that so?"

"Yeah, yeah…" Cole squirmed in his high-back swivel chair. "I even told Retegi that we should go there sometime soon. I hear the place is very nice."

"Indeed, it is," Rick commented and nodded. Then he thought to himself: *You lying bastard…have any friends with a black off-road pickup truck?!*

"Okay..." Cole tried to change the subject hoping it would throw Rick off-balance. "Now, tell me about your prospects."

"What prospects?" Rick answered with a question.

"You know..." The gambit had been unsuccessful and another stumble.

"Huh?" Indeed if Cole had had a spy on Rick, and knew Rick and Gail were at Pier Sixty-Six the night before, Cole also might have received a report that Rick was wining and dining sales prospects. If any of the conversation with Santelli had been overheard, the "prospect" label would apply, even to the untrained ear. However, Rick decided to play dumb. "I'm not sure what you mean, Dan."

"You know, prospects, the ones you hope to sell airplanes to, my boy."

"Dan, I've got to hand it to you," he said, forcing a grin at the man he despised, "you're a very perceptive man."

"Ah-haa..." Cole smiled and began to relax. Rick's apparent compliment fed into Cole's gigantic ego. Cole never even paused to consider if he himself was being played.

Rick stood, ambled toward the wall of windows behind Cole's desk, and gazed out at the airport's runways and taxiways in the distance. "Prospects, huh?" he said, still peering out the windows.

"Yes, prospects, my boy!"

"Well, Mister Cole, if I have prospects, they are exactly that." Rick placed his right hand into his pants pocket and palmed the micro transmitter Tommy Maxwell had given him that morning. Turning away from the windows, he took a few steps back toward Cole, and sat on the edge of the cantilevered desk. Rick gripped the edge of the desk, inclining his body toward Cole. "To be perfectly clear, my prospects are just that—MY prospects." He raised his eyebrows maintaining drilling eye contact with Cole, shrugged, and covertly pressed the bug onto the undersurface of the desk. Caught in Rick's hard stare, Cole was oblivious.

"Now, now, Mister Harris," Dan Cole spoke up, confident enough to add an admonishing tone, "as managing director of this division, you need to work with me. Remember, I sign the payroll checks here."

"That may be true, Dan," Rick said with an air of condescension as he leisurely walked around to the front of the desk and reseated himself. "And, I'm sure that you have a very important position with RioAero. But like it or not, your realm of authority does not include sales."

Cole frowned. Regardless of what his official position was with any airframer, Dan Cole always had been involved with sales—always.

Rick flashed a self-assured smile, then slowly sat back into his chair. "You see, Dan, I report directly to Salo Montero and no one else. Because of the highly competitive nature of this business, the only one who actually knows what I'm up to at any given point in time is me, and perhaps Salo, that is, if he asks. Does that clear everything up for you?"

"HA," Cole grunted arrogantly, "all that's gonna change. If RioAero wants to stay in business, inventory has to be moved. To do that, RioAero needs me and my connections. Mark my words young man, without Dan Cole, it's *adiós* WindStar."

"We'll just have to see about that, Mister Cole." Rick got to his feet and walked to the door. He paused and turned to Cole. "In the meantime, Dan, a word to the wise, stick your nose in sales and you might lose it."

"You sonovabitch," Cole bellowed. "You, threatening me?" His face seethed with anger. "Nobody threatens Dan Cole. I'll do what I goddamn please."

Harris briskly walked back to Cole, stopping abruptly in front of the desk. Maintaining hard eye contact with Cole, Rick's hands clenched the forward edges of the desk. Rick's knuckles whitened. His body tensed. He flexed, arching his back. Cole's eyes widened; he froze in his high-back chair. Clearly, Rick was about to overturn the desk onto Cole. Rick wanted to. Rick really wanted to. It was written all over his face. He despised the man. Then, tension snapped; Rick backed away. His better sense prevailed; aggression now against Dan Cole would be counterproductive. If Cole was indeed a player in the sabotage conspiracy as Rick strongly suspected, Cole needed to be capable of continuing on in his role in the plot against the WindStar. Having Cole briefly out of commission with a few broken ribs would, for the time being, only delay uncovering a prime suspect and complicate matters for Rick.

Inwardly forcing restraint upon himself, Rick allowed his thinly controlled rage to be fully appreciated as he glowered at Cole. Breaking the moment, Rick slammed his right palm down hard onto the center of the desk. The sound of the sharp slap hung in the air. Rick's tightly pursed lips hid the grimace of pain as he flared his nostrils and acerbically challenged, "Do whatever you goddamn think you need to do, Mister Cole. I've got more important things to do with my time than hassle with you."

Rick turned on his heel, strode purposefully out of the room, slamming the door behind himself.

Dan Cole, visibly shaken, finally exhaled. His relief was quickly punctuated by the sound of shattering glass. In true form, Cole had flung a coffee mug against the closed door.

Rick heard the crashing sound and smirked as he walked the few steps to his own office just two doors down the hallway. He settled into the chair behind a cluttered desk. His mood quickly changed as he thought about what he had just done. With the window blinds drawn and overhead lighting extinguished, his office had the same gloomy aura he now felt. Rick leaned forward, anchored his elbows to the desktop, and buried his face into his hands. He groaned, chastising himself for losing control and antagonizing Cole, bemoaning how he had now cast himself. He hoped the brief confrontation would quickly pass from the man's mind. Rick wanted Cole to proceed with whatever activity Cole might be ramrodding. Intuition told him that Cole was indeed a player in the conspiracy against the WindStar. Now, it only had to be proven.

FORTY-ONE

Suriname

T he spotlight remained trained on Svensson as the vehicle came to a stop just beyond the nose of the WindStar. There was a shout comprised of multiple voices; the sound of Army boots hitting the tarmac at a fast-pace. Svensson shielded his eyes from the beam of brightness, glimpsing the silhouettes of two young soldiers rushing toward him.

Before Svensson could react, the soldiers were upon him. Their child-like faces were expressionless. Their penetrating gazes unlocked from his eyes and shot up to the aircraft's open doorway, then back to him—once, twice, three times. The brandished submachine guns were intimidating—riveting Svensson's attention, continuing to freeze him in place. He was not sure how to act; what to do. Anything could happen next. He expected the worst.

Then as suddenly as the soldiers had arrived, they retreated. The spotlight extinguished.

"*Tudo bom?*" came the voice of Franco Rameros asking if everything was okay.

"Dunno," Svensson replied as he turned back toward the WindStar, his eyes immediately noticing the image of the khaki-clad pseudo-general standing on the upper step of the airstair door with his hat cocked well down on his forehead.

"Those kids were intimidating, were they not?" Rameros remarked with a smirk while climbing down the airstairs. "When they spotted me, they scurried away…probably for reinforcements."

"Reinforcements?" Svensson's voice quivered.

"You Swedes are too nervous." Rameros placed his hand on Svensson's shoulder in a comforting fraternal gesture. "The last thing Suriname wants is to piss off its big neighbor to the south with some inane incident."

The sound of muffled voices in the distance refocused Rameros' and Svensson's cautious attention onto the military vehicle. Out of the shadows of the dimly lit ramp, Rameros and Svensson spied a huge silhouette big enough to be a sumo wrestler waddling toward them. The two young soldiers trailed the advancing shape.

"Good evening, gentlemen," came a deep wheezy voice from the silhouette.

"Good evening, sergeant," now able to discern details about the man, Rameros replied with an accompanying casual military salute that was summarily returned.

"So," the fat man grunted, all the time breathing heavily, "what brings you to my fair country?"

"Just a refueling stop."

"No one comes here for fuel," the fat man immediately responded. "It is always Georgetown or Cayenne, never Zanderij."

"And, why not Zanderij?" the smooth-tongued Rameros quickly returned. "This is a wonderful country."

Stunned by the reply and comment, the fat man's face went blank with puzzlement. His eyes darted from side to side as he tried to figure out the angle and how to respond. Indeed, both he and Rameros knew exactly why few visitors came to Suriname. But no one dared to mention that the recent military coup was responsible for creating such an unpredictable environment that transient aircraft seldom chose to land at Zanderij.

A brief transmission through the radio that the sergeant wore clipped on the left side of his belt was a temporary distraction. The sergeant quickly replied to the transmission, and then returned his attention to his visitors.

Rameros had a sudden tinge of apprehension. "There is kerosene here, yes?" Without fuel, the WindStar and its passengers would be indefinite guests of a country that was as unstable as a vial of nitroglycerin.

"Kerosene, huh?" The fat man indifferently stared at the WindStar, unhurried to reply and seemingly unmotivated to provide any assistance.

With measures calm, Rameros took a cigar from the right breast pocket of his epaulette decorated jacket and gripped the cigar between his teeth. He snapped open a silver-tone Zippo that was embossed with the RioAero logo. A cloud of smoke lazily drifted up into the still evening air. He slowly removed the cigar from his mouth. "Montecristo," Rameros said, approvingly eyeing the cigar, "hand rolled and aged in Santo Domingo. A very fine cigar." He reached back into the same pocket, fished out another, and offered it to the sergeant.

The fat man's eyes widened as his stubby fingers greedily grasped the cigar.

"Here, take the lighter," Rameros said, handing over the Zippo. "It is yours to keep."

The fat man's face glowed with appreciation. "Very nice," he said, examining the lighter. The cigar was quickly lit and the Zippo hurriedly pocketed.

Rameros nodded and continued on to ingratiate his position with the sergeant. He needed assistance in obtaining fuel. Befriending the fat man would be his ticket to success. "You know, my friend, noncommissioned officers like you do not get enough recognition." Rameros briefly lingered to appreciatively puff twice on his own cigar. "Unfortunate, but it is very much the same in my country. Still, noncoms are the backbone of the military. They have my admiration." Rameros took a step closer to the sergeant and placed another cigar into the sergeant's open breast pocket. "You will help us get fuel, will you not?" He slowly reached out and smoothly pressed an American twenty-dollar bill into the fat man's palm.

The sergeant smiled. He motioned for the two young soldiers to return to the Jeep. "Yes, that can be arranged. It may take some time. How quickly do you need fuel?"

Rameros pressed a second twenty into the fat man's hand.

The sergeant grinned. "I will personally handle your request." He paused, cocking his head toward the terminal building. "Now, you must clear customs and immigration, and then register your flight plan with the Tower. Remember, only American dollars. Cruzeiros are worthless here."

"You are a good man, sergeant," Rameros said, hiding his distaste.

The fat man lumbered off to the Jeep and departed.

"This is one scary place," Svensson whispered to Rameros.

"It has not always been this way," Rameros returned. "Suriname is a poor country that recently has been turned upside down. Nowadays, it is anybody's guess as to what will happen next." He reached into his left pants pocket, pulled out a wad of greenbacks, and peeled off about two-dozen of the bills. "Here's a couple thousand. You will need it for the refueling. Give the line chief a twenty when he arrives. Then watch him like a hawk." He took two steps toward the terminal and then turned back to Svensson. "Do not—I repeat—do not under any circumstances leave the aircraft. Tell our engineers to stay put as well. We want to keep a low profile." He paused, and with a quick wink he facetiously said, "BJ, try not to get yourself shot."

Svensson's pinched expression spoke volumes.

During the short walk to the terminal, Rameros quickly glanced at paperwork attached to a clipboard that Svensson had prepared: General Declaration; Aircraft Manifest; ICAO Flight Plan for the next segment to the Dominican Republic. Just the standard fodder airport officials routinely process.

The terminal layout, though modest by most standards, was more than adequate for the handful of international airline flights that were once regularly scheduled to arrive in a country populated by less than half a million. The building's simple Dutch architectural design reflected a burgeoning colonial period of the past. Now, times had changed. International flights were a rarity. The one-story terminal building had become a ghost of even its spartan yesteryear. Its poorly maintained exterior mirrored the dreary ill-kept landscape surrounding it.

As Franco Rameros was about to step up into the entrance portico, he heard a chilling metal-to-metal snapping click. Within the shadows, a soldier had just closed the chamber of an Uzi.

Casting his eyes to the right, he picked out a young soldier sitting on a wrought iron bench. Rameros' response was to slow stride only enough to exchange a casual salute while continuing to make his way into the terminal. He knew that from this location, the soldier had most likely witnessed the convivial encounter Rameros had had with the sergeant only moments before. This, he hoped, would imply tacit approval to freely move about the terminal area. The assumption was correct.

The silence within the desolate and poorly-lit terminal was eerie. The once carefully positioned, brightly colored modular passenger seating arrangements were in disarray. Several stacks of water-stained cardboard boxes, piled five high, were clustered near an airline's gatehouse. The dank smell of a mausoleum permeated the building. Fluorescent light tubes, recessed within the suspended ceiling, periodically flickered as if in dismay. A small pack of startled rats scurried amidst clutter and grime on the white-and-black tiled floor.

Franco Rameros walked on, following a path clearly marked with signs that provided directions to customs and immigration. He ambled down the corridor to his right, then turned to his left. Each step he took on the tiled floor echoed off the walls of the narrow dingy hallway. He turned left again, then came to a stop. Over a closed door was a sign containing the word IMMIGRATION in both Dutch and English. He tried the doorknob. It was locked. He proceeded farther down the corridor to the open doorway of a brightly lighted office.

"CUSTOMS," he mouthed the word reading the office signage from above the door. He glanced into the office and focused past its plain furnishings to the dignified, dark-skinned man in his mid-forties who sat behind a long wooden table facing the doorway. Like most customs officials, this inspector held a prominent position within his country, and he was fastidiously dressed for the part. Dark brown pants were topped with a white blouse complete with lanyard and wide epaulette boards striped in the national colors of red, white and green. The official gold badge identified him as Inspector of Customs. His impressive uniform was immaculate in every way. It bespoke power and authority over anyone entering or re-entering the country. Rameros strode into the room.

"Good evening," the inspector said as he looked up from the newspaper he was reading. "You are pilot-in-command of the aircraft that just landed?"

"Yes, I am."

The inspector placed his newspaper aside and carefully eyed Rameros' uniform. "Brazilian general?"

"That is correct." Rameros answered with both conviction and pretense.

"You are on military business?"

"No, this is a private flight." He seated himself in a chair across from the inspector. "I am ferrying the aircraft to the United States where I will visit with friends. Our stopping here is for fuel only."

"I see, I see..." the inspector responded, using both hands to preen his shirt collar. He cocked his left wrist and pointedly glanced at his Rolex President.

Rameros noticed the watch and other gold jewelry the inspector wore. Gifts and other offerings were common bribes to high level customs personnel in third world countries. Also common was a flair for pretention and ostentation among senior inspectors.

The inspector continued, "Now, please be aware that I am here after-hours to process you and your aircraft."

Rameros nodded, fully understanding that additional and perhaps excessive fees would apply. He handed the inspector the completed customs forms. "And, your fee?"

The inspector glanced at his watch once again. He groaned, then punched a few numbers into a handheld calculator. "Only one hundred American dollars, no cruzeiros."

"Why, of course." Rameros handed the inspector the fee. "Would you care to inspect the aircraft?" he asked as he casually placed a twenty-dollar bill onto the table.

"No, no," the inspector responded, matter-of-factly pocketing the bribe as if it were normal business. "You are a transient aircraft. I see no need for a physical inspection."

"Thank you." Rameros cracked a thin smile, knowing he had just reduced his ground time by at least half an hour.

With the typical flamboyance of a customs official, the inspector assertively stamped the documents and then took a slow seven seconds to sprawl his ornate signature halfway across each page before returning copies to Rameros. "Now, I must leave. I have business elsewhere."

At the summary dismissal, both arose from their chairs and simultaneously exited the office.

"The immigration official should be arriving shortly," the inspector commented. "He will also charge you with an after-hours fee." The inspector closed and locked the office door. "In the meantime, I will show you to the Tower on my way out."

"Thank you, I certainly appreciate your time and effort," Rameros said, displaying all the true diplomacy he could muster, knowing full well how to play the bureaucratic airport arrival game on an international scale. He followed the inspector down the corridor to a passageway and stairs leading to the Control Tower. There the two departed each other's company.

After climbing three levels of narrow metal stairs, Franco Rameros arrived at the locked entrance door to the Tower cab. He pressed the lighted call button. A moment later the controller opened the door.

A dimly-lit Control Tower cab is among the most isolated places on earth. While a fish bowl of sorts, always in plain view, the cab is off limits except to a select few. Even though pilots are normally welcomed to visit the Tower, pilots typically shun controllers, disdainfully viewing controllers as unnecessary complications in their professional lives. Pilots invariably regard controllers as meddlers who either create delays or question a pilot's authority. It is generally an oil and vinegar relationship, resignedly tolerated by pilots only by necessity. There are, of course, exceptions.

"Welcome, welcome," the controller said, honestly enthusiastic at the opportunity to have a visitor break the many hours of solitude and sheer boredom that accompanied his job. The short slightly-built East Indian native, who like many of his countrymen had made Suriname his home, extended his hand.

Franco Rameros forced an obliging smile as he grasped the controller's extended hand and pumped it several times.

"I am always excited to have a visitor. Few aircraft land at Zanderij these days," the controller lamented. "This morning, it was just a twin Cessna from Caracas. Earlier this afternoon, it was a Queen Air from Cayenne. You were unexpected. I had incomplete flight plan information on your aircraft. Your stated destination was Georgetown." The controller shrugged. "That has been happening a lot these days. Communication system problems." His smile broadened. "Still, I am glad you chose to land at Zanderij."

Rameros politely nodded.

"Come with me," the controller eagerly said. He led Rameros to the section of the cab that overlooked the terminal ramp. "You see," he continued, "your aircraft is being refueled. You are very lucky to have located the lineman. I tried earlier, but to no avail."

"Thanks for trying," Rameros acknowledged. "I was fortunate enough to convince the sergeant to assist me in obtaining fuel."

"Aah, yes, the sergeant," the controller said with a less than complimentary tinge to his tone. "He thinks he owns the airport; nonetheless, he can get things done when he is motivated."

"Yes, indeed," Rameros admitted, "but why so much hostility among the troops? Why does everyone carry a machine gun?"

"The revolution, you know. It was an unfortunate occurrence," the controller said with chagrin. "There was no reason for it, just a power play. Of course, the new regime found out very quickly that their action put the economy into a tailspin. Now, there is little money for anyone. So, to maintain a position of power and show a force of strength, every kid in uniform is given a toy. It bestows the aura of authority and importance. Still, I seriously doubt if half the guns you see are either loaded or in proper working order. If the guns were, there would be a lot of accidental shootings as boy soldiers tried to figure out how to use them." The controller solemnly grinned.

"Well, those young soldiers are very intimidating."

"Yes, that is exactly the point."

Rameros nodded as he handed his flight plan to the controller who carefully reviewed the information written onto the form.

"Everything appears to be in order. I will enter it into the system immediately." The controller glanced out the window one more time as he made his way to the computer terminal. "That aircraft you fly—the WindStar—it is a very fine aircraft, very beautiful."

"Thanks," Rameros said. He spotted the controller's binoculars lying on a ledge at the foot of one of the massive glass windowpanes. "May I?"

"Certainly."

Rameros focused the binoculars on the WindStar, and quickly noted that the engineers were still conducting the detailed walk-around inspection he had mandated. He saw the lineman replace the cap on the refueling point atop the left wing tank, climb down from the stepladder, and begin to reel his hose into the fuel tender. He observed Svensson scurrying around the WindStar like a mother hen, being sure everything was in proper order for their departure.

Then, over a speaker in the Tower came a transmission from an inbound aircraft: "Zanderij Approach, Saberliner Hotel-Kilo-Five-Five-One-Zero."

Rameros cringed, his mind immediately identifying the registration prefix and its possible implications for him.

"Saberliner calling Zanderij Approach, please standby," the controller matter-of-factly responded to the incoming aircraft. He turned to Rameros and almost gleefully said, "Another visitor. Not many Colombian aircraft fly into Suriname these days."

"I see," Rameros hastily acknowledged. He paused, reseating his hat, now more anxious than ever to depart as soon as possible. "From what I saw through your binoculars, it looks like my aircraft has been refueled and is ready to go," he commented to the controller who was making some entries with a keyboard to relay Rameros' flight plan data to Santo Domingo.

"Yes, I understand," the controller said, making the last of his keystrokes, "I am sorry that you must leave so soon." He escorted Rameros to the door. "I trust you will have a very safe and swift flight."

Franco Rameros scrambled down the metal stairs to the terminal below, made his way through the corridor maze, and exited the building in a fast-paced walk toward the WindStar.

"General..." came a deep, wheezy voice from the shadows of the portico.

Rameros stopped in his tracks. The voice was familiar. It was the sergeant.

"General..." The fat man approached from the shadows. His two young soldiers followed closely behind. He puffed on his cigar. "May I presume everything is to your satisfaction?"

"Very much so," Rameros responded, knowing full well that the sergeant's presence was not happenstance.

"Your aircraft is a very beautiful, but also a very delicate machine."

Rameros quickly read between the lines. He was sure he knew what the sergeant was implying. Extortion came to mind. This time it would be more than just cigars. "Yes," he responded to the sergeant, "she is a true lady who deserves the best possible treatment that both you and I can provide."

"Indeed, she is," the fat man said in accord.

Rameros took two steps toward the fat man and lowered his voice to a whisper. A long minute passed. The bribe was paid. This time it was a C-note. "You are a gentleman," Rameros spoke, cringing at the words he felt he had to say.

"Enjoy your flight."

Rameros walked on to the WindStar. The fuel tender was just pulling away from the aircraft. The engineers were climbing up the airstair door. Svensson hopped to attention and flashed a salute to his pilot-in-command.

"*Tudo bom*, BJ?"

"Everything is fine, we are ready to go."

"Excellent."

Within minutes, the WindStar was taxiing out for departure with an IFR clearance to Santo Domingo. Rameros had just completed the takeoff checklist and was setting up his navaids. Svensson was at the controls of the aircraft.

"I cannot get out of this place too soon," Svensson said over the cockpit intercom.

"Roger that, BJ, I am in total agreement with you this time. Things went almost too smoothly, did they not?" He made no mention of the incoming Saberliner with a Colombian registration.

"They certainly did." Svensson nodded. "The fuel tender was here in a flash. I gave the lineman a twenty, just like you said to do, and he hustled like there was no tomorrow."

"Yes, as the saying goes, cash is king, but this place is getting pretty damn expensive." He paused, shaking his head in disgust. "Okay, BJ, you do the takeoff and I will back you up."

Svensson nodded in acknowledgement.

Rameros switched to the Tower frequency. "Good evening, Tower, Sierra-Bravo-Yankee is ready for takeoff, Runway One-One." He avoided using the two letter Brazilian registration prefix or identifying his aircraft with the word WindStar. He knew that the Saberliner might now be monitoring the frequency.

"Roger, Sierra-Bravo-Yankee, taxi into position and hold, Runway One-One."

"Into position, Sierra-Bravo-Yankee."

Svensson rolled the WindStar out onto the runway, lining up with the centerline. Rameros switched on the wingtip strobes, and then the landing lights.

"We are on our way," Svensson said over the cockpit intercom, relieved that Suriname was about to become just another episode in a day filled with more tension and stress than he had ever experienced in his life.

"Just keep your fingers crossed, young man," Rameros cautioned. "We are only on our way when the gear is up and we are climbing through three thousand feet."

Svensson held the brakes and slowly advanced the power to twenty percent torque, anticipating a takeoff clearance within the next few seconds.

The controller keyed his mic, "Sierra-Bravo-Yankee, standby one."

Here we go again, Rameros thought remembering the fiasco in Brasilia earlier that afternoon.

Ten seconds later, the Tower made a further transmission, "Sierra-Bravo-Yankee, immigration advises your presence is required."

Svensson, perplexed, reduced the power levers back to flight idle and awaited Rameros' response to the Tower.

No response was transmitted.

From his left side window Rameros saw the sergeant and his two men scramble for their Jeep at the terminal boulding.

"Okay, BJ," he said over the cockpit intercom, "I think you had better let me take control of the aircraft."

The controller's voice came again over the Tower frequency, this time with a tone of urgency, "Sierra-Bravo-Yankee, immigration needs to see you."

Still, no responding transmission from Rameros.

Svensson remained silent.

"Screw him," Rameros blurted out over the cockpit intercom. "I do not have all goddamn night to wait for some pompous scumbag immigration inspector just so he can collect a hundred dollar fee plus whatever bribes he can suck out of me. I have had enough of this damn place." In his mind, he had a strong feeling that the immigration inspector's temporary absence was not accidental.

He held the brakes and aggressively advanced the power levers, being sure not to over temp the engines. The airframe shuddered as the prop wash peppered the empennage. From his left window, he saw the Jeep speed away from the terminal building. He knew the sergeant had most certainly been monitoring the Tower frequency on his radio.

"Sierra-Bravo-Yankee, this is the Tower, you must return to the ramp, you are not cleared for takeoff. Sierra-Bravo-Yankee, I repeat, you are not cleared for takeoff."

That was exactly what Rameros needed to hear. It further inspired his ire. He keyed his mic on the Tower frequency. "Roger, Tower, cleared for takeoff." On the avionics control panel, he punched off the Tower frequency. There was no need to hear anything further from Zanderij.

As Rameros released the brakes the WindStar surged forward, gaining momentum as it began its takeoff roll.

Near the opposite side of the airfield, the Jeep sped along a taxiway and entered onto the runway. It was now racing toward the WindStar, head on.

Forty knots…fifty knots… The fully fueled aircraft steadily accelerated, bobbing along down the runway's uneven surface.

The Jeep was quickly closing ground.

"They have machine guns," Svensson blurted out. "Abort, ABORT!"

"Worry not, my friend, the machine guns will not be used," Rameros said, confident that his bribes to the sergeant were all the insurance he needed.

Sixty knots…seventy knots…

Suddenly, a rapid burst of flashing light came from the Jeep. The initial visual appearance, amplified and three dimensional, was such as if seen through a kaleidoscope. Indeed, an automatic weapon had opened fire.

"Shit," Rameros said, "guess I was wrong about the sergeant."

Almost instantaneously, the Jeep became unstable, swerving erratically, uncontrollably. Its direction changed by ninety degrees. The Jeep was sliding sideways, wheels skidding on the pavement. Then suddenly, upon hitting a wide crack in the tarmac, the vehicle pivoted longitudinally and began rolling over and over—again and again—on the runway surface.

The young inexperienced soldier who had been standing in the back section of the Jeep had apparently triggered his Uzi from the hip. The rounds from the automatic weapon, while intended for the WindStar, instead inadvertently blasted directly through the windshield of the Jeep, totally missing the aircraft.

A wide grin spread across Rameros' face as he realized what had just happened in the Jeep. "Ninety knots," he said, "ROTATE."

The aircraft leapt into the air, hurdling over the still tumbling Jeep, rocketing into the darkness of night.

"Unbelievable!" Svensson was aghast.

"The sergeant was a greedy man," Rameros said, shaking his head. "He took my cigars, my lighter, my money, and then when he had a choice, it was still not enough. He still wanted more. The sonovabitch got what he deserved."

"But what if they come after us?"

"HA!" Rameros laughed aloud. "In what? Suriname does not really have an Air Force. Well, maybe a few helicopters and a couple of Cessna mix-masters, but that is probably about it. We will be long gone before they can scramble. I will have someone at the factory smooth things over later."

Rameros panned the surrounding darkness, searching for any airborne traffic. Perhaps it was nothing, he kept saying to himself, just a coincidence. Still, the inbound Saberliner loomed large in his mind. He switched off the aircraft's landing lights and strobes, and then paused before extinguishing the navigation lights and rotating beacon.

Cloaked in obscurity, the WindStar forged ahead into the darkness of night.

FORTY-TWO

RioAero, NA

Rick Harris opened the briefcase he had dropped off in his office just prior to the confrontation with Dan Cole. He removed from it the UHF repeater that would receive and then re-transmit signals to Tommy Maxwell from the bug freshly planted under Cole's desktop. Rick flipped on the small switch of the repeater, then picked up his telephone handset and dialed Maxwell's office.

"MacroScientific," the female voice announced.

"Monica, this is Rick Harris," he said, pausing as he eyed the slowly pulsating small red light on the repeater, "tell Tommy we're on the air."

"Very well, Mr. Harris," came her professional response.

"Thanks." He hung up the phone and began to shuffle through some of the paperwork on his desk. Two pink message slips immediately caught his eye. Both had been written up by his secretary within the hour after he had left the facility the day before. A smile crept across his face. The first message was from Salo's daughter. Apparently she had forgotten to retrieve a tennis racquet she had stowed in the cabin of the WindStar. He shook his head and thought: Who has time for tennis anymore. He glanced up noting that someone had retrieved the racquet from the aircraft and had laid it atop a double stack of files on his desk. "Thanks, Joey," he murmured.

Rick put the receiver of the phone to his ear and dialed Victoria's number. It was nice to hear her cheerful, though apologetic, voice. During their brief conversation, he agreed to deliver the racquet to her later that day at The Embers, a lounge in Hollywood just fifteen minutes south of the airport. He thought the diversion would do him good.

The next message was from a Ramon Segundo. The message was marked urgent. It read: NEED TO MEET WITH YOU IMMEDIATELY! The name was familiar but at that instant Rick could not identify why he knew it. Then, his mind connected. Ramon Segundo was the ever-pleasant, politically attuned president of BASA, the well-established Barcelona airframe manufacturer. These days, Segundo was also temporarily heading up BASA's North American subsidiary. Segundo's focus was to flood the deregulated airline industry with his aircraft—the Avio-23. Although Rick had had little occasion to interface with Segundo, the BASA president's projected image was of a classy, confident gentleman. Segundo was creative and articulate. At CAAA conventions, Segundo's mannerisms distinguished him from all other airframe executives. Rick admired what little he knew of the man. He would soon learn much, much more.

Rick dialed the Fort Lauderdale phone number written on the message. The number was not for BASA's North American offices.

"*Buenas Tardes, ésta es LA BASA,*" came the voice over the telephone. "*¿Cómo puedo le ayudo?*"

"*Rick Harris está volviendo la llamada telefónica del Señor Segundo.*"

"*Un momento por favor.*"

Thirty seconds later, Ramon Segundo spoke into the telephone. "Thank you for the callback, Rick." His voice was upbeat. "*¿Cómo va?*"

"I am doing well, Ramon." Rick was cautiously guarded, trying to speculate why Segundo had contacted him. "After a few weeks in Brazil, I'm back in town and just cleaning up the paperwork mess that comes with being out of the office."

"Yes, I know what you mean," Segundo sighed. "Selling aircraft is a very detailed and time consuming activity. Unfortunately, the paperwork never seems to end."

"Very true," was Rick's sparse response letting Segundo direct the conversation.

"Ah, by the way," Segundo continued, "I want to congratulate you on your new position with RioAero. Director of aircraft sales, is it?"

"Why yes, that's correct. Thank you."

"So, you are going to be the man who tries to take sales away from both BASA and Fairchild with that new WindStar of yours?"

Rick chuckled. "Nothing personal, but with the WindStar I won't have to try that hard."

"*Bueno,* I like a straightforward man." Segundo paused.

Rick waited.

Segundo's tone turned paternal. "You know, aircraft sales can be a very demanding and frustrating job. A young company, a new aircraft…indeed, you have a formidable task on your hands."

"I very much understand what you're saying, Ramon," Rick began. "When I accepted this position, my eyes were wide open. I know that breaking into a market with a new product can be very difficult. But there is one thing I am very sure of…" He smiled to himself at what he was about to say. "The WindStar is the most impressive aircraft I've ever had the pleasure to fly. It's leagues above the Fairchild Metro. And, please excuse my candor, it makes your Avio-23 seem like a Model-T."

Segundo gave a hearty laugh. "Very good, Mr. Harris, very good. I admire your positive attitude. Indeed, that is one of the reasons I gave you a call."

"And, the other reasons?"

"Well, that is a bit more complex, that is what I would like to discuss with you."

Rick waited for him to continue. The ball was in Segundo's court.

"The truth of the matter, Rick, is what I need to talk with you about is difficult to discuss on the phone." He hesitated before continuing. "Would it be possible for you to meet with me?"

The request did not surprise Rick. It was clearly written on the message in front of him. Still, the tone was urgent; it had to be a matter of importance. "Sure, why not," Rick responded. "I'll need about an hour or so to finish up here. Where would you like to meet?"

"Do you know Bahia Mar?"

"Yes."

"Well, we have our company boat—*LA BASA*—docked there."

"Fine. Shall we say a little after five o'clock?"

"That will be excellent, Rick. I shall look forward to seeing you."

"Until then." Rick hung up the phone, still clueless as to why Ramon Segundo wanted the meeting. He glanced at his watch. Just past four in the afternoon, *damn*, he said to himself, remembering his conversation earlier that morning with his wife. He had told her he would be back at the ranch by mid-afternoon and they would spend a quiet evening home, alone. That was not going to happen. Not today.

He dialed the number for the ranch. After four rings, the answering machine picked up the call. The message he left apologized and said he would try to get home as soon as he could. He ended by saying: "Put on your party dress, we have some business and pleasure at September's tonight."

In the following hour, Rick feverishly worked on drafting a Letter of Intent for the aircraft order he was proposing to Sammy Santelli. His fingers flew across the keyboard as he entered information into a template on his Commodore computer. Although much of what he set forth was industry boilerplate, Rick took great care to incorporate all of the terms and conditions discussed earlier that day with Sammy.

To distinguish his offer from the competition, Rick had to be creative as well as aggressive. He knew that his aircraft and its acquisition program were superior to anything that the competition could offer. Better performance, lower cost of operation, and the enhanced FINEX financing tied to LIBOR, all gave him a substantial edge. Still, Santelli's concerns were very legitimate. The inexplicable incidents recently plaguing the aircraft, the young company's lack of a track record in airline product support, and Brazil's economic woes had to be addressed.

Rick read and re-read the document he was preparing. He closed his eyes and began thinking to himself. What if the WindStar really did have serious component flaws that were causing the rash of calamities? What if RioAero were to have funding cut off by the government and be shut down? What if Brazil's hyperinflation caused a catastrophic economic crisis within the country? Where would that leave Sammy Santelli and his new airline? How could he insure Sammy against these possible scenarios? If all hell broke loose, how could he insure Sammy's airline would be financially insulated from it all?

Rick was stumped. What he needed was a mechanism to give Santelli confidence despite the all too real scenarios Santelli rightfully knew could be anticipated.

He moaned. There had to be a solution to this problem. *Think*, he said silently to himself, *be creative.*

Nothing.

Then, inspiration. A smile crept across his face, broadening as his mind tapped his earlier thoughts and accelerated ahead. "That's it," he said aloud, "INSURANCE...why not?"

No airframe manufacturer had ever proposed such a concept to a customer. Insurance. It usually worked the other way around. Insurance. New or financially stressed airlines were frequently required to obtain letters of credit or other insurance mechanisms to reduce the risk exposure an airframe manufacturer had in placing equipment with them. But why had not airframers employed the same mechanism themselves? It had never been necessary. When acquiring a Boeing, McDonnell Douglas or Lockheed aircraft, an airline simply banked on the long-established reputation of the manufacturer. The pedigree of well known smaller aircraft manufacturers was not dissimilar: BASA had been in business for nearly half a century; Fairchild Aircraft had the backing of its renowned parent, Fairchild Industries.

RioAero lacked a history an airline could bank on. The company had only been in business for a short thirteen years. So, could an insurance policy help to lift the cloud of doubt created by the circumstances now weighing on RioAero? Absolutely! Initially, RioAero might have to institute such a program to generate sales of the WindStar. Of course, it would be a temporary measure, needed only until the company established itself as a mainstream player in the regional airline marketplace. Rick hesitated. Would insurance truly be the answer? Would insurance even be wise to offer? It might not be needed. After all, Sammy Santelli would ultimately decide what was truly critical to the deal.

Rick's fingers made the decision for him by attacking the keyboard again. The sentence he added, without ever mentioning the word insurance, was: "RioAero shall provide *assurances* to the Buyer that all terms and conditions represented herein, and hereafter in the definitive purchase agreement, will be fulfilled to the satisfaction of the Buyer." This left it to Santelli to determine whatever assurances were necessary to consummate the deal.

He hit the print button and waited amidst the clatter as his state-of-the-art matrix dot machine churned out copies of the document.

"Good," he said aloud. He hastily examined the pages.

Rick glanced at his watch. "Damn," he moaned. It was just after five o'clock. He was already running late for his meeting with Ramon Segundo.

He stuffed the paperwork into his briefcase and dashed out the door.

FORTY-THREE

Bahia Mar Marina

Rick Harris eased the old Chevy into a left turn off of Seabreeze Boulevard and drove beneath the canopy of towering royal palms that lined the narrow driveway leading to the gated entrance of the Bahia Mar complex. The truck slowed, then came to a stop. A young attendant dressed in a fitted bright white shirt with nautical epaulettes, tan shorts, and boat shoes without socks stepped out of the gatehouse.

"Good evening, sir, may I help you?" he questioned, carefully eyeing Rick in the well-weathered pickup truck. His cool polite tone was ready to instantly rebuff Rick's entrance to the marina.

Harris grinned, understanding the attendant's skepticism. An old beat-up truck driven by an apparent proletarian who was about to request entrance into one of the area's most posh resorts was indeed cause for pause. Rick certainly did not look like a yachtsman or, for that matter, anyone who could be associated with a yacht.

"I have a meeting with Mr. Segundo on his yacht, *LA BASA*," Rick responded. "Would you be so kind as to direct me to its whereabouts?"

The attendant's raised eyebrows knit together into a frown. "And, he is expecting you?"

"He certainly is," Rick said quickly glancing at his Omega Speedmaster. It was just past 5:30 p.m. "Unfortunately, I'm running a tad late."

"I see," the attendant said, his frown remaining. "One moment, please." The young man turned and re-entered the gatehouse, only to shortly reappear after verifying Rick's statement. Now convinced that Rick was more likely an eccentric than a tramp, the attendant forced a polite smile and said, "You will need to go to slip number one. It's to the south on the Intracoastal."

"Thank you, Robert," Rick said, reading the attendant's nametag. "Must be a big boat to be berthed there, huh?"

"Yes indeed, she's a hundred twenty-five footer," the attendant commented. "You can't miss her. Her color is, well, you'll see...very distinctive."

"What do you mean?"

"Uh, not your typical motor yacht white." The attendant reached into the gatehouse and pushed a button. The wooden gate arm pivoted ninety degrees upward to allow Rick entry into the marina's parking area.

Rick motored the Chevy along the narrow access way and through the jam-packed lot. "Damn snowbirds" he muttered. There was not a space to be had. Large sedans, mostly light in color, interspersed with a good number of Ferraris, Porsches, Lambos, and other exotic cars, crammed the limited parking area. "Ah-haa..." He eyed a silver Bentley backing out of a space to his left. He waited and promptly pulled into the newly vacated area. "Lucky!" He snatched the briefcase lying on the seat beside him, popped out of the pickup truck, and quickly walked toward the Intracoastal.

The broad asphalt pathway narrowed then transitioned to pressure-treated pine boards that gently inclined, snaking around the ground's subtropical flora, funneling onto a catwalk supported by the marina's telephone pole-size pilings. To the left, an arrangement of boardwalks fanned finger-like, jutting off and slightly below the main walkway to create a maze of slips. Sportfishermen, cruisers, and other powerboats of various shapes and sizes peacefully commingled at their moorings along with an assortment of sailboats. Rick laughed to himself, amused by reading some of the names that adorned the boats' sterns. Mostly names of women—real or fictional—and slogans—some boastful, others rather bizarre—fancifully accommodating to each owner's personality. Few slips were unoccupied. During the high season in a city known as the Venice of America, there would be no "vacancy" to be filled; an advance reservation was required.

Along the way, Rick sidestepped a group of lobster-red tourists ogling a Bertram 46. The flash of the tourist's camera was impotent in the still bright, late afternoon sun. Nonetheless, a memento of their vacation was hopefully captured. Though running late, Rick paused, turned back toward the tourists, and offered to take their picture with the marina as a backdrop. The offer was gratefully accepted.

He crouched to frame the picture in the viewfinder and said, "Say mahi-mahi" The group's smiles transitioned to giggles. A good deed was done.

Rick continued along his way on the wooden walkway to the main dock on the Intracoastal. Ever the friendly ambassador, a slight wave of his hand acknowledged eye contact from two strangers passing by on the walkway, a well-groomed man in his mid-forties accompanied an attractive young woman. She stumbled, but quickly recovered, when one of her high heels slipped between the boards of the decking as she came abreast of Rick. Age-wise, she could easily have been the man's daughter. Rick guessed she was not. Typical Fort Lauderdale, he thought.

Finally, Rick reached the premier main pier that the marina reserved for the largest of yachts. Three glistening white motor yachts each in excess of one hundred feet quietly rested, secured to their moorings. To his far left at the end of the pier, Rick's eye immediately caught sight of *LA BASA*. The attendant was certainly correct in saying that Rick could not miss her. The boat was eye-popping canary yellow. Her sleek hull also sported an unconventional broad red stripe above the lower deck port holes running horizontally for almost one hundred feet with each end tapering to a dagger-thin point. Not only was the boat's color dramatically different from the traditional white, but its design was an even more radical departure from all the other boats at the docks.

Before Rick made his way down the pier, he paused, slightly awestruck. The sleek low-profile boat was a unique, custom-built, tri-deck motor yacht. Her glistening hull and superstructure were designed for one obvious reason—piercing wind and wave with the least possible resistance. The boat looked fast just floating dockside, and as Rick would soon learn, she was even faster than appearances. *LA BASA* was a one-of-a-kind, hyper-fast motor yacht. She was like something out of a James Bond thriller, only more impressive because she was real.

Rick walked up the red-carpeted gangway and pressed an ivory button inset into an ornately designed brass fixture attached to the right gangway rail. A faint yellow light within the ivory button began to slowly flash.

Moments later a tall young man appeared from a doorway amidships. His massive upper body snugly filled a white three-button collarless polo shirt. The shirt was neatly tucked into a pair of equally form-fitting navy blue shorts. As the man moved forward, his imposing appearance was undercut by the comic chirping of his white Sperry Topsiders with each step he took on the decking.

Rick reflexively smiled.

"Mr. Harris, I presume?" The young man spoke clearly and distinctly with a slight Spanish accent.

"Yes indeed, Rick, Rick Harris."

"My name is Orlando, I am first mate." A well-rehearsed smile smoothly crept across the man's face. "Mr. Segundo has been expecting you."

Rick bent over to remove his roper boots as he was accustomed to doing before boarding any pristine boat.

"No need for that, Mr. Harris," the first mate was quick to intercede. "If the ladies who visit with us in stilettos keep on their pumps, your ropers will be just fine where they are."

Rick shrugged. "Whatever you say, Orlando."

"Please follow me."

The man removed the stainless steel chain to unblock access from the gangway and led Rick through the main foyer.

LA BASA was a stunning example of the liberties designers could take when artfully merging the traditional with the avant-garde. Just inside the spacious entry foyer, a striking staircase with a gilded banister linked the main deck to decks above and below. Slightly aft of the foyer and to the starboard, a light gray marble bar was flanked with five tall padded chairs.

"Please make yourself comfortable, Mr. Harris," Orlando said, offering Rick a seat at the bar by swiveling one of the dark blue leather-covered chairs toward Rick. "Mr. Segundo is on the afterdeck taking a telephone call, he should only be a few minutes. He prefers to do most of his business out-of-doors as the weather permits."

"I see," Rick said, seating himself on the offered chair while taking in the yacht's formal, yet not overbearing, ambiance. Farther aft, beyond an etched glass divider, he glimpsed the expansive main salon with its large open dining area. Huge walls of windows edged the sides of the salon, extending upwards from a thin waist-high sill of glistening maple burl veneer to join an ornate ceiling casement that encircled the room's dimensions. The combination of pastel upholstery fabrics, neutral carpeting, highly polished lightwoods, and strategically placed down-lighting all lent a feeling of spaciousness.

"Care for a drink, Mr. Harris?"

"Yes, thanks, Orlando," Rick said, quickly redirecting his attention back to the man behind the bar. "A Coke or Pepsi would be nice."

The first mate switched on the overhead lighting. The bar surface glistened in a shower of bright halogen light.

"Here you are, sir," he said as he placed the tall, cut crystal glass of cola on a gold-framed leather coaster in front of Rick.

"Thanks so much," Rick replied, and then took a sip. "Tell me, Orlando, how long have you been with *LA BASA?*"

"Since she was commissioned." After a thoughtful pause, he added, "A little less than a year."

"Well, this is one impressive motor yacht," Rick opined, gazing again at his surroundings.

Orlando beamed. "You don't even know the half of it."

At that moment, the telephone under the bar beeped twice. Orlando quickly picked up the handset and uttered his name into the mouthpiece. He paused listening, and without a further word placed the handset back onto its cradle beneath the bar.

"*El Capitán* will see you now. Please follow me."

Orlando led Rick past the dining area, through the salon, and on to the large open area abaft. The main afterdeck was overhung by a structurally reinforced extension of the bridge deck that had the capability of holding a twenty-five foot tender, or allowing for helicopter operations.

Upon seeing Rick, Ramon Segundo immediately rose from his seat at the huge, highly polished teak table to greet his visitor. From his thick black hair and his well-chiseled facial features, to his six-foot-two athletic frame, Ramon Segundo's presence conveyed an aura of confidence and style. Now in his mid-fifties, Segundo was very much of a politician and a diplomat. He was also one very intelligent and highly competitive individual. All these skills were brought to bearing in his position as president of a major airframe manufacturer where he had recently felt pressure from his board of directors to take a more personal role in accelerating aircraft sales around the globe.

"*¿Cómo estás, Señor Harris?*" Segundo enthusiastically said as he strode from behind the table toward Rick.

"*Muy bien, Señor Segundo...te ves bien, Ramon.*"

"Haaa," Segundo laughed. "Thank you, Rick, you flatter me." Any trace of a Spanish accent was now almost imperceptible.

They shook hands.

"This is one helluva boat you have Ramon. *LA BASA*, huh?"

"Yes indeed," Segundo said with evident pride. "We could not name her *La Barcelona Aeronáuticas, SA*...too long, you know. So, just like the company, we shortened it to BASA. And if *LA BASA* had wings, she would probably fly...just like an aircraft."

Rick nodded, but quizzically.

"Oh," Ramon addressed Rick's puzzlement as he offered his visitor a seat at the table, "I see Orlando did not have the chance to fully inform you about this gem?"

Rick shook his head no.

"Well, then..." Excitement spread across Ramon's features. "*LA BASA* is a state-of-the-art, lady-of-the-seas. She is actually the new big sister to the *FORTUNA*." He paused to see if Rick caught the essence of what he was saying. Rick did not.

"Okay," Ramon continued, "let me give you some background. I think you will find this fascinating." He sat down across the table from Rick. "A few years back, PalmerJohnson—the renowned custom yacht builder—was commissioned by the Crown Prince Fahd of Saudi Arabia to construct a special gift for our King, Juan Carlos, who is a yachting aficionado. Indeed, the gift was special...very special. In 1979, the *FORTUNA*—a hundred foot, all-aluminum motor yacht—was presented to the King. The *FORTUNA* was lighter and faster than any yacht in its class by a wide margin. Her engine room contained a state-of-the-art propulsion system combining gas turbine-powered waterjets with wing diesels for lower-speed maneuvering. In fact, water jets and gas turbine power had never before been combined on a private yacht."

"Her speed?" Rick inquired.

"Fifty-two knots, nearly sixty miles per hour."

"Very impressive." Rick knew that most motor yachts in the hundred-foot class typically cruised at less than half that speed.

"Indeed, impressive." Ramon paused building emphasis. "Anyway, not to be outdone, another Middle Eastern potentate, who must remain nameless, wanted something bigger, better, and faster. Those guys are like that, you know. So, the same naval architects and designers were retained, but this time a ship builder was selected that was located in Barcelona—our backyard. To make a long story short, things did not work out quite as expected. The boat was bigger and grander, but it was not fast enough to please. The technology just was not there to push a one hundred twenty-five footer much more than fifty-five miles per hour. So, the rich camel driver walked away from the deal and forfeited his advance payments, which some say were close to ten million dollars. Pocket change to him, I suppose."

"How did an aircraft manufacturer like BASA wind up with the yacht?"

"Simple," Ramon answered with a conspiratorial grin, "as a high profile company involved in selling rather expensive capital goods like aircraft, we regularly come in contact with those who have very deep pockets and are looking for a new diversion. Essentially, we struck a deal with the builder to showcase the yacht around the world and collect a modest fee for ourselves if we generated any interest that resulted in a sale."

"In the meantime," Rick interjected, "*LA BASA* is yours to use as you see fit."

"Exactly," Ramon crowed. "This motor yacht and the dinghy moored behind it are, as Malcolm Forbes would say, our capitalist tools...at least for now."

Rick briefly stood and glimpsed the striking yellow silhouette of a forty-one foot Cigarette OffShore racer tied up near the stern of *LA BASA*. "Some dinghy!"

"Admittedly an understatement," Ramon said in return. "Now that little gem can top out at over ninety. And when the seas are fairly calm, she almost floats above the water." He shook his head, remembering other times. "Of course, in three to four foot seas, it is much less comfortable. Still, that boat can do rough seas better than anything else in its class."

Rick smiled, well aware that driving a powerboat offshore at high speed in rough seas could be more punishing than breaking a bronco. He was also aware that the Cigarette 41/OS was truly the best there was.

"So, Rick," Ramon segued, suddenly serious, "tell me, how are you doing, really doing?

Puzzled at the familiarity of the query, Rick raised his brow. "Fine, I guess."

"You seem a bit stressed."

"It shows?"

"Not so obvious, but I can sense it."

"Well, the truth is," Rick admitted, "I am somewhat stressed. Right now, I'm pretty much a one-man show at RioAero."

"I figured that was probably the case," Ramon said with compassion. "Perhaps I can help. I think I can, that is why I wanted you to visit with me. There is something important I would like to discuss with you." His voice trailed off.

Rick waited.

Ramon clasped his hands together, leaned across the table, and then began to speak again, "Mr. Harris, Rick, I have a proposition for you. I do not need an answer right here and now. Still, I would like for you to consider what I say very carefully—as carefully as you would any other major business decision."

"Fine." Rick thought, why not. He was very much interested in what was going through Ramon Segundo's mind.

"But first, let me give you some perspective."

Rick raised his open hands slightly, gesturing Ramon to proceed.

"Now, I do not know how much you really know about BASA, except for what you read in the press. So, let me fill you in," Ramon began to explain. "As you are most certainly aware, we are one of your competitors in this very hot marketplace. And, as you are probably aware, we have also been making aircraft for a long, long time…a bit over fifty years. In some ways we have changed a lot, in others we have not. Nonetheless, we are a solid company with a worldwide reputation second to none.

"Today, our business is growing beyond our wildest forecasts, thanks in part to your country's airline deregulation. Demand for the Avio-23 is at an all-time high. Last year, we had the best sales ever. Our backlog is over one hundred sixty aircraft. Our factory has more than doubled its production. We are running three shifts. And, we are making a handsome profit—very handsome indeed." He was earnestly enthusiastic.

Rick nodded, wishing that he and his company were in a similar position. Unfortunately, RioAero was not.

"Just minutes before we sat down together today, I received word from Spain that we officially received funding authorization to increase our production facility by sixty percent. And that will, from our program plans, be completed within the next eighteen months. It is a huge step for BASA."

"I'm glad for you," Rick honestly intoned.

"But that is not all," Ramon said, pressing on. "Although it has not yet been announced, a go-ahead decision has been made to design a high-speed fifty-seat turboprop aircraft for regional airlines around the world." He paused for the impact of his next statement. "But what is even better, is that we have located a partner to share the risk in developing this new airframe. A risk, which you know, is rather high for any such venture these days."

"I understand." Rick nodded slowly. But why was Ramon telling him all of this? There had to be a reason. Rick had little idea where Ramon Segundo was going with the conversation.

"Of course, nothing comes without strings attached," Ramon moaned as he slowly began to get at the crux of the situation. "Our board of directors has, in consideration of its major investment in the company's future, mandated that we further increase our worldwide market share. For starters, our new goal is to capture seventy percent of the available seat miles of the regional airline market in North America. We already have the largest market share of any of our competitors, but you know that. So, our goal is something that we feel is..." He stammered for the word, "...something that, as you would say, is *doable*."

Rick smiled. Maybe possible, he thought, but not probable given the nature of the competition that was evolving among airframe manufacturers.

"But, Rick, I do have a problem, and here is where you come in to play. There are certain critical tools which I need to accomplish my goal. And, tools can be difficult to obtain." He paused, noting Rick's silence. "Are you following me?"

Rick thought for a second. "Well, to be honest, maybe not fully."

"I see." Ramon clasped his hands tightly together and took a moment of silence. "Okay, let me get to the point. The tools I need to be successful are talented people. People who can sell aircraft."

Now, the picture was becoming very clear to Rick.

"My proposition to you, Mr. Harris, is for you to join BASA as vice president of sales and marketing for our North American division."

"But—"

"Yes, I know you have just signed on with RioAero, and yes, I know the positions are very similar. But think about it...think about what you are now enduring. Your job with RioAero will not get any easier. It will not get any better."

"Well—"

"You do not know the half of what you are up against," Segundo said, sadly shaking his head. "There is no way your company can be successful in this market. Yes, you will work hard, but nothing will come of your efforts. Our mission, and probably that of Fairchild as well, is to block and counter any initiatives you take in the marketplace. Trust me, Rick, we have the product and financial backing to do it."

"Mr. Segundo," Rick finally spoke, "I respect your candor. I understand your intent to be aggressive and extremely competitive against any inroads RioAero may attempt to make in the marketplace. But believe me, it is my intent to be even more aggressive than BASA in making sales and obtaining market share."

"I expected you to say that, Rick." A broad smile filled Segundo's face. "You have a reputation for being a tenacious salesman. You are well respected in the industry. But once again, you must believe me...your company is in over its head. RioAero may have a potentially fine aircraft, but it is too new, it is too advanced, it is unproven. Add to that the fact that your company originates from a country full of economic turmoil, and your aircraft has had severe, unexplained problems..." Ramon paused, staring past Rick with unfocused eyes. "Rick, everything I see puts you behind the proverbial eight ball. From the outset, the odds are stacked against you. A host of systems problems are plaguing your new WindStar. The gear up incident reported in the morning paper is just one example. I am sure that is just the tip of the iceberg. When the press is finished dragging RioAero through the mud, you will wish you never heard the name WindStar."

Rick shrugged. "I guess that's just a matter of opinion, Ramon," he said, summoning all the politeness he could.

"No, Rick," Segundo responded quickly with a slightly raised voice, "it is more fact than opinion." He paused, looked Rick straight in the eye, and then reached for a large manila envelope that was on the far side of the table. "Perhaps one more piece of information may more clearly illustrate that you are between a rock and a hard place."

Rick furrowed his brow.

"The only North American customer currently scheduled to take deliveries of the WindStar is Highland Airlines out in Seattle. Of course, the Highland deal was set up while you were still with Fairchild, before you joined RioAero."

"Yes, I know." Rick was very familiar with the Highland Air operation. Increased load factors out of SeaTac required that the airline upgrade its old fleet of Beech-99s to larger aircraft. Early last year at the CAAA convention, Jim Highland, the airline's owner, met Salo Montero. The two immediately hit it off. Two months later when Highland visited the factory in Brazil, an aircraft purchase agreement was signed. Fairchild and BASA were stunned. Highland Airlines' first WindStar delivery was planned for late April.

"But, what you do not know," Ramon continued, "is that Jim Highland is not as bullish on the WindStar as you may have been led to believe."

"What do you mean?"

"Well, I hate to be the one to break this news to you, Rick," he said gloomily, "but Highland has changed his mind." He paused, assessing Rick's reaction.

Rick blinked and nervously shifted his eyes away from Ramon. What he had just heard was a total surprise.

"You see," Ramon went on with an apologetic tone, "Highland will be joining the BASA team. Late last night, he formally sent notification to cancel his contract with RioAero."

Rick's jaw dropped. He paled. He was blindsided, and he could not hide the depth of his utter shock.

"BASA has agreed to take all six of his Beech-99s in on trade for twelve Avio-23s."

Rick pursed his lips and closed his eyes for a two second count.

"Nothing personal, Rick, but BASA has made a strategic decision to defeat RioAero by doing whatever it takes. And when I say whatever it takes, I mean exactly that—WHATEVER IT TAKES."

Ramon opened the manila envelope he had been holding. He fished out a single sheet of paper. It was a copy of the press release announcing the Highland Airlines/BASA deal. He pushed the sheet of paper across the table to Rick. It read:

PRESS RELEASE
FOR IMMEDIATE RELEASE: FEBRUARY 20, 1981

HIGHLAND AIRLINES SELECTS
BASA AVIO-23 AIRCRAFT

BARCELONA, SPAIN, FEB. 20, 1981—Seattle-based Highland Airlines has signed a firm contract placing orders for twelve Avio-23 aircraft manufactured by BASA in Barcelona, Spain. The document includes an equal number of options. Highland is the thirty-second airline to order the popular Avio-23. Deliveries will begin June 1, 1981, and continue at a rate of one per month.

"We chose the Avio-23 aircraft because it has an excellent reputation among travelers and it lends itself well to our route structure," said Jim Highland, president of the airline. "The aircraft's reliability is second to none. Our comfort level in making the decision to go with the Avio-23 is extremely high," he added. The airline's fleet of six Beech-99 aircraft will be replaced by the new Avio-23.

Ramon Segundo, President of BASA, emphasized: "It is truly satisfying to supply our aircraft to an airline with the reputation of Highland. Highland's aircraft selection decision further reinforces why the Avio-23 continues to be the overwhelming choice of commuter and regional airlines around the world."

Highland Airlines' prior contract to acquire six WindStars has been terminated.

###

Rick could not believe what he had just read. But it had to be true. The real clincher was Jim Highland's handwritten note on the bottom of the page: "Ramon...The draft looks good to me. Let the press have at it. Regards, Jim."

"Damn," Rick softly muttered. He knew Salo Montero would be devastated. It was Salo himself who had closed the WindStar deal with Highland just over nine months ago. Now, there was no launch WindStar operator for North America. Losing a sale was one thing; losing a customer to the competition was something else—disaster.

Rick shook his head in dismay as an awkward moment of silence filled the afterdeck of *LA BASA*. He cleared his throat with a swallow from the glass of cola he had brought out from the bar. "May I have a copy of the press release?" he finally asked.

"Why certainly," Ramon quickly responded. "Indeed, you should have a copy." He handed Rick another copy of the release without Jim Highland's handwritten note.

Rick re-read the document again, then slowly, still disbelievingly, shook his head. Perhaps an omen, he thought.

The sun had already kissed the horizon across the Intracoastal to the west. The late afternoon's colorful brightness began turning to shades of evening purple. Soon dusk would transition to darkness. A different scenario was unfolding.

Ramon observed Rick was obviously shaken. Just exactly the effect planned. While Rick was still off-balance, Segundo measuredly pressed on in a consoling manner, "Like I said, Rick, it is just business...nothing personal."

Rick did not answer. Instead, he bent over and opened the top of his briefcase which he had placed on the deck under the table. He shuffled through the contents longer than was really necessary to file the document, and while still fumbling around beneath the table, said to Ramon, "I wish I had a press release or at least something to give you in exchange." He continued to fidget in his briefcase for a few seconds longer, and then sat back up in his chair.

Segundo momentarily diverted his eyes, sympathetically ignoring the clumsy fumbling. Something like pity was welling in him for the plight into which he had cast Rick. The feeling was brief. The situation was intentional, and effect had been desired and studiously well-crafted. Ramon kindly smiled. "I will accept whatever you might have to offer, whatever decision you make. But please, please think very carefully about what has transpired here this afternoon."

"I will," Rick responded, then consciously paused before going on. "Ramon, let me ask you this: Why would you think that I'd be ready to abandon RioAero and the WindStar? Like you said, I've only just signed on with the company."

"Aah, Rick," he said confidently, "you are a smart man. In fact, you remind me of myself when I was your age. I think by now you probably have been able to accurately assess the situation. I think you know where you stand. Be honest with yourself. Your company and your aircraft simply will not make it in this market. Not today, anyway. Part of my job is to be sure you fail. It is not a pleasant thing for me to do; and, again, it is not personal, mind you. But, it is going to happen. There is nothing anyone can do to stop it. The script has been written. The players have rehearsed. Everything is now coming together for me; everything is falling apart for you and RioAero."

Ramon seemed overly confident and too comfortable with the picture he was painting. He also seemed to know far too much about what was happening at RioAero—what was happening to the WindStar. Something was wrong, but Rick was unable to put his finger on it. He quickly replayed in his mind his meeting with Segundo. There was a lot of new information—information he would need time to digest. For now, though, he realized there was nothing to lose by playing along. In fact, playing along might even work out to be an advantage.

Rick took a slow calculated breath and said, "What you're saying may well be true, Ramon. I certainly must admit I did not expect to be faced with the avalanche of events that threaten both the WindStar and RioAero."

"Rick," Ramon spoke again with a slight paternal tinge, "believe me, RioAero's misfortunes are not over…not yet. You do not have a chance of succeeding. The WindStar is a dead program. Take it from me, Mr. Harris, D-E-A-D." Segundo allowed a brief moment of silence for the ominous words to sink in. Then, he resumed the pressure on Rick. "Please give my offer due consideration. You would be an asset to BASA, and BASA would be an asset to you. You will have access to all the necessary resources—this yacht, for example. I am confident you will make many aircraft sales at BASA. Rick, the right decision will make you a wealthy man."

Harris let several seconds wordlessly pass before speaking up. "Okay, Ramon, your point is well made." He nodded with a half smile. "I'll certainly give your proposition due consideration. Indeed, why should I make my life miserable by trying to dream the impossible dream if I now realize that it may never come true."

Ramon laughed aloud. "I like that, Rick…like Cervantes, there is much Spaniard in you."

Rick's smile broadened. "Very well, for now let's say we have an understanding. I'd be foolish not to accept your offer in light of what I already know. RioAero may have misled me. Perhaps BASA would be a better home for me. Let me sleep on it. You'll have my firm decision tomorrow."

"Thank you, Rick," Ramon said continuing in a reassuring tone. "You will not regret switching horses. RioAero is foundering."

"It seems that could very well be true," Rick commented with implied agreement.

"Okay…" Ramon stood.

Rick pushed back his chair, grabbed his briefcase from the deck, and rose to his feet.

Segundo smiled warmly. "Okay, say we get together tomorrow afternoon." He wanted to pounce quickly and pin Rick down on a decision. "Four o'clock?"

"That'll be fine, Ramon."

They shook hands.

"I will have a bottle of '71 Dom Perignon iced up."

"You really know how to close a deal, Ramon."

"*Gracias, Señor Harris.*"

Together, they walked forward to the starboard gangway.

"Damn, this is one exquisite motor yacht." Rick could not help but blurt out his thoughts. Well-placed exterior lighting showcased every facet of her bold and beautiful presence.

"*LA BASA* will serve you well, my friend," Ramon said with sincerity, counting on the fact that Rick would be joining his company, and with underpinnings gone, a competitor would fall by the wayside. "And, thank you for taking the time to visit with me today."

"No, Ramon," Rick was quick to respond, "I thank you. It has been my pleasure in more ways than you can imagine."

"I am glad you feel that way, Rick. I think we will work together very well."

They shook hands again.

Rick disembarked *LA BASA.*

"*Hasta mañana*," Ramon called out.

Rick acknowledged with a backwards wave of his hand as he walked down the dock.

In the stillness of the early evening air, Rick's mind kept flashing back on various parts of the meeting: how persistent Segundo was; how persuasive he could be; how much current knowledge he had about RioAero and the WindStar. But there was something that troubled him more than anything else. It was something that the BASA president had said—something that had been emphasized. It was one sentence. The words were unnerving to Rick. The words continued to play over and over again in his mind. The words echoed along with each step he took: Defeat RioAero by doing whatever it takes…whatever it takes…whatever it takes…

FORTY-FOUR

The Embers

Thirty minutes after the highly enlightening and all too unsettling meeting with Ramon Segundo, Rick Harris arrived at The Embers on Dixie Highway in Hollywood, just south of Fort Lauderdale. Over the years, the nightspot had been many things to many people. Its most recent reincarnation was as a discotheque—a pulse-pounding, strobe-lighted, smoke-filled tribute to that music's genre.

At the club's entrance, a stylishly attired doorman/bouncer disapprovingly eyed Rick's approach. Faded jeans, a khaki shirt, and well-worn ranch boots were beyond limits of the dress code, even during a relaxed happy hour.

Rick quickly intuited the man's thoughts, knowing that for the second time today his attire was being scrutinized, judged, and found wanting. Clothes make the man, and his clothes were definitely not vogue for this place, at this time. He flourished the tennis racquet he was carrying and said, "I just need to return this to a friend waiting inside. Promise, I won't be more than a few minutes."

The doorman's face scrunched up into a look of pained forbearance, then with a slight nod, cocked his head to the right indicating taciturn approval of the request.

"Thanks."

Rick strode through the open door into a sea of cool air that churned with the pulsating beat of Alicia Bridges' Nightlife. The club's low-level lighting dramatized periodic flashes from randomly rotating striplights and the occasional strobe burst. The milieu was infused with a slew of artificial pheromones and the haze of cigarette smoke.

As Rick's eyes adjusted to the surroundings of the bustling, yet far from overcrowded nightclub, he began to search for Victoria. Through massive ceiling mounted speakers, the song's vocals transitioned to a brief saxophone intermezzo with the subtle strings of ever-present violins in the background. The snappy crisp sound of the music was uplifting. A smile broadened across his face. He thought: *How could anyone say disco sucks?*

The DJ segued to a track from Chaka Khan and the dance floor thickened with activity. Voices buzzed, struggling to compete with the music. There was a shout here, a wave of clapping there, a guffaw from someone at the bar. It was wholesale energy. Tourists and locals were spooling up for what would be another lively Saturday night on the Gold Coast.

Rick scanned the swarm of faces, all unfamiliar. There was no sign of Victoria. He moved forward, weaving his way past tables, then continued along the perimeter of the elevated bar. Ahead and slightly to the right, he spotted her at one of the small tables near the dance floor. She was seated across from two athletic-looking young men.

After snaking his way toward her, Rick unobtrusively commandeered an empty chair from another table and slid it beside her.

"Hello, good-looking," he said with a big smile as he seated himself.

"Hello to you, handsome stranger." She wrapped her arm around his.

The young men at the table were taken back with Rick's arrival. One of them, speaking for both, gruffly parried, "She's a little young for you, old man. What say you just bug-off."

Rick raised an eyebrow. "Old man...bug-off," he quizzically repeated the words, as if not believing he had heard right. Without missing a beat Rick went on, "Why gentlemen, your remarks, rather boorish, are they not?" A half smile and a furrowed brow etched on his face. His eyes fixed on the two young men.

The young men, while unfamiliar with the word *boorish*, were quite sure it was not an apology nor an indication that Rick was about to leave. Rick's presence at the table was an unfriendly intrusion. Taken back, they puffed up their chests like gamecocks ready for the ring. The one who had verbally accosted Rick glared across the table, poised for a confrontation.

Rick coolly regarded the two's demeanor as he casually crossed his legs, twirled the tennis racquet by its handle and bounced its face off his knee half a dozen times. He had been served up enough frustration throughout the day. Unnerving a couple of punks would be a welcome diversion for him and release pent-up tension. He took the racquet by the throat and spun it around his index finger before allowing the grip to slide back into his hand.

A devilish grin spread across his face. "You guys like tennis?" he queried.

Before the young men could react in any way, Victoria spoke up. "Mr. Harris is a good friend of mine. He also just happens to be associated with the F-L-P-D." She paused.

The young men's eyes widened. All vestiges of aggression instantly evaporated. Their minds backpedaled to assemble damage control.

"So," she continued, "if you insist, I am sure he would entertain having a private conversation with both of you, if that is what you would really like."

Silence blanketed the table. The quiet was oppressive with the brief pause in the music as the DJ transitioned to the next track.

The young men, now only wanting to escape as promptly as possible, slid back their chairs and eased away from the table, muttering between themselves not quite audibly, as they headed for the bar.

"Fort Lauderdale Police Department, huh?" Rick remarked with a chuckle.

"It was the first thing that came to mind."

They both laughed.

"So, Rick, how does it feel to be back home?" She smiled, knowing that several weeks away in Brazil must have been a tiresome strain.

Rick shook his head. "You don't want to know," he responded bemoaningly.

Confounded at his response, she probed, "Family problems?"

"Hell no," he answered decisively, and then paused for a second. "Anyway, not yet. But if things continue on their present course, who knows."

"What is going on?" she asked.

His eyes fell to the tabletop with a slight shake of his head. "You don't want to know," he repeated.

"What is wrong?" She probed further, "What is troubling you?"

He interlaced his fingers, clasping his hands together. "Well, if you insist, if you must know…" His words dropped off.

"Rick, what is it?" He was a friend, and she was truly becoming alarmed.

He momentarily gathered himself. There was no reason for her not to know. "It's RioAero…the WindStar. I've got one hot potato on my hands." He nodded in deep accordance with his own words.

"Huh?" she retorted, not truly understanding what he meant. "I am not sure I am following you, Rick."

"It's a tricky situation…complicated…difficult to comprehend," he began. "Vicky, there's a real problem brewing." He scratched his head, an unconscious reaction to his frustration. "And, I'm afraid I'm stuck with it…got to deal with it."

"What do you mean?" She pressed him for an explanation.

A waitress appeared through the crowd and leaned over the table offering to take a drink order. Victoria requested a Long Island iced tea. Rick stammered for a second, and then with a wink, he asked for a gin and tonic, without the gin, heavy on the lime.

As the waitress departed, Rick deftly sidestepped Victoria's question and posed one of his own. "Tell me, Vicky, how much do you know about RioAero, about the WindStar?"

"How much do I know?" she haltingly repeated his question.

"Yeah, about what's happening."

She scanned his face for any additional clues to his query, what he was really interested in learning.

Rick pressed on, "Vicky, you're part of Salo's inner circle, you're family, he must talk to you about his company from time to time." He was hopeful, fishing. Now, he had subtly taken back control of the conversation.

She shrugged. "Yes, I suppose we talk quite a bit. My father and I are very close. He confides in me." She cocked her head to the side. "I guess I probably know more about RioAero and the WindStar than you do." She smiled. "You see, I have been living with RioAero as the undercurrent for most of my life. And the WindStar, well that is a relatively new program, but it is all Salo has had on his mind for the past three years. So yes, we talk about the aircraft and the company. Salo is a driven man like you; and like you, he intends to succeed in whatever he chooses to do."

"Yes, I know Salo is that way," Rick said, flattered with being compared to the chairman and CEO of RioAero.

"But you, Rick Harris," Victoria reminded him, "you have only been involved with the company and the aircraft for a month—one short month."

"That's very true," Rick agreed and then countered, "but let me tell you this, Vicky, during that very brief period of time I've learned a lot and I've seen a lot. These past few days—especially the past thirty-six hours—have been a real experience." He paused, pressing his palms together in a prayerful fashion. "Some of what I've seen I don't like, and some of what I've learned doesn't make any sense. There's something happening, and it's not very good. Even with what knowledge I have, I'm pretty sure I don't know the half of it." He was carefully mining for any missing information she could supply.

"What do you mean?"

There were a few yells from the crowd as the DJ faded in a cut from Loleatta Holloway. The song's opening, a penetrating percussive instrumental staccato, was followed by the lyrics: "Crash…Crash…"

Rick, momentarily distracted by the eerie prompt from the vocals, directed his focus back to Victoria. "Remember that electrical problem we encountered just before landing at Fort Lauderdale?"

"How could I forget?"

"Exactly," Rick said, regretting Victoria had personally experienced the incident, but thankfully all were well and accounted for. "Vicky, the reason for that harrowing event may not have been as cut and dry as it seemed at the time. It wasn't just a black box failure. Its cause...well, there's a real possibility it could have been intentional."

Victoria briefly looked away, but her reaction was not as shocked as it should have been. Her silence seemed more to do with being uneasy that he had come to this revelation than surprise at his words.

Rick continued, "There have been other even more perplexing incidents, incidents that could easily point to a well planned effort to..." He paused considering whether or not to say what was on the tip of his tongue—the word sabotage.

Victoria quickly jumped on his unfinished thought, "A well planned effort to what?" She too had had concerns of her own.

"That's the question, and I'm not sure I have the correct answer. But right now, I'm beginning to feel there's an effort underway to..." he paused again, and then quietly said the next few words, "sabotage the WindStar."

"Sabotage?" she carefully pronounced the word as she raised an eyebrow, but otherwise her face remained expressionless.

"Yes, sabotage." He looked intently for any further reaction from her. There was none.

"Go on," she said with interest, but again without any significant shock or surprise.

"Victoria, I believe there's an ongoing effort to prevent the WindStar from making it to the marketplace."

Her eyes began to rapidly dart from side to side. She did know something, though she was trying to act nonchalant about his words. Rick saw her neck muscles tense, and realized her whole body was taut.

"Can you think of anything that's going on," he coaxed, "anyone who might want the WindStar or RioAero to fail? Vicky, I need all the help I can get to understand what I'm up against. I need to sell this aircraft or..." Rick abruptly cut himself off.

Victoria's eyes had strayed. She was in deep thought about something.

"Vicky," he said softly, "are you with me?"

"Oh, sorry." Her eyes shot back to him. "I do know something about what you are saying."

"You do?" He purposefully acted surprised, though he really was not. He had already decided she did know something—something she was coming to grips with, something she would soon divulge.

She sharply inhaled. "Apparently Salo's greatest fear may be coming true."

"Huh?" Her weighty statement caught him off-guard. She really knew even more than he had thought. He was sure of it. Now, he had to find out what it was.

"Dear, dear," she went on, "Salo must not have told you about it."

Uh-oh, flashed through his mind. He steeled himself for the worst, with no idea what Victoria was about to reveal—what the impact would be on him personally; what dangers he and Tommy Maxwell could face during their investigation. Rick prompted Victoria to go on by saying, "Salo didn't tell me about what?"

"Well," she said, about to throw another log on the bonfire already blazing beneath the WindStar, "I guess Salo has not told you about the power play that is going on in Brazil—how it is affecting RioAero. If he had, I am sure you would probably have taken the next flight home to the States on the day you arrived in Rio."

"Great," he grumbled, "exactly what are you talking about, Vicky?"

"It really should come from him."

Neither one spoke.

The DJ's music blared over the speakers. The disco beat pounded throughout the room.

The waitress served their drinks.

Rick sensed he was about to learn something very important from Victoria—something that could conceivably lead him to the root of what was plaguing RioAero and the WindStar. "Let's move to the back of the club," he said, "to another table so we don't have to shout…where I can better hear what you're saying."

She nodded in agreement.

They collected their drinks, got up together, and inched through the happy hour crowd, making their way to the far end of the club. There it was much less busy and they quickly found a vacant booth.

"This is better," Rick said, seating himself across from Victoria. He leaned forward and continued, "Vicky, I'm up to my neck in quicksand, and now you tell me I need to talk with Salo." He shook his head in dismay. "Vicky, I'm committed to RioAero and the WindStar. I need help now, not later. I'm the one who has to make this aircraft reach the marketplace. I'm the one who has to make a major sale. And, I'm the one who has to make it all happen soon—very soon."

Rick had been convincing. "Okay, okay," she said, "I am sure Salo would want you to know, at least now."

"Good," he said in relief, "tell me about it." He looked at Victoria, whose face seemed uncharacteristically morose. He briefly bridled his drive to learn the truth, and gently said, "It can't be as bad as you think."

"Oh, yes it can," she replied with conviction.

Rick gave a comforting, reassuring smile. "Go ahead, Vicky. I'm here to help."

She fidgeted with her drink for a second, then the words tumbled out, "As you know, Brazil—my beloved country—is in turmoil."

Rick nodded. He had heard more than enough of that today—first from Santelli, later from Segundo. It seemed as though anything associated with Brazil was doomed to be weighted down with an albatross.

"Brazil has been under military rule for some time," Victoria went on, "since the revolution in 1964. We have no popular vote like in your country. Brazil is not a democracy, it is a military dictatorship. Our presidents—yes, that is what they are called—are always hand picked by their predecessors and then rubberstamped by an electoral college. General Joao Baptista Figueiredo is the man now in charge. He came from the Army...the cavalry, in fact. When he was a young lieutenant colonel, he played an active part in the revolution. As a result of that participation, he was rewarded time and again and eventually came to head up what those outside of Brazil call the National Information Service. Brazilians, however, know it as the SNI—*Serviço Nacional de Informações*—the feared military security arm where many of the dictatorship-era presidents are groomed.

"So," he impatiently pushed, "what does this have to do with RioAero and the WindStar?"

"I am getting to that Rick," she replied, slightly irritated with the interruption. "Be patient," she pouted, now breaking into a slight smile.

He took a sip of his drink.

"General Figueiredo," Victoria noted, "is a different type of man...different than all the others who came before him."

"What do you mean?"

"The general is a complex and highly intelligent man. He has his own views and is frequently outspoken." She leaned over the table toward him and slightly lowered her voice. "Believe it or not, he has a basic dislike for politics and politicians. In fact, he never really wanted to become president. He was pressured into it. Although not a person who believes in democracy, he freed the country from the straight jacket of the two-party system and allowed for a diversity of opinions to be made public. He even granted amnesty to thousands of political exiles. Now, he is focused on scientific and technological self-sufficiency. He wants the country's economy to expand. He strongly believes that RioAero will some day become a major industrial force—one that even Western Europe and the United States will have difficulty competing with. He and Salo think very much alike. Even with the severe financial problems RioAero is experiencing, Figueiredo supports Salo's initiative. That means you too, Rick."

Rick had carefully listened to every word Victoria said. Still, he had no answers. "The general sounds like a good man. So, what's the problem?"

"One word," Victoria said lowering her voice once again, "Cardella."

"Cardella?" Rick repeated.

"Yes, Cardella," Victoria emphasized. "A man named Carlo Vicente Cardella—General Cardella."

"I'm sorry," Rick admitted, "but I'm not up to speed with your country's political infrastructure or its players. Why is this Cardella guy important? Where does he fit into the RioAero/WindStar puzzle?"

"He is Figueiredo's nemesis."

"Nemesis, huh?"

She nodded.

He thought for a second. "Oh, I see, it's a political thing. Figueiredo has an archrival. That person is this Cardella guy who wishes he were the president, but he is not."

"Exactly," Victoria went on to explain, "only Cardella is much different than Figueiredo. He is more like many previous leaders my country has had in recent times. He is unprincipled, ruthless, and corrupt. He has little interest in helping the people of Brazil, or even the nation. Cardella is interested only in himself. From everything I know, he is an evil man—a man to fear. He is one of those people who would smile in your face as he slashes your throat." Now having set up the stage for Rick, she paused, and got to the point of it all. "Cardella wants to reorganize RioAero, possibly shutting down the WindStar program."

"What?" Rick was stunned to speechlessness. Several moments passed. "How do you know all this?"

"My father," she said. "Salo is very much involved with the military-industrial state. As you know, Salo used to be in the military. And, in many ways because of his connections, he was appointed to undertake a major initiative for Brazil—its entry into the aviation industry. With the government's backing, he created RioAero. It has become a part of him. Now that the company's very existence is in jeopardy, he is compelled to keep RioAero alive. He and General Figueiredo have the same philosophy. They both believe in time that the company and its products will be successful. But time is running out. Cardella is breathing down their necks. Cardella has convinced other powerful people in Brazil that RioAero must make some sales outside the country or else."

"Salo has his hands full, doesn't he?"

"He definitely does."

"Has Cardella actually approached Salo about cutting the WindStar program?"

"Yes and no. Cardella mercilessly grilled Salo about RioAero's shortcomings for months with the implied threat of termination due to inadequacies. Then, it seemed as though Cardella had disappeared. He was never around. Word had it that he was traveling abroad. No one knows why. Now, he is back, and his interest in RioAero's performance is more keen than ever. He phones Salo two and sometimes three times a week. The discussions are frequently less than pleasant."

"Turning up the pressure, huh?"

"Very much so. Cardella maintains that the WindStar has drained nearly a billion dollars from the country's treasury. And, he is right. He maintains that the WindStar will never sell well enough to pay back what has been invested in it. This is arguable. Salo says Cardella is shortsighted. Cardella is vile but not stupid, so there must be a reason why Cardella is highly adamant about his position; however, this is something Salo cannot quite figure out."

"I see," Rick said, trying to absorb all this newly gained information. "So, that's why Salo needs me to make a major sale as soon as possible."

"Exactly," Victoria reaffirmed. "Although Cardella is not the president, he is very powerful and has a very large following. He is looking for anything to make General Figueiredo look bad. Cardella is now zeroing in on the money-losing RioAero like a vulture over a dying animal."

"He certainly can make a strong case," Rick begrudgingly conceded. "Salo's company has produced little revenue over the past several years, and it has spent hundreds of millions on R&D and production tooling."

"Yes, all that is very true," Victoria admitted. "But Salo believes that a thousand WindStar's can be sold during the next ten years; and, beyond that, new aircraft now under development will assure profitability well into the future."

"I think he's right," Rick said, "but, then again, I'm biased. I'm already sold on the company and its aircraft."

"I was hoping you felt that way."

"I do, I really do."

"Not everyone feels the same way you do," Victoria cautioned, "and that is the problem."

"Of course, there will never be total agreement within a government or within a company," Rick offered. He paused to gather his thoughts. "Who else have you talked with about RioAero? Who else gives you reason to believe that something negative may be happening that could soon cripple the WindStar?"

"Cardella has a son, Raul." Victoria shook her head. "He is as sinister as his dad. But he was not always that way. We grew up together: private schools in Rio; special programs abroad. He had a crush on me." She self-consciously laughed. "We used to date, but that was a long time ago, and it was brief. He used to be a nice boy, then he became a young man. His personality changed. Maybe it is because he is following in his father's footsteps. He is a lieutenant in the Army now and works at *Centro de Informações do Exército* or CIE for short. That is the Army intelligence center, an autonomous service agency similar to the SNI. And his father, General Cardella, heads up the CIE."

"Cardella heads up the CIE, huh?" Rick groaned.

"Yes, I know what you are thinking, and you are probably right."

"You should keep your distance from that Raul," Rick advised. "If Salo remains unresponsive to General Cardella's agenda, the lieutenant may step in. You may become an expendable pawn in the game they're playing. They might use you to further pressure Salo."

"I know, but I hope that will not be the case. I suppose being here in the U.S. is fortunate for me."

"Maybe yes, maybe no." Rick did not like the scenario Victoria was painting. "Still, be careful, the world has gotten much smaller these days. If Cardella and his clan are as ruthless as you have depicted them to be, they'll stop at nothing to get their way."

"I know," she repeated, and then shifted back to the topic of Cardella's son. "Anyway, the last time I saw Raul was two weeks ago when I was with my club, hang gliding off the cliffs just southwest of Rio."

"And?"

"Well, for someone who does not work for RioAero, he seemed to know far too much about what was going on within the company."

"Yes?"

"About how poorly WindStars were selling; about how quickly company debt was mounting."

"Interesting, very interesting…" Rick began thinking aloud, "it seems like a few people out there know more than they should about what's going on at the factory." He recollected that Ramon Segundo was another one.

"Anyway," Victoria returned to her train of thought, "Raul mentioned that because of the disastrous economic situation in Brazil, the country would probably be better off without having a company like RioAero that was just sucking the treasury dry. Then, he said something I remember very well." She paused, eyes boring straight into Rick's eyes. "He said the WindStar was a dead program...DEAD."

Victoria's words penetrated Rick's very soul. The choice of words echoed loudly in his mind. Ramon Segundo had said exactly the same thing.

"You told Salo about the conversation, right?" Rick spun back.

"Oh yes, and he was extremely upset. He and Cardella are very much at odds concerning the fate of RioAero and the WindStar. Of course, Cardella has the upper hand...he out-ranks Salo in more ways than one."

Rick deeply inhaled and then his breath hissed out through tight lips. "Looks like there's real trouble brewing in River City."

"Music Man?" Victoria immediately questioned.

He laughed, breaking the tension. "You Brazilians know about that?"

"You forget I have spent many years as a student in your country."

"Yes, yes I remember."

"Tell me, Rick," she sincerely asked, "are you going to be able to put together a sale before it is too late?"

He thought for a few seconds. "That's a tough question. Yesterday evening, I came across a hot prospect. Early this afternoon, I felt even more confident. Then things quickly started to fall apart. I haven't given up, mind you, but it's going to be an uphill battle. With a little luck and proper timing, I just might pull a rabbit out of the proverbial hat."

"Timing is everything, is it not?"

"It's certainly a big part of the equation." He glanced at his watch. "Speaking of timing, it looks like I'm running late again."

"Oh?"

"I have a business meeting in less than two hours and must prepare for it."

She smiled, more at ease after unburdening her thoughts to Rick. "Do all aircraft salesmen work around the clock?" she asked, shifting her focus.

"The successful ones do."

"Well, I am certainly not going to stand in your way." She continued smiling. "Besides, I see my friends have arrived to join me for an evening of clubbing."

"Thanks for everything." Rick eased out of the booth and stood. "It was good to see you again, Vicky. You've very much helped me to understand what I'm up against. Please give my regards to Salo when you speak with him."

"I will," she said, "I will."

He leaned over and kissed her on the forehead, said good-bye in Portuguese, and then continued on in English. "Now, Victoria," he said, somewhat paternalistically, "I want you to be careful. Strange things have been happening. More could be on the way."

"I will," she quickly said, "and good luck to you."

"Thanks," Rick replied. He took two steps toward the door and briefly turned back. He pointed to the pillar beside the booth where he had propped the tennis racquet. "Don't forget again to take your sports equipment with you."

She affected a pained expression, then winked, and stood to greet her approaching friends.

Rick smiled as he departed the club.

FORTY-FIVE

Pasador Ranch

G ail glanced at her wristwatch. It was nearly nine o'clock in the evening and she had no idea where Rick was, or when he eventually would be coming home. Typical for an aircraft salesman, she thought.

Without warning, the rottweilers lunged to their feet. Their muscular black and tan bodies alertly mobilized. With hackles raised and paws slipping and sliding trying to gain traction on the smooth kitchen floor, the dogs madly dashed toward the entry door. Deep-throated barks resonated throughout the room. This was no drill. All was not as it should be outside the house—an encroachment or worse. The dogs were not sure. Not yet.

The startling alert sent Gail rushing to the pantry, yanking open its door. She reached for the stainless steel Walther PPK/S that was strategically wedged between two large blue canisters on the bottom shelf. Grasping the semi-automatic pistol by its black grip and lifting the gun from the shelf, she was smoothly ready for the threat: safety, off; hammer, uncocked.

The dogs' frenzy continued unabated. Gail's pulse quickened.

"Bruce, Jessica," she said in a firm tone, "what is it?"

The dogs' barking transitioned to a low rumbling growl. Their hackles were still raised; their undocked tails stiffly erect and motionless. An interlude of silence to hone in on the threat was followed by more ominous guttural growling.

Gail switched off the lights. She sidled to the kitchen door and peered through its small eye-level windowpanes into the darkness outside. Slowly, she cautiously opened the door just a few inches, all the while clutching the Walther, pointing it to the side and away from the dogs. Her index finger was posed on the trigger guard.

The dogs' alert status intensified. Growls again resonated throughout the room.

In the distance, she saw the pale yellowish headlights from a vehicle at the entrance to the ranch. The light was much different than that from Rick's BMW.

Gail's eyes widened as she watched the vehicle begin to creep up the driveway.

"Bruce…Jessica…" she said once again, this time in a commanding tone. "SIT…STAY!"

Both dogs sat instantly on command and fell silent. They awaited her next cue, taut and ready, with only an occasional soft threatening growl.

The vehicle continued onward, its headlights piercing the darkness.

Gail's mind flashed back to the night before—to the harrowing high-speed chase by an unknown pickup truck. Her body tensed. Her adrenalin flowed. The possibilities that swirled through her mind were pulse-pounding.

CLICK. She cocked back the hammer of the Walther.

At the sound, the dogs rose to their feet. Intermittent echoing growls were accompanied by an occasional snort. Their wet noses now sampling the air through the cracked doorway; their mirrored eyes cutting through the distant darkness.

The vehicle was drawing closer. She could hear the deep-throated rumble of its poorly muffled engine exhaust. She mentally girded for whatever might happen next. Her heart raced.

The vehicle was closer yet. Its engine noise grew louder, menacingly near. There was no attempt made to hide its approach.

Gail thought of the previous night's chase again. Tonight, she was without Rick. But the dogs were with her. While she knew how to use the Walther, she had never fired it at another person in self-defense— when her life depended on it. She hoped this would not be the night to find out how to do so.

Abruptly, the dogs again fell silent. The hush knotted her stomach worse than their growls had done. She knew rottweilers attacked silently.

As she steeled herself for what she had to do, an excited whining bark filled the void. The dogs' bodies trembled. Their backs slightly arched. Thick undocked tails thrashed against the doorsill.

Gail was momentarily stumped by the change in the dogs' behavior. They were even more excited than just seconds before, but now with intense anticipation.

Whining barks turned to outright barking. The dogs were eager to charge out of the house.

Only briefly baffled by the dramatic change, Gail instantly snapped to the reason for the dogs' new behavior. Her tension evaporated and relief flooded her mind. She decocked the Walther. She pulled the door wide open.

"Go get 'em!" she commanded the dogs.

The rottweilers rocketed from the house to greet the old Chevy that had just pulled into the parking area.

As Rick slid out of the pickup, the dogs happily leapt into the cab.

"You guys like trucks, huh?" he posed the question to the dogs, knowing full well that the words, except for "trucks," were meaningless to the dogs, but their joy at his return was shameless. "Come on, let's go see mommy."

The dogs dashed from the truck toward the door to the kitchen. Rick followed, briefcase in hand.

Gail sheepishly smiled. "You scared the bejesus out of me...out of us all. I thought that you had taken the BMW this morning. I had totally forgotten it was the truck."

Rick gave her a firm comforting hug and a long kiss on the lips. "Sorry to have startled you. Are you okay?"

"Yes," she said taking a relaxing breath, "yes I am." She paused. "Since you flew home on Friday afternoon, things have been a bit stressful. RioAero, the WindStar, Brazil...I don't know, maybe you shouldn't have taken that—"

"Don't say it, Gail," Rick interceded, "please don't even think it. Everything will work out...soon, I promise."

She turned on the lights they strolled into the kitchen. Rick seated himself at the table.

"So, Mr. Harris, how was your day?" she inquired, now at ease. Her calmness in stark contrast to the emotional tension riveting her body only moments before.

"Well," Rick began, "my day was interesting and then some."

"Go ahead, fill me in." She poured two glasses of iced tea and joined him at the table, the ever-present rottweilers at her side shadowing each and every move she made. "If I'm going to have to live through this with you, I need to know what's happening." She paused, recollecting that one of his agenda items for the day had included a visit with a private investigator. "How did things go with your friend, Tommy Maxwell?"

"He's one different kind of guy, that Tommy Maxwell..." Rick could not hold back a broad smile. "...but a really bright fellow."

"Did he agree to help you?"

"It took some convincing since he's not in the PI business anymore, but yes, he took the case."

"Good." Gail breathed a sigh of relief, and followed up with a question, "If he's not doing PI stuff, what business is he in these days, and how did you get him to work with you on what's happening to the WindStar?"

"Tommy's into some kind of high-tech oceanography—actually, marine cartography—the kind of work I think he used to do with the Company up north. His new operation—MacroScientific, Ltd—seems to be doing very well." Rick slugged down half of his iced tea.

"Anyway, after I gave him my pitch about the WindStar, I think he felt that it would be a fun thing to temporarily get back in the PI business."

"Fun?"

"Yeah, Tommy likes being challenged. And, there's no doubt about it," he said with a nod, "getting to the bottom of what's going on with the WindStar will be a real challenge. This is going to be a difficult case to crack. While I do have my suspicions about what's happening and why, as soon as I think I have a handle, everything changes. There seems to be more than one spider weaving a web in hopes of snagging the WindStar and pulling it from the air."

"What's the latest?"

"Well, you know there's Dan Cole, who you know I don't trust even as far as I can see. He has to be involved, and Tommy should be helpful in snaring him. I bugged Cole's office.

"Rick!"

"The stakes are high, Gail. Ya gotta do whatcha gotta do."

She just shook her head in obvious disapproval.

"Then, there's BASA."

"BASA?" she questioned, remembering the name of the competitor of RioAero. "Another airframer could be responsible for what has been happening to the WindStar?" Incredulous, she thought.

"Maybe," Rick said with a shrug. "Earlier this afternoon, I had a meeting with Ramon Segundo, their president, at his request. He comes across as a classy kind of guy, but he's as slick as a snake and as devious as one, too."

"What do you mean?"

"Well, after telling me that he was personally going to kill the WindStar program—doesn't want any new competition screwing up his sales—he offered me a job heading up sales and marketing for his company's North American division."

"What?" Gail was stunned and baffled as to why. "And, you said?"

Rick laughed. "What do you think?"

"That you'd sleep on it?" She figured that a blunt "no" was too unimaginative a reply for Rick.

"Aah, Gail," Rick said with a grin, "you know me too well. Actually, I told him—without ever saying the word yes—that I'd be foolish not to accept his offer, and that I'd give him my answer tomorrow."

"Why? Are you serious? You mean you're considering leaving RioAero? Already?"

"No, no," Rick quickly responded, "that's not the case, not at all. Although I really wanted to, I knew that I couldn't say: I'm so sorry,

Mr. Segundo, but I wouldn't sell that piece of crap you call an airplane if my life depended on it!"

"Well, of course not," Gail said with grimacing distaste at his coarse language. "But you could have used a bit more tact by thanking him for the offer and then politely turning him down."

"I suppose I could, but I chose not to do it right then and there."

Gail furrowed her brow in confusion.

"You see, I have this hunch," Rick began his reasoning out loud. "I think that BASA just might be involved with the current spree of sabotage that's plaguing the WindStar." He paused. "Segundo seemed too confident about beating a new player even before the game had actually begun. I want him to continue on being confident in his position. I don't want him to divert from whatever activity he may be undertaking. If he and his company are somehow behind any of the incidents that have occurred, I certainly don't want him to cover his tracks. Now that he thinks that I'm about to join his team, he should be relaxed. Hopefully he'll get sloppy and make a mistake. Maybe he'll reveal something he shouldn't."

"So, you really think BASA is a more likely culprit than Fairchild or some other airframer?"

"Interesting question. But the more I think about it, the more I zero in on BASA. I really don't think it's Fairchild Aircraft. Their parent company is a big player in government contracts. Fairchild Republic Division is known for its famed A-10 Warthog. And, they're working on a new jet trainer to replace the Air Force's fleet of aging T-37s. I don't think they'd be stupid enough to jeopardize everything they've got going for themselves just to stop RioAero from entering the market with the WindStar. Remember, I know the folks at Fairchild. While they're as competitive as hell, it just isn't their style to act as the mafia would against a new pizza joint in North Jersey."

Gail nodded, listening intently.

Rick continued, "However, just when I thought that I was coming to grips in isolating who might be behind sabotaging the WindStar, I learned of yet another spider spinning a web."

"You're suggesting there could be independent and unrelated parties involved with what's happening?"

"That could very well be the case. Each one could be unaware of the others; and each one could have a separate agenda. But, this new spider is big—really big. And, its involvement is almost impossible to believe." Rick drained the remaining iced tea from his glass.

"Go on," she said, intrigue fueling her interest.

"I came across some new information during a quick visit with Victoria, Salo's daughter, when I returned a tennis racquet she'd mistakenly left on the aircraft. She mentioned that there's a power struggle going on within the Brazilian government. She said that the country's president has an archrival named Cardella, and that this archrival is maneuvering to quite possibly restructure RioAero."

"Oh my," Gail groaned, "that's not good."

"For sure."

"But, Rick," she asked, "what does all of this have to do with you? I still can't understand why you're getting involved with it. You're a salesman, not a James Bond. Why don't you just pick up the phone and tell Salo it's his problem, because it really is. Then, let Salo sort everything out."

"Well..." Rick slowly said.

"Well?" Gail grilled.

"Well, it's just not that easy."

"Rick, I'm your wife. I know you. There has to be something going on inside that head of yours. You owe me an explanation."

"Okay, okay," Rick said, unabashedly. "You know I like a contest...I like to compete. And, you know if I believe in something, I'll do the best I can for that something. Right?"

She nodded.

"Unfortunately," he continued, "Salo isn't in a position to do what must be done to save RioAero. Salo is in a viper pit. He has to tread very carefully. He can't continue to forge ahead with the WindStar program, and he can't buy any more time. There are some very powerful people in the military establishment who would oppose any kind of proactive initiative he might undertake. Indeed, if he became too burdensome for them, they could easily strike him down. Vipers are like that."

"Sounds grim."

"It is."

"Rick, you're really sticking your neck way out on this one. You must have other compelling reasons than just accepting a challenge or helping out Salo."

"Damn, you're awesome, Gail." Rick smiled genuinely. His wife could read him almost like a book. "It's hard for me to to put into words why I'm doing what I'm doing. But the truth of the matter is that I do like Salo, and I respect him, too. In fact, in many ways he and I are similar. Like him, I want to do the right thing. Unlike him, I'm not in Brazil. I'm in a much safer position to do whatever it takes, or at least give it a try." His eyes briefly fell to the two rottweilers quietly lying on the floor near his wife's feet. "Gail, my life has been privileged. My aircraft sales career has been good to me...good to us. Now, it's payback time. I feel I have the opportunity to do something important—something I believe in—even though it may be difficult, painful, and perhaps dangerous. I don't want to see thousands of factory workers get laid off in a week or two because some greedy sonovabitches don't give a damn about anything else except themselves. I don't want to see a fantastic aircraft fail and not even be given the opportunity to make it to the marketplace."

"Rick—"

"I'm sorry, Gail, but I really need to finish what's on my mind. Please hear me out. Then, if you truly think I should back off and tell Salo this is his problem, I will."

She pursed her lips and nodded for him to proceed with his thoughts.

"Years ago, when I was getting my MBA, we used the case study method to learn many of the key principles of marketing, management, and the like. It showed why some companies succeeded, yet others failed. RioAero should succeed. They have a lot going for them. But the problem is that they have been failing—miserably failing. Fortunately, they recognized it. So, steps were taken to rectify their weaknesses, which pretty much were centered in sales. Now, if given just a small amount of time, RioAero will be back on track and become a success. I'm sure of it."

He was waxing pedantic, Gail thought. He did that from time to time. She bit her tongue and listened, having agreed to hear him out.

"What RioAero is now experiencing are the negative effects from what I call externalities—things that are beyond its control; things that are outside the marketplace of supply and demand. There are many instances where this sort of thing has happened in the past to other companies in other industries. But to my mind, one case stands out— Preston Tucker."

She shrugged, not sure what he was talking about or how it tied in with RioAero's dilemma.

"Just after the war—The Big War—this guy out in Detroit decided to build a better mousetrap while the legacy automakers simply treaded water. The Tucker '48 was an advanced automobile—so advanced that it threatened the major automobile powerhouses in Detroit and the politicians who slept with them. To make a long story short, Tucker and his company were stonewalled, smeared, spied upon, and sabotaged to such an extent that the car never really made it to market even though it was revolutionary and should have been a big seller in the long run.

"Now I'm not saying that RioAero and the WindStar exactly parallel the Tucker case, because that is not so, but there are some strong similarities. I just don't want to see the WindStar get bushwhacked like the Tucker did. This is another good product with good people behind it. Since RioAero is paying me to sell their product, I can see an implied authorization for me to do what I can—to get to the bottom of whatever is going on; to stop the WindStar's graveyard spiral. Even though no one told me I had to take it upon myself and do what I'm doing, I believe it's the right thing to do." He paused and searched his wife's eyes. "Gail, I ask for your support."

She drew her breath in while slowly shaking her head from side to side for what seemed to be an agonizingly long time to Rick. Finally, she spoke up, "What you're doing is not wrong, Rick. Maybe way out of bounds. Maybe a little crazy. Now that I understand your reasons, I can't stand in your way—I won't. I support your decision."

"Thanks, I was hoping you'd say that."

"Rick, please, please be careful," Gail said with genuine concern. "This is a very high stakes game you're playing. Your adversaries undoubtedly have much to gain if successful. They also have much to lose if they fail, and much, much more to suffer if they are found out. Be careful," she repeated.

"I will," he said from the heart, "I will." Then, with a raised and cheerful voice, he switched gears. "Now, are you ready to join me for some business and pleasure at September's?"

The weighty atmosphere dissipated. Pleasant anticipation buoyed their spirits.

"Why certainly, Mr. Harris, I thought you might have forgotten."

"Not tonight." Rick beamed. "I can't wait to hear what Tommy Maxwell has found out. Hopefully, he'll have some good information to share with us."

"Oh, speaking of information," she abruptly interjected, "Bob Waterman at the *Sun-Sentinel* called late this afternoon. He said he'd like for you to give him a call as soon as you got in. He has some information he'd like to review with you."

"Good, I'd like to talk with him too," Rick affirmed. "Even though his byline wasn't on that brief gear-up blurb in this morning's paper, he might be able to tell me how the story and photo made it to print so quickly. Did he give you a number?"

Gail handed him the message note with the phone number and left the room to dress for the evening.

R ick glanced at the note and mumbled, "I wonder how Bob's golf game is doing these days." He grabbed the phone and started dialing.

Bob Waterman, a short, pudgy, far from athletic man in his late twenties, had migrated south after graduating from NYU with a degree in journalism. After a brief stint with the *Miami Herald*, Waterman found his home at the *Sun-Sentinel* and was just digging in his heels as an investigative reporter when he met Rick Harris. Their introduction was slightly over four years ago during a charity golf tournament partially sponsored by the *Sun-Sentinel* at the Doral. Rick and Bob had been paired together in the same foursome. After five blistering hours under a South Florida summer sun, a relationship was melded that endured to this day. Perhaps due to their conversations, Waterman developed an interest in aviation and even began taking flying lessons. He wrote several award-winning stories dealing with various aspects of the subject— *MIA Counterfeit Parts, Negril Beach Drug Runners,* and his latest, *Mayday in September.* On aviation feature stories, he invariably relied on Rick for background information or to check on content accuracy. Bob Waterman was as diligent and principled as a reporter could get. Rick admired the young man.

The phone rang twice. "Waterman," came the voice from the other end of the line.

"Bob, it's Rick Harris."

"Hey, Rick, good to hear from you. My, it's been a while, hasn't it?"

"Yes, five or six months—something like that," Rick said.

"So, how are you doing?" Waterman inquired.

"I've been better but, then again, I've been worse. My golf game is still in the tank. That's life, I guess." Rick's comments were intentionally non-committal.

"Still selling airplanes? With Fairchild, right?"

"Actually, yes and no. Airplanes, yes; Fairchild, no. I've been with RioAero for just about a month now. That's why I thought you were calling."

There was dead silence on the other end of the line.

"Bob, you still there?"

"You caught me off-guard, Rick. I, uh, I..." he stammered, "I had no idea you were with RioAero. I, uh, was just calling to get some background information on a story we're going to run about the, uh..."

"The WindStar?"

"Yes, the WindStar. Perhaps you may be more helpful than I had initially thought."

Rick chuckled. "That may very well be the case. You see, I just came back home this Friday after three weeks at the factory in Brazil. So, I've got plenty of background information, if that's what you really need."

"Great."

"But before you begin asking away, I've got a quick one for you."

"Shoot."

"On page one of this morning's Metro Section, the paper ran a photo and a few lines on the WindStar." Rick hesitated, waiting for a response.

"Uh…yes, yes we did," Waterman said almost apologetically. "It, uh, wasn't very flattering, was it?"

"HA, flattering?" Rick's voice boomed. "That's the understatement of the year. Tell me, Bob, how did you guys come by that photo?"

"Rick, I can't say."

"Do you mean can't or won't?"

"Can't," Waterman quickly responded. "I mean I don't know exactly who submitted it. All I can say is that the photo and some copy were delivered to us via a messenger service just before press time. That's about it. No credits were listed."

"And you ran it with no questions asked?" Rick posed the query with a tinge of suspicion.

"Of course not!" Waterman brusquely shot back, and then relaxed his tone. "Come on, Rick, you know we're not that kind of a paper. I called a friend at the airport to check it out. He's one of those bored-out-of-your-mind fire/rescue guys whose job it is to pretty much just hang out in the city's plush facility at the airport and wait for disaster to happen. Anyway, at my request, he nosed over to the south ramp and verified what had happened. Only then did we choose to run the piece."

"And the copy?"

"We did some heavy editing on what came with the photo. Apparently, whoever submitted the stuff to us wasn't a big fan of your aircraft."

"I could imagine that," Rick said with more than a hint of sarcasm. "So, no other ideas on who may have submitted it?"

"Not really, most likely a plane spotter. You know, those crazy folks who are keen on observing, photographing, and recording anything dealing with aircraft. Sort of like modern bird watchers, if you ask me."

"Hmmm…" Rick moaned, at a loss for any other comment. "I guess that will have to do." Rick knew better. No damn plane spotter would have done that, he thought. Still, Bob was probably divulging all he knew. "Now, what can I do for you, my friend?"

"I have another disturbing story that we're getting ready to run in this Sunday's edition."

"Oh?" Rick's intuition told him what story Waterman might be planning to write. "More on the WindStar?"

"Yes, but this time it's worse."

"Go on," Rick said. He had little choice.

"There seem to be some serious problems with that new bird of yours."

"What do you mean?" Rick felt compelled to play dumb.

"This time, what I've got is even more damning."

"Uh-huh…"

"It's another photo of the WindStar—a really bizarre photo. This time, the aircraft has one propeller totally missing and the other…" he paused, closely examining the photo on his desk. "Wow, the other prop looks like it separated from the engine and impaled itself into the fuselage."

"Goddamn." Rick knew exactly what Waterman was referring to.

"Aptly put, Mr. Harris. It's damning alright. What can you tell me about it?"

"On the record or off?"

"Both," Waterman answered. "But before you make any comments, I need to tell you that I've already had a discussion with the head of RioAero here in Fort Lauderdale. I've incorporated some of what he told me into a brief story we're about to run."

"Head of RioAero?"

"Yes, a very pleasant and knowledgeable gentleman named Dan Cole. You know him, I assume."

Rick blanched in disgust, only imagining what kind of damaging information Cole could have supplied to the reporter. "Oh yes, I know Mr. Cole. He's brand-new with the company. Actually, he's only been with RioAero for a few days."

"Interesting, somehow I got the impression that he'd been in the industry all his life."

"That's history alright, but he knows very little about RioAero or the WindStar."

"Well then, I'm glad I have you on the phone, Rick. I need to be sure that my information is accurate."

"What did Cole have to say?"

"Let's see what he said." Waterman reviewed his notes and began speaking in sentence fragments: "It's a new airplane…problems are bound to occur…RioAero is a young company…the WindStar is its first airframe design…there is always a learning curve with our production workers…the company is currently investigating its quality control…there is no cause for alarm, new aircraft always go through a teething process…" He paused, shuffling through paper on his desk. "Okay, then there's just some basic info on the commuter and regional airline industry. Cole made it a point to fill me in on the excellent working relationship the factory has with the Brazilian airworthiness agency, which, like the factory itself, is controlled by the government. Sorta like one hand washing the other, wouldn't you say?"

Rick avoided answering the direct question and its damaging implications. "Well, Mr. Waterman, some of what Cole said is correct, and some not. There's no doubt that RioAero is a young company and that the WindStar is its first major airframe design. For your information, the company spent over three years in designing and then testing the aircraft. Many hundreds of hours of pre-production test flights on three different aircraft were required prior to receiving type certification from the FAA and their Brazilian counterpart, the CTA. Everything was flawless—no hiccups, no delays."

"I see." There was the sound of typing in the background.

Rick continued, "We, as well as all airframers, make a product which we call an aircraft like Keebler makes its product called cookies. Only we make our product in a more exacting manner than Keebler makes its cookies. We have to—our product is made to last for twenty, forty, and even sixty years. Yes, we have an approved recipe or design specification just like Keebler does, but we use significantly higher levels of technology, and spend much more time testing every rib, stringer, and rivet than you could possibly imagine. Our lead production people are highly trained and certified. Independent technicians inspect every stage of the production and assembly process. If there is a learning curve, it only means that our initial production rate is slower than it will be later on, not less safe. Every aircraft that rolls out the factory door is 100 percent, not 99.99 percent. And, that's all on the record, Bob."

"Uh-huh..." There was the sound of more typing in the background.

"There's no aircraft better designed than the WindStar," Rick pressed on. "There's no safer aircraft than the WindStar. There's no aircraft currently being used by commuter or regional airlines that is more advanced than the WindStar. Because of all of this, I elected to leave Fairchild and join RioAero."

"Uh-huh..." The typing sound stopped. "But why does the WindStar seem to have such significant problems?" Before Rick could answer, the reporter punctuated his thought. "Somehow, I get the feeling that what I know is only part of the story."

"Indeed, Bob, you do only know part of the story. At this juncture, even I only know part of the story."

"What do you mean?"

"I can't go on the record with unconfirmed suspicions. All I will say is that a far-reaching, in-depth investigation is currently being undertaken. And, I can assure you that when our investigation is over, there will be nothing found to label the WindStar as a compromised aircraft."

"You sound pretty sure of yourself, Rick."

"I am sure, Bob. But I can't tell you anymore right now. In twenty-four hours, I'll lay all the cards on the table. Then, you'll understand why I'm saying what I'm saying. Then, you'll understand why I could not say anything further at this time. For now, though, I do have one favor to ask of you."

"Go ahead."

"Kill the story. Give me twenty-four hours, and I'll give you a story that will knock your socks off."

"It's not that easy, Rick," Waterman lamented. "It's on the wire. Everyone is going to run some kind of story to go along with the photo."

Damn, Rick thought. "I know publishers like a headline that sells, but could you tone this one down a bit? Could you avoid running a story that makes the reader jump to an unfair conclusion? Could you report without slamming the WindStar or RioAero?"

There was silence on the other end of the line.

"Look, Bob, just say there is an unknown irregularity with a vendor item...that it's currently under high-level investigation...that it has nothing to do with the aircraft's certification. All of this is totally accurate."

There was no response from Waterman.

"Bob, you're a damn good investigative reporter, and the *Sun-Sentinel* is an honest paper." Rick held his breath and paused, trying to somehow figure out how to convince Waterman to tread lightly on the WindStar incident. The answer came to him. "Maybe I can whet your appetite. I have a proposition for you."

The silence was broken with two words from Waterman: "I'm listening."

Good, Rick thought, I have not struck out yet. "Okay, try this on for size. I have a brand-new WindStar coming up from the factory. It should be arriving here mid-morning tomorrow. The aircraft is being expressly ferried up for a high-level flight demonstration to key executives from three different airlines who are all but totally convinced that this is the aircraft for them."

"Go on."

"I'd like for you to join us for that flight demonstration. See what the WindStar is all about. Get a first hand view of why some major airline people and I are excited about the aircraft. Then, after you've seen it with your own eyes, write your story. Say anything you like."

"Rick, are you sure you really want to do this? It could backfire on you."

"I'm absolutely sure about it. Talk with the folks during and after the demo. Ask whatever questions you like. Just don't get too pushy with your questions. These are my customers, my friends. Do let them know that you are a reporter. Do let them know that you have more than a passing interest in the WindStar. Do not identify them or their airlines in your story unless they expressly authorize you to do so. And please, don't write about any unconventional flight maneuvers we might demonstrate since that could give my friends at the FAA heartburn if they were to read about it. Do we have a deal?"

There was a brief silence, then came Waterman's response: "We do, Rick, we have a deal."

"Good." Rick was relieved. "Meet me at the RioAero hangar tomorrow on the South Ramp at 10:45 a.m., SHARP."

"See you then."

Rick hung up the phone. He exhaled loudly in relief.

G ail re-entered the room. She saw a thin smile of satisfaction on his face. "Is everything working out for you?"

Rick glanced up and begging the question said, "My, my, my...you are one strikingly beautiful woman."

Gail smiled and did a three-sixty. She was dressed in a gold halter-top, tight black silk pants, and red pumps with three-inch heels. She looked nothing like an equine veterinarian who had just hours before been tending to a mare in a nearby paddock that was due to foal sometime later this weekend.

She carefully eyed what Rick was wearing and announced, "You had better clean up. You can't go to September's looking like a horse farmer."

"Right you are." Rick slid his chair back from the table and got to his feet. "I do suppose I should slip into something more appropriate for the evening."

Rick exited the kitchen to take on another persona.

FORTY-SIX

September's

Ignoring the raised eyebrows, Rick and Gail moved forward as politely as possible. The two weaved to the front of the line, squeezing through the menagerie already queued up and patiently waiting to enter one of the most popular nightclubs on the Gold Coast.

For the past several years, September's had been widely known as the place to be and be seen, especially on a Saturday night. It was stylish. It was fast-paced. It was high energy. The clientele: very upscale or at least pretending to be. The music: disco, of course.

At the entrance stood the club's sergeant-at-arms—a towering iron man who chose to wear a lightly-tinted pair of sunglasses even in the darkness of night. Although Rick had enjoyed visiting the club from time to time, he was far from a regular and certainly not considered a VIP.

The man in the sunglasses took a side-step to center himself in the doorway when he saw Rick and Gail approaching. "The wait is thirty to forty-five minutes," his deep bass voice boomed, although his face never turned from the waiting line of people.

Rick smiled winningly. "Pretty much normal for a Saturday night, huh?"

The man mechanically rocked his head forward and back in a habituated response, his face remaining expressionless.

Undaunted, Rick explained he had an invitation to join a friend in the club's cloistered *haute cuisine* restaurant.

The man imparted a resounding laugh. "Everybody says that!" He motioned with his chin for them to take a place at the end of the line.

"No, no," Rick quickly came back. "My name is Rick Harris. I'm here to have dinner with Tommy Maxwell."

"Maxwell, you say..." the man slowly mouthed the name. He slid the sunglasses down the bridge of his nose to fix an intimidating stare into Rick's eyes. The formidable man's eyes narrowed, his brow knit into a frown, the tight muscles on his neck were brought into sharp relief in the glare of the lighting that framed the club's entrance. His face contorted, eyes initially squinting, adjusting to the bright glare. "Maxwell..." the man repeated the name. "And, he is a friend of yours?"

Rick was taken back by the man's question. He hoped that when Maxwell had entered the club earlier that evening, mention had been made of Rick Harris as an expected dinner guest. If not, Rick and Gail would have a long wait in line and possibly miss their meeting with Tommy. Did the glowering hulk of a man confronting him simply not know Tommy Maxwell, or did bad blood exist between the two. Perhaps Tommy had had an earlier encounter with this man. With Maxwell, Rick thought, you could never be quite sure about anything. Remaining optimistic that the gatekeeper was just being intimidating in order to verify Rick's claim of knowing Tommy Maxwell, Rick nodded a "yes" to the question but said nothing else.

The man stared long and hard at Rick, then shifted his eyes to Gail. The story was true. They were expected inside. He had fulfilled his duty. His body relaxed. A wide grin promptly filled his face. "Aah, Mr. Maxwell, he is one different kind of guy."

Relieved, Rick agreed, "He certainly is."

The man reseated his sunglasses with one firm shove of a finger and spoke as if he were addressing an old friend. "Mr. Maxwell arrived about thirty minutes ago. He told me to expect you." The black velvet rope that cordoned off the entranceway was swiftly removed. The man stepped to the side and motioned them through. "The restaurant is—"

"Behind and to the right of the lower bar."

"Yes, Mr. Harris. Have an enjoyable evening."

They walked through the entranceway and past the overly thin, heavily made-up, young blonde woman who was seated within a small enclosed booth and responsible for collecting cover charges from those entering only the club and not the restaurant. She had overheard Rick's earlier conversation and simply said, "Enjoy your dinner, sir."

Rick flashed a quick acknowledging smile in the young woman's direction as he led Gail through the foyer.

The nightclub's own musical ensemble, also named September's, actually more closely resembled a small sixteen-piece orchestra than a band. The group had just finished its first set of the evening and was on a break. In its absence, the percussive thump of recorded music piped through the club's state-of-the-art audio system and fused with heavy scents of perfume, cologne, and the always-present cigarette smoke. The ambiance was typical for any discotheque of the day.

The posh club was both old and new. Every few years, mysterious fires caused enough damage to require a near total renovation. Still, September's was always pristine and always open for business during the high season. You could count on that.

As Rick and Gail moved past the foyer, the club's massive interior fanned out ahead of them. They eased around one of the half a dozen, strategically placed telephone pole-sized columns that supported the lofted ceiling's skeleton of rough-hewn rafters and purlins. They skirted the slightly elevated upper level and its expansive oval bar that was packed three deep with weekend revelers. Pausing now and then as a courtesy to allow meandering patrons to ease past them, the twosome continued toward the rear of the club, following along a carpeted pathway. After descending a short series of steps that led down to the dance floor and the lower level bar to its right, Rick and Gail slipped into a short hallway that led to the entrance of the restaurant.

In front of the restaurant's huge mahogany and stained glass double doors stood a stocky, nattily-clad man in his mid-thirties. He smiled warmly. "You have reservations?"

"Yes, indeed," Rick spoke up. "We're with Tommy Maxwell."

"Aah yes, Mr. Maxwell," the man immediately responded with the familiar party line phrase. "He did mention that he would be joined by some guests. Please step inside." He pulled open one of the doors allowing entrance into an entirely different world.

The restaurant was truly the antithesis of the club. Heavily insulated from the sound and activity they had just transited, the restaurant was an oasis of tranquility and a culinary nirvana. A hint of classical music whispered in the background. Frescoed walls and a broadly arched pale-blue ceiling set up the ambiance for the venue. Carefully designed cove lighting diffused golden-orange hues for the sensation of an early evening piazza during Renaissance times. Curiously, September's nightclub and restaurant, considered together, fused to create reflections of both times present and times past.

From out of nowhere the maitre d' appeared. *"Monsieur et Madame, bonsoir."*

"Good evening," Rick Harris returned. He identified himself and said that he had arrived to join Tommy Maxwell.

"Certainement." The maitre d' turned briefly to survey the restaurant. "Aah, there is *Monsieur Maxwell.* Please follow me."

Rick's eyes searched the restaurant. He did not see Tommy.

The maitre d' briefly paused, allowing two other guests to depart the restaurant. As he moved forward again, he whispered to Rick, *"Monsieur Maxwell*...he is a *connoisseur*...he is one of our best patrons...he truly appreciates our fare."

Again Rick scanned the area, still unable to spot Tommy.

The maitre d' continued on toward the back of the restaurant, eventually stopping near a recessed alcove that was bustling with activity. Half a dozen people, all dressed in very formal attire, stood surrounding a table. There was a loud burst of laughter. Then, the conclave dissolved and the group filed out of the restaurant.

From within the shadows of the alcove, a man in a white Panama hat rose from his chair.

"You're a bit tardy, Mr. Harris," Tommy Maxwell said, removing his hat.

Rick's jaw dropped. This was not the Maxwell that he knew, not at all the person with whom he expected to be meeting.

More dapper and even more bizarre than the funkiest bachelor to ever cross the cover of GQ magazine, Maxwell was dressed to the nines: open collared bright-pink shirt, framed by a heavy gold chain that hung from his neck, and swathed in an expertly tailored creamy linen jacket and flared trousers. Everything about him screamed: Let's party tonight. He was certainly not the conservative man Rick had visited earlier that day.

"Sorry about being late," Rick apologetically said. "It has really been a crazy day for me."

"HA," Tommy retorted, "no more so than mine." His eyes quickly settled on Gail. A broad smile spread across his face accentuating his perfect sparkling white teeth. "My, my, my," the words came slowly at first, "and who is this unbelievable beauty?"

Tommy extended his open hand to her. She politely grasped it. Then with a flourish, he lowered his head and lightly kissed the back of her hand.

"Gail Richmond," came her response to his question. "I am Rick's—"

"Why, of course..." Maxwell interrupted as he recollected the name. "It's Doctor Richmond, right?"

She smiled and nodded.

"Mr. Harris," his two words flowed, eyes still focused on Gail, "you are a very fortunate man to have such an attractive and intelligent woman for a partner in life." Then, remembering the presence of his associate who was now quietly standing at his side, he said, "Oh, excuse me, Gail, this is Monica Rice. She's my gal Friday, Saturday, Sunday, and the rest of the days of the week. She makes sure my company ticks like a clock."

Monica's studied indifference quickly brightened with the compliment.

Tommy gestured for Rick and Gail to join the table. "Sit, sit..." He signaled with two nods to the hovering maitre d' who snapped his fingers at the table captain. Tommy reseated himself and continued on, "I've already ordered for us all, good food takes time to prepare. I hope you don't mind. Unfortunately, I'm on a rather tight schedule. This last minute investigation of yours is really cutting into my weekend's activities."

"Thank you for ordering for us," Rick spoke up as he and Gail settled into their chairs. "Sorry about your weekend's activities, but you know the urgency of this case. And, I can't even begin to express to you how deeply I appreciate your efforts."

The appetizers began to arrive within seconds.

"I hope you like fish," Tommy said, briefly directing his attention to the food. "This restaurant prepares the very best seafood I've ever had. Your palate will be delighted when the entrée arrives." He paused briefly to transition back to business. "So, Rick, tell me what you've been up to since you called Monica earlier today…just after, shall we say, you left my ears in you-know-who's office." He laughed, rubbed his hands together with anticipation and glee, then promptly dug into the smoked salmon appetizer the waiter had just served.

Rick took the next several minutes to provide essential details of his meetings with Cole, Segundo, and Victoria.

Tommy listened intently, occasionally making a comment here and there. By the time Rick had finished speaking, so too had Tommy finished his appetizer.

"No wonder you're late," Maxwell said. "You've been busier than a one-armed paperhanger." He laughed at his own analogy. "From what you say, this investigation is going to be pretty complex." He took a sip of chardonnay, then eyed the label on the bottle, which read: Grgich Hills, Special Reserve, 1978. "Excellent wine, one of the best." Then, Tommy arched an eyebrow in Rick's direction. "You know, Mr. Harris, complex usually means expensive."

"Cost is irrelevant," Rick quickly responded. "We need to do whatever it takes, and the sooner the better. I believe we will only have one shot at solving this debacle, and time is quickly running out."

"Don't worry, one shot is all we'll need," Tommy said confidently. "But the question is, just who do we shoot and when? From what you tell me, there could be several targets we need to line up in our sights. It's apparent that more than one campaign is being undertaken against the WindStar. These initiatives could easily be independently spawned. And, of course, those who are involved most likely have different motives. This makes the case very complex."

"Yes, so it seems." Rick crunched a bite of tangy capers between his teeth. His lips puckered. He took a swallow of water. "Have you and Monica been able to uncover anything?"

Tommy glanced at his watch and quickly began spooning down the lobster bisque he had just been served. He did not answer Rick's question. "I love this bisque. Enrico, the executive chef, is a magician when it comes to food." He cast a glance to Monica and snapped a quick nod, handing the conversation off to her.

"Well, Mr. Harris," Monica began, getting right to the point, "transmissions from Mr. C's office were at first almost nonexistent, but the pace picked up as soon as you left the building, that was slightly after 5:00 p.m.—5:12 to be precise. I know, because that is when he had his first telephone contact. In fact, he referred to you as 'that sonovabitch who had been hanging around.'" She smiled thinly.

Rick laughed, briefly closing his eyes and shaking his head. "The feeling is mutual, and I'm sure he knows it."

"Anyway," Monica proceeded, "he had no visitors, made two international and two local calls, and also received one local call."

Tommy broke in, "Of course, we have everything he said on tape. It's not wiretapping, mind you, it's just eavesdropping. There's no law against that." He returned to his lobster bisque.

Monica continued, "Let's see…" Her eyes darted from side to side as if sorting data she had previously stored for recall. "Although I only was able to hear one side of his telephone conversations, I think I was able to get the gist of some of his discussions.

"His first call was most likely to someone in Brazil. I surmised that because he said, 'Hey listen, Dan Cole doesn't have time to learn any goddamn Portuguese.' The conversation was brief, but heated. Cole was animated and profane. I was able to deduce that whoever was on the other end of the line made mention of things that had been planned, but did not pan out. Then Cole came unglued—he started yelling into the phone. He said that things needed to be wrapped up real soon. In his own words, 'the deal has to be done and now.' He said that you, Rick Harris, were becoming a major problem. That's all I got."

Rick shook his head. He had no idea to whom Cole might have been speaking, or what the conversation was all about. Then, for a brief moment, he felt flush. The word "deal" stuck in his mind. For that instant, he thought Cole might have become aware of his efforts to sell to Santelli. He quickly shook off the thought as too unlikely. There had to be some other deal to which Cole was referring—some other plot with which Cole was involved.

Monica continued, "Next, Cole received a call from some newspaper reporter. I heard him repeat the words '*Sun-Sentinel.*' It was obvious that the reporter was fishing for information concerning some kind of propeller problem with the WindStar. Cole spent about ten minutes chatting with the reporter. He—"

"I know," Rick politely interrupted. "I talked with that same reporter earlier this evening. I've known him for several years. He filled me in on the conversation. I think I've convinced him to be as fair as possible in running the story. I did, however, promise to take him on tomorrow's flight demonstration."

"Oh, okay," Monica matter-of-factly said before continuing on. "After about five minutes of silence in his office, Cole placed another international call to a man he called Jeffe. He congratulated the man for some kind of good work that had just been completed. Then, he asked the man how everything else was going. Cole seemed pleased with what he heard. The conversation lasted just under two minutes."

"Jeffe," Harris repeated the name. "It doesn't ring a bell. I wish it did." He shook his head. "Were you able to tell what country Cole was calling?"

"Unfortunately, I was not," Monica responded. She briefly paused. "But come to think of it, Cole did ask: 'How's it going *down there*?' Perhaps he was calling Brazil again. I can't say for sure."

"I'll check it out," Rick said. "Maybe there's someone at the factory named Jeffe. What's next?"

"He called a man to whom he referred only as *El Capitán*. Cole tried to speak Spanish, but he just bastardized some English words, thinking it sounded like Spanish. He asked how the meeting went. I deduced that whatever meeting to which he referred had gone well. He seemed surprised. Then, he asked when the deal was scheduled to go down. I surmised there was going to be another meeting—an important meeting—sometime tomorrow afternoon. Cole said, 'See you then.' The conversation ended."

"Does any of this make sense to you, Rick?" Tommy asked.

"Not sure," Rick responded, "it's sort of cryptic." But again, the word "deal" stuck in his mind. Something big was going to happen tomorrow. He had to discover exactly what it was. His attention turned back to Monica. "Who was his last call to?"

"He checked in with a man named Felipe, possibly the Felipe you asked for information about. He said he'd meet him at the club on Federal Highway at 8:30 p.m. That's all the intelligence I have been able to gather from Cole's office, at least so far. We are, however, automatically recording any further transmissions that may be sent over the repeater to our office."

"All very interesting," Tommy said as he slowly sat back into his chair. "As you can hear, lots of things are happening and Cole seems to be right in the thick of it."

The waiter began serving the sole Veronique entrées. Conversation momentarily ceased.

"Monica," Rick spoke up, "were you able to do that background check on Cole's friend, Felipe Retegi?"

"Yes, indeed." Monica smiled. "Originally from Andorra, a tiny country between France and Spain, Retegi attended college in the United States–mechanical engineering at the University of Pittsburgh. He briefly worked for Lockheed on the L-1011 program, and then went to Spain, perhaps to be closer to home. Most recently, he returned to the States to work for an aircraft leasing company called ComJet up in Boca."

"Who did he work for in Spain?" Rick asked.

"*Barcelona Aeronáuticas, SA,*" Monica said in perfect Castilian.

"Bingo," Rick said immediately, "BASA! And, did you happen to stumble across anything about his current employer—ComJet?"

"I couldn't find very much," she said with a wink, knowing better. "ComJet is a very private company, but I did find it listed as a subsidiary of a Bahamian corporation that was oddly enough called BASA Holdings, Ltd."

Rick's eyes lit up. "Now we're cooking with gas," he declared. "Some of the pieces to this puzzle are coming together. To me, at least one part of it is becoming increasingly clear."

"Good." Tommy grinned, realizing exactly what was going through his friend's mind.

Rick pressed on with his thoughts. "From what you've just told me, I'd say that Cole, Retegi, and Segundo are on the same team. They all directly or indirectly work for BASA. Even though Cole was recently appointed as managing director of RioAero here in the States, my bet is that he's also on the BASA payroll."

Gail finally joined the conversation. "Rick and I talked about BASA earlier this evening. He has a strong suspicion that BASA is somehow involved with what's happening to the WindStar. Monica's information certainly strengthens that suspicion." She paused, making eye contact with everyone at the table. "I could be wrong, but..." She paused again. "Okay, now think about this: Remember when Cole telephoned the person he referred to as *El Capitán*?"

She saw three staggered nods.

"Well," she continued, "maybe he was calling someone on a boat." She turned toward Rick. "Maybe, just maybe *El Capitán* is a man named Ramon Segundo."

Rick's eyes widened. He slowly smiled, then said, "Why yes, of course, I remember the first mate referring to Segundo as *El Capitán*." He chuckled, then ruefully shook his head. "So now, Cole thinks I'm ready to switch horses and join BASA. Maybe he spoke too soon when he called me a sonovabitch. He probably thinks we'll soon be playing on the same team." Rick now thought that the meeting and the deal Monica had heard Cole refer to probably involved Rick's scheduled return visit to Segundo on *LA BASA*.

"But there's more. BASA is certainly spinning a tangled web," Monica interjected. "Remember you also asked me to check out AeroMech, the aviation services company in Opa Locka?"

"Yes," Rick said, and then offered a minor correction, "but really it was Tommy's idea to profile AeroMech."

Monica shrugged. "Anyway, that's how I stumbled across the connection between ComJet and BASA."

All eyebrows shot up. Everyone at the table was lost for a second.

"Oh sorry, I've gotten ahead of myself." She regrouped, and then went on to explain, "AeroMech is a major overhaul and repair facility for older 707s and DC-8s. They also service smaller aircraft, and, among other things, are a factory authorized service center for the Avio-23. But, and get this, they are also owned by BASA Holdings, Ltd."

Rick took a sharp breath.

"Wow," Gail declared, "those were the people Joey called to help get the geared-up WindStar back on its feet. Only they put a screwjack through a wing tank, accidentally on purpose. Poor Joey, I'm sure he had no idea about AeroMech."

Tommy was just swallowing the last bite of his sole Veronique. "Shall we go to the videotape?"

"Interesting, I hope," Rick said, very pleased with what he had learned so far.

"Mr. Harris…" Tommy chidingly intoned. He patted his lips with a linen napkin and took a long swallow of chardonnay before continuing. "Now, I purposefully saved the best for last. Our man Cole should get an award for best actor in a short videotape travesty." He snickered.

"Tell me about it," Rick said.

Tommy began a brief narrative. He noted that a man approached the WindStar at 6:00 p.m. "Fortunately," Tommy stated, "even though the sun was just dipping below the horizon, the bright security lights from the Administration Building allowed the camera to adequately capture the man and his movements. Unfortunately, the video showed a wide view of the entire ramp area; it was not just narrowly focused on the aircraft. Still, I was able to obtain some good intelligence by enlarging and scrutinizing each frame on the tape. As you suspected, the man was none other than Dan Cole—the man in the tangerine guayabera shirt. Cole opened the cabin door and quickly—well, as quickly as a short, fat old man could—climbed up the airstairs, went directly to the cockpit, and settled into the left seat. After about a minute, he exited the aircraft. Now I can't say what, if anything, Cole did while he was in the cockpit, but he was certainly there, that's for sure." Tommy paused, glancing at Rick. "Any comments?"

Rick narrowed his eyes, pursed his lips, and glanced at Gail.

She shrugged.

Rick shook his head. "Not really, Tommy. There's nothing the surveillance tape can really prove except that Cole entered the cockpit and was there for a brief minute. My bet is that he was setting up the WindStar to take a fall. But there's no evidence to prove it."

"Sorry," Tommy said facetiously, "but there's more." He cleared his throat with another swallow of chardonnay. "Later that evening at 8:15, Cole and his friend pulled up in a black Lincoln Town Car. This, of course, was after the WindStar had fallen to the tarmac, and was while you and Gail were in the Administration Building. The tape showed the two of them standing about forty-five degrees off the left front side of the WindStar. One frame showed a congratulatory handshake—which was odd—and then the tape captured the flash of a strobe. Regeti had taken a photo of the aircraft. After placing the camera into the trunk of the car—also rather odd—they entered the aircraft. This was when you turned off the lights to the ramp area, removed the video tape and exited the building." Tommy paused. "You know the rest."

Gail smiled. "That's undoubtedly where the *Sun-Sentinel* got the gear-up photo of the WindStar. Cole and Retgi's position near the aircraft at the time of the camera's flash proves it. The photo in the newspaper was taken from that angle."

Rick remained silent, deep in thought. He was processing what Tommy had said—what the videotape contained.

"Are you with me, Rick?" Tommy asked.

"Yes, yes I am," Rick said, quickly organizing what he had just reviewed in his mind. "Perhaps we can go even further and now actually implicate Cole as being responsible for the gear-up incident after all."

"How so?" Tommy queried.

"Try this scenario on for size," he confidently began. "Gail and I know that the gear lever was in the up position immediately following the incident. We saw it. We also know that the downlock override switch was armed."

Gail nodded in agreement.

"And," Rick added, "Joey Delgada told me that shortly after Cole and his friend departed the area, he personally checked the cockpit, but found nothing abnormal. When I visited with Joey at the hangar earlier today, he told me he was positive that the gear lever was in the down position and that the override switch was safety-wired. We also know that no one entered the aircraft after Gail and I left it and before Joey performed his inspection, except..." Rick, abruptly stopped, his eyes widened, a broad smile spread across his face. "Except for Dan Cole and Felipe Retegi. So, we really don't have to speculate anymore. Cole and Retegi were responsible for rigging the WindStar so the gear would retract when the master power switch was flipped on. And then later, cleaning up the crime scene after the fact."

Tommy, pleased his intelligence had tied events together so well, flashed a timeout signal with his hands. "Yes, your conclusion appears to be valid, but we must be cautious," he warned. "Even though what we've just pieced together implicates Cole and Retegi in the sabotage against the WindStar, blowing the whistle on them now would prove counterproductive. There's a lot more we need to learn about what's going on. We need to know why. We need to continue to build our case. We need to identify all those involved with any aspect of the sabotage. That's the only way to save your aircraft and your company."

Everyone at the table nodded in agreement.

Rick spoke up, "So far, everything we know points to BASA. Still, there are other incidents involving the WindStar that need to be traced to someone—the electrical failure and the double propeller separation."

"Perhaps our continued eavesdropping on Cole's office will provide us with more intelligence," Tommy suggested.

"Or," Rick interjected, "perhaps eavesdropping on Segundo would help."

"That would be nice," Tommy said, "but, Rick, we just can't slip onto his boat at midnight and plant a bug."

"I know, but it would certainly be helpful if *LA BASA* were bugged, wouldn't it?"

"Indeed it would."

"Well," Rick offered, "let me give you some information that should prove to be helpful. Near the end of that meeting I had with Segundo earlier today, he gave me a copy of a rather disastrous press release, presumably intending that I fax it down to Salo in Brazil." Rick paused, no foreshadowing emotion on his face. Then, he continued acting out the rest of his story. "As I leaned over and began to stuff the document into my briefcase, which was under the table on the yacht's afterdeck, I realized that the second bug you had given me was right at my fingertips. So..." Rick beamed as his words trailed off and he thumped the underside of the table with his open hand in a pantomime of planting a listening device.

Tommy applauded. "Good show, Mr. Harris."

Rick grinned. "Now, Mr. Maxwell, you have two ears to help you gather intelligence."

"Right you are," Tommy said. "But there's a slight problem."

"Oh, what's that?" Rick asked, slightly taken back.

"You see," Tommy began his explanation, "the two bugs I gave you are sort of related. They were intended to be placed together—to complement each other—at the same location. They transmit on the same low powered frequency; they use the same repeater."

"What does all that mean?" Gail asked.

"Not to worry," Tommy said, easing the apprehension that was quickly mounting. "It's merely a logistics problem. We can work around it."

Still not convinced, Gail posed another question: "But if both bugs transmit on the same frequency, couldn't dissimilar yet simultaneous transmissions from different locations create just a bunch of gibberish?"

"Yes, that very well could occur, but the bugs themselves have an extremely low microwatt transmission power. Their range is only about three hundred feet. This helps to avoid detection as well as to conserve battery power. That's why we typically use a significantly higher-powered repeater to scramble and then re-transmit signals to our base of operations. But considering where they have been placed, there should be no interference between the bugs. The second bug certainly can't reach the repeater at RioAero. It would be best, however, to station someone very close to *LA BASA* to monitor anything that that bug transmits."

"Fine," Rick said, "let's do it."

"There are complications, though," Tommy added. "I have limited manpower. Remember, Rick, I'm not in the PI business anymore."

"So, what do we do?" Rick asked.

Tommy answered, "What we're working on is certainly too sensitive to share with anyone else. We can't bring in an outsider."

"How about the Feds—the FAA, the FBI?" Gail inquired. "They'll need to know about this sooner or later. After all, Cole was involved with the sabotage of an aircraft, and that's a Federal offense."

Tommy smiled at her naiveté, holding back a laugh. He glanced at his watch. "It's late Saturday night, tomorrow's Sunday. By the time we contact and then convince the Feds to jump on this case it will be Tuesday or Wednesday, if we are lucky. That would probably be too late for any significant help. Besides, with all of the bureaucracy, they'd probably be totally ineffective in accomplishing our objective: Saving the WindStar program. The focus would be narrowly on Cole and screw up the big puzzle we're trying to solve."

"Any suggestions?" Rick asked.

Tommy's eyes shifted to Monica. He winked. "How would you like to spend tomorrow hanging around Bahia Mar, sunning yourself on the bow of one of those beautiful offshore racers I could borrow for the day?"

Monica's face lit up. She knew Tommy was referring to the high performance class of offshore powerboat that he had developed a passion for since he began working on the contract with PetroMar, the Colombian oil producer. Three of the boats owned by PetroMar were currently based at Anderson's Marina on the New River.

"Well?" Tommy posed the question to Monica again. He knew that although two of the Don Aronow-built Cigarette 41/OS boats were in dry-dock, a Scarab 38 was available.

"Seriously?" There was excitement in her eyes.

"Absolutely," he instantly replied. "You've been offshore with me over a dozen times. I'm confident you can handle the Scarab. I'll call Hal Anderson and have him ready it for you by 10:00 a.m. Then, just motor it over to Bahia Mar. I'll join you around midday." He paused. "Oh, do remember to stop by the office before you go. You'll need to bring the gray receiver and the tape recorder that are on my credenza. And, please be sure to pick up some refreshments at Winn-Dixie. What do you say?"

"Great," Monica blurted out, happily surprised at the chance for fieldwork.

Tommy turned to Rick and asked, "How much cash are you carrying?"

"Two or three hundred, may be a little more."

"I guess that will have to do for now." He motioned for Rick to give the money to Monica. "We'll need some decent cash to grease the dockmaster's skids. The closer we tie up to Segundo's boat, the better for us. I have confidence Monica can make it happen."

Monica took the money Rick handed over and carefully placed the cash into her purse. "I have a feeling that tomorrow is going to be a very long day." She excused herself from the table.

Tommy turned and watched her stroll out of the restaurant. He commented, "They don't come any better than Monica."

"You're a lucky man, Mr. Maxwell," Rick affirmed.

"Indeed, I am." Tommy rose from his chair. "Now, if you'll also excuse me, I've got some business to conduct out in the club. Enjoy the rest of your meal. And, do join me later at the lower bar. They have one excellent band here." He took two steps over to Rick and whispered, "Thanks for dinner. Be sure to leave a generous tip."

Tommy seated his hat low on his head before making his way to the club.

Rick and Gail leisurely finished their dinner.

Ten minutes later, the bill was presented at the table. Rick quickly reviewed it, and then glanced toward Gail. "Tommy was right, a complex case means an expensive case."

The tip was well over a hundred dollars.

Outside the restaurant, the nightclub was jam-packed—wall-to-wall people, generally singles looking to connect. The September's orchestra had just begun its second set of the evening. Their music mixed Latin rhythms with elements of funk to produce the strong, steady disco dance beat that energized the crowd.

At the lower bar near the dance floor and stage, Tommy Maxwell threw back his second shot of Crown Royal. He grimaced slightly and exhaled. As soon as the burning sensation began to abate, he motioned for the bartender to serve up another.

"Take it easy, my friend," a voice from behind spoke up above the music.

Tommy, caught off guard, involuntarily flinched. He quickly turned to face the voice.

It was Rick Harris.

"Damn…" Tommy extorted, instantly recognizing Rick along with Gail.

Rick clasped Tommy on the shoulder and said, "Remember, we've got a long and important day ahead of us tomorrow."

"I know, I know," Tommy quickly responded. "Something else was preoccupying me." He paused, self-consciously shaking his head. "I always get wired just before a gig—stage fright I guess."

"Don't worry," Rick reassured, "we'll do the best we can. I'm confident tomorrow will turn out just fine for us."

"HA," Tommy echoed above the music, "that, my friend, is not what I'm worried about."

A confused look spread across Rick's face.

Tommy threw back his third Crown Royal, shook his head hard, and noisily exhaled. He filled his lungs with a deep breath and said, "Now, that's better." He moved away from the bar. "Take my seat. I'll be back." He disappeared across the dance floor.

Rick offered the barstool to Gail and reiterated his comment from earlier that evening: "Maxwell is one different kind of guy."

She nodded in agreement, then ordered Campari and sodas for them both.

The band had just finished an opening medley of songs and was rearranging the set for its next number.

"Earlier," Gail said, "Tommy seemed fine. Now, he seems awfully uptight."

"You never can tell about that guy," Rick remarked. "There's something going on with him. He mentioned something about stage fright."

"Really?"

"Maybe he's getting cold feet about this WindStar investigation."

"That's not the impression I got over dinner."

The stage faded to black. Within moments, borderlights hanging from high above the bandstand painted the set in dramatic crimson red. Striplights, inset within the stage floor, steadily stepped-up to soften the mood with an amber hue. A tight spotlight briefly illuminated an empty microphone, then widened, lessening the intensity to further set the tone for the upcoming musical arrangement.

A high-octave chord from an electric guitar sang through the club's speakers. Almost simultaneously, the drummer began a light rhythmic tapping on the cymbals. A keyboard syncopated its notes. Three violins effortlessly added a smooth flowing undertone. A second guitar began the melody. A bass thumped in the background.

Rick turned away from Gail to regard the orchestra.

From upstage left, a violinist broke ranks with the others and slowly began a dance-like stroll. He moved forward toward the center stage microphone. The tall lean man swayed with the music as he bowed.

Rick recognized the man immediately. His jaw dropped. "Gail, look at this," he said in disbelief. "Is that who I think it is?"

Her eyes followed his to the bandstand. "Why...why yes," she responded, and then smiled.

It was Tommy Maxwell on stage and beginning to perform a major hit song—Native New Yorker from the group Odyssey. And, he was doing well—very well—despite his pre-performance anxiety. Both he and his voice had a striking presence.

The dance floor filled. Rick and Gail mixed in with the footloose crowd. The music flowed with all of its artistic complexities.

Tommy performed one more number, and then rejoined Rick and Gail who were back at the bar. "Just a tall glass of water, please," he said to the bartender. Tommy was soaked with perspiration. His performance had drained every ounce of energy from his body. He was temporarily exhausted, but, at the same time, revitalized.

"You're a man of many talents, Mr. Maxwell," Rick said complimenting his friend.

"Thanks, an interesting diversion," he nonchalantly replied. "I like to push myself and do things on the edge of my level of comfort. Mostly it works fine, sometimes not, but it always tests the nerves."

"That's life," Rick philosophized. "If you wait until you're truly ready to do all the things you dream about, the opportunities to do so tend to pass you by."

Gail nodded and smiled.

After a few minutes of idle conversation, everyone was ready to leave the club. All knew full well that the coming day would be pivotal for the WindStar and RioAero. But no one could know just how pivotal it would be—how critical the next day would be for them, the aircraft, and the company that built it.

No idea.

None.

FORTY-SEVEN

Rio de Janeiro

T he silence of the midnight hour was broken.

From just inside the doorway to the study at the general's private retreat near Rio de Janeiro, a well-trained SNI agent caught the sound. He craned his neck to the left to lock in on the origin. Even though forewarned, his eyes strained as he intensely peered down the narrow dimly lit corridor.

The faint distant click of hardened heels on tiled flooring grew closer, louder. The crisp purposeful sound resonated with each step.

The agent quickly glanced at his charge in the study, then back down the hallway. He squared his shoulders for the necessary visual identity confirmation—standard protocol. Seconds later, he made it.

Within the study, the general was totally detached from his surroundings—indeed from all reality. He had been that way for nearly twenty minutes now. Ensconced in his favorite high back leather chair, he sank deeper and deeper into another world—a world potent to the imagination, but totally fiction. His eyes flickered from side to side as the story leapt from the paper to unfold in his mind. Pages turned without thought, effortlessly, almost automatically. He momentarily paused from reading to think: There certainly must be some military application for this. He was sure that Crichton's *The Terminal Man* had a deeper message for him; it was more than just an exercise in creative writing. His absorption proved it had to be.

The general's involvement in so many cloak and dagger activities throughout his long military career made his mind keen to seek any and every angle that could be used for tactical advancement. In Brazil, everything was about control and repression. The country's leadership structure had preserved its position utilizing those tactics, beginning with the military coup in 1964. Power periodically bounced from one general to another as each claimed the office of the presidency under a pseudo-democratic process laced with a mixture of coercion and control. However, once in office, some autocrats proved to be more benevolent than others. These moderates aroused suspicion and discontent among hard-liners. The current president had come into office hand-selected by the previous moderate president. Both men shared many of the same philosophies. The churning was inevitable among the hungry-eyed-wannabes. The grumblings among hard-liners were now beginning to cause waves that threatened to become a groundswell. This could very easily lead to an unseating of the general—the president.

The friction developing was no secret. While not yet desperate, the general sought to explore any concept that could strengthen his position or mitigate any weakness, lest it be used against him. Perhaps Crichton had that concept. The general closed his eyes tightly as he pondered the thought.

Just then, the SNI agent audibly cleared his throat.

Instinctively, the general glanced up, abruptly pulled back into the real world from which, through fiction, he had temporarily departed. Brief eye contact with the agent and a single nod were the only communication needed to be mustered for the moment.

The general decisively uncrossed his legs, snap-closed the book he was reading, and rose to his feet in preparation to greet the arriving visitor. Shaking the last vestiges of the fiction from his mind, he filled his lungs with air and stretched his arms backwards, flexing his upper body much like a large bird preparing to soar into flight. Even at the seasoned age of sixty-three, his movement was more like the strong athletic young man he had once been than the aging potentate he had now become—a man who, unbeknownst now to anyone, would suffer a major heart attack before year-end.

He waved off the ever-present SNI agent, who dutifully exited the room. Then, he refocused on the approach of his visitor. A thin practiced smile was replaced with an actual warm welcoming grin, etching itself into his leathery face. He extended his right hand.

"You look well, Mr. President," the visitor said with an enthusiastic shake of hands. "You have always had a firm grip, sir."

"Thank you, Salo. Strength is power, you know." The general's once mirthful eyes still had sparkle. Then, he sighed. "Sometimes I wonder what I have gotten myself into by taking up the reins of this country." He glanced toward the now vacant doorway to the study as he slowly shook his head. "I started off in charge of a bunch of horses with the cavalry, and before I knew it…" He gestured palms up to the surrounding room. "Damn."

General Figueiredo had never intended to become President of the Republic, but now he was. The career path he had taken made this outcome almost unavoidable. As head of the national SNI, the die had been cast. The position he had held with that agency had evolved to become a traditional stepping-stone to the presidency; and, as always, the regime in power was very persuasive—it made certain he would accept the nomination to succeed President Ernesto Geisel. In Brazil, an individual had few choices and still fewer freedoms. Even a powerful minister of the SNI who harbored no political aspirations could be manipulated by the proper application of pressure and an appeal to sense of duty.

Once anointed, Figueiredo, as Geisel before him, had then become the target to topple by hard-line, anti-politics military underlings. Indeed, he agitated many by signing the *Lei da Anistia* (Amnesty Law), which unlatched the country's door to thousands of Brazilians who had been disenfranchised by being jailed or banished. This essentially led to a gradual opening of the political system which years later would eventually become a real democracy. Hard-liners reacted in-kind with an orchestrated series of terrorist bombings. To add insult to injury, the booming economy of the early 1970s had waned. Now, the bleakest of times that ever existed became more so with low productivity, heavy debt, and triple-digit inflation. There was discord within all sectors of the military-industrial state; and, of course, Figueiredo was caught in the center of the maelstrom.

Although his helmsmanship of the country had only been for the brief period of time elapsing since 1979, Figueiredo was proving to be more unpopular as each day passed. He was averse to the traditionally accepted pomp and ceremony. He was labeled by many as a quintessential curmudgeon. Even as president, he could never hide his distaste for the machinations of politics. He frequently avowed that he preferred the smell of horses to the smell of people. But nowadays, he was the man not only in charge of all the country's horses, but all of its people as well—like it or not. As repugnant as he found the Office of President, his sharp competitive edge would not allow him to vacate it without a struggle. Indeed, at the end of his time in office, his very life might depend on what remnants of the vestiges of power he managed to hold onto on his way out, regardless of when that might be.

The General turned away from Salo and strolled over to the main entrance of his study. He flashed a conspiratorial grin to the expressionless SNI agent stationed in the hallway, quietly said a few words, and slowly closed the door, latching it.

"That is better," he said, returning to Salo. "I like my privacy, now and then." He laughed. "I know, I know…when you are president, there is very little privacy." He sighed, resignedly.

Intuiting that this visit might be an unwelcome disruption, Salo spoke up, "It was good of you to see me, Mr. President. I trust I am not intruding. I know the hour is late."

"Nonsense," the general's voice immediately retorted. "I still sleep as soundly as ever, and I still only need five hours of sleep each night. At least that is one thing that has not changed in my goddamn life."

The two men's friendship had been cultivated over many years. It was as a direct result of what was called the "great leap forward," a period of time when Brazil had embarked upon an ambitious program of scientific and technological self-sufficiency. Huge sums had been invested to develop an infrastructure and an industrial base to propel the Republic upwards to heights that no other third world country had ever achieved.

Shortly after Salo Montero was tapped by the military to form RioAero, Figueiredo was promoted from an Army colonel and chief of the SNI's bureau in Rio to general and military chief of staff by President Emílio Garrastazú Médici. Figueiredo was then tasked with working closely with Salo in orchestrating the important role an aviation company would have in a military-industrial state. Their acquaintanceship had proven mutually advantageous as the years passed. RioAero doubled in size, time and again. Figueiredo went on to become chief of the entire SNI, and then President of the Republic.

After a reflective pause, the general began to speak again. "Anyway, Salo, you look good...you look good." He offered his visitor a drink, which was graciously declined. The general grasped a small-stemmed glass and casually poured some tawny port for himself. "So, how is that beautiful young daughter of yours?"

Salo beamed with pride. "She is about to enter medical school in the United States."

"My, my," the general said, shaking his head in disbelief, "why it was just yesterday that she was in grade school."

"Yes, Mr. President, time does pass by very quickly, does it not?"

"Indeed, it does." The general took a slow sip of his port and then continued, "I take it that your visit with me is more than just social."

"That is true..." Salo said, and was about to go on.

The general put his index finger to his lips, prompting an immediate halt to the flow of Salo's words. "Come, let us take a stroll out to the stable. The night is beautiful. My horses are always so peaceful during this time. It gives me much joy to be near them. That is one of the reasons why I leave that godforsaken place called Brasilia every chance I can."

The two men exited the study through a sliding glass doorway to a garden pathway leading to the stable.

The typical unsettled weather of the day had transitioned to a clear, still, star-studded night. A brilliant full moon illuminated the meandering pathway. The two strolled in the calm of the midnight hour.

"Your visit has to do with RioAero," the perceptive general said breaking the silence. "I trust you have good news for me, Salo. It is important that you do."

"Well..." Salo hesitated.

"You are very close to making a major sale, no?"

"Well..." Salo tried to begin again.

"Hmmm..." the general groaned, disappointedly.

"Mr. President," Salo nervously admitted, "things are not going well."

"Yes, I see," the general said. "Although I felt that could be a possibility, I hoped it would not be so." He grimaced. "This is why I wanted to leave the study." He briefly glanced back toward the building they had just left. "We can talk freely here. In the study, and almost everywhere else, there is always the possibility of eavesdropping. I know the SNI very well. Even though that organization reports only to me, it has become somewhat fragmented during the past few months. There are those who would prefer I not be president. And while the CIE has weakened, it is persistent in its attempts to make inroads to undermine the SNI and my administration."

The general broke off his commentary, lost in his own thoughts, nodding to himself as the pair continued strolling toward the stable in silence. "Hell," he finally blurted out, refocusing again on the CIE and SNI, "they might just be doing me a favor. Still, I do not like the idea of being pushed aside. If and when I step down, it will be on my own terms and not because of any underhanded intelligence that the CIE or anybody else may gather against me or my initiatives. Besides, I still have many plans for after my term ends; and, one must be alive to fulfill one's dreams."

Salo forced a rueful smile. He fully understood the general's tenuous predicament. Independent military intelligence agencies like the Army's powerful CIE were autonomous, always seemingly at odds with the SNI. It was a perennial power struggle, much like that of the FBI, CIA, and NSA in the United States. But now with tension growing throughout Brazil due to the worst economic times ever experienced, greater and greater opportunities existed for factions of dissidents within an intelligence agency to make a power play against the current regime.

Nearing the first stall in the stable area, the general looked Salo in the eye. "Speak your mind, my friend, in this place our words are safe—my horses are more loyal to me than any person I have ever known. I would trust any one of my steeds with my life." He turned away and scratched the ear of a black, but soon to be gray, young gelding. The horse further extended its neck over the closed lower stall door, pressing its ear closer to the general's hand.

"Mr. President," Salo slowly began, "when we last met, you had given me four weeks to pull RioAero out of its tailspin, four weeks to consummate a major WindStar sales contract."

"That was over ten days ago," the general sternly reminded.

"Yes, of that I am very much aware," Salo acknowledged, "bu—"

"No 'buts,' *Sr. Montero*," the general warned, "little more than a fortnight remains. There is much pressure being placed upon me by the ministers. RioAero cannot, they say, continue as it has in the past. Times have changed. Both money and patience have worn thin. The Army has its own agenda, and, as you know, that includes a plan to reorganize the company. They want RioAero to redirect its focus toward subcontract manufacturing rather than the actual production of finished aircraft."

"But—"

The general raised a silencing eyebrow.

"But," Salo imperviously persisted, "something insidious is happening." He paused.

The general said nothing.

"During the past twenty-four hours I have learned of several seemingly unrelated, deeply disturbing incidents involving the WindStar."

The general still said nothing.

"No one has, as yet, determined the cause of these incidents." Salo paused. "I believe these otherwise unexplained incidents are the result of a well-crafted effort against RioAero and its aircraft programs."

The General's eyes narrowed.

"Sa-bo-tage," the word quietly rolled off Salo's tongue. Montero had independently come to the same conclusion that Lou Biega, Ronnie Trilliano, and Rick Harris had all been separately considering, but whom none as of yet had voiced suspicions to Salo.

The General remained silent.

"And," Salo continued, "I have a feeling—a gut feeling—that behind all of it could be a man we both distrust." He paused again and tilted his head toward the general. "Cardella...General Carlo Cardella."

"Cardella," the general distastefully spat the name. He furrowed his brow. "That is a serious accusation, Montero. Tell me, what makes you think he would be involved with any of this?"

A rustle from within the hedges that landscaped the stable area startled the gelding. Its ears pricked toward the sound; its body tensed. The two men's attention immediately redirected away from the topic of RioAero. Their eyes searched into the darkness for any sign of motion. For the moment, both feared their conversation might have been overheard. The CIE and SNI could be anywhere.

The gelding snorted alarm. From within the stall a thudding sound ricocheted off of the rough-cut timber walls. The horse reared in panic. Its hooves madly pounded down upon the hard rubber matted flooring. The horse blindly sought any avenue of escape, though none existed. Salo instinctively backed away from the stall, but the general lunged forward to the horse's aid. A dark object hurtled out of the stall directly toward the general's face. Only the general's quick agile dodge averted the explosive escape of a startled, just-awakened bird which was rocketing to freedom from smashing into the general's face.

"Only a bird!" The general heartily laughed. With the tension thoroughly broken, he continued, "Lucky we were not inside that stall. It would have been rather interesting, to say the least." His attention turned to comforting the gelding, which was still wide-eyed and breathing heavily, but slowly calming down. "Cardella, huh?" he almost whispered to Salo. "You think so?"

"Yes, Mr. President." Salo continued, stepping forward to approach the general at the stall door. "Earlier this evening, I was summoned to the CIE headquarters in Rio by Cardella himself. When I arrived, however, I was met only by two of his lieutenants. After a few minutes of mindless chitchat, one of the lieutenants advised me that I was expected to join Cardella on a flight tomorrow morning. At that time, the lieutenant said, I would be briefed by Cardella himself." Salo momentarily regarded the gelding, and then returned his attention to the general. "I know Cardella is up to something that involves RioAero, but I really do not understand exactly what it might be. I know I might learn more than I want to learn."

"Hmmm..." the general intoned as he continued to stroke and soothe the gelding.

Salo went on, "Over the past few weeks, Cardella has called me quite frequently—sometimes twice a day. Of course, because he is who he is, I have to take his calls. He mostly presses for information about sales prospects for the WindStar. He also seems very interested in the special missions derivatives of the WindStar that are nearing completion in Hangar One."

"The retrofits involving surveillance and armament?"

"Yes, Mr. President."

"Interesting." The general raised his brow.

"What I need, sir, is any guidance you could provide, any further information that could help me understand what I may be up against. I need to know what might be brewing in Cardella's mind." Although the general had earlier authorized Salo to tap the SNI for a profile of Cardella, Salo felt he needed more information.

The general thought hard. He shook his head. "Unfortunately, Salo, there is nothing I can tell you that I think you do not already know."

Salo nodded, dissatisfiedly.

"All I can say is that Cardella is a very aggressive man. He is dissatisfied with his lack of power—hates the fact that he was passed over to head up the SNI when I vacated that position to take over the presidency. I think he remains bitter about that." The general was in silent thought for half a minute. "Still, I do not think he would be behind any effort to sabotage RioAero. Cardella is a smart man; he knows the facts. All he has to do is just wait a few more weeks and hope that no sales come through for the WindStar. Then, the Army will likely have its way and reorganize the company."

"But why is Cardella so focused on RioAero? Why not Petrobrás, Telebrás, Eletrobrás, or some other company the state controls?"

The general laughed. "Frankly, I do not know and I do not care. I am fully aware of your personal attachment to RioAero, but I am also in a much different position. I have a country, not a company, to run. If Cardella takes over RioAero and he and his CIE become less acrimonious with my administration, then fine."

"But like you said, Mr. President, Cardella is an aggressive man, and aggressive men tend to have insatiable appetites. RioAero might just be an appetizer for him."

"Not Cardella," the general said, shaking his head. "Tell me, Salo, do you remember the fable about the dog with a bone who saw his reflection in the water?"

Salo knew the fable and nodded, but he could not agree with the general's assessment of Cardella.

"Well, when the dog grabbed after the bone being reflected in the water, he lost the bone he had in his mouth and, of course, wound up with no bone at all, right?"

"Yes."

"Well, Cardella is not that stupid. Trust me, Salo. He may be greedy, but I do not believe he is a fool. One fat bone will be fine for him."

The general walked away from the gelding and toward the training ring in front of the stable. Salo followed.

"Tell me, Montero," the general once again probed, "just how are your sales prospects coming? How close are you to actually making a major sale?"

"Not to be evasive, Mr. President, but that is hard to say. I have a highly qualified, tenacious man heading up our North American effort. I feel very confident that he will make something happen. The real question is when. Will he be able to do it in time?" Salo paused for a moment. "In all honesty, sir, I cannot say. Aircraft sales are like that. It takes time, something we do not have."

"Well," the general remarked with genuine sadness, "that is very true. With the country's economy almost out of control and my adversaries on a witch-hunt, it looks doubtful that RioAero can be saved. Still, I gave you four weeks, you now have two weeks remaining. Use that time well, my friend."

In silence, both men stared upward into the star-studded summer night sky as if delving divine inspiration. Both knew that RioAero in its current form was critical to the future of their country. Both knew that huge investments had been made to develop RioAero into the company it was today. Unfortunately, both knew that unless a near miracle occurred, RioAero could be relegated to a mere low-cost production machine for the Boeings and Airbuses of the world.

Salo closed his eyes, lowered his head, and rubbed his brow hard. Running out of options, he was very much ill-at-ease at what the future could bring. He desultorily thanked the general for hearing him out.

As they began to walk back toward the main residence, Figueiredo placed his hand atop Montero's shoulder, first kindly, and then firmly clamping down with a powerful grip. Salo's trapezius muscle cramped. He held back a wince.

"Remember, my friend," the general said, relaxing his fingers, "this is not the end of the world. You do have two weeks remaining. Regardless of what Cardella and others may think, you are still the master of RioAero. The fate of the company lies in your hands. Although you do have my support, please know that this is the time to do whatever it takes to preserve your dream. Make something happen, or..." The general removed his grip from Salo altogether and reclasped his hands behind his own back.

Salo reacted with a nod and a forced smile. The general had made his point very clear. He could support Salo only so long. Time was running out. Although two weeks officially existed before major changes would likely be made at RioAero, Salo doubted that he actually had that much time available to turn his company around. Somehow he felt as if only hours, not weeks or days, remained.

Salo Montero was right, but he had no idea how close to the truth he really was.

FORTY-EIGHT

Pasador Ranch

SUNDAY, FEBRUARY 22, 1981

It was just past two in the morning and inside the ranch house the rottweilers' muscular bodies began quivering. Then, brief snorts transitioned to incessant whining. The dogs had detected the distinctive sound of Rick's BMW even before it had passed through the gated entrance to the ranch. The eagerness sprang from the innate behavioral trait of dogs to greet returning pack members.

Harris wheeled his car up the driveway and into a parking area beside the house. He shut off the engine, glanced toward Gail, and sighed. "It's good to be home again." He shook his head in disbelief before continuing. "Damn, this day seemed like it would never end— NEVER."

She smiled, turned, and planted a kiss on his lips. "I think we both could use some rest," she commented, soothingly. Then remembering what had been said during their visit with Tommy Maxwell at September's, her smile changed to a slightly worried frown. "Somehow, Mr. Harris," she declared, "I have this uneasy feeling that your upcoming day will prove even more challenging than the one that has just finally ended."

Rick chuckled, briefly closed his eyes, and then quipped, "That's the aircraft sales business, I guess."

"Well," Gail immediately came back, "if you were an airplane that had been put through all of the maneuvers you were put through today, you'd be in the shop for a major overhaul."

"Ain't that so!" he laughingly acknowledged.

Leaving the car, the couple made their way along the paved walkway toward the side entrance door of the kitchen, beaming as the sounds of the dogs' excitement intensified. The day's tension was broken, at least for now.

Reaching for the door knob, Rick turned to Gail and asked, "Now tell me, good doctor, which are your favorites: dogs or horses?"

Smiling, she shook her head. "I love both equally…for what each is, of course. But you know that, don't you?"

And he did. Even though this was a frequent query, her response was invariable. Gail was very sensitive to making judgments about animals. She was protective of them all, even lowly insects and slithering reptiles.

Rick turned to the door, which was generally left unlocked. He did not see the need for the precaution. He steadfastly maintained that two well-trained rottweilers could provide better security than any deadbolt ever made. But as soon as he grasped the doorknob, he suddenly jerked back his hand. Something was wrong.

Gail quickly noticed his odd demeanor. "What is it, Rick?"

Open-mouthed, he drew his stained palm toward his face for close inspection. "I...I don't know what this is," he said knitting his brow, perplexed. The fingers of his right hand were coated with a viscous substance—somewhat like thick saliva, but with a darkish tinge.

"Let me see," Gail said, concerned. She took hold of his hand and guided it near her eyes for a close examination. "Odd," she admitted, her mind unsure of what to make of seeing this substance on his hand. "Let's go inside where there's more light."

Pushing open the door and flipping on the lights, the always-happy-to-see-you rottweilers were only briefly acknowledged. "Relax, guys," Gail sternly said to the dogs as she led Rick to the kitchen sink, "mommy has a mystery to solve."

She thoroughly examined Rick's right hand, washed it with water, and inspected it once again. No evidence of injuries. Good, she thought. Then, on the countertop to her left, she glimpsed a smear of the same substance that had been on his hand. Nearby the smear, several crumpled paper towels were also speckled with the fluid. She well knew the crimson dark tinge. It was fresh blood, and lots of it.

Even before Gail confirmed the identity of the substance, it came to Rick like a thunderclap. His thoughts raced...blood, where blood should not be. Why? The dogs seemed fine. The house appeared to be undisturbed—everything, at least in the kitchen, was in order.

Near the balled-up towels, Gail zeroed in on a similarly stained handwritten note. She picked it up and read aloud. It was in Domingo Sanchez's handwriting. It simply said: *COME TO STABLE.*

As she flipped the note back down onto the countertop, they both heard shouts coming from the stable. The words were undecipherable. But the message was clearly urgent.

The worst of fears intruded on Rick's mind. With all the odd events occurring to the WindStar, perhaps someone had gone too far—maybe it had become personal. The horses, Rick thought. Perhaps some unthinkable harm had come to them. That was the explanation he sensed was behind Domingo's cryptic message. Someone could be making a statement to Harris. Maybe he was getting too close to uncovering what had been happening to the WindStar and why. It was an unnerving thought that he did not have time to ponder.

Gail had already kicked off her high-heeled pumps, grabbed and pulled on the coveralls she kept on a hook near the door, and was almost out the open door as she pushed her feet into her barn boots. Rick joined her on the dash from the kitchen, rushing toward the stable with the dogs in hot pursuit.

"¡*Vienes rápidamente!*" Domingo's voice grew louder as they drew closer.

With pounding hearts, the two raced ahead, closing the distance between themselves and the answer they were not sure they wanted to know. Beams of incandescent light streamed from the cluster of stalls. As they ran, everything seemed surreal—a dream-like distortion, slightly suspended in time.

"¡*Vienes!*" Domingo called out once again. There was intensity in his voice. He urged them to hurry with the beckoning of his hand. His face was turned away from them; he was staring into a stall.

As Rick and Gail neared, a haggard and disheveled Domingo Sanchez turned briefly away from the stall to face them. His light khaki work clothes were heavily soiled, soaked with blotches of wet darkness.

"What is it?" Gail gasped out, breathing heavily; her eyes fearfully regarding his blood-stained clothing.

"Look, you look..." He pointed into the stall, and then stepped back.

Gail clenched her teeth, steeling herself for the worst. She sucked in a deep gasp of air as her eyes beheld the sight in the stall.

Still blocked from a view into the stall, Rick's heart sank. Forcing himself to do so, he angled around Gail to see for himself. There, standing toward the back of the box stall, was a very weary mare—sweat drenched and exhausted, but peaceful and seemingly content. In the shadows to her left, a newborn foal.

"*Primera del año,*" Domingo spoke proudly. "*Muy difícil,*" he groaned as he continued, "she take much work, hang up foot, but she okay, I think." He smiled.

Gail nodded, fully understanding what Domingo was saying. "*Muchas gracias, Mingo. ¿Bonita, sí?*"

"*Sí, señora.*" His voice had the passion of a man who truly loved the Paso Fino horse. His face radiated pride. Domingo stretched his arms out in an air-caress of the foal as Gail entered the stall.

Enormous relief flooded through Rick Harris. The mysteries of a few moments ago were explained. His sense of alarm evaporated. His tension broke with an almost audible snap, but just as immediately, his mind coiled back to tautness. It could have been different, very much different. For the first time, the true ramifications of his involvement with RioAero struck home with sobering instant clarity. His mind's eye perceived what could have happened. Rick immediately understood that the stakes of this game in which he and Salo Montero were involved were astronomically high—a game where life and death mattered little to their adversaries, whoever those adversaries actually were. Suddenly everything became personal. His focus narrowed to a laser point, sparking even greater determination to uncover exactly what was happening to the WindStar and why. This is hardball, he thought.

He ripped his thinking back to the here and now. "How are they?" Rick asked, returning to the mother and foal.

"I'll let you know in a minute," Gail distractedly responded as she continued to thoroughly examine the mare and foal, completely unaware of Rick's epiphany.

Gail had expected the mare to foal within a few days, but not at two o'clock this morning. The zinc turbidity test she had performed on the mare the day before yielded negative results. She felt comfortable that yet another twenty-four hours would pass before the mare would foal. She had been wrong.

Fortunately, Domingo Sanchez was at the ready. He had assisted in the delivery of hundreds of foals during his lifetime. He knew that foals were typically delivered front feet and head first—coming into their new world diving stancewise. But what Domingo had witnessed this time was a malpresentation. The foal's front right foot was turned backwards from the knee, essentially hanging it up in the mare's birth canal. To prevent injury or death to both the mother and foal, Domingo had struggled for nearly fifteen minutes to push the foal back inside the mare's birth canal to allow for careful repositioning of the leg, therefore steering the normal chain of events back on course. It was a delicate, tedious, and messy procedure, but tonight it was a successful one.

Gail came to the stall door. "Thanks so much, Mingo. You're a lifesaver," she said appreciatively. "They're both fine."

"You're sure?" Rick broke in.

"Absolutely." Gail nodded. "The mare is a bit weary from the whole process, but our new daughter is as sound as any newborn foal I've ever seen."

The foal was already standing in the corner of the box stall, trying to balance herself on trembling, stilt-like legs.

"Good," a reassured Rick said.

Domingo spoke up, "I will stay here with them."

"Thanks," Gail said. "I'll check in with you at sunrise."

Rick and Gail departed the stable for some much needed rest at the ranch house.

FORTY-NINE

Pasador Ranch

Rick Harris kicked off his shoes and, fully dressed, collapsed onto the king-size bed. "Awww, that feels so..." he mumbled out loud, heavy lids falling over his eyes even before finishing the sentence.

"What time should I set the alarm for?" Gail's question fell on deaf ears.

Harris just moaned, totally oblivious. It was nearly three o'clock in the morning.

"How about eight o'clock?" she persisted.

He groaned again.

"Fine," she said, "eight o'clock it will be."

Rick was dead to the world.

Gail quietly disappeared into the bathroom. Regardless of the hour, she was too disciplined to forego her normal pre-slumber routine. Upon returning to the bedroom only five minutes later, she was greeted by the ring of the telephone.

"Damn," she said, seriously considering letting the answering machine pick up. She hesitated. The call could be important, if not for her, for Rick. Maybe Tommy Maxwell had stumbled onto something important; maybe it was Salo Montero or someone at the factory. Then like the night before, it might be Franco Rameros. He was ferrying up a WindStar from Brazil that Rick was counting on for his upcoming flight demonstration with Santelli. "Damn," she said again, forcing herself to reach for the handset. Quickly composing herself, she snatched up the handset and spoke into the mouthpiece, "Hello."

"Sorry to bother you, Doctor Richmond," came the words above the static on the line, "but I need a brief word with Rick." It was Franco Rameros. She recognized his voice.

"Now? Are you sure?" she asked, glancing at Rick's motionless body as it emitted a gurgling snore. "At this hour?"

"Unfortunately, yes."

"Okay, then, just one minute, please." She punched on the mute button. It was not a good sign that Rameros was calling this late. And the words, "unfortunately, yes," did not sound promising either. She dashed into the bathroom, dampened a hand towel with cold water, and returned to place it on Rick's forehead.

"Err...aah..." Rick grunted, his eyes first squinting, then opening more widely as he struggled to throw off the haze of his slumber.

Before he could utter a word, Gail spoke up, "It's Franco Rameros, he's on the phone."

Rick grumbled, wiped his face with the damp towel, propped himself up against the headboard of the bed, and grasped the phone that Gail was presenting to him. He pressed off the mute button, and with a composing breath said, "Good morning, Mr. Rameros. Having a splendid flight, are you?" It was the wrong query.

Franco rolled his eyes. In response to Rick's innocent, but under the current circumstances thoroughly grating question, Rameros removed the handset from his ear, held it in front of himself, and briefly glared at it. He turned the handset to the side and sharply rapped it several times against the sill of the glass-enclosed phone booth in which he was standing.

Rick quickly jerked the receiver away from his ear.

Only partly satisfied that Rick understood his displeasure, Rameros lit into Rick as only Franco Rameros could. "What is all this *having a splendid flight* crap? I have been to hell and back trying to get this bird up to you in one piece. So, the answer is no…NO, I have not been having a goddamn SPLENDID flight, Mr. Harris."

Taken back, Rick ventured diplomatically, but it proved to be another blunder. "Problems?"

"'PROBLEMS?'" Rameros thundered back Rick's question, the sneer icily slicing over the telephone line. "Hell no, no problems at all…just one friggin' disaster after another, with a near catastrophe thrown in for good measure."

"What's happened? Tell me, Franco."

"Well, do you want the good news or the bad news?"

"The good, of course."

"Okay, in that case, I will be arriving right on schedule. I expect to be in the chocks at the RioAero hangar by nine o'clock or so. Of course, it all depends on how long your customs and immigration guys want to screw around with me and the aircraft."

"That's great." But Rick's pleasure was brief. It was tempered by the thought of the other information that Franco had alluded to. "So, what's the bad news?"

"Oh, you really do not want to know. You have enough problems on your hands trying to sell airplanes. Anything I could mention would just be trivial to you and is best left unsaid."

"Listen, Franco," Rick pressed on with a mixture of curiosity and irritation, "you call me in the middle of the night to say you're going to arrive on time, and then you add: Oh, by the way, I have some bad news that I don't want to talk about. What is going on, Franco?"

"It has been a long twenty-some hours," Franco said with a tone almost apologetic. "Even though I have a young copilot on board, it has been a bit difficult to get more than a catnap now and then. Indeed, there have been some harrowing moments, my friend."

"Like what?"

"Oh, let me just see..." Any sound of apology in his tone was replaced by biting sarcasm. "My, my, where should I start? Hey, how about in Brasilia when line service almost put the wrong fuel in our tanks, and then some CTA inspector wanted to ground the aircraft over some imaginary paperwork irregularity." Rameros paused.

There was no response from Rick.

"Or how about in Zanderij, where some Army guys in a Jeep opened fire on us with a machine gun and then almost crashed head-on into the WindStar during its takeoff roll." He paused again.

Rick winced hard, making no audible response.

"Damn," Rameros forged ahead, "how could I almost forget the most exhilarating experience we had when a Colombian Gulfstream jet, specially equipped with Sidewinder missiles, tried to shoot us out of the sky over the Amazon."

Rick was dumbfounded. Other than the typical static of an international call, there was now total silence on the line. Harris was now convinced—absolutely convinced—more than one spider was weaving a web to ensnare RioAero and the WindStar. That had to be the case.

Rameros continued, "From my recital, Mr. Harris, you can hear that I have had nothing but a very splendid flight. So, how was your day, my friend?"

Rick ignored the pointed barb. "Franco, you are lucky to be alive."

"No shit," Rameros quipped, "goddamn lucky. Hell, that double prop separation on Friday was a lark compared to what I have been through since."

"Quite unbelievable," Rick said and then quickly switched gears. "By the way, where are you now?"

"Santo Domingo. It is rather peaceful here—not the tropical storm season yet, if you know what I mean." The country had been devastated by a hurricane just two years earlier.

"Good," Rick responded, "at least you won't have to over-fly Cuba."

"That would not be much of a challenge. I cannot remember the last time Cuba had anything faster than a '55 Chevy to chase anybody in."

"Okay," Rick said, obligingly laughing at Rameros' humor, but realizing the conversation had to be redirected from Rameros' recent perils to the larger situation as Rick now understood it. "Franco, listen...please just listen, for once." Rick paused.

Rameros fell silent.

"RioAero is in the throes of a disaster," Rick began. "I think that is obvious to both of us by now. There are some complex and what appear to be independently directed initiatives being aimed at RioAero and the WindStar. I cannot exaggerate the seriousness of the situation. What you experienced on your trip is only part of it. I have a full-blown investigation going on up here." He paused, organizing his thoughts. "Have you been able to relay any of what you just told me to the factory?

"No, not at all. This has been my first opportunity to contact anyone."

"Franco, I'm glad you got this call out. And while I do appreciate being first on your list, it is critical that we get all of these details back to the factory as quickly as possible. They need to be forewarned. Anything can happen next." Indeed, Rick knew the words were only too true; anything could happen next, and the factory was a prime target. "I'll get Salo into the loop. He's at his lake house this weekend. I have his number."

"Good," Rameros responded, "better you than me. I would sure hate to be the one to wake up Salo in the middle of the night, only to tell him that everything he spent the better part of his life constructing is about to crater."

"Yeah, I know," Rick groaned at the thought. "I don't look forward to it either, but it has to be done. Salo has to be fully informed in order to have a chance at saving the company he built. In fact, he may know more about what is happening than we do." Rick quickly segued to the next question: "You're what, about another three flight hours away?"

"Probably a little less."

"Okay, why don't you get some rest before leaving there. In fact, why don't you plan on arriving at ten o'clock, and get some extra shut-eye. You'll need it. Once you arrive here, it will be non-stop activity until the sun sets."

"Rest, that is exactly what I intend on doing. And a little extra sounds great." Rameros hesitated. "So, it will be me, not you, doing the demo flight with your customers, right?"

"That's affirmative, if you're up to it."

Rameros laughed and only half-jokingly said, "Try not to irritate me anymore than I already am. Harris, you cut your deal with your customers; I will make sure they are impressed enough with the WindStar to sign on the dotted line."

"I'm with you on that, Franco." Rick paused collecting his thoughts to fill Rameros in on the details for the flight demonstration that was scheduled for noon. "When you arrive at our hangar, Joey Delgada will be there to coordinate unloading the cargo and preparing the aircraft for the demonstration. I'll join you shortly after that." He thought for a second. "Please be sure to have only two hours of fuel on board...nothing more. I want the aircraft to be very light for unbelievable performance. There will just be three customers and you and me on board for the flight. And, oh yes...I almost forgot, a reporter will also be joining us as well."

"Reporter?" Rameros hated reporters. Their probing questions always made his skin crawl. He viewed reporters as more of a liability than an asset.

"Yes, he's a long-time acquaintance of mine. You'll like him."

"HA," Rameros immediately shot back, "we will see."

"Anything else?" Rick asked.

"No, not really." But Rameros, still ire inspired, could not resist baiting Rick a little further. It had been a long and periolous trip. "Oh, by the way, these prospects of yours, they are not flakes, I hope."

Rick's answer choked in his throat. He thoroughly recognized that he needed Rameros on his side, so he bit back his ready retort and evenly responded, "Indeed not, Franco, and with your help, we will sell a new airline a fleet of WindStars before the day is out."

"You are a good man, Harris," Rameros said warming to the compliment. It was a well known fact that not all salesmen were willing to share customer contact with factory pilots—even damn good pilots like himself. He added, sincerely, "We are going to wow them."

"Roger that, my friend," Rick came back. "I'll be counting on you."

"You bet," Franco responded. "See you around ten o'clock."

Rick switched off the portable phone, grabbed his wallet from the nightstand and fished out the business card with Salo's lake house phone number scrawled onto it. He switched the phone back on, punched the digits into it and waited anxiously as the circuits processed his call. Fifteen seconds later, the connection was made and the phone in Brazil began ringing, and ringing, and ringing, and ringing...

"Damn," Rick mumbled, "answer the phone." But no one answered, and no answering machine picked up the call. He glanced at his watch. It was 4:00 a.m. in Brazil. He hung up the phone knowing he would have to try to reach Salo later. At this hour on a Sunday morning, it would be senseless to try to alert anyone at the factory. He was sure.

"Problems?" Gail asked, having heard only one side of the conversation and not knowing to whom he had just tried to place a call.

"That's putting it mildly," Rick said with a great deal of frustration. "I was just trying to contact Salo; there was no answer."

"How is Franco doing? Your conversation didn't seem totally congenial."

"He's fine, the aircraft's fine…it could have been much different. It seems like all hell is breaking loose."

"What do you mean?"

"Franco has had nothing but obstacles placed in the way during his flight." Rick hesitated. "In fact, I would say he is lucky to be alive."

"That bad?"

"That bad."

"So, the plot against RioAero and the WindStar grows larger," Gail said, not truly understanding how bad things had really gotten.

"Very much so. There appears to be a full-scale war going on now, and it's intensifying—getting extremely nasty. Earlier sabotage efforts seem minor compared to what is currently happening." Rick went on to briefly highlight what Rameros had just conveyed.

Gail contemplated what Rick had related, not being sure how to react. "This kind of activity seems well beyond anything Dan Cole or even Ramon Segundo could orchestrate."

Rick nodded. "I believe you are correct."

"A Colombian jet with missiles?" Gail's eyes widened in disbelief.

"That's what Franco said." Rick shrugged. "I have no reason to disbelieve him, even though it seems rather bizarre."

Gail thought for a moment, her eyes now narrowed. "A cartel?"

"Interesting you should say that. My thoughts exactly. Cartels are about as ruthless as ruthless comes."

"But why would a cartel go after RioAero?"

"Good question. Not sure." He shook his head in frustration. "Still, a cartel is the only organization I can think of with the chutzpah and wherewithal to attempt something that bold."

Gail nodded. "RioAero must be developing something they fear, something that could compromise their business…their future." She paused. "Think about it, Rick, what could RioAero be involved with that would cause a cartel to respond with such deadly intent?"

"I don't know." He wiped his face again with the damp towel. "There's nothing I can think of." He silently sunk into contemplation as his mind tried to glean any aspect of his three-week visit to the factory that might prove helpful. He knew that the GEA's work was top secret, yet there were ongoing rumors that some of their programs involved new satellite and laser technology. Nonetheless, all of those programs had to be in the very early R&D stages. Certainly, aerospace companies in the United States were far more advanced with this technology than RioAero. But then again, Brazil was a neighbor of Colombia, and the Brazilian government was slowly becoming less insensitive to the drug trade than it had been in the past. The current

Brazilian regime disliked Brazil being known as a burgeoning transshipment area for Colombian cocaine headed for the U.S. and Europe.

"Think hard," Gail prodded.

"I just don't know," Rick spoke up. But just as he finished uttering those words, his features lit with comprehension. "Wait, wait...there might be something here." He paused to formulate his thoughts.

"What is it?"

"Maybe it could be..." He grinned. "Yes, it has to be."

"What?"

"It's not super high-tech, but it is high-tech enough."

"And?" She felt as though she was pulling words out of his mouth.

"The factory is very close to completion on two military derivatives of the WindStar. One aircraft has been modified to carry short-range air-to-surface missiles. It could easily be sold to Colombia and used against the cartels."

"But the Colombian Air Force must already have some type of aircraft in their fleet that is missile equipped."

"They certainly do, but nothing they have has the range, low-level capability, and accuracy as this version of the WindStar."

Gail shrugged, not being able to dispute his knowledge of aircraft.

"Still, there's something else, something even more threatening than a missile equipped WindStar."

"Yes?"

"The second military project that RioAero is nearing completion on is a WindStar with the latest technology in air-to-ground radar." Rick began nodding to himself as his mind filled with a picture of what he had seen in Hangar One. "Almost half of the aircraft's lower fuselage is taken up by its radar antenna. I have been told that it can detect a small band of men with pinpoint accuracy up to a hundred miles away. And with its extended-range tanks, the aircraft can loiter for more than eight hours. This WindStar would be a serious threat to drug trafficking—to any cartel."

"Wow, sounds plausible, and a really good reason for Rameros to have had a serious engagement with unfriendlies on his ferry flight."

"It sure might be," Rick agreed and went further, "What this theory of ours does, however, is to really complicate matters. Not only do we have to worry about Cole and Segundo, but now a cartel could be threatening RioAero."

"And, don't forget about Cardella," Gail reminded. "Salo's daughter told you that Cardella is lobbying to shut down the WindStar program and reorganize RioAero. Maybe he could be the mastermind behind it all."

"Maybe, I'll have to run that past Salo later this morning, that is, if I can reach him."

"Mr. Harris," she asked metaphorically, "what kind of hornet's nest have you stirred with this new job of yours?"

Her comment had its intended effect; he ruefully laughed. "I don't know, but I have this feeling we are both going to find out fairly soon."

"I'm sure we will," she agreed, "but for now, we are both going to sleep. Tomorrow is going to be another crazy day for you. I am certain of it."

Gail turned off the light in the bedroom.

FIFTY

RioAero, SA

Big Lou's body twitched. His eyelids fluttered. The voices grew louder. The images, first in shades of gray, quickly transitioned into full color, now vividly so. To his left in the conference area of his office, he saw a dozen of his most senior GEA engineers seated around the huge table for a special early Sunday morning meeting. And there, at the head of the table, was Jeffe Martinez. He had just put another transparency on the overhead projector.

"Let's quiet down, now," Martinez said above the din of voices at the table.

The inattentive engineers ignored Martinez and continued their chatter.

Martinez frowned and raised his hand to take control. It was to no avail.

Across the room, the man sitting in the dark blue leather chair behind the immense reddish-brown mahogany desk placed his fingers between his lips and gave two piercing whistles. "*Silêncio!*" he commanded.

An immediate hush spread throughout the group.

Salo Montero pushed himself away from the massive desk and rose from the chair. He glowered at the engineers as he slowly paced toward them. "We are resolving a goddamn crisis here!"

The engineers cowered, their eyes quickly taking refuge within their notebooks on the table.

"Your attention is needed," Montero angrily spoke up, "all of your attention." He stared at two of the engineers seated near the head of the table who were avoiding eye contact at all costs. They nervously fiddled with their mechanical pencils. "Now," Montero heatedly continued, "if any of you have a problem with the organizational changes that have been made, you are free to get the hell out of here." He paused.

There was no movement in the room. Not a sound.

"Okay, then..." Montero went on, toning his voice down somewhat. He proceeded to the front of the group and stood next to Jeffe Martinez. With crossed arms and pointedly looking at the assembled engineers, Salo took a long minute before going on. He inhaled sharply, and again began: "Listen up, and listen carefully..." Salo slowly mouthed the words. "Because of goddamn incompetence and the problems these men created for the WindStar program, Biega and Trilliano are no longer in positions of authority." He lingered for effect. "As I am sure you all know by now, Mr. Martinez is our new director of engineering. He is in charge. He reports directly to me. You all will do whatever he asks, or…" Salo paused, allowing his audience to briefly dwell on the unfinished statement. "Do we have an understanding?"

There were staggered nods of agreement from the group at the table.

Montero glanced at his watch. "Damn," he groaned, "I must leave you now. There is a press conference over at my office with the CTA, FAA, and President Figueiredo. Major changes at RioAero will be announced. The company will be much stronger, but it will also be much different. Martinez has all the details. He will share those with you. In the meantime, I expect you to give Jeffe your total support."

Montero stalked out of the room.

"Gentlemen," Martinez said, picking up from the point where he had previously been unable to garner attention, "as the new director of engineering, I am pleased to take an active role in this reorganization. Although painful to some, it is in the best interests of everyone. Brazil has suffered too long and too much from the inadequacies of RioAero. All that will change. First and foremost, I am today announcing the immediate termination of the WindStar program…the termination of the WindStar program…the termination…the termination…the termination…"

Biega's body twitched violently. His pulse pounded. He began taking a series of short shallow breaths. His hands chilly and clammy. So much was happening, and all of it was wrong. Big Lou had to make it stop—that is, if he indeed could. His body twitched again; eyelids fluttered. His eyes racing from side-to-side behind closed lids.

The telephone rang.

Biega's upper body suddenly jerked upright from the sofa. His eyes were now wide open with dilated pupils. He was briefly confused. His heart still racing. His breathing rate still increasing—faster, shallower.

His eyes scanned the room. The scene streaming through his mind from only moments before had totally changed. Where there had been chaos was now serene. There was no bustle of activity in his office. There were no chattering voices; no engineers at the conference table; no Montero; no Martinez. Only Ronnie Trilliano, sitting in the chair behind Biega's desk; only Ronnie's voice speaking into the telephone handset glued to his ear. Trilliano's thin, raspy voice was quietly saying, "Yes, the connection is clear. I can hear you very well."

Big Lou swung himself into a sitting position on the sofa and touched his own damp face with both hands. He slowly got to his feet and carefully re-surveyed the office. It was just as he remembered it from before his slumber. The conference table was littered with paper. He saw the cardboard boxes filled with file folders and large black binders. He shook his head—hard—in both disbelief and relief. He noticed the early morning sunlight diffusing through the bank of heavily tinted windows to his left.

Biega now realized it had all been a dream—an intense, bone-chilling nightmare. Nothing was changed. He was still faced with a very critical and highly complex situation. Even worse, he did not yet have any of the answers that were so desperately needed.

"...Lou...Lou..." Trilliano said for the fifth and sixth time.

Biega groggily swung his head toward the desk and made eye contact with the slightly built engineer.

"You okay, Lou?" Trilliano asked, genuinely concerned.

Biega took a deep head-clearing breath, then exhaled. He cracked a thin smile. "I am okay, Ronnie." Biega tried to muster a laugh, but could not. "It has been a rough night, a very rough night."

Trilliano nodded, these had been difficult hours for them both. "Willie Roth is on the line," he said cupping the mouthpiece. "They have been up all night in Dayton. From his tone, I think he may have some information, some answers for us."

"Good," Biega said. His body felt like it had been run over by a truck; his mind, a muddle. "Tell him I will be with him in half a minute, then put him on hold."

Trilliano relayed the information to Roth, punched in the hold button on the telephone, and placed the handset into its cradle. Biega quickly disappeared into a small kitchen adjacent to the office. After a long thirty seconds, he returned. He was drying his face with a damp towel that he held in one hand while carrying a tall glass of orange juice in the other.

"Put him on the box," a partially revitalized Biega said. He took a long swallow from the glass.

Trilliano punched the speaker button.

"Good morning, Mr. Roth," Big Lou's voice boomed out as he made his way to the chair that Trilliano had just vacated. "I trust you have some goddamn answers for the questions that the Feds are going to nail my ass with come Monday."

"Good morning, Lou," Willie Roth was quick to respond, dismissing Biega's belligerence and being as diplomatic as any vendor could. "I'm not used to pulling all-nighters with my guys," he affected a laugh, "but the problem you presented to us needed to be solved, and it needed to be solved fast." Willie paused for a moment.

Biega said nothing.

"Lou, I understand what you are up against. And, I know our prop appears to be responsible for what you are going through."

"Good, I am glad we are all in agreement on that minor friggin' detail." Biega was back to his normal self. "What did you find out?"

"Lou, it is highly suspect. We have never seen anything like it. It is not a defect in material; it is not a defect created by our manufacturing. This is all very suspicious. There was no way that shaft could have done anything else but fail."

"How so?"

"The consensus here among us is that it looks like sabotage—high-tech sabotage."

Trilliano knowingly nodded to Biega. Ronnie had raised the theory of sabotage from the very beginning.

Roth went on, "Remember those near-microscopic irregularities that you and Franco Rameros spotted on the sheared shafts?"

"Yes."

"Well, it appears some very advanced method was used to fatigue those shafts to insure failure in flight."

"What do you mean, Willie? How?"

"The integrity of the prop shaft was intentionally compromised. Our mass spectrometry analysis confirms it. We feel certain it was done with a highly sophisticated laser—state-of-the-art stuff. We double-checked everything with an ion microscope for verification."

"How could that have happened?"

There was a long silence. "I have absolutely no idea," Willie Roth finally responded.

"Maybe it occurred during your manufacturing process."

"No way, Lou," Roth began his defense. "We are still old fashioned about the way we mill our shafts. Our work with this level of laser technology is still in the R&D phase. It will be years before we employ lasers in production. Besides, Lou, it's our prop. Why in the hell would we want it to fail?"

Biega thought for a second. "So, when did did the laser tampering happen?"

"Honestly, Lou, I don't know. It had to have been done after the shaft was inspected at our facility and certified as airworthy. From an analysis of what you sent up to us, the shaft never would have passed our stress test. It would have failed just as it did on your aircraft."

"So, it was done after the shaft left your factory."

"Yes."

"But where?"

"Perhaps at your facility," Roth too quickly answered, and then regretted it.

"You sonovabitch!" Biega came unglued. "There is no goddamn way. You are up to your ass in alligators and you are trying to put the bite on us. You sonovabitch! You goddamn sonova—"

"Willie," Trilliano broke in, "bear with us for a moment." He quickly punched the hold button on the telephone and looked Big Lou in the eye.

"I know, I know," Biega admitted. "I will calm down. It is counterproductive to vent my frustrations on Willie."

Trilliano's firmly closed lips cracked a thin affirming smile.

Biega punched on the speaker button. "Sorry, Willie, things are rather stressful down here on the front line."

"I understand, Lou," Willie Roth empathized, "we are under the gun up here as well."

"Late last night," Biega began, now more constructively, "Ronnie was digging through some stacks of paperwork associated with the particular WindStar that was involved in the incident. He was also reviewing the last shipment of components we received from your factory back in December. He discovered that the two failed shafts, as well as two others that so far have not failed, had serial numbers that were significantly older than others on the delivery manifest. The failed shafts were a year old, maybe more." Biega paused. "The question is: Why did we get them? Were they returns? Where did they come from?"

"Hmmm..." Willie groaned on the other end of the line. "Interesting observation. My guys did not and probably would not have spotted that, at least not right away. You have a sharp eye."

"Ronnie has a really sharp eye," Biega emphasized. "Last night after Ronnie discovered those older serial numbers, we were able to correlate them to the failed shafts. At that point, Ronnie and I had some unsettling thoughts." Biega paused only long enough to gulp down the remaining orange juice. "We thought that if those shafts were returns from another airframer, or perhaps an overhaul shop, the returns could have been because of damage that was overlooked before the shafts were sent to us. Or..." Biega said with a wince, "there is the possibility that the shafts could have been sabotaged by whoever sent them back to you—perhaps another airframer. You know this is a dog-eat-dog business, Willie. A competitor could easily have sent the shafts back, for whatever reasons, in anticipation that the shafts would later be delivered to us, for example."

"Give me just a minute, and I'll track down the history of the failed shaft you sent us."

Biega and Trilliano remained silent, listening to Willie's fingers clicking away on his keyboard, accessing data from the mainframe at Dayton-Standard.

"Okay," Willie's voice came back over the speaker, "your assessment that the shaft was over a year old is correct—it was manufactured on October 28, 1979. It was placed in inventory about a week later after our final inspections. It stayed in inventory for just over three months. Then it was shipped out to a customer."

"Who was the customer?"

"Let's see." Roth began tapping on the keyboard again. "Stand by. Okay, here we go. Ah-ha, it was BASA."

"So, how did we end up with the component?"

"Well, on November 19 of last year, we received it back from BASA."

"Why?"

"Dunno, our computer records don't say, but that's not odd. Sometimes airframers overstock. Sometimes engineers change specifications and therefore require a different part number. Sometimes production damages the engine mount flange." He cleared his voice. "The bottom line is that it's hard to second guess why it was returned. Maybe I can find out, maybe I can't."

"But if it was returned due to damage, there would be a paper trail detailing that it was remanufactured and yellow tagged, right?"

"That's correct, Lou, let me check a little further. I'll go into the BASA account and see what kind of return history they had during the fourth quarter of '80." More tapping on the keyboard. "Okay, here we go. Yes, they returned a bunch of stuff during that timeframe. Blades, pistons, seals, shafts.

"How many shafts?"

"I see one...two...three...four...that's it. Four shafts were returned."

"In the same shipment?"

"Yes."

"Any reason listed?"

"A variety of reasons for the different components, but they basically cited wanting more recent serial numbers. BASA has a stated policy of returning items that are more than twelve months old that have not been installed on the production line. Components in their huge inventory can sometimes get temporarily lost." He paused. "However, they rarely implement that policy. I can't recall the last time they invoked the twelve month clause in our vendor contract for any component returns."

"Strange, is it not?"

"Why yes, yes it is."

"Okay, Willie, let me ask you this: How much do you know about the type of technology BASA currently has?"

"Not much, Lou. They are pretty much a low-tech manufacturer, just like de Havilland and Fairchild. But from what I understand, BASA is advancing fairly rapidly. Their relationship as a supplier to Airbus has allowed access to the latest stuff."

"One more question, Willie..." Biega glanced up at Trilliano and then back to the speaker. "Do you think BASA has the type of laser technology to compromise a propeller shaft?"

"That's a tough one, Lou, I really can't say. But with the significant share of the market their Avio-23 enjoys, it doesn't seem likely that BASA would do anything like you're implying. If they did, I can't understand what their motivation would be. BASA can't feel threatened by the WindStar, certainly not at this stage of the game."

"Fine, Willie, just thought I would ask while I had you on the line." Biega paused for a second. "Tell you what, fax me your findings. I will need that info for the Feds. For now, though, we will call it a suspicious defect in the prop shaft unrelated to the WindStar's certification or operation."

"Yes, Lou, that's the way I see it."

"Thanks, Willie, I truly appreciate what you have done," Biega said, then punched off the speakerphone.

There was silence in the office.

"So," Trilliano began, "that is it?"

"Yes," Biega added, both pleased and displeased with the knowledge he had just gained. "Of course, Dayton-Standard will continue trying to find out the particulars involved in the tampering with those shafts. For now, I think we have enough information to keep the fleet from being grounded by the authorities."

"That is good news," Trilliano agreed. "And, since the other two old shafts were installed on S/N-34, I will be sure to call Delgada up in Fort Lauderdale and have him pull the shafts while the aircraft is under repair. Dayton-Standard should take a look at those as well."

"Good," Biega concurred and then shifted gears. "You know, it is a miracle that Rick Harris did not have a prop failure during his long trip up to the States. He and the WindStar could have disappeared into the Atlantic Ocean, never to be found."

"It could have been luck," Trilliano noted, "or maybe there was no tampering done to the shafts on his aircraft."

"Or," Biega quickly came back, "maybe, just maybe, any tampering with those shafts was less severe. Maybe the intended failure was to be at a later point. Maybe someone wanted there to be a problem with the aircraft when Rick Harris had a plane load of airline executives up for a flight demonstration."

"Maybe."

FIFTY-ONE

Aeroporto de Nova Iguaçu

A cross from RioAero on the far south side of *Aeroporto de Nova Iguaçu*, the Brazilian Air Force ramp area was virtually silent except for the droning hum of a fuel tender engine. Here, a variety of different aircraft types were strategically clustered on the tarmac. Half a dozen four-engine turboprops stood idle in the morning sun. A large group of fighter and low-level attack jets, which the military had acquired over the past decade, were chocked and tied down. Brazil was not in a state of alert. Neighboring countries had scant airborne military resources. It was just another sleepy Sunday morning for the Air Force command center in the Sarapuí River Valley.

Near the massive operations hangar, a KC-137 quietly stood as it took on fuel from the large drab-green tender. This military transport version of the venerable Boeing 707 had been repositioned during the early morning hours from *Base Aérea do Galeão*, which was located only a short distance away to the north of Rio de Janeiro. Soon it would be flying a mission—a mission that would hold the fate of RioAero.

The aircraft, an intercontinental series 320B, was both similar and dissimilar to the three other KC-137s recently acquired by the Brazilian Air Force from Varig and subsequently modified to replace the problematic Lockheed KC-130E Hercules as tankers for in-flight refueling. While still maintaining the probe-and-drogue in-flight refueling retrofit capability, this specific aircraft had a much different status. That, however, was not readily apparent to the untrained eye.

The aircraft's exterior had the same appearance as the other KC-137s. Its long, seemingly endless fuselage was bright white on the upper surfaces with the words *Força Aérea Brasileira* (FAB) in bold black lettering centered at the wing root and displayed above the cabin windows. A lateral blue cheat line demarcated its lower "air superiority" gray surfaces. Just forward of its tall white rudder, a small upright two bar fin flash in the country's green and yellow national colors was dwarfed by the huge vertical stabilizer; below in black, the ship's serial number read: FAB 2401.

The racing sound of the fuel tender's engine abruptly returned to a normal idling rpm; a line service technician had just disengaged the PTO. The underwing pressure refueling had taken almost thirty minutes of connect time. Today, the aircraft had taken on a full load of fuel. It would be necessary.

Three flight officers from the *Grupo de Transporte Especial* (GTE) squadron waited patiently in the cockpit. A flight attendant manned his station near the forward cabin entrance door. The GTE had the official duty of providing air transportation for the President of the Republic, ministers, secretaries of the presidency, high-ranking members of the congress and justice, as well as the military high-command officers. Today's flight would be official, but unsanctioned by the president. General Carlos Cardella had unilaterally requisitioned the aircraft. He had more than enough clout to do so.

From the left seat of the cockpit, the captain spotted a black Cadillac Fleetwood pass through the security checkpoint and drive onto the ramp. He immediately flipped on the switch to the APU. The small turbine engine quickly lit off, providing pre-start auxiliary power to the aircraft.

"*Atenção!*" came the captain's command to crewmembers. He wanted everyone on high alert. Even though he had flown Cardella to Europe on several occasions during the past six months, all uneventfully, the captain was very much aware of the reputation the general had for being difficult. The captain intuitively sensed that today would be a difficult day for him and his crew.

Typically, the GTE had extensive advance notice for any assigned KC-137 airborne mission. Today's flight, however, was different. Only a few hours notification had been provided. But even more unusual, the flight crew had not been given a destination. The orders had been to reposition the aircraft, load three sealed LD3 containers into the cargo hold, have maximum fuel on board, and be prepared for takeoff anytime after zero eight-hundred hours. That was all.

The Cadillac slowed as it approached the aircraft, stopping opposite the large movable stairway leading up to the main cabin entrance doorway. The driver, a staff sergeant, quickly exited from the vehicle, promptly opened the left rear door, and snapped to attention. General Carlos Cardella donned his mirror-finished aviator sunglasses and stepped out of the car. He nodded to the sergeant, rounded the car toward the aircraft, trotted up the stairs, and disappeared into the cabin.

Close behind was Salo Montero with the strap of his leather travel bag slung over his shoulder. The general's attaché, a powerfully built Army major, was unloading two suitcases and a large briefcase from the trunk of the car. He soon trudged up the stairway with the luggage and onto the aircraft behind the two primary passengers.

FAB 2401 was, in many respects, patterned after the VC-137B/C Stratoliner which entered service in 1962 and carried the President of the United States. Like the Stratoliner, it had a specially designed interior from Boeing's Wichita facility. This FAB KC-137 interior arrangement consisted of three major cabin compartments, subdividable with additional moveable partitions available for privacy. The most forward and most commonly used section contained the galley, communications center, and club seating arrangements to accommodate sixteen passengers. Farther back, the conference area section had a long mahogany veneer table with twelve high-back swivel chairs, a projection screen, and a double sofa seating arrangement. The most aft section was outfitted with reclining passenger seats and convertible sofa berths.

Cardella had selected a forward facing window seat in the first club arrangement on the right side of the aircraft. He eyed the late morning edition of *O Globo* that the flight attendant had placed upon the table in front of him. He unfolded the paper and scanned the front page, looking over the top of his mirrored sunglasses. He repressed a smile as his eyes fixed on a large black and white photo. The propless WindStar had made page one. Cardella promptly refolded and stowed the paper just as Salo Montero eased into the adjacent aisle seat.

The table-mounted FliteFone beeped twice.

"Shall I?" Montero offered.

Cardella nodded.

Salo removed the phone from its cradle, pressed the receive button, and listened. "It is the captain," he said, removing the handset from his ear. "He says he needs to speak with you."

"Is he too lazy to take a few steps back here and greet me?" Cardella reclined his seatback, eyes closed behind the sunglasses in a show of disdain and power.

Montero relayed the essence of the general's comment to the cockpit. Immediately the captain appeared, nervously concerned.

"To where shall we proceed?" the captain inquired of Cardella, seeking the flight's destination.

Cardella was unresponsive. For him, the Air Force was merely an adjunct to the Army. The Army itself was the military establishment. It ran the country; it had the power.

"General, sir," the captain implored, "I need your directive, please."

Cardella slowly removed his sunglasses, casually laying them on the table. "Montero," he said to Salo, "would you please excuse us? I need to have a word with this confused pilot."

Montero relocated to a seat across the aisle.

The captain placed a clipboard containing an incomplete flight plan form on the table. He leaned over to the general and quietly asked, *"Destino, senhor?"*

"*Pontos norte, capitão.*" Cardella shot a condescending glance at the captain. "Check in with me when we are over Belém for further instructions."

"But, we cannot—"

"Cannot!" Cardella glared at the captain. "While in Brazil, I can do anything I damn well please." He paused waiting for a reaction from the pilot. There was none, just downcast eyes. "Am I understood?"

The captain nodded and swiftly retreated to the cockpit.

Cardella grinned to himself. He loved to be in control. Many times like today, he went out of his way to show the power of his position. As head of the highly autonomous CIE, no one questioned his judgment...ever. And, only rarely would any information from the CIE flow up to the head minister of the SNI. But times were changing.

Since Figueiredo took over as President of the Republic less than two years earlier, a new generation of officers within the SNI began meddling with the autonomy of the CIE and other intelligence service agencies. Cardella was now finding that his activities were being monitored, and occasionally even the unthinkable happening—his directives challenged. Recognizing that his position of power was slowly eroding, Cardella developed a plan of action. And, his plan was quickly coming together. Soon he would be more autonomous than ever before. That was exactly what he wanted. He would stop at nothing to achieve this goal.

Across the aisle, Salo Montero sat quietly, biding his time. He knew this trip was directly related to RioAero, but as yet, he did not know exactly how. When Cardella had summoned him to the CIE headquarters in Rio the night before, Salo expected the worst—a reassignment to another government controlled company, or even a possible reorganization of RioAero itself. At the very least, he expected an explanation for why his presence was required. Nothing. Cardella was absent. Montero was merely greeted by two of the general's lieutenants who summarily disclosed that Montero would be joining Cardella on a flight the next morning during Salo would be briefed. Aside from cursory conversations about the operational status of RioAero, nothing was discussed. Even when Cardella picked Salo up at the Air Force reception center this morning, few words were exchanged. Montero could tell something was weighing heavily on the general's mind. Still, Salo decided to patiently wait until the timing was right before probing.

FAB 2401's four powerful Pratt and Whitney JT3D engines spooled up for breakaway thrust. The heavy aircraft moved forward, beginning its taxi to Runway 21. From his seat, Salo's eyes fixed on the factory in the distance. He glimpsed the large inventory of unsold

WindStars that were tied down on the factory's ramp. For an instant, he thought he might have been too aggressive in pushing the WindStar production rate as high as he had. He quickly shook off the thought. "It is a good aircraft," he quietly said to himself, "the best on the market. It will sell, it will."

Salo glanced over at Cardella. The flight attendant had just finished pulling down the window shades on the right side of the aircraft at the general's request.

The captain sounded a two bell signal indicating that the takeoff would shortly commence. The one hundred-fifty foot long KC-137 turned onto the takeoff runway. Its kerosene-guzzling turbojet engines roared, spooling up to the required 18,000 pound takeoff thrust. Expansion joints of the concrete runway thumped beneath the rolling wheels, first slowly, then more rapidly, as the aircraft accelerated down the runway.

Cardella grabbed the FliteFone from the table. He punched in a few numbers and placed the handset to his left ear.

Twenty seconds later, the KC-137 pitched up and began its initial climb-out.

Cardella reached for the window shade near his right armrest. He slid it open partially, peering out at the factory below. He glanced across the aisle to Salo, who was engrossed in a magazine, and then the general turned back to the window.

"Wait until after the pilot leaves the Tower frequency," Cardella spoke softly, but assertively, into the mouthpiece. "Make sure he contacts Rio Departure Control." He paused, slowly nodding. "Then, do it!" Cardella firmly placed the handset back into its cradle on the table.

Nearly thirty seconds went by. The plane passed through three thousand feet, transitioning to an enroute climb attitude with a slight power reduction. It entered a shallow bank to the right, turning to a heading of three-six-zero. It continued climbing.

The general leaned down on his right armrest and crooked his neck, once again peering out the sliver of open window at the factory below. Amidst the sprawl of buildings, he focused specifically on Hangar One—the R&D hangar that housed the two military prototypes and the propless WindStar. The sun's rays glistened off of the dew on the hangar's roof. The factory complex was still peaceful—asleep on a lazy Sunday morning.

Cardella began slowly nodding in anticipation. He clenched his fists, and slightly thrust his chin forward as if goading on some intended action below.

And, something did happen.

Suddenly.

Within the quiet confines of Hangar One below, a large mangy rat began scurrying across the gray concrete floor. Midway across the hangar, it froze in its tracks. A metal-to-metal sound caught its attention. CLICK. CLICK. If the rat were wiser, the noise would have been foreboding. As it was, the unfamiliar sound made the rodent's beady eyes bulge and sent its nose frantically twitching.

It was too late to sense anything; everything was set into motion. There was no stopping it. The rodent moved not a muscle, but it could not have been saved even by a mad dash.

There was a silent, split second delay.

Then detonation set off an abrupt rumble and a massive blast. First once, then again.

An immense fireball expanded from the center of the hangar, totally engulfing the structure. Instantaneous, uncontainable pressure built up. Within a blink of an eye, the massive doors at both ends of the hangar violently blew off their tracks. Simultaneously, long sections of the corrugated roof were uplifted from the rigid I-beam rafters to float momentarily like huge sheets of paper in a fiery swirl of air. There was a brief surge of golden orange flames; next, an ominous cloud of heavy black smoke cloaked the entire hangar. Over sixteen thousand gallons of both jet fuel and avgas had been detonated.

The KC-137's engines continued to roar on its climb out. The general's plan was coming together. He smiled to himself, closed the window shade, and turned to Salo, who was oblivious to the rat's fate.

"Montero," he abruptly said with a face devoid of expression, "today will mark a turning point for all of us."

Not knowing what response was expected, Salo Montero briefly looked up from his magazine toward Cardella and gave a nod of acknowledgement.

The flight had just begun.

It would be nearly seven hours before their destination was reached.

FIFTY-TWO

Pasador Ranch

"My, my…look who's finally up and about this morning," Gail remarked derisively as Rick entered the kitchen for his customary pint-sized glass of cold milk mixed with Ovaltine. She eyed his clothes as he approached her. "Why Mr. Harris, you look rather preppy today."

Rick sneered. "It's resort casual, by the way," he said, quickly correcting her. "Aircraft salesmen are never preppy." Then after a pause, he allowed, "Well, maybe if you were a Brit, the term could apply."

Rick's mind was already in high gear. He was bright-eyed, seemingly well-rested and either resort casual or preppy, depending upon one's viewpoint. Dressed in a bright pink Ralph Lauren Polo shirt, freshly pressed khaki slacks, and taupe Sperry Topsiders on his sockless feet, he looked more like a Florida yacht broker than an aircraft sales executive.

Gail continued honing in on his attire. "Going yachting today, captain?"

"You know," he retorted without hesitation, "sometimes I wish I was born a dog whose owner was a veterinarian. Now, that's the life." He squatted to scratch behind the ears of one of the two rottweilers stationed near Gail's feet at the kitchen table. "You are always kinder to them than you are to me," he said, playfully chiding her as he stood. He leaned over, kissed her on the forehead, and casually glanced at the newspaper she was reading.

Gail laughed at his comment without diverting her eyes from the newsprint. "Maybe in your next life you'll be lucky enough to be a dog. For now, though, you'll just have to be satisfied as a preppy—err, resort casual—aircraft marketeer."

"Maybe." He nodded, zeroed in on the newspaper, and hesitated before strolling to the refrigerator for his milk. "Anything interesting in the *Sun-Sentinel*?"

"Well, I thought you'd never ask." She handed him Section A, which contained national and world news. "At least this time you're prepared for it. Check out page twelve."

Rick thumbed through the paper to page twelve, and just as expected, there it was—a three-column quarter-page story that included a photo of the propless WindStar in Hangar One at the RioAero factory.

"Hey, that's a very striking photo," he noted, his eyes capturing every aspect of the aircraft, but paying particular attention to the left propeller that was embedded in the fuselage. "Those props can sure cause some damage, can't they?" He hummed to himself as he began to scan the story Bob Waterman had written.

Gail looked up. "You're awfully chipper for a salesman whose product looks like a total disaster."

Rick shrugged. "How am I supposed to act, morose?"

"Well..."

"Even the best of products can get bushwhacked. The WindStar did, and, don't get me wrong, I'm not pleased about it." Rick punctuated his remark by abruptly handing the newspaper back to Gail. He turned and pulled the refrigerator door open, retrieved the carton of milk, poured a glass and then promptly stirred in five teaspoons of Ovaltine. "This is excellent stuff," he said after taking a large gulp. He paused. "Waterman did a nice job with the story, don't you think?"

"Why yes, I suppose." Gail was still trying to figure out why Rick was so upbeat.

"Bob is a good journalist. He couldn't have been more reportorial. He just presented what few facts were known and didn't editorialize—indeed, he could have. I certainly like that page twelve placement." Rick took another slug of his chocolate milk and reached into a huge cookie jar for some Stella D'oro Breakfast Treats.

"Are you still planning on taking him on that flight demo with your customers?"

"Absolutely!" Rick's eyes widened with his thoughts. "I'd be real disappointed if he didn't show up." He briefly paused to shake his head at the notion. "Oh, I know he'll be there. This opportunity is too big for him to pass up." Rick chomped down on half of a Breakfast Treat, promptly washing it down with the milk. "This is going to be a good day," Rick said with heightened enthusiasm, "a really good day. I can feel it in my bones. Everything will go down like clockwork; nothing will go wrong." He rubbed his hands together briskly.

Gail just shook her head in amazement. With all the potential adversity still lurking around the corner, she was confounded with his extraordinarily positive attitude. "Ovaltine does that?" she quipped.

Rick frowned, genuinely taken back. "A salesman has to have a proper outlook, otherwise he might as well never get out of bed. Just like an actor in a leading role who's striving for that Oscar, I must captivate my audience." He raised his hands in the classical style of a true thespian and intoned in his best Shakespearian accent, "I will sell many—MANY—WindStars today." With a broad smile and a flourish, he bowed.

"Bravo!" Gail theatrically applauded, proud of his pluck and his determination.

"Thank you, thank you…" Rick bowed again. "I am just warming up, you know. I will get even better as the day goes on." He paused. "Now, if you would be so kind as to excuse me, I must retire to prepare for Act One—The Flight Demonstration—and Act Two—The Sale." He blew kisses from his palm to his adoring audience of one. "Adieu." He left the room for his home office to undoubtedly work on his script.

Under her breath, Gail said, "Amazing." She had seen his performances before. When the chips were down, Rick somehow energized himself like no one else she had ever known. This morning was no exception. He was on an adrenalin high. It could easily last all day.

Within the quiet of his small office at the opposite end of the house, Rick reflected upon the presentation he had made to Santelli and friends the previous day. His mind flashed back to the details…to his prospect's apprehensions. He could almost hear Santelli expressing his concerns anew: "My main problem deals with betting our brand-new airline on a brand-new aircraft manufactured by a relatively young company located in a third world country which is currently having some serious economic difficulties. I feel ill-at-ease putting so many of our eggs into one basket." Rick further considered another statement made the previous day. Aside from the gear-up incident Rick had disclosed, Santelli and partners were collectively concerned that the WindStar could easily be plagued by other additional and equally troubling incidents. Rick grimaced. He knew Santelli was already right.

He rifled through his briefcase and fished out a copy of the Letter of Intent he had prepared back in his office at RioAero shortly after his meeting with Santelli. Would what he had then composed satisfy Santelli and the others?

Rick pursed his lips and closed his eyes, tight. He felt as if he and the WindStar were in an indefinite holding pattern and running low on fuel. He snapped open his eyes, shook his head hard, and focused upon the first page of the LOI. The typical inane pablum language of the opening paragraph brought a lighthearted smirk to his lips. It broke the anxiety bearing down upon him to which he would never admit feeling. Indeed, chasing a deal involving a total of sixty aircraft was a justifiable cause for tension. He buckled down to take his time to thoroughly review each major category of what he had composed the day before:

◆AIRCRAFT DEFINITION & CONFIGURATION
◆FIRM AIRCRAFT & DELIVERY SCHEDULE
◆OPTION AIRCRAFT & EXERCISE DATES
◆PRICING & FINANCING
◆WARRANTIES & PRODUCT ASSURANCE
◆SUPPORT SERVICES

Everything seemed in order. He nodded to himself. He liked what he had just re-read. It was a highly aggressive proposal. It had to be. Rick knew that he would only have one shot at landing the deal. He particularly liked his concept of tying the whole deal up with an insurance policy of sorts to allay Santelli's concerns about uncertainties in Brazil and the unexplained incidents that had afflicted the WindStar. But would that lone sentence he had added to the Warranties and Product Assurance section be enough? Would it be what Santelli was looking for? He read the sentence again: *RioAero shall provide assurances to the Buyer that all terms and conditions represented herein, and hereafter in the definitive Purchase Agreement, will be fulfilled to the satisfaction of the Buyer.*

What had seemed like such a brilliant idea the day before looked tarnished in the morning's light. The statement was gray, lifeless, unimaginative, and without punch. It could easily be overlooked among the other warranty and assurance provisions. Not good, Rick thought. It has to be more prominent. Santelli would certainly be looking for something more, something specific, something containing the words AIRWORTHINESS and INCIDENTS.

Now came the hard part: crafting some targeted verbiage to specifically abate Santelli's concerns involving the gear-up event and other troubling incidents that, as yet unknown to Santelli, had already occurred.

Rick ratcheted a blank sheet of paper into the electric typewriter at his desk and flipped the switch to on. He started by entering the word CONTINGENCIES, centered at the top of the page, and then paused. "Now, what?" he mumbled aloud. "What would it take to be sure?" His insurance policy concept was certainly innovative, but it would be months before an underwriter was found and the legalese drafted. Even then, Santelli could be dismissive of the entire idea.

He stared ahead at the wall for nearly two minutes, his mind searching for a brainstorm that would drive his proposal home. It would have to allow Sammy to walk away from the deal if Rick could not assure him that the WindStar was a sound well-engineered aircraft without airworthiness problems. It also would have to be reasonable and straightforward. It could not contain sentence after sentence of convoluted mumbo jumbo. He needed something simple, something concise. He groaned, then shifted his IBM Selectric to all capital letters and began typing again. The sole sentence he had written as the contingency read:

ANY AND ALL AIRWORTHINESS INCIDENTS THAT MAY HAVE OCCURRED TO THE WINDSTAR SINCE ITS CERTIFICATION SHALL BE FULLY EXPLAINED TO THE SATISFACTION OF THE CUSTOMER; AND FURTHER, SHOULD THE CUSTOMER DEEM THAT ANY INCIDENT WAS THE RESULT OF IMPROPER DESIGN, ENGINEERING OR MANUFACTURING, THE CUSTOMER MAY UNILATERALLY TERMINATE THIS AGREEMENT WITHOUT PENALTY AND HAVE ANY AND ALL DEPOSITS PROMPTLY RETURNED WITH INTEREST.

A bit long for a sentence Rick thought re-reading it three times, but the typed words said it all. If Sammy Santelli was not happy with any explanation for any airworthiness incident, the deal could be nullified. It was that simple, but that would not—could not—happen. Rick knew the WindStar was a sound aircraft. He was now positive all the misfortunes that had befallen the aircraft were a direct result of sabotage. Indeed, explaining would have to be done. And as yet, Rick did not have the answers. But he knew he would. There was no alternative. He had to have the answers, and he had to have those answers soon.

After making two copies of what he had just composed, he stuffed the Letter of Intent along with some additional paperwork into his briefcase and ambled back toward the kitchen. He looked at his watch and moaned. It was nearly ten o'clock. Franco Rameros would hopefully be taxiing a WindStar to the RioAero hangar by now, or at least be in the final stages of clearing Customs and Immigration.

"I'm late, I'm late…" he said to Gail in Alice-in-Wonderland mimicry as he re-entered the kitchen.

"Got your script together, Mr. Harris?" Gail inquired.

"Absolutely, positively!" Rick beamed. "Santelli has to bite. The WindStar is perfect for his route structure. And, he's in the right place, at the right time. He'll never get a better deal."

"I sure hope he agrees with you."

"He will," Rick confidently affirmed. He briefly paused, remembering a minor detail of his upcoming performance that had not yet been totally arranged. "But, I need your help."

"My help?" Gail, of course, had no idea what he was talking about. She was as yet unaware of the supporting role she would play in his sales effort.

"Yes, your help," Rick reiterated. "You see, Gail, I volunteered you, but forgot to ask if you would be so kind as to pick up my customers at the Pier Sixty-Six Marina." He looked at her with soulful, playfully pleading eyes. "You will do me this big favor, won't you?" He gave her his best sad puppy look.

"Me, alone with those three big guys?" She feigned apprehension.

"Why all of them together still weigh less than a Paso Fino stallion, and they have less kick."

"Well..." she drew out her answer.

"Gail, please," he whined in a pathetically contrived sorrowful tone.

She laughed. "No need to overact with me, Mr. Harris. Of course I will, but only if you promise to continue polishing those thespian skills of yours and swear to use them very sparingly with your customers."

"Love you," he said heading to the kitchen door, but then stopping and returning to give her a hug and a kiss on the lips. "The guys will be waiting for you near the parking area at the end of the marina's C-Dock at 11:15."

She nodded an acknowledgement.

Rick continued, "When you get them back to the ranch, offer the guys some drinks that Domingo will have iced up out at the picnic area. Then walk them over to the stable—show off the new foal." He mentally reviewed the timing of his arrival. "But be sure to have the fellows back to the picnic area by twelve noon. That's where Domingo will be preparing a barbecue lunch. Franco and I will be arriving at EXACTLY that time. We'll meet you out there. I want to impress the hell out of Santelli and his pals. I know we will. Franco is one damn excellent pilot."

"Consider it done," Gail confirmed.

"Remember," Rick emphasized, "have the guys out at the picnic area by twelve noon and nowhere else."

"Yes, Rick, I heard you the first time." She paused, recognizing his serious tone and re-emphasized her answer, "Aye, aye, sir! We will be there."

"Good, Gail." He passed through the doorway, and then poked his head back into the room. "The picnic area at HIGH NOON."

She fashioned an imaginary six-shooter with her hand and pointed the extended forefinger straight at his chest. Gail said, "Get out of here while you still can. This kitchen ain't big enough for the two of us, pilgrim."

"Thanks again, but I'm not sure Gary Cooper would be happy being mis-characterized as John Wayne." Rick grinned. "Anyway, I'm gone." He turned and dashed to the stable where he met Domingo and quickly reconfirmed all the details that had discussed the day before. Satisfied that all the elements were in place, he fired up the old Chevy pickup and left the ranch for the airport.

As he drove along, he said aloud, "This is going to be one hell of an interesting day!"

Rick grinned and gunned the Chevy down SR-84.

FIFTY-THREE

Over the Brazilian Highlands

At thirty-four thousand feet above the country's vast central plateau, the KC-137 continued on its way north-northwest toward an as yet undisclosed destination. Slicing through the tranquil bright blue morning sky at just over five hundred knots, the military transport's four powerful turbojet engines ejected a mixture of spent hydrocarbons and moisture into the dry frigid high-altitude air. Almost instantaneously, the aircraft's hot exhaust morphed into four cloud-like ribbons of ice crystals that streamed from behind each engine, gradually converging into one huge contrail, lazily floating for hundreds of miles, slowly churning, ultimately dissipating into thin air. Inside the aircraft's forward cabin, the highly muffled but still noticeable engine roar and constant low-level fuselage vibration produced a soothing hypnotic effect.

Salo Montero yawned, blinked open his eyelids, then quickly remembered where he was. But he was still not totally sure why. His brow furrowed as he glanced across the aisle to his right at the Army's powerful CIE chief who appeared to be in a state of serene repose. General Carlo Cardella's slightly built frame was ensconced in the large plush blue-leather seat. His chest gently rose and fell with each breath. His russet acne-scarred face was slack behind mirror-finished aviator sunglasses. While Salo was still not sure why Cardella had insisted being accompanied on this trip, Salo knew it had to involve RioAero. And, Salo felt so with foreboding.

To most people, Cardella seemed the same as any other Army general—authoritarian, single-minded, often rash. Montero had greater insight. Cardella's recent and keen interest in the financially plagued RioAero had prompted Salo to seek assistance from his longtime acquaintance, President Figueiredo. Salo mentally reviewed the dossier subsequently supplied by the SNI.

Aside from the SNI report's caustic narrative about the general's life-long and rather tumultuous military career, the document made specific reference to frequent international travel and to extensive contacts with nefarious factions in other third world countries. Perhaps this was not to be unexpected; Brazil's successful military régime had become a model for other Latin American countries. Between the lines, the report also painted Cardella as an egocentric middle-aged man who cared little about anyone or anything else outside of his own goals. The general fervently subscribed to the hard-liner philosophy of a military autocracy. This was considered a serious character flaw by the current more moderate administration. It was the key reason for Cardella being bypassed to head up the SNI. Montero thought it was easy enough to connect the dots and grasp the basis for what made the man tick. The more he thought about it, the more sure he was that Cardella had a covert vendetta with Figueiredo. Nonetheless, Montero was unable to find what he was really looking for in the SNI report. The document contained no obvious reason for Cardella's intense, if not compulsive, interest in RioAero.

Salo's brief glance toward Cardella transitioned to a trenchant stare. Salo very much wished he had the supernatural power to make the man across the aisle evaporate just like the contrails of the jet in which they were traveling were fated to do.

Quite suddenly, the general twitched almost as if Montero's thoughts had goaded him. The general's body briefly shuddered. Cardella moaned, his face contorted. Unintelligible, monotone words rapidly spewed from his lips. The mumbling continued for nearly a minute.

Salo grinned, hoping that a nightmare was ensuing and continued his glaring stare.

Cardella's body twitched again. A series of short, shallow breaths, then a sudden gasp for air. The general's fingers clutched the armrests of his seat. His head abruptly jerked forward. He moistened his lips with his tongue as he became fully conscious. Awakened, yet still not quite oriented to his current surroundings, he tore off his sunglasses, flipped them onto the table, and glanced about, only to be greeted by the fixated perplexing gaze of Salo Montero from across the aisle.

The general slapped his clammy palms to his damp forehead and ran his hands down the sides of his face. He looked up, canted his body to the left and raised his right hand, straining to reach a WEMAC eyeball vent located on the passenger service panel above. His fingers fumbled, unsuccessfully trying to reach and twist open the knurled aluminum collar which seemed just out of his grasp. He swore in Portuguese, then in English, when finally realizing that his fastened seatbelt had held him back from the task. He snapped open the belt's metal tongue from its buckle, raised himself up, and forcefully opened the vent to a whoosh of cool air.

His satisfaction was short-lived. He was now acutely mindful of Salo's presence across the aisle. Discomforted that his gaffe had been so obvious, he reseated himself and went on the offense. "What the hell are you looking at, Montero?"

Sidestepping the barbed comment, Salo tactfully segued, "You were having a dream, sir." Salo fluttered his eyelids and averted his gaze away from the general's penetrating eyes. "It was seemingly intense, sir." In a further attempt to mollify Cardella, he continued, "I dream all the time. People tell me it is one of the joys—but, sometimes annoyances—of an intellectual mind." He smiled collegially.

"Yeah, yeah..." Cardella gruffly replied, still deeply gripped by the thoughts that had only moments before passed through his subconscious. He briskly shook his head to clear his mind, pressed the flight attendant call button, and refastened his seatbelt.

Seconds later, the flight attendant appeared. *"Senhor?"* the handsome young man eagerly inquired.

"Suco de goiaba...café, preto," the general brusquely demanded.

"Certamente, senhor," the attendant said. He subserviently glanced toward Salo, who nodded a compassionate reassurance and quietly said, *"O mesmo, por favor."*

As the attendant dutifully disappeared up the aisle toward the forward galley, the FliteFone at the general's table beeped twice. Cardella snatched the phone from its cradle, placed it to his ear and listened. Without a word, he slammed the phone back down into its cradle. "Damn Air Force pilots," he said, infuriated. "Thank God the Air Force does not run this country."

Cardella noticed the thin smirk on Salo's pursed lips. He once again unfastened his seatbelt, slid over to the aisle seat, and leaned toward Salo. "You were Air Force, were you not?" the general more accused than asked, his tone intimidating.

"Why yes, general." Salo nodded.

"Pilots are a pain in the ass, are they not?"

Salo smiled, unabashedly. Some pilots were. "Why yes, general." He paused briefly. "I should know, I was a pilot."

"Transport?" Cardella baited the hook, knowing more about Salo than Salo could have ever imagined.

"No." Salo shook his head. "Fighter."

"Hmmm...that is quite different," an apparently taken back Cardella said, seeming to warm to Montero. "You guys have balls. Transport and tanker pilots are worthless scum. They could not qualify for fighters...they know it, and they are forever pissed about it. Maybe that is why they are such royal pains in the ass. They ask too many questions. They have too much time on their hands. I would like to be rid of the lot of them, and would, but unfortunately they serve a necessary function."

Salo nodded an acknowledgement. Some of what the general said was true.

"So, Mr. Montero..." Cardella switched gears in his questioning. "What destination should I tell that dumb-ass pilot of ours to aim for today?"

Playing along, Salo thought for a second and replied, "Our actual destination, of course, sir."

"And that is?" Cardella pressed for an answer.

"Points north, sir," Salo said, summing up the general's pre-takeoff instructions to the pilot and couching the answer as diplomatically as possible. He hoped it was the right tactic.

Cardella laughed heartily. "You are a smart man, Montero…points north." He laughed again, then abruptly stopped. His eyes narrowed to a steely gaze. "Exactly which point north, Montero?"

Salo raised his eyebrows. "With all due respect, sir, that is not for me to say." He calculated the length to hesitate. "This is your mission, sir, I am only here at your request to support you."

Cardella grinned. "I like your attitude, Montero. You know what to say, and you know how to say it." His grin widened. "I do believe that we will work well together."

"Why thank you, sir. I appreciate the compliment." Salo smiled with all the politeness he could muster at the man he had come to despise—a man whom he believed was about to try to extract the very heart out of RioAero.

"But you do know exactly where we are going, do you not, Montero?"

"Why—" Salo bit off his response as the flight attendant returned with servings of guava juice and black coffee for them both.

"That will be all." Cardella impatiently waved off the attendant after having been served.

Salo continued with his answer as the attendant departed. "Fox-Lima-Lima." It had to be RioAero's operation in Fort Lauderdale, he thought.

The general grinned. "Ultimately, yes, but we will be landing at Oscar-Papa-Fox." He gulped down the chilled guava juice.

OPF was the IATA (International Air Transport Association) identifier for Opa Locka. The airport, which was located just seven miles north of Miami International and some twenty miles southwest of Fort Lauderdale, had been founded by aviation pioneer Glenn Curtiss in the mid-1920s. It was later heavily used by the Navy Training Command during World War II as the hub of six training bases. Aging Quonset huts, huge dirigible hangars, and lackluster barracks that even predated The Big War still dotted the airport grounds. Whereas the primary commercial airports at Miami and Fort Lauderdale heavily focused upon air carrier activity, Opa Locka was a misfit and still concentrated upon flight training, now of a civilian nature, and general aviation services. Unbelievable but true, during the late 1960s, Opa Locka was the world's busiest airport with over

650,000 annual flight operations. Today it was still the busiest airport, but now in the area of flight training activity.

"Opa Locka," Salo said curiously, wondering at the destination. "Why Opa Locka?"

"Logistics reasons," Cardella said smugly. He took a sip of his coffee. "People there cater to our needs. They make sure that customs and immigration are handled, that we may come and go freely, that the aircraft is never inspected." He smiled with self-approval. "It is smart business."

Salo nodded, his mind flashing back to their arrival at the aircraft earlier that morning. He remembered briefly glimpsing the three LD3 containers stowed in the cargo hold just as the line crew began to secure the aft compartment door. At that time he thought it was rather unusual for a passenger flight to be carrying large containers of cargo. Now, Salo believed he understood what Cardella was saying. Not only was the general a military man, but he was a businessman as well. It was hardly an uncommon occurrence—corruption was rampant in Brazil. It was not a stretch for Salo to believe Cardella had a streak of ruthless avarice running through his very soul. But the actual contents of the three sealed containers aboard the KC-137 were beyond Salo's wildest imagination.

The general casually eyed the Rolex wristwatch on his arm. It was time. With the single snap of his fingers, he summoned his attaché. The major arrived almost instantaneously.

"Major Alverez," Cardella spoke in an official tone, "tell the pilot that our destination is Oscar-Papa-Fox—Opa Locka. I do not want to have the idiot begin a holding pattern so as not to leave Brazilian airspace without a flight plan destination."

The attaché nodded without saying a word.

"Tell him that this trip is highly confidential, that all arrangements have been made for our arrival, that his only responsibility is to get us there without crashing the goddamn aircraft." The general beckoned the major closer with a crook of his finger. The major leaned over to Cardella who continued speaking in a whisper.

When the conversation ended, the attaché nodded again, without saying a word, and proceeded forward to the cockpit.

"The major is a highly trusted aide," Cardella commented to Salo while watching the powerfully built man gracefully stride up the aisle. "The best of any we have at the CIE, better than anyone at the SNI. His mind is brilliant; his body, a lethal weapon."

Salo could tell by way of the major's carriage that the man was self-assured and unpretentious. "Martial arts?" he queried the general.

Cardella laughed. "Better than martial arts, Gracie martial arts master."

"I see," Salo said slowly, his eyes widening, fully understanding the implications of the general's statement. "Impressive."

Salo had heard of the renowned Carlos Gracie, who as a brash young man had studied jujitsu under the great Japanese champion, Mitsuyo Maeda. Although a mere 135 pounds, Gracie modified the classical techniques he had learned from Maeda into a deadly form of "no rules" fighting which he subsequently took to the streets of Rio and used to remain undefeated for decades. Now in his eighties, the legendary Gracie and his sons continued to refine and teach their highly effective form of martial arts. Many intelligence agency officers had sought out Gracie to learn his Brazilian-style jujitsu. Becoming a master under Gracie's tutelage merited respect; Cardella's attaché had become just that.

The general continued, "Alverez has been with me for just over five years. He handles many details very effectively."

Salo sipped his coffee. After a few minutes he looked up and saw Alverez returning from the cockpit. A troubled expression knitted the brows on the major's formerly stoic face. Alverez studiously avoided eye contact with Salo, and with a subtle cock of his head motioned for Cardella to join him in the conference area. The general immediately rose from his seat and followed the major down the aisle to the aircraft's center section.

Five, ten, fifteen minutes went by. Neither the general nor the major had returned. Salo concluded that there had to be a problem, something they were struggling to resolve. Perhaps the pilot had some difficulty with the destination. Perhaps Cardella had overstepped his bounds in making this trip. Perhaps the head minister of the Army had ordered the aircraft to return to Rio. Perhaps, perhaps... Salo shook his head. There were many possibilities. He craned his neck to look back toward the aircraft's conference area. There was no sign of anyone standing in the aisle. As he turned his head forward, he noticed a steady red light on the FliteFone that was attached to the table across the aisle. It was in use. The general was obviously in contact with someone, somewhere. Something was happening. Salo wanted—needed—to know what it was.

FIFTY-FOUR

RioAero, NA

Franco Rameros glanced across the cockpit toward Bjorn Svensson who was controlling the aircraft from the left seat. "We are almost there, BJ," Rameros said quite casually.

Svensson smiled, his eyes focused on the expanses directly ahead. There was only a very short distance remaining in their journey to RioAero, NA, on the south ramp at FLL.

Rameros nonchalantly moved his left hand toward the cockpit's center control pedestal, resting his hand on the engine condition levers. He nakedly grinned, curled his fingers around the red gear-knobbed tops, and with one abrupt motion yanked both levers back into the fuel cutoff positions. The WindStar's gas-turbine engines immediately lost power and began spooling down. The aircraft's propellers windmilled, losing rpms by the second, slowly going into feather.

"What the—" a startled Svensson gasped, not sure why Rameros had done what he did.

Rameros just smirked. "Do you think you can make it?"

Svensson's eyes widened as he fixated on a point a short distance over the nose of the WindStar. "Duh, dunno," he stammered. It was too close to call.

"Well, we can," Rameros said reassuringly. "Just do not do anything to slow the aircraft down."

"Ah, okay, but it would be very embarrassing if we did not make it."

Rameros laughed. "Yes, it would, would it not?"

There was complete silence within the cockpit. Both propellers were fully feathered and had almost totally ceased rotating.

"Just keep on trucking," Rameros coached Svensson. A few seconds later he instructed, "Make a slight turn to the right."

The aircraft's forward momentum allowed it to continue on, though its speed was rapidly bleeding off.

"Now, what?" Svensson asked as the aircraft came to a crawl.

The taxi from customs and immigration to the hangar was not yet completed.

"Ehh, just continue on coasting. When your wingtip is abeam the second hangar door, ease on the brakes, that is, if you need to."

A few seconds later, the WindStar came to a full stop exactly where Rameros had intended. No braking needed.

Rameros beamed. "Not bad, huh?"

"I really did not think we would make it," an amazed Svensson said. "You know this aircraft pretty well."

"It is my job to know everything about the WindStar," Rameros said confidently. "And, there are some things I know that even the guys who designed it do not know."

"Roger that," Svensson said with a nod. In his book, Franco Rameros walked on water.

From inside the cockpit, Rameros surveyed the quiet, nearly vacant ramp area in front of RioAero's new hangar. He smiled as he saw a familiar face. Joey Delgada had appeared from the hangar's shadows and began trotting out to greet them. Rameros saw no one else. He scanned the area again to be sure. Still, no one. "Where the hell is Harris?" he said under his breath. "Damn, I bust my tail to make his schedule and…" His words trailed off.

Svensson firmly pressed the tops of both rudder pedals forward with the balls of his feet to set the parking brake. He flipped off the master power switch on the overhead panel, and then began making an entry in the aircraft's log.

"Looks like you are about to have a day off, BJ," Rameros noted, unbuckling his seatbelt and removing his shoulder harness. "After we off-load the cargo, you and the guys in the back can unwind at wherever Delgada has decided to put you up."

"What about you, Franco?"

"My day is far from over," he replied, his tone less than pleased. "I am scheduled to fly a demo for Rick Harris, but after that, I will be taking the next damn week off."

They exited the cockpit together. The two engineers who had accompanied them from the factory to help repair the damaged WindStar had already disembarked down the open airstair door. Svensson and Rameros followed onto the ramp where Joey Delgada was already introducing himself.

"*Como vai, Franco?*" Joey said extending his hand. "It has been a while."

Franco grasped Joey's hand and pumped it three times. "It could not have been that long, maybe four or five months," Rameros commented.

Joey shrugged.

"Anyway," Rameros said, continuing with his natural acerbic manner, "looks like you have gained some weight, huh?" Delgada had always been on the chubby side.

"Nah, just maintaining what I already have," Delgada said, then quickly returned the jab. "But you, Franco, are getting uglier by the day."

Rameros turned the scarred left side of his face away. "Maybe so," he came back, "but it is my personality that endears me to people."

"HA..." Joey guffawed.

They both laughed at the friendly no-holds-barred verbal sparring match.

"It is good to see you, Joey," Rameros said, his eyes scanning the hangar and ramp area. "Where is that Rick Harris fellow? He was supposed to be here by now."

Just as Joey was about to say Harris' whereabouts were an equal mystery to him, Rick's old Chevy pickup truck slowly rumbled across the ramp, tired brakes screeching it to a stop just inside the shadows of the hangar. "There is your man, Franco." He pointed to the truck.

"You must be kidding me, Joey," Rameros said in amazement. "You mean to tell me that our director of sales drives that piece of junk?"

"It is his ranch truck," Delgada began explaining, as they both watched Rick Harris exit from the cab and stroll toward them. "He has had it forever, I think he is attached to it." He paused. "For sure, Harris sometimes does not seem to care about the image it may project."

"Hmmm..." Rameros snorted in disapproval without commenting further.

"Good morning, guys," Rick shouted out as he crossed the distance between himself and Joey and Franco.

"You are late!" Rameros threw out the first jab.

"And I suppose you'll try to tell me that you've been here for hours," Harris said with a smirk. He could see the mirage-like presence of heat still shimmering from the WindStar's stainless steel exhaust stacks, and that Svensson and the others were just beginning to unload the aft cargo compartment.

"Nah," Rameros said with a smile as they shook hands, "just got here five minutes ago."

Rick took two steps back, cocked his head to the side, and carefully eyed Franco's unusual attire. He quickly keyed in on the four gold pentastars embroidered on Rameros' epaulettes. "You look like some high ranking military officer, maybe a starship commander."

"You hit the nail on the head, Harris," Rameros said with a grin. "Starship commander, as in WindSTAR." He paused. "You like it?"

"Well..."

"Hey, it intimidates the hell out of customs and immigration officials in most Latin American countries." Rameros snickered. "I get a kick out of screwing with their heads."

Joey excused himself and walked to the rear of the aircraft to check out the type of support equipment that had been transported up from the factory. Rick and Franco continued their banter for a brief while longer, then the conversation took on a serious note.

"You've been at the factory for a while, haven't you Franco?" Rick asked.

"Something over ten years by now."

"So, you pretty much know most of the people down there."

"For better or for worse, that is correct."

"Maybe you can help me out with a name?"

"By all means, who do you want to know about?"

"Well, I'm not sure what he does down there, and frankly I'm not even sure he actually works at the factory. But his name came up the other day when someone was talking about aviation and Brazil in the same breath."

"Go ahead."

"Now, uh, I don't know whether it's his first name, last name, or nickname." Rick paused, briefly remembering the name that Monica had mentioned the night before. As a result of the bug he had placed in Dan Cole's office, she had been able to hear Cole's end of the telephone conversation. She speculated that one of the telephone calls Cole had made was to someone in Brazil, quite possibly someone at the factory. And from what she had overheard, whoever Cole was speaking to was a likely player in the conspiracy against the WindStar. She was confident of that. Rick posed the critical question, "Have you ever heard of a man named Jeffe?"

"Who?" Rameros asked with a scowl, although he had clearly heard Rick.

"Jeffe," Rick repeated himself, and then said the name once again.

"That is what I thought you said." Rameros glowered. "A friend of someone you know?"

"Well, yes, a friend, a colleague, an acquaintance..." Rick responded, not being sure exactly what kind of relationship existed between Jeffe and Cole.

"And, who is this person you know that made mention of the name 'Jeffe?'"

Rick rolled his eyes. "Why the third degree, Franco?" He briefly hesitated. "Do you know a guy named Jeffe or not?"

Rameros glanced down at the tarmac, shaking his head vigorously. Then he spat out, "The guy is a goddamn friggin' snake!"

Harris was taken back by the unexpected forceful outburst.

Franco Rameros took a sharp breath, looked Rick straight in the eye, and began nodding. "Yes, I know of the man, and yes, he works at the factory. So, what would you like me to tell you about the bastard?"

"Everything you can."

Rameros began shaking his head again. "Jeffe is a goddamn—"

"Franco," Rick quickly interrupted, "it's obvious that there is some kind of friction between you and this Jeffe character, but try to simmer down so I can understand what you know about the man." Rick paused momentarily.

Rameros tightly folded his arms across his chest and gritted his teeth.

Rick continued, "Although I don't have all the facts as of yet, I'm rather certain that Jeffe is somehow involved in the plot against the WindStar."

That was all Rameros needed to hear. "I knew it," he roared out. "I could sense there was something devious about that weasel."

"Tell me about it," Rick pressed on.

"Well, his name is Martinez, Jeffe Martinez," Rameros began, regaining his composure. "He is the head of QA at the factory."

Rick Harris paled. A red emergency warning light began flashing in his mind: QA—Quality Assurance. That said everything to him. It reconfirmed his earlier speculation.

The quality assurance department was an ideal place to be for someone who wanted to undertake subversive activities against an airframe manufacturer. QA inspectors had the final say on releasing an aircraft from production. They were empowered to delay the issuance of an airworthiness certificate if any deviations from prescribed assembly procedures were discovered. In fact, QA could immediately shut down the entire production line if it discovered critical errors in the manufacturing process affecting, for example, flight safety. That is the way the system was supposed to work. Checks and balances were in place. But the system could also work the other way around. QA inspectors could also easily overlook production errors. Even more far reaching, an inspector could covertly sabotage an aircraft that would have otherwise conformed to production specifications as it progressed down the assembly line.

As director of quality assurance, Jeffe Martinez was the man who ultimately controlled the fate of each and every aircraft. He himself, or through a handpicked inspector, could control the specific serial numbers of parts that were incorporated into each aircraft. He could also secretly modify any component's installation after the fact. The propeller separation experienced by Rameros, as well as the in-flight electrical failure and gear retraction incident with which Rick had been involved, all could easily have been the result of QA negligence, or outright sabotage.

Pieces to at least one part of the puzzle were finally beginning to fit into place for Rick Harris. He remembered Monica saying that Cole congratulated the man he called Jeffe for some kind of good work that had just been completed. Harris felt sure the "good" work involved sabotaging the WindStar, but he needed more information to support his conviction.

"Tell me, Franco," Rick inquired, probing further, "how long has Jeffe Martinez been in his current positionat the factory?"

"Not very long," Rameros paused momentarily, trying to recollect the length of time. "When we were well into the WindStar flight certification program and just started tooling up for full-scale production, Lou Biega saw the need to have someone with first-rate experience for QA. That was back in mid-1979, a little less than two years ago. Of course, Big Lou's recruitment process took some time. So, I would say Martinez has been at the factory for a year, maybe slightly more."

"Where did Martinez come from?"

"Not sure." Rameros thought hard. "Airbus rings a bell." He thought again. "Yes, I believe it was Airbus, but I cannot be absolutely positive about it."

"And before that?" Rick knew that people in the airframe business tended to move around—from one project or company to another. Airbus Industrie was a fairly new player among the heavy iron airframers. He was fishing for the name of a specific manufacturer with which he felt Martinez still had an alliance.

"Before Airbus?" Rameros shook his head. "Beats the hell out of me."

"How about BASA?" Rick persisted.

Rameros shrugged. "Maybe, but I honestly cannot say." He thought for a moment before continuing. "Of course, Lou Biega will know, he hired Martinez." Franco glanced at his wristwatch. It was past noon in Brazil. "Why not give Big Lou a call? He is usually in his office at the factory around midday on Sunday to put out fires or catch up on paperwork. Besides, I am sure he would be interested in hearing what you have to say, especially considering that Martinez could be the source of the problems we have been having."

"Good idea."

In the distance, Rick glimpsed a young Bob Waterman strolling across the ramp, his head swiveling as he took in his surroundings, his mind storing every aspect of his present environment for later recall in drafting the story he had planned. Spotting Rick by the WindStar, Bob hastened his pace.

Rameros followed Rick's gaze, zeroing in on the approaching man who was dressed in a pair of dark blue Farah polyester slacks and an open collar white shirt. Tucked under his arm was a small black leather satchel. "Shit," Rameros said under his breath. To Rameros, Waterman looked like a Fed. "Guess we are in for a ramp check."

"No, no," Rick corrected his friend, "he's the press guy I invited to join us on the demo flight."

"Oh, oh yeah," Rameros said in temporary relief. Then viscerally reacting to his general aversion to the media, he groaned. Rameros remembered Rick's heads-up about Waterman during the telephone call from Santo Domingo. With some effort, Rameros shook off his disgust to quickly change the subject back to the previous topic. "By the way, when you talk with Big Lou, tell him about my experiences in Brasilia and in Zanderij. And do not forget to mention the air show I performed with that Gulfstream over the Amazon."

Rick nodded an acknowledgement and smiled. "But you'll have to be a kind host to Waterman while I use Joey's office to make the call."

"Well, since you are in a bind..." Rameros grinned, cracked the knuckles of his left hand, leaving his intent clear but unspoken.

Rick raised an eyebrow.

"Not to worry, Rick, I will put on my RioAero ambassador's hat and dazzle the young lad."

"Thanks, Franco, I owe you."

Rameros shrugged off Rick's appreciation. "This is just a small favor, Mr. Harris. When we sell your customers because I impressed the hell out of them on the demo flight, then you will owe me big time. Then, I will collect. Hmmm...how about a big bottle of Jack Daniels?"

"Agreed," Rick quickly said. Focusing on Waterman who was within shouting distance, he yelled out, "Good morning, Bob."

Waterman acknowledged with a wave of his hand, all the time carefully eyeing the pristine WindStar as he approached.

"Looks better with both props on the engines, doesn't it, Bob?" Rick was referencing the WindStar story in the morning's *Sun-Sentinel* that Waterman had penned, but had also been kind enough to alert Harris about the day before.

"Sorry about that, Rick," Waterman said apologetically. "I had little choice but to run the story."

"I know," Rick said with total understanding, "and I do appreciate the way you put the story together." Quickly dropping the subject, he introduced Waterman to Rameros.

"Now, Bob," Franco Rameros said enthusiastically, taking the lead, "I am going to show and tell you more than you ever imagined you would learn about what is undoubtedly the finest aircraft ever made. Come with me, young man, you are getting the cook's tour."

Waterman smiled, followed Rameros up the airstair door and into the cabin of the WindStar.

Rick disappeared into the hangar, grabbed his briefcase from the Chevy, and made his way to Joey Delgada's office for an important phone call to the factory.

FIFTY-FIVE

Departing the Brazilian Highlands

Just as Salo unfastened his seatbelt and was preparing to go to the center section conference area, he was startled by the sudden appearance of Major Alverez quietly standing in the aisle beside him.

"Mr. Montero," the major said in an official, but polite voice, "General Cardella has asked for you to join him."

"Thank you, major," Salo replied in his most professional tone while his curiosity piqued. "I would be pleased to join the general."

Salo walked down the aisle, passing by two small communications compartments before reaching the massive center section bulkhead that was covered on both sides by a specially commissioned ornate tapestry. The bulkhead's impressive display of Brazil's coat-of-arms filled Salo with an uplifting feeling of national pride. His steps slowed as his eyes took in a sight he never tired of seeing.

The success of RioAero was the success of Brazil. Salo knew seeing the coat-of-arms at just this moment was a sign his efforts with RioAero were indeed righteous. For the sake of Brazil, he could not fail. Buoyed up, Salo Montero smiled to himself as he entered the center fuselage conference area. However, his euphoria and certainty would only be temporary.

At the far end of a long mahogany veneer table, sat the general with elbows firmly anchored to the table and forehead buried in the palms of his hands. Salo approached Cardella, coming to a stop behind one of the dozen leather swivel chairs that surrounded the table. There, Salo stood motionless, only an arm's length from the general, as the minutes stretched uncomfortably long. Salo considered speaking up, but was unsure of what to say. The general seemed detached from the here and now. The distress in the air was almost palpable.

Finally, Cardella took a deep breath, leaned back into his chair, and folded his arms tightly across his chest. His unfocused eyes gazed aimlessly at the media center at the far end of the table. After another audible breath, Cardella finally acknowledged Montero's presence by asking him to be seated. Salo complied. The general continued to stare absently ahead.

"All is not well," the general said, not meeting Salo's eyes and now taking on the role of a heavily dejected bearer of bad news. He slowly shook his head, turned to Salo, and exclaimed, "You have no idea what we are up against, Montero."

Salo, confused by the general's declaration, remained respectfully silent. This was not the time to chance asking the wrong question. Cardella appeared to be visibly shaken, very much out of character for the man. Whatever had happened had been momentous. At least that was the distinct impression conveyed to Salo.

There was an intermittent flicker from one of the fluorescent tubes in the overhead cove lighting. A slightly more noticeable vibration within the aircraft was only temporary as the pilot synchronized the kerosene-guzzling engines. The jet rumbled on, still heading north-northwest, now leaving Brazilian airspace.

"Salo," the general began, using Montero's first name for the first time, "we need to talk." He hesitated. His eyes momentarily wandered before refocusing upon Salo. "A distressful event has occurred, an event that will have significant impact upon us both." Cardella went silent for a moment. "Damn," he blurted out, "politics is a dirty business. One can never be sure who one can trust. Everyone in politics, regardless of initial integrity, always becomes reprogrammed by the system, their values compromised and frequently corrupted." He snorted in frustration. "During the past few years, our country has been ravaged by politics. On one hand, there are military hard-liners like me, and hopefully you; on the other hand, there are the moderates who are evermore receptive to the left-wing and populist influences. It is cut-throat, with even the military now becoming fragmented and divided. Our country is being torn apart."

Salo nodded, not quite sure where Cardella was going with the conversation, but knowing full well that it was important to hear this out without interruption. Indeed, he had noticed a distinct difference in the general. The brash, insensitive personality was waxing philosophic. For once Cardella seemed reasonable and logical. Why?

Cardella continued, "The chaos we see developing today is nothing compared to what it will be in the future." He rose from his seat at the head of the table and, in silence, measuredly moved forward toward the media center as if he were going to make a full-blown presentation, which he was not.

Salo's eyes followed him.

"We must briefly step back in time. We must retool," Cardella insisted, firmly placing the fist of one hand into the palm of the other with a twist, much like a pestle in a mortar. "What Castelo Branco first began with the coup in 1964, and what was continued with Costa e Silva and Médici, provided our country with a truly glorious period. Many major long-needed projects were completed, scientific and technological advancement soared, the economy boomed." He pointed his index finger at Montero. "And you, Salo Montero...you launched an important new company. RioAero came from absolutely nowhere to become an airframe manufacturer with impressive capabilities." He stopped near the far end of the long conference table, and with both hands, grasped the top of one of the high-back swivel chairs. His knuckles whitened as his fingers gripped the soft black leather covering, sinking deeply into the polyfoam padding.

"But now," the general despondently continued, "the pendulum has lost its momentum. With successive moderates like Geisel and Figueiredo taking over the helm, the economy has gone to hell. We have labor strife, high inflation, and heavy debt—soon the country will be borrowing money just to pay off interest on prior loans. It is an economic and political nightmare. For you, though, it has a more personal impact. All the years you spent building RioAero into what it is today will mean nothing—nothing at all—unless changes are made."

"Sir," Salo interjected, unable to hold his tongue any longer, believing that Cardella was about to discuss a plan to drastically restructure RioAero, "much of what you say may very well be true. Still, I do not—"

"Salo, please," the general interrupted firmly, but courteously, "please hear me out. What I have to say is very important."

Salo slightly shrugged in equally polite acquiescence, allowing Cardella to continue.

The general lowered his head, then turning on his heel he continued his slow methodical stroll around to the other side of the conference table as he regathered his train of thought. "You have had a longtime relationship with Figueiredo—from the early days when he was the Army's liaison to RioAero."

Salo nodded.

"Well, you may or may not have noticed, but Figueiredo is a different man these days. He is older, he is slower, he is over his head. He does not have any idea what he is up against, what he is doing." The general paused.

Salo nodded again, reserving any comment. There was much truth in what Cardella had said. The current administration was seemingly inept. Many felt the country was being led down a dead-end, one-way street. Figueiredo had always readily admitted that he was a bad choice for the country's top office. That was no secret. And yes, during his recent visit with Figueiredo, Salo had noticed the pressure beginning to take its toll.

"Mark my words, Salo..." Cardella temporarily stopped in his tracks. With both forearms, he leaned onto the back of one of the conference table chairs. "Figueiredo will go down in history as the least popular and worst president the Republic of Brazil has ever had. He is letting the country get out of control. He heeds little advice from those who know what is best. He has come to be a despicable piranha, willing to say anything to your face, but then gobbling off your arm when you turn your back. On one hand, he and his SNI have tortured, murdered, and oppressed thousands of Brazilians; on the other hand, he is slowly opening the doors to democracy, which will create further chaos because the country simply is not ready for democracy. The man is a goddamn fool—a charlatan. He is worse than the hard-liners he now despises, even though he was once one of us. His policies profess to be progressive, yet his implementation is without finesse. The man still uses the hard-line tactics that he always has used to repress opposition. The difference is hard-line autocrats have had a record of economic achievement, he and his kind have not.

"Today, we have a leader who lacks resolve. He has no backbone. He acquiesces to populist influences. Because of him the country is foundering. Everything the current administration now attempts to do only digs a deeper hole. Soon the hole will be so deep no Brazilian will be able to crawl out of it." He paused, nodding in agreement with his own words, then continued his steps toward Salo. "Anarchy is not an impossibility." He lowered his voice. "I and a few select allies in the military aim to prevent that occurrence. We must, for the good of the country, for the good of the people."

Salo had quietly listened to all of Cardella's political commentary and was now ready to speak out in defense of his friend, Figueiredo. "I understand what you are saying, general, but—".

"No, Salo," the general broke in sharply, "you may think you understand, but you are too far removed from the political machinery of the country, you simply cannot truly understand. For too long you have been mired in RioAero. And unless things change very quickly, RioAero will cease to exist. You and your company will be buried."

"What do you mean, general?" A frown creased Salo's face.

Cardella seated himself next to Montero. "Salo, what I am about to tell you is distressful enough for me, but for you, it will be devastating."

Salo paled. The word "devastating" boomed in his mind. Still, he had no way of knowing what Cardella was about to say. How personally it would affect him.

"When Major Alverez called me away from the forward cabin, it was because he had obtained some unconfirmed information that the flight crew had heard over a frequency they monitor in the cockpit." Cardella grimaced, woefully shaking his head. "I just spoke to my operations chief in Rio who confirmed the report." He hesitated, obviously troubled. "This is difficult for me to say, Salo, but earlier this morning there was a big problem at RioAero."

Montero's pulse pounded. So this was what Cardella had taken his time leading up to. He tried to imagine what Cardella was about to say. If Salo could guess, he could lessen the news' impact. He wanted to avoid a verbal roundhouse; he had to keep his wits about himself. Perhaps the problem was a labor strike. He quickly dismissed the idea. It was Sunday morning, workers would never consider beginning any kind of protest then. He thought again. Perhaps a factory aircraft had had another in-flight incident, or worse, an accident. Still, it was Sunday morning when no sanctioned activity was ever conducted. What else, what else could it be?

The general looked Salo straight in the eye. He wanted to be sure what he was about to say would be readily understood. He cleared his throat, then spoke up. "There was an explosion." He paused for impact. "In one of your hangars." He paused again, savoring the drama he was creating. "The destruction was total."

Salo's jaw dropped, his face in shock. His eyes closed, tightly. He felt the pain, the reality of the words. But he kept saying to himself that it could not have happened. No, somehow Cardella had to have been mistaken. He opened his eyes and scanned the general's face, looking for any sign of uncertainty. There was none. All he saw was Cardella ever so slowly nodding his head up and down.

"Yes, Salo," the general reconfirmed, "unfortunately it is true." He paused. "I am terribly sorry to be the one to have to tell you. I feel your pain." He firmly placed a comforting hand on Salo's shoulder. "Do know that I have directed the CIE to undertake an immediate investigation. The Army, as well as the Air Force, has a vested interest in the success of RioAero." He hesitated, temporarily averting his eyes from Salo, allowing Salo to regain his composure, and then asked, "Can you think of anyone who might have—"

"Nuh-no…" Salo stammered. "No one."

"Think carefully, very carefully," the general persisted. "Anything, anything could be of value."

Salo's eyes took refuge on the tabletop. He slowly shook his head left to right several times, remaining silent.

"There is something else you need to know, Salo," Cardella went on, his tone compassionate and slightly conspiratorial. "From what little we do now know, it does not appear to be an accident. There is a strong suspicion of sabotage."

Salo's pupils dilated. His mouth went dry. He initially had thought of the possibility of sabotage when Biega had first apprised him of the propeller separation incident. At that time, he had quickly—perhaps too quickly—dismissed the idea. However, he had not been able to totally squelch the thought. The concept of sabotage had still lurked in the back of his mind, raising its ominous head from time to time. In fact, during his visit with Figueiredo the night before, he had suggested sabotage and Cardella in the same breath. Figueiredo, however, was dismissive of the idea. Now, Cardella himself was advancing the thought that RioAero could indeed be the target of sabotage. Salo was forced to reconsider what he had intimated the night before. It was difficult for him to believe that a saboteur would actually raise the issue of sabotage.

"Sabotage?" Salo finally spoke up. "How? Why?"

The general was quick to respond. "My sources say that the cause of the explosion was due to significant quantities of fuel that somehow ignited."

"No way," Salo shot back immediately. "None of our hangars contain large quantities of fuel. Production aircraft are only fueled after leaving the hangar." He thought for a few seconds. "Do you know which hangar it was?"

"Yes, Hangar One."

Salo moaned. "Damn, that is our R&D hangar. That is where we were just finishing up work on two military prototypes, where long-term fatigue testing is ongoing with S/N-003. That is also where we parked the WindStar that suffered the double prop failure this past Friday. Damn!" He slammed his fist down on the conference table. Shock and dismay had turned into anger. Salo was now fuming. Many thousands of hours of R&D work had gone up in smoke. He knew that except for the four aircraft, the hangar was virtually empty. There could not have been enough fuel in or near the hangar to cause the event that Cardella had depicted. Sabotage was the only explanation.

"It is a real setback, I know," Cardella said sorrowfully as he empathized with Salo. "But we must look at the brighter side. The factory and its production capability remain unscathed." He smiled reassuringly.

"Very true," Salo agreed, now less incensed, still visibly frustrated. "Although future programs certainly have been impacted, current production capability remains unchanged."

Cardella acknowledged with a nod, but remained silent.

"Why?" Salo's mind was now in high gear, trying to rationalize any motivation for what had happened. "Why Hangar One? Why RioAero at all?"

The general sat back in his chair and clasped his hands together tightly. He was confident that the timing was right to lure Salo further into his hard-liner camp. He viewed Salo as a man who could very much assist implementing the plans he had for RioAero.

"Why?" Salo repeated the question, totally at a loss for the answer and saddened by that fact.

Cardella's response was just one word: "Politics."

"What?" Salo blurted out.

"It is like I was saying earlier," the general self-assuredly said, "politics is undermining the country. Figueiredo is over his head. It would not surprise me if he and his SNI were somehow involved."

"What are you talking about?" Salo furrowed his brow, thrown off-balance by the suggestion. He had had the distinct impression that it was Cardella—not Figueiredo—who had been putting the pressure on RioAero to perform or be dramatically restructured. Could his judgment have been off-base? Figueiredo did indeed admit that the ministers were pressuring him to more effectively deal with the RioAero situation. Perhaps Cardella's recent interest in RioAero was an effort to save it rather than to undermine the company. Montero had never even considered the thought that Figueiredo could have been the instigator of egregious acts against his company. Now, it seemed a possibility.

"I know you may find this hard to accept," Cardella began, "but one of the ways politicians can restore order and thus regain lost power is to do just the opposite—create havoc." He raised his brow, pursed his lips tightly. "Then, a witch-hunt ensues. The blame is cast onto others and off of themselves." He rocked his head back and forth. "Yes, it is a highly deceptive tactic. On the other hand, it is also highly effective. So, whoever is responsible for the explosion in Hangar One will certainly implicate some predetermined soul—someone to roast in their stead. My best guess is that the current administration played a role in the sabotage. Figueiredo has been criticized too long for feathering RioAero's nest for naught. And yes, the current administration could as well have been behind that propeller separation you mentioned. Anyway, if the ploy succeeds, Figueiredo's position of power will, for the moment, increase dramatically. The people will rally behind the 'discoveries' from a one-sided investigation. The truth of the explosion may never be known."

Salo's mind grasped onto what Cardella was saying. It made sense to him. Cardella had identified a possible motive for Figueiredo. But Figueiredo had been Salo's friend, or so Salo thought. They had worked closely together during the early days of RioAero. Salo trusted Figueiredo, and within the past twenty-four hours he had even met with him for counsel. Unfortunately, Salo knew that times had changed, and so had people. He had found Figueiredo to be much different—more guarded, more distant—since assuming the presidency. It was a true but disappointing fact.

"There is more..." Cardella pressed on. He was sure he had swayed Salo. "When you have had the opportunity to study a person for as long as I have studied Figueiredo, you get to know that person pretty well. In fact, you can almost second guess what is going through their minds, what direction will be taken next."

"You think you know him that well?" a disbelieving Salo asked.

"Absolutely," Cardella responded almost before Salo had finished his question. "For several years he and I have been at odds. That is no secret. We have different philosophies, you know. And because Figueiredo is neither a very bright nor complex man, he is not hard to figure out."

"Uh-huh." Salo, though still somewhat guarded, was now eager to learn what Cardella thought was going through Figueiredo's mind.

"I am sure you are not prepared for what I am about to say," the general remarked with conviction, "but I know what his next move will be."

"Really?" Salo said, regaining some skepticism.

"Figueiredo and his goon squad will single out a scapegoat. This will finally allow the president to provide closure to the RioAero situation and the fiscal embarrassment that has haunted him ever since he took office."

"And from how well you say you know Figueiredo, you probably have a pretty good idea who this scapegoat may be, right?"

"Yes, I do," Cardella said assuredly.

"Who?"

"Trust me, Salo, you do not want to know. Not right now anyway. With all you have been through today, tomorrow would be a better time to drop the name on you."

"I know him, huh?"

"Indeed you do, very well."

"Okay, then maybe tomorrow if you insist, general."

"No, I am not insisting. I am just saying that right now might not be the best time."

"Well, if that is the case, and if you do not mind, I would prefer to know now. I would rather swallow another painful pill than have the thought hanging over my head for yet another day."

"Fine then," the general said. "It is your choice." He consciously paused, then spoke decisively: "The man Figueiredo intends to hang is a man named…a man named…Salo Montero."

"WHAT?" The thought was incredulous to Salo. It could not be true. No way. Not after everything Salo had done to bring RioAero to where it was today. "You are dead wrong, Cardella," Salo burst out.

The general simply shrugged, his face expressionless. "For your sake, I hope I am wrong, but I do have high level sources. I know every move Figueiredo and his SNI henchmen make. Well, maybe not every move, but certainly the important ones, the ones I care about. At this juncture, Mr. Montero, I would say you have been screwed."

Salo felt numb, like a bantamweight that had gone two rounds with a heavyweight...battered by each detail Cardella had thrown at him. The last punch was truly bone chilling. He never saw it coming. Everything Cardella had said was woven together with threads of credibility. But why had Cardella revealed as much as he just had? There had to be a reason—something in it for Cardella.

The general eased himself up from his seat next to Salo and said, "There is more you need to know." He took a few steps away from the table into the aisle.

Salo's eyes followed the general. He thought, what more could there be? Disaster had already struck—twice. Could he even dare hope this time it would be good news for a change?

Cardella glanced back toward the aft compartment where the major had stationed himself. He gave a quick nod upon making eye contact with his attaché. The major immediately rose to his feet and came forward. The brief words they exchanged were inaudible to Salo. Then, the major disappeared up the aisle and past the forward bulkhead.

The general began speaking as he strode back to the table. "I have something to show you, Salo, but first there is an explanation you need to have."

"Fine." Indeed, Salo Montero was learning far more than he thought possible from a man he had once distrusted enough to despise.

Cardella reseated himself at the conference table and began his explanation. "Follow me through this scenario, Salo. After you hear me out, disagree with me if you can...if you think what I say is implausible."

Salo simply nodded. He had already committed himself to hear the general out.

Cardella continued, "Every year RioAero sucks billions of cruzeiros out of Brazil's treasury. And every year RioAero creates little revenue to offset that investment. Much of the money pumped into RioAero has been under the moderate leadership of Figueiredo and his predecessor. They, and only they, are responsible for what many call a blatant misappropriation of funds. Of course, the current administration will not allow itself to accept culpability for, shall we say, poor judgment. So you have been singled out, and through you, they will unburden themselves from this 'RioAero problem.'"

"How?"

"It has already started."

The major returned from the forward compartment, handed the general the Sunday morning edition of *O Globo*, and then backed away from the table.

Cardella quickly unfolded the front page, placed it face up on the table and slid it over to Salo. One of the two headlines that shared billing as top stories of the day was about RioAero. That headline read: *WINDSTAR: AVIÃO INSEGURO?* It was accompanied by a large damning photo of the referenced "unsafe aircraft" with a propeller assembly embedded in its left fuselage.

Salo Montero absorbed the headline, then he glanced over to Cardella who simply shrugged. Salo closed his eyes and buried his face in his hands. He groaned in dismay. This was certainly not what he had anticipated seeing. He gritted his teeth, opened his eyes, and leaned forward to more closely study the photo. Like it or not, he had to. His mind quickly flashed back to the telephone conversation he had had with Lou Biega shortly after the incident. And yes, the photo he was now perusing was a vivid snapshot of the incident Big Lou had so cursorily described. He closed his eyes once again for a moment, and then plunged into the story itself. Just from gleaning the headline he anticipated the worst. He would not be wrong.

What he began to read was highly critical of RioAero, its engineering and its management. It questioned the aircraft's airworthiness. It suggested that, in the public interest, the CTA and FAA could easily justify issuing an emergency directive to immediately ground every WindStar, everywhere.

He read on and on, following the story as it continued to page five. There in the second paragraph, his eyes froze on a statement attributed to President Figueiredo. He was stunned and angered as well. When he had met with Figueiredo the night before, he clearly remembered asking for guidance and requesting any information that he needed to know—information that would help him understand what he might be up against in his efforts to turn RioAero around. At that time, Figueiredo had made no mention of the upcoming *O Globo* story. No mention at all, though Salo now believed that the president had to have known about it. He clearly recalled the president's words: *There is nothing I can tell you that I think you do not already know.* Now, as Salo absorbed Figueiredo's statement in the paper, he felt betrayed. And, he had every reason to feel so. Comments in the story attributed to Figueiredo were scathing.

Salo read the statement once again. "I am greatly disturbed by the incident that has occurred," the reporter quoted Figueiredo as saying. "This administration will take immediate and decisive action. We will re-evaluate our position in RioAero. Top-level changes will be made."

"Damn…damn…damn," Salo spoke out, enraged. He could only conclude that the president had intentionally deceived him. As he studied the statement more closely, something clicked. The words did not sound anything like those Figueiredo would say. Not at all. It had to be the SNI—the masters of intelligence and information—who all too frequently spoke words for the president which the president would only later learn he had said. Maybe not this time; then again, maybe so. The more Salo thought about it, the more confused he became.

He read on. The story was disparaging. It was more editorial than reportorial. It inferred that the WindStar was under-engineered and patently unsafe. It commended President Figueiredo's involvement and initiatives for immediate action.

Salo Montero saw his life's work unraveling—quickly disintegrating before his very eyes. He pushed the newspaper aside and glanced toward Cardella. "What next?"

The general spread his arms apart, palms up. "Hard to say…it is your move." A devious smile crept across his face. "I do, however, have a plan."

"What kind of plan?"

"Not so fast, Salo." Cardella sat back into his chair, folding his arms across his chest. "My plan is complex and highly confidential. I had anticipated that something like this might happen to RioAero. That is why I have been so involved with your company during the past few months. Remember, I know Figueiredo very well. But before I reveal anything else to you, I want you to think about everything you now know. Then, I want you to look into the future. Try to visualize what will likely happen to RioAero—and you—if you try to go it alone."

Salo groaned. Cardella's point was well taken. There seemed little he could do in face of what Figueiredo and his SNI henchmen had apparently put into motion. His only choice was to join up with the man who had an alternative plan—a plan that would preserve RioAero in some form and have him remain at the helm. But could he trust Cardella? After all, Cardella was the man who he had loathed—the man who he had thought was out to dismember his company. Was Salo wrong with his assessment of Cardella? Was he wrong with his assessment of Figueiredo? He had to make a decision, and soon. And, he had to make it himself. There was no one he could depend upon to discuss his options. There was no one he could rely upon to even verify the information Cardella had presented.

"Think about it," Cardella said again. He rose from his chair and glanced at his Rolex. "We still have a few more hours before reaching our destination. I will need to know what your position is by then. I will be in the forward cabin."

The general turned his back on Salo and flashed a clandestine wink at his ever-present major, who held back a smile. The major followed the general up the aisle toward the forward cabin area.

Salo's eyes despondently followed their movement as they disappeared past the conference area bulkhead. The ball was now in his court. How he played it would determine the game, set, and match for RioAero...and himself.

FIFTY-SIX

RioAero, NA

The smell of fresh latex paint greeted Rick Harris as he entered Joey Delgada's office in the rear section of the recently completed hangar. The highly polished off-white industrial tiled floor was outlined by a border of deep blue squares. A dozen beige Steelcase filing cabinets lined an equally beige sidewall.

As Rick closed the door behind himself, he noticed that attached to the backside of the door was a large full-color poster of a Harley Sportster, identical to one Delgada owned, but with a bikini-clad blonde sprawled across this bike's seat and handlebars. He casually eyed the poster, noticing it was personally inscribed. It read: "Joey…Always think of me when you open your throttle, Love Julie." He grinned, wondering if the "Julie" who had signed the poster was really named "Joey." As skilled as the genre of men were who worked in product support, more than a few were also crude and boastful and given to swagger about women. Truth be told, the women in some of their lives were only the fantasy of a pinup. Displays such as this one were not an uncommon fiction.

Rick navigated past half a dozen aluminum-framed chairs scattered around a conference table while making his way to Joey's desk. He slid the castered chair back from the desk, swiveled it to the left, and plopped his body down into it. Not relishing the task ahead, he paused for several minutes while looking out into the nearly empty hangar through the wide picture window that framed the entire upper half of the office's front wall. After gathering his thoughts, he broke his own pensive silence by snatching up the telephone handset and punching in a long string of numbers. His first call was to Salo Montero's lake house retreat.

After a slight delay, the connection was made; he patiently listened to the echoing double-beep tone on the line until the call was answered.

"*Esta é a residência do Sr. Montero,*" the housekeeper's voice faintly came across the line through the static.

"*Boa tarde…*" Rick began in the best Portuguese he could muster. "*Este é Ricardo Harris chamando Salo Montero, por favor.*"

"*O Sr. Montero não está aqui,*" she said, and continued on to say that Salo had departed the night before, possibly to Rio, but she was not certain.

"*Obrigado...adeus,*" Rick said thanking the woman and hung up the phone. "Well then," he said aloud to himself in the empty office, "I guess Big Lou is next."

He picked up the handset once again and punched in the number of RioAero's director of engineering. He hoped Franco Rameros was correct in his comment that Biega had a habit of being in the office around midday on Sunday.

"Biega," Big Lou's voice boomed through the static.

"Hello, Lou, this is Rick Harris in Fort Lauderdale...*Como é tudo?*"

There was a long silence on the other end of the line. Then Biega spoke up with irreverence and irritation, "I guess you could say everything is just friggin' great, considering all the problems I have staring me in the face."

"Problems?"

"Yeah, Harris, big problems," Biega growled back into the phone. Without hesitation he supported his opening salvo with a blockbuster. "Earlier this morning, some goddamn sonovabitch blew the friggin' hell out of Hangar One. It is totally wasted."

"Shit," Rick immediately said in reaction. He could tell that Biega was dead serious. "Damn!" he exclaimed, understanding the impact of the event. "Why? How?"

"Why, not sure," Biega responded. "How, I have my suspicions."

"Suspicions?"

"Yes, the source of the explosion appears to be rather obvious. It was a result of the ignition of a significant quantity of fuel. There were huge amounts of dense black smoke after the explosion as the fire went on for hours. But how the fuel got into the hangar, and then how it ignited, remains unanswered."

"Well," Rick spoke up, feeling awkward about changing the subject, "the reason I called is about other problems we've been experiencing—problems about which you may be unaware."

"Go ahead," Biega said, his frustration momentarily stayed by his curiosity. The word "problem" itself no longer held sway with him. "I am sitting down. Whatever you have to say cannot be any worse than the smoldering ruins I see when I look out of my windows and across the ramp below."

"First, one quick question," Rick began. "Have you talked to Salo Montero within the past twenty-four hours?"

"No, not since late afternoon on Friday, just after Rameros' propeller separation. Salo seems to have mysteriously disappeared. I have no idea where he is." Biega paused briefly. "By the way, has Franco arrived up there yet?"

"Yes, safe and sound, though he had a rather tense and nerve-racking trip."

"Really?" Biega was genuinely surprised. Rameros was virtually unflappable when it came to flying an aircraft. "Tell me about it."

Rick went on to relay an executive summary of the incidents experienced by Rameros on his flight up from the factory. When he finished, there was thick silence on the other end of the line.

"Wow," Biega finally spoke up, "shit is really happening!"

"That's an understatement, Lou," Rick declared. "It seems like holy hell has broken loose and RioAero and the WindStar are at the epicenter."

"Yeah," Biega replied with a slight tinge of despondency, "and somehow we will deal with it. I am not sure how just yet, but we will...we have to." He sighed, then yawned, audibly. It had been a long night for him.

"I'm confident you can handle it," Rick said in an effort to bolster the obviously weary Biega, "but let me get to the real reason I called." He briefly hesitated before going on. "Lou, I need some information, information on a man who I understand you hired a year or so ago." He paused, realizing that where the conversation was headed could very well ignite another major explosion for Biega to handle. "The man's name is Martinez, Jeffe Martinez."

"Yes, I hired the man," Biega immediately confirmed, unaware of why Rick was asking the question. "What is it you want to know?"

"Where did you hire him from?"

"Airbus."

"Yeah, that's what Franco thought. How long was he with Airbus and where did he work before that?"

"If memory serves me well," Biega said, "Martinez was with Airbus as assistant director of quality assurance for a year or two. He had the QA background and experience we needed for the WindStar program."

"And, before that?"

"He came from one of the companies in the Airbus consortium, as did many Airbus engineers. His former company supplied Airbus with some major airframe components for the A300."

"Which company was it, Lou?" an impatient Rick pressed for an answer.

"Oh, sorry," Biega said, sensing urgency in Rick's voice, "the company Martinez worked for before transferring to Airbus was BASA."

"Bingo," Rick said jubilantly.

"Huh?" Lou was confused.

"Bingo," Rick repeated himself. "It's a word us gringos shout out when winning a game we play up here in the States. It's a game of chance, and as luck would have it, you helped me become a winner."

"Winner?" Biega was now totally confused. "And, just what did you win today?"

"Oh, it's a big prize," Rick said, delighted with his newly found information. "The prize is Jeffe Martinez."

There was another silence on the other end of the line from a bewildered Biega.

Rick continued, "Jeffe Martinez is the burr under your saddle. He is the man who has been sabotaging the WindStar. He is also the man who is most likely responsible for blowing up your hangar."

"What?" Biega shouted out in disbelief.

Rick then began explaining about Dan Cole and his involvement in RioAero. He went on to divulge that he had bugged Cole's office, and went further to reveal the details of what Monica had learned from eavesdropping on Cole's conversation with Jeffe.

"Hmmm..." was Biega's only response. "Hmmm..." he said again, his engineering mind analyzing the data with which he had been presented.

Rick waited, expecting more than just a grunting acknowledgement from the never-at-a-loss-for-words director of engineering.

As Biega began to correlate everything Rick had disclosed, Biega said, "Damn...goddamn...I think you have something there, Harris."

Big Lou mentally flashed back to the night before in his office when he and Trilliano were doggedly trying to ferret out the cause of the double propeller separation incident. He remembered walking over to the bank of windows that lined the wall of his office and gazing into the darkness only to chance focusing upon the lights of two 8,500-gallon tanker trucks slowly rolling across the ramp below, disappearing as they reached Hangar One. At that time, he had presumed that the trucks were headed to the fuel farm. So, he quickly dismissed the unusually late weekend delivery without any concern.

A little later, Biega recalled seeing four men walking at a fast pace toward the employee parking lot, which he thought was rather strange for the hour. Although recent troubling events briefly raised alarm in his mind, he quickly rejected the ominous thoughts when he identified one of the men as a security guard and another as Jeffe Martinez.

But after all Rick had just said, Lou had a decidedly different perspective on what he had witnessed the night before. It all began to make sense to Big Lou. Martinez could have easily planned for the delivery, and then diverted and parked the fuel trucks in Hangar One. And beyond the explosion, since Martinez was the head of QA, he could also have easily orchestrated any one—or all—of the recent problems involving the WindStar.

Finally Biega spoke up again, "Rick, I think you have definitely uncovered something here." He paused. "Martinez could very well be behind the recent rash of disasters we have been experiencing, but he cannot be in this alone. What is his motivation? By himself, he stands little if anything to gain from these acts. So, who is behind him?"

Rick chuckled. "A really big fish," he confidently replied. "It's BASA, a former employer with whom Martinez undoubtedly has maintained ties."

"Why would BASA be behind this type of activity?"

Rick briefly reflected upon the conversation he had the previous afternoon with Ramon Segundo, then he spoke up, "It's quite simple, Lou, BASA wants to put us out of business. They want to keep a highly competitive aircraft like the WindStar from dealing a fatal blow to the sales of their aging Avio-23."

"That is a heavy accusation, Rick."

"I know, but I'm convinced that BASA is behind it."

"You have ironclad proof?"

"For me, yes; for you, maybe it's not ironclad enough just yet. By the end of the day, I'm sure I'll have everything I need to convince even the King of Spain that BASA is involved in a high level conspiracy to sabotage the WindStar and RioAero."

"Okay," Biega said in accord. "For now, I will have the CIE detain and interrogate the hell out of Martinez." He laughed, knowing the ways and means of that intelligence agency. "In fact, CIE agents are onsite as we speak. They are taking the lead in investigating the explosion."

"The CIE…" Rick said skeptically, knowing that Cardella headed up that agency. "Hold off on that action for now."

"Why?"

"Well…" Rick began, but then stopped, realizing that he could be treading on thin ice. He had no way of knowing with which political faction Biega might be aligned, so he offered a rather ambiguous watered-down answer. "Letting the CIE loose on Martinez at this juncture could prove counterproductive."

"Counterproductive? What do you mean?"

Just as Rick had expected, Biega was no fool. Harris had to take the chance that however politically inclined Big Lou was, his primary loyalty was to RioAero—a company that he and Salo Montero had spent over a decade building from the ground up. "Lou," Rick said, "what I have to say is very sensitive and must be held in the utmost confidence."

"I understand," Biega acknowledged, "I will keep it that way."

Rick took a deep breath. "Okay..." he said, exhaling, "I have reason to believe that the CIE may be a party to this entire fiasco."

There was no initial response as Biega pondered the statement. Trilliano had mentioned that politics could be a force behind the problems RioAero was experiencing. Although it was a seemingly bizarre comment at the time, it now seemed more plausible to Lou. CIE agents were on site at RioAero within minutes of the explosion. The response time was too quick. It almost seemed as if the CIE knew about the explosion before it happened.

Rick continued, "After the explosion and all that has happened during the past few days, my guess is that there will be a period of calm until the dust settles. I seriously doubt our adversaries will undertake any other type of action until being able to assess the degree of damage we have sustained. Just play it cool for now, Lou, and don't do anything to rattle their nerves. I'm in the middle of a very serious investigation of my own up here. I can't say anything else just now."

"Fine, Rick, I will be on red alert and continue doing my own quiet engineering investigation on the prop separation from down here." Biega paused before interjecting a key piece of information into the conversation. "By the way, I almost forgot to mention the discussion I had with Dayton-Standard earlier this morning. Willie Roth, their president, told me that the propeller shafts that failed on Rameros' WindStar flight on Friday were returns from BASA. Somehow those shafts got shipped out to us without a re-inspection. Dayton-Standard's initial analysis of the damaged shaft we air expressed up to them detected signs of laser tampering. Willie Roth believes that this alone resulted in metallurgical fatigue and therefore the structural failure Rameros experienced."

"BASA again." Rick smiled, knowing he was very much on the right track.

"So it seems," Biega returned. "Anyway, give me a call if you need anything else and be sure to let me know when you have the evidence to nail the asses of whoever was responsible for blowing up my goddamn hangar."

"Don't worry, Lou, you'll hear about it. I promise you that." Harris hung up the phone.

FIFTY-SEVEN

RioAero, NA

Nearly thirty minutes had elapsed since Rick Harris had left Franco Rameros and the WindStar for Joey's office. A quick glance at his wristwatch revealed it was 11:15 a.m. Gail would just now be picking up Santelli and his associates at the marina. Rick groaned, realizing that he was getting slightly behind schedule.

He snatched up his briefcase, left Joey's office, and began jogging the length of the hangar toward the parked WindStar on the ramp ahead. His mind raced forward with each springing step he took on the gray concrete floor.

As he consciously regulated his breathing, he could not help but wonder where in the hell Salo Montero was. He puffed out a quick exhale and continued thinking about the possible whereabouts of the chairman and CEO of RioAero. Salo's company was literally blowing up, but Salo was nowhere to be found. Strange…very strange…very strange, indeed.

He exited the hangar, slowed to a walk, took another glance at his wristwatch, and once again began jogging to cover the last hundred feet to the WindStar. "Franco," he shouted out.

There was no sign of Franco Rameros. The only person he spotted was Joey Delgada who was securing the aft cargo door.

He paused at the airstair door, and before ascending into the cabin, fell to a squat, searching beneath the fuselage to the other side of the aircraft. He smiled in relief. There, by the opposite engine nacelle, he spotted a cluster of feet. He placed his briefcase onto the tarmac, gathered himself up, and, at a normal pace, proceeded around the aircraft's streamlined nose to a position where he was able to immediately identify three men with their backs turned toward him— Franco Rameros, Bob Waterman, and…Dan Cole.

Rick Harris froze. The last thing he needed to be confronted with at this juncture was a meddling Dan Cole. There was no time for that.

He retraced his steps back around the aircraft, making his way to the aft cargo door and Joey Delgada. "Cargo off-loaded? Tow bar secure?" he asked.

"All taken care of, Rick," Joey responded. "And, as Franco had requested, I ordered some additional fuel to be taken on so you guys will have about two hours of flying time."

"Great," Rick said. "Now, how do we get rid of Cole?"

"You mean he is not going on the demo with the rest of you?"

"Hell no!" an infuriated Rick Harris shot back.

"Well," Joey said, raising his brow, "he seems to think he is."

Rick angrily shook his head. "How the hell did he find out about the demo?"

"Rameros…Waterman…I really have no idea." Joey shrugged. "Cole just showed up and I guess everybody assumed he was going along for the ride."

"Damn!" Rick pounded an imaginary table with his fist. He was at a loss as to what to do about Cole's presence. "How do I cut him loose, Joey?"

Delgada shrugged. "He is the company's managing director, and I guess rank has its privileges."

"Not in sales, not today," Harris snapped back.

"Whatever you say, Rick," a taken back Joey responded. "I know that sales is your bag, and so maybe you do not have to report to him, but right now, he is here, there is no doubt about that."

"Sorry, Joey," Rick said in earnest, "I didn't mean to jump all over you. You're right, Cole is my problem." Rick momentarily closed his eyes and briefly covered his face with the palms of his hands. He would have to find a way to dump Cole. "Okay, Joey," he said, his thoughts regathered, "where did you stow the spares you just off-loaded?"

"Oh, in a secure area, Rick, if that is what you mean."

"Huh?"

"We have a climate controlled spares storeroom on the left side of the hangar." Joey paused. "It is a long, big room with not much in it yet; nonetheless, all aircraft parts we receive are placed in that room and are logged into our inventory." Joey smiled. "I even stowed two of those cases of Brahma Chopp you brought back on your ferry flight there."

"Hmmm…" The gears were turning inside Rick Harris' mind. "I need the key to the room."

"What for?"

"Joey, please," Rick implored, "no questions. I don't have time to explain."

"Well—"

"You'll have it back before we leave."

"Okay, then." Joey unclipped a large key ring from his belt and handed it to Rick. "The green one is for the padlock on the outside, the silver one next to it works the deadbolt."

"Thanks." Rick stuffed the wad of keys into his pants pocket. Then without a moment's hesitation, he walked around the aircraft to where the others were standing.

Dan Cole was first to spot Rick. "Howdy there, Rick Harris, and a good morning to ya," Cole's good-old-boy, southern drawl cut through the air like a rusted saber making Rick clench his jaws while forcing a smile.

"Good morning, Dan," Rick returned as he gave Rameros a quick nod and cock of the head indicating it was time to depart.

The group began walking around the front of the aircraft toward the airstair door.

"It's a beautiful day for a demo flight, isn't it Rick, my boy?" Cole spoke out, glancing up at the cloudless blue sky. Cole was well informed that Rameros was ferrying a new WindStar to FLL for a flight demonstration this via yesterday's telecom with Jeffe Martinez. Cole was keenly interested in observing Rick Harris' reaction to his own presence at the RioAero hangar during the arrival of Rameros and the new WindStar, especially in light of the acrimony that had flared between them in Cole's office. Of course, Cole was also privy to the details of Rick's meeting with Ramon Segundo the day before. He was looking for any and all cues as to Rick's allegiance.

"Indeed it is, Dan," Rick said, being unusually cordial to the man he despised. "It's going to be as smooth as silk up there...a perfect day."

Cole was delighted to note Rick's unusually friendly tone, especially after their confrontation the day before. It now seemed to him that Rick must be switching sides. As a further test, Cole shot out a barrage of questions: "So, where are we flying to? Who are the customers? How close are they to buying? How many aircraft are we talking about?"

"Easy, Dan," Rick said, holding up the palms of both hands, "slow down for a second. I promise you'll learn about everything soon enough, but first I've got something to show you." He paused for a brief second. "And trust me, Dan, you're going to be impressed, very impressed."

"Yeah?" Cole said, curious and eager to be in on a confidence with Rick.

Rick grinned. Cole had taken the bait. "Come walk with me, it will take just a minute. Then, we'll launch the WindStar on that demo flight."

They walked away from the aircraft and into the hangar toward the parts storeroom.

"What do ya have to show me?" Dan Cole inquired. "Are ya sure there's nothing ya want to tell me first?"

"Dan...Dan..." Rick said, placing his hand upon Cole's shoulder as the two walked on, "if I said anything now, it wouldn't be a surprise, would it? And, that's what's in store for you."

Cole grinned, his eyes twinkling with confident anticipation. Rick had joined the BASA team. He was sure of it.

They reached the parts storeroom, which was locked as Joey said it would be. Rick fished out the key ring from his pants pocket, unlocked the padlock, and then the deadbolt. As he opened the door, Rick heard a turbine engine light off. Franco Rameros had just started up the right engine on the WindStar.

"We'd better hurry," an eager Cole advised.

"Don't worry, Dan," Rick said, reassuringly placing his hand once again upon Cole's shoulder as they both entered the room, "they wouldn't dare leave without me. They'd have no idea where to go."

The storeroom was huge in size—nearly eight thousand square feet. However, since construction of the hangar itself had only been completed within the past few weeks, the storeroom was mostly empty. Indeed, there was little need for a huge spares inventory to support a fleet of WindStars that did not as yet exist in North America. Although a partial Erector Set look-alike maze of shelving and parts bins had already been assembled, many long cardboard boxes of steel frames, shelves, and mounting brackets remained scattered about the room's perimeter. The few shelves already assembled contained only a smattering of parts.

Cole's eyes surveyed the area. "What should I be looking for?" he asked.

Rick pointed to a stack of boxes at the far corner of the room. The two cases of Brahma Chopp were among the boxes. "Over there, see for yourself," Rick said urging Cole on.

Cole's grin turned to a beam. He promptly marched toward the boxes. He read the name off the cases of beer. "Brahma Chopp," he said aloud, "this is really good stuff." He turned toward where he had left Rick Harris and said, "Thanks." But Rick was nowhere to be seen. "Harris," Cole shouted out. "HARRIS."

There was no response.

Cole started walking back past the shelving that obscured the entrance door, but a sound stopped him in his tracks.

He heard a loud metal clang echoing within the mostly empty storeroom. The door through which he had entered had just slammed shut. Now, there was total silence. Though perplexed for a moment, Cole continued on toward the entrance door, but stopped again. He heard a solid heavy metal CLICK. The deadbolt lock was engaged. CLICK. The padlock was engaged.

"Goddamn!" Cole shouted out. He raced to the door, but found it securely locked. "Harris, you sonovabitch, I'll have your ass." His words echoed within the room. Then there was silence once again. Dan Cole realized he had been had.

Rick Harris had already dashed out of the hangar and was now sprinting the last twenty yards to the WindStar and Joey Delgada, who was positioned at the bottom of the airstair door. He gave Joey a thumbs-up signal. "Thanks," he yelled over the engine noise. Rick retrieved his briefcase from the tarmac, tossed Joey back the ring of keys, and loudly spoke up, "Somehow, Cole got himself locked in the parts storeroom." He winked at Joey. "Do be sure to let him out after we've departed, but be careful, he's going to be one wild animal, if you know what I mean."

Joey rolled his eyes and nodded an acknowledgement.

Rick continued on, plying Joey with misinformation for Cole's benefit. "Tell him we're going up to West Palm, then offshore…that we won't be back until late afternoon."

Joey nodded again and shouted, "Good luck, I'll secure the cabin door for you."

Rick scampered up the airstairs and made his way directly to the cockpit. He smiled at Waterman who was already strapped into the right seat. "Let's boogie," Rick said to Franco Rameros.

"What about Cole?" Rameros returned.

"He's locked into other commitments and can't take the ride," Harris responded with a devious wink.

Almost immediately, the WindStar rolled away from the hangar with a taxi clearance to Runway 27-L. Rameros started up the left engine during the brisk taxi. He quickly began going through his pre-takeoff checklist by rote. "Where to, Rick?" he asked.

"Take a straight-out departure, maintain two thousand for some air work just southwest of the airport traffic area. Tell the Tower we'll guard Approach on one-twenty-eight-six and be squawking twelve-hundred in Mode-C."

Rameros shrugged and said, "Fine." It seemed a rather unusual departure for positioning an aircraft for a flight demonstration.

Rick clasped Waterman on the left shoulder and smiled once again. "Enjoy the takeoff, Bob, though I'll need to borrow your seat shortly after we level off at two thousand."

"Thanks," a wide-eyed Bob Waterman said. "This will be my first time up front for a takeoff in a plane this size."

"Have fun, I'll see you later." Rick strolled back down the aisle to the cabin, buckling himself into seat 2-A.

FIFTY-EIGHT

Pasador Ranch

Questions, questions…non-stop questions…seemingly endless. First, about Brazil; then, about RioAero; then, the WindStar.

"How about that Mardis Gras in Rio? They call it Car-nee-vaal, right? Coming up pretty soon, huh?"

"What do you think about Brazilian Music? Samba? Bossa nova?

"The girl from Ipanema…fiction, right?

"Now, how come they decided to make airplanes in Brazil?"

Questions. More questions.

Gail wondered what she had been cajoled into. Mentally, she kicked Rick in the shins more than once for assigning her the task of chauffeuring Sammy Santelli and his associates from the Pier Sixty-Six Marina to Pasador Ranch. Still, she knew the inane banter was better than periods of awkward silence.

She smiled when Kelly Long asked her what she thought of *cachaça*, the Brazilian liquor distilled from sugar cane. "It's different, alright," she tactfully answered. *Nasty firewater*, she thought to herself, remembering the bottle Rick had brought home for her to taste. *Yuck!*

The brief drive droned on for what seemed much longer than its thirty minute duration. Fortunately, Gail knew more than enough about RioAero, the WindStar, and Brazil to provide entertaining and enlightening answers. She knew how to further Rick's sales efforts. She also knew what not to say, especially in light of the recent events that had begun to cast a dark cloud over the WindStar. Her years as an aircraft salesman's wife had primed her well for her mission today. Nonetheless, she was glad Rick was the aircraft salesman and not she herself. Gail was plenty happy to draw the line with her version of sales support. Sales, for better or worse, was Rick's job. Period.

Sammy Santelli finally asked a probing question. "Gail," he began, "when we were together the other night, I never did get around to asking Rick why he actually left Fairchild and took the job with RioAero. Wasn't he happy at Fairchild?"

"Well, yes and no." She admitted that it was a difficult decision for Rick to make. She went on to say, "Rick had finally come to the conclusion that the Fairchild people were not as capable as he had once thought—the new Metro III had not effectively resolved certain problems of the older Metro IIA. He felt that when Ed Swearingen finally sold his remaining interest in the company to Fairchild

Industries, engineering simply went into hibernation. The final contributing factor was that Fairchild began to push for its sales executives to move to San Antonio. While that would have been fine several years ago, we're now happily settled in Florida."

"I see." Santelli absorbed her words for a moment. "Rick sure does have a formidable challenge on his hands with the WindStar."

Gail nodded, taking a long inhale. "That's for sure. He certainly didn't expect to land in a hornet's nest. But you know Rick, if he believes in something, it's hard to hold him back." She paused. "And in case you haven't figured it out yet, he truly believes in the WindStar and the engineering capability at RioAero."

"Yes, I gathered that," Santelli slowly said.

There was an awkward moment of silence as Gail waited for the next question. Then her eyes sparkled. She quietly drew in a breath of relief as the first section of the ranch's black pipe fencing came into view. Slowing the BMW, she pointed ahead and said, "We're here, guys."

Her passengers gazed through the car's tinted windows. In the pasture to their left, they spotted four Paso Finos standing motionless. The horses basked in the late morning sun with bellies full of fresh grass and hay.

From the back seat, John Andreas commented, "Ah-ha, your Paso Finos, no doubt."

"Why yes." Gail genuinely smiled, glancing up into the rearview mirror back at John, pleased that horses were now the object of his attention. "You remembered the breed."

"And, you thought I would not?"

"Well," she chuckled, "the drinks were certainly flowing freely that night at Pier Sixty-Six."

"You can say that again," Kelly Long added with a snicker. "Our dear friend Sammy took half of the next day just to get his head straight."

"C'mon, guys," Santelli cut in, "it was a special occasion, what with running into Rick and meeting his highly intelligent and extremely beautiful wife." He grinned and continued with the most *bon vivant* flair he could muster, "Gail, am I saying the right things to help get a brother-in-law deal on some of those Brazilian machines your husband is trying to sell us?"

"Oh, I'd say that you're getting close," she said to Santelli, who was sitting in the front seat. "Keep flattering his wife and I'm sure he'll go the extra mile for you." She pretended to hold back a smile. "Anyway, for his sake, I hope you can agree on a deal. In fact, it was just this morning that I told him if he didn't sign up you guys for some

WindStars, he'd better start looking for another job in another industry altogether...maybe used cars." She laughed.

"Don't worry," Sammy said, "regardless of whether or not we buy any of his airplanes, Rick is the finest salesman I've ever met. When you shake his hand, you never have to cringe, and then later wipe off your own hand in disgust. And, you can pretty much take whatever he says to the bank." He nodded. "Yes, we all like what we know about the WindStar so far. While there are still a couple areas of concern that need to be worked out, there's no doubt that his aircraft is on our short list." He paused. "You know, I'm really looking forward to this demo flight."

"That's great to hear," Gail said emphatically as she pulled the BMW through the entrance to the ranch.

"Nice place," Kelly Long commented with genuine admiration, effectively steering the discussion away from business. He eyed the ranch house and stable in the distance as Gail proceeded down the driveway. "How long have you folks lived out here?"

"Well, we bought the land in 1975," she began, again launching into the ever-accommodating hostess that she naturally was. "Almost immediately, we began the consuming project of building the house and stable. Thankfully, the entire project was completed in a little less than a year." She paused momentarily. "So, I guess that makes it about five years since we moved in."

"And the horses," John Andreas spoke up, "all of them are yours...you don't do boarding, do you?"

"No, no, John, the horses are all ours, it's just a private, family affair," Gail said, and then went on. "About four years ago we started off with three Pasos, now we have ten." She hesitated, remembering the latest addition and hastened to add, "Make that eleven, one of our mares had a foal late last night."

"Congratulations," Kelly Long chimed in. "You've certainly got a lot of mouths to feed, Gail."

"Oh yes," she said, briefly glancing up into the rearview mirror. "And a lot of feet to trim, too."

The conversation continued about horses as Gail steered the car past the ranch house, then slowed the car at the south end of the stable to come to a stop near a huge banyan tree and the picnic area. The group exited the car.

"So, when will Rick be arriving?" Sammy asked, rubbing his hands together in eager anticipation as he surveyed the area.

Gail glanced at her wristwatch. She grinned, stuck her thumbs into the front pockets of her jeans, lowered her voice and replied in her best, Western drawl: "High Noon, pardner."

"I see." Santelli smiled. "And, will the price of lunch include the purchase of an airplane?"

"Well, if ya don't buy a passel," she continued on with her pantomime, "we may be having a necktie party under that banyan tree rather than a barbecue."

They all laughed.

"Hey, how about a cold drink?" she asked. "Then, I'll give you a glimpse of our new foal before we settle down to some lunch."

"C'mon boys," Santelli said, taking the lead and following his hostess' directions.

The group sashayed over to the picnic table and the large iced cooler filled with beer and soft drinks from which they happily grabbed frosty bottles.

"Will you look at this!" Kelly Long said in surprise as he examined the label of the bottle he had fished out. "Brockton Ale, brewed and bottled by Andreas and Sons, Norwood, Mass."

John Andreas, who had opted for a Diet Coke, snatched the bottle out of Kelly's hand. "Where did you ever get this, Gail?"

She smiled. "A good aircraft salesman knows how to make his customers feel at home."

"Wow," John said, still amazed, "we haven't even begun to distribute our brews in Florida yet." He kept shaking his head, amazed and quite impressed.

Out of the corner of her eye, Gail spied Domingo Sanchez arrive to slather on yet another thick coating of barbecue sauce to the ribs he had been ever so slowly cooking on the grill since almost sunrise. As she parted her lips to introduce him, Sammy spoke up first. "*Buenas días, compadre*," he shouted out to Domingo. "*¿Como va?*"

"*Muy bien*," Domingo responded, then rattled off a string of words in Spanish.

Sammy laughed and replied back in Spanish. He popped the top off of a bottle he had fished out of the cooler, walked over to Domingo and introduced himself. "Spanish is a beautiful language." He paused. "I enjoyed studying it at *la universidad*." He paused again, and was about to go on.

Gail interrupted to introduce John and Kelly to, as she put it, "*Señor Sanchez*, a man of two great talents: the world's best trainer of Paso Fino horses; and, equally impressive, a man who can barbecue the finest ribs you'll ever sink your teeth into."

Domingo's dark deeply tanned face hid his blush.

John Andreas spoke up. "So, as you promised, Gail, let's see that new baby of yours."

Gail glanced at her wristwatch. It was ten minutes before noon. "Sure," she replied.

The group navigated the short distance over to a small paddock behind the stable where the mare and foal had earlier been relocated. There, the mare was blissfully revitalizing herself after her early morning ordeal by rhythmically tearing away mouthfuls of hay from a feeder attached to the fence. The foal, exhausted from earlier stumbling explorations of the paddock on gangly legs, was napping on the ground near her mother.

Gail entered the paddock, and, for the next five minutes, enchanted her guests by explaining and showing what the process of imprinting a foal was all about. She slowly approached the foal, and, with a reassuring tone, began quietly talking to it as she proceeded to gently touch every part of the foal's body with her hands. She told her audience that her actions essentially were conditioning the foal to the human species and programming it not to fear or flee mankind. For the foal, having already experienced human contact, this was simply another lesson in becoming more acclimated to people. This young filly was well on her way to accepting people as a type of odd and distant in-law relative.

"We do this with every foal born on the ranch," she said, exiting the paddock and shepherding the group back to the picnic area. "When this baby grows up, she'll be more trusting like a dog and less flighty like a horse." She paused for effect. "But, it won't be a total transformation, there is one thing we would never want to change about a horse…he or she will still be a vegetarian."

The mental image that Gail had conjured of horses as thousand pound carnivores brought brief grimaces to John and Kelly's faces before Santelli's segue brought the group back to the day's real business. "Almost high noon," Santelli said, glancing at his wristwatch. "I suppose we'll see Sheriff Harris moseying down that road…comin' toward us any moment now."

Gail nodded. "Any moment now."

FIFTY-NINE

Landing Pasador Ranch

T he WindStar, now in level flight at two thousand feet, was operating at reduced power to comply with the two hundred-fifty knot speed limit that existed below ten thousand feet. Franco Rameros had just departed the airport traffic area's five-mile radius and was guarding the Approach Control frequency for traffic advisories.

"Where to?" he asked Rick, who had just entered the cockpit.

Rick squatted down between and slightly behind Rameros and Waterman. "Oh, just maintain heading and I'll give you a hand." He nodded to Waterman in the right seat.

Bob Waterman unbuckled his safety belts and stepped out of the cockpit, allowing Rick to slip into the seat.

"Thanks, Bob," Rick said, turning back toward Waterman with a smile. "Feel free to take any seat in the cabin that strikes your fancy. And, do be sure to buckle up securely...we'll be doing some abrupt maneuvering in a few minutes." He paused. "Please keep what we are about to do off the record. Don't worry, though, everything we do will be perfectly safe."

Waterman grinned. "It's a deal." He made his way back into the cabin with wide-eyed anticipation, truly having no idea what Rick Harris meant by "abrupt maneuvering." No idea at all.

"Okay, Captain Rameros, let me fill you in on the details." For the first time, Rick divulged his plan for the WindStar and his customers. To isolate this particular aircraft from any possible sabotage efforts, Harris had decided to promptly fly the aircraft away from FLL and land it on the rarely used, but still licensed, private airstrip at his ranch.

"Hmmm...different," Rameros said with a smirk. "I suspect our arrival will impress the hell out of your boys."

"Yes, that was certainly part of the intent." Rick scanned the ground ahead and to the left of the aircraft. He quickly spotted his thirty-five acre ranch and the three thousand foot long pasture that was once used by the previous owners as a landing strip for drug runners. He glanced at his wristwatch. It was just a few minutes before twelve o'clock. "Mind if I take over and do the landing, Franco?"

"You feel comfortable with it?"

Rick grinned. "Franco, this is a WindStar, not a jet fighter about to land on an aircraft carrier."

Rameros released his hands from the controls. "All yours, call out for anything you want me to do."

Rick took over the controls after readjusting his seat and flipping down his left armrest. "Thanks, Franco." He eased the power levers back slightly, reduced the airspeed to two hundred-twenty knots, and pitched the nose down five degrees. "Have you got the grass strip in sight, Franco?"

There was no windsock or other identification to reveal that the grassy strip of land on Pasador Ranch was indeed a runway. For even an experienced pilot, locating an unmarked landing area sometimes required luck as well as skill.

"Hmmm…" Rameros scanned the terrain ahead and to his left. "How about that grassy area that runs north and south, the one just west of the orange-roofed house?"

"Excellent," Rick acknowledged with surprise, "you have the eyes of an eagle." He paused. "Okay, here's what we're gonna do." He further pitched the aircraft down, slightly reduced the power to maintain his target airspeed, and placed the WindStar into a shallow bank to the left. The altimeter passed through one thousand feet, descending. "I'll make a low-level high-speed pass down the runway to the south with the power almost at flight idle. All those on the ground will hear is a whooshing hum as the aircraft glides by." He again paused, further easing the power levers back and increasing the aircraft's pitch down. "Then, expect an abrupt pitch up as I break right on climb-out to position for a left wingover to a short final with landing to the north."

Rameros shrugged. "Why not a split-S? That would really impress the hell out of everyone."

"Well…" Rick hesitated. While confident with his flying skills, he also respected his own limitations. "A low altitude split-S is a tad more than I feel comfortable with. After all, Franco, I've only recently been introduced to the WindStar. And besides, I'm an aircraft salesman and not a test pilot."

"I can do it, if you like."

"Fine." Rick obligingly handed the controls back to Rameros. "Split-S to a landing is fine with me." He reconsidered, now conceding that it was indeed smarter to have Rameros do the flying anyway. A split-S was an aerobatic maneuver that was rarely, if ever, performed in transport category aircraft like the WindStar. Although relatively simple, it did require a higher level of skill and had less tolerance for error than a simple wingover, especially at low altitude.

Franco Rameros rested both hands on the control yoke and shot a quick glance at the altimeter. It read five hundred feet. The runway elevation was ten feet above sea level. He reduced the power, pitched down the WindStar, and maintained the two hundred-twenty knot airspeed. At a quarter mile from the runway, he retarded the power to a torque setting that equated to zero thrust. Now fifty feet above the ground and advancing at just over two hundred knots, he eased the aircraft's nose down. The WindStar swooped over a hedgerow that marked the property boundary and settled to within ten feet of the grass runway as it streaked along.

Midway down and off to the east side of the grass strip, stood Gail with Rick's customers. They had been continuing their casual conversation about horses, occasionally glancing up the driveway in anticipation of Rick's arrival. Sammy Santelli caught a glimpse of the WindStar first. "Holy cow, will you look at this," was all he could say.

Domingo Sanchez grinned, fully aware of the surprise arrival Rick had planned for his customers.

The others' eyes followed Santelli's stare. Their jaws dropped in awe as they focused upon the hushed approach of the WindStar. Their eyes took in the glossy white fuselage with its sleek pinstripe accenting. Even in the bright of day, the illuminated landing lights and pulsating wingtip strobes gave the WindStar an added radiance. Wide smiles filled their faces. The group swiveled in unison to watch the aircraft whisk past them. Its propellers just keeping stride with the advancing relative wind; its powerful engines gently resonating, ready to spool up at a moment's notice.

Near the end of the runway, Franco Rameros pitched up the aircraft and gradually increased the power. He held a shallow climb for a ten-beat count in order to distance himself from what would soon be his landing threshold.

"Here we go," Rameros said, pulling back on the control yoke.

The aircraft pitched up thirty-five degrees, airspeed rapidly bleeding off. One-eighty knots...one-sixty...one-forty... Smoothly, the angle of attack was decreased to level flight at one-twenty knots— the speed he had chosen to enter the maneuver. The altimeter read fifteen hundred feet.

Rameros retarded the power levers to flight idle. There was near silence within the cockpit. With both hands on the control yoke, he immediately rolled the WindStar inverted where it hung for only a split second. As he allowed gravity to take over and slowly draw the aircraft's nose down through the horizon, he began adding back pressure on the yoke. "GEAR DOWN," he called out to Rick while the aircraft was still partially inverted.

With the aircraft pointed straight down, airspeed began building...the altimeter unwinding. The hissing sound of airflow filled the cockpit through the open landing gear doors. Rameros pulled further back on the yoke, tightening the downward arc of the maneuver, coaxing the WindStar out of its near-vertical nose down attitude. He was pressed deeply into his seat; his sunglasses slid down the bridge of his nose. Just over two G's were being pulled—well within the aircraft's operating limits.

In response to Rameros' commands, what had been the beginning of an inverted dive toward the ground, smoothed out to a rounded arc, ending with the plane upright. The WindStar was once again in level flight, directly lined up with the runway and on a half-mile final approach at five hundred feet.

"FULL FLAPS," Rameros called out to Rick. As the flaps extended, the aircraft began to slow to its minimum short/soft-field target approach speed of ninety knots. He added forward pressure on the control yoke, nosing the aircraft down to maintain airspeed. A steep power-off approach was required to lose the excess altitude that Rameros had built into the split-S maneuver as a safety cushion. Knowing the aircraft's high sink rate, Rameros simultaneously pitched the nose up to reduce his descent and added a slight amount of power to maintain his targeted ninety-knot airspeed.

Hovering at a mere ten knots above stall speed, the WindStar staggered over six foot sawgrass that formed the southern boundary of the landing area. Rameros rolled in elevator trim to reduce the amount of back pressure required on the yoke. Then suddenly, the unexpected occurred. A brief low-level gust of wind from over the Everglades changed the relative wind. The stall warning horn began to trumpet a foreboding alert.

From his seat in the first row of the cabin, Bob Waterman heard the stall warning horn. He well knew what the sound meant. His heart pounded. He had been unnerved by the unannounced aerobatics. From what little he knew about the WindStar, he braced for the catastrophic event he was sure was about to happen.

But the warning horn fell silent. Rameros had the aircraft under positive control and continued his now shallow, power-on approach down to the runway. Waterman gulped down a breath of air.

The stall warning horn blared to life again. It droned an ominous warning throughout the cockpit and on into the cabin. This time the sound was not temporary. It was unrelentingly sustained. Waterman pressed the palms of his hands over his ears to block the bone-chilling noise. He did not want it to be the last thing he remembered.

The airspeed indicator hovered just below eighty knots. Rameros calmly eased up the power levers momentarily for an added burst of thrust, but the stall warning horn continued its penetrating drill. Suddenly, the airframe began to quiver, then shudder. The main landing gear had made a smooth but positive contact with the uneven grassy turf, causing a rapid vibration to run through the fuselage.

With both hands on the yoke, Rameros continued adding back pressure to keep the nose wheel just off the grass runway for as long as possible. The WindStar continued to lose speed, its throbbing vibration slowing. As the airspeed indicator fell below forty knots, Rameros gently eased the nose wheel down onto the turf.

The aircraft needed only light braking and no reverse thrust to come to a stop just halfway down the runway. Waterman erupted in enthusiastic hand clapping, unaware that the aircraft had been under complete control and had behaved flawlessly throughout its last maneuvers.

With the addition of power, Rameros steered the WindStar to the right and taxied toward the side of the pasture before promptly cutting both engines and coming to a full stop.

"Not bad, Franco," Rick complimented his friend.

"Of course, not bad," Rameros parroted Harris. "Hopefully your customers will see the versatility we engineered into this bird. She goes three hundred knots at cruise, but can land short and soft as well. You have got yourself one hell of a product, Mr. Harris. It almost sells itself."

"I have no complaints, Captain Rameros. That's why I left Fairchild to join RioAero."

"HA…Fairchild," Rameros spat out. "The only reason Fairchild has been able to sell its Metro aircraft is because there has not been any real competition until now." He disdainfully shook his head, then spied Domingo Sanchez who was tending the ribs on the grill. It had been twenty-four hours since Rameros had had a decent meal. "I think I see a man grilling some meat with my name on it. You promised me lunch, right?"

"Let's do it," Rick said unbuckling his seatbelt and removing his shoulder harness.

"And, let's sell some airplanes today!" Rameros added as he watched Rick's smiling customers striding up to the WindStar.

Unfortunately, Rameros temporarily had to postpone satisfying his hunger pangs. Customers always had priority. An obligatory tour of the WindStar for Sammy Santelli and associates was the first course of business. After a brief orientation to the group, Rick and Franco excused themselves and exited the aircraft.

Over the years, Rick had learned that a good salesman needed not be a hovering, always-in-your-face salesman. He found it much more productive to allow customers to talk among themselves in private and, for better or worse, formulate their own perspectives about an aircraft. He knew that later over a casual lunch, and during the flight demonstration, he would have the opportunity to more clearly shape those perceptions, and better address any concerns.

SIXTY

Flight Demonstration

One by one, Domingo Sanchez began turning the almost-ready slabs of ribs on the grill. The tantalizing smells and sizzling hiss as juices hit the glowing charcoal combined with periodic flare-ups created a culinary atmosphere that made Franco Rameros almost drool. Franco poured Bob Waterman a tall glass of iced tea from the pitcher on the table, then poured one for himself. Franco licked his lips, then shot an evaluating glance toward Domingo. Barbecuing in Brazil is even more of a tradition than it is in the States.

Sitting at the end of the picnic table with Gail, Rick popped the top off of a bottle of Coke and took a long swallow. He glanced up into the cloudless blue sky. The early afternoon sun had brought the temperature up into the eighties. It was a truly beautiful afternoon.

Rick turned to Gail. "So, how was our arrival received?" he eagerly inquired.

"Dramatic and unexpected," she responded. After a brief pause, she added, "I was impressed, they had to be, too."

"Good." Rick was pleased. He turned to Waterman. "And Bob, were you okay with everything?"

"Well," Waterman admitted, "when the aircraft leveled off after the aerobatics and safely landed, it was only then that I realized I wasn't going to be the lead story in the *Sun-Sentinel* obits tomorrow and could start breathing again." He laughed, now relaxed. "Yes, Rick, impressive."

Rameros affably slapped Waterman on the back. "The WindStar is one hell of an aircraft."

Bob Waterman nodded.

Inside the WindStar, Sammy Santelli had just emerged from the cockpit to join John Andreas and Kelly Long in the cabin. "What do you think, guys?"

"Not bad, not bad at all," Kelly Long replied. He had pulled up a section of the aisle carpeting and was using his Swiss Army knife to remove an inspection panel on the floor. "This looks like a solidly built, well-engineered aircraft." His background in the construction business always pressed him to closely examine how things were built. He lifted up the panel, slid it to the side, and peered down into the channel that held the control cable run.

"Here you go." John Andreas offered a flashlight to Kelly that Andreas had snatched from its attachment on the forward bulkhead.

Kelly switched on the light. He let out a soft breath as he contorted his body for a better look at the area under the floorboards. "No metal shavings; excellent corrosion protection; high-quality stainless steel cables; nice wire bundling…"

The ringing of a cowbell from outside the aircraft interrupted the inspection. The group looked up to see Rick entering the cabin. "Lunch, guys," Rick announced. He noticed the in-depth examination. "Remember, if you break it, you buy it," he jested.

"Seems like you've got one beautiful aircraft, even beneath the skin," Long said replacing the inspection panel and rising to his feet.

"You guys are thorough, aren't you?" a pleased Rick commented.

"Well, it's a big move for us," Santelli said. "We need to be sure about everything we do. We're a small organization, we can't afford to make mistakes."

"I understand," Rick said with a nod. "This aircraft will withstand the type of scrutiny that no other aircraft in its class can."

Rick beckoned the group down the airstairs and over to the picnic table where lunch was being served.

During lunch, the conversation almost exclusively centered upon the WindStar—performance data, fuel burn, direct and indirect operating costs, optional equipment, maintenance intervals, spares provisioning, ground support equipment, technical support, crew training. All the typical topics that Rick would have expected to be discussed were indeed discussed. The information exchange flowed freely. Everything sounded positive. Not once was concern raised about the Brazilian economy or the WindStar's unexplained misfortunes. Rick was savvy enough to know that these concerns were as yet only just unspoken. The group was for now more focused on details about the aircraft itself and the upcoming flight demonstration.

Rick was pleased and slightly surprised about how smoothly Franco Rameros interacted with his customers. After Sammy Santelli's initial badgering of Rameros over the rather unusual looking flight uniform, the group attentively listened, almost in awe, as Rameros confidently spoke about the WindStar's flight characteristics and the relative ease with which a pilot could transition to it from even a lowly Navajo Chieftain or Cessna 402.

"It is an advanced machine," Rameros spoke of the WindStar, "but it is also a simple and rather forgiving machine. From the very beginning, the WindStar was designed with the regional airline industry in mind. Great lengths were taken to engineer the aircraft to airline standards of comfort, safety, and maintainability. The resulting product, gentlemen, is a reliable aircraft that passengers will love. The WindStar is also a dream for pilots to fly and a joy for technicians to maintain." Rameros went on to note that in addition to the flight simulator currently operating in Brazil, an identical simulator was under construction for Fort Lauderdale. And further, that maintenance training could be conducted at any site an airline selected.

The more Rick listened, the more he thought that Rameros would make a damn good aircraft salesman. All too often, factory pilots and technicians were just that—niche professionals who rarely stepped out into the real world. A salesman being accompanied by one of these cloistered professionals could never be quite sure what might be said next or what interaction might occur with customers. However, Rameros was making Rick's job of selling easy. And since Rameros was a pilot and not a salesman, his endorsement was viewed more as from an accommodating ambassador than a pushy marketeer. He had even a further distinct advantage over Rick Harris: Franco Rameros spoke with the authority and first-hand knowledge of a man who had been with the company for ten long years—before the WindStar program had even been a twinkle in Salo Montero's eye. All could sense that Rameros knew the WindStar as well as the back of his own hand.

"Now that everyone is more familiar with the aircraft and the company behind it," Rick said, finally speaking up, "I'd like to show you first hand what Franco has been talking about." He paused, nodding. "Gentlemen, a flight demonstration is in order. This will be your first opportunity to put the WindStar through its paces—to ask from it pretty much whatever you want." He paused again. "Any special requests?"

"Well, not really," Sammy Santelli spoke for the group. "Just the normal stuff: steep turns, slow flight, a few stalls, a take off and landing…that sort of thing. I'm current in the Beech 99; John knows the Beech 99 as well as the Shorts 330; and, Kelly has just upgraded from Otters to Dash 7s. So, we know turbine equipment, but aside from military jets in Nam, we haven't flown anything as hot as the WindStar in quite a while."

"Fine," Rick said. "Franco will handle the cockpit and I'll be in the cabin to answer questions about anything that comes to mind." He glanced over to Waterman. "And, let's try not to scare Bob too much. I'm counting on a favorable story from his experiences with us today."

Sammy Santelli eyed Waterman. "Since he appears to have weathered the maneuvering you did just before landing, I don't think there's much we can do to spoil his day. Right, Bob?"

Waterman, who had been attentively taking notes, just grinned.

"Okay, then," Rick said, "let's mount up."

The group rose to their feet, extended their appreciation to both Gail and Domingo for the splendid lunch, followed Rick out to the WindStar, and climbed up the airstairs. Franco Rameros entered the aircraft last, secured the airstair door behind him, and made his way to the cockpit where he found Sammy Santelli sitting in the right seat.

"Uh-hmmm..." Rameros cleared his throat to gain Santelli's attention. "If you are serious about buying this aircraft, you will need to move over to the left seat and get a captain's perspective." Rameros paused, then added, "Don't worry, over time I have become so comfortable with the WindStar that I could almost fly her from the cabin using ESP."

Santelli laughed as he accepted Rameros' offer and moved into the left seat. Rameros, tapping into his many years of experience as a flight instructor, began guiding Sammy through the engine start and taxi. Over the cockpit intercom, he reviewed the takeoff configuration needed for the short grassy runway. He went on to detail what Santelli would physically feel on the controls and in the seat of his pants.

At little more than a snail's pace, Santelli began the WindStar's taxi down to the departure end of the runway. The aircraft's high-pressure, nitrogen-filled tires transmitted every nook and cranny of the uneven grassy surface to the fuselage through stiff landing gear struts. Bodies joggled in their seats; heads slowly—almost rhythmically— bobbed first forward, then back. An occasional jolt compressed the struts as the tires rolled over a deeper recess in the turf, causing Waterman to reflexively wince. Santelli continued the WindStar's taxi and, upon reaching the departure end, added power to turn the WindStar into position for takeoff in the opposite direction.

"Okay, we are about ready to go," Rameros said, detailing last minute takeoff instructions. "You fly the aircraft; I will take care of the power, gear, and flaps. Since this is your first time in the WindStar, I will call out airspeeds and give you pointers on what to do and when." He reached over, about to advance the power levers, then paused. "Oh, there is one more thing I want to make clear." His words arrested Santelli's motions just as Santelli had pulled back on the yoke to add full up elevator and lessen the load on the nose wheel during the soft-field takeoff roll. Sammy's eyes riveted on Rameros' face as Rameros added, "If I see anything going wrong—not that I expect it to—I will shout out I GOT THE AIRCRAFT, and will take over the controls." He smiled to lighten the moment and raised his brow. "You know, there can only be one PIC (Pilot-in-Command) of an aircraft, and today, I am it." The wink that followed broke any remaining tension from Rameros' announcement.

"Understood," Santelli acknowledged. That element of the briefing was an often-overlooked part of standard cockpit protocol. Not infrequently, in both corporate and airline aircraft, two captains occupied the cockpit, thus creating doubt, especially under emergency situations, as to who was actually in command of the aircraft. Two pilots struggling against each other on the controls could easily make a bad situation worse. That type of scenario, though rare, had caused more than one aircraft to go out of control in the past. Today, Franco Rameros wanted to be sure that would not happen.

Finally ready for takeoff, Rameros double-checked to be sure that the prop and condition levers were full forward, and that the flaps were set at fifteen degrees to reduce the takeoff run. "Here we go," he said, smoothly advancing the power levers. The aircraft almost immediately surged forward, pitching up slightly and lessening the load on its nose wheel as it began accelerating down the runway. What began as a thudding and clunking of the landing gear struts repeatedly compressing and decompressing over the uneven grass surface, transitioned to a more rapid vibration throughout the entire fuselage as speed increased.

Forty knots…

Fifty knots…

The nose noticeably pitched up, continuing to rise higher. The stall warning horn blared within the cockpit.

"Nose down," Rameros commanded, as he instantly jabbed his control yoke forward to initiate the similar response from a hesitating Santelli.

Swiftly recovering, Santelli adjusted to the controls and applied just the right amount of control yoke back pressure to provide the nose wheel with positive but light ground contact.

"Good," Rameros quietly reinforced Santelli's actions.

Sixty knots…

Seventy knots…

The WindStar's nose tried to pop up again, seemingly wanting the aircraft to soar into the sky, yet the airspeed was still too low. This time Santelli was ready without any cue from Rameros. He eased off the back pressure he was holding on the control yoke and kept the nose wheel just skimming the grassy turf.

Halfway down the runway, now at ninety knots and slightly above V_{MC}—Velocity Minimum Control, the speed below which an engine failure would result in a catastrophic and uncontrollable situation—the vibration within the fuselage structure ceased. The WindStar was airborne.

"Doing great," Rameros said in an upbeat tone. "Just hold the aircraft in ground-effect until we hit one-ten knots and then begin your initial climb-out." He paused, reaching for the gear handle. "Gear is coming up, be sure the aircraft does not settle back down."

Santelli briefly eased back on the control yoke to maintain his five-foot margin above the runway as the gear retraction changed the aircraft's aerodynamics. As the WindStar rapidly accelerated, Santelli added further elevator to initiate climb-out. The aircraft easily cleared the low-level boundary of hedges at the runway's end.

"Excellent, Sammy, you are getting the hang of this bird." Rameros smiled. He always got a kick out of making a pilot feel at home in the cockpit of a WindStar.

Despite his heavy concentration on the task at hand, Santelli grinned appreciation to Rameros' kind words. Still completely focused, his eyes repeatedly scanned the instrument panel and then the outside horizon as he made small adjustments in pitch so as to maintain his best-rate-of-climb speed.

Rameros relaxed back into his seat and folded his arms across his chest. The aircraft had performed exactly as expected. Sammy Santelli had done a remarkable job at the controls, especially since this was his first time flying a WindStar and getting the "feel" of any new aircraft type required some time to achieve.

With the WindStar's powerful rate of climb, it was soon high over the Everglades at twelve thousand five hundred feet and trimmed for level flight. After adjusting the power levers and prop rpm for maximum cruise, Franco Rameros directed Santelli's attention to the airspeed indicator on the instrument panel. "Check out our true airspeed," he encouraged. "Use an OAT (Outside Air Temperature) of ten degrees and see what you get."

Sammy focused on the airspeed indicator, rotated a small black knob on the instrument's lower right side to align the pressure altitude with the OAT in its upper area cutout. Simultaneously with rotation of the knob, a bezel that was integrated within the outer section of the lower left side of the instrument automatically adjusted itself to accurately translate the aircraft's indicated airspeed into true airspeed—an airspeed adjusted primarily for temperature and pressure altitude. "Three hundred ten knots," Santelli called out, almost in disbelief.

"Better than advertised," Rameros happily remarked, and then continued on. "We are that fast right now because we are pretty light. At gross weight, she will do an honest three hundred knots."

Santelli nodded with pursed lips, still highly impressed.

"Ready for some air work?" Rameros asked, retarding the power levers to slow the WindStar to its one hundred eighty-five knot maneuvering speed.

"Absolutely."

They both scanned the sky for traffic. There was none.

"Try a seven-twenty to the left with sixty degrees of bank," Rameros suggested. Left turns were always easier for a pilot in the left seat. Still, a sixty degree banked turn was steeper than anything required by the FAA to demonstrate pilot proficiency.

Sammy Santelli grinned. Without saying a word, he glanced to his left and smoothly rolled into the turn, slowly increasing back pressure on the yoke to maintain the nose slightly above the horizon. At thirty degrees into the turn, they both sank down into their seats feeling the effects of the two-G maneuver. On the instrument panel, just below the attitude indicator, the azimuth card of HSI sped past headings as it made one complete rotation in less than twenty seconds.

When Santelli continued on for his second of the two complete turns that made up the seven-twenty maneuver, the WindStar suddenly shuttered. The sensation was dramatic—almost like an automobile speeding over a never-ending series of railroad tracks on a country road. The shaking continued, but Sammy paid no heed to what the WindStar was signaling to him. His eyes flashed inside the cockpit, to be sure he maintained twelve thousand five hundred feet on the altimeter and sixty degrees of bank on the attitude indicator. He fleetingly glanced outside as the aircraft's nose swept around the pale blue horizon. His eyes darted inside to the instrument panel and then outside to the horizon...inside and then outside...again and again. He intently maintained sixty degrees of bank and twelve thousand five hundred feet of altitude. The shaking and shuddering did not stop. He clenched his jaw. His concentration intensified; he forced himself to ignore the shaking and shuttering.

Rameros smiled.

Fifteen seconds after the shuddering had commenced, it ceased altogether. Santelli had rolled the WindStar out of its steeply banked turn and directly back onto the heading from which he had initiated the maneuver. He smiled, pleased with his performance. His tense body relaxed.

"That, my friend, is as good as you can get." Rameros was beaming and nodding. "To hold an aircraft in its own wake turbulence during the entire second turn is the mark of perfection." He also knew that the calm winds aloft had accommodatingly held the turbulence in place.

"Thanks." Santelli let out his pent-up breath and ran a palm across his damp forehead. With confidence whetted by success, he wanted more. Not unlike video game junkies, many pilots thrive on opportunities to test their skills. "How about some slow flight, then an approach-to-landing stall?"

"Fine," Rameros acknowledged, then diligently scanned the horizon for possible traffic. "Maintain twelve thousand five hundred and slow to one hundred knots. I will set up the configuration for you." He slowly retarded the power levers to flight idle. The WindStar began slowing. "Approach flaps coming down." There was a slight pitch up as the wing's aerodynamics changed, creating an increased camber and slightly more lift. "Gear down." The aircraft continued slowing. "Full Flaps." The WindStar pitched up again, now slowing dramatically as a result of the significant drag created. Rameros added just enough power to stabilize the airspeed at ninety knots.

Throughout the configuration transition, Santelli made constant adjustments to control yoke pressure so as to maintain altitude and heading. The WindStar was now flying at nearly a seven-degree pitch up attitude. The reduction in engine and airstream noise created a hush within the cockpit.

"Good," Rameros said, "this is the configuration and speed used over the fence on a short approach to landing." He briefly paused. "As you make some relatively shallow turns to the left and right—twenty degrees of bank or so—you will notice that the controls are a bit sluggish, but still quite responsive."

Santelli made the suggested turns. The WindStar handled just as Rameros said it would. A further reduction in power was made in anticipation of Rameros' next command.

"Okay, go to V_{S0} at the bottom of the white arc on your airspeed indicator—eighty knots," Rameros coached, and waited as the WindStar further slowed. "You will get the stall warning indicator right about…now."

The stall warning horn blared within the cockpit. Rameros dropped his right hand down to the circuit breaker panel and popped the breaker to silence the warning horn.

"Thanks," Santelli said, "that sound gets real irritating, real fast."

"Roger that," Rameros said in agreement and then continued on. "Now, try some more turns, but keep them very shallow."

Santelli rolled in to a shallow ten-degree bank to the left. The aircraft began to slightly buffet.

"Good," Rameros said reassuringly, "you are right on the edge of a stall, but as you can see, the WindStar is still very stable, still very controllable." He watched as Sammy leveled the wings and initiated a shallow turn to the right. "Okay, give me a heading of two-seven-zero." He briefly paused. "When we roll out on the heading, I will ease the power back and have you put the aircraft into a power-off stall. But do not try to make any recovery from the stall. Keep the control yoke full back…use rudder and aileron to control yaw and roll."

"Huh?" Santelli said, confused, still in the midst of turning to the heading. Except in flight training, pilots always avoided placing an aircraft into a situation where a stall could occur. And even in flight training, when a stall occurred, a prompt recovery was always implied. It seemed strange to Sammy for Rameros to suggest that an aircraft the size of the WindStar should be held in a stall.

"Oh..." Santelli's concerns suddenly clicked into place for Rameros. He understood why Sammy was perplexed. "The WindStar is a docile lady. She needs no stick shaker like the Metro—certainly, no stick pusher—and there is no need for added aerodynamic paraphernalia to make her behave properly. You can stall her all day long and she will always treat you right. She is as predictable as a Cessna 150, and that is mighty hard to beat. I want you to see this for yourself."

"Fine," Santelli said, deeply skeptical, but trusting Rameros.

"Okay," Franco continued, about to reduce the power to flight idle, "just keep applying back pressure to the control yoke and continue to hold the aircraft in the stall. But, be prepared for a surprise."

"Uh-oh..." Santelli protested, still in slow flight, not yet having followed the directive to initiate the deep power-off stall.

"Not to worry," Rameros reassured Sammy, "it is a pleasant surprise. You see, the WindStar is designed to have positive aileron control throughout the stall in addition to positive rudder control. The controls may be sloppy but still effective." He retarded the power levers to flight idle.

Within a split second, the WindStar experienced aerodynamic buffet. Its aluminum skin began to vibrate—first slightly, then more severely. The shaking and shuddering penetrated deeper. From stringer to rib to spar, the aircraft's entire structure was affected. It was almost as if the WindStar itself was unsure, and nervously shivering and quivering—uncontrollably—in fear of a harrowing fate.

It seemed that an animated WindStar was instinctively fighting for its life. Beginning to gyrate like an enormous bucking bronco, the aircraft pitched down as if attempting to wrest control away from the pressure Sammy Santelli held on its reins. Then it pitched up as if to regain its footing, then down in another dash to escape.

With repetitive oscillations, the WindStar acted as if it were truly struggling for its very existence, battling to avoid an ominous fate.

Santelli was aggressive on the controls and resolute in his command. He continued to effectively hold the aircraft in its highly agonized state.

"RECOVER," came the word from Rameros as the power levers were slowly advanced.

Santelli reduced the aircraft's angle of attack. The buffeting abated as airspeed built up.

Rameros milked up the flaps and, when a positive rate of climb was established, he retracted the gear.

During the protracted process of holding the aircraft in the approach-to-landing stall maneuver, the WindStar had lost nearly a thousand feet. It was now climbing back to its original altitude.

"What do you think, Sammy?" Rameros posed the question.

"Very nice, indeed impressive," Santelli responded as Rameros had expected. "You'd almost have to fall asleep at the controls to have the WindStar hurt you."

"Want to give the other guys a chance at the controls?"

"Good idea." Santelli reluctantly nodded. It was only fair.

During the next thirty minutes, Kelly Long and John Andreas took turns flying the WindStar. Rick sat in the back section of the cabin with Sammy Santelli, initially discussing how beautifully the WindStar handled. Sensing the timing was right, Rick took the next step and handed Sammy two copies of the newly drafted Letter of Intent.

As Santelli paged through the document, Rick said, "This is our best and final offer. I know that neither of us wants to play cat-and-mouse over nickels and dimes." He paused, seeking a reaction from Santelli. There was none. "Let me call your attention to page six. I've included a provision that gives you 'favored nation status.' Just for clarification, that means that no one—NO ONE—will ever get a better deal than I've given you."

Sammy nodded slowly, perusing the page.

Rick continued on, "I also want to proactively address concerns about the misfortunes that have occurred to the WindStar." Rick hesitated, awkwardly, as Santelli looked up from the page he was reading. "In the appendices, I've included a statement I believe will provide satisfactory closure to that issue."

Santelli remained silent as he flipped through the pages to the appendix section.

"I'd appreciate it if you and your associates would review what I've drafted and let me know what you think."

The WindStar turned to the east and began its enroute descent for landing at FLL.

Rick went on, "Why don't you head up to the cockpit and do the landing. I've arranged for ground transportation to take you back to your boat at the marina." He hesitated briefly. "I would join you myself, but I want to help navigate Franco back to the ranch and then give him a hand in pulling the WindStar into my hay barn. After that—"

"Hay barn?"

"Yes," Rick admitted, "I know it might seem strange to you, but I don't want anything mysterious happening to this aircraft. I'm very close to figuring out why incidents inexplicable until now have occurred to other WindStar aircraft...to RioAero."

"And, you're still convinced that it's sabotage?"

"Even more so, Sammy."

"Hmmm..." Santelli skeptically intoned.

"As I was saying," Rick said, picking up where he had left off, "after I tuck this WindStar into my barn, I'd like to meet with you and John and Kelly. I may have more information that will ease your concerns about the WindStar incidents." He paused making direct eye contact with Santelli. "The WindStar is the right aircraft for you. I'm sure of it."

Sammy closed his eyes briefly and squeezed his lips tightly together. "Rick..." he began, then went silent. He shook his head. He stood up in the aisle of the cabin. "Rick," he said again, "you're free to come by later and continue the dialogue." He paused, looking toward the cockpit before refocusing upon Rick. "I can't guarantee anything, Rick. Our foremost concern is flight safety. No WindStar has crashed and burned yet."

Rick's expression was crushed. He swallowed very hard.

Sammy saw the impact his words had upon Rick and tried to mute the blow. "Listen, we've known each other for a long time, and I've come to trust you and have regard for you as a friend. There is no other reason Kelly, John, and I are in a WindStar now than our confidence in you." Santelli abruptly stopped, shifted his thoughts and continued, "I know you want to make a sale. And, I know you believe the aircraft's problems are sabotage and not integral. The guys and I will review what you've drafted. That's all I can promise for now."

"Fine," Rick said with a forced smile, "that's all I can ask."

Sammy nodded once, strolled up the aisle and disappeared into the cockpit.

Damn, a frustrated Rick thought, trying to be as positive as possible. Getting closer, but no cigar. What will it take? Sammy liked the WindStar—he had to, it showed. Rick asked himself if he was reading too much into Santelli's reticence. Maybe Santelli was just positioning for further negotiations. But then again, maybe Santelli was not.

Rick knew he needed to make a sale. He knew he needed to make this deal happen...and make it happen fast.

The key question was: How?

SIXTY-ONE

Bahia Mar Marina

Only a stone's throw away from *LA BASA*, the sleek thirty-eight foot Scarab floated tranquilly in the still waters of the Bahia Mar Marina. Its moorings, slack; its glistening black gel coat both reflecting and absorbing the bright mid-afternoon sun.

Tommy Maxwell sweated. He turned from the helm and made his way back to the fuchsia-colored bench seat just forward of the Scarab's aft engine compartment. First gulping down an Orange Crush soda he had grabbed from the cooler, then slathering more suntan lotion onto his dark brown skin, preventing a burn would be the least difficult thing he would face today.

"Damn black boat," he muttered with contempt. It was definitely not his favorite maritime color, and he still could not believe nor agree with the PetroMar PR folks' decision to choose black. Tommy Maxwell scoffed at the thought this Scarab was actually black by design. The color was chosen in part because of PetroMar's product—crude oil; and partly to play on the imagery of the watercraft's namesake—the scarab, a sacred beetle of ancient Egypt that symbolized immortality. To Tommy, the choice of black only meant that the boat was always hot—sometimes hot as hell. In fact, during the summer, a cheese omelet could be fried on its slick forward deck within minutes. "Damn sizzling B-L-A-C-K," he growled, this time enunciating each letter of the word.

Monica ignored his castigation. Like a subtropical lizard, she lay comfortably atop the foredeck on a thick beach towel, basking in the winter sun and absorbing its warmth. Behind her dark wraparound sunglasses she directed her gaze toward *LA BASA*. The headset she wore was not piping in top forty tunes, it relayed conversations from the bugging device Rick Harris had planted under the massive table on the yacht's afterdeck.

Tommy grabbed a large white towel from a stowage locker, stepped up onto the aft bench seat, and cat-walked along the narrow starboard rail of the Scarab to the forward deck and Monica. He shot a momentary glance toward *LA BASA*, making out the silhouettes of two men seated at the shaded table on the yacht's afterdeck. He assumed Ramon Segundo and Dan Cole were still discussing the possibilities of what Rick Harris might have been up to during his flight demonstration. Tommy unfolded the towel and placed it down next to

Monica. "What's happening?" he asked as he sat down on the towel with his back to the yacht.

She pushed one side of the headset slightly forward of her ear and said, "Yeah, that Dan Cole guy is a real piece of work. For the past few minutes, all he's done is rant and rave about being locked up in a storage room just prior to the demo flight." She snickered. "Rick's maneuver really infuriated him." She paused, cocking her head to the left in a move reminiscent of the RCA dog, as she concentrated on the sound coming through her headset. "Okay, the talk is back to those expected visitors who were first mentioned when you were monitoring the transmissions a little earlier."

Tommy nodded, raising his brow in anticipation.

Monica fell silent—her attention rapt on the conversation from *LA BASA*. She shook her head. "Nothing, Cole's just chattering away, obviously sucking up to Segundo. But before, during your ongoing tirade about the color of this Scarab, there were specifics about the expected visitors." She grinned. "Looks like there's going to be a very high-level meeting this afternoon. General Carlo Cardella and Salo Montero have flown up from Brazil and should be arriving just about anytime. From what I can gather, some pretty big deal is expected to go down."

"Hmmm..." Maxwell was deeply puzzled. Still, not enough information to know what deal. He did know that Rick was scheduled to make an appearance on *LA BASA* within a few hours, so perhaps the mysterious deal involved Rick Harris. Lots of interesting possibilities about what might happen aboard the yacht...very interesting, to say the least. "You're taping everything, right?"

Monica nodded. She advanced her hand forward, briefly patting the fishing tackle box into which the UHF receiver and the tape recorder had been stowed.

"Good," Tommy said, noting the strand of black wire snaking from the tackle box to her headset. Now satisfied, he changed the subject. "That's one super motor yacht they have."

"Yes, it looks fast just sitting there tied up at the dock." Monica's eyes had been almost exclusively focused on *LA BASA* for the past several hours.

"And, how about that Cigarette 41/OS moored along side?" Tommy queried.

"Indeed, impressive."

Not content to let an opportunity for discussing racing to go by, Tommy added: "Yeah, and it is even faster. Except for being yellow rather than black, it's a virtual cousin to the ones we have...err, PetroMar has at Anderson's Marina. If it's stock—and you can never tell—it has a pair of 475 hp engines that can probably push its speed close to triple digits. We might get eighty or so out of this Scarab if we're light and lucky."

Monica grinned as she both monitored the transmission from *LA BASA* and conversed with Tommy. "Expect to go racing today?"

"Nah, at least I hope not. That Cigarette would eat our lunch." He paused. "Speaking of lunch, have you had any yet?"

Monica did not respond, her interest piqued by what she was now hearing through her headset.

"Well, I'm hungry again." He continued on, "Can I get you anything?"

She slid her sunglasses slightly down the bridge of her nose. Her eyes squinting in the bright sunlight as she focused on *LA BASA*. "Don't move," she whispered to Tommy, who had not yet gotten to his feet. "Don't turn around."

"Huh?"

"Shush…" Her eyes darted as she listened through her headset. Her body language revealing the intensity of her attention.

"What's happening?" Tommy Maxwell was usually not one to obediently follow anyone's instructions. Still, he did not turn to follow her gaze.

A long minute passed by. Maxwell began to fidget.

The ongoing conversation which Monica had been intently monitoring through her headset had ceased. Her body remained tense as she bit down on her lower lip, it paled. "What's happening," she softly said to Tommy, "is what we expected to happen." She pushed her sunglasses back into place. "Take a look for yourself, but don't make it obvious. We're not really that far away from them, you know."

SIXTY-TWO

Landing Pasador Ranch

With the WindStar back aloft and on its way to Pasador Ranch from FLL, Rick Harris reclined his seat in the cabin and tried to relax. He closed his eyes and struggled to totally blank his mind, at least for the moment.

"Ehh…" he uttered aloud in frustration, "no way." It just was not going to happen. His mind was spinning with details: what had happened during the past few days; what he hoped would happen during the next few hours. His mind was aswirl with flashing thoughts, none of which he could fix upon. His mind kept returning to focus upon the deal he was trying to put together with Sammy Santelli. This was the most crucial deal of his aircraft sales career. And not only personally, the pressing need to solidify a major sales contract for the WindStar had far-reaching implications.

Harris consciously forced his eyes shut as he kept asking himself how, how…how could he get Sammy Santelli to commit to a major order for the WindStar? So very much rode on the wings of that order. How could he move forward to quickly unravel the web of sabotage that was draining the very life out of RioAero? How could he ensure that come Monday morning the gates to the factory would not be locked shut, leaving thousands of workers without, and workers already with so very little? How could he do it? How could he be sure? How?

He felt the pressure, the onus. He felt these problems were his alone to resolve.

Rick jerked his head forward and snapped open his eyes. There had to be a way. He stared ahead at the aircraft's standard mahogany veneer bulkhead as if trying to summon inspiration from it. Nothing.

Agitated, he unbuckled his seatbelt, strode up to the cockpit, and lowered himself to one knee between Franco Rameros and Bob Waterman. "How are we doing?" he affably asked.

"Hmmm…" Franco Rameros began, his voice already dripping sarcasm. "Do you mean can I find that backwater strip of pasture you call a runway?"

Rick hesitated, trying to decide whether to take offense. "Well—"

"Relax, Harris," Rameros abruptly cut Rick off. "Remember, it was my eyes that found that strip the very first time, and without much help from you. I certainly can do it again." He smirked, immodestly joggled his head as he pointed to the RNAV computer, and then to the radar screen at the bottom of the avionics stack on the instrument panel. "That white diamond on the CRT is the waypoint I set in when we taxied out with Santelli and his boys for the demo flight. Your pasture—my runway—is five miles dead ahead." He paused, glancing over to Waterman, and uncharacteristically said, "Ain't technology neat!"

Bob Waterman grinned. It was great to be inside the story. He felt like a barn mouse that had fallen into a bin full of grain. What he was experiencing today was a reporter's dream. There was going to be one hell of a story here. He was sure of it. Besides, it was just damn fun to be a part of the adventure.

"Okay, captain," Rick said as he rose to his feet and clasped Rameros on the shoulder, "looks like you have everything under control." He leaned over toward Franco and continued, "Normal landing...no split-S, agreed?"

"Normal landing on an abnormal runway?" Rameros responded, sarcasm again coating his words. He glanced over his shoulder and up toward Rick. A smile crept across his face. "Hey, Harris, like I said, relax. I certainly do not need any more aerobatic practice. Besides, I do not want to give my new friend, Bob, the idea that I am some kind of hotdog pilot. I want his story to make me look good." He grinned at Waterman, before cocking his head to the left and haughtily intoning, "As the factory's most senior pilot, my image has to be more bedrock."

Rick raised his brow and squeezed out a smile at Rameros. Before proceeding back to the cabin, he turned to Waterman and whispered in jest, "He's a damn hotdog, Bob, and don't ever forget it."

Waterman tried to hold back a snicker.

In the cabin, Rick fastened his seatbelt and leaned down on his armrest to gaze out the double-paned Plexiglas window at the flat, subtropical vista below. Thus far today, Franco Rameros had performed well and professionally in demonstrating the WindStar. Now, however, Rameros seemed to be reverting to his standard of a horse's ass.

As Rick felt the WindStar pitch down, he instinctively grasped his armrests. With the reduction in power, he waited. He heard the expected groan from the hydraulic system as the landing gear extended. Good, within a few minutes he would be on the ground. His mind fast-forwarded: within the hour he would be on Sammy Santelli's sportfisherman. He clenched his jaws. He knew this meeting with Santelli was all or nothing—the big cigar. There would be no prize for coming close, in aircraft sales there never was.

He heard the propellers go to high pitch, and noted an increase in engine power. All standard procedure for short-field landings. Rick instinctively tugged on the loose end of his seatbelt, snugging the belt down against his hips.

Rameros expertly guided the WindStar through its smooth, uneventful approach to a soft landing on the grassy turf. He made his turn to the right, taxied to the same position he had earlier held that day, and shut down both engines. He glanced back down the aisle into the cabin and hammed it up over the aircraft's public address system: "This is the termination of WindStar Flight-102. Please come back and fly with us again."

Rick flashed him a thumbs-up acknowledgement.

Safe landing. Services rendered. Franco Rameros could finally allow himself to begin spooling down. It had been a long event-filled flight from Brazil, and the tension had continued on with the demands of a top-notch demo flight for Rick's customers. Rameros would not admit how physically drained he was. The promise of those upcoming five days of vacation on the Gold Coast were now all that kept him mentally keen and pumped up. Rameros exited the cockpit with Waterman close behind. Rick followed the two out of the aircraft.

Standing at the bottom of the airstair door, Rameros perfunctorily commented to Rick, "I guess you're pretty much finished with my services, huh?"

"Pretty much," Rick casually responded, "and I really appreciate everything you've done. After we put this bird to bed, I've got to disappear for maybe an hour or so and see if I can pull a rabbit out of my hat. Why don't you and Bob have a couple of beers and continue your discussions about RioAero and the WindStar." He paused. "Don't worry, I'll be back to fill you in on what I hope will have been a successful visit with Santelli and his associates. Then, you two, it's dinner on me wherever you'd like. How's that sound?"

"Fine with me," Rameros agreed.

Waterman nodded. He still needed to obtain a host of background information from Rameros. A longer visit suited him fine, especially since in an unexpected turn of events he had taken a liking to Franco, despite the man's egotistical personality.

From around the right side of the nearly empty hay barn came the distant chugging rumble of a diesel engine. Moments later, Domingo Sanchez appeared guiding the old Massey-Ferguson toward them. Its heavy metal attachment fittings rhythmically clanked together as the tractor bounced over uneven ground.

"Okay," Rick took the lead and said to Rameros, "why don't you and Bob retrieve the tow bar from the aft cargo compartment? I'll disconnect the steering linkage from the strut so the nose wheel will caster freely during the tow."

"Will do," Rameros acknowledged.

"Good." Rick took a few steps forward and stooped down to disconnect the nose wheel steering for the tow. Rameros and Waterman disappeared behind the left wingtip to retrieve the tow bar from the cargo compartment.

A few minutes later after the tow bar had been attached between the Aircraft's nose wheel axel and the tractor, Domingo revved the rpm of the Massey-Ferguson's engine. Blurps of oily dark-gray smoke puffed from its stack. The throaty diesel hum deepened, resonating a vibration that chopped through the air as the tractor strained to move the ten thousand pound aircraft. As if entranced by the stubborn deep bass chortle of the diesel engine at work, the WindStar acquiesced and followed the tractor along to the hay barn.

With careful maneuvering, Domingo Sanchez reduced the engine rpm and eased on the tractor's brakes. The rumbling engine growl changed to a mechanical sandpaper-coarse purr that was punctuated by a metallic clash as Domingo selected the low reverse gear. With the addition of power, the exhaust stack flapper rattled open and the engine once again roared to life. The WindStar inched its way up a slight incline and backed into the barn. Rick chocked the nose wheel, removed the tow bar, and signaled Domingo to drive the tractor away.

Franco Rameros surveyed the expansive unobstructed interior of the post-and-beam structure that was clad in corrugated steel. It could easily have passed for a general aviation hangar at any airport, though Rick was quick to point out that this was the first time any aircraft had ever been parked inside his barn.

To his far right, in the south section of the barn, Rameros eyed a wall of some four hundred bales that were neatly stacked fifteen high. He dragged his foot across the gravel floor stirring up stray wisps of hay, all that remained from nearly nine hundred bales that had been fed to the horses during the past six months. The sweet smell of well-cured coastal grass permeated the warm air.

"They eat a lot, huh?" Rameros surmised.

"Indeed, they do." Rick's eyes had followed Rameros' gaze. "Horses are veritable eating machines. They never seem to truly get their fill. The hay we stow in this barn supplements pasture grazing, especially in the winter when grass grows slowly." He paused, sadly reflecting upon Gail's favorite stallion, now a gelding. "We unfortunately have one horse that eats hay almost exclusively."

A perplexed Waterman furrowed his brow. "Why not fresh pasture grass?" he asked.

"It may seem hard to believe," Rick said, slowly shaking his head as he began explaining, "but there are a few horses that actually sicken if allowed to eat fresh grass. At some point in their lives, maybe ten percent of horses develop various adverse reactions to fresh grass.

We've got one of those horses. When he eats fresh grass for more than half an hour or so, he founders."

"Well," Rameros broke into the conversation in his typical acerbic habit, "I certainly hope that Santelli and his boys have not as yet developed an adverse reaction to the WindStar."

"Franco," Rick quickly rebuked, "if anyone is developing an adverse reaction today, it might be me to you because of your mindless blather."

Rameros raised his hands, palms up. "No offense, Rick. It has just been a long couple of days for me."

"Yeah, I know," Rick conceded, however Rameros' negative words bruised Rick's already shaky confidence. "Anyway, I've got to go." He reached into the briefcase he had brought along from the aircraft and pulled out one of Tommy Maxwell's small black Alinco transceivers. He turned on the transceiver, dialed 444.135 MHz into the frequency window, and adjusted the squelch. "Here," he said, handing it to Rameros.

"What is this for?"

"It's to hear that announcement I will be making in an hour or so," Rick said. "Then, you will know that Sammy doesn't have a WindStar allergy, and that we've landed a deal for sixty aircraft. How's that?"

"You are pretty damn optimistic," Rameros archly replied.

"Yes, I am," Rick said assertively, squaring off with Rameros. "In this business you better be an optimist. If you're not, you're working with one hand tied behind your back." He paused.

Rameros did not retort. It was obvious his last few remarks had worn Rick's patience thin.

Waterman slowly backed away from Rick and Franco, trying to quietly fade into the background.

"Sorry, Rick," Rameros said, now with genuine regret. "Sometimes my mouth disconnects from my thoughts."

"Apology accepted," Rick said with a genuine smile as he extended his hand, which Franco grasped and shook. "Wish me luck, my friend, I need your support."

"You have got it, Rick. I will be guarding that transceiver for your announcement."

"Thanks." Rick clasped Franco on the shoulder, then turned and walked away.

SIXTY-THREE

On Board *LA BASA*

Tommy Maxwell's eyebrows shot up. His mind replaying Monica's last comment: *What's happening is what we expected to happen.* Heeding her instructions, he knelt down on the white beach towel he had placed on the Scarab's forward deck, casually stretched out his body, and languorously turned to face *LA BASA*.

As Maxwell's eyes zeroed in on the afterdeck of the yacht, Ramon Segundo abruptly ended his conversation with Dan Cole. Something had captured Segundo's attention. Segundo quickly rose to his feet and walked from behind the table where he and Cole had been seated. A quick glance but accurate—in fact, perfectly clear. "It's show time," Segundo quietly said as he strode forward, gripping his hands together in anticipation.

The expected guests had just boarded his yacht. Led by the first mate, the entourage walked single file along the starboard passageway toward the afterdeck.

"Gentlemen, gentlemen," Segundo enthusiastically said with open arms in an exaggerated thespian fashion, "welcome to *LA BASA*. I am so glad you could come." Segundo beamed, shaking hands first with General Cardella and then with Salo Montero. He nodded to Major Alverez, in the background as always.

Dan Cole moved from behind the table, stood beside Segundo, and cleared his throat impatiently waiting for recognition.

"Oh, yes," Segundo continued, first directing his attention to Cole and then to Montero, "do correct me if I am wrong, but I believe you two have not formally met."

Not waiting for a formal introduction, Dan Cole stepped forward, offered his hand and a loutish grin, and said, "Howdy, Salo, I'm Dan Cole."

"Well..." Montero began, knowing now this was the man for whom Rick Harris held such extreme angst. He hesitated as he eyed the short, over-weight, middle-aged man who could easily have passed for a retired plumber. To Salo, the man's unimposing presence was diametrically opposed to the typical airframe industry executive. "Well," Montero continued, "your repute certainly does precede you."

Cole guffawed. "I trust everything you've heard is good."

"Good?" Montero laughed, and for dramatic punctuation he simultaneously slapped Cole on the shoulder with his hand. "You have no idea how well-known your reputation is." He kept a frozen smile in place as he turned to the general and then back to Cole. "You are an industry icon, Dan. I consider myself fortunate to have had General Cardella play a part in convincing you to join our North American operation." Salo was playing his chosen role to the hilt. He intended to appear as positive about everything as he could and began implementing that strategy with the introduction to the reputedly contemptible Dan Cole. Like it or not, that was the way high-stakes corporate politics was played. When all participants were good-humored and relaxed, conversation flowed easily and people tended to drop their guard. Salo was not sure what he would be up against, but he knew positioning was important from the outset. And, he needed every advantage he could muster from the very start.

"Sit, sit..." Segundo motioned for all to join him at the table, which everyone did. "Again, thank you for coming." He turned to Montero. "I know it was an imposition for you to breakaway from the factory on such short notice, and so I must apologize for that and perhaps the secrecy behind it. But it was important that we get together. This you will see." He paused, briefly glancing at the general before redirecting his attention to Montero. "Salo, I want you to know that before this day is done, both of our companies will have changed. Trust me, Salo, Brazil—and of course you—will be better off because of it."

Montero flashed an obligatory smile to Segundo. During the flight from Brazil, and then during the drive from AeroMech's impressive facility at Opa Locka, he and the general had discussed a great many things. Salo knew Cardella was poised to make a move involving RioAero that seemed to have the support of a select group of key ministers within the country's current administration. And for all Salo knew, Figueiredo had even tacitly approved whatever action Cardella was about to undertake. Still, he could not be certain what Cardella was about to do, or if Cardella truly had the authority to do it. As of yet, Salo had not made a commitment to join the general in whatever action was about to be undertaken. Soon, he knew he would have to declare himself.

The major remained standing, absorbing his surroundings. He scanned the marina, briefly focusing upon the black Scarab a short distance away. He backed away from the table and seated himself just within the yacht's main salon to stay within earshot of Cardella. The first mate joined him.

"So, Salo," a conciliatory Segundo began, "things have been a bit difficult for you and your company, have they not?"

Montero sighed, then forced a disconsolate laugh. Segundo was wasting no time in getting down to business. "Why yes, yes things have." He paused in expectation for Segundo to pick up the conversation.

Ramon Segundo's face was expressionless. An awkward silence overcame the table.

Montero was being forced to expound, so he chose careful words. "As you know, we are a relatively new company with a brand-new aircraft in a highly competitive market. So yes, these times have been a bit difficult for us."

Segundo raised a seemingly sympathetic brow. "More difficult than you had expected?"

"Unfortunately, that is true."

"Perhaps we can find a way to work together, to the benefit of both of our companies," Segundo offered.

"Well, I suppose that is one of the reasons I am here today," Montero admitted. "It never hurts to explore every avenue. Certainly, the timing is right. There is no doubt that the difficulties RioAero is experiencing must be addressed." With pinched lips, he slowly nodded. "There is only so much my company can weather before alternative actions must taken. General Cardella has been kind enough to take me into his confidence...to help me reassess my program plans...my priorities as they relate to RioAero." Salo gazed out at the calm Intracoastal Waterway and watched a paddleboat replica loaded with tourists motoring by.

"Good, then," Segundo said underscoring Montero's vulnerability. He flashed a surreptitious wink in the direction of the general.

The sightseeing boat tooted its horn. Segundo and Montero waved to its passengers.

"You like boats, Salo?"

"Yes, indeed. In fact, I have a small ski boat on a lake a few hours drive from Rio."

"Well, how about if I have Orlando, my first mate, give you and the general's attaché a tour of *LA BASA*. She is in a class of her own—turbine powered, of course."

"Turbines, huh?" Salo repeated, seemingly impressed, even though he could not have cared less. His mind was timing to process more important things. He did, however, gather that Segundo and Cardella wanted to speak together in private. "Sure, I would be delighted to take a closer look at your yacht." He rose from his seat and leaned over the table toward Segundo. "I would even bet that *LA BASA* is for sale, right?"

"Why, of course." Ramon smiled, and then turned to Cole. "Dan, why not join the group?" he urged. "See if you can sell my Brazilian friend a super motor yacht."

Taking his cue from the conversation, Orlando appeared from the salon. "Gentlemen, please follow me to the helm where I will begin our tour of this impressive motor yacht."

The group followed the first mate through the salon and up the staircase to the bridge deck.

After a moment of silence, Segundo quietly said to Cardella, "I take it that all is well, Carlo."

The general shrugged, then nodded. "More or less."

"Hmmm…" Segundo furrowed his brow and narrowed his eyes. "Tell me about the less."

"Well," Cardella began, "the CTA and our Colombian friends were unable to prevent the second WindStar from coming up here to support Mr. Harris' sales efforts. It seems as though we underestimated the skill of the pilot who was ferrying the aircraft."

"This, I know." Segundo clenched his jaws. "Cole and I were just discussing that matter before you arrived." He shook his head. "That mistake could be very costly for us. You see, Harris is already using that very aircraft for a flight demonstration as we speak."

"Damn," the general blurted out. "Real prospects?"

"It is hard to say," Segundo slowly responded, "but I doubt it. Rick Harris would have to be some kind of wizard to sell the WindStar to anybody, especially considering all of the events in which we have made the WindStar a star." He paused. "Hell, a customer would have to be a damn idiot to select an aircraft that has been cursed with the types of problems the WindStar has shown."

"Good." The general smiled. "Oh, by the way, my sources at RioAero tell me that those modifications your guys in Barcelona made to a couple sets of prop shafts are driving engineers at the factory crazy."

"State-of-the-art lasers." Segundo grinned. "We recently stole that technology from Airbus. RioAero will never know why those props failed." His own remark prompted an additional inquiry from Segundo to Cardella. "And, how is everything at the R&D hangar?"

The general raised his hands and brow in a feigned expression of resignation. "Not too well," he said shaking his head. "It seems that a freak explosion totally devastated the hangar and the two special mission prototypes housed there. Very, very inopportune for something like that to have happened to a foundering airframe manufacturer." He grinned. "Oh well, I guess sometimes shit happens." He laughed. "Hell, you should have seen it from the air— one humongous inferno. Damn impressive if I may say so myself." The general paused. "Missiles from a Gulfstream may not have hit their target, but two big tanker trucks full of fuel and a couple of small detonators made one hell of a mess."

"The Colombians should be happy about that."

"They damn well better be." The general sat back in his chair and unwrapped a Quai d'Orsay Corona Claro he had pulled out of his breast pocket. "Those guys owe us…big time. The military prototypes that were destroyed in Hangar One were destined for use against them." He mouthed the corona from tip to tip before nipping off its double cap with his thumb nail.

"And, speaking of those guys owing us…" Segundo's words trailed off as he saw a smug smile etch itself onto the general's face.

"All taken care of…for now." The general chomped down on his cigar. He leaned forward in his chair, grasped the handle of the large briefcase he had straddled with his legs, and lifted it up onto the table. "A small gift from the boys in Medellín to you, Ramon."

Segundo's pupils immediately dilated. He hefted the case. "Ten keys?"

Cardella nodded, now firing up his corona with a small gold butane lighter. Grayish smoke filled the air.

Segundo unlatched the case and opened its top halfway. He beamed. "Very thoughtful."

Cardella nodded again, then removed the cigar from between his lips. "It is just a personal offering to you, Ramon. We flew three sealed LD3 containers full of the stuff up here in the president's KC-137. Diplomatic protocol made it a no-brainer. Customs would not dare create any problems for us. Additionally, to forestall concerns, there is an understanding with the chief agent, if you know what I mean. Anyway, the containers probably have been off-loaded at your company's facility at Opa Locka by now."

Segundo looked up at the clear blue sky. "Aah, it is a beautiful day, my friend."

"Yes, indeed it is."

"Now," Segundo asked, switching gears, "what is your take on Salo Montero? Is he in? How much does he know?"

"He is in," Cardella said confidently, taking a pull from his cigar, briefly hesitating before going on. "But he has not actually said so yet. You see, Salo really does not have much of a choice. His R&D hangar is a bunch of twisted metal and smoldering debris; he distrusts Figueiredo; and, his company is basically broke. He has no sales. He has no one else to turn to."

"But how much does he know?" Segundo repeated.

"Nothing, nothing at all." Cardella wiped his mouth with the back of his hand. "He has no idea what we have been up to."

"You sure?"

"Absolutely."

"Good."

"When he comes back from the tour of your boat, we will just lay out the deal to him. He will have no choice but to go along with it."

Segundo nodded. "Everything we have been planning during the past few months?"

"Exactly," the general said. "By the end of the day, the WindStar program will be owned by BASA. Soon, all the jigs and other production tooling will be transferred to Barcelona, and you will have a brand-new aircraft in your stable." The general paused, his eyes narrowing. "But of course, as we have discussed, RioAero and the Brazilian government will need something from BASA. That, my friend, is where you give them the sleeves from your vest." The general laughed heartily. He slowly rolled the lit end of his corona in the ashtray in front of him. "RioAero will become the risk-sharing partner on that new fifty-seat aircraft you are developing. They will manufacture the wing and maybe even the empennage. And, they will also get some of the subcontracting work BASA does for Airbus. Essentially, they will work for you...no longer will they be a competitor. You will profit well on selling a damn good aircraft that they took years to develop."

"Indeed we will." Segundo smiled. "We already have covert approval for our program from the powers in Spain, but how about your people in Brazil. Have they agreed?"

"HA," Cardella responded, "they, like Salo, have no choice. The two most powerful ministers in Figueiredo's administration have quietly given me the green light. The rest will fall in line when pressure is put upon them. The key motivator will be the end of that constant bleed of billions of cruzeiros into a foundering RioAero. Fortunately, the short term is their focus. The huge long-term gain otherwise to be reaped many years down the road when RioAero would have become a global force in aviation will be lost. But what the hell do I care about that."

"And, President Figueiredo?"

"To hell with him. He is the least of my worries. If he does not go along with our program, he will be replaced. He is already the least popular president the country has ever had. Still, Figueiredo is no fool. He too will fall in line."

Segundo interlaced the fingers of his hands. "Damn, I love to see a plan come together."

"Yes, it is a nice feeling, a very nice feeling," Cardella said, and then he once again chomped down on his cigar. Its scarlet tip glowed. Plumes of grayish smoke wafted into the still air of the yacht's afterdeck, slowly rising, slowly dissipating.

SIXTY-FOUR

Destination: Pier Sixty-Six

Rick Harris wheeled his BMW out the gated entrance to the ranch and headed east toward Pier Sixty-Six and the meeting he would soon have on Sammy Santelli's sportfisherman. As he drove along, he could not help but wonder how Tommy and Monica were doing on their stakeout at Bahia Mar. Was the bug he had placed under the table on the afterdeck of *LA BASA* providing any useful information? He hoped it was. Perhaps their eavesdropping might have uncovered something that would be useful in his meeting with Santelli.

He glanced at his watch as he drove on. It was thirty minutes past two in the afternoon. No time to stop by and briefly speak with Tommy at Bahia Mar prior to the visit with Santelli. Even if he had had the time to do so, there was always the possibility Ramon Segundo or one of his crewmembers might spot him. If that happened, his entire plan would be upended. He needed to meet with Santelli first, and then with Segundo. That was the way it had to be. It could not change.

A broad smile suddenly lit Rick's face. But it was fleeting. His eyes narrowed; his brow knit into a frown. He had had an idea, though he was not so sure it would pan out. He thought about it once again. "What the hell," he said aloud, "why not give it a shot...nothing to lose."

He reached over to the passenger seat and into the briefcase resting there. He fumbled momentarily among its contents before fishing out the second transceiver Tommy Maxwell had given to him the day before. Now, if he could only raise Maxwell on the radio.

Rick switched on the transceiver and checked the frequency window. It was semi-duplex programmed to match the transceiver that he hoped Tommy would be monitoring. This programming allowed the transceivers to alternatively send and receive on different frequencies, thus making eavesdropping on the entire conversation much more difficult. Still, transmissions were not encrypted. Rick keyed his mic: "Hello Tommy...Hello Tommy..." When he released the mic button, the transceiver automatically broadcasted its hallmark *bud-a-leep* tone, signifying the transmission's end.

He paused, waiting for a response. There was none.

He tried again, "Hello Tommy...Hello Monica...This is Rick." ...*bud-a-leep*.

Still no answer.

"Damn," Rick said under his breath as he placed the transceiver on the passenger seat and turned the BMW onto SR-84. Maybe Monica had had a problem with the boat she was to have picked up at Anderson's Marina earlier that morning. Maybe she was not able to obtain a slip from the dockmaster at Bahia Mar. Or, just maybe neither she nor Tommy Maxwell had turned on their transceiver.

Temporarily frustrated by his inability to reach Tommy or Monica, Rick gunned the BMW through an intersection where a traffic signal had just changed from yellow to red. Guiltily, he scanned the road ahead and to the sides. He glanced into his rearview mirror. This was not the time for him to be delayed by a Broward County Deputy Sheriff for running a red light. He eased off of the accelerator and began to more carefully focus upon his driving. Maybe as he got closer, he would be able to raise Tommy or Monica on the radio.

"*Bud-a-leep.*" At the sound, his eyes flashed to his right—to the transceiver. Someone had keyed their mic on the frequency.

Tommy's voice came through loud and clear on the VHF frequency. "Rick, you there?" ...*bud-a-leep.*

Rick quickly snatched up the transceiver and pressed down on the mic button. "Roger that." ...*bud-a-leep.*

"Damn," came back Tommy's voice, "where the hell have you been? I've tried to raise you for the past hour or so." ...*bud-a-leep.*

Rick keyed his mic. "Sorry, I've been taking care of business out here." ...*bud-a-leep.*

"Well, so have we, and there's a hell of a lot going on. You need to get your ass down here, pronto." ...*bud-a-leep.*

"Wish I could, but I really can't join you for awhile. I've got a critical meeting to attend." He paused intrigued by what Maxwell had said, continuing to depress the mic button. "But, what do you mean by 'there's a hell of a lot going on?'" ...*bud-a-leep.*

"I can't go into it with you on the air. Is there a landline I can call you back on?" ...*bud-a-leep.*

Rick quickly shifted his weight to the right, reached back to his left hip pocket, and pulled out his wallet. He flipped it open and retrieved the portion of the cocktail napkin he had saved with Sammy Santelli's phone number at the marina written onto it. He read the number to Maxwell and said, "Give me a call here in about twenty minutes." ...*bud-a-leep.*

"Will do, and like I said, there's a lot going on down here. I think our puzzle may almost be complete. So now, some important decisions need to be made, and you're the man who needs to make them. Talk to you later, over and out." ...*bud-a-leep.*

"Hot damn," Rick said aloud, his widened eyes sparkled as he accelerated the BMW. His mind now raced ahead considering all the possibilities. A smile spread across his face. Maybe, just maybe, things were finally falling into place for him.

Even from the very first meeting with Ramon Segundo, Rick had suspected Segundo was a key player in the sabotage against RioAero. That was one of the reasons Rick had agreed to the second meeting Segundo had suggested for this afternoon. Indeed, Rick had no intention of accepting Segundo's offer to leave RioAero and join BASA. He thought of the second meeting only as an opportunity to gain further information about Segundo and Cole, and whoever else was allied with them against RioAero. But from reading between the lines of Maxwell's transmission, Rick knew the next meeting with Segundo would escalate beyond the purpose of just fact finding. Certainly, he would have to hear what Tommy was anxious to disclose. And then, he would have a decision to make: What to do next?

As Rick continued driving on toward the marina at Pier Sixty-Six, he had little idea how earth-shattering Tommy Maxwell's information would prove to be.

SIXTY-FIVE

Pier Sixty-Six Marina

"Damn," Sammy Santelli barked out, slapping the palm of his hand down onto the table in the main cabin of his sportfisherman. He jutted out his jaw and closed his eyes, hard. "There are just too many unknowns, too many uncertainties." His shoulders slumped forward as he grappled with the situation at hand. "I'm just not sure what the hell we should do."

After intensely reviewing, and then discussing the terms and conditions contained in the Letter of Intent (LOI) Rick Harris had presented, Santelli and his partners were still unable to reach a decision. The three men were highly impressed with the WindStar. Indeed, it was the type of aircraft that would satisfy their newly forged airline's requirements well into the future. No other presently available aircraft could do what the WindStar could do for them. And, the comprehensive bottom-line acquisition package Rick had constructed was very attractive—astoundingly so. It was almost perfect. But there was just one problem—a major problem.

John Andreas, who had finished carefully reviewing the LOI for a third time, resignedly shrugged. Like the others, he was well aware of the dilemma. In the back of everyone's mind lurked the possibility that somehow the WindStar was flawed—perhaps irresolvably. The situation into which they had been thrust was distressfully unsettling. Yet, Santelli and his partners had to come to grips with it. A decision had to be made, one way or the other.

"Damn," Santelli said again, "what the hell are we going to do? Harris will be here any minute. I just can't say, 'Duh, we don't have a clue as to how we want to proceed.'" He paused, glancing first at Kelly Long, then at John Andreas. "We need airplanes, and we need them soon. The merger of our airlines doesn't make any sense unless we can standardize our fleet. There are tremendous opportunities out there for us. We just can't sit on the sidelines and let the world pass us by." He paused again, his frustration mounting. "C'mon, guys, what the hell are we going to do?"

Kelly Long sank back into his chair on the left side of the table and slowly crossed his arms. "I say we go for it, Sammy," he said. "Sign Rick's LOI. It has bailout provisions bigger than a barn door. Should any of our concerns come true, we can walk away from the deal, and while we won't be totally unscathed, we'll be whole."

John Andreas echoed Kelly's remarks. "Kelly's right, Sammy. If you look at the alternatives, there's not much of a choice. Remember, the WindStar is fully certificated by the FAA. Fundamentally, it has to be a sound and safe aircraft otherwise the Feds would not have signed off on it. Rick may well be correct in believing that sabotage is at the root of his aircraft's problems."

"Yeah, yeah," a flustered Santelli said, "Rick isn't the type of guy to try to pull the wool over our eyes. We've all known him too long for that. It's just not his style."

Andreas and Long nodded in agreement.

"But sabotage is a rare bird in this business," Santelli continued on. "I can't recall a single case of it."

"Well, it might be because we just never hear about it," Kelly offered.

"Or," John Andreas added, "it's very possible that past incidents could never be proven as sabotage."

"Or, on the other hand," Santelli finally conceded, "sabotage may never have been undertaken on such a large scale to make it as significant as it is with the WindStar. Here, we're not just talking about one isolated incident undertaken by some disgruntled employee."

"You might be right," Andreas concurred.

There was a moment of silence as the group pondered their next move.

"I'm sure Rick will understand our predicament," Santelli said. "Let's see if he has any further information that may set our minds at ease."

"Fine with me," Andreas said. "But Sammy, I think the issues are only ours at this point. I really doubt Rick will have anything new or compelling enough that would convince you to sign up for the WindStar today. Remember, we were with him just an hour or so ago. Nothing much could have changed."

"Okay, okay…" Santelli said at wits end. "We'll just have to pass on his deal for now. We can't afford to make a mistake by selecting an aircraft that's plagued with disaster. Even though I'm not a big fan of the Fairchild Metro, that aircraft may be our only alternative."

"You must be crazy, Sammy," an incensed Kelly Long blurted out, "the Metro sucks. I'd rather make do with the equipment we currently have and delay our planned route expansion than to go with that maintenance hog from Fairchild. I have serious concerns with the Metro." He paused, then pointed his finger directly at Santelli. "And don't even suggest BASA's Avio-23 or I'll have to—"

"Or you'll have to *what*?" Santelli roared back.

"Enough, enough..." John Andreas raised his hands into the air. "Let's simmer down now. Remember, we're on the same team here." He paused as Santelli and Long just shook their heads at each other. "Okay, I say let's wait." Andreas offered. "We obviously need more time. I'm sure the deal Rick is now offering us won't go away if we delay for a week or two. We're talking about buying airplanes, not automobiles. I say wait, can we agree?"

Kelly Long shrugged. "I guess there's no other choice. What say you, Sammy?"

"We'll wait. We can't afford to make a mistake on such an important decision."

The three sat around the table in awkward silence.

SIXTY-SIX

On Board *LA BASA*

"Here he comes now," General Cardella turned and whispered to Ramon Segundo. He had just glimpsed Salo Montero leave the main salon and walk out onto the afterdeck.

"Well, well, well," Segundo said, glancing up toward Montero without rising from his seat at the table, "what do you think? Do we have a new owner for this gem of a motor yacht?"

Montero politely smiled, approached the table, but remained standing. "She is very nice, you know." He paused and then facetiously added, "But I really need a pair of matched yachts—one for our operation up here and one for down in Rio." To Montero, expensive motor yachts were a least important agenda item, especially today. For the moment, he played along and continued his banter with Segundo. "So, since this yacht is one-of-a-kind, I am afraid I will have to pass. One yacht just would not do. I hope you understand."

"What a shame, my friend," Segundo said laughingly, "I somehow figured you would have to take a pass. Nonetheless, you would look good at the helm of *LA BASA*...yes indeed, you certainly would." His eyes focused past Salo and into the relative darkness of the main salon. "By the way, where are Cole and the others?"

"Having a drink at the bar." Montero motioned back to the salon door with his head. "Orlando is explaining the yacht's navigation system." That was true, but only part of the story. The fact of the matter was that Montero had told the others he needed some time in private with both Segundo and the general. And, he had been adamant about it.

"Salo Montero," the general spoke up, getting right down to business, "you know why we are here. You know what needs to be done. Please sit. Let us go through the details."

Montero ignored the general's request and walked past the left side of the table and to the abaft sea rail of the yacht. He gazed below at the sleek canary yellow Cigarette 41/OS that was moored parallel to the stern of the yacht with its bow pointed out toward the Intracoastal. "That is the kind of boat I could use," he said turning to Segundo. "I suppose it is for sale as well, right?"

"Why, of course, Salo, everything is for sale, you know..." Segundo stopped mid-sentence, having noted the general's growing irritation with Montero's insolent dismissal. It was time to talk business. The general was getting agitated.

Montero forged on, still temporarily skirting the conversation at hand. "Aah yes, I suppose almost everything is for sale." He then turned away from the stern, strolled back around the table, and seated himself across from Segundo and the general. "You know, for a moment I thought you were truly interested in selling boats." He chuckled, a smile briefly on his lips. "I do imagine you would prefer to focus upon aircraft instead."

"Mr. Montero…" General Cardella brusquely took over the conversation. "Airplanes are why you are here. Airplanes are what this meeting is all about. Airplanes… Airplanes."

Salo sat back into his chair and crossed his legs. "Very well, then…" He paused for effect before making his next comment, which was intended to further goad the general. "Now, tell me what is on your mind—what you can do for me."

The general's eyes widened, then he snapped, "What *I* can do for *you*? HA, Mr. Montero, you do not get it, you just do not get it. It is what *you* can do for us, and, in the process, save your own goddamn ass." Cardella's body tensed.

Salo shrugged, fighting to maintain his own cool demeanor. Cardella's true colors were coming to light, and with such little provocation. Exactly as, but somewhat sooner than Salo had surmised it would happen.

The tour of *LA BASA* had given Montero the opportunity to mentally review everything that had transpired since being called away from his lake house retreat by the general slightly less than twenty-four hours earlier: the meeting at the CIE headquarters in Rio; his visit with President Figueiredo; and, his discussions with Cardella aboard the KC-137. Conclusions he had drawn were quickly being validated. Now, as he sat across the table from Cardella and Segundo, he knew any semblance of control he may have thought he had over the situation was evaporating. The atmosphere was overtly hostile toward him. He clearly saw the relationship between the general and the president of BASA as chummy—too chummy. He sensed whatever the two were about to propose would be totally one-sided—totally unacceptable to him. However, at this point, he had little choice but to listen.

"Salo," Segundo began in a reassuring tone, "the general and I have devised a plan to save RioAero—and you, of course—from total disaster." He paused to allow his words to have the effect of smoothing over the general's heated initial outburst. "You know, it is just a matter of time before the current administration in Brazil simply pulls the plug on RioAero. Then, everything will be over—*fini*. The aircraft company you spent the better part of your life building will be shut down, most probably never again to function as it does today."

Salo's face remained tautly expressionless. Segundo's words were all too true. Indeed, there was not much time left to pull RioAero out of its tailspin.

Segundo briefly looked to the general for agreement to continue. Cardella nodded his consent.

"So," Segundo went on, "what we have decided to do is have BASA help you. It is the only way to keep RioAero from being shut down. It is the only way to keep you as head of the company you founded." Segundo proceeded to detail their plan to transfer the entire WindStar production to Barcelona, to have RioAero focus exclusively on subcontract production work, and, lastly, to have RioAero become a supporting, risk-sharing partner in BASA's new fifty-seat regional airliner. When Segundo was finished, he smiled and asked, "Now, Salo, how does that sound to you?"

Salo Montero slowly rocked his head back and forth, though his face still remained expressionless. He had heard Segundo loud and clear. He was surprised; but then again, he was also not surprised. Events of the past few days had toughened his skin.

"I thought you would like it," Segundo said, rather pleased with himself. "Any comments? Questions?"

Salo Montero slowly shook his head from side to side, his mind weighing the words he had just heard. He briefly closed his eyes. Then, he spoke up. "Mr. Segundo, General Cardella, with all due respect..." He measured his words to flow confidently, unhurriedly. He smiled, momentarily directing his gaze to the heavily lacquered teakwood table prior to refocusing first upon Segundo, then Cardella. Without warning, Salo launched into a full verbal assault. His voice boomed out the words: "Do you guys think that I am some kind of friggin' idiot! There is no goddamn way I would ever go along with such a lame program. Hell, you must be out of your minds."

Far from intimidated, the general glared across the table at Salo. "Montero, you have no choice," he spit out.

"The hell I don't!" Montero struck back.

"No, no, you are dead wrong," the general buttressed his stance. He glanced up toward the doorway to the main salon. Alert to the raised voices, Major Alverez had just appeared, standing ready to respond to any instruction from Cardella. Making sure Salo had noted Major Alverez's implied threat, Cardella waved his attaché off and continued on with Montero. "You have no idea what you are up against. The die has been cast. Either you go along with our program or—"

"Or what? You will have your CIE goons break my legs?"

The general laughed. "You know me too well, Salo, but you really do not know me well enough. That type of action would be far too mundane for me. So no, that is not my plan. What I have in mind is much different...much more far-reaching...much more, shall we say, unpleasant for you."

"And I suppose that Figueiredo and the ministers will approve of whatever action you are about to undertake?"

"Do not be naive, Montero," the general smugly said. He sat back and folded his arms across his chest. "While I pretty much have been given carte blanche from a few key ministers, President Figueiredo knows nothing. You see, Salo, Figueiredo and I do not see eye-to-eye. When all is done, he may have his suspicions, but his hold on the presidency is much too tenuous for him to expose his throat by helping you. Forget Figueiredo. Anyway, you better be concerned with your own skin. If you do not go along with what I have arranged for RioAero, you will pay dearly."

"And just how do you intend to make me do that?"

"Simple," the general said with a smile, "you will take the fall for the miserable failure of RioAero. A team I personally selected from the CIE has taken the lead on investigating the explosion of Hangar One. They have already made their determination. Their findings will be accepted as conclusive. All I need to do is pick up the phone and have the report released. If you are not on our side, you will definitely be on the outside."

"What do you mean?"

"Salo, Salo, Salo...you ask many questions—too many questions for a man in your position. Still, I will answer you." The general leaned forward, anchoring his elbows onto the tabletop and clasping his hands together. He smiled, almost with portentous glee. "You, Salo Montero, will be singled out...singled out as the one who orchestrated the devastation of your own R&D hangar."

"*I what?*"

"I thought you would be surprised," the general said with a smirk, and then sat back in his seat. "And, you did it all as a cover-up for your bumbling attempts to sabotage the WindStar—a ploy to distract others from your total mindless incompetence as CEO of RioAero."

"That is absurd," Salo said scornfully. "No one will believe you."

"You think not, Mr. Montero, I know so. For too long you and your management team have drained the country's treasury without ever generating one lousy cruzeiro of profit." He paused, briefly glancing toward Segundo. "Hell, North America is the world's hottest market for the WindStar and you do not even have a customer up here anymore."

"WHAT?" Salo was stunned. What he had heard could not be true, but it was.

Segundo further clarified the general's statement. "I guess you have not read the press release yet. You see, Jim Highland just signed up for twelve BASA Avio-23s and nullified your WindStar contract."

"Damn," Salo groaned. He felt the world collapsing around himself.

"That news is nothing compared to the evidence my CIE boys have conjured up against you," the general said arrogantly. "If you choose not to side with us, you could never again set foot in Brazil. If you did, you would be arrested on the spot and stand trial—as a formality, of course—and then be locked up in one of our less than pleasant detention centers. You would never again see the light of day."

"You sonovabitch!" Salo leaned forward and grasped the edge of the table with both hands, trying to restrain his ire. Furiously grinding his teeth, he rapidly shook his head in disbelief.

"Thank you for the compliment," came the general's wry response. "I do take pride in my work." He grinned.

Montero shrunk back into his seat at the table. He believed every word the general had spoken. Indeed, Cardella had the power and the motivation to destroy Salo Montero; and, as Salo could see, Cardella was savoring every aspect of his task.

"What say you now, Salo?" Segundo posed the question. "Accepting our offer is far better than suffering the consequences. Either you work with us, or...well, I think you understand the alternative."

Salo Montero was torn. He could not accept their offer. He knew that RioAero would essentially be transformed into a mere satellite operation for Segundo. BASA would gain significant benefits from the cutting-edge technology RioAero had developed during the past several years. BASA would also eliminate a competitor and gain a brand-new state-of-the-art aircraft. Regardless of what decision Salo made, Segundo and the general were going to have their way. There was no doubt about it.

"Well, Mr. Montero?" the general pressed.

Salo said nothing.

"I do not have all day, Montero."

Salo finally responded, "I need more time." Then he went silent again; stalling, waiting, willing some form of salvation to come to his aid. "This is a major departure from anything I could have anticipated."

Cardella leaned forward and spoke in a slow, deliberate tone: "YOU HAVE NO TIME."

Salo rose from his seat at the table, his eyes first searching for an escape route in the Intracoastal to his right, then at the pier to his left. "Fine, make your own goddamn decision. I am out of here." He hastily turned and disappeared forward along the starboard passageway.

"You cannot let him leave," Segundo quickly said to the general.

"Do not worry," the general said confidently, "he will not."

Moments later, Salo Montero reappeared, slowly walking back to the yacht's afterdeck. Major Alverez, who was directly behind him, had apparently been effectively persuasive.

"I see you had a change of heart," the general said, almost gloating.

Salo Montero remained silent. He reseated himself at the table.

Segundo spoke up, "So, where do we go from here?"

SIXTY-SEVEN

Pier Sixty-Six Marina

S uddenly, the uncomfortable silence was broken. From the lower stern deck of the Hatteras, a rapid clanging din rang out. It was a familiar sound, but not a maritime sound.

Santelli smiled, followed by Long and Andreas. The tension among the three evaporated. Rick Harris' arrival was being announced by the vigorous ringing the cowbell he had brought along from the ranch.

"Ahoy, ahoy..." Rick called out from the bottom of the stairs leading to the cabin.

Santelli rose from his seat at the table and strode toward the open cabin door. "Come on up, we've been expecting you."

Rick climbed up the stairs, entered the cabin, and placed his briefcase onto the table. "Good afternoon, gentlemen," he said, "I've got just what the doctor ordered."

He opened the top of his briefcase and pulled out a twelve-inch high mahogany woodcarving. He placed it in the center of the table, and then stepped back.

"What is this?" Santelli asked, curiously eyeing the sculpture.

"Something I brought back from Brazil." He paused with a grin. "It was actually Gail's idea for me to present it to you."

The dark reddish brown wooden sculpture depicted an almost to scale fist of a hand extending from its forearm base. The thumb of the hand was interposed between the middle and forefinger.

"But, but what is it?" Santelli repeated the question. "Some kind of voodoo icon?"

"No, no," Rick was quick to respond, "it's a *figa*—a symbol of good luck in Brazil." He fashioned his own hand into the pose as depicted in the sculpture. "We can never have enough good luck, right?"

"That's for sure," came the response from Santelli. "You and your WindStar could use a couple dozen of those *figa* things right about now."

Rick sucked in his lower lip and nodded. "I know what you mean, Sammy. It seems as though luck hasn't been on our side...until now."

Until now? The words held his audience's rapt attention in anticipation of what he meant.

Rick too fell silent while casually picking through his briefcase, plucking out three thin file folders. He so loved the center stage and making the moment last. "Well, how do you all feel about the WindStar?" he asked seating himself at the table and opening the top file folder.

A sharp intake of breath from Kelly Long, a deep sigh from John Andreas, and a nondescript groan from Sammy Santelli were his only responses.

"Hmmm…" Rick moaned, "that bad, huh?"

"No, no," Kelly spoke up, "we—"

"We like your aircraft, Rick," John quickly interjected. "The WindStar is exactly what we need."

"But?" Rick prodded.

"But," Sammy began, "we're not sure." He grimaced, awkwardly pausing. "We're not sure about those problems the WindStar has been experiencing. Without explanations, without understanding why these incidents have occurred…well, we feel ill-at-ease at making a firm decision."

Rick smiled, which given the circumstances seemed rather odd to Santelli.

"What's up?" Andreas asked Harris.

"A lot," was all Rick said. He took four sheets of paper out of the open file folder, kept one for himself, and passed the others out.

"What do we have here?" Sammy Santelli asked, glancing at the document Rick had passed to him. Across the top of the page in bold lettering were the words: CONFIDENTIALITY AGREEMENT.

Rick said, "It's a standard document that says whatever you hear from me and whatever I hear from you stays between us, or else I and my lawyers might own this boat, or you and your lawyers might own my ranch."

"Why do we need this?" Kelly Long asked.

"Is there a problem?" Rick replied with a question of his own.

"No, no," Kelly answered back.

"Sammy, John…are you okay with this?" Rick asked.

"Sure, we're fine with it," Santelli answered for both himself and Andreas.

"Good." Rick signed his copy and placed it in the center of the table. Santelli and the others followed suit with their copies. Rick knew that any contract or agreement was only as good as the integrity of the people who executed it. Rick trusted that Santelli and the others would hold anything discussed in the strictest confidence even without a confidentiality agreement. But he also knew that formal confidentiality agreements imparted a strong note of official sanction to the forthright exchange of information. Rick Harris was poised to disclose every bit of information he had concerning RioAero and the WindStar, however damning it might be. He also wanted to provide

Santelli and his partners with the same unencumbered opportunity—to speak freely about their program plans.

"Now, who wants to go first?" Rick asked.

"Why don't you, Rick," Kelly replied.

"Fine with me," Rick said. "There's more you need to know about RioAero and the WindStar, especially considering what's been happening this afternoon." He paused, making eye contact with everyone at the table, noticing puzzled stares. "Before I do, though, there's one important question I need to ask you. I think I have the answer, but I'd like to hear it from you."

"Go ahead, Rick," Santelli said, "whatever you'd like to know is yours for the asking.

"Okay…" With clasped hands, Rick placed his elbows onto the table and leaned forward. "When you first disclosed that you were consolidating your three airlines, it didn't seem to make any sense. But the more I thought about it, the more sense it made. Follow my thought process for a moment, then tell me if I'm right."

Santelli nodded.

Harris continued, "Since deregulation, the industry has been slowly but dramatically evolving. Point-to-point air travel is changing to hub-and-spoke. Major airlines are setting up hubs—essentially their fortresses—to better position for the type of competition never before experienced under government regulation. The sharing of passenger revenue through today's interline agreements will soon be a thing of the past. Each airline wants every passenger that boards one of its airplanes to be its very own. An airline doesn't want to share even a penny of revenue with one of its competitors. Just plain business sense, right?"

Santelli nodded again, still not knowing where Rick was going with his treatise.

"But a major airline can't be all things to all people," Rick continued on. "A major airline can't fly everywhere, so partners are needed that otherwise do not pose a competitive threat to the major's very existence—smaller commuter or regional airlines are what I mean. Of course, too many partners can become a managerial nightmare for any major airline. So, a select group of small to medium sized operators feeding passengers to the majors at their hubs would be preferable. Do you follow me now?"

There were blank stares from the group.

"Okay, let me cut to the chase. You guys are merging your airlines together for a single reason: to feed passengers to *one* major airline, right?"

There was silence at the table.

Rick waited for a response.

Finally, Santelli spoke up, "Well, we can't confirm or deny that." He fumbled with a pen before abruptly placing it onto the table. "You know, there just could be another confidentiality agreement that precludes commenting on our new airline's program plans."

Rick grinned. He knew he was on the right track. "I understand. But it would add a ton of credibility if you could disclose it."

"Sorry, Rick, we just can't disclose anything, not yet."

"Well then, do you mind if I tell you what your plans are?"

"No, not at all, still we won't be able to tell you if you are right or wrong."

"Fine, try this on for size." Rick proceeded to detail his final thoughts. "Only one major airline has a presence and a strategic expansion plan for the three markets in which your three airlines are currently based. Let me go through the Greek alphabet for you: Alpha, beta, gamma, DELTA." He hesitated, intentionally emphasizing the last word. "Need I say more?"

The group smiled almost in unison. "I can't tell you anything, Rick Harris," Santelli reiterated his position, "but there is one thing I can say: You are one hell of an intuitive aircraft salesman."

"Thank you," Rick said, "thankyouverymuch." Although Santelli had not formally confirmed Rick's suspicions, it was not a stretch for Rick to surmise that the new airline the group was forming by combining their three operations was intended to exclusively serve Delta Airlines. And that was big news—really big news. It was very likely that within a two year period over a hundred WindStars could be flying passengers from small outlying cities to Delta's major hub in Atlanta as well as to its planned expansions for hubs in Cincinnati and Boston.

"Okay," Sammy Santelli said to Rick, "now we have some questions for you."

"I'm ready."

Just then, the telephone rang. Sammy casually arose from his chair and took three steps toward the forward bulkhead to grasp the handset and pull it away from its wall-mounted cradle. "Hello, Santelli..." He listened for a few seconds, then motioned to Rick. "It's for you."

Rick moved to take the handset from Sammy. He spoke his name into the mouthpiece, and then listened intently for nearly a minute. "Hold on for a second," he said assimilating the news and pondering his next move. There were risks involved with what he had in mind, but he felt there really was no choice. "I'm going to put you on the squawker." Rick punched the speaker button and re-cradled the handset. To his airline friends he said, "Gentlemen, I have my private investigator on the line. He has some important information concerning RioAero and the WindStar that I think we all need to hear."

From the other end of the line, the voice spoke over the speaker, "Rick, are you really sure you want others to hear what I've got to say? It's highly sensitive stuff. This is the first time you yourself will be hearing it." Concern was heavy in Tommy Maxwell's voice as he spoke from a public telephone near the dockmaster's offices at the Bahia Mar Marina.

"I'm absolutely sure, Tommy," Rick said decisively. "Tell us everything you've learned. For better or worse, my customers need full disclosure."

"Fine, if you say so, you're the boss." Maxwell paused as a go-fast boat at the marina revved up one of its big block engines. When the thundering noise subsided, Maxwell continued, "Okay, Rick, the bottom line is just as you suspected. The WindStar is a sound aircraft. All the problems have been the direct result of a well-orchestrated plot of sabotage."

"Excuse me," Sammy Santelli spoke up, astounded and skeptical, "how do you know all this?"

Maxwell laughed. "I guess Rick hasn't filled you in on everything he's been up to. Anyway, thanks to him, I've been able to monitor certain conversations that have been highly enlightening, to say the least. These conversations, without a doubt, verify that sabotage has been undertaken against the WindStar and RioAero. It's pretty heavy stuff, almost unbelievable. Fortunately, I have everything on tape to boot."

Tommy Maxwell went on to quickly explain the major elements of what he and Monica had overheard from conversations on the afterdeck of *LA BASA*. He identified the key players involved with the sabotage plot and their plan to strip RioAero of the WindStar and relegate the Brazilian airframe manufacturer to being a mere subcontractor. He noted that sabotage was the cause of each and every crippling problem that the WindStar had experienced over the past few days. He mentioned the explosive destruction of Hangar One and the involvement of the Medellín Cartel, which apparently feared that RioAero's military prototypes would soon be used against its operations. Lastly, he added Salo Montero had made an appearance on *LA BASA*, but looked quite unhappy with the assembled group. When Maxwell had finished, there was a long period of silence.

Finally, Santelli roared out, "Those goddamn sonovabitches. They almost forced me to pass on signing up for the WindStar. I'd like to go over there and kick their friggin' asses."

Kelly Long and John Andreas remained quiet, though vigorously nodding in agreement with Santelli.

"Okay, Tommy," Rick spoke up, "get back with Monica and continue on with your work. I should be arriving at the marina in about twenty minutes."

"Will do," Maxwell said, "but I've got one more phone call to make."

"Phone call? To whom?"

"The Feds, who else?"

"No Tommy, not yet," Rick said. "I'd like to have the personal satisfaction of confronting Segundo myself. Besides, he's expecting a visit from me this afternoon to formally accept an executive position with BASA in the U.S."

"Yeah-yeah, I almost forgot about that meeting; but I didn't mean calling up the Feds to come to the marina," Tommy clarified. "I meant arranging for them to visit the AeroMech facility at Opa Locka."

"Huh?"

"You see," Tommy went on, "not only did General Cardella bring up Salo Montero from Brazil, he also brought up some ten thousand pounds of cocaine—three LD3 containers full of the stuff—for his cartel friends. Unfortunately for him, the general had to brag about it to Segundo, and I have that on tape as well. I'm just going to call up the customs guys and suggest they take their beagles out for a walk around the AeroMech hangar. Who knows what might be found." Maxwell laughed.

Rick smiled. "Go for it, Tommy, I'll be on board *LA BASA* shortly." He paused. "Do stand by, though, I may need your assistance if things get ugly on their yacht."

There was a brief silence on the other end of the line. "Ugly?" Maxwell asked. "What do you have planned, Rick?"

"Well," Harris was slow to respond, "that depends on what I can accomplish here with Santelli."

"Remember, Rick," Maxwell warned, "Segundo has a gorilla-type for a first mate, and the general brought along one eerie attaché who looks like he can handle anything."

"I'll keep that in mind."

"Good luck. See you soon."

The conversation ended. Rick turned back to the group.

"Your hunches were right, Rick," Santelli began somewhat apologetically. "The WindStar seems to be everything you said it was. Sabotage on such a large scale is hard to believe, but apparently it's true."

"Yes, yes it is." Rick walked back to his seat at the table and sank down into the chair. "So, now you guys know everything."

There were slow nods of agreement from everyone.

"Rick Harris," Kelly Long spoke up, "this is one big can of worms you've opened up."

"It's a real mess alright," Rick said, "but I didn't open it. The can was already spewing out worms. I just slapped a label on the can and called it what it was."

"Indeed you did," Andreas noted. "Still, none of us envy your current position one bit."

Santelli asked, "How can we help?"

"Do you really want to know?" Rick quickly responded with his own question.

"Absolutely," Santelli said in earnest.

"Well this may be rather presumptuous, but I'm a salesman, so I've got to ask." Rick opened the second file folder on the table in front of him and stared at it momentarily before going on. He pointed to the document that the folder contained. "If you sign this LOI, which I'm sure you all have carefully reviewed, it just might blow Segundo and his cronies out of the water."

"Hmmm…" Santelli dubiously asked, "You think so?"

Rick emphatically nodded. "It's my only chance to save the WindStar. It's your only chance to get the aircraft you really need, and within the timeframe you'd really like."

Sammy looked to Long and Andreas for approval. They cocked their heads forward. "Okay," Santelli said, "but the deal has changed."

Rick's heart sank. He had already gone as far as he could go with what he had pulled together for Santelli—no further concessions could be made. None. Still, he needed to hear Santelli out. If there was any possible way to make this sale today, Rick had to do it. "Go on."

"There are two things, really three things that we need."

"Yes…" Rick said as he sat back in his chair. This truly was not what he had expected. Three more items needed to be addressed. Well, there was no choice. He had to deal with whatever Santelli threw at him.

"The first item could be a bit of a problem. It essentially changes the entire contract." Santelli paused. "But, you're a creative salesman. Somehow, I think you can handle it."

Rick waited, his mind ominously dwelling upon what Sammy had said: It essentially changes the entire contract. Damn.

"Since you're already sitting down," Santelli went on, "I'll get right to the point." He paused for what seemed to be forever to Harris. Finally, Santelli continued on, "I want the order doubled."

Rick's eyes flew open. "What? You must be kidding. Is this some kind of a joke?"

"No, no," Santelli said, seemingly taken back, albeit slightly, "you heard me right. I want the order doubled."

"Forty aircraft, with two options of forty each?"

"That's correct." Sammy grinned. "We'll need them. I'm sure of it." He glanced toward Andreas and Long. They shrugged, then nodded. "I know this order will be the largest order ever made by a regional airline. It will certainly astound everyone—General Cardella, Segundo, Cole, and Montero. Brazil could never let RioAero tank with a deal like that on the books." Santelli grinned. "What say you, Mr. Salesman? Do you have a problem with it?"

"Sammy, Sammy..." Rick beamed. "You know my situation, and you think I'd have a problem with it?"

"Nah," Santelli scoffed, "I just wanted to have some fun with you before we penciled in more aircraft to the order and then signed on the dotted line. Sometimes I like center stage too."

"Okay," Rick smiled, then tempered his enthusiasm and forged ahead, "what else?"

"The next two items are not slam-dunks, but I don't think there should be a problem with agreement. First, I don't happen to have a checking account with two million dollars—now probably four million—to cover the required deposits. So, what I propose is—"

"A promissory note in lieu of hard currency."

"Exactly." Santelli's eyes appraisingly evaluated Rick. He was both surprised and relieved that Rick had read his mind.

Rick slid the third file folder across the table to Santelli. It contained the promissory note Rick had anticipated would be needed.

Santelli opened the folder and quickly glanced at the document. "Damn, you're one hell of an aircraft salesman!"

"Thanks, but it's just my job. All we'll need to do is just change the two million dollars to four, and that's it."

"Good," Santelli said and continued on to his next point. "Now, the third item might require some weasel-wording modifications, but then again, maybe not."

"Fine." Rick was now feeling confident that he could accept Santelli's final request, whatever it might be.

"Well, Rick, in order to feel comfortable about this entire deal, we need an assurance we currently don't have. You see, even though we have been given the capability to walk away from the deal if RioAero doesn't meet its contractual provisions, it would still be painful for us—a logistics nightmare. We don't want that to happen. So, here's what I propose." Sammy handed Rick a piece of paper entitled ATTACHMENT-1. Scribbled upon it were two paragraphs written in longhand by Santelli.

Rick carefully read the attachment. "I'm flattered," he said.

"It's important to us," Santelli remarked. "With everything that's been happening, and with everything that you've done on your own to save the WindStar and rescue your company, we all want to be sure that you'll be there in the future to serve as our advocate."

The attachment that Rick was now reading for the second time essentially stipulated that a long-term employment contract exist between Rick Harris and RioAero.

John Andreas began adding his commentary: "You know, sometimes a salesman can be a real pain in the ass." He paused for effect. "But, then again, sometimes a salesman can be a real asset to both his company and his customer. We all want to be sure that you'll stay at RioAero. And hell, unless the Brazilians are damn fools, they should want the same thing."

"Fine," Rick said, "I'll incorporate it into the agreement." He paused. "So, gentlemen, do we have a deal?"

"Yes, yes we do." Santelli picked up the pen from the table, initialed each change, each page, and finally scrawled his signature across the final page of the document. He tapped the pages together on the table, was about to hand them to Rick, but hesitated. He placed the document back down in front of himself. "There is, however, one more thing. It's more of a personal nature."

"Okay, Sammy." Rick said with a chuckle. "Now, what?

"Well, since this deal of ours almost didn't get done because of that goddamn Segundo guy and his scumbag cohorts, I'd like to join you at Bahia Mar and rub this contract in their pathetic faces."

Rick firmly shook his head. "While I'd love for you to join me, I really can't have you do so. Once Segundo and his cronies realize they've been had—that everything they've said has been tape recorded—things could get a little weird, maybe dangerously so. Anything could happen. I wouldn't want you to get caught up in the crossfire just to gain some personal satisfaction."

"Still, I'd like—"

"Sammy," Kelly Long broke in, "Rick's right. We have an airline to organize. Besides, Rick has done one excellent job so far without any meddling from us. Let him continue on. If you got involved with this just for the sport of it, things could get screwed up."

"My vote is with Kelly," Andreas added. "This is Rick's baby, and it ain't over yet. Let our advocate be our advocate. That's what we wanted, what we agreed to, right?"

"Well, I suppose so." Santelli said, his ego temporarily deflated. "Okay, Rick, you've got the conn. We'll be on this Hatteras if you need us. Just give a signal."

"Thanks for understanding." Rick signed a second copy of the agreement and exchanged it with Santelli. He glanced at his watch. It was nearly four o'clock in the afternoon. "Now, if you'll excuse me," he said, stuffing one signed copy of the agreement into his briefcase,

"I have an important meeting to on that big, flaming yellow motor yacht at Bahia Mar. I'll be back as soon as I can. Hang loose and save me a cold beer."

"Will do," Santelli said. "Good luck."

Rick rose from the table, fashioned his right hand into the likeness of a *figa* for the group, and departed the sportfisherman for the short drive to Bahia Mar. He strode down the pier to the parking area in the warmth of the late afternoon sun as yet another weekend in Fort Lauderdale was coming to a peaceful end. But for Rick Harris, peaceful was far from a near-term reality.

SIXTY-EIGHT

On Board *LA BASA*

"So, where do we go from here?" Salo Montero slowly rocked back and forth on his chair as he parroted Segundo's question. But before he could say anything else, a rapid clanging sound rang out interrupting his question to Ramon Segundo.

Standing on the dock below was Rick Harris enthusiastically ringing his cowbell.

"Ahoy, ahoy *LA BASA*..." Harris shouted out. "Anyone happen to have a cold beer for a tired, over-worked aircraft salesman?"

Ramon Segundo immediately recognized the voice. "Good," he uttered confidently to Cardella, "it is that WindStar sales guy I spoke to you about earlier." He turned to Montero and said, "This will be a surprise for you, but Rick Harris is here this afternoon to formally accept an offer I made to him yesterday. He intends to join BASA as vice president of sales and marketing for North America." He paused awaiting a response from Montero.

Salo swallowed hard at the news—another unexpected setback. He was quite certain an offer had been made that Rick simply could not refuse.

"Perhaps this Mr. Harris will help you come to grips with the decision you know you must make," the general interjected.

The cowbell rang out again.

Segundo instantly rose to his feet and hurried to the starboard passageway. "*Buenas tardes*, Mr. Harris," he said, looking over the sea rail and down to Rick. "Do come aboard, my friend. I will have Orlando bring us both some cold cerveza."

"*Gracias*, Ramon." Rick retraced his steps back toward *LA BASA's* amidships gangway where he boarded the yacht and confidently strode onto the afterdeck. Once there, he immediately froze for effect, feigning surprise at seeing Salo Montero.

"Hello, Rick," Montero said acidly as he turned toward Harris.

"Why, why..." Harris forced a stunned stammer. "What are you doing here, Salo?"

"Unexpected, huh?"

"I'll say. I certainly—"

"Rick," Segundo interrupted, "I would like you to meet my friend, General Carlo Cardella, from Brazil."

They shook hands and exchanged brief pleasantries.

The general said, "Ramon has told me that you are an excellent aircraft salesman."

"Why thank you, General Cardella," Rick replied with a respectful smile. "I work hard at it, and sometimes good fortune smiles upon me."

"Orlando, Orlando..." Segundo called for his first mate who promptly came out from the salon and onto the afterdeck. Ramon was about to request some cold beers, but after a second of thought, he changed his mind. "Beer, Mr. Harris? No, I think not. Given the circumstances, I believe beer would certainly be inappropriate." He paused, briefly making eye contact with Salo Montero. "But Rick, first let me ask you this: Do you have an announcement to make today?"

"Oh yes, yes I certainly do." Harris placed his briefcase and the cowbell down onto the table. He grinned. "Gentlemen, I have an announcement that, depending upon who you are, will either be delightful or—"

"Then, champagne it will be," Segundo said, confident in Rick's upcoming proclamation. "Orlando, bring us two bottles of our finest."

"But don't you want to hear my announcement first?" Harris asked.

"No, no," a smug Segundo responded, "we will toast you as you make your announcement. I know what is best, young man."

"Fine, then." Rick let Segundo remain smug. The scene was evolving just as Rick had hoped it would. "Anyway, I'm pleased Salo Montero is here for what I have to say." He glanced toward the general. "And of course, having a high ranking representative from the Brazilian government on hand is equally opportune."

"Yes, indeed," Segundo added, "today will be an important day in the history of RioAero. Many people have spent much time and effort to arrive at this juncture."

Still playing mister innocence, Rick contrasted General Cardella and Ramon Segundo's relaxed good spirits with Salo Montero's tense brink of despair countenance. *"Tudo bom?"* Rick continued his charade with Montero who was now meekly standing behind his chair at the table.

Montero ignored the question as he avoided eye contact with Rick.

Harris redirected his attention to the general. "So, General Cardella, will you be visiting with us in Fort Lauderdale for a few days?"

"Unfortunately, not," Cardella said affably, "I must depart for Rio later this evening. There are many details involving RioAero that require my attention."

"That is regrettable," Harris said. "I would have hoped you could have spent the night and then taken a tour of our new facility at the airport."

"Yes, that would have been nice. Dan Cole offered me a tour as well. He too was disappointed when I had to decline his invitation."

"So, Dan Cole, is he here too on *LA BASA?*"

"Why yes," Segundo answered for the general, "since he is part of the new RioAero team, it was important for him to be here." He turned to the salon, glimpsed the silhouette of Cole lurking just inside the doorway, and shouted out, "Dan, join us, please."

Dan Cole, very much aware of Rick's presence, begrudgingly drifted out of the salon and onto the afterdeck. He was followed by Major Alverez, who carried a tray of glasses, and Orlando, who was clutching two bottles of chilled Dom Perignon.

"Dan, Dan," Rick said with a grin as he approached Cole and extended his hand, "I sort of expected you to be here."

"Yes," was the only word Cole uttered. He perfunctorily shook Rick's offered hand.

The slight whooshing kiss of a sound made as Orlando expertly opened each bottle was almost indiscernible. The long-stemmed narrow flutes were filled halfway, and everyone on the afterdeck was handed a glass of bubbly.

Ramon Segundo took center stage. "Gentlemen, I will propose a toast, but first, Rick Harris has an announcement to make." He turned to Harris and said, "Rick."

"Thank you, Ramon," Rick commenced. "Although I'm generally a long-winded type of guy, I'll try to keep this announcement as brief as I possibly can." He paused temporarily, quickly gathering his thoughts for what he knew would be one dramatic announcement. His performance was going well, so far.

"All of us here today are somehow involved with RioAero, a company that because of Salo Montero came from nowhere to become what it is today. As you know, I am very new to this company, being in my position for just one short month. As you may not know, I elected to join this company due to my respect for Salo Montero and the fantastic aircraft he and his engineers have developed—the WindStar."

Ramon Segundo audibly cleared his throat. What Rick Harris was saying was beginning to unnerve him. He shot Rick a stern glance.

Harris nodded conciliatorily to Segundo and continued on, "But during the past couple of days, things have changed. A series of seemingly inexplicable problems occurring to the WindStar have caused some to question its integrity...its airworthiness. These questions can only further worsen the disastrous sales record the

WindStar has experienced over the past several months. And, compounding matters even more is the fact that RioAero can no longer tout Highland Airlines as its North American launch customer. So, gentlemen, things look bleak—very bleak—for RioAero."

Segundo, now regaining his confidence, whispered something to Cardella. The general smiled, and then almost laughed.

"But remember, gentlemen, it always seems darkest before the end of a storm, and now that storm has passed for RioAero. So, I am here today to make an announcement, an announcement that will affect RioAero. An announcement that, for better or worse, will affect each and every one of us here today." Rick opened the briefcase he had placed onto the table and pulled out a manila file folder. He handed the folder to General Cardella, and said, "General, as a trusted representative of the Republic of Brazil, I give you this document to present to your president and his ministers."

The general was caught off-guard, initially not knowing exactly what Rick had handed to him nor why. The moment was at hand for everything to be revealed.

"Gentlemen," Rick raised his voice, "I am pleased to announce that RioAero has just consummated an aircraft sale for forty WindStars with eighty options. Deliveries will begin in thirty days. The customer has pledged a deposit in the amount of four million dollars. Now for your toast, Mr. Segundo." Rick hoisted his glass into the air.

Rick's words met slack-jawed wide-eyed stares from everyone except Salo Montero who tried, but could not stifle his exclamation of joy.

The stunned pause was broken when an enraged general shouted out, "What the hell is this shit? Segundo, what the hell is going on here?"

Salo spoke up first, "It is simple, Cardella. The last thing you thought could happen, actually happened." He paused staring the general directly in the eye. "Now, see if your minister friends in Brasilia think it is such a good idea to essentially give the WindStar away to BASA and turn the country's only airframe manufacturer into a lowly subcontractor."

"Screw you, Montero," the general bellowed. He grabbed the pages from the file folder angrily tearing those pages in half and in half again, then letting the pieces flutter to the deck. "This is what I think of your goddamn announcement, Harris."

Rick raised the palms of his hands into the air. "Fine with me, general, make the paper into confetti. The agreement is still an agreement; the paper upon which it was written is just the formality. That's Business Law 101, in case you didn't know."

"Go to hell, Harris," the general scoffed. "This agreement means nothing."

Segundo immediately said, "Rick, you disappoint me, I thought we had a deal."

"No, Ramon, we had an understanding, a tentative agreement. I said I'd give you my firm decision today after I slept on it. And, I have. Since saying I might consider joining you and BASA yesterday afternoon, I learned it was you, and not RioAero, who misled me. So, now you have my firm decision. I elect not to accept your offer to join BASA."

Cardella took a step back toward the right edge of the table and said to Rick, "You are making a big mistake by siding with Montero and not joining BASA."

"Mistake? No, general, I am not the one making a mistake, you are siding with the ones making mistakes."

"I do not make mistakes," the general shot back. "I will still accomplish my mission, with or without you."

"You will accomplish nothing, general," a tenacious Rick Harris took issue. "And, you have made more mistakes in the past few days than I have made during my entire life."

"Young man," the general warned, "you should listen to Segundo, you do not know what you are getting yourself into."

"Oh, I know exactly what I've gotten myself into," Rick affirmed. "It's you, general, who don't know what you've gotten yourself into." He glanced over to Segundo who was zeroed in on their conversation. "And that goes double for you, Ramon."

Segundo recoiled. He stammered a few unintelligible words.

Cardella fumed, "You insolent bastard. You goddamn insolent bastard." He gave a quick nod to his attaché who stepped from behind, reached out with his right hand, and firmly grasped the back of Rick's neck.

Harris felt the major's grip crushing down. The pressure that was applied made Rick wince. The pain was sudden and searing. He flexed his knees, half turning, trying to dislodge the major's grasp, but to no avail.

Cardella cocked his head to the right. The major immediately released his hold and backed away.

Segundo quickly interceded. "Rick," he said, "you do not know what you are up against. I strongly suggest that you reconsider your position and go along with our program." He paused, watching Rick rub his neck and roll his head from side to side assessing for possible damage. "Rick, what I am suggesting is in your best interests…trust me."

Harris turned and walked to the left side of the table. He wanted to be sure he had a total view of his surroundings, and that included Major Alverez and Orlando. He glanced toward the pier as a possible exit for escape. He was instinctively programming himself for a jump to safety in the very likely event another forceful move were to be made against him. In the near distance, behind and to the left of *LA BASA*, he glimpsed Tommy Maxwell who was crouching like a tiger ready to spring into action from the bow of the Scarab. Somewhat more reassured in his current position, but significantly angered at both Segundo and the general, Rick lashed out: "Trust you, Ramon?" His words dripped fire. "Hell, I'd trust a lowly pit viper that hadn't had a meal in six months before I'd trust you. But Cardella is worse." He glared at the general, still keenly aware of the major and Orlando out of the corner of his eye. "Not only does General Carlo Cardella have no principles, he is also selling his country down the river for personal gain."

"Mr. Harris, this is your last—" the general began his response with ultimatum in his voice.

"No, General Cardella," Rick brashly said, "you're finished. I'm not going to let you and Segundo get away with what you're planning."

The general raised his hand to stop Major Alverez who had already taken two steps forward and was about to once again collar Rick Harris. Cardella's questions came rapid-fire at Rick. "What the hell are you talking about? What do you mean? Get away with what?"

Rick laughed boldly. "You know what the hell I mean. You know exactly what the hell I mean."

"Major—" Cardella was about to have his attaché take decisive control of Harris.

"No, no, major..." Rick quickly turned toward Alverez. "The general will want to hear what I've got to say before you strong-arm me again."

The general shrugged and motioned his attaché to back off, at least for now.

"I certainly have to hand it to you and Ramon," Rick said, moving into deeper water. "You two have taken much time and effort to plot and implement your sabotage against RioAero and the WindStar."

"Sabotage?" the general spoke with rehearsed disbelief. "Ramon and I? That is ludicrous."

Rick Harris grinned. "Clever—yes; shrewd—that too; but ludicrous—no." Rick was about to throw everything he knew back into their faces. It was a high-risk gamble, but he felt he had to take it. When put under enough pressure, he sensed his adversaries would snap—do something irrational; something they would later regret. At least, that was what Rick Harris hoped.

The major stared at Harris like an animal posturing to attack. Rick's words were far from kind; but his words would grow worse.

Rick continued, "You guys just could not wait." He sadly shook his head. "RioAero was so close to being comatose, but your combined greed got in the way. So, you had to act, and act you did. Having BASA use laser technology that it stole from Airbus to fatigue prop shafts..." Rick shook his head. "Having Dan Cole set up the aircraft's gear to collapse on our very own ramp and then send photos off to the media..." Rick shook his head. "Having your Colombian friends try to shoot down a WindStar with air-to-air missiles..." Rick shook his head. "Having the factory's R&D hangar blow sky high so you, general, and your CIE goons could frame Salo Montero..." Rick shook his head. "Goddamn, guys, did you really think you'd get away with it?"

The general and Segundo were totally caught off-guard with Rick's fusillade of revelations. Dumbfounded, they uncertainly regarded each other with suspicious eyes, remaining frozen in time just long enough for Rick to move a few steps forward, reach under the table, and remove the listening device he had planted the day before during his initial meeting with Segundo.

Ramon Segundo's eyes followed Rick's movements and then focused upon the small black device Rick casually held up for all to see. "What the hell is that, Harris?"

"It's a listening device I planted when I was here the other day." He paused, then forcefully underlined the implications. "So, gentlemen, everything you've said—everything—has been overheard."

"Shit," Segundo groaned.

"But that's just part of it," Rick added. "You see, I went one step further. Every word has also been recorded on tape."

"Tape..." Cardella scoffed. "You are bluffing, Harris."

"I don't bluff," Rick said calmly. He placed the bug down on the far side of the table, just out of everyone's reach. Then, he spoke in a normal tone as he directed his eyes to the device. "Hello out there, guys. Please standby."

"Who the hell are you talking to?" the general demanded.

Rick shifted his gaze to Cardella, then to Segundo. "This place is surrounded by Feds," he lied, suddenly realizing that he was at a complete disadvantage with all he had disclosed, especially with the major and Orlando breathing down his neck. "Agent Maxwell," he said looking in the distance to his left, "wave a hello to our resourceful saboteurs." Rick pointed to the black Scarab and Tommy Maxwell who haltingly stood up and waved back.

Earlier, in his sweeping search for escape routes, Rick had noticed a large white sportfisherman lazily idling just off the wide main channel of the Intracoastal. He had recognized the orange with black parallelogram pennant flying from its tuna tower. It was Santelli and partners. Rick pointed to the sportfisherman and said, "Out there on that boat, we have half a dozen special agents." He pumped his fist into the air three times. The sportfisherman blasted its horn thrice.

Rick waved the Hatteras on in toward *LA BASA*. Then, he turned and spoke what would be his final words to Cardella and Segundo. "Gentlemen, I'd say the jig is up. You came close, but in this business, close doesn't cut it."

SIXTY-NINE

Escape from Bahia Mar Marina

O n board the Hatteras, Sammy Santelli advanced the throttles; the sportfisherman's twin Detroit Diesel engines roared to life. A modest 850 hp slowly overcame the inertia of the once stationary, massive boat as its props churned below. Gracefully easing up out of the water from dead-start acceleration, the 55,000-pound boat began a wide sweeping turn toward *LA BASA*, steadily gaining speed all the time.

Dan Cole was first to react. He eased himself into the shadows of the salon and scurried away like a frightened cat.

Segundo hurriedly made his way back behind the table on the afterdeck. He snatched the large briefcase that the general had earlier presented to him, and then dashed toward the stern stairway.

A visibly shaken general slammed his fist down onto the table. He saw his plan unraveling before his very eyes. "Goddamn you, Harris." He took three steps to the stern sea rail of the yacht. "Major," he shouted, "take care of this sonovabitch, then we are out of here."

Major Alverez cast a sinister smile toward Rick, but then briefly refocused upon the route Segundo and the general were using in order to follow and join them. The major's eyes watched the general tread behind Segundo down the integrated staircase at the stern that led to the lower swim platform and the moored Cigarette. This was all the advantage Rick Harris needed. Turning away from the major, he feigned an explosive sneeze, grabbed his cowbell from the tabletop, and, with all the strength he could muster, pivoted to swiftly slam it into the advancing major's forehead. A muted clanging din rang out, then a dull thud. The general's attaché slumped onto the table, writhing, grimacing in pain, but nonetheless resolutely regathering himself.

A short distance away, Tommy Maxwell was very much aware of the melee that had just begun aboard *LA BASA*. He tore off his headset and hollered out to Monica, "Crank up the Scarab and bring her around." He leapt off its forward deck onto the marina's catwalk below and sprinted toward the yacht.

Simultaneously, the Cigarette's first engine churned over with a resonating rumble, followed by its second engine's start. Segundo left the controls, which he turned over to Cardella, and placed the large briefcase that he had cradled in his arms into an empty stowage locker to the port side of the aft engine compartment. He hastily began casting off lines and fenders. Above the engines' idling growl, he yelled to Cardella, "Have the major bring Montero."

The general shouted out a few words up the staircase to his attaché who had not yet made his way down to the Cigarette.

The now regrouped major promptly acknowledged his orders, shifted his attention from Rick who had been snared by Orlando, and quickly spotted Salo Montero trying to dash past into the salon. He grabbed Montero by the right wrist, spun him around into a hammerlock, throwing him facedown onto the massive teakwood table. "You come with me," the major commanded through clenched teeth, "or I kill you now."

Salo struggled in vain to escape from the major's commanding hold.

The major briefly laughed, and then intensified his pressure down upon Salo's back. He was forcefully making his point known. With a quick jerk, he ripped the arm further up Montero's back. Salo felt a sharp intense pain, then a penetrating pop as his shoulder dislocated. Alverez breathed hotly on Salo's neck. Blood dripped down onto the side of Salo's face from the gash on the major's forehead. Alverez repeated his command one final time. There was no choice but for Montero to comply.

The major narrowed his eyes to reacquire Rick's whereabouts. The ever so dutiful attaché wanted to be sure that all of the general's commands were being executed. What he saw brought on a self-satisfying grunt. He pushed Montero toward the staircase at the stern without a backwards glance.

To the port side of the afterdeck, Rick Harris struggled with Segundo's burly first mate who had restrained him from behind just after Harris had slammed the cowbell into the major's forehead. With both of Rick's arms trapped under a bear hug, Orlando ratcheted up his purchase, momentarily lifting Rick off of the deck. The bloodied cowbell fell clangorously down onto the deck as Rick violently thrashed to no avail.

Harris felt his chest begin to cavitate under the immense pressure. He gasped for air. His field of vision narrowed, graying. His arms went limp.

The last sound Rick heard was a cracking, splintering sound.

Suddenly, he and Orlando were jolted forward and to the side before both collapsed down onto the deck.

Rick rolled himself free from the now loose limbs of the hulk of a man who had nearly crushed his ribs. He looked up, glimpsing the silhouette of a tall, thin, black man holding the splintered handle of a wooden baseball bat.

"You okay?" a concerned Tommy Maxwell asked. It was with full force that Maxwell had swung the bat, squarely connecting with Orlando's lower back, effectively striking the blow that saved Rick Harris.

Rick took in a gasp of air. Though his chest throbbed with pain, he struggled to his feet. He stumbled, momentarily, and then said, "Just bruised, I think."

"Well, you almost bought the farm, my friend," Tommy said.

A stern and below the afterdeck on the swim platform, the major and Salo Montero had just boarded the Cigarette, its engines thumping melodically, ready to rocket its passengers away from the marina. Segundo yelled to the major, "Where is Orlando?"

With an evil grin, the major returned, "Taking care of business." He pushed Salo down onto the deck and against the portside of the Cigarette.

Segundo grimly nodded and scanned for the position of the sportfisherman.

Less than a mile dead ahead, Sammy Santelli's boat was rapidly closing in at just under thirty miles per hour.

The general's eyes followed Segundo's glance, and the general barked out, "We must go, Orlando or not."

Segundo shrugged, then confidently grinned as he threw off the last line. "HIT IT," he yelled out to the general, who advanced the throttles full forward. There was a momentary lag as the pair of 475 hp engines transferred power to the props.

As the fleeing men braced for the powerful thrust forward, the unimaginable occurred.

An explosive thud, immediately followed by a smashing, crashing, bone-chilling sound. The fiberglass transom buckled under the pressure.

The Cigarette had forcefully slammed backwards into one of the marina's massive concrete pilings.

"Goddamn, Cardella," an enraged Segundo shouted out, picking himself up off of the boat's deck. The major had been knocked to his knees; Salo had been slammed into the aft side of the boat.

The bewildered general had already retarded the throttles.

Segundo rushed forward and took command of the Cigarette. In the heat of the moment, the general had blindly added power at Segundo's command. The general overlooked that the engine transmissions had been left in reverse from when the boat had been positioned and docked the previous day.

Across a quickly narrowing expanse of waterway, Santelli's rock-solid sportfisherman loomed large, now having closed to less than half a mile. A frothy wake spewed out nearly one hundred feet to either side of its hull.

Segundo slammed the shifters through neutral to full forward positions—a heavy metal-to-metal clunk verified the Borg-Warner transmissions were properly engaged. As he aggressively advanced the throttles, the Cigarette's engines once again sprang to life with its KELSO Performance exhaust system bellowing a tribute to an awesome escalation of power. The combined 950 hp was effectively channeled through a 1.5:1 reduction gear to a pair of 17x28 Alpha-3S stainless steel racing props. The initial generation of thrust from the twin props plunged the stern of the 10,000-pound boat downward into the water.

Now that the propellers were spooling up in the proper direction, the Cigarette sprang forward, steadily gaining speed. With its bow quickly dropping, time to plane would be under five seconds. Acceleration would then be rapid.

Segundo could not have cared less about the tethered buoy to his right identifying the marina's no-wake zone. His total focus was upon the intimidating, fast-approaching Hatteras. He knew it would be close, yet his options were few. He instinctively reacted by veering the Cigarette to the left—toward Port Everglades and his escape to the open sea.

But Santelli had anticipated that very move and swung his sportfisherman to parry in concert.

With the distance between the two boats rapidly closing, and a huge rusted-out dredging barge moored directly in his path, Segundo's pulse quickened. Doubt entered his mind. In a drastic split-second change in plan, he immediately arced the Cigarette instead to the right. In this direction, he calculated there would be greater margin for error.

He confidently leaned into the turn as the Cigarette's deep-V hull sliced through the water with very little sideslip, even at its current speed of fifty miles per hour. But that greater margin for error Segundo had hoped to achieve swiftly vanished. He had underestimated the speed of the oncoming Hatteras. Within a blink of the eye, all he could see was a massive wall of glistening white fiberglass. For a split second, time stood still—all seemed lost. There was nowhere to go.

Segundo's reaction was out of sheer desperation. With engines growling under wide-open throttle (WOT), he wheeled in more rudder, canting the offshore racer dangerously to its side, aiming to narrowly miss the Hatteras' menacing bow. It would not be enough.

Almost instantly, the Cigarette painfully ricocheted off the sloping side of the Hatteras. The smaller craft's hull emitted an anguished groan. The impact had been severe. Segundo felt his boat being forced to the point of capsizing. A torrent of water rushed over its starboard gunwale.

Ramon Segundo tightened his grip on the steering wheel. He used his legs to press his body back into the form-fitting stand-up racing bolster. His heart pounded. His eyes widened. He knew there was little he could do to compensate for the Cigarette's tenuous position. Miraculously, though, the offshore racer's powerful engines missed not a stroke, accelerating the boat forward and into the sportfisherman's churning wake.

Perilously leaning to its side with its bow angled up as it entered the turbulent coiling mass of water, the Cigarette was momentarily thrust upward and into the air. Its stern and fixed-shaft drives remaining only partially submerged; its propellers fighting to grip back deeply into the liquid blue medium they knew so well. Then, BLOWOUT.

The rpm of the twin 475 hp engines streaked upwards, redlining. The ratio of air to water around the props had instantly climbed so high that only air—not water—was available. With no water to grab onto, the props lost their bite. Instantaneously, the steering loosened; the Cigarette angled further to the right. Total disaster was certain.

The general yelled out a string of unintelligible Portuguese words.

Major Alverez clutched the injured Salo Montero between his legs and, using both hands, locked on to a set of portside stainless steel grab handles with a grip so strong only death could break.

Segundo, oblivious to the plight of his passengers, reacted to the perilous situation by immediately jerking the throttles back to idle. The Cigarette leaned to the left, though slightly. Now gliding toward the turbid center of the Hatteras' wake, the Cigarette's hull regained positive water contact. With a battering, bouncing slam, the boat chine-walked away from the edge of doom under Segundo's guidance and a perfectly timed advance of the throttles.

SEVENTY

The Chase Begins

Still at the marina, Rick Harris and Tommy Maxwell impatiently waited on the lower stern platform of *LA BASA* for an inexperienced Monica to carefully motor the black Scarab along side. Tommy hurdled aboard the boat. Rick Harris followed with his briefcase in one hand and lucky cowbell in the other. Maxwell immediately took over the helm, advanced the power to WOT, and the pursuit began.

"Where are they headed?" Maxwell shouted to Rick over the Scarab's thundering engine roar.

"Anywhere away from us."

"No, seriously."

"Not sure. Probably Bimini; maybe Andros."

Though the Cigarette had almost a forty-five second advantage, Tommy Maxwell still had it in sight. He commented, "Their boat sure took one hell of a pounding back there at the marina. I'm amazed it's still in one piece."

"Yeah, those Cigarettes are truly amazing. They're built to take a pounding, but what that one went through should certainly have caused some structural damage."

"Hell, I'm sure they don't give a damn about any damage so long as they can get to wherever they're going."

"Probably so," Rick admitted, and then added, "I just hope it is enough to slow them down. They're much faster than us, you know."

Tommy nodded in grim agreement.

SEVENTY-ONE

The Intracoastal

Segundo aggressively weaved the Cigarette through the late Sunday afternoon Intracoastal Waterway traffic, which at this point, seemed rather light. A mile farther up the waterway, just beyond the marina at Pier Sixty-Six, the long staccato ring of a bell indicated the impending opening of the Seventeenth Street causeway drawbridge. There would certainly be a bottleneck of marine traffic waiting to funnel up the Intracoastal from the south, as well as out to sea from the north, through the narrow no-wake zone below the causeway. The congested causeway area was the very place Segundo was heading.

In the distance: towers and outriggers of sportfishermen dotted the waterway; mastheads of daysailers and ketches bobbed near the channel; four huge motor yachts stood at idle; dozens of smaller power boats slowly meandered along. All were eager to pass under the causeway. Yet, the canary yellow Cigarette streaked onward with single-minded reckless abandon.

The general looked abaft toward Salo Montero, whose face was contorted in pain from both the dislocated shoulder and the battering his body had taken just moments ago during the life-risking escape from the marina. "Take him below," Cardella shouted to his attaché, who had a firm purchase on Montero's waistband, "and find some damn life jackets for all of us." Then directing his attention to Ramon Segundo, he said, "When we clear the inlet, I will radio AeroMech on a private frequency and have them coordinate an aircraft for us on Bimini. In a few hours we will be in Medellín and have safe refuge. There, we will plan our next move." He paused, craning his neck aft, glimpsing the Scarab a mile behind. "Rick Harris is a dead man, I guarantee it. Let his people try to catch us. It is a futile chase." He gnashed his teeth, donned one of the offshore Lifeline jackets the major had retrieved from below, and again scowled back at the black boat.

Segundo nodded, his eyes intently focused upon the clutter of boats below the causeway. "It will be tight up ahead," he said, subconsciously using his legs to temporarily press himself back into the stand-up racing bolster. He retarded the throttles slightly, slowing the Cigarette to fifty miles per hour. He knew that passing through the boat traffic and under the causeway at this hour would be like threading a needle in the darkness of night; moreover, he would only have one shot at doing so.

Segundo veered the Cigarette to the right, paralleling the seawall just before the new Marriott resort. His intent was to stay as far away from channel traffic as possible—at least for now—at least until he had to face it.

A Donzi Sweet-16 appeared out of nowhere, directly in their path.

"Watch OUT!" Cardella shouted wildly, pointing to the small boat.

It was too late. The Donzi's occupants dove from their boat to safety. The Cigarette's bow caromed off the stern of the tiny craft, destroying the Donzi's transom.

"Damn!" Ramon Segundo grimaced. He swerved the Cigarette to the left, just missing making contact with a near-by Boston Whaler.

Traffic was getting worse. Idling and slow-moving boats appeared everywhere—the Intracoastal almost seemed like a marina.

"Goddamn, Ramon, slow the hell down," the general ordered. "If you trash this boat, we are dead meat."

Segundo knew Cardella was right. He eased the power further back. The engines quieted, thumping a growl-like purr. Down to twenty-five miles per hour, he felt the rudders become sluggish—the heavy Cigarette was almost off plane.

Segundo S-turned the Cigarette, first around a Zodiac loaded with scuba divers and their equipment, then around an older Chris-Craft fisherman. Each time the boat responded slowly, almost begrudgingly answering to turns of the wheel.

The general focused ahead to where the Intracoastal further narrowed at the causeway. He zeroed in on the heavy immovable support structure that took up vast amounts of precious marine real estate he wished instead was available for maneuvering. He noticed a thick wet barnacle and algae coating on abutments and pillars that climbed some three feet above the water. He saw the swirling flood current forcefully slapping up against the causeway superstructure. "Low Tide," he called out to Segundo. It meant that only the narrow center channel could assure safe passage.

Segundo was all lined up to make his run under the open causeway bridge and into Port Everglades when a wide Bertram cruiser blasted its horn and entered the channel. Segundo had little choice but to abort. Now, he had to make a wide three-sixty to his right and weave through more wake-idle traffic.

As the Bertram passed the causeway's northern-most pilings, impatience emboldened Segundo to go to WOT and make his move to sprint through the narrow passage. The Cigarette's engines trumpeted their brute power. Its speed escalated. Its wake widened. The only obstacle now between Segundo and Port Everglades was a lumbering old fishing trawler that obstinately crowded the channel, yet taking up less water than the previous cruiser.

Segundo mentally calculated there would be enough daylight for the Cigarette to slip past the trawler. He had been wrong before when he misjudged the sportfisherman at the marina. This time he felt confident. The Cigarette leapt forward. Segundo had committed himself. There was no turning back.

The trawler seemed motionless—slowly bobbing and weaving beneath the causeway as it lazily chugged northward. Once again Segundo's body tensed. His fingers clutched the steering wheel, tightly. He flexed his legs, pressing himself deeply into the snug racing bolster.

Seconds later, the Cigarette was directly within the causeway's swirling eddying currents. The water formed fists that smashed against the surrounding superstructure's pilings. Massive abutments abruptly shrouded the light of day. The slovenly trawler loomed larger than life.

"Oh...oh...oh—" a suddenly unsure Segundo stammered.

At the Cigarette's speed, there was no time to allow for hesitation or reconsideration. It had been a frantic gamble, and time seemed to stop as the unavoidable result played itself out.

Zipping past the trawler like a greased pig, the Cigarette continued on to zig-zag its way through a motley assemblage of marine traffic on the southern side of the causeway and rocket on into the expanses of Port Everglades.

"Ha-Haaa..." Segundo exclaimed in relief. He beamed. The rest of the trip would be a cakewalk, he thought. He steered to the left for the Port Everglades inlet and the open sea.

The Cigarette hit seventy miles per hour...then eighty...ninety... The noise was deafening—Segundo had switched to bypass the mufflers to attain extra power and speed. The wind whipped tears from the corners of his eyes that then streamed obliviously down and back along his cheeks.

Cardella shot a fleeting glance aft. No sign of the black Scarab. He motioned to Segundo with a palm down signal that it was safe to drop to a somewhat lower cruising speed.

Segundo obligingly eased the power back slightly from WOT, and then trimmed out the Cigarette to optimize the hull's wetted area. Riding on top of the wave it created, the offshore racer effectively used hydrodynamic lift to smoothly skim across the occasional chop created by other marine traffic. "Now," Segundo said to the general, "we are in for a pleasant trip—the seas should be flat. We should hit Bimini in about forty minutes and be at the airport within another fifteen."

SEVENTY-TWO

The Gulf Stream

Two miles behind the Cigarette, the black Scarab blended in with the deep blue waters and became virtually undetectable. "You still got them in sight?" Rick shouted to Tommy.

Maxwell grinned. "Out there at eleven o'clock, just exiting the inlet. Canary yellow makes them easy to spot."

"Can we overtake them?"

"HA, I doubt if we can even keep up with them."

"Damn," was Rick's singular, disconsolate response.

Tommy Maxwell noticed it first. "Oh, shit," he moaned.

"What is it?" Rick asked.

"Fuel," Tommy shouted out in dismay, disgusted, shaking his head. "We've only got quarter tanks…not enough to get us to Bimini, let alone get back." He paused, bitterly angry with himself. "I never told Anderson's Marina to fill up the Scarab—never thought we'd get into an offshore pursuit like this."

Rick Harris went silent. The thought of Segundo and Cardella escaping was worse than upsetting. Segundo easily could have the connections to take temporary refuge on the island, perhaps at the very private, old Rockwell estate at Paradise Point on North Bimini. Then again, he simply could arrange to fly out of the airport on South Bimini to points unknown. Rick could not let that happen, especially not with Salo's abduction. Having limited fuel aboard the Scarab, the escape of the Cigarette and its passengers seemed imminent. There was nothing that could be done.

"We can follow them for another twenty minutes or so before we have to turn back," Maxwell dejectedly announced.

Rick's mind raced in every direction. He had to come up with a solution to the problem. He glanced abaft at Monica. Her eyes squinted through the oncoming wind that peppered her face. Her long dark hair wildly streamed in the turbulent air. She had herself securely anchored into one of the bolstered seats just forward of the engine compartment. Rick's focus deflected away from Monica and down onto the deck. He smiled. "Keep on truckin'," he said to Maxwell, "I have a plan."

"It had better be a good one," Tommy commented, all the while focused straight ahead, not letting the Cigarette out of his sight.

Harris quickly moved abaft to a seat next to Monica. "Having fun yet," he shouted over the engine noise.

She drilled him with her eyes.

Rick reached down onto the deck to his left and retrieved his briefcase.

"Looking for your lucky cowbell?" she shouted crossly.

"Nah, not right now," Rick responded, "but I could really use your help."

"How so?"

Rick cocked his head forward, toward the helm. "Go up front and contact the Coast Guard." He paused, glancing toward her. "They monitor Channel 16. Be sure that channel is what is set into the radio. Tell them there's a high profile kidnapping in progress. Give them a description of the Cigarette, its location, heading, and speed. My guess is that the Cigarette's destination is Bimini. See if the Coast Guard has a cutter in the area."

"Will do." Monica cautiously made her way forward as the Scarab skimmed across the water at just under eighty miles per hour.

Rick opened his briefcase, sorting through its contents until grasping hold of what he had been searching for. "This better work," he said aloud to himself. "This damn well better work."

Up front at the helm, he could see Monica speaking into the microphone Tommy had handed to her. As she completed her final transmission, Rick made his way forward. "Any luck?" he asked.

"Yes and no," she answered. "The Coast Guard has no patrol boats in our area, but an 82-foot Point-class cutter is being dispatched out of Port of Miami. They've requested we keep our position updated with them via radio contact."

"Thanks, Monica," Rick said. "Even though that cutter is fairly slow, it's reassuring to have the Coast Guard in the wings."

"So, I guess it's up to us to stop them," she said.

Rick nodded.

Monica returned to her seat abaft.

"Okay, Mr. Harris," Maxwell began, "how's that plan of yours coming?"

Rick shrugged. "I guess we'll know in a few minutes." He flipped on the switch to the dual-band Alinco transceiver he had retrieved from his briefcase. He reset the frequency to match that of the transceiver he had given to Franco Rameros earlier that afternoon. "Here goes nothing," he said to Tommy Maxwell, keying and releasing the mic...*bud-a-leep.*

SEVENTY-THREE

Pasador Ranch

"Aah, now I am relaxed, totally relaxed." Franco Rameros had just finished off his third beer of the afternoon. He crushed the aluminum can in half between the palm and fingers of his left hand and then hooked it over his head toward the green Rubbermaid trash bucket near the far end of the picnic table. It glanced off the rim and fell to the ground. "Well, Bob, I am certainly glad I am not flying this afternoon," he said to Waterman, who was intently scribbling words into his spiral notebook.

"Huh?" Waterman acknowledged hearing his name, but was totally oblivious as to what Rameros had just said. "Oh, sorry," he added apologetically, "perhaps I've been concentrating too heavily on entering my notes."

"No issue, Bob," Rameros said as he got up from the picnic table and ambled over to the bucket. "I like a man who takes his work seriously." He picked up the flattened beer can, flipping it into the trash bucket. "Too many people try to cut corners these days with everything they do."

"Yeah, I know what you mean Franco. I see it all the time in the newspaper business, but the *Sun-Sentinel* is different. We try harder." He watched Rameros disappear behind the huge banyan tree.

A long minute later, Rameros returned. "Now that's better," he said matter-of-factly. "Beer has diuretic properties, you know."

Bob Waterman grinned. He had been in Franco's situation before.

"So," Rameros said reseating himself across from Waterman at the table, "any further questions, Bob? Anything else you'd like to know about the WindStar or RioAero?"

"Thanks for asking," Waterman said closing his notebook and placing it into his small leather satchel, "but I think I've got all the material I need. In fact, I've probably got more than I need." He paused. "Newspapers like pith. As my editor says: 'Just the facts, Bob. Your opinion ain't news.'"

Rameros laughed. "I guess that's what news editors are supposed to say. Anyway, for just the facts, be sure to ask Rick for a press kit. It will give you just that. Do use it as the final word. My memory may not always be as accurate as I would like."

"Thanks, Franco," Waterman said appreciatively. "Rick was kind enough to have already provided me with a press kit while you and his customers were putting the WindStar through its paces."

"Good." Rameros thought for a moment and then switched gears. "By the way, how did you come to know Harris, and what kind of story are you working on?"

Waterman smiled, briefly remembering the first time he met Rick Harris at the Doral. "Rick and I met at a charity golf tournament that my paper began sponsoring a few years ago. Since then, he's sort of become my unofficial aviation consultant. So, when I was doing some follow up work on a WindStar incident that came over the wire service, I gave him a phone call. I thought he was still with Fairchild." He shook his head and laughed twice. "I quickly learned he had recently joined RioAero. At any rate, Rick pleaded with me to give him the opportunity to present the WindStar as a safe and reliable aircraft that had been rigorously tested. He wanted me to present the other side of the story—to reveal there's more to the WindStar than a bunch of crazy incidents that made the headlines during the past two days. So, here I am."

"Interesting, but do you think your paper will run the story?"

"Well," Waterman said, hesitating with a shrug, "I'm not sure. What I now have seems more like an advertisement for the aircraft. I guess that's a compliment, but unfortunately there's really no headline news in it. As my editor would put it: There's no fire to inspire."

"Hmmm..." Rameros groaned. Then trying to be helpful, he said, "I really cannot speak without Rick's nod, you know this is his territory, but..." he paused, then said it anyway, "there just might be more to those WindStar incidents than meets the eye."

"You don't say." Waterman's interest piqued. "Like what?

"I truly cannot go into it," Rameros responded, holding his ground. "Still, when Rick arrives back here, you need to have a chat with him. Maybe he can give you some inside information—you know, some fire to inspire."

A scoop, Waterman thought. "Thanks, Franco, I'll be sure to approach him about it." He paused, momentarily dwelling upon the meeting Rick Harris would now likely be finishing up with Sammy Santelli. "Hey, maybe he will have even made that sale he's gunning for."

"Yeah, that certainly would give you a lead-in for the story."

"It would probably work okay." Waterman's vicarious enthusiasm for Rick's big sale waned. At this moment, he was consumed by Rameros' comment: *There might be more to those incidents than meets the eye.* That would be news—big news.

Just then, interrupting the conversation, both Rameros and Waterman heard a strange sound—an electronic sound: *bud-a-leep.*

Each looked at the other, initially perplexed.

It repeated: *bud-a-leep.*

"The radio," Waterman said, identifying the source of the sound. Someone had keyed a mic to the frequency on the transceiver Rick had left with them.

Rameros curiously eyed the small Alinco transceiver on the far side of the picnic table.

"It could be Rick," Waterman prompted.

"Maybe," Rameros said with a shrug, "let's see if he comes back." He reached over, picked up the transceiver, turned up the volume, and then waited.

Amidst a muffled drone of background noise came Rick's words, "Franco, Franco...you there?" ...*bud-a-leep*.

"Yes, that is Rick alright," Rameros said to Waterman. He moved the transceiver toward his mouth and directed his voice to the tiny built-in microphone at the top of the unit. "Hey there, good buddy, what is your ten-twenty...ten-four, over." ...*bud-a-leep*. He grinned, glanced over to Waterman, and proudly said, "I am a big fan of *Smokey and the Bandit*. I know the lingo."

"That's CB talk." Waterman snickered. "I think what you're now using is very close to a VHF amateur radio rig."

"Whatever," Rameros indifferently said.

"Franco, Franco," Rick's voice came through on the frequency, "I need your help. I've uncovered the cause of the WindStar's problems...the web of sabotage that has been plaguing RioAero. I need your help." ...*bud-a-leep*.

"What's going on? How can I help?" ...*bud-a-leep*.

While Tommy piloted the Scarab out of Port Everglades and into the open sea, Rick quickly brought Franco up to speed on what was happening. As Rick spoke, the larger and more powerful Cigarette continued to pull farther away from the Scarab. Rick knew they would likely lose sight of the boat in a matter of minutes. But there was something that was even more troubling to Rick than losing sight of the Cigarette. It was something even more disturbing than the limited fuel on board the Scarab. Within the next hour, night would be falling over the Caribbean. The Cigarette would essentially disappear into the darkness. And no one could do anything about that.

Rameros said, "I understand the situation. What do you want me to do?" ...*bud-a-leep*.

"Fire up the WindStar. Fly out here and monitor where they're going. I have a Coast Guard cutter on its way up from Miami." ...*bud-a-leep*.

"Consider it done, Rick. I'll be out there within fifteen minutes." ...*bud-a-leep*.

"Wow!" Waterman exclaimed.

"Yeah," Rameros replied without a hint of enthusiasm. He rose from his seat at the table and stuffed the small transceiver into his breast pocket. Franco Rameros did not want to fly. Really. It was not his style to pilot an aircraft after he had one, let alone three beers, even though he had done that very thing many times before during his brash youth. That was a long time ago, a very long time ago. Today, though, there was little choice—he had to fly.

"You'll be taking me with you, right?" Waterman stated more than asked with keen anticipation.

Rameros answered back, matter-of-factly, "Not this time, young man." He turned away from Waterman and began his walk toward the WindStar in the hay barn.

Waterman's heart sank, but the tenacious reporter persisted. He hastily snatched his leather satchel off the table and quickly followed. "Why not?" he called out from behind.

"Might be dangerous out there," Rameros said, looking straight ahead. He quickened his pace and extended his stride. "Remember, the guys in the boat that Rick is chasing are running for their lives."

"Yeah, but I could use the material for the story," Waterman said, struggling to match steps with Rameros.

Rameros smiled, recollecting Waterman's earlier comment. "Bob, remember it was only a few minutes ago when you said you had all the material you needed for the story."

"I said *that*?" he asked in an incredulous tone. He knew he had.

"Absolutely," Rameros said with a quick glance toward Waterman. "In fact, you said you probably had more material than you needed. Now, do you remember?"

"Well, Franco..." Waterman said, then paused, avoiding the question. "What's happening out there on the water is the type of eyewitness fire I really need for my story."

Rameros walked on, expressionless and remaining silent.

"Listen, Franco, listen," Waterman continued, his voice faltering, "you, Rick, RioAero...you need a journalist to capture everything that's happening." He paused, noting Rameros' still expressionless face as they reached the hay barn.

"Not this time, young man," Rameros said for a second time. He stooped down to remove and toss the nose wheel chocks to the side; he verified that the nose wheel steering linkage had been reconnected.

"But..." Waterman knew he was losing the battle. "But I'm sure you could use an extra set of eyes, and maybe an extra set of hands up front in the cockpit. It couldn't hurt."

Rameros' austere features cracked a small smile. He turned and looked the journalist directly in the eye. "You really want this story, huh?"

"More than you could ever imagine, Franco." Sincerity was etched into his every word.

Rameros shook his head, walked away from Waterman toward the WindStar, and opened airstair door. He paused for a moment, then turned back to Waterman and said, "What the hell, Bob, let's fly!"

Inside the cockpit, Franco began rapidly flipping switches like an automaton, being sure that engine inertial separators were in the bypass mode. Within ten seconds, the compressor section of the right engine began rotating. He adjusted his headset and spoke to Waterman through the cockpit intercom: "It will get a bit messy here in about thirty seconds."

A justifiably confused Waterman asked, "What? Why?"

Rameros ignored the questions as he initiated the second engine start and monitored its ITT peak and then fall off. Out of habit, he kicked the rudder to its full left and right stops and then moved the control yoke through its limits to check aileron and elevator freedom of movement. "Here we go, Bob. Close your eyes."

Waterman did not.

Rameros advanced the power levers, obtaining the breakaway thrust needed to move the WindStar from its stationary position on the compressed gravel floor inside the hay barn.

Instantly, the heavy dust and hay wisps that had been littering half an inch deep across the barn floor filled the air—churning, swirling—bringing visibility to zero, much like a lake-effect blizzard on a blustery winter's day near Buffalo, New York. Instantly, the wings of the aircraft disappeared from sight. It was worse than flying under most IFR conditions. Strands of hay stirred up by the props pelted the fuselage.

Rameros immediately released the brakes. He relied upon his HSI for the split second it took to safely maintain direction and exit the hay barn.

"That was really weird," Waterman said through his headset over the cockpit intercom.

"Certainly not good for the aircraft or its engines," Rameros said as he briskly taxied the WindStar for a departure to the north. "We had no time to tow her out properly."

"No damage, right?" a concerned Waterman questioned.

"We will see soon enough."

Rameros advanced the power levers and began his takeoff roll.

SEVENTY-FOUR

On Board the Cigarette

T he wind: a light onshore breeze. The sky: cloudless, interminably blue with a golden orange sun lazily drifting down to the west. The seas: almost like glass—small wavelets with glossy non-breaking crests provided only a slight definition to the surface. The conditions offshore were perfect.

The Cigarette raced on, still at over ninety miles per hour. Its unmuffled engines violating the silence of the tranquil aquamarine Gulf Stream.

A much more relaxed Segundo turned to his left and grinned. "Another twenty minutes and we will be there."

General Carlo Cardella forced a smile as he stared out ahead into the expanses of the open sea. The day had not gone well, and he knew it. The endless months of furtive planning, the intricacies of coordination, and the final implementation of each detail intended to discredit the WindStar and effectively destroy RioAero had come off flawlessly; that is, except for one unanticipated factor—Rick Harris.

The general grimaced, his eyelids briefly fluttered. The sinking, depressing feeling that had overcome him now extended to the very pit of his stomach. He tried to rationalize the blame as Ramon Segundo's. After all, it was on Segundo's yacht that Cardella's entire scheme had begun unraveling. As much as it pained him, he understood that what Rick Harris had accomplished by successfully planting a listening device on *LA BASA* was totally unexpected—it would have foiled anyone.

Now, both Cardella and Segundo had little choice. They, like an aircraft unable to complete a successful landing, were executing a missed approach. The last minute failure to successfully navigate past Rick Harris caused them to abort their mission. They had no alternative but to flee, and then hopefully disappear into the foothills of the Andes. Once there, Cardella felt confident a major benefactor would provide safe haven. Still, the failure was a crushing blow—a blow that would endure for some time to come. However, the escape was not yet assured, there were still many miles to travel: another forty miles to Bimini; nearly fifteen hundred miles to Colombia.

So, the Cigarette raced on.

From below, Major Alverez opened the cabin door. "General Cardella..." he shouted tentatively. Concern was written onto his face. "I think we may have a problem."

The general, immediately finding a lightning rod for his disheartened mindset, glared down at his long-time attaché. "What the hell are you talking about, major?" he barked out in glacial tones. He did not want to consider the possibility of any further complications. The fact that Alverez had even uttered the very word "problem" infuriated him. "We damn well better not have any more problems."

The major visibly cowered in response to Cardella's rebuke. "General," he said with a slight stammer, "you need to come take a look." The fact that the major would persist despite the general's ferocious mood truly meant something was wrong—apparently dreadfully wrong.

Cardella scowled. "If the goddamn problem is Montero, I could not care any less."

"No, no..." the major quickly retorted. He paused, then said the very last words the general would have wanted to hear: "We are taking on water below."

"Shit," Cardella hissed through clenched teeth. That sinking feeling in the pit of his stomach had returned with a vengeance. He closed his eyes tightly and slowly shook his head a half a dozen times. Turning to Segundo, he said, "You heard what the major said. I am going below. This could be a big problem."

Segundo was aghast. He glanced back in the distance past the Cigarette's churning wake. The black Scarab was not in view. Reacting to the situation at hand, he slightly retarded the throttles, slowing the boat down to seventy miles per hour.

Alone at the helm, the formerly relaxed Ramon Segundo agonized. Taking on water below was a grave matter. It was an ominous problem that clearly could worsen—a problem that could thwart their escape. What could have caused it? His mind flashed back to incidents at the marina and on the Intracoastal: the catastrophic slamming of the Cigarette's transom into the marina's massive concrete piling; the harrowing blow to its hull from the Hatteras; crashing off the stern of the small Donzi. Either singly or together, these events could easily have seriously compromised the superstructure of his boat. Then again, perhaps the major had overreacted. Perhaps the unusual attitudes the Cigarette had been put into during the getaway had caused its onboard potable water supply to leak into the cabin, or perhaps the torrent of water that had earlier rushed over its starboard gunwale during the collision with the Hatteras had made its way below. Perhaps...perhaps. It could not be that bad, he thought...or could it? For now, though, he would have to wait for Cardella's assessment.

After a torturous period of time, the general returned to the helm. Only two minutes had elapsed.

"Was the major right?" Segundo impatiently asked, but he hoped the answer would be no.

Cardella scowled. "There is water down there," he said, "no doubt about it." He paused, shooting a glance aft to the horizon. "No sight of the Scarab, huh?"

"No," Segundo said, then quickly returned to the situation at hand. "What did you see below?"

"Well, we tore up the carpet to inspect the inside of the hull." He shrugged. "There are significant cracks in the interior gelcoat. Looks like the structure has been severely compromised…stressed…fatigued. The core, side bulkheads, and stringers are also likely to have problems. It is hard to identify the total extent of the damage. The worst damage is probably in the engine compartment, but at our speed there is no way to check that out."

"How much water are we taking on?"

"Not that much. My feeling is that most of it—perhaps all of it—came aboard when you almost capsized us after hitting the Hatteras."

"Good."

"Not so fast." Cardella's early engineering background gave pause to consider the extent of the damage. "I said the structural integrity was likely compromised by the hell you put this boat through earlier. While the water below is unlikely a significant consideration, there has to be some ply separation, and that could lead to a major fracture."

"What are you getting at?"

"Well, with the calm seas we have today, not much. If I were you, I would take great care not to run over or slam into anything else."

Segundo nodded and smiled. The pressure was off. He advanced the throttles forward. The Cigarette accelerated above eighty miles per hour as it again sliced through the water, expanding its wake to each side.

"Major," the general shouted down into the cabin, "bring Montero up on deck. I seriously doubt if he would be interested in jumping off at this speed. Besides, I would like to see his goddamn sorrowful face."

The major complied with Cardella's directive.

SEVENTY-FIVE

On Board the Scarab

Some four miles behind, the Scarab continued on its magnetic heading of 120 degrees to Bimini. The Cigarette was out of sight. "We've just got to trust our intuition and believe that they're only a couple of miles ahead," Rick said to reassure both Tommy and himself.

"They're more than a couple of miles," Maxwell corrected Rick. "At our eye height, the distance to the horizon is three point five nautical miles. The Cigarette has to be beyond that or I would have glimpsed its flaming yellow paint job."

"Three point five miles to the horizon, huh?"

"Yeah," Maxwell grinned, proud to show off his knowledge. "I've done the calculation before, but if you're interested in the math, the distance to the horizon is one point one seven times the square root of nine, where nine is currently the height of your eye above the water."

"Thanks, Einstein."

"By the way," Maxwell segued, "where the hell is that WindStar pilot of yours?"

Rick turned, searching up into the sky toward the beaches to the west. "Dunno, but he should be in the area by now. Let me try to raise him on the radio."

Rick was about to press the mic button on his handheld VHF transceiver when he heard Rameros' voice come through its speaker. "Hey, Harris, where are you now?" ...*bud-a-leep.*

"We're in a black Scarab about fifteen miles out of Port Everglades tracking direct Bimini," he responded, continuing to depress the mic button. "And, there should be a canary yellow Cigarette four or five miles ahead of us. You should see four guys on board—one of them is Salo Montero." ...*bud-a-leep.*

"Roger that, just passed over the beaches at three thousand, descending. You should see us fly by in the next few minutes." ...*bud-a-leep.*

Rick paused, keying in on a single word that Rameros had uttered. "US?" ...*bud-a-leep.*

"Yes, I brought along that reporter friend of yours for the ride." ...*bud-a-leep.*

"Damn," Rick muttered in reaction to learning of Waterman being on board the WindStar. Then he reasoned that the reporter's presence could be a godsend, regardless of the outcome of the chase. "Let us know when you locate the Cigarette." ...*bud-a-leep.*

"Wilco, good buddy." ...*bud-a-leep.*

Rick glanced over toward Tommy Maxwell and then focused on the speedometer. It read just under eighty miles per hour. "Can't you push this Scarab any harder?"

"Unfortunately, no. What you see on the speedo is all you get." He paused momentarily. "Hey, let your pilot do the work. He should have an easy time spotting them from above."

Rick nodded. He was confident that Franco Rameros would soon make visual contact with the canary yellow offshore racer. Then, what? The Coast Guard was likely still forty or fifty miles away. And worse, the Coast Guard had no authorization to take any action once the Cigarette entered Bahamian waters. Unless the Cigarette simply died in the water within the next fifteen minutes, Segundo and the general would be virtually home free. That thought was unnerving to Rick Harris. "Tommy," he began by asking, after a quick glance toward the instrument panel, "how's our fuel situation?"

"In another ten minutes we'll have to turn back."

"If we don't?"

"Well, the answer to that question is simple. We won't make it back under our own power."

Rick's eyes sparkled. He grinned. "Is that so?"

Tommy quickly glanced toward Rick. He had read his friend's mind. "You know, Mr. Harris, it will be a very expensive tow-in from out here."

Rick grinned again. "Put it on my tab, Tommy. We've come too far not to at least try to snatch the brass ring."

Tommy nodded. "I know what you mean."

Rameros' voice came through the transceiver's speaker once again, "Wow, that is one yellow Cigarette." ...*bud-a-leep.*

Rick and Tommy looked skywards spotting the WindStar almost directly overhead at fifteen hundred feet.

"How far ahead of us are they? And, uh, can you see a Coast Guard cutter coming up from Miami?" ...*bud-a-leep.*

"The Cigarette, oh, maybe five or six miles ahead of you...distance over water is difficult to judge. Bimini is probably another twenty-five miles beyond them. And, uh, no cutter is visible to the south." ...*bud-a-leep.*

"Okay, keep the Cigarette in sight. I guess there's not much else we can do." ...*bud-a-leep.*

SEVENTY-SIX

On Board the WindStar

F ranco Rameros smiled to Bob Waterman in the right seat, and in typical Rameros form said, "HA, not much else we can do...do not believe that for a second."

"Huh?" a baffled Waterman questioned from behind a knitted brow and narrowed eyes.

Rameros dismissed Waterman's bewilderment, and without missing a beat, he asked, "You got a camera with you, Bob?"

"I sure do. In fact, I already took a few shots of the WindStar interior with it."

"Got a zoom lens on it?"

"Uh-huh."

"Well, get the damn thing out, Bob. Some action photos should give that story you are working on some more fire to inspire."

Bob Waterman quickly reached to the right side of his seat where he had placed his leather satchel, pulled out a small camera, and held it up for Rameros to see.

"Hey, that is a nice one. Olympus, huh?"

Waterman nodded, beaming at the compliment.

Rameros then focused on the Cigarette in the distance on the water below. He knew with the boat's engines loudly thundering, its passengers would be oblivious to any sound from the WindStar. Franco set his jaw and shot a quick glance over to Waterman. "Be sure your seatbelt and shoulder harness are snug." But before Waterman could respond, Rameros rolled the WindStar into a sixty-degree bank and shoved the nose down thirty degrees below the horizon. The aircraft entered a diving spiral to the left.

Waterman's pupils dilated. His windshield was filled with nothing but the sight of pale blue Gulf Stream water. The airspeed rapidly increased, the hallmark whooshing hiss swiftly swelling within the cockpit and cabin. "Wha...what's happening?"

"Oh," Rameros casually responded as he concentrated on his outside references, "going on down for a closer look." He paused. "I want to give you the opportunity to take a few shots of the bad guys." For now, that was the only clue he wanted Waterman to have as the WindStar swooped down from behind the Cigarette like a hungry bird of prey.

"This is going to be fun, Bob," Rameros commented over the cockpit intercom.

"Ye-ye-yes," Waterman stammered, tightly clutching his camera close to his chest, highly conscious of the rapidly approaching water below.

Rameros leveled the WindStar at twenty feet above the Gulf Stream waters and headed directly for the Cigarette, which was now less that a mile ahead. He retarded the power levers to flight idle, added approach flaps, dumped the landing gear for added directional stability, and began slowing the WindStar to one hundred knots. "We will be passing just a hair off the boat's left side. Everything is going to happen pretty fast. So, get ready, Bob."

Waterman's body was taut, but not numb. He automatically reacted by raising the camera up to eye level and pointing it toward the cockpit's side window even though there still was nothing to capture on film except endless blue water.

What Rameros had in mind was more than just arranging a photo shoot for Bob Waterman. His intent was to unnerve whoever was at the helm of the Cigarette. He wanted to do whatever he could to slow down or temporarily divert the boat from its direct course to Bimini. Capturing shots of the yellow offshore racer on film was just a ploy to occupy Waterman and ease the reporter's tension.

As the WindStar slowed to one hundred knots, Rameros inched up the power levers to maintain his target airspeed. He banked the aircraft slightly to the left and positioned it for a fly-by just off of the port side of the boat. "Here we go," he said to Waterman who was poised with index finger on the shutter button.

"I'm ready," Waterman said over the cockpit intercom.

Flying at only twenty miles per hour faster than the Cigarette was traveling, the WindStar emerged barely half a wing length away from the boat.

Waterman began pressing down on the shutter button.

Rameros could hear the motorized film drive advancing each frame within the cockpit's quiet hush.

Waterman saw the startled faces: Segundo and Cardella at the helm; Major Alverez and Salo Montero nested in the aft bolster seats. The WindStar overshadowed the relatively smaller forty-one-foot Cigarette.

Rameros' concentration intensified. There was no margin for error. Timing would be critical. "NOW," he grunted aloud as he snapped the ailerons to the right, eased back on the yoke, and advanced the power levers. The WindStar banked steeply, its wingtip passing just ahead and slightly below the bow of the boat. The stall warning horn chirped out, then silenced.

Segundo reacted just as Rameros had anticipated. The Cigarette swerved off course to the right.

Waterman kept punching the shutter button. With each passing frame, the motorized film drive ground away.

Rameros further advanced the power levers to their maximum ITT-limited torque. He felt the surge of power. The WindStar sprang from just above the water and began its climbout as Rameros retracted its gear and milked-up its flaps. "How was that?" he asked Waterman who was craning his neck backwards and to the right as he followed the Cigarette until it disappeared behind the wing.

Bob Waterman turned to Rameros. "I'd say you shocked the hell out of them," he said with beaming approval.

"Excellent, that is exactly what I wanted to do."

The WindStar leveled off at five hundred feet and made a wide, circling left turn from its southern heading. Rameros held his airspeed to one hundred sixty knots. "Get anything good with that camera of yours?" he asked Waterman.

"Bound to have gotten at least one out of the dozen or so I must have shot."

"Good."

"Now, what?"

"Well, I am just going to swing around, descend, and try to spook them with a head-on pass. Maybe they will veer off course again."

A now seasoned-for-the-unexpected Waterman said, "Fine, I'll be ready with my camera."

Rameros smiled, but said nothing. He thought to himself: *This time, I will take the paint right off that damn Cigarette.*

SEVENTY-SEVEN

On Board the Cigarette

"What the hell was that? Segundo finally shouted out.

The general shouted back, "A goddamn friggin' WindStar...probably the one our Colombian friends failed to shoot down over the Amazon."

After a slight delay, Segundo steered the boat back on course to Bimini. He asked the general, "You think he will be back?"

"You can count on it."

"What can he do to us?"

"It depends on how crazy the pilot is."

"Crazy?"

"Yes, crazy. Some of those flyboys think they are invincible." Cardella briefly shot a glance aft toward the major, then he asked Segundo, "You got any guns on board?"

Segundo broadly smiled and flashed an assertive thumbs-up sign. The Cigarette was well outfitted for the high seas where maritime law could easily lie only in the hands of the captain and crew. "A semi-automatic shotgun and an Uzi with a mag of thirty-two," he answered.

"Very nice, Ramon," Cardella said with a smirk. "Slow down the boat to sixty." He paused, very pleased with the situation at hand. "At least this time we will not be caught ill-prepared."

Segundo dismissed the general's derisive comment and went on, "The guns are stowed in a locker under the starboard lounge seating down in the cabin. You will find a key to the locker under the seating cushion."

Cardella disappeared into the cabin below, returning only a minute later with a fully automatic Uzi and a twelve-gauge Browning Automatic-5. He motioned Major Alverez forward and handed him the Uzi.

It was obvious to the major. He knew precisely what the general had in mind.

The major's eyes were first to catch the reflection of the Windstar's glossy white wings as the aircraft made its turn back toward the Cigarette. He pointed it out to General Cardella. They both watched the WindStar begin its descent and fly directly toward them.

"A sitting duck," Cardella scoffed, pushing off the cross bolt safety on the trigger guard of his Browning. "We are going to nail that sonovabitch's ass." He paused following the aircraft's flight path, then briefly turned to Alverez and said, "Major, on my command, you take out the right engine—the one to your left. I will blast away at the cockpit. Remember to keep your gun low until you fire, and lead him plenty. Our closure rate is very high."

Alverez nodded, happily. He was now back in familiar territory. With glee in his eyes, the major methodically unfolded and extended the sub-machine gun's steel stock and then moved the safety/fire selector switch on the left side of the receiver to full automatic. He widened his stance and positioned his left foot forward while all the time focusing upon the approaching WindStar. His concentration intensified. He waited for the general's order as the distance between the Cigarette and WindStar rapidly closed.

One half mile...

One quarter mile...

The WindStar was inching closer to the water.

Twenty feet...

Fifteen feet...

The general snapped the Browning to his shoulder, much like a hunter would for a bird on the wing. His eyes squinted down the barrel's ventilated rib. He leaned into the shotgun and steadied himself against the side of his bolster as the Cigarette smoothly floated atop the path its deep-V hull was carving out of the water.

"NOW!" Cardella shouted after taking a deep breath. He pulled back the trigger once, twice, thrice...

The resounding blasts made even a well-prepared Segundo flinch.

Almost simultaneously, the major's gun fired three rapid bursts at the WindStar's engine. The Uzi's 9mm parabellum shell casings spewed out of its chamber and onto the deck.

The shooters' actions spelled DISASTER. Their assault on the WindStar had been PRECISE.

Segundo smiled and said to the general, "Nice shooting."

The general nodded as his eyes followed the WindStar's struggle to stay alive. "The aircraft will never make it back," he said, self-assuredly. "NEVER."

SEVENTY-EIGHT

On Board the WindStar

"Goddamn bastards," Franco Rameros blurted out.

Waterman had bent over into a tucked position when he realized what was about to happen, just before the first shotgun blast smashed through the safety glass panel of his front windshield. Hurricane-like wind tore into the cockpit. Deafening.

After the WindStar hurdled over the Cigarette, its airspeed rapidly bled off, its nose edged further down toward the water.

"GODDAMN..." Franco Rameros blurted out once again. He kicked in full left rudder and slammed both power levers to their forward stops. The WindStar staggered in ground-effect just a few feet above the water's surface as Rameros fought the controls, struggling to keep it alive. He had precious little time to do what had to be done. He felt like a juggler with a dozen balls in the air. Too many things were happening—happening all at once.

Just below the center glare shield, the master caution panel was flashing like a Vegas slot machine. Rameros tore off his David Clark headset to silence the earsplitting warning alarms directed into it. Indeed, he knew he had a multitude of problems on his hands. What he did not need was the blatant distraction of blaring alarms that well designed sensors were urgently trying to communicate. To him, it was obvious: the right engine was engulfed in flames. The explosive potential was very real.

Almost faster that a blink of an eye, he slammed the right power lever back to its aft flight idle stop, jerked the right condition lever to fuel cutoff, and ripped the right prop control to feather. Next, he automatically grasped the illuminated T-shaped fire handle on the center instrument panel just below the glare shield that read: FIRE (R ENG) PULL. He yanked it out, hard. Through a maze of suppression nozzles that snaked within the right nacelle, a high-rate discharge of Halon-1301 gas immediately flooded the engine. The gas chemically reacted with the combustion process and effectively smothered the fire.

Rameros continued to tackle various other items critical to damage control. He had just trimmed in a generous amount of left rudder to compensate for the asymmetrical thrust. He eased back on the yoke to pitch up the aircraft. The WindStar began a shallow climb at one hundred knots as the wind continued to tear into the cockpit through

Waterman's shattered windowpane. "You okay, Bob?" Rameros shouted out.

Waterman instinctively touched himself on various parts of his body to see if indeed he was okay. He nodded yes, he was. He angled toward Rameros and, with intense personal concern, shouted out, "Can we make it back to the airport?"

Rameros' answer was instantaneous. "Not a problem," he said, but at this point he was not really sure. Still addressing damage control, he glanced over toward the fuel control panel and switched on cross-feed to move fuel from the right wing tank to the opposite side of the aircraft. He intuited that if the right engine had been rendered inoperative by the gunshots, the right fuel tank had likely been hit as well. However, what complicated matters even more was that the WindStar had had very little fuel on board to begin with. It had only taken on enough Jet-A at FLL that morning to provide a total of two hours worth of flight time for the demo with Santelli. Considering all the flying done earlier in the day, Rameros estimated that he had just thirty minutes of time remaining before the left engine would flameout. And, he could not be sure how much fuel might have been lost if indeed the right wing tank had been damaged.

The WindStar labored, slowly climbing past five hundred feet. Rameros could see the Scarab in the distance below; he knew they could see him. He plucked the Alinco transceiver out of his left breast pocket and pressed the mic button. "Do NOT ask," he shouted above the cockpit noise, "I am rather busy right now." ...bud-a-leep. He flipped the transceiver off and re-pocketed it.

Out of the corner of his eye, Rameros saw Waterman squinting his eyes, leaning toward the center of the cockpit and away from the gaping hole in the windshield. "You sure you are okay, Bob?" he asked.

By now, Waterman had had the time to dwell upon what had just happened. The normally reserved, but presently harried reporter hollered back, "Hell no, I almost got killed!"

"Good, almost does not count," was all Rameros said in response.

As the WindStar leveled out at one thousand feet, Rameros began a turn to the southeast—away from the airport.

"Where are you going?" a thoroughly panicked Waterman shouted the question.

Rameros shrugged, then grinned. "Unfinished business."

"What? You're going back?" Waterman could not believe it. He uncharacteristically shouted, "Are you goddamn crazy?"

Rameros laughed heartily. "Crazy? No. Stubborn? Yes. Pissed-off? Very much so. Those friggin' scumbags made Swiss cheese out of *MY* aircraft."

"I hope the hell you know what you're doing," Waterman shouted back. It was insane, he thought.

"I do, Bob, I do. Just hang in there. We are going to put a real bang into that story of yours."

Waterman was too shaken to reply. Another bang was not what he wanted or needed. What he had already experienced was plenty. However he knew a protest would fall on deaf ears. He had no choice but to weather whatever RioAero's chief test pilot was about to serve up.

Franco Rameros extended his right hand and was about to grasp the landing gear handle. But his hand stopped in mid-air. Two red lights that just began flashing on the master caution panel gave him cause for pause. "Shit," he moaned.

One light was labeled L HYDR PRESS, the other was labeled L HYDR RES. There was no doubt in Rameros' mind what the lights indicated—no hydraulic pressure, no hydraulic fluid. It was a total hydraulic failure. In addition to a loss of hydraulics that resulted from shutting down and extinguishing the fire in the right engine, the aircraft's secondary system, which was run off of the left engine accessory gearbox, had failed as well. Somewhere, hydraulic lines had been cut. He knew it had to have been a delayed effect of the gunfire assault, the engine fire, or both.

In a quandary, Rameros hesitated. He needed to extend the landing gear as he had done before during his first pass on the Cigarette. But the landing gear was electro-hydraulic. He pondered the alternatives for a split second, then dropped his right hand down to the floorboards and glanced at a small access door a few inches aft of the center control pedestal. It was placarded in red: EMERG LG EXT. He hesitated again. A separate, backup system that was isolated from the main hydraulics had been engineered into the WindStar to extend the landing gear in the event of a complete hydraulic system failure. He knew it would work, but it was a bold move for him to take. The parasitic drag generated by an extended landing gear with just one engine operating created a significant risk. The WindStar's performance would be virtually nil, especially considering that the failed engine's seriously damaged propeller had not feathered and was creating an immense amount of drag in and of itself. That was not his only concern. He knew that once the gear was extended through the emergency system, it could not be retracted. Period.

Franco Rameros took a deep breath, held it for a second, and then fiercely shook his head. The decision was made. He placed the gear selector handle into the down position, then opened the access door to the emergency landing gear extension switch and moved it to the ON position. He waited. Five seconds later, he felt three sequential thumps and saw three small green lights illuminate near the gear handle. All three gear struts were down and locked.

From one thousand feet above the Gulf Stream waters, Rameros could see the yellow offshore racer speeding ahead. It was just five miles in the distance. He grinned, pitched the WindStar down slightly, and maintained maximum continuous power on the left engine. The aircraft accelerated to one hundred twenty knots. In a little more than three minutes he would once again be confronting the archenemy. This time he hoped the outcome would be different from the previous experience. For both his and Bob Waterman's sake, it had to be.

SEVENTY-NINE

On Board the Cigarette

Cardella and Segundo gloated in mutual admiration. Their assault on the WindStar had been successful—devastatingly so. The aircraft was gone—gone for good. They were totally convinced. Now, any remaining angst held for the earlier failure to ruin RioAero had temporarily evaporated. Ten to twelve miles ahead lay Bimini. There was nothing that could stop them.

"So, Carlo," Segundo said to the general above the thundering roar of the Cigarette's engines, "what kind of reception do you think we will get in Colombia?"

"Mixed, I suppose." The general shrugged. "Certainly, there will be disappointment we failed in our plan against RioAero. That goes without saying. But those military derivatives of the WindStar that were destined to be used against the cartel are dead...at least for now. And, there will be delight that we moved three LD3 containers of product for them." He grinned. "Indeed, several hundred million dollars from their wholesale distributors should provide a great deal of satisfaction."

"Good," Segundo said, unaware this assessment was in error. Neither Segundo nor Cardella could have known that U.S. Customs agents were only minutes away from storming the AeroMech facility at Opa Locka.

"Do not worry, Ramon, we are not finished yet." The general began nodding. "We will regroup; we will restructure. I have not abandoned plans for RioAero. Next time, we will prevail."

Segundo glanced to the left side of his instrument panel and checked the boat's navigation system. He pointed into the distance beyond the bow. "Less than ten miles ahead. Keep an eye out for the island."

On the aft seating arrangement of the Cigarette, both Salo Montero and the major stared ahead into the wind through squinting eyes.

EIGHTY

On Board the WindStar

From behind and above, Franco Rameros guided the WindStar to within half a mile of the Cigarette, descending through five hundred feet. "Okay, Mr. Bob Waterman..." There was excitement in his voice. "It is showtime—the fat lady is singing. Oh, yeah!"

Waterman tugged down on the loose ends of his already snug seatbelt and shoulder harness. He tugged again—hard—trying to make himself part of the seat frame to which the straps were attached. He had no idea what Rameros had planned, but he knew whatever Rameros was about to do would be dramatic. Bob Waterman could never have fathomed how breathtaking it would be.

Franco Rameros did indeed have a plan—a flawlessly calculated plan. This time he had no intention of toyfully sparring with the Cigarette. He knew exactly what he had to do. He knew there would be zero margin for error. It was all or nothing. It was his last chance. His intent was to stop the Cigarette, regardless of risk, regardless of cost.

With both hands on the control yoke, Rameros pitched down the nose of the WindStar—now, radically. His eyes locked onto the canary yellow offshore racer like the sensor on a heat-seeking missile. Nothing within the cockpit could distract him. Although the wind's intensity increased as it howled through the gaping hole in Waterman's windshield, Rameros obstinately focused only on the yellow watercraft ahead and below.

Three hundred feet above the Gulf Stream waters...

One hundred forty knots of indicated airspeed...

Fifteen hundred feet behind the Cigarette...

The WindStar made its approach.

Franco Rameros tightened his grip on the control yoke as he began slowing the aircraft. The cloudless sky and even heating of the water's surface provided a smooth descent without convection or turbulence. He set his jaws. His eyes narrowed. He was totally absorbed by the offshore racer that sped onwards, all the time closing its distance to Bimini. He continued to make small adjustments to his flight path. The wounded WindStar unwaveringly complied with each and every input of the controls. Flying doggedly despite significant handicaps, the aircraft, like Rameros, seemed resolutely intent upon obtaining vengeance from those below.

One hundred feet above the Gulf Stream waters…
One hundred twenty knots of indicated airspeed…
Five hundred feet behind the Cigarette…
The WindStar continued its approach.

Rameros glimpsed Segundo and the others on board the boat. They were staring out into the distance ahead, totally oblivious to the presence of the WindStar, certain that the aircraft had either already ditched at sea or was limping back to FLL only to become a spectacle on the six o'clock news. "Just one more second," Rameros slowly muttered through still clenched jaws as he guided the WindStar to its mark.

At first, the shadow of the WindStar engulfed the Cigarette from behind. It was the type of ominous predatory specter that would instantly cause staggering fear to any prey animal. But the shadow hardly had time to register before Segundo and Cardella heard the high-pitched whine from the propeller of the aircraft's lone operating engine from less than twenty feet away. The glimpse of a blur from the WindStar's nose wheel just to the starboard side of the boat. Next, the lower fuselage.

"NOW!" Rameros explosively barked at five feet above the boat. He cut the power, dipped the left wing down, and aggressively shoved the yoke full forward for a split second. The WindStar fell from the sky like a hawk that had suddenly tucked its wings.

Waterman clutched the armrests of his seat, bracing himself. His face frozen in absolute terror. He closed his eyes, tight. His mouth began moving without saying words.

Rameros' timing had been precise.

The impact, impressive.

The WindStar's left main landing gear forcefully struck down upon the apex of the Cigarette's bow. A crushing, smashing, structurally destructive blow. The powerful jolt thrust the bow of the ninety-mile-per-hour boat deeply down into the water. The boat's stern angled sharply upward to the sky; its direct-drive propellers ineffectively sliced through thin air. The engines red-lined.

The crushing impact from the aircraft's landing gear strut combined with the force of the surrounding water made the Cigarette first spin vertically, then tumble end-over-end, further fracturing the already weakened superstructure. The fiberglass layers, the balsa core laminate, the stringer buildups, and the composite bulkheads, all experienced inexorable stress. Cataclysmically, without warning, the watercraft's deck and hull broke apart, splintering into pieces, flinging away from each other, tumbling laterally atop the water, slowly coming to a stop. Within seconds, the speeding offshore racer had been transformed into ravaged, stationary junk—some bobbing in the swirl of its own slowly dissipating wake, some immediately sinking to the depths below. The occupants, who had been flung away and clear of the breakup, now floated among the watercraft's other debris in the warming Gulf Stream waters.

In the cockpit of the WindStar, there was no time to absorb the sight. Franco Rameros' eyes remained riveted to the open water ahead. Though he had leveled the wings, added full power to the aircraft's lone operating engine and a slight amount of positive elevator just after making contact with the Cigarette, he had not yet achieved the response he needed. A fully extended landing gear, which could not be retracted, created an immense amount of drag. The aircraft's speed had significantly slowed. Suddenly, without warning, the WindStar's wings began an oscillating roll from side to side. The aircraft shuddered. Rameros grimaced. As he eased off on some of the back pressure he held on the control yoke, he felt the nose wheel jab into the water's glossy surface. Helpless, he knew there was little that could be done. He had to wait for the aircraft's response to his control inputs. There was nothing else he could do. Nothing.

"Come on...COME ON," he shouted out, hoping to coax the WindStar into a climb while taking great care to prevent a deep, devastating stall.

Although the WindStar's initial pent-up inertia had caused the massive, accelerated downward force that was instrumental in splintering the boat's deck and hull, the aircraft should have been poised to leap back into the air soon after its left gear strut had bottomed out. But now, with its landing gear glancing off the water and the aircraft hovering in ground effect at under ninety knots, all Rameros could do was patiently wait for the response while split seconds stretched out to seem like hours. The airspeed had to build up. Controllability had to improve.

It had to...

It needed to....

It would.

The aircraft sluggishly inched itself above the water. The airspeed crept up to ninety-five knots, ever so slowly accelerating. Franco Rameros' tense body relaxed slightly. He gently eased the WindStar into a shallow climb and followed with a delayed, equally cautious, shallow bank to the right. Even though he was well aware that he had made solid contact with the Cigarette, he had no idea of the true damage he had caused.

Rameros retrieved his headset from where he had earlier tossed it down onto the cockpit floor, adjusted its spring headband, fitted its large gel seals over his ears, and positioned the noise-cancelling boom mic directly onto his lips. He motioned for Waterman to don his own headset as well. The headset attenuated the loud growling hiss of the wind that continued to blast through Waterman's smashed windowpane.

Over the cockpit intercom Rameros said to Waterman, "Let's see if we were fortunate enough to slow that Cigarette down." The background noise, while apparent, was no longer deafening.

They both gazed out through the right cockpit side window, and, in disbelief, glimpsed only floating pieces of the once sleek canary yellow boat.

"Incredible!" an astonished Waterman exclaimed.

Rameros widely grinned. He circled the area to assess the damage more closely and to verify that all four souls on board the Cigarette had survived the disastrous event. They had.

Waterman had luckily retrieved his camera and began snapping away. "This is unbelievable," he said, savoring the once-in a-life-time photo-journalistic moment.

"Well," Rameros came back, "it would be even better yet if we could save this aircraft and quietly slip it back into the hangar at RioAero for a major overhaul."

Waterman had no response. The true reality of it came back full force. Their offshore journey was far from over.

Only having climbed to a mere two hundred feet, the WindStar struggled under the heavy parasitic drag being created by an unfeathered right propeller and fully extended landing gear. Rameros needed every foot-pound of torque the WindStar's lone engine could generate. But fate would not have it so.

On the master caution panel, a yellow light flickered: L ENG OVERTEMP.

Rameros uttered a disconsolate groan. Somehow the left engine's turbomachinery had also been damaged. Its internal turbine temperature sensors were indicating that it was running hot. For now, though, it was running, and that was all Franco Rameros really cared about. But it had to continue to run.

Rameros retarded the power lever just slightly. The ITT gauge reading dropped fifty degrees. The warning light extinguished. The best performance he could now obtain from the WindStar's operating engine was a marginal one hundred foot per minute rate of climb with an airspeed of one hundred ten knots. And, there was no assurance that he could maintain even that performance for long. Further power reductions to offset a deteriorating engine hot-section would likely be needed.

Waterman had noticed the concern on Rameros' face. He too was aware of the marginal rate of single-engine climb from the laboring WindStar. He asked, "Are we gonna be okay, Franco?"

Rameros remained silent for a moment, though the obvious answer was no. "Worry not," he said in his perennially confident tone, "if I cannot get this bird home, nobody can."

Bob Waterman forced a nervous smile. He knew enough about aviation to sense the gravity of the problem they faced. Still, if he had to be in the right seat of this WindStar, he knew there was no one other than Franco Rameros he wanted in the left seat.

As the WindStar fought its way up through three hundred feet, Rameros fished out the Alinco transceiver from his left breast pocket and handed it to Waterman. "Turn it on and give Rick Harris a call. Tell him the Cigarette is dead in the water about five miles ahead of them and slightly to the right of their course. Tell him Salo Montero and the others are treading water. Tell him he owes me a case of Jack Daniels. Then, tell him whatever else you like."

Waterman took the transceiver, flipped its switch to on, and began communicating with Rick Harris on the Scarab.

Rameros reached up to the center avionics stack on the instrument panel, opted to bypass Fort Lauderdale Approach Control altogether, and tuned the Tower frequency into COM-1. He began monitoring communications on that frequency to assess the runways in use and the traffic activity. In short order he was able to glean some good news and some bad news. Although airline arrivals and departures were steady, general aviation activity was only intermittent. Unfortunately, though, an onshore breeze of five to seven knots dictated a takeoff and landing pattern to the east. The very last thing Rameros wanted to do was fly the WindStar several miles past the airport to the west, then turn around for a landing to the east. He was convinced there was not enough fuel in the tanks to stay in the air that long. As it was, he could only hope that his lone engine would run long enough to make it to the airport itself. He could certainly declare an in-flight emergency and receive priority for landing. That, however, was not Franco Rameros' style—at least not yet.

EIGHTY-ONE

On Board the Scarab

Rick Harris held the transceiver close to his ear, listening intently to the information Waterman was transmitting. Rick was both elated and concerned by what he heard. When the conversation ended, he motioned with the palm of his hand for Maxwell to begin slowing down the Scarab. "They're out there, dead in the water, somewhere right of our course."

With an understanding nod, Maxwell powered back the throttles, slowing the Scarab to forty miles per hour.

They both scanned the Gulf Stream waters.

Rick spotted it first. "Two o'clock and half a mile," he yelled out.

A second later, Tommy Maxwell spotted the Cigarette's debris field. "Wow! How the hell did that happen?"

"I'll explain it to you later," Rick answered, "but first, let's focus on locating Salo. The Coast Guard can deal with the others, unless the sharks get them first." He pulled off his polo shirt, kicked off his Sperry Topsiders, and dropped his khaki slacks to the deck.

"Red Jockey briefs," Maxwell quipped.

Rick pretended not to hear the comment. First, he spotted Segundo in a red life jacket who was thrashing about in the water, swinging one hand wildly into the air. Then, he zeroed in on a motionless red object floating three hundred feet off to the left. He directed Maxwell to steer the Scarab in that direction.

Monica had brought up bright orange life jackets from the cabin below. She handed one of them to Rick.

"It's him," Harris yelled out to Maxwell as the Scarab approached the seemingly lifeless body that was floating on its back. "It's Salo." Rick tossed the life jacket over toward the body, dove into the water, and swam the twenty feet to Salo.

Montero grabbed the life jacket with his left hand and hung on. He coughed, then asked, "What took you so long, Harris?" He tried to force a smile, but could not.

"Good to see you, too," Rick came back. "You okay?"

Montero coughed again, clearing his throat. "Except for a dislocated right shoulder, bruises over a hundred percent of my body, and halfway drowned, I am fine."

With assistance from Monica and Tommy, Rick carefully eased Salo up into the Scarab.

"Thanks," Montero said in a weak voice. He looked and acted like a welterweight who had gone ten rounds with Sugar Ray Leonard.

"Just try to relax," Rick said. "We'll take it slow going back to shore."

Montero eased his battered body down into one of the aft bolster seats. "What about the others?" he asked.

"Don't worry about them," Rick said. "Earlier, we radioed the Coast Guard about what was happening. They dispatched a cutter out of Miami. I expect they'll be arriving here in about ten minutes or so."

Montero nodded. He watched as Tommy Maxwell motored to the vicinity of the other men and dropped additional life jackets into the water. "I suppose those guys deserve to tread water a bit longer, and then suffer whatever consequences the authorities may impose upon them."

"That's for sure," Rick said with a smile, then paused while he surveyed the damage Rameros had caused to the Cigarette. "That Franco Rameros can be one ruthless pilot with a WindStar."

Montero nodded, then winced in pain as he repositioned his body in the seat.

"Tommy, let's head on back and get Salo some medical care. I'll radio the Coast Guard on the Cigarette's position."

Maxwell advanced the throttles and turned the Scarab to the northwest.

Salo Montero asked, "By the way, Rick, where is Franco Rameros now?"

"Hopefully he's limping back to FLL. His aircraft got shot up pretty bad."

Salo Montero's face paled. "Yes, I know." His tongue moistened his lips and he closed his eyes momentarily. "I hope he makes it. I know he will make it." Still, his voice quivered with uncertainty.

EIGHTY-TWO

Destination: Fort Lauderdale

"Eastern Eleven-Sixty-Two is ready to go, Runway Nine-Left," the captain's heavy southern accent made his unhurried words flow like poetry over the Tower frequency.

"Eleven-Sixty-Two, taxi into position and hold," the Tower shot back in a typical rapid-fire communications exchange sequence as airport activity began picking up. "Citation Two-Two-Fox-Charlie, expedite rollout Runway One-Three, hold short of Nine-Right." Pause. "Delta Four-Fifty-Five, contact Departure on one-twenty-eight point six." Pause. "American Three-Fourteen report the Marker." Pause. "Gulfstream Ten-Echo-Mike, contact Ground Control, point seven."

A long caravan of airliners slowly taxied to the west, parallel to Runway 9-L, the primary air carrier runway on the north side of the field. This was all very typical for a late Sunday afternoon. The 5:15 "push," in airline-speak, was in progress. "Banks" or large numbers of commercial jets were simultaneously being pushed back from terminal gates. The ramp areas and taxiways quickly became congested as each airliner vied for departure sequencing, generally to destinations in the Northeast and upper-Midwest. Most of the planes were full of snowbirds interested in spending as much of their limited vacation time as possible in South Florida, opting for late afternoon flights, needing to be back on the job come Monday morning.

The heavily loaded Eastern Airlines Lockheed L-1011 proceeded to taxi out onto the runway, aligned its nose wheel with the centerline, and then awaited takeoff clearance.

The controller continued to rattle off a succession of instructions to a host of other aircraft from his perch in the Tower cab on the far northwest side of the field nearby the departure ends of Runways 9-L and 13. Although the controller had a clear enough view to almost count the number of antennas on the close-by Lockheed 1011 on Runway 9-L, his view of Runway 9-R, which was well over a mile away on the south side of the airport, was severely limited. Ground Control, also located in the Tower cab, had the same imprecise view of the airport's southern-most runway.

"Eastern Eleven-Sixty-Two is ready," the captain mellifluously repeated to remind the Tower that *the wings of man* were eager to soar.

"Haven't forgotten about you, Eastern," the harried controller's tone, gruff. Safely and efficiently juggling dozens of departing and arriving aircraft of varying sizes and speeds was a major responsibility. "Power up, Eleven-Sixty-Two." Pause. "Twin Cessna Ten-Tango-Xray, report a two mile final for Nine-Right." Pause. "Citation Two-Two-Fox-Charlie, Ground Control, point seven." Pause. "Eastern Eleven-Sixty-Two, cleared for takeoff." Pause. "Aircraft calling Fort Lauderdale Tower say again, you were cut out."

Franco Rameros groaned. The airport had suddenly come alive with traffic. It appeared highly unlikely that the Tower could accommodate his request for a landing to the west, since it would directly conflict with the established traffic flow. He keyed his mic, making sure his tone only coolly broadcasted his position and landing preference: "WindStar Papa-Tango-Sierra-Bravo-Yankee is five miles east, squawking twelve hundred, requesting a straight in for Two-Seven-Left."

"American Three-Fourteen cleared to land." Pause. "Lear Two-Five-Juliet-Lima, hold short of Nine-Right." Pause. "Sierra-Bravo-Yankee, unable to approve request, report a midfield right downwind for Nine-Right."

In response, a frustrated Rameros double-clicked his mic button rather than reading back the Tower's instructions as was standard protocol for airlines but sometimes shunned by some in general aviation. He slowly shook his head in disappointment. He had really hoped for approval to land on Runway 27-L; it would have significantly lessened his time in the air. Now he could only mentally review what few remaining options he had before running out of fuel.

The Tower controller continued his no-nonsense communications on the frequency. All aircraft flying at or below three thousand feet within a five-mile radius of the airport, or positioned on the runways, relied upon his directives. However, as had been intended by Franco Rameros, the controller remained oblivious to the WindStar's perilous in-flight condition. Rameros had purposefully neglected making mention of the WindStar's damage in the hope of avoiding adverse publicity that would certainly be generated if the true condition were known. Despite its condition, the aircraft was successfully continuing to maintain its thousand-foot altitude at one mile from the Dania Pier, three miles from the airport.

Then, not unexpectedly, an audible alarm came through the cockpit headsets with the simultaneous FUEL LOW light flashing on the master caution panel. Rameros quickly jabbed the light to silence the alarm.

A panicky Waterman squirmed in his seat. "Can we make it?" There was real doubt in his mind.

EIGHTY-THREE

On Board the Scarab

Offshore, with the seas remaining calm, Tommy Maxwell elected to ease the power slightly forward on the Scarab, escalating its speed to fifty miles per hour. The boat forged ahead, now fifteen miles east of Port Everglades, its deep-V hull riding atop a smooth cushion of water. He glanced down at the fuel gauges and scowled. The Scarab's fuel condition was identical to that of the WindStar. In another few minutes the Scarab's big-block engines would begin sputtering and then stop from fuel starvation. However for those on the boat, running out of fuel would simply be an inconvenience rather than the fatal plunge of disaster faced by Rameros and Waterman.

Over the frequency Maxwell had earlier entered into his marine radio, he and Rick listened in as an officer on the Coast Guard cutter informed operations in Miami that they had just arrived at the Cigarette's location and were retrieving its passengers from the water. The transmission further advised that several packages of a suspicious substance found floating among the debris had been retrieved and taken aboard. Miami operations ordered the cutter to maintain its current position until a U.S. Customs watercraft could arrive on the scene.

Rick grinned. "I'd say Segundo, Cardella and the major are in deep trouble."

Maxwell nodded. "Serves them right."

The Scarab's engines sputtered and slowed, initially misfiring, then totally silent from an absence of fuel.

Rick shrugged. "I guess you'll want my MasterCard now."

"Nah, hang on to it for awhile," Tommy insisted. "We're probably only ten or so miles from the inlet. Maybe we'll get lucky enough to hitch a ride in with some trawler or sportfisherman."

"That would be nice," Rick said in accord.

On the heel of Rick's words, a loud horn sound blasted out in the distance, causing all to swivel their heads, searching the horizon for the source.

Monica scrambled onto the higher foredeck for a better vantage point. A long minute later she began waving both arms high into the air. Sammy Santelli's relatively slow moving sportfisherman had just come into view. Santelli, after finally leaving the Intracoastal and exiting Port Everglades, had also made a course toward Bimini in search of Rick and the black Scarab. Because his speed was too slow to catch up to the Scarab, Santelli had manned the tuna tower in hopes of spotting the boat he was pursuing. Just now, he had spied the Scarab from atop his boat's tall tower. Knowing that from their low vantage point the occupants of the Scarab could not see him, he had blasted his proximity with the horn.

"Well, I knew they'd show up," Rick said, trying to be convincing.

"Yeah, sure," Tommy responded with a quick wink of the eye and knowing nod. "At any rate, it looks like we've got our ride home."

"Roger that."

The Hatteras neared. "Ahoy, black Scarab," came the amplified words over the sportfisherman's public address system. "How about a little welcoming cowbell, please?"

Tommy broke up laughing.

A perplexed Salo Montero made his way forward. He glanced toward Maxwell who was still doubled-over in hysterics, then commented to Rick, "Cowbell?" The word was foreign to him.

Rick began laughing as well. He stooped over to his left, opened a stowage locker, and pulled out his now well-used cowbell. He held it up to Montero, said, "Cowbell," and began to ring it vigorously.

Salo smiled, immediately recognizing what the cowbell was all about.

Again, the sportfisherman's public address system boomed forth with Santelli's amplified voice: "A little cowbell goes a long way, Harris."

Rick Harris feigned dejection as he silenced the clanging cowbell.

EIGHTY-FOUR

Destination: Fort Lauderdale

A t an altitude of one thousand feet and abeam the Dania Pier, a tense Waterman repeated his question: "Can we make it?"

"Who the hell knows," frustration wearing him thin, Rameros snapped back shrugging off the reporter's legitimate concern.

Chastised and fraught with worry, Waterman grasped the armrests, sank into his seat, and turned away.

Rameros knew Waterman's concern was valid. Indeed, it seemed more and more likely that the WindStar's engine would flameout prior to landing. Though too busy working on a solution and too crusty to have much empathy, Rameros still fished for some words to calm the passenger he had come to like. "No worries, Bob, as long as Franco Rameros is at the controls, you'll live through this one." He flashed a wink at Waterman, then grinned. There was one last strategy that might convince the Tower controller to approve his landing request. It was a long shot, but...

Rameros waited for a brief pause on the Tower frequency, then keyed his mic. "Sierra-Bravo-Yankee is a test flight aircraft, requesting the option for Two-Seven-Left."

Rameros knew test flight aircraft in Brazil were usually accorded special courtesies from air traffic controllers. In most cases, CTA inspectors were on board to supervise the aircraft and its transmissions while the pilot's skills were assessed during a routine recurrency check or for an additional aircraft rating. And further, CTA inspectors held rank and status that was above many of the lower echelon CTA employees in air traffic control. Rameros also knew that a similar accord existed within the analogous FAA fraternity in the U.S. He hoped this gambit would get his request for landing on Runway 27-L approved.

Almost immediately, the Tower controller replied to Rameros' request by saying, "Unable to approve, report midfield downwind. I've got a twin Cessna comin' up on a final, Nine-Right."

He double-clicked his mic button in response, then shouted out, "DAMN!" Rameros was now even more frustrated than before.

Bob Waterman had heard and understood everything. "Now, what?"

The silence was thick and dark within the cockpit of the WindStar.

"You would think the Tower would cut me a little slack," Rameros said, glaring ahead through the windshield. "But no, not today when I really need it."

An emboldened Waterman suggested, "Tell them we've got problems."

Well," Rameros said, "it is not that simple." His voice rose as he began explaining, "I would really like to land this damaged bird without having to declare a GODDAMN EMERGENCY." He briefly paused to gather himself. "It would be a lot easier on everyone. You see, if I told the Tower we were in a Mayday situation, they would scramble the fire/rescue guys and drag FAA inspectors out here on a late Sunday afternoon. Nobody would be happy. There would be a detailed inspection of the aircraft and its documents, a ton of questions would be asked, and a ream of reports generated. Can you just try to imagine what this aircraft must look like from the outside?"

Waterman nodded. The WindStar had been shot up pretty bad. The right nacelle showed obvious signs of the earlier engine fire.

"Anyway," Rameros continued, "in addition to being greeted by a rash of hubbub, we would be at the airport for hours and hours, going through our story again and again. Hell, if I can help it, I am not going to go through that today. Monday morning maybe, but not today."

"Yeah, but declaring an emergency sure beats crash landing on a crowded highway or into a subdivision."

"Damn it, Waterman, that will not happen. My intent is to make as normal of a landing as possible, and then slip this bird into the hangar. To do that, we really need to keep a low profile, you know." He paused to drive his point further home. "Besides, do you want some ambulance chasing reporter from another paper to scoop your story?"

Waterman shook his head, no.

"Good," Rameros said, "for now, I will keep that emergency trump card in my hand. If need be, I can always play it." He nodded. "I will certainly use it if they extend my downwind past the landing threshold, or if the engine flames out."

"You only have maybe another minute before that happens."

"I know, that is why I am keeping us real close to the runway on our downwind." Rameros keyed his mic and reported a midfield downwind to the Tower. As if trying to coax the controller into the right decision, he silently mouthed the words to the closed mic: *Landing clearance, Now!*

The Tower fired instructions off to three other aircraft, and then simply acknowledged Rameros' position report.

Rameros cocked his head to the side and gritted his teeth. *Now! Landing clearance, NOW!*

After a slight pause that seemed years long to the pilot of the crippled WindStar, the controller said words that were music to his ears: "WindStar Papa-Tango-Sierra-Bravo-Yankee is cleared to land, Runway Nine-Right."

Great, Rameros thought, allowing himself a deep exhale of relief. "Request short approach to Nine-Right," he quickly said back to the Tower.

"Approved," came the controller's response.

"Thank you Tower, Sierra-Bravo-Yankee," he said with barely suppressed exultation. Clearance to land with a short approach was everything he had hoped for, and not a second too soon. Rameros smiled. The WindStar pressed on, still noisily churning out power on its lone operating engine and maintaining its one thousand foot altitude above the airport, when suddenly…

FLAMEOUT.

Now everything changed. Dramatically.

No roaring sound from an operating engine.

No high pitched droning buzz from an active propeller.

The cockpit silenced. Even the sound of the wind gushing through the gaping hole in Waterman's windshield had subsided.

The WindStar had quickly slowed to one hundred knots.

Soon, the aircraft would drop from the sky like a rock.

EIGHTY-FIVE

On Board the Hatteras

At the stern of the Hatteras, Sammy Santelli began snaking a heavy-duty braided nylon line around two bolt-through cleats to fashion a tow bridle. John Andreas tossed Tommy Maxwell the end of another line to fasten to the Scarab's bow eye attach-point. Meanwhile, Monica and Rick helped a still soaking-wet Salo Montero onto the sportfisherman.

After Rick introduced Salo to Sammy, Rick appreciatively said, "Thanks for coming after us, Sammy."

"Hey," Santelli came back with swagger, "even though we only cruise at just over twenty knots, from up there," he pointed to the tuna tower, "I can see things over six miles away." He briefly paused. "Anyway, what the hell did you expect us to do, sit around the marina drinking rumrunners? We have a vested interest in getting airplanes from you, Rick Harris." He clasped Rick on the shoulder and lowered his voice. "Tell me, how in the hell did you nail those sonovabitches?"

"Air raid." Rick beamed. "I called on that WindStar you had a demo in earlier today so we could bird-dog the Cigarette." He shrugged, quickly glanced toward Montero then back to Santelli. "But the bird dog turned terrier and attacked. Salo told me that the guys on the boat had firearms aboard and took a bead on and shot up the aircraft pretty bad when it made a second low-level pass on them." He shook his head woefully. "One engine caught on fire, and later, the gear did not seem to be able to be retracted. So, it looks like the hydraulic system was hit too. But Cardella and Segundo made a strategic error. They, and I as well, thought the WindStar was a goner as it struggled back toward land. He hesitated with a slight laugh. "What they had unintentionally accomplished was to really piss-off Franco Rameros. He reacted with extreme prejudice. Salo said that no one expected it. When everyone on the boat figured the WindStar had ditched at sea, Rameros roared back at the Cigarette with everything he had. He slammed his left main landing gear down onto the boat's bow. He literally broke its back—smashed it to smithereens."

An incredulous smile filled Santelli's face. "You've got to be kidding me."

Salo shook his head. "You should have seen it, but you would not have wanted to be there."

"Unbelievable," Santelli said, "and where's Rameros now?"

Rick said, "Being the optimist that I am, I assume he's on an approach to Two-Seven-Left at FLL."

Santelli held up an open hand to Rick requesting a temporary pause in the conversation. He shouted up to Kelly Long at the helm, "Slowly ease us on forward to tension the towline, then go to about ten knots." He hesitated before giving more instructions remembering that the transceiver on the bridge had a full spectrum of both VHF and UHF frequencies. "Wait, why don't you also..." He turned to Rick. "What's the Tower frequency at FLL?"

"One-nineteen point three."

"Kelly," Santelli continued, "switch the radio to the VHF band, set in one-one-niner point three, and put it on the speakers down here."

Kelly Long shot an aye-aye salute to Santelli.

Moments later, Tower frequency chatter came through speakers on the fishing cockpit of the Hatteras as everyone watched the twin Detroit Diesel engines slowly take slack out of the line and begin towing the Scarab at a leisurely pace of ten knots.

Rick said, "The WindStar's registration is Papa-Tango-Sierra-Bravo-Yankee."

Everyone listened intently. There was no mention of "WindStar" in any of the controller's transmissions, and there was no mention of its registration number.

John Andreas asked, "Do you think Rameros might have had to ditch at sea?"

"No, no," Salo Montero spoke up as he eased his battered body against the starboard gunwale, "Franco Rameros is the best pilot I have ever known. He will make it, he will."

Everyone continued to carefully listen to transmissions coming over the speakers. Still, they heard nothing but mundane airport chatter.

EIGHTY-SIX

Runway Nine Right

Without any engine or propeller noise, the cockpit of the WindStar took on an eerie, almost coffin-like aura. But not for long.

Like a brick of lead, the WindStar plummeted from the clear blue sky. For Bob Waterman, it was another horrifying moment. He should not have trusted Rameros' judgment. He should have demanded Rameros declare an emergency earlier—much earlier. But now, it was too late for that—too late for anything.

The corners of Franco Rameros' mouth curled up. "This is what I live for," he growled over the cockpit intercom with raw excitement in his voice.

Waterman cringed as the thought hit him. He absorbed Rameros' tone and the words that had come through the headset. Earlier, he had decided that Rameros was an eccentric rogue when Rameros crashed the WindStar's left main gear down onto the Cigarette. Now, he was convinced that the man was a dangerous raving lunatic.

Rameros aggressively shoved the nose of the WindStar well below the horizon and snapped its wings into a seventy-degree bank to the right. The aircraft angled toward the landing threshold of the relatively short, fifty-two hundred foot runway.

The airspeed had increased to one-twenty knots.

Waterman's body was shivering in uncontrollable fear. It was another diving spiral, almost exactly like the one just prior to the first low-level run on the Cigarette. This time, though, expanses of crypt-like concrete and ominous grayish tarmac, not the warming blue waters of the Gulf Stream, filled his field of vision.

Franco Rameros' concentration grew deadly intense. His dilated eyes focused exclusively outside of the cockpit. There was only an occasional glance inside to the airspeed indicator. This was "seat-of-the-pants" flying. His judgment calls had no protocol to follow. He had to act based completely on what he saw outside the cockpit. The WindStar's sophisticated array of instruments and indicators were totally irrelevant. His inputs to the flight controls would be drawn instead from deep within himself. He would be tapping into years and years of actual flight experience that allowed for intuitive reaction. There was no procedure in the Pilot's Operating Handbook for what he was about to attempt. He would have just one chance at landing. There could be no missed approach. It was all or nothing. Everything would be over in less than a solitary minute.

The WindStar continued its drop to the ground, its wings steeply banked, its nose pitched sharply down.

The parasitic drag on the aircraft was enormous. Although the undamaged left engine had shut itself down due to fuel starvation and had its prop feathered by Rameros, the severely damaged right engine's unfeathered propeller acted as a circular eight-foot speed brake that fought against the relative wind with the intent of tearing the WindStar from the sky. The fully extended landing gear only added to the misery of an aircraft that was struggling to stay aloft.

Franco Rameros ignored these obstacles with unyielding determination. His eyes darting, occasionally narrowing to absorb every visual cue. He knew he could not land short—there was no power to carry him onto the runway. He knew he could not land long—the dual master cylinders of the hydraulic brake system were likely shot up—braking capability might be only the few pedal applications that remained. His rate of descent was breathtaking, making it almost impossible not to fly directly down into the ground. His airspeed was high—extending flaps for landing was impossible; that, too, called for use of now defunct hydraulics from powerpacks. And then again, if he were fortunate enough to safely land, his nose wheel steering would be inoperative—it was electro-hydraulic as well.

The WindStar continued its free fall from the sky, with objects on the ground looming larger all the time.

Rameros muscled the control yoke to the left to level the wings and line up with the runway centerline from two hundred feet above the landing threshold. He consciously maintained the aircraft's one-hundred-twenty-knot speed and the associated extreme rate of sink. A split-second later, he abruptly hauled back on the heavy yoke in a final attempt to harness the tremendous power of the aircraft's crashing descent.

The WindStar's wings flexed, its superstructure groaning under the heavy G-force loading. A warning horn blared from within the cockpit, announcing the onset of a deadly, incipient accelerated stall.

In the right seat, Waterman knew this was certainly the end of his life. He muttered a quick prayer and crossed himself in the name of the Father, Son, and Holy Ghost.

In the left seat, Franco Rameros continued to be focused, not even taking a breath. His actions and reactions seemed totally programmed. He responded to the impending stall by momentarily shoving the nose down, then smoothly bringing it up slightly above the runway.

The stall warning horn silenced.

The aircraft's downward plummet was arrested by ground effect—the compressed cushion of air created between the wings and the runway. But the crash had only been forestalled, not averted. Now, another problem reared its ugly head. With drag greatly reduced in ground effect, the WindStar's airspeed surged past one hundred thirty knots.

To safely land, Rameros had to somehow slow the WindStar. And, he had to do it quickly while there was still runway ahead to land on.

Without having to think, Rameros entered a forward slip. He automatically applied aileron to lower the aircraft's left wing to within inches of the runway surface, canting its nose to the right by easing off on some of the left rudder he had held to offset the drag from the unfeathered prop. With the aircraft's left side exposed to the relative wind, the WindStar's aluminum skin shuddered as its fuselage literally skidded sideways through the air while tracking directly down the runway. The instantaneous drag that the fuselage created could now be used by Rameros to finely tune his forward speed.

The lowered left wing tip briefly scraped the runway's surface...once...twice...

The airspeed rapidly bled off to ninety knots.

The stall warning horn blared once again in the cockpit.

Instinctively, Rameros leveled the wings and simultaneously kicked in enough left rudder to re-position the aircraft's nose down the runway, aligning once again with a forward direction of motion.

The main landing gear made firm, jolting contact with the runway. The nose wheel immediately followed.

Eighty knots.

Now, it would only be a guess as to how much braking ability Rameros could coax out of the hydraulic cylinder reservoirs. He pressed the balls of his feet down atop the rudder pedals, hard. The tires skidded. The brake caliper on at least one of the main gear wheels momentarily locked up. The right inboard tire blew out.

Seventy knots.

Rameros avoided the brakes, using right rudder to exit the runway on a high-speed taxiway that led to the RioAero hangar. He dropped his left hand down to the side panel and instinctively grasped the small, round, nose wheel steering control, but he quickly remembered that it too needed hydraulic pressure from the failed system. Directional control could only be had through differential braking—that is, whatever braking might be left.

Fifty knots.

The new RioAero hangar loomed large ahead, a mere four hundred feet away. He briefly tapped on top of the right rudder pedal to steer the aircraft.

Forty knots.

The hangar, two hundred feet dead ahead.

Rameros' voice growled with determination. "One more time, PLEASE."

He slammed his feet down onto the tops of the rudder pedals and pressed himself back into his seat. The brake pads froze on their respective rotating discs, blowing out the remaining, undamaged main gear tires.

The WindStar rolled to a thumping, wobbling stop less than twenty feet from the hangar's closed entrance doors.

For the moment, the only sound other than the two men's ragged breaths in the cockpit was the controller's fast-paced instructions on the Tower frequency. Rameros keyed in to the words meant for his aircraft: "WindStar Sierra-Bravo-Yankee, contact Ground Control on point seven."

Franco Rameros double-clicked his mic. He tried but could not hold back a triumphant guffaw. It seemed as though the busy controller was totally oblivious to Rameros' frantic last-minute maneuvering in the WindStar from the vantage point of the Tower cab over a mile away. Rameros promptly switched to the preset Ground Control frequency in COM-2. He pressed down on his mic button. "Ground, Sierra-Bravo-Yankee is clear."

"Roger," came the controller's indifferent solitary word in response.

From within the totally silent cockpit of the stationary WindStar, Franco Rameros flashed a huge, victorious grin to Waterman. "Well?" he said to the reporter.

"Aha..." Waterman began in response, his knuckles not yet unclenched from his armrests, his chest still heaving in deep breaths of relief, his mouth dry and trying to form words. "That...that was one wild ride." He paused, trying, but failing to summon up composure. "That...that was something I would never—EVER—want to go through again."

Rameros nodded. "It has certainly been a long and hectic day."

Indeed, it had.

EIGHTY-SEVEN

On Board the Hatteras

Offshore and ten miles away from the RioAero hangar, a boisterous cheer arose from all on Santelli's sportfisherman.

Monitoring the Tower frequency had paid off. All were now exuberantly aware that Rameros and the WindStar had safely landed.

"I knew it," Salo Montero said, pumping the fist of his uninjured arm. "Way to go, Franco!"

Rick Harris shook his head and said, "Amazing, truly amazing how everything worked out."

"Not at all," Sammy Santelli remarked. "You guys at RioAero had, and fortunately still have, a very good thing going. Unfortunately, some other folks simply could not handle the thought of it. Despite their best wicked efforts to destroy the WindStar and RioAero, they failed miserably." He turned with a smile and a nod to Rick. "They could not squelch your resolve to succeed, Mr. Harris." He then turned to Montero and said, "Salo, I want you to know that you have a damn fine aircraft and a damn fine aircraft salesman. I am proud to be a customer of RioAero."

"Why thank you, Mr. Santelli—

"It's Sammy, Salo."

"Why, why yes, Sammy..." Montero stammered embarrassingly, quickly correcting himself. "And tell me, Sammy, what is the name of our North American launch airline?"

Santelli groaned. "Well, it was only this weekend that my partners and I formally committed to merge three companies into one. So right now, we're still debating the name thing. I guess you could say that we're currently at loggerheads."

John Andreas and Kelly Long had just come down from the main cabin with two six packs of beer and began passing the beverages out.

"That's true, for better or worse," Andreas spoke up. "Our new airline remains nameless, and that might be the case for some time to come. You see, Salo, we all feel very strongly about carrying forward our old airlines' name into the merged company."

Kelly Long woefully nodded. "Ehh, we'll come to terms, hopefully sooner than later."

"Gentlemen," Montero began, "I do believe I know someone who can solve yet another of your problems."

Santelli narrowed his eyes. "Really? Who?"

Montero glanced expectantly toward Rick who nodded in approval. One evening while in Brazil, Rick Harris had floated a thought to Salo. Both agreed it was an idea that could be used given the right circumstances and the right time. It involved a name for an airline—an airline that had placed a major fleet order for the WindStar. Salo sensed that now was the time. "Rick," he prodded, "I bet you have a tie-breaker of a name for your customers' new airline."

Rick grinned, immediately seizing center stage. He said two words: "WindStar Airlines."

There was a contemplative hush among the group.

"WindStar Airlines?" Santelli slowly mouthed the name. Then he said it again with conviction, "WindStar Airlines." He paused and searched his partners' faces for approval. They both cocked their heads forward in full agreement. He beamed. "I like it...I like it!"

Santelli flashed a wink at Rick. "You know, Salo," he said, "I believe WindStar Airlines and RioAero will be an unbeatable team."

Salo nodded. "I am sure that we will both be formidable companies as the future unfolds." He paused, briefly glancing toward Rick. "But in the meantime, there is still much work to do and many challenges to be met. Lasting success never comes easily."

Salo gently rubbed his throbbing shoulder, but the smile on his face was megawatt bright.

Sabotage Plot Exposed
Reckless Sea Chase Ends In Disaster

By Robert Waterman
Sun-Sentinel Staff Writer
February 23, 1981

Fort Lauderdale — Alberto Garcia, head of the Miami office of the FBI, announced late yesterday evening that the Coast Guard, U.S. Customs, the FAA, and the FBI were jointly investigating "one of the most complex cases of industrial sabotage ever to have been uncovered." While Garcia could only provide scant details concerning the investigation, he did credit local resident Rick Harris as being instrumental in discovering "an elaborate and ruthless conspiracy" against Brazilian aircraft manufacturer RioAero, SA.

Rick Harris, a well-regarded aviation industry executive and recently appointed sales director for RioAero, had been working to improve the weak sales record for his company's new-generation regional airliner when he came across a number of highly suspicious incidents. It was then that Harris realized weak sales were the least of his problems.

While RioAero recently endured a rash of unusual and seemingly unrelated mishaps, the company's misfortunes crescendoed over this past weekend. Suddenly, RioAero's very existence was in question. In the nick of time, Harris unraveled the common thread to the unfortunate events that had been dogging his employer.

The climax occurred late Sunday afternoon with a pair of thundering offshore racers dueling it out in a perilous cat-and-mouse chase. Their reckless high-speed clash began along the Intracoastal Waterway and damaged several other boats—one severely—before the chase spilled out into the open waters of the Gulf Stream. Ten miles west of Bimini, the pursuit came to an abrupt end with the total destruction of a Cigarette 41/OS.

A Coast Guard cutter dispatched from Miami rescued three survivors and recovered ten kilos of cocaine. Even though the FBI would provide little information due to their ongoing investigation, a source exclusive to the *Sun-Sentinel* disclosed that this event was the culmination of an intricate plot of international proportions.

Arrested by the FBI on multiple charges of kidnapping, attempted murder, and drug trafficking were the following alleged perpetrators…

(See Archives, #81-2-2364-9. SABOTAGE, A10, Col. 1)

Acknowledgements

Although *Missed Approach* is totally a work of fiction, it does draw heavily upon the author's intimate knowledge of the commuter/regional airline industry—an industry essentially created by the Airline Deregulation Act of 1978. As such, the author would be remiss to not recognize those colorful, real-life characters who helped form that industry during its early years. Indeed, these pioneers—and there were many—inspired the concept of *Missed Approach*.

Among airlines, appreciation is extended to a host of noteworthy executives: Joel and Gloria Hall (Chautauqua Airlines), Angelo and Ann Koukoulis (Aeromech Airlines), Gary Adamson (Air Midwest), Curt Coward (Air Virginia), Preston Wilbourne (Air Wisconsin), George Pickett (Atlantic Southeast Airlines), Bill Best and Lou Sutton (Atlantis Airlines), Al Caruso (Bar Harbor Airlines), Bill and Marilyn Britt (Britt Airways), Jim McManus (Business Express), Roy Hagerty (CCAir), Clark Stevens (Chaparral Airlines), Tony von Elbe (Clinton Aero), Chuck Colgan (Colgan Airways), Dave Mueller (Comair), Kingsley Morse (Command Airways), John Sullivan (Crown Airways), Paul Quackenbush (Empire Airlines), Doug Voss (Great Lakes Aviation), Dick Henson (Henson Airlines), Milt Kuolt (Horizon Airlines), Larry Risley (Mesa Air), Rob Swenson (Mesaba Aviation), J. L. Seaborn (Metro Airlines), Bryce Appleton (Midstate Airlines), Bill Clark (Pennsylvania Airlines), Walt and Suki Fawcett (Precision Valley Aviation), John Van Arsdale (Provincetown-Boston Airlines), Dawson Ransome (Ransome Airlines), Hulas Kanodia (Resort Air), D.Y. Smith (Royale Airlines), Joel Murray (Simmons Airlines), Jerry Atkin (Skywest Airlines), Mike Brady (Southeastern Airlines), Don Young (Southern Jersey Airways), Art Horst (Suburban Airlines), Stu Adcock (Tennessee Airways), Jim Dent (Trans Air), Neal and Ruth Frey (Vee-Neal Airlines), Tim Flynn (WestAir Airlines), and Carl Albert (Wings West Airlines).

Among airframe manufacturers, special recognition is given to the following instrumental people of the then nascent industry: Earl Morton (Fairchild Aircraft), Colonel Ozires Silva (Embraer, SA),

Newton Berwig (Embraer, NA), Ove Dahlen (SAAB Aircraft of America), Chet Schickling (Beech Aircraft), Jack Cook (Piper Aircraft), and Oakley Brooks (Short Brothers, USA).

The author is privileged to have known many of the people who were along during the wild ride of developing and then rapidly expanding this segment of America's air transportation system. To all of these amazing people, and others involved but not listed above, many thanks from this author for those exciting times.

And lastly, I give my most important thanks to my wonderful and remarkable wife, Marguerite, who supported the project from the initial thought to the final editing draft. Without her continued support and editorial prowess *Missed Approach* would not exist as it now does.

About the Author

Mack Adams is well acquainted with his subject matter. He has over two decades of experience in aviation as a pilot, flight instructor, FBO operator, FAA designated pilot examiner, and aircraft sales executive. Among other airframe manufacturers, the author enjoyed being a part of Embraer, the now renowned Brazilian aircraft manufacturer. The author draws broadly from the challenges and heady excitement of the early days of Embraer in creating the fictitious RioAero.

Now retired from the industry that took him to dizzying heights, Mack Adams enjoys spending time with his veterinarian wife and a couple of horses as he spins tales as a writer. He combines a degree in speech, theater and English writing from the University of Pittsburgh along with experience as an associate editor (trade books) and advertising copywriter to serve as the launch point for his fiction. He has been a freelance contributor to the *Washington Post*, where he has published both feature and non-feature material.

The author's depth is enhanced by his further studies resulting in an MBA in microeconomics (Temple University), as well as his work-world experience as a CFO and as an undergraduate and graduate-level adjunct faculty member. Mack Adams' broad range of interests outside of aviation allow for diverse subject matter to be interspersed throughout his stories.

Mack Adams' expansive, firsthand knowledge of aviation, airframe manufacturers, and airlines make *Missed Approach* as accurate as it is compelling. No detail was left to chance. The author has personal experience with most of the elements contained in the story. But, of course, the author's work is fiction.

Pilot Licenses/Authorizations Earned

Airline Transport Pilot Certification #2139471
Flight Instructor: Airplane, Instruments, Gilder
Ground Instructor: Basic, Advanced, Instrument
Ratings: Airplanes (Single/Multi-engine, Land/Sea), Glider
Type Rating: EMB-110 (Embraer Bandeirante)
FAA Pilot Examiner: Private, Commercial, Instrument, ATP
FAA Recognition: Flight Instructor of the Year: District Award
Flight Time: 8,000+ hours

Made in the USA
San Bernardino, CA
16 November 2015